WILLIAM SAROYAN

The Saroyan Special

SELECTED SHORT STORIES

Illustrated by Don Freeman

HARCOURT, BRACE AND COMPANY, NEW YORK

To the Memory of My Father

ARMENAK SAROYAN

Bitlis, Armenia, 1874–San Jose, California, 1911

Contents

Myself upon the Earth   3

Seventy Thousand Assyrians   9

Aspirin   16

A Curved Line   20

1, 2, 3, 4, 5, 6, 7, 8   23

Laughter   30

The Shepherd's Daughter   34

The Daring Young Man on the Flying Trapeze   36

Five Ripe Pears   40

The Oranges   42

Two Days Wasted in Kansas City   45

Going Home   48

The Horses and the Sea   52

World Wilderness of Time Lost   56

Fresno   58

The Broken Wheel   62

The War   69

The Death of Children   71

The Barber Whose Uncle Had His Head
Bitten Off by a Circus Tiger   75

Antranik of Armenia   78

Little Miss Universe   84

Our Little Brown Brothers the Filipinos   90

The Dark Sea   96

Malenka Manon   97

The Proletarian at the Trap Drum   100

The Black Tartars   104

The Little Dog Laughed to See Such Sport   111

Train Going   115

The Whistle   117

Finlandia 122

The Armenian and the Armenian 127

The Man with the Heart in the Highlands 129

Bitlis 135

Baby 137

The Beggars 149

Quarter, Half, Three-Quarter, and Whole Notes 152

The Living and the Dead 164

Laughing Sam 178

The Sunday Zeppelin 181

Corduroy Pants 191

The First Day of School 195

The Man Who Got Fat 198

The Messenger 201

My Uncle and the Mexicans 206

Countryman, How Do You Like America? 210

Where I Come from People Are Polite 214

The Trains 220

One of the Least Famous of the
 Great Love Affairs of History 226

The La Salle Hotel in Chicago 228

Ah Life, Ah Death, Ah Music, Ah France,
 Ah Everything 233

The Genius 234

The Fire 237

The Filipino and the Drunkard 240

Jim Pemberton and His Boy Trigger 242

The Insurance Salesman, the Peasant,
 the Rug Merchant, and the Potted Plant 247

The Year of Heaven 250

1924 Cadillac for Sale 252

The Love Kick 255

The Warm, Quiet Valley of Home 257

A Number of the Poor 262

Peace, It's Wonderful 265

Piano 266

The Sweet Singer of Omsk 268

The Russian Writer 270

The Journey and the Dream 272
The Tiger 275
Sweetheart Sweetheart Sweetheart 284
The Brothers and the Sisters 290
The Ants 294
The Great Leapfrog Contest 297
The Acrobats 301
Citizens of the Third Grade 305
A Prayer for the Living 311
Memories of Paris 312
The Job 315
The Vision 319
We Want a Touchdown 322
Saroyan's Fables, IX 327
Saroyan's Fables, XXIV 329
Dear Baby 329
The Hummingbird That Lived Through Winter 336
The Stolen Bicycle 339
The Story of the Young Man and the Mouse 341
The Struggle of Jim Patros with Death 343
Sailing Down the Chesapeake 347
I Know You Good 350
How It Is to Be 353
The Declaration of War 357
Highway America 360
My Home, My Home 362
The Grapes 364
My Witness Witnesseth 367

Note

THE stories brought together here have been selected by the writer from all of his books of short stories so far published. These nine books appeared over a period of ten years, from 1934 to 1944. Most of them are out of print and several of them came out in limited editions. The stories appear in the chronological order of first book publication because that has seemed the natural order in which to make them available in one volume. If it is true that the writer would not today, at forty, write such stories as these, it is also true that he could not if he would, and therein no doubt lies the greater part of their worth, for they are youth's stories written in youth.

W. S.

The Saroyan Special

Myself upon the Earth

☼ ☼ ☼

A BEGINNING is always difficult, for it is no simple matter to choose from language the one bright word which shall live forever; and every articulation of the solitary man is but a single word. Every poem, story, novel and essay, just as every dream is a word from that language we have not yet translated, that vast unspoken wisdom of night, that grammarless, lawless vocabulary of eternity. The earth is vast, but vastest of all is the ego, from which is born God and the universe. For myself, I say, *Rejoice in this*.

I am a young man in an old city. It is morning and I am in a small room. I am standing over a bundle of yellow writing paper, the kind that sells at the rate of one hundred and seventy sheets for ten cents. All this paper is bare of language, clean and perfect, and I am a young writer about to begin my work. It is Monday, September 25, 1933. How glorious it is to be alive, to be still living. (I am an old man; I have walked along many streets, through many cities, through many days and many nights. And now I have come home to myself. Over me, on the wall of this small, disordered room, is the photograph of my dead father, and I have come up from the earth with his face and his eyes and I am writing in English what he would have written in our native tongue. And we are the same man, one dead and one alive.) Furiously I am smoking a cigarette, for the moment is one of great importance to me, and therefore of great importance to everyone. I am about to place language, my language, upon a clean sheet of paper, and I am trembling. It is so much of a responsibility to be a user of words. I do not want to say the wrong thing. I do not want to be clever. I am horribly afraid of this. I have never been clever in life, and now I do not want to utter a single false word. For months I have been telling myself, "You must be humble. Above all things, you must be humble." I am determined not to lose my character.

I am a story-teller, and I have but a single story—man. I want to tell this simple story in my own way, forgetting the rules of rhetoric, the tricks of composition. I have something to say and I do not wish to speak like Balzac. I am not an artist; I do not really believe in civilization. I am not at all enthusiastic about progress. When a great bridge is built I do not cheer, and when airplanes cross the Atlantic I do not think, "What a marvelous age this is!" I am not interested in the destiny of nations, and history bores me. What do they mean by history, those who write it and

3

believe in it? How has it happened that man, that humble and lovable creature, has been exploited for the purpose of monstrous documents? How has it happened that his solitude has been destroyed, his godliness herded into a hideous riot of murder and destruction? And I do not believe in commerce. I regard all machinery as junk, the adding-machine, the automobile, the railway engine, the airplane, yes, and the bicycle. I do not believe in transportation, in going places with the body, and I would like to know where anyone has ever gone. Have you ever left yourself? Is any journey so vast and interesting as the journey of the mind through life? Is the end of any journey so beautiful as death?

I am interested only in man. Life I love, and before death I am humble. I cannot fear death because it is purely physical. Is it not true that today both I and my father are living, and that in my flesh is assembled all the past of man? But I despise violence and I hate bitterly those who perpetrate and practise it. The injury of a living man's small finger I regard as infinitely more disastrous and ghastly than his natural death. And when multitudes of men are hurt to death in wars I am driven to a grief which borders on insanity. I become impotent with rage. My only weapon is language, and while I know it is stronger than machine-guns, I despair because I cannot single-handed annihilate the notion of destruction which propagandists awaken in men. I myself, however, am a propagandist, and in this very story I am trying to restore man to his natural dignity and gentleness. I want to restore man to himself. I want to send him from the mob to his own body and mind. I want to lift him from the nightmare of history to the calm dream of his own soul, the true chronicle of his kind. I want him to be himself. It is proper only to herd cattle. When the spirit of a single man is taken from him and he is made a member of a mob, the body of God suffers a ghastly pain, and therefore the act is a blasphemy.

I am opposed to mediocrity. If a man is an honest idiot, I can love him, but I cannot love a dishonest genius. All my life I have laughed at rules and mocked traditions, styles and mannerisms. How can a rule be applied to such a wonderful invention as man? Every life is a contradiction, a new truth, a new miracle, and even frauds are interesting. I am not a philosopher and I do not believe in philosophies; the word itself I look upon with suspicion. I believe in the right of man to contradict himself. For instance, did I not say that I look upon machinery as junk, and yet do I not worship the typewriter? Is it not the dearest possession I own?

And now I am coming to the little story I set out to tell. It is about myself and my typewriter, and it is perhaps a trivial story. You can turn to any of the national five-cent magazines and find much more artful stories, stories of love and passion and despair and ecstasy, stories about men called Elmer Fowler, Wilfred Diggens, and women called Florence Farwell, Agatha Hume, and so on.

If you turn to these magazines, you will find any number of perfect stories, full of plot, atmosphere, mood, style, character, and all those other things a good story is supposed to have, just as good mayonnaise is supposed to have so much pure olive oil, so much cream, and so much whipping. (Please do not imagine that I have forgotten myself and that I am trying to be clever. I am not laughing at these stories. I am not laughing at the people who read them. These words of prose and the men and women and children who read them constitute one of the most touching documents of our time, just as the motion pictures of Hollywood and those who spend the greatest portion of their secret lives watching them constitute one of the finest sources of material for the honest novelist. Invariably, let me explain, when I visit the theatre, and it is rarely that I have the price of admission, I am profoundly moved by the flood of emotion which surges from the crowd, and newsreels have always brought hot tears from my eyes. I cannot see floods, tornadoes, fires, wars and the faces of politicians without weeping. Even the tribulations of Mickey Mouse make my heart bleed, for I know that he, artificial as he may be, is actually a symbol of man.) Therefore, do not misunderstand me. I am not a satirist. There is actually nothing to satire, and everything pathetic or fraudulent contains its own mockery. I wish to point out merely that I am a writer, a story-teller. I go on writing as if all the periodicals in the country were clamoring for my work, offering me vast sums of money for anything I might choose to say. I sit in my room smoking one cigarette after another, writing this story of mine, which I know will never be able to meet the stiff competition of my more artful and talented contemporaries. Is it not strange? And why should I, a story-teller, be so attached to my typewriter? What earthly good is it to me? And what satisfaction do I get from writing stories?

Well, that is the story. Still, I do not want anyone to suppose that I am complaining. I do not want you to feel that I am a hero of some sort, or, on the other hand, that I am a sentimentalist. I am actually neither of these things. I have no objection to *The Saturday Evening Post,* and I do not believe the editor of *Scribner's* is a fool because he will not publish my tales. I know precisely what every magazine in the country wants. I know the sort of material *Secret Stories* is seeking, and the sort *The American Mercury* prefers, and the sort preferred by the literary journals like *Hound & Horn,* and all the rest. I read all magazines and I know what sort of stuff will sell. Still, I am seldom published and poor. Is it that I cannot write the sort of stuff for which money is paid? I assure you that it is not. I can write any sort of story you can think of. If Edgar Rice Burroughs were to die this morning, I could go on writing about Tarzan and the Apes. Or if I felt inclined, I could write like John Dos Passos or William Faulkner or James Joyce. (And so could you, for that matter.)

But I have said that I want to preserve my identity. Well, I mean it. If in doing this it is essential for me to remain unpublished, I am satisfied. I do not believe in fame. It is a form of fraudulence, and any famous man will tell you so. Any honest man, at any rate. How can one living man possibly be greater than another? And what difference does it make if one man writes great novels which are printed and another writes great novels which are not? What has the printing of novels to do with their greatness? What has money or the lack of it to do with the character of a man?

But I will confess that you've got to be proud and religious to be the sort of writer that I am. You've got to have an astounding amount of strength. And it takes years and years to become the sort of writer that I am, sometimes centuries. I wouldn't advise any young man with a talent for words to try to write the way I do. I would suggest that he study Theodore Dreiser or Sinclair Lewis. I would suggest even that, rather than attempt my method, he follow in the footsteps of O. Henry or the contributors to *The Woman's Home Companion.* Because, briefly, I am not a writer at all. I have been laughing at the rules of writing ever since I started to write, ten, maybe fifteen, years ago. I am simply a young man. I write because there is nothing more civilized or decent for me to do.

Do you know that I do not believe there is really such a thing as a poem-form, a story-form or a novel-form? I believe there is man only. The rest is trickery. I am trying to carry over into this story of mine the man that I am. And as much of my earth as I am able. I want more than anything else to be honest and fearless in my own way. Do you think I could not, if I chose, omit the remark I made about Dos Passos and Faulkner and Joyce, a remark which is both ridiculous and dangerous? Why, if someone were to say to me, "All right, you say you can write like Faulkner, well, then, let's see you do it." If someone were to say this to me, I would be positively stumped and I would have to admit timidly that I couldn't do the trick. Nevertheless, I make the statement and let it stand. And what is more, no one can prove that I am cracked; I could make the finest alienist in Vienna seem a raving maniac to his own disciples, or if I did not prefer this course, I could act as dull and stupid and sane as a Judge of the Supreme Court. Didn't I say that in my flesh is gathered all the past of man? And surely there have been dolts in that past.

I do not know, but there may be a law of some sort against this kind of writing. It may be a misdemeanor. I hope so. It is impossible for me to smash a fly which has tickled my nose, or to step on an ant, or to hurt the feelings of any man, idiot or genius, but I cannot resist the temptation to mock any law which is designed to hamper the spirit of man. It is essential for me to stick pins in pompous balloons. I love to make small explosions with the inflated bags of moralists, cowards, and wise men. Listen and you will hear such a small explosion in this paragraph.

All this rambling may seem pointless and a waste of time, but it is not. There is absolutely no haste—I can walk the hundred yard dash in a full day—and anyone who prefers may toss this story aside and take up something in the *Cosmopolitan*. I am not asking anyone to stand by. I am not promising golden apples to all who are patient. I am sitting in my room, living my life, tapping my typewriter. I am sitting in the presence of my father, who has been gone from the earth so many years. Every two or three minutes I look up into his melancholy face to see how he is taking it all. It is like looking into a mirror, for I see myself. I am almost as old as he was when the photograph was taken and I am wearing the very same moustache he wore at the time. I worship this man. All my life I have worshipped him. When both of us lived on the earth I was much too young to exchange so much as a single word with him, consciously, but ever since I have come to consciousness and articulation we have had many long silent conversations. I say to him, "Ah, you melancholy Armenian, you; how marvelous your life has been!" And he replies gently, "Be humble, my son. Seek God."

My father was a writer, too. He was an unpublished writer. I have all his great manuscripts, his great poems and stories, written in our native language, which I cannot read. Two or three times each year I bring out all my father's papers and stare for hours at his contribution to the literature of the world. Like myself, I am pleased to say, he was desperately poor; poverty trailed him like a hound, as the expression is. Most of his poems and stories were written on wrapping paper which he folded into small books. Only his journal is in English (which he spoke and wrote perfectly), and it is full of lamentations. In New York, according to this journal, my father had only two moods: *sad* and *very sad*. About thirty years ago he was alone in that city, and he was trying to earn enough money to pay for the passage of his wife and three children to the new world. He was a janitor. Why should I withhold this fact? There is nothing shameful about a great man's being a janitor in America. In the old country he was a man of honor, a professor, and he was called Agha, which means approximately lord. Unfortunately, he was also a revolutionist, as all good Armenians are. He wanted the handful of people of his race to be free. He wanted them to enjoy liberty, and so he was placed in jail every now and then. Finally, it got so bad that if he did not leave the old country, he would kill and be killed. He knew English, he had read Shakespeare and Swift in English, and so he came to this country. And they made a janitor of him. After a number of years of hard work his family joined him in New York. In California, according to my father's journal, matters for a while were slightly better for him; he mentioned sunshine and magnificent bunches of grapes. So he tried farming. At first he worked for other farmers, then he made a down payment on a small farm of his own. But he was a rotten farmer. He was a man of books, a professor; he loved good clothes. He loved leisure and comfort, and like myself he hated machinery.

My father's vineyard was about eleven miles east of the nearest town, and all the farmers near by were in the habit of going to town once or twice a week on bicycles, which were the vogue at that time and a trifle faster than a horse and buggy. One hot afternoon in August a tall individual in very fine clothes was seen moving forward in long leisurely strides over a hot and dusty country road. It was my father. My people told me this story about the man, so that I might understand what a fool he was and not be like him. Someone saw my father. It was a neighbor farmer who was returning from the city on a bicycle. This man was amazed.

"Agha," he said, "where are you going?"

"To town," my father said.

"But, Agha," said the farmer, "you cannot do this thing. It is eleven miles to town and you look . . . People will laugh at you in such clothes."

"Let them laugh," my father said. "These are my clothes. They fit me."

"Yes, yes, of course they fit you," said the farmer, "but such clothes do not seem right out here, in this dust and heat. Everyone wears overalls out here, Agha."

"Nonsense," said my father. He went on walking.

The farmer followed my father, whom he now regarded as insane.

"At least, at least," he said, "if you insist on wearing those clothes, at least you will not humiliate yourself by *walking* to town. You will at least accept the use of my bicycle."

This farmer was a close friend of my father's family, and he had great respect for my father. He meant well, but my father was dumbfounded. He stared at the man with horror and disgust.

"What?" he shouted. "You ask me to mount one of those crazy contraptions? You ask me to tangle myself in that ungodly piece of junk?" (The Armenian equivalent of junk is a good deal more violent and horrible.) "Man was not made for such absurd inventions," my father said. "Man was not placed on the earth to tangle himself in junk. He was placed here to stand erect and to walk with his feet."

And away he went.

Ah, you can be sure that I worship this man. And now, alone in my room, thinking of these things, tapping out this story, I want to show you that I and my father are the same man.

I shall come soon to the matter of the typewriter, but there is no hurry. I am a story-teller, not an aviator. I am not carrying myself across the Atlantic in the cockpit of an airplane which moves at the rate of two hundred and fifty miles per hour.

It is Monday of this year, 1933, and I am trying to gather as much of eternity into this story as possible. When next this story is read I may be with my father in the earth we both love and I may have sons alive on the surface of this old earth, young fellows whom I shall ask to be humble, as my father has asked me to be humble.

In a moment a century may have elapsed, and I am doing what I can to keep this moment solid and alive.

Musicians have been known to weep at the loss of a musical instrument, or at its injury. To a great violinist his violin is a part of his identity. I am a young man with a dark mind, and a dark way in general, a sullen and serious way. The earth is mine, but not the world. If I am taken away from language, if I am placed in the street, as one more living entity, I become nothing, not even a shadow. I have less honor than the grocer's clerk, less dignity than the doorman at the St. Francis Hotel, less identity than the driver of a taxi-cab.

And for the past six months I have been separated from my writing, and I have been nothing, or I have been walking about unalive, some indistinct shadow in a nightmare of the universe. It is simply that without conscious articulation, without words, without language, I do not exist as myself. I have no meaning, and I might just as well be dead and nameless. It is blasphemous for any living man to live in such a manner. It is an outrage to God. It means that we have got nowhere after all these years.

It is for this reason, now that I have my typewriter again, and have beside me a bundle of clean writing paper, and am sitting in my room, full of tobacco smoke, with my father's photograph watching over me—it is for this reason that I feel as if I have just been resurrected from the dead. I love and worship life, living senses, functioning minds. I love consciousness. I love precision. And life is to be created by every man who has the breath of God within him; and every man is to create his own consciousness, and his own precision, for these things do not exist of themselves. Only confusion and error and ugliness exist of themselves. I have said that I am deeply religious. I am. I believe that I live, and you've got to be religious to believe so miraculous a thing. And I am grateful and I am humble. I do live, so let the years repeat themselves eternally, for I am sitting in my room, stating in words the truth of my being, squeezing the fact from meaningless and imprecision. And the living of this moment can never be effaced. It is beyond time.

I despise commerce. I am a young man with no money. There are times when a young man can use a small sum of money to very good advantage, there are times when money to him, because of what it can purchase, is the most important thing of his life. I despise commerce, but I admit that I have some respect for money. It is, after all, pretty important, and it was the lack of it, year after year, that finally killed my father. It wasn't right for a man so poor to wear the sort of clothes he knew he deserved; so my father died. I would like to have enough money to enable me to live simply and to write my life. Years ago, when I labored in behalf of industry and progress and so on, I purchased a small portable typewriter, brandnew, for sixty-five dollars. (And what an enormous lot of money that is, if you are poor.) At first this machine was strange to me and I was annoyed by the racket it made when it was in use; late at night this racket was unbearably distressing. It resembled more than anything else silence which has been magnified a thousand times, if such a thing can be. But after a year or two I began to feel a genuine attachment toward the machine, and loved it as a good pianist, who respects music, loves his piano. I never troubled to clean the machine and no matter how persistently I pounded upon it, the machine did not weaken and fall to pieces. I had great respect for it.

And then, in a fit of despondency, I placed this small machine in its case and carried it to the city. I left it in the establishment of a money-lender, and walked through the city with fifteen dollars in my pocket. I was sick of being poor.

I went first to a bootblack and had my shoes polished. When a boot-black is shining my shoes I place him in my place in the chair and I descend and polish his shoes. It is an experience in humility.

Then I went to a theatre. I sat among people to see myself in patterns of Hollywood. I sat and dreamed, looking into the faces of beautiful women. Then I went to a restaurant and sat at a table and ordered all the different kinds of food I ever thought I would like to eat. I ate two dollars' worth of food. The waiter thought I was out of my head, but I told him every-thing was going along first rate. I tipped the waiter. Then I went out into the city again and began walking along the dark streets, the streets where the women are. I was tired of being poor. I put my typewriter in hock and I began to spend the money. No one, not even the greatest writer, can go on being poor hour after hour, year after year. There is such a thing as saying to hell with art. That's what I said.

After a week I became a little more sober. After a month I got to be very sober and I began to want my typewriter again. I began to want to put words on paper again. To make another beginning. To say something and see if it was the right thing. But I had no money. Day after day I had this longing for my typewriter.

This is the whole story. I don't suppose this is a very artful ending, but it is the ending just the same. The point is this: *day after day I longed for my typewriter*.

This morning I got it back. It is before me now and I am tapping at it, and this is what I have written.

Seventy Thousand Assyrians

✿ ✿ ✿

I HADN'T had a haircut in forty days and forty nights, and I was begin-ning to look intellectual. You know the look: genius gone to pot, and ready to join the Communist Party. We barbarians from Asia Minor are hairy people: when we need a haircut, we *need* a haircut. It was so bad, I had outgrown my only hat. (I am writing a very serious story, perhaps one of the most serious I shall ever write. That is why I am being flippant.

Readers of Sherwood Anderson will begin to understand what I am saying after a while; they will know that my laughter is rather sad.) I was a young man in need of a haircut, so I went down to Third Street (San Francisco), to the Barber College, for a fifteen-cent haircut.

Third Street, below Howard, is a district; think of the Bowery in New York, Main Street in Los Angeles: think of old men and boys, out of work, hanging around, smoking Bull Durham, talking about the government, waiting for something to turn up, simply waiting. It was a Monday morning in August and a lot of the tramps had come to the shop to brighten up a bit. The Japanese boy who was working over the free chair had a waiting list of eleven; all the other chairs were occupied. I sat down and began to wait. Outside, as Hemingway (*The Sun Also Rises; Farewell to Arms; Death in the Afternoon; Winner Take Nothing*) would say, haircuts were four bits. I had twenty cents and a half-pack of Bull Durham. I rolled a cigarette, handed the pack to one of my contemporaries who looked in need of nicotine, and inhaled the dry smoke, thinking of America, what was going on politically, economically, spiritually. My contemporary was a boy of sixteen. He looked Iowa; splendid potentially, a solid American, but down, greatly down in the mouth. Little sleep, no change of clothes for several days, a little fear, etc. I wanted very much to know his name. A writer is always wanting to get the reality of faces and figures. Iowa said, "I just got in from Salinas. No work in the lettuce fields. Going north now, to Portland; try to ship out." I wanted to tell him how it was with me: rejected story from *Scribner's*, rejected essay from *The Yale Review*, no money for decent cigarettes, worn shoes, old shirts, but I was afraid to make something of my own troubles. A writer's troubles are always boring, a bit unreal. People are apt to feel, *Well, who asked you to write in the first place?* A man must pretend not to be a writer. I said, "Good luck, north." Iowa shook his head. "I know better. Give it a try, anyway. Nothing to lose." Fine boy, hope he isn't dead, hope he hasn't frozen, mighty cold these days (December, 1933), hope he hasn't gone down; he deserved to live. Iowa, I hope you got work in Portland; I hope you are earning money; I hope you have rented a clean room with a warm bed in it; I hope you are sleeping nights, eating regularly, walking along like a human being, being happy. Iowa, my good wishes are with you. I have said a number of prayers for you. (All the same, I think he is dead by this time. It was in him the day I saw him, the low malicious face of the beast, and at the same time all the theatres in America were showing, over and over again, an animated film-cartoon in which there was a song called "Who's Afraid of the Big Bad Wolf?", and that's what it amounts to; people with money laughing at the death that is crawling slyly into boys like young Iowa, pretending that it isn't there, laughing in warm theatres. I have prayed for Iowa, and I consider myself a coward. By this time he must be dead, and I am sitting in a small room, talking about him, only talking.)

I began to watch the Japanese boy who was learning to become a barber. He was shaving an old tramp who had a horrible face, one of those faces that emerge from years and years of evasive living, years of being unsettled, of not belonging anywhere, of owning nothing, and the Japanese boy was holding his nose back (his own nose) so that he would not smell the old tramp. A trivial point in a story, a bit of data with no place in a work of art, nevertheless, I put it down. A young writer is always afraid some significant fact may escape him. He is always wanting to put in everything he sees. I wanted to know the name of the Japanese boy. I am profoundly interested in names. I have found that those that are unknown are the most genuine. Take a big name like Andrew Mellon. I was watching the Japanese boy very closely. I wanted to understand from the way he was keeping his sense of smell away from the mouth and nostrils of the old man what he was thinking, how he was feeling. Years ago, when I was seventeen, I pruned vines in my uncle's vineyard, north of Sanger, in the San Joaquin Valley, and there were several Japanese working with me, Yoshio Enomoto, Hideo Suzuki, Katsumi Sujimoto, and one or two others. These Japanese taught me a few simple phrases, *hello, how are you, fine day, isn't it, good-bye*, and so on. I said in Japanese to the barber student, "How are you?" He said in Japanese, "Very well, thank you." Then, in impeccable English, "Do you speak Japanese? Have you lived in Japan?" I said, "Unfortunately, no. I am able to speak only one or two words. I used to work with Yoshio Enomoto, Hideo Suzuki, Katsumi Sujimoto; do you know them?" He went on with his work, thinking of the names. He seemed to be whispering, "Enomoto, Suzuki, Sujimoto." He said, "Suzuki. Small man?" I said, "Yes." He said, "I know him. He lives in San Jose now. He is married now."

I want you to know that I am deeply interested in what people remember. A young writer goes out to places and talks to people. He tries to find out what they remember. I am not using great material for a short story. Nothing is going to happen in this work. I am not fabricating a fancy plot. I am not creating memorable characters. I am not using a slick style of writing. I am not building up a fine atmosphere. I have no desire to sell this story or any story to *The Saturday Evening Post* or to *Cosmopolitan* or to *Harper's*. I am not trying to compete with the great writers of short stories, men like Sinclair Lewis and Joseph Hergesheimer and Zane Grey, men who really know how to write, how to make up stories that will sell. Rich men, men who understand all the rules about plot and character and style and atmosphere and all that stuff. I have no desire for fame. I am not out to win the Pulitzer Prize or the Nobel Prize or any other prize. I am out here in the Far West, in San Francisco, in a small room on Carl Street, writing a letter to common people, telling them in simple language things they already know. I am merely making a record, so if I wander around a little, it is because I am in no hurry and because I do not know the rules. If I have any desire at all, it is to show the brotherhood of man. This is a big statement and it sounds a little precious. Generally a man is ashamed to make such a statement. He is afraid sophisticated people will laugh at him. But I don't mind. I'm asking sophisticated people to laugh. That is what sophistication is for. I do not believe in races. I do not believe in governments. I see life as one life at one time, so many millions simultaneously, all over the earth. Babies who have not yet been taught to speak any language are the only race of the earth, the race of man: all the rest is pretense, what we call civilization, hatred, fear, desire for strength. . . . But a baby is a baby. And the way they cry, there you have the brotherhood of man, babies crying. We grow up and we learn the words of a language and we see the universe through the language we know, we do not see it through all languages or through no language at all, through silence, for example, and we isolate ourselves in the language we know. Over here we isolate ourselves in English, or American as Mencken calls it. All the eternal things, in our words. If I want to do anything, I want to speak a more universal language. The heart of man, the unwritten part of man, that which is eternal and common to all races.

Now I am beginning to feel guilty and incompetent. I have used all this language and I am beginning to feel that I have said nothing. This is what drives a young writer out of his head, this feeling that nothing is being said. Any ordinary journalist would have been able to put the whole business into a three-word caption. Man is man, he would have said. Something clever, with any number of implications. But I want to use language that will create a single implication. I want the meaning to be precise, and perhaps that is why the language is so imprecise. I am walking around my subject, the impression I want to make, and I am trying to see it from all angles, so that I will have a whole picture, a picture of wholeness. It is the heart of man that I am trying to imply in this work.

Let me try again: I hadn't had a haircut in a long time and I was beginning to look seedy, so I went down to the Barber College on Third Street, and I sat in a chair. I said, "Leave it full in the back. I have a narrow head and if you do not leave it full in the back, I will go out of this place looking like a horse. Take as much as you like off the top. No lotion, no water, comb it dry. " Reading makes a full man, writing a precise one, as you see. This is what happened. It doesn't make much of a story, and the reason is that I have left out the barber, the young man who gave me the haircut.

He was tall, he had a dark serious face, thick lips, on the verge of smiling but melancholy, thick lashes, sad eyes, a large nose. I saw his name on the card that was pasted on the mirror, Theodore Badal. A good name, genuine, a good young man, genuine. Theodore Badal began to work on my head. A good barber never speaks until he has been spoken to, no matter how full his heart may be.

"That name," I said, "Badal. Are you an Armenian?" I am an Armenian. I have mentioned this before. People look at me and begin to wonder, so I come right out and tell them. "I am an Armenian," I say. Or they read something I have written and begin to wonder, so I let them know. "I am an Armenian," I say. It is a meaningless remark, but they expect me to say it, so I do. I have no idea what it is like to be an Armenian or what it is like to be an Englishman or a Japanese or anything else. I have a faint idea what it is like to be alive. This is the only thing that interests me greatly. This and tennis. I hope some day to write a great philosophical work on tennis, something on the order of *Death in the Afternoon*, but I am aware that I am not yet ready to undertake such a work. I feel that the cultivation of tennis on a large scale among the peoples of the earth will do much to annihilate racial differences, prejudices, hatred, etc. Just as soon as I have perfected my drive and my lob, I hope to begin my outline of this great work. (It may seem to some sophisticated people that I am trying to make fun of Hemingway. I am not. *Death in the Afternoon* is a pretty sound piece of prose. I could never object to it as prose. I cannot even object to it as philosophy. I think it is finer philosophy than that of Will Durant and Walter Pitkin. Even when Hemingway is a fool, he is at least an accurate fool. He tells you what actually takes place and he doesn't allow the speed of an occurrence to make his exposition of it hasty. This is a lot. It is some sort of advancement for literature. To relate leisurely the nature and meaning of that which is very brief in duration.)

"Are you an Armenian?" I asked.

We are a small people and whenever one of us meets another, it is an event. We are always looking around for someone to talk to in our language. Our most ambitious political party estimates that there are nearly

two million of us living on the earth, but most of us don't think so. Most of us sit down and take a pencil and a piece of paper and we take one section of the world at a time and imagine how many Armenians at the most are likely to be living in that section and we put the highest number on the paper, and then we go on to another section, India, Russia, Soviet Armenia, Egypt, Italy, Germany, France, America, South America, Australia, and so on, and after we add up our most hopeful figures the total comes to something a little less than a million. Then we start to think how big our families are, how high our birth-rate and how low our death-rate (except in times of war when massacres increase the death-rate), and we begin to imagine how rapidly we will increase if we are left alone a quarter of a century, and we feel pretty happy. We always leave out earthquakes, wars, massacres, famines, etc., and it is a mistake. I remember the Near East Relief drives in my home town. My uncle used to be our orator and he used to make a whole auditorium full of Armenians weep. He was an attorney and he was a great orator. Well, at first the trouble was war. Our people were being destroyed by the enemy. Those who hadn't been killed were homeless and they were starving, *our own flesh and blood*, my uncle said, and we all wept. And we gathered money and sent it to our people in the old country. Then after the war, when I was a bigger boy, we had another Near East Relief drive and my uncle stood on the stage of the Civic Auditorium of my home town and he said, "Thank God this time it is not the enemy, but an earthquake. God has made us suffer. We have worshipped Him through trial and tribulation, through suffering and disease and torture and horror and (my uncle began to weep, began to sob) through the madness of despair, and now he has done this thing, and still we praise Him, still we worship Him. We do not understand the ways of God." And after the drive I went to my uncle and I said, "Did you mean what you said about God?" And he said, "That was oratory. We've got to raise money. What God? It is nonsense." "And when you cried?" I asked, and my uncle said, "That was real. I could not help it. I had to cry. Why, for God's sake, why must we go through all this God damn hell? What have we done to deserve all this torture? Man won't let us alone. God won't let us alone. Have we done something? Aren't we supposed to be pious people? What is our sin? I am disgusted with God. I am sick of man. The only reason I am willing to get up and talk is that I don't dare keep my mouth shut. I can't bear the thought of more of our people dying. Jesus Christ, have we done something?"

I asked Theodore Badal if he was an Armenian.

He said, "I am an Assyrian."

Well, it was something. They, the Assyrians, came from our part of the world, they had noses like our noses, eyes like our eyes, hearts like our hearts. They had a different language. When they spoke we couldn't understand them, but they were a lot like us. It wasn't quite as pleasing as it would have been if Badal had been an Armenian, but it was something.

"I am an Armenian," I said. "I used to know some Assyrian boys in my home town, Joseph Sargis, Nito Elia, Tony Saleh. Do you know any of them?"

"Joseph Sargis, I know him," said Badal. "The others I do not know. We lived in New York until five years ago, then we came out west to Turlock. Then we moved up to San Francisco."

"Nito Elia," I said, "is a Captain in the Salvation Army." (I don't want anyone to imagine that I am making anything up, or that I am trying to be funny.) "Tony Saleh," I said, "was killed eight years ago. He was riding a horse and he was thrown and the horse began to run. Tony couldn't get himself free, he was caught by a leg, and the horse ran around and around for a half hour and then stopped, and when they went up to Tony he was dead. He was fourteen at the time. I used to go to school with him. Tony was a very clever boy, very good at arithmetic."

We began to talk about the Assyrian language and the Armenian language, about the old world, conditions over there, and so on. I was getting a fifteen-cent haircut and I was doing my best to learn something at the same time, to acquire some new truth, some new appreciation of the wonder of life, the dignity of man. (Man has great dignity, do not imagine that he has not.)

Badal said, "I cannot read Assyrian. I was born in the old country, but I want to get over it."

He sounded tired, not physically but spiritually.

"Why?" I said. "Why do you want to get over it?"

"Well," he laughed, "simply because everything is washed up over there."

I am repeating his words precisely, putting in nothing of my own. "We were a great people once," he went on. "But that was yesterday, the day before yesterday. Now we are a topic in ancient history. We had a great civilization. They're still admiring it. Now I am in America learning how to cut hair. We're washed up as a race, we're through, it's all over, why should I learn to read the language? We have no writers, we have no news— well, there is a little news: once in a while the English encourage the Arabs to massacre us, that is all. It's an old story, we know all about it. The news comes over to us through the Associated Press, anyway."

These remarks were very painful to me, an Armenian. I had always felt badly about my own people being destroyed. I had never heard an Assyrian speaking in English about such things. I felt great love for this young fellow. Don't get me wrong. There is a tendency these days to think in terms of pansies whenever a man says that he has affection for man. I think now that I have affection for all people, even for the enemies of Armenia, whom I have so tactfully not named. Everyone knows who they are. I have nothing against any of them because I think of them as one man living one life at a time, and I know, I am positive, that one man at a time is incapable of the monstrosities performed by mobs. My objection is to mobs only.

"Well," I said, "it is much the same with us. We, too, are old. We still have our church. We still have a few writers, Aharonian, Isahakian, a few others, but it is much the same."

"Yes," said the barber, "I know. We went in for the wrong things. We went in for the simple things, peace and quiet and families. We didn't go in for machinery and conquest and militarism. We didn't go in for diplomacy and deceit and the invention of machine-guns and poison gases. Well, there is no use in being disappointed. We had our day, I suppose."

"We are hopeful," I said. "There is no Armenian living who does not still dream of an independent Armenia."

"Dream?" said Badal. "Well, that is something. Assyrians cannot even dream any more. Why, do you know how many of us are left on earth?"

"Two or three million," I suggested.

"Seventy thousand," said Badal. "That is all. Seventy thousand Assyrians in the world, and the Arabs are still killing us. They killed seventy of us in a little uprising last month. There was a small paragraph in the paper. Seventy more of us destroyed. We'll be wiped out before long. My brother is married to an American girl and he has a son. There is no more hope. We are trying to forget Assyria. My father still reads a paper that comes from New York, but he is an old man. He will be dead soon."

Then his voice changed, he ceased speaking as an Assyrian and began to speak as a barber: "Have I taken enough off the top?" he asked.

The rest of the story is pointless. I said so long to the young Assyrian and left the shop. I walked across town, four miles, to my room on Carl Street. I thought about the whole business: Assyria and this Assyrian, Theodore Badal, learning to be a barber, the sadness of his voice, the hopelessness of his attitude. This was months ago, in August, but ever since I have been thinking about Assyria, and I have been wanting to say something about Theodore Badal, a son of an ancient race, himself youthful and alert, yet hopeless. Seventy thousand Assyrians, a mere seventy thousand of that great people, and all the others quiet in death and all the greatness crumbled and ignored, and a young man in America learning to be a barber, and a young man lamenting bitterly the course of history.

Why don't I make up plots and write beautiful love stories that can be made into motion pictures? Why don't I let these unimportant and boring matters go hang? Why don't I try to please the American reading public?

Well, I am an Armenian. Michael Arlen is an Armenian, too. He is pleasing the public. I have great admiration for him, and I think he has perfected a very fine style of writing and all that, but I don't want to write about the people he likes to write about. Those people were dead to begin with. You take Iowa and the Japanese boy and Theodore Badal, the Assyrian; well, they may go down physically, like Iowa, to death, or spiritually, like Badal, to death, but they are of the stuff that is eternal in man and it is this stuff that interests me. You don't find them in bright places, making witty remarks about sex and trivial remarks about art. You find them where I found them, and they will be there forever, the race of man, the part of man, of Assyria as much as of England, that cannot be destroyed, the part that massacre does not destroy, the part that earthquake and war and famine and madness and everything else cannot destroy.

This work is in tribute to Iowa, to Japan, to Assyria, to Armenia, to the race of man everywhere, to the dignity of that race, the brotherhood of things alive. I am not expecting Paramount Pictures to film this work. I am thinking of seventy thousand Assyrians, one at a time, alive, a great race. I am thinking of Theodore Badal, himself seventy thousand Assyrians and seventy million Assyrians, himself Assyria, and man, standing in a barber shop, in San Francisco, in 1933, and being, still, himself, the whole race.

Aspirin

✿ ✿ ✿

REMEMBER above all things the blood, remember that man is flesh, that flesh suffers pain, and that the mind being caught in flesh suffers with it. Remember that the spirit is a form of the flesh, and the soul its shadow. Above all things humor and intelligence, and truth as the only beginning: not what is said or done, not obviousness: the truth of silences, the intelligence of nothing said, nothing done. The piety. Faces. Memory, our memory of the earth, this one and the other, the one which is now this and the one that was once another, what we saw, and the sun. It is our life and we have no other. Remember God, the multitudinous God.

Remember laughter.

There were nights in New York when my hair would freeze on my head, and I would awaken from sleeplessness and remember. I would remember stalking through print, the quiet oratory of some forgotten name, a quiet man who put something down on paper: *yea* and *yea* and *yea*. Something wordless but precise, my hair frozen, and the small attic room in the heart of Manhattan, across the street from the Paramount Building, and myself in the room, in the darkness, alone, waiting for morning. I used to leave my bed sometimes and smoke a cigarette in the darkness. The light I disliked, so I used to sit in the darkness, remembering.

One or two faces I saw coming across the Continent: the boy with a bad dose, riding in the bus, going home to his mother, taking a bad dose with him from a South American resort, talking about the girl, just a young kid and very beautiful, and God, what a pain, every moment and nothing to do about it. He was eighteen or nineteen, and he had gone down to South America to sleep with a girl, and now he had got it, where it hurt most, and he was drinking whisky and swallowing aspirin, to keep him going, to deaden the pain. York, Pennsylvania, a good town, and his people living there. Everything, he said, everything will be all right the minute I get home. And the sick girl, going back to Chicago, talking in her sleep. The language of fear, the articulation of death, no grammar, exclamations, one after another, the midnight grief, children emerging from the grown girl, talking.

And the faces of people in the streets, in the large cities and in the small towns, the sameness.

I used to get up in the middle of the night and remember. It was no use trying to sleep, because I was in a place that did not know me, and whenever I tried to sleep the room would declare its strangeness and I would sit up in bed and look into the darkness.

Sometimes the room would hear me laughing softly. I could never cry, because I was doing what I wanted to do, so I couldn't help laughing once in a while, and I would always feel the room listening. Strange fellow, this fellow, I would hear the room say; in this agony, he gets up, with his hair frozen, in the middle of the night, and he laughs.

There was enough pain everywhere, in everyone who lived. If you tried to live a godly life, it didn't make any difference, and in the end you came up with a dull pain in your body and a soul burning with a low fire, eating its substance slowly. I used to think about the pain and in the end all I could do was laugh. If there had been a war, it would have been much easier, more reasonable. The pain would have been explicable. We are fighting for high ideals, we are protecting our homes, we are protecting civilization, and all that. A tangible enemy, a reasonable opposition, and swift pain, so that you couldn't have time enough to think about it much: either it got you all the way, carrying you over into death and calm, or it didn't get you. Also, something tangible to hate, a precise enemy. But without a war it was different. You might try hating God, but in the end you couldn't do it. In the end you laughed softly or you prayed, using pious and blasphemous language.

I used to sit in the dark room, waiting for morning and the fellowship of passengers of the subway. The room had great strength. It belonged. It was part of the place. Fellows like me could come and go, they could die and be born again, but the room was steady and static, always there. I used to feel its indifference toward me, but I could never feel unfriendly toward it. It was part of the scheme, a small attic room in the heart of Manhattan, without an outside window, four dollars a week: me or the next fellow, any of us, it didn't matter. But whenever I laughed, the room would be puzzled, a bit annoyed. It would wonder what there was for me to laugh about, my hair frozen, and my spirit unable to rest.

Sometimes, during the day, shaving, I used to look into the small mirror and see the room in my face, trying to understand me. I would be laughing, looking at the room in the mirror, and it would be annoyed, wondering how I could laugh, what I saw in my life that was amusing.

It was the secrecy that amused me, the fact of my being one of the six million people in the city, living there, waiting to die. I could die in this room, I used to say to myself, and no one would ever understand what had happened, no one would ever say, Do you know that boy from California, the fellow who is studying the subway? Well, he died in a little room on Forty-fourth Street the other night, alone. They found him in the little room, dead. No one would be able to say anything about me if I died, no one knew I was from California and that I was studying the subway, making notes about the people riding in the subway. My presence in Manhattan was not known, so if I came to vanish, my vanishing would not be known. It was a secret, and it amused me. I used to get up in the middle of the night and laugh about it quietly, disturbing the room.

I used to make the room very angry, laughing, and one night it said to me, You are in a hurry but I am not: I shall witness your disintegration, but when you are destroyed I shall be standing here quietly. You will see.

It made me laugh. I knew it was the truth, but it was amusing to me. I couldn't help laughing at the room wanting to see me go down.

But there was an armistice: what happened was this: I moved away. I rented another room. It was a war without a victor. I packed my things and moved to the Mills Hotel.

But it isn't so easy to escape a war. A war has a way of following a man around, and my room in the Mills Hotel was even more malicious than the other. It was smaller and therefore its eloquence was considerably louder. Its walls used to fall in upon me, with the whiteness of madness, but I went on laughing. In the middle of the night I used to hear my neighbors, old and young men. I used to hear them speaking out against life from their sleep. I used to hear much weeping. That year many men were weeping from their sleep. I used to laugh about this. It was such a startling thing that I used to laugh. The worst that can happen to any of us, I used to laugh, is death. It is a small thing. Why are you men weeping?

It was because of remembrance, I suppose. Death is always in a man, but sometimes life is in him so strongly that it makes a sad remembrance and comes out in the form of weeping through sleep.

And it was because of the pain. Everybody was in pain. I was studying the subway and I could see the pain in the faces of everybody. I looked everywhere for one face that was not the mask of a pained life, but I did not find such a face. It was this that made my study of the subway so fascinating. After months of study I reached a decision about all of us in Manhattan. It was thus: the subway is death, all of us are riding to death. No catastrophe, no horrible accident: only slow death, emerging from life. It was such a terrific fact that I had to laugh about it.

I lived in many rooms, in many sections of the city, East Side, West Side, downtown, uptown, Harlem, the Bronx, Brooklyn, all over the place. It was the same everywhere, my hair frozen at night, alien walls around me, and the smile of death in my eyes.

But I didn't mind. It was what I had wanted to do. I was a clerk in one of thousands of offices of a great national enterprise, doing my part to make America the most prosperous nation on earth, more millionaires per square inch than all the other nations put together, etc. I was paying cash for my sleeplessness, for the privilege of riding in the subway. I was eating in the Automats, renting vacant rooms all over the place, buying clothes, newspapers, aspirin.

I do not intend to leave aspirin out of this document. It is too im-

portant to leave out. It is the hero of this story, all of us six million people
in New York, swallowing it, day after day. All of us in pain, needing it.
Aspirin is an evasion. But so is life. The way we live it. You take aspirin
in order to keep going. It deadens pain. It helps you to sleep. It keeps you
aboard the subway. It is a substitute for the sun, for strong blood. It stifles
remembrance, silences weeping.

It does not harm the heart. That is what the manufacturers say. They
say it is absolutely harmless. Maybe it is. Death does not harm the heart
either. Death is just as harmless as aspirin. I expect casket manufacturers
to make this announcement in the near future. I expect to see a full page
advertisement in *The Saturday Evening Post*, making a slogan on behalf of
death. *Do not be deceived . . . die and see your dreams come true . . .
death does not harm the heart . . . it is absolutely harmless . . . doctors
everywhere recommend it . . .* and so on.

You hear a lot of sad talk about all the young men who died in the Great
War. Well, what about this war? Is it less real because it destroys with less
violence, with a ghastlier shock, with a more sustained pain?

The coming of snow in Manhattan is lovely. All the ugliness is softened
by the pious whiteness. But with the snow comes the deadly cold. With the
snow death comes a little closer to everyone. If you are pretty rich, it
doesn't bother you much: you don't have to get up in the morning in a
cold room and rush out to an Automat for a cup of coffee and then dive
into the subway. If you are rich, the snow is only beautiful to you. You get
up when you please, and there is nothing to do but sit in warm rooms and
talk with other rich people. But if you aren't rich, if you are working to
make America a nation of prosperous millionaires, then the snow is both
beautiful and ghastly. And when the cold of the snow gets into your bones
you are apt to forget that it is beautiful; you are apt to notice only that
it is ghastly.

A few evenings ago I was listening to the radio out here in San Francisco. Aspirin days are over for me. I depend on the sun these days. I was
listening to a very good program, sponsored by one of America's most prosperous manufacturers of aspirin. You know the name. I do not intend to
advertise the company. It does enough advertising of its own. The radio
announcer said the cold and sore throat season had come, and of course it
had. I could see snow falling over Manhattan, increasing the sales of aspirin
all over the city. Then the announcer said, Aspirin is a member of the
National Recovery Act.

It made me laugh to hear that. But it is the truth. Aspirin *is* a member
of the N.R.A. It *is* helping everyone to evade fundamentals, it *is* helping
to keep people going to work. Aspirin *is* helping to bring back prosperity.
It *is* doing its part. It *is* sending millions of half-dead people to their jobs.
It *is* doing a great deal to keep the spirit of this nation from disintegrating.
It *is* deadening pain everywhere. It *isn't* preventing anything, but it is deadening pain.

What about the National Recovery Act? Well, I leave that to you.
Maybe the N.R.A. is a member of aspirin. Anyhow, together they make a
pretty slick team. They are deadening a lot of pain, but they aren't preventing any pain. Everything is the same everywhere.

All I know is this: that if you keep on taking aspirin long enough it
will cease to deaden pain.

And that is when the fun begins. That is when you begin to notice that snow isn't beautiful at all. That is when your hair begins to freeze and you begin to get up in the middle of the night, laughing quietly, waiting for the worst, remembering all the pain and not wanting to evade it any longer, not wanting any longer to be half-dead, wanting full death or full life. That is when you begin to be mad about the way things are going in this country, the way things are with life, with man. That is when, weak as you are, something old and savage and defiant in you comes up bitterly out of your illness and starts to smash things, making a path for you to the sun, destroying cities, wrecking subways, pushing you into the sun, getting you away from evasions, dragging you by your neck to life.

It made me laugh, the way I used to laugh in New York, when I heard that radio announcer say that aspirin was a member of the N.R.A., and it made me remember. It made me want to say what I knew about aspirin.

A Curved Line

✿ ✿ ✿

I WAS living next door to the high school. In the evenings the lights would go on and I would see men and women in the rooms. I would see them moving about but I wouldn't be able to hear them. I could see that they were saying something among themselves and I thought I would like to go among them and listen. It was a place to go. I didn't want to improve my mind. I was through with all that. I was getting a letter from the Pelman Institute of America every two weeks. I wasn't taking their course. I wasn't even opening the envelopes. I knew exactly what they were saying. They were saying Chesterton and Ben Lindsey had taken their course and now had fine big brains, especially Chesterton. I knew they were telling me I too could have a fine big brain, but I wasn't opening the envelopes. I was turning the matter over to my niece who was four years old. I was thinking maybe she would like to take the course and have a brain like the wise men of the world. I was giving the letters to my niece, and she was taking them and sitting on the floor and cutting them with a pair of scissors. It was a fine thing. The Institute is a great American idea. My niece is cutting the letters with a small pair of scissors.

It was a place to go at night. I was tired of the radio. I had heard NRA speeches, excerpts from Carmen, Tosti's "Goodbye" and "Trees" every night for over a year. Sometimes twice a night. I knew what would happen every night. It was the same downtown. I knew all the movies, what to expect. The pattern never changed. It was the same with symphonies even. Once a lady conducted, but it was the same. Beethoven's Fifth, "The Sorcerer's Apprentice" and "The Blue Danube Waltz." It's been going on for years and years. The thing that worries me is that my great-grandchildren are going to have to listen to "The Blue Danube Waltz" too. It's gotten so that even when the music isn't being played, we hear it. It's gotten into us. Years ago I used to like these fine things, but lately the more pathetic things interest me.

I thought I would go among the people at the night school and listen to them. Going to the school was like walking from one room into another, it was so close. I liked the idea of walking headlong into a group of people who were either very lonely or pathetically ambitious.

The night I went was a Tuesday. The classes were English for Foreigners, Sewing, Dressmaking and Millinery, Leather Work, Wood Work, Radio, Arithmetic, Navigation, Theory of Flight, Typewriting and Commercial Art. I had the printed schedule.

I went to the class in Commercial Art. Beauty with a motive. Practical grace. I didn't know what to expect, but I walked in and sat down. There was a fat woman who gasped when she talked, and always talked. She was the teacher, and she had memorized a number of things from books about art and when I was in hearing distance I heard her gasp, "There are five arts, painting, sculpture, architecture, music, and poetry." She was telling this to a middle-aged, dried-up little lady who was amazed, almost astounded. The little lady had just come to class, and she hadn't heard. It was news to her, and she was amazed that there were five arts. It appeared as if she believed one might have been sufficient. There was a sheet of white paper on the table before her, pencil, bottle of ink and pen. She was delighted with the whole idea. She began to draw a picture of Marlene Dietrich. She had a ten-cent movie magazine to copy from, but her sketch didn't look like Marlene Dietrich. Everything was out of proportion. It looked like a very good Matisse. Only a very shrewd art critic would have been able to tell that it was not an original Matisse. It had all the artless subtlety. It was certainly the face of a woman. The dried-up lady couldn't think of anything else to draw. There were three other women drawing pictures of Marlene Dietrich. It was part of the course.

The men were painting display cards. They were thinking of increasing their incomes.

I heard the women talking about inspiration, and one of the younger women actually looked inspired, but I suppose she was slightly ill.

One of the men was making a pen and ink sketch of Lincoln. He was *absolutely* inspired. The instant I saw him I could tell he was aflame with wonderful sentiments. Every student of art draws Lincoln. There is something about the man. If you start to draw him, no matter how poorly you draw it will look exactly like Lincoln. It's the spirit, the inspiration. No one remembers how he looked. His face is like a trade-mark. The man had worked his sketch to the point where it was all but finished, and he was amazed. He was a man in his late thirties, and he wore a small Hitler-style moustache. I have reason to believe, however, that he was not a Nazi. It is simply that people, unknown to one another and separated by oceans and continents, are apt, now and then, to come upon the same sort of revelation in regard to some great human problem, such as sex, or to grow the same style of moustache. There is the well-known case of Havelock Ellis and D. H. Lawrence, beards and all. I sat at the table behind the man with the Nazi moustache. The teacher had said that she would be with me in a moment. I sat and watched the man who was sketching Lincoln. He was looking about nervously to see if anyone was noticing what he had done. He expected something to happen. He hadn't known he had had it in him. The others were mere sign painters.

There was a young girl on the opposite side of his table. She was doing a charcoal portrait of a pretty girl. I thought it was someone she knew. It was Clara Bow. I hadn't noticed the movie magazine she was copying from. She had already made her sketch of Marlene Dietrich. All over the class it was this way.

The man who was sketching Lincoln wanted the girl to notice what he had done, but she was busy putting the finishing touches on Clara Bow. Finally, with the will and impetuosity of the true artist, he got up and walked past the girl to get to the pencil sharpener. He wasn't using his pencil. He was making a pen and ink sketch of Lincoln. On his way back to his seat, he stood over the girl, studying carefully her sketch of Clara Bow. The girl couldn't draw with the man looking over her shoulder. She couldn't move her hand. She was embarrassed. The man said her sketch was very good, but that she hadn't shaded the eyes just right. Having made a sketch of Lincoln, he had become a graduate art critic. He wanted to talk about art first. The girl didn't know what to say. She said something I didn't quite hear. It was something apologetic and not well articulated. I felt sorry for the man. His idea hadn't worked. He had expected something to happen. He had expected a warm interest in him from the girl. He had hoped she would ask to see what he had done, and then he would have thrilled her with his sketch of Lincoln. It hadn't worked. He sat down sullenly and began to put the last touches to Lincoln. Then he signed his name to the work and ran a heavy line beneath his name, giving it force and character. When the roll was taken I found out that the girl's name was Harriet. I didn't get the last name. She looked to be a clerk in the basement of some big department store. She was probably lonely too.

Now the teacher was free to introduce me to art. She stood over me and gasped, and I got a strong odor from her. She began with the five arts and kept on. She had a schedule. She enjoyed going through the schedule, or else it was simply that, like so many teachers, she was unmarried and had to do something, had to talk at least. The first thing I began listening to was about line. It took me that long to get used to her odor.

"By line," she gasped, "we mean the boundaries of shapes. A vertical line denotes activity and growth. A horizontal line denotes rest and repose." She had it pat. "A straight line is masculine," she said. "A curved line is feminine." She went on gasping. I couldn't tell what pleasure she got from it. I certainly hadn't encouraged her. "A vertical line," she said, "slightly curved is considered a line of beauty." There was an exclamation mark in her voice.

"Considered?" I said. "How do you mean?"

Then she understood that I was a radical, and that I was out for no good. She became confused for a moment, then blushed with bitterness, then walked away to get me paper and a pencil. She placed the paper and pencil before me and told me I could draw anything I liked. I tried to draw the dried-up lady who had been amazed about art, and while I was doing so I could hear the teacher gasping to someone else, "There are three fundamental forms. They are the sphere, the cone, the cylinder, or modifications of them." My sketch of the amazed lady was very poor. I hadn't been able to get her amazement into it.

After an hour there was a short recess. Everyone sighed and went into the hall or out on the school steps. I offered the man who had sketched Lincoln a cigarette. He didn't smoke, but he got to talking. He talked in a low dreary voice. We stood on the school steps and I listened to him while I smoked a cigarette. It was February. The evening was mild. I was standing there smoking, listening to the man. I didn't get a word of what he was saying. I told him his sketch of Lincoln was as good as the one he had copied it from, maybe better. When the bell rang we walked back to the room and sat down again.

The genius of the class came at eight for the second period only. She was a woman of about forty with a well-rounded body and gold teeth in her mouth. She wore a green sweater tight, and she was the only artist in the class who worked standing. She stood at the front of the class with her legs apart, one of those forty-year-old women who have young bodies. She was sketching a small plaster reproduction of a nude Grecian youth. With her back to me I could admire her, and there are women who are lovely from this point of view and unbearable from any other. One could sit and look at her for a long while, thinking about lines and which were feminine and which masculine, which denoted activity and which repose. It was a thing to do, a way to kill time. She had an old face, but from where I sat I couldn't see her face.

It felt splendid to be among such a group of people, and walking home after class I decided I would go back the next evening and find out more about the man who had sketched Lincoln, and the girl he secretly loved, and the lady in the green sweater, and the amazed one, and the fat teacher who gasped. It would be something to do for a while, a place to go in the evening.

1, 2, 3, 4, 5, 6, 7, 8

✿ ✿ ✿

WALKING through Woolworth's in 1927, he saw a small crowd of shoppers working swiftly with their arms over a table stacked high with phonograph records. He went over to find out what it was all about, and it was a special, new Victor and Brunswick records, five cents each, and a wide choice of titles to choose from. Well, he hadn't heard the phonograph in months. He might wind it up again and listen to it. The phonograph was pretty much himself. He had gotten into the machine and come out of it, singing, or being a symphony, or a wild jazz composition. For months he hadn't gone near the phonograph, and it had stood in his room, dusty and mute.

These five-cent records reminded him that he had been silent through the phonograph for a long time, and that he might again enjoy emerging from it.

He selected a half dozen records and took them to his room. He was certain that none of the records could be very good, but he wasn't seeking anything good and he didn't mind how trivial or trite the music might be. If a thing is terribly bad, anything, a man or a piece of music, it is a form of exploration to go through the thing. He knew that he could do this with the worst sort of American jazz. The melody could be idiotic, the orchestration noisy, and so on, but somewhere in the racket he would be able, by listening carefully, to hear the noblest weeping or laughter of mortality. Sometimes it would be a sudden and brief bit of counterpoint, several chords of a banjo perhaps, and occasionally it would be the sadness in the voice of some very poor vocalist singing a chorus of a very insipid song. Something largely accidental, something inevitable.

You could not do this with the finer music. The virtues of the finer music were intentional. They were there for everybody, unmistakably.

It was early August, I think. (I am speaking of myself.) For many months he had not listened to himself through the phonograph, and now he was taking these new records home.

In August a young man is apt to feel unspeakably alive: in those days I was an employee of a telegraph company. I used to sit at a table all day, working a teletype machine, sending and receiving telegrams, and when the day was over I used to feel this unspeakable liveliness, but at the same time I used to feel lost. Absolutely misplaced. I seemed to feel that they had gotten me so deeply into the mechanical idea of the age that I was doomed eventually to become a fragment of a machine myself. It was a way to earn money, this sitting before the machine. I disliked it very much, but it was a way.

He knew that he was lost in it and that they were taking out the insides of him and putting in a complicated mass of wheels and springs and hammers and levers, a piece of junk that worked precisely, doing a specific thing over and over again, precisely.

All day I used to sit at the machine, being a great help to American industry. I used to send important telegrams to important people accurately. The things that were going on had nothing to do with me, but I was sitting there, working for America. What I wanted, I think, was a house. I was living in a cheap rooming house, alone. I had a floor and a roof and a half dozen books. The books I could not read. They were by great writers. I could not read them: I was sitting all day at the table, helping my country to become the most prosperous one in the world. I had a bed. I used to fall asleep sometimes from sheer exhaustion. It would be very late at night or early in the morning. A man cannot sleep anywhere. If a room has no meaning for you, if it is not a part of you, you cannot sleep in it. This room that I was living in was not a part of me. It belonged to anybody who could afford to pay three dollars a week rent for it. I was there, living. I was almost nineteen, crazy as a bat.

He wanted a house, a place in which to return to himself, a space protected by lumber and glass, under the sun, upon the earth.

He took the six records up to his room. Looking out of the small window of his small room, he saw that he was lost. This amused him. It was a thing to make slurring conversation for entertainment. He walked about in his room, his hat still on his head, talking to the place. Well, here we are at home, he said.

I forget what he ate that night, but I know he cooked it on a small gas-range that was provided by the landlady for cooking as well as suicide. He ate something, washed and wiped the dishes he had used, and then turned to the phonograph.

There was a chance for him to find out what it was all about. There was a chance that the information would be hidden in the jazz music. It was a thought. He had learned something about machinery, American machines working, through jazz. He had been able to picture ten thousand humpback New York women in an enormous room, sewing on machines. He had been able to see machines bigger than mountains, machines that did big things, created power, conserved energy, produced flashlights, locomotives, tin cans, saxophones.

It was a small phonograph, not a portable, but a small Victor. He had had it for years, and he had taken it with him from place to place. It was very impractical to carry such a phonograph around, and he knew it was impractical, but he always carried it with him when he moved from one room to another, or from one city to another. Even if he hadn't used the phonograph for months, he would take it away with him. He liked to feel that it was always there and that whenever he liked he could listen to it. It was like having an enormous sum of money in the bank, a sum so large that you were afraid to touch it. He could listen to any music he liked. He had Roumanian folk songs, Negro spirituals, American westerns, American jazz, Grieg, Beethoven, Gershwin, Zez Confrey, Brahms, Schubert, Irving Berlin, *Where the River Shannon's Flowing*, *Ave Maria*, *Vesti La Giubba*, Caruso, Rachmaninoff, Vernon Dalhart, Kreisler, Al Jolson. It was all there, in the records, himself in the music, and for months he had not listened to the phonograph. A silence had come over him and the phonograph, and as time went by, it had become more and more difficult to break the silence.

He had begun to feel lost months ago. One evening, from a moving streetcar, he had suddenly noticed the sky. It was a terrific fact, the existence of the sky. Noticing it, looking up into it, with night coming on, he had realized how lost he had become.

But he hadn't done anything about the matter. He had begun to want a house of his own, but he hadn't done anything to get a house.

He stood over his phonograph, thinking of its silence and his own silence, the fear in himself to make a noise, to declare his existence.

He lifted the phonograph from the floor and placed it on his small eating table. The phonograph was very dusty, and he spent a leisurely ten minutes cleaning it. When he was through cleaning it, greater fear came over him, and he wanted for a moment to put it back again on the floor and let it remain silent. After a while he wound the machine slowly, hoping secretly that something inside of it would break, so that he would not be able, after all, to make a noise in the world.

I remember clearly how amazed I was when nothing in the machine snapped. I thought, after all these months of silence, how strange. In a moment sound will be emerging from the box. I do not know the scientific name for this sort of fright, but I know that I was very frightened. I felt that it would be best if my being lost were to remain a secret. I felt certain that I no longer wanted to make a noise, and at the same time I felt that, since I had brought home these new records, I ought at least to hear them once before putting them away with the other records I had accumulated.

I listened to the six records, to both sides of them, that night. I had purchased soft needles, so that the phonograph should not make too much of a noise and disturb the other dwellers in the rooming house, but after months of silence, the volume of sound that emerged from the phonograph was very great. It was so great that I had to smoke cigarettes all the time, and I remember the knock at my door.

It was the landlady, Mrs. Liebig. She said, Ah, it is you, Mr. Romano. A little music, is that it? Well . . .

Yes, I said. Several new records. I shall be done with them in a moment.

She hadn't liked the idea of my playing a phonograph in her rooming house, but I had been with her so long, and I had paid so regularly and kept my room so orderly that she hadn't wanted to come right out and tell me so. I knew, however.

The records were all dull and a little boring. All except one. There was one passage of syncopation in this record that was tremendously interesting to me. I played this passage three or four times that night in an effort to understand its significance, but I got nowhere. I understood the passage technically, but I could not determine why it moved me so strangely. It was a bit of counterpoint to a rather romantic and therefore insipid melody. It was eight swift chords on the banjo, repeated fourteen times, while the melody grew in emotional intensity, reached a climax, and then dwindled to silence. *One two three four five six seven eight,* swiftly, fourteen times. The sound was wiry. There was something about the dogged persistence of the passage that got into me, something about it that had always been in me, but never before articulated. I won't mention the name of the composition because I am sure the effect it had on me was largely accidental, largely inevitable for me alone, and that anyone else who might listen to the passage will not be moved by it the way I was moved. The circumstances would have to be pretty much like the circumstances of my own existence at the time, and you would have to be about nineteen years of age, crazy as a bat, etc.

He put away the records and forgot them. Their music joined all the other music he had ever heard and became lost. A week went by. One evening suddenly, in his silence, he heard the passage again, *one two three four five six seven eight,* fourteen times. Another week went by. Every now and then he would hear the passage. It would be when he felt unspeakably alive, when he seemed to possess strength enough to smash everything in the earth that was ugly.

There was nothing for me to do in the city Sundays, so I used to work. Sitting at the teletype machine had become the major business of my life, so I used to work on Sundays too. But on Sundays business would be very slow, and most of the day I would sit around in the office, moping, dreaming, thinking about the house I wanted to get for myself. The teletype machine sends and receives messages. It is a great mechanical triumph, and it put thousands of old-time telegraphers out of work. These men used to get as much as a dollar an hour for their work, but when the teletype machine was perfected and put into use these men lost their jobs and young fellows like me who didn't know the first thing about regular telegraphy got their jobs. It was a great stroke of efficiency, the perfection of this machine. It saved the telegraph companies millions of dollars every year. I used to earn about twenty-eight cents an hour, and I used to be able to send and receive twice as many telegrams as the fastest telegraph operator would have been able to receive and send in the same length of time. But on Sundays business would be very slow and the teletype would be silent sometimes for as long as an hour.

One Sunday morning, after a long silence, my machine began to function, so I went over to it to receive and check the message, but it was not a message, not a regular telegram. I read the words, *hello hello hello.* I had never thought of the machine as being related in any way to me. It was there for the messages of other people, and the tapping of this greeting to me seemed very startling. For one thing, it was strictly against company rules to use the machine for anything other than the transmission of regular business. It was a breach of company discipline for a teletype operator, and it was because of this fact that I began to think a great deal of the other operator who had sent me the greeting. I typed the word *hello,* and we began a conversation.

It seemed very strange for me to be using the machine in a way useful to myself. I talked with the other operator for about an hour. It was a girl, and she was working in the operating room at the main office. I was working in one of the numerous branch offices in the city. We did a lot of talking for about an hour, and then suddenly I read the words *wire chief,* so I knew that the big shot had returned to the room and that we would not be able to go on talking.

Suddenly, in the silence, he began to hear the passage again, *one two three four five six seven eight,* over and over again, and it began to have specific meaning for him: the house, the clean earth around it, the warm sun, and another, *one two three four five six seven eight,* himself and this other and the house and the earth and the sun and clear senses and deep sleep and *one two three four five six seven eight,* and meaning and fullness and no sense of being lost and no feeling of being caught.

I began to try to visualize the girl. I began to wonder if she would go out with me to this house I wanted and help me fill it with our lives, together. After a while the teletype machine began to tap again, and again I read *hello hello, wire chief gone.*

It was very splendid, the way it happened, a breach of company discipline and so on.

At five o'clock in the afternoon she came down from the main office and walked into the office where I was working. She hadn't said she was coming down, but the moment she stepped into the office I knew who she was because as soon as I saw her face I began to hear the music, *one two three four five six seven eight,* swiftly, and it was so bad with me that I wanted to leap over the counter and embrace her and tell her about the house.

We talked politely instead.

At six o'clock, when he was through working for the day, he walked with her out of the city to her house, talking with her, hearing the music over and over again. For the first time in months he began really to laugh. She was splendid. Her mind was deliciously alive; she loved mischief, and in her eyes he seemed to see the earth, the bright earth, full of light and warmth, and the strength of growing things. It was a place to build the house and to be alive and himself.

That evening he played the record over and over again, and finally the landlady came to his room and said, Mr. Romano, it is almost half past eleven.

They got to be pretty good friends, and he began to tell her about the house. At first she didn't really listen to what he said; she merely listened to the way he said it, but after a while she began to listen to everything he had to say, all the insane things about the machines getting into them and destroying them and destroying everything decent in them.

They stopped working Sundays and began going across the bay to Marin County. Every Sunday they walked into the hills of Marin County, talking about the house. All during September and October, 1927, they were together on Sundays, walking in the hills across the bay from San Francisco.

The feeling of being lost began to leave him. There was at least one person in the world who knew that he was alive and attached some importance to the fact, and for a while it looked as if the house he had wanted so long would actually materialize, and he would enter it with this girl, laughing, and they would be in it together, forever and forever.

I have said that he was nineteen.

Forever and forever, this is the amusing part. All day long at the teletype machine he would hear the music, *one two three four five six seven eight*, forever and forever and forever, and this girl and this music and the house that was to be, all mingled, and for a while he believed in the inevitability of his hope.

I am coming now to the truth. I am not permitting myself to make a story.

In August and September and October, because of something inexplicable, atmospheric if you like, they were splendidly one, melody and counterpoint, precisely, perfectly, and the dream of eternity was not a fantastic dream.

The house, they wanted. They wanted it desperately. In August and September and October. They wanted themselves desperately. And so on.

Things happen. They happen subtly, quietly, strangely. Everything for a moment is thus: then when one looks again, everything is changed and is now *thus*: a new configuration, the blood thus, the earth thus, and the meaning of life thus. There is nothing you can do about it. Only art is precise and everlastingly itself: everlastingly dependable.

They did not quarrel. The girl did not get sick and die. She did not run off with another young man or with an older rich man.

All of a sudden, the melody was silenced, the counterpoint faded away. It was November.

I used to sit in my room, trying to understand what had happened to us. The house. Why, it was laughable. How would I ever be able to own a house on my salary? The feeling of being lost. That was nonsense. It was absolutely stupid. I used to walk up and down my room, smoking one cigarette after another, trying to understand the sudden toppling of the edifice we had built for ourselves. I wanted to know why we no longer wanted to go away from the city. It was not the girl alone. I myself had stopped talking about the house. I myself had stopped hearing the music, and suddenly the silence had returned, and I was standing in the midst

of it, again lost, but now without the wish to return to myself. Let it go,
I felt. Let it stand as it is. And so on.

During the winter they gradually fell away from one another, and then
suddenly in March, 1928, he knew that the whole business was a thing of
the past, that it was dead.
Something happened to her. She lost her job. She moved away, to
another address, to another city, he didn't know which. He lost track of
her.
In June something happened to him.

One afternoon I was sitting at the teletype machine, working it, and
all of a sudden I began to hear the passage, *one two three four five six seven
eight*, swiftly, and I began to see her face and the landscape that was her
eyes, and I began to hear her laughter, *one two three four five six seven
eight*, and as I worked the machine this music and the remembrance of this
girl and the resurrection of the house we were to have made for ourselves,
all these things began to be in my mind the way they had been in the
summer, as truth and reality, and I began to feel lost and bewildered and
confused.

That evening he played the record, but he listened to it only once because it brought tears to his eyes. He had laughed at the tears, but he had
not dared to listen to the music a second time. The whole thing was really
very amusing, he thought. He had got the music and the girl and the house
together as one significance in his mind, and it was amusing.

But the next day I began trying to locate her. It happened automatically.
I was taking a walk and before I knew it I was at her old address, asking
the people who had moved into the house if they knew where she had gone.
They did not know. I walked until one o'clock in the morning. The music
was getting into me again, and I was beginning to hear it very often.

Whenever he sat down to operate the teletype machine, he would begin
to hear the music, emerging from the machine, *one two three four five six
seven eight*. Every Sunday he found himself begging the machine to bring
her to him again. It was preposterous. He knew that she was no longer
with the company, and yet he found himself expecting the machine to
tap out her old greeting to him, *hello hello hello*. It was preposterous.
Absolutely.
He had never known a great deal about her. He had known her name
and what she had meant to him, but nothing more.
And the music: over and over again.
One afternoon, he got up from the teletype machine and removed his
work jacket. It was a little after two, and he quit his job and went away
with his money. I don't want any of the prosperity, he said. He went up to
his room and put all the things he wanted to take away with him into two
suitcases.
The phonograph and the records he presented to Mrs. Liebig, the landlady. The phonograph is old, he told her, and it is apt to groan now and
then, especially when you put on anything by Beethoven. But it still runs.
The records aren't much. There is some decent music, but most of the
records are monotonous jazz. He was feeling the music while he was

speaking to the landlady, and it was really paining him to be leaving the phonograph and the records in a strange house, but he was sure he didn't want them any longer.

Walking from the waiting room of the depot to the train, I could feel the music tearing out my heart, and when the train began to get under way and when the whistle screamed, I was sitting helplessly, weeping for this girl and the house, and sneering at myself for wanting more of life than there was in life to have.

Laughter

☼ ☼ ☼

YOU want me to laugh?"
He felt lonely and ill in the empty class-room, all the boys going home, Dan Seed, James Misippo, Dick Corcoran, all of them walking along the Southern Pacific tracks, laughing and playing, and this insane idea of Miss Wissig's, making him sick.
"Yes."
The severe lips, the trembling, the eyes, such pathetic melancholy.
"But I do not want to laugh."
It was strange. The whole world, the turn of things, the way they came about.
"Laugh."
The increasing tenseness, electrical, her stiffness, the nervous movements of her body and her arms, the cold she made, and the illness in his blood.
"But why?"
Why? Everything tied up, everything graceless and ugly, the caught mind, something in a trap, no sense, no meaning.
"As a punishment. You laughed in class, now as a punishment you must laugh for an hour, all alone, by yourself. Hurry, you have already wasted four minutes."
It was disgusting; it wasn't funny at all, being kept after school, being asked to laugh. There was no sense in the idea. What should he laugh about? A fellow couldn't just laugh. There had to be something of that kind, something amusing or pompous, something comical. This was so strange, because of her manner, the way she looked at him, the subtlety; it was frightening. What did she want of him? And the smell of school, the oil in the floor, chalk dust, the smell of the idea, children gone; loneliness, the sadness.
"I am sorry I laughed."
The flower bending, ashamed. He felt sorry, he was not merely bluffing; he *was* sorry, not for himself but for her. She was a young girl, a substitute teacher, and there was that sadness in her, so far away and so hard to understand; it came with her each morning and he had laughed at it, it

was comical, something she said, the way she said it, the way she stared at everyone, the way she moved. He hadn't felt like laughing at all, but all of a sudden he had laughed and she had looked at him and he had looked into her face, and for a moment that vague communion, then the anger, the hatred, in her eyes. "You will stay in after school." He hadn't wanted to laugh, it simply happened, and he was sorry, he was ashamed, she ought to know, he was telling her. Jiminy crickets.

"You are wasting time. Begin laughing."

Her back was turned and she was erasing words from the blackboard: *Africa, Cairo, the pyramids, the sphinx, Nile*; and the figures 1865, 1914. But the tenseness, even with her back turned; it was still in the class-room, emphasized because of the emptiness, magnified, made precise, his mind and her mind, their grief, side by side, conflicting; why? He wanted to be friendly; the morning she had entered the class-room he had wanted to be friendly; he felt it immediately, her strangeness, the remoteness, so why had he laughed? Why did everything happen in a false way? Why should he be the one to hurt her, when really he had wanted to be her friend from the beginning?

"I don't want to laugh."

Defiance and at the same time weeping, shameful weeping in his voice. By what right should he be made to destroy in himself an innocent thing? He hadn't meant to be cruel; why shouldn't she be able to understand? He began to feel hatred for her stupidity, her dullness, the stubbornness of her will. I will not laugh, he thought; she can call Mr. Caswell and have me whipped; I will not laugh again. It was a mistake. I had meant to cry; something else, anyway; I hadn't meant it. I can stand a whipping, golly Moses, it hurts, but not like this; I've felt that strap on my behind, I know the difference.

Well, let them whip him, what did he care? It stung and he could feel the sharp pain for days after, thinking about it, but let them go ahead and make him bend over, he wouldn't laugh.

He saw her sit at her desk and stare at him, and for crying out loud, she looked sick and startled, and the pity came up to his mouth again, the sickening pity for her, and why was he making so much trouble for a poor substitute teacher he really liked, not an old and ugly teacher, but a nice small girl who was frightened from the first?

"Please laugh."

And what humiliation, not commanding him, begging him now, begging him to laugh when he didn't want to laugh. What should a fellow do, honestly; what should a fellow do that would be right, by his own will, not accidentally, like the wrong things? And what did she mean? What pleasure could she get out of hearing him laugh? What a stupid world, the strange feelings of people, the secretiveness, each person hidden within himself, wanting something and always getting something else, wanting to give something and always giving something else. Well, he would. Now he would laugh, not for himself but for her. Even if it sickened him, he would laugh. He wanted to know the truth, how it was. She wasn't *making* him laugh, she was *asking* him, *begging* him to laugh. He didn't know how it was, but he wanted to know. He thought, Maybe I can think of a funny story, and he began to try to remember all the funny stories he had ever heard, but it was very strange, he couldn't remember a single one. And the other funny things, the way Annie Gran walked; gee, it wasn't funny any more; and Henry Mayo making fun of Hiawatha, saying the lines wrong; it wasn't funny either. It used to make him laugh until his face got red and he lost his breath, but now it was a dead and a pointless thing, *by the big sea waters, by the big sea waters, came the mighty,* but gee, it wasn't funny; he couldn't laugh about it, golly Moses. Well, he would just laugh, any old laugh, be an actor, ha, ha, ha. God, it was hard, the easiest thing in the world for him to do, and now he couldn't make a little giggle.

Somehow he began to laugh, feeling ashamed and disgusted. He was afraid to look into her eyes, so he looked up at the clock and tried to keep on laughing, and it was startling, to ask a boy to laugh for an hour, at nothing, to beg him to laugh without giving him a reason. But he would do it, maybe not an hour, but he would try, anyway; he would do something. The funniest thing was his voice, the falseness of his laughter, and after a while it got to be really funny, a comical thing, and it made him happy because it made him really laugh, and now he was laughing his real way, with all his breath, with all his blood, laughing at the falseness of his laughter, and the shame was going away because this laughter was not fake, and it was the truth, and the empty class-room was full of his laughter and everything seemed all right, everything was splendid, and two minutes had gone by.

And he began to think of really comical things everywhere, the whole town, the people walking in the streets, trying to look important, but he knew, they couldn't fool him, he knew how important they were, and the way they talked, big business, and all of it pompous and fake, and it made him laugh, and he thought of the preacher at the Presbyterian church, the fake way he prayed, O God, *if it is your will,* and nobody believing in prayers, and the important people with big automobiles, Cadillacs and Packards, speeding up and down the country, as if they had some place to go, and the public band concerts, all that fake stuff, making him really laugh, and the big boys running after the big girls because of the heat, and the streetcars going up and down the city with never more than two passengers, that was funny, those big cars carrying an old lady and a man with a moustache, and he laughed until he lost his breath and his face got red, and suddenly all the shame was gone and he was laughing and looking at Miss Wissig, and then bang: jiminy Christmas, tears in her eyes. For God's sake, he hadn't been laughing at her. He had been laughing at all those fools, all those fool things they were doing day after day, all that falseness. It was disgusting. He was always wanting to do the right thing, and it was always turning out the other way. He wanted to know why, how it was with her, inside, the part that was secret, and he had laughed for her, not to please himself, and there she was, trembling, her eyes wet and tears coming out of them, and her face in agony, and he was still laughing because of all the anger and yearning and disappointment in his heart, and he was laughing at all the pathetic things in the world, the things good people cried about, the stray dogs in the streets, the tired horses being whipped, stumbling, the timid people being smashed inwardly by the fat and cruel people, fat inside, pompous, and the small birds, dead on the sidewalk, and the misunderstandings everywhere, the everlasting conflict, the cruelty, the things that made man a malignant thing, a vile growth, and the anger was changing his laughter and tears were coming into his eyes. The two of them in the empty class-room, naked together in their loneliness and bewilderment, brother and sister, both of them wanting the same cleanliness and decency of life, both of them wanting to share the truth of the other, and yet, somehow, both of them alien, remote and alone.

He heard the girl stifle a sob and then everything turned up-side-down, and he was crying, honest and truly crying, like a baby, as if something had really happened, and he hid his face in his arms, and his chest was heaving, and he was thinking he did not want to live; if this was the way it was, he wanted to be dead.

He did not know how long he cried, and suddenly he was aware that he was no longer crying or laughing, and that the room was very still. What a shameful thing. He was afraid to lift his head and look at the teacher. It was disgusting.

"Ben."

The voice calm, quiet, solemn; how could he ever look at her again?

"Ben."

He lifted his head. Her eyes were dry and her face seemed brighter and more beautiful than ever.

"Please dry your eyes. Have you a handkerchief?"

"Yes."

He wiped the moisture from his eyes, and blew his nose. What a sickness in the earth. How bleak everything was.

"How old are you, Ben?"

"Ten."

"What are you going to do? I mean—"

"I don't know."

"Your father?"

"He is a tailor."

"Do you like it here?"

"I guess so."

"You have brothers, sisters?"

"Three brothers, two sisters."

"Do you ever think of going away? Other cities?"

It was amazing, talking to him as if he were a grown person, getting into his secret.

"Yes."

"Where?"

"I don't know. New York, I guess. The old country, maybe."

"The old country?"

"Milan. My father's city."

"Oh."

He wanted to ask her about herself, where she had been, where she was going; he wanted to be grown up, but he was afraid. She went to the cloakroom and brought out her coat and hat and purse, and began to put on her coat.

"I will not be here tomorrow. Miss Shorb is well again. I am going away."

He felt very sad, but he could think of nothing to say. She tightened the belt of her coat and placed her hat on her head, smiling, golly Moses, what a world, first she made him laugh, then she made him cry, and now this. And it made him feel so lonely for her. Where was she going? Wouldn't he ever see her again?

"You may go now, Ben."

And there he was looking up at her and not wanting to go, there he was wanting to sit and look at her. He got up slowly and went to the cloakroom for his cap. He walked to the door, feeling ill with loneliness, and turned to look at her for the last time.

"Good-bye, Miss Wissig."

"Good-bye, Ben."

And then he was running lickety split across the school grounds, and the young substitute teacher was standing in the yard, following him with her eyes. He didn't know what to think, but he knew that he was feeling very sad and that he was afraid to turn around and see if she was looking at him. He thought, If I hurry, maybe I can catch up with Dan Seed and Dick Corcoran and the other boys, and maybe I'll be in time to see the freight train leaving town. Well, nobody would know, anyway. Nobody would ever know what had happened and how he had laughed and cried.

He ran all the way to the Southern Pacific tracks, and all the boys were gone, and the train was gone, and he sat down beneath the eucalyptus trees. The whole world, in a mess.

Then he began to cry again.

The Shepherd's Daughter

✿ ✿ ✿

IT is the opinion of my grandmother, God bless her, that all men should labor, and at the table, a moment ago, she said to me: You must learn to do some good work, the making of some item useful to man, something out of clay, or out of wood, or metal, or cloth. It is not proper for a young man to be ignorant of an honorable craft. Is there anything you can make? Can you make a simple table, a chair, a plain dish, a rug, a coffee pot? Is there anything you can do?

And my grandmother looked at me with anger.

I know, she said, you are supposed to be a writer, and I suppose you are. You certainly smoke enough cigarettes to be anything, and the whole house is full of smoke, but you must learn to make solid things, things that can be used, that can be seen and touched.

There was a king of the Persians, said my grandmother, and he had a son, and this boy fell in love with a shepherd's daughter. He went to his father and he said, My lord, I love a shepherd's daughter, and I would have her for my wife. And the king said, I am king and you are my son and when I die you shall be king, how can it be that you would marry the daughter of a shepherd? And the son said, My lord, I do not know but I know that I love this girl and would have her for my queen.

The king saw that his son's love for the girl was from God, and he said, I will send a message to her. And he called a messenger to him and he said, Go to the shepherd's daughter and say that my son loves her and would have her for his wife. And the messenger went to the girl and he said, The king's son loves you and would have you for his wife. And the girl said, What labor does he do? And the messenger said, Why, he is the son of the king; he does no labor. And the girl said, He must learn to do some labor. And the messenger returned to the king and spoke the words of the shepherd's daughter.

The king said to his son, The shepherd's daughter wishes you to learn some craft. Would you still have her for your wife? And the son said, Yes, I will learn to weave straw rugs. And the boy was taught to weave rugs of straw, in patterns and in colors and with ornamental designs, and at the end of three days he was making very fine straw rugs, and the messenger returned to the shepherd's daughter, and he said, These rugs of straw are the work of the king's son.

And the girl went with the messenger to the king's palace, and she became the wife of the king's son.

One day, said my grandmother, the king's son was walking through the streets of Bagdad, and he came upon an eating place which was so clean and cool that he entered it and sat at a table.

This place, said my grandmother, was a place of thieves and murderers, and they took the king's son and placed him in a large dungeon where many great men of the city were being held, and the thieves and murderers were killing the fattest of the men and feeding them to the leanest of them, and making sport of it. The king's son was of the leanest of the men, and it was not known that he was the son of the king of the Persians, so his life was spared, and he said to the thieves and murderers, I am a weaver of straw rugs and these rugs have great value. And they brought him straw and asked him to weave and in three days he weaved three rugs, and he said, Carry these rugs to the palace of the king of the Persians, and for each rug he will give you a hundred gold pieces of money. And the rugs were carried to the palace of the king, and when the king saw the rugs he saw that they were the work of his son and he took the rugs to the shepherd's daughter and he said, These rugs were brought to the palace and they are the work of my son who is lost. And the shepherd's daughter took each rug and looked at it closely and in the design of each rug she saw in the written language of the Persians a message from her husband, and she related this message to the king.

And the king, said my grandmother, sent many soldiers to the place of the thieves and murderers, and the soldiers rescued all the captives and killed all the thieves and murderers, and the king's son was returned safely to the palace of his father, and to the company of his wife, the little shepherd's daughter. And when the boy went into the palace and saw again his wife, he humbled himself before her and he embraced her feet, and he said, My love, it is because of you that I am alive, and the king was greatly pleased with the shepherd's daughter.

Now, said my grandmother, do you see why every man should learn an honorable craft?

I see very clearly, I said, and as soon as I earn enough money to buy a saw and a hammer and a piece of lumber I shall do my best to make a simple chair or a shelf for books.

The Daring Young Man on the Flying Trapeze

✼ ✼ ✼

I. SLEEP

HORIZONTALLY wakeful amid universal widths, practising laughter and mirth, satire, the end of all, of Rome and yes of Babylon, clenched teeth, remembrance, much warmth volcanic, the streets of Paris, the plains of Jericho, much gliding as of reptile in abstraction, a gallery of watercolors, the sea and the fish with eyes, symphony, a table in the corner of the Eiffel Tower, jazz at the opera house, alarm clock and the tap-dancing of doom, conversation with a tree, the river Nile, Cadillac coupe to Kansas, the roar of Dostoyevsky, and the dark sun.

This earth, the face of one who lived, the form without the weight, weeping upon snow, white music, the magnified flower twice the size of the universe, black clouds, the caged panther staring, deathless space, Mr. Eliot with rolled sleeves baking bread, Flaubert and Guy de Maupassant, a wordless rhyme of early meaning, Finlandia, mathematics highly polished and slick as a green onion to the teeth, Jerusalem, the path to paradox.

The deep song of man, the sly whisper of someone unseen but vaguely known, hurricane in the cornfield, a game of chess, hush the queen, the king, Karl Franz, black Titanic, Mr. Chaplin weeping, Stalin, Hitler, a multitude of Jews, tomorrow is Monday, no dancing in the streets.

O swift moment of life: it is ended, the earth is again now.

II. WAKEFULNESS

He (the living) dressed and shaved, grinning at himself in the mirror. Very unhandsome, he said; where is my tie? (He had but one.) Coffee and a gray sky, Pacific Ocean fog, the drone of a passing streetcar, people going to the city, time again, the day, prose and poetry. He moved swiftly down the stairs to the street and began to walk, thinking suddenly, *It is only in sleep that we may know that we live. There only, in that living death, do we meet ourselves and the far earth, God and the saints, the names of our fathers, the substance of remote moments; it is there that the centuries merge in the moment, that the vast becomes the tiny, tangible atom of eternity.*

He walked into the day as alertly as might be, making a definite noise with his heels, perceiving with his eyes the superficial truth of streets and structures, the trivial truth of reality. Helplessly his mind sang, *He flies through the air with the greatest of ease; the daring young man on the flying trapeze;* then laughed with all the might of his being. It was really a splendid morning: gray, cold, and cheerless, a morning for inward vigor; ah, Edgar Guest, he said, how I long for your music.

In the gutter he saw a coin which proved to be a penny dated 1923, and placing it in the palm of his hand he examined it closely, remembering that year and thinking of Lincoln whose profile was stamped upon the coin. There was almost nothing a man could do with a penny. I will purchase a motorcar, he thought. I will dress myself in the fashion of a fop, visit the hotel strumpets, drink and dine, and then return to the quiet. Or I will drop the coin into a slot and weigh myself.

It was good to be poor, and the Communists—but it was no good to be hungry. What appetites they had, how fond they were of food! Empty stomachs. He remembered how greatly he needed food. Every meal was bread and coffee and cigarettes, and now he had no more bread. Coffee without bread could never honestly serve as supper, and there were no weeds in the park that could be cooked as spinach is cooked.

If the truth were known, he was half starved, and yet there was still no end of books he ought to read before he died. He remembered the young Italian in a Brooklyn hospital, a small sick clerk named Mollica, who had said desperately, I would like to see California once before I die. And he thought earnestly, I ought at least to read *Hamlet* once again; or perhaps *Huckleberry Finn*.

It was then that he became thoroughly awake: at the thought of dying. Now wakefulness was a state in the nature of a sustained shock. A young man could perish rather unostentatiously, he thought; and already he was very nearly starved. Water and prose were fine, they filled much inorganic space, but they were inadequate. If there were only some work he might do for money, some trivial labor in the name of commerce. If they would only allow him to sit at a desk all day and add trade figures, subtract and multiply and divide, then perhaps he would not die. He would buy food, all sorts of it: untasted delicacies from Norway, Italy, and France; all manner of beef, lamb, fish, cheese; grapes, figs, pears, apples, melons, which he would worship when he had satisfied his hunger. He would place a bunch of red grapes on a dish beside two black figs, a large yellow pear, and a green apple. He would hold a cut melon to his nostrils for hours. He would buy great brown loaves of French bread, vegetables of all sorts, meat; he would buy life.

From a hill he saw the city standing majestically in the east, great towers, dense with his kind, and there he was suddenly outside of it all, almost definitely certain that he should never gain admittance, almost positive that somehow he had ventured upon the wrong earth, or perhaps into the wrong age, and now a young man of twenty-two was to be permanently ejected from it. This thought was not saddening. He said to himself, Sometime soon I must write *An Application for Permission to Live*. He accepted the thought of dying without pity for himself or for man, believing that he would at least sleep another night. His rent for another day was paid; there was yet another tomorrow. And after that he might go where other homeless men went. He might even visit the Salvation Army—sing to God and Jesus (unlover of my soul), be saved, eat and sleep. But he knew that he would not. His life was a private life. He did not wish to destroy this fact. Any other alternative would be better.

Through the air on the flying trapeze, his mind hummed. Amusing it was, astoundingly funny. A trapeze to God, or to nothing, a flying trapeze to some sort of eternity; he prayed objectively for strength to make the flight with grace.

I have one cent, he said. It is an American coin. In the evening I shall polish it until it glows like a sun and I shall study the words.

He was now walking in the city itself, among living men. There were one or two places to go. He saw his reflection in the plate-glass windows of stores and was disappointed with his appearance. He seemed not at all as strong as he felt; he seemed, in fact, a trifle infirm in every part of his body, in his neck, his shoulders, arms, trunk, and knees. This will never do, he said, and with an effort he assembled all his disjointed parts and became tensely, artificially erect and solid.

He passed numerous restaurants with magnificent discipline, refusing even to glance into them, and at last reached a building which he entered. He rose in an elevator to the seventh floor, moved down a hall, and, opening a door, walked into the office of an employment agency. Already there were two dozen young men in the place; he found a corner where he stood waiting his turn to be interviewed. At length he was granted this great privilege and was questioned by a thin, scatterbrained miss of fifty.

Now tell me, she said; what can you do?

He was embarrassed. I can write, he said pathetically.

You mean your penmanship is good? Is that it? said the elderly maiden.

Well, yes, he replied. But I mean that I can write.

Write what? said the miss, almost with anger.

Prose, he said simply.

There was a pause. At last the lady said:

Can you use a typewriter?

Of course, said the young man.

All right, went on the miss, we have your address; we will get in touch with you. There is nothing this morning, nothing at all.

It was much the same at the other agency, except that he was questioned by a conceited young man who closely resembled a pig. From the agencies he went to the large department stores: there was a good deal of pomposity, some humiliation on his part, and finally the report that work was not available. He did not feel displeased, and strangely did not even feel that he was personally involved in all the foolishness. He was a living young man who was in need of money with which to go on being one, and there was no way of getting it except by working for it; and there was no work. It was purely an abstract problem which he wished for the last time to attempt to solve. Now he was pleased that the matter was closed.

He began to perceive the definiteness of the course of his life. Except for moments, it had been largely artless, but now at the last minute he was determined that there should be as little imprecision as possible.

He passed countless stores and restaurants on his way to the Y.M.C.A., where he helped himself to paper and ink and began to compose his *Application.* For an hour he worked on this document, then suddenly, owing to the bad air in the place and to hunger, he became faint. He seemed to be swimming away from himself with great strokes, and hurriedly left the building. In the Civic Center Park, across from the Public Library Building, he drank almost a quart of water and felt himself refreshed. An old man was standing in the center of the brick boulevard surrounded by sea gulls, pigeons, and robins. He was taking handfuls of bread crumbs from a large paper sack and tossing them to the birds with a gallant gesture.

Dimly he felt impelled to ask the old man for a portion of the crumbs, but he did not allow the thought even nearly to reach consciousness; he entered the Public Library and for an hour read Proust, then, feeling himself to be swimming away again, he rushed outdoors. He drank more water at the fountain in the park and began the long walk to his room.

I'll go and sleep some more, he said; there is nothing else to do. He knew now that he was much too tired and weak to deceive himself about being all right, and yet his mind seemed somehow still lithe and alert. It, as if it were a separate entity, persisted in articulating impertinent pleasantries about his very real physical suffering. He reached his room early in the afternoon and immediately prepared coffee on the small gas range. There was no milk in the can, and the half pound of sugar he had purchased a week before was all gone; he drank a cup of the hot black fluid, sitting on his bed and smiling.

From the Y.M.C.A. he had stolen a dozen sheets of letter paper upon which he hoped to complete his document, but now the very notion of writing was unpleasant to him. There was nothing to say. He began to polish the penny he had found in the morning, and this absurd act somehow afforded him great enjoyment. No American coin can be made to shine so brilliantly as a penny. How many pennies would he need to go on living? Wasn't there something more he might sell? He looked about the bare room. No. His watch was gone; also his books. All those fine books; nine of them for eighty-five cents. He felt ill and ashamed for having parted with his books. His best suit he had sold for two dollars, but that was all right. He didn't mind at all about clothes. But the books. That was different. It made him very angry to think that there was no respect for men who wrote.

He placed the shining penny on the table, looking upon it with the delight of a miser. How prettily it smiles, he said. Without reading them he looked at the words, *E Pluribus Unum One Cent United States Of America*, and turning the penny over, he saw Lincoln and the words, *In God We Trust Liberty 1923*. How beautiful it is, he said.

He became drowsy and felt a ghastly illness coming over his blood, a feeling of nausea and disintegration. Bewildered, he stood beside his bed, thinking, *There is nothing to do but sleep.* Already he felt himself making great strides through the fluid of the earth, swimming away to the beginning. He fell face down upon the bed, saying, I ought first at least to give the coin to some child. A child could buy any number of things with a penny.

Then swiftly, neatly, with the grace of the young man on the trapeze, he was gone from his body. For an eternal moment he was all things at once: the bird, the fish, the rodent, the reptile, and man. An ocean of print undulated endlessly and darkly before him. The city burned. The herded crowd rioted. The earth circled away, and knowing that he did so, he turned his lost face to the empty sky and became dreamless, unalive, perfect.

Five Ripe Pears

✧ ✧ ✧

IF old man Pollard is still alive I hope he reads this because I want him to know I am not a thief and never have been. Instead of making up a lie, which I could have done, I told the truth and got a licking. I don't care about the licking because I got a lot of them in grammar school. They were part of my education. Some of them I deserved and some I didn't. The licking Mr. Pollard gave me I didn't deserve, and I am going to tell him why. I couldn't tell him that day because I didn't know how to explain what I knew.

It was about spring pears.

The trees grew in a yard protected by a spike fence, but some of the branches grew beyond the fence. I was six, but logical. A fence, I reasoned, can protect only that which it encloses.

Therefore, I said, the pears growing on the branches beyond the fence are mine—if I can reach them.

It happened during school recess. The trees were two blocks from the school.

I told the Jewish boy, Isaacs, that I was going to the trees, and he said it was stealing. This meant nothing, or it meant that he was afraid to go with me. I did not bother at the time to investigate what it meant, and went running out of the school grounds, down the street.

I reached the trees breathless but alert and smiling. The pears were fat and ready. The sun was warm. The moment was a moment of numerous clarities, air, body, and mind.

Among the leaves I watched the pears, fat and yellow and red, full of the stuff of life, from the sun, and I wanted. It was a thing they could not speak about in the second grade.

The pears were mine if I could reach them, but I couldn't. It was almost enough to see them, but I had been looking at them for weeks. I had seen the trees when they had been bare of leaf. I had seen the coming of leaves and the coming of blossoms. I had seen the blossoms fall away before the pressure of the hard green shapes of unripe pears.

Now the pears were ripe and ready, and I was ready.

But it was not to eat. It was not to steal. It was to know: *the pear*. Of life—the sum of it—which *could* decay.

I was determined to get them, and remain innocent.

Afterwards, when they made a thief of me, I weakened and almost believed I *was* a thief, but it was not so.

A misfortune of youth is that it is speechless when it has most to say, and a fault of maturity is that it is garrulous when it has forgotten where to begin or what language to use. Oh, we have been well educated in error, all right. We at least know that we have forgotten.

I couldn't reach the pears, so I tried leaping. At first I leaped with the idea of reaching a branch and lowering it, but after I had leaped two or three times I leaped because it was fun to do so.

I was leaping when I heard the school bell ring, and I remember the ringing sickened me because I knew I was going to be late. A moment afterwards, though, I thought nothing of being late, having as justification both the ripe pears and my discovery of leaping.

I believed it was a reasonable bargain.

I didn't stop to think they would ask me questions, and I wouldn't have the words with which to answer them accurately.

I got five pears by using a dead tree twig. There were many more to have, but I chose only five, those that were most ready. One I ate. Four I took to class, arriving ten minutes late.

A sensible man is no less naïve at six than at sixty, but few men are sensible. Four pears I took to class, showing them as the reason for lateness.

This caused an instantaneous misunderstanding, and I knew I was being taken for a thief. I had nothing to say because I did have the pears. They were both the evidence of theft and the proof of innocence. I was amazed to discover that to Miss Larkin they were only the evidence.

She was severe and said many things. I understood only that she was angry and inclined toward the opinion that I should be punished. The details are blurred, but I remember sitting in the school office, feeling somewhat a thief, waiting for Mr. Pollard to put in an appearance.

The pears·were on his table. They were cheerless and I was frightened.

There was nothing else to do: I ate a pear. It was sweet, sweeter than the one I had eaten by the tree. The core remained in my hand, lingering there in a foolish way.

I ate also the core, keeping in my hand only a number of seeds. These I pocketed, thinking of growing pear-trees of my own.

One pear followed another because I was frightened and disliked feeling a thief.

The Principal of the school came at last. His coming was like the coming of doom, and when he coughed I thought the whole world shook. He coughed a number of times, looked at me severely a number of times, and then said: I hear you have been stealing pears. Where are they?

I imagined he wanted to eat a pear, so I felt ashamed of myself because I had none to give him, but I suppose he took it the other way around and believed I was ashamed because I was a thief who had been caught.

I could see him taking advantage of my shame, and I knew I would be punished.

It was not pleasant, either, to hear him say that I had stolen the pears. I ate them, I said.

You *ate* the pears? he said. It seemed to me that he was angry.

Nevertheless, I said: Yes, sir.

How many pears? he said.

Four, I said.

You *stole* four pears, he said, and then *ate* them?

No, sir, I said. Five. One I ate by the tree.

Everything was misunderstood, but all I could do was answer questions in a way that would justify his punishing me, which he did.

I cried for all I was worth, because it seemed very strange to me that no one could even faintly understand why I had picked the five ripe pears.

I know Miss Larkin is dead, but if old man Pollard is still alive I hope he reads this because I want him to know that I did *not* steal the pears, I created them, and took four to class because I wanted others to see them. No hard feelings, Mr. Pollard, but I thought I ought to tell you how it really was with me that day.

The Oranges

✿ ✿ ✿

THEY told him, Stand on the corner with two of the biggest oranges in your hand and when an automobile goes by, smile and wave the oranges at them. Five cents each if they want one, his uncle Jake said, three for ten cents, thirty-five cents a dozen. Smile big, he said. You *can* smile, can't you, Luke? You got it in you to smile once in a while, ain't you?

He tried very hard to smile and his uncle Jake made a terrible face, so he knew it was a bad smile. He wished he could laugh out loud the way some people laughed, only they weren't scared the way he was, and all mixed-up.

I never did see such a serious boy in all my life, his uncle Jake said. Luke, he said.

His uncle squatted down, so he could look into his eyes, and talk to him.

Luke, he said, they won't buy oranges if you don't smile. People like to see a little boy smiling, selling oranges. It makes them happy.

He listened to his uncle talking to him, and he understood the words. What he *felt*, though, was: *Jake is mixed-up, too.* He saw the man stand up and heard him groan, just as his father used to groan.

Luke, his uncle Jake said. Sometimes you can laugh, can't you?

Not him, said Jake's wife. If you weren't such a coward, you would be out selling the oranges yourself. You belong the same place your brother is, she said. In the ground. Dead, she said.

It was this that made it hard for him to smile: the way this woman was always picking on his uncle Jake. How did she expect him to smile or feel all right when she was always telling them they were no good, the whole family no good?

Jake was his father's younger brother, and Jake looked something like his father. Of course she always had to say his father was better off dead just because he was no good at selling stuff. She was always telling Jake, This is America. You got to get around and meet people and make them like you. And Jake was always saying, Make them like me? How can I make them like me? And she was always getting sore at him and saying, Oh, you fool. If I didn't have this baby in my belly, I'd go out and work in Rosenberg's Packing House and keep you like a child.

Jake had the same desperate look his father had always had, and he was always getting sore at himself and wanting other people to be happy. Jake was always asking him to smile.

All right, Jake said. All right, all right, all right. Ten boxes of oranges and not a penny in the house and nothing to eat. Should I stand in the street, holding oranges? Should I get a wagon maybe and go through the streets? I should be dead, he said.

Nobody was ever that sad in the world, and he wished he didn't want to cry because Jake was so sad. On top of that Jake's wife got sorer than ever and began to cry the way she cried when she got real sore and you could just feel how terrible everything was because she didn't cry sad, she cried sore, reminding Jake of all the bills and all the hard times she had had with him and all about the baby in her belly, to come out, she said, Why, what good is another fool in the world?

There was a box of oranges on the floor, and she picked up two of them, crying, and she said, No fire in the stove, in November, all of us freezing. The house should be full of the smell of meat. Here, she cried, eat. Eat your oranges. Eat them until you die, and she cried and cried.

Jake was too sad to talk. He sat down and began to wave back and forth, looking crazy. And they asked *him* to laugh. And Jake's wife kept walking in and out of the room, holding the oranges, crying and talking about the baby in her belly.

After a while she stopped crying.

Now take him to the corner, she said, and see if he can't get a little money.

Jake didn't even lift his head. So then she shouted.

Take him to the corner. Ask him to smile at the people. We got to eat.

What good is it to be alive when everything is rotten and nobody knows what to do? What good is it to go to school and learn arithmetic and read poems and paint eggplants and all that stuff? What good is it to sit in a cold room until it is time to go to bed and hear Jake and his wife fighting all the time and go to sleep and cry and wake up and see the sad sky and feel the cold air and shiver and walk to school and eat oranges for lunch instead of bread?

Jake jumped up and began to shout at his wife. He said he would kill her and then himself, so she cried more than ever and tore her dress and she was naked to the waist and she said, All right, better all of us were dead, kill me, but Jake put his arms around her and walked into the other room with her, and he could hear her crying and telling him he was a baby, a great big baby.

He had been standing in the corner and it all happened so swiftly he hadn't noticed how tired he had become, but he was very tired, and hungry, so he sat down. What good is it to be alive if you're all alone in the world and no mother and no father and nobody to love you? He wanted to cry but what good is it to cry?

After a while Jake came out of the room and he was trying to smile.

All you got to do, Luke, he said, is hold two big oranges in your hand and wave them at the people when they go by in their automobiles, and smile. You'll sell a box of oranges in no time, Luke.

I'll smile, he said. One for five cents, three for ten cents, thirty-five cents a dozen.

That's it, said Jake.

Jake lifted the box of oranges from the floor and began walking to the back door.

It was very sad in the street, Jake holding the box of oranges, and him walking beside Jake, listening to Jake telling him to smile big. There were no leaves on the trees, and the street was sad, and it was very funny. The smell of the oranges was clean and good and they looked so nice it was very funny. The oranges looked so nice even though they were so sad.

They came to Ventura corner, where all the automobiles went by, and Jake put the box on the sidewalk.

It looks best with only a small boy, Jake said. I'll go back to the house, Luke.

Jake squatted again and looked into his eyes. You ain't afraid, are you, Luke? I'll come back before it gets dark. It won't be dark for two hours yet. Just feel happy and smile at the people.

I'll smile, he said.

Then Jake jumped up, like maybe he couldn't get up at all unless he *jumped* up, and he went hurrying down the street, walking so fast it was almost running.

He picked out two of the biggest oranges and held them in his right hand and lifted his arm over his head. It didn't seem right. It seemed crazy or something. What good is it to hold two big oranges in your hand and lift your arm over your head and get ready to smile at people going by in automobiles?

It seemed a long time before he saw an automobile coming up the street from town, right on his side, and when it got closer he saw there was a man driving and a lady in the back with two kids. He smiled very big when they got close, but it didn't look as if they were going to stop, so he waved the oranges at them and moved closer to the street. He saw their faces very close, and smiled just a little bigger. He couldn't smile much bigger because it was making his cheeks tired. The people didn't stop and didn't even smile back at him. The little girl in the automobile made a face at him as if she thought he looked cheap. What good is it to stand on a corner and try to sell oranges to people who make faces at you because you are smiling and want them to like you?

What good is it to have your muscles aching just because some people are rich and some people are poor and the rich ones eat and laugh and the poor ones don't eat and always fight and ask each other to kill them?

He brought his arm down and stopped smiling and looked at the fire hydrant and beyond the fire hydrant the gutter and beyond the gutter the street, Ventura, and on both sides of the street houses and in the houses people and at the end of the street the country where the vineyards and orchards were and streams and meadows and then mountains and beyond the mountains more cities and more houses and streets and people. What good is it to be in the world when you can't even look at a fire hydrant without wanting to cry?

Another automobile was coming up the street, so he lifted his arm and began to smile again, but when the automobile went by he saw that the man wasn't even looking at him. Five cents for one. They could eat oranges. After bread and meat they could eat an orange. Peel it and smell the nice smell and eat it. They could stop their automobiles and buy three for ten cents. Then another automobile went by while he smiled and waved his arm, but the people just looked at him and that was all. If they would just smile back it wouldn't be so bad, but just going by and not even smiling back made it seem crazy or something. A lot of automobiles went by and it looked as if he ought to sit down and stop smiling. They didn't want any oranges and they didn't like to see him smile the way his uncle Jake said they would. They just saw him and didn't do anything else.

It began to be pretty dark and for all he cared the whole world could end. He just guessed he would be standing there holding up his arm and smiling until the end of the world.

He just guessed that's all he was born to do, just stand on the corner and wave oranges at the people and smile at them till the end of the world, everything black and empty and him standing there smiling until his cheeks hurt and sore at them because they wouldn't even smile back at him and for all he cared the whole world could just fall into the darkness and end and Jake could be dead and his wife could be dead and all the streets and houses and people could end and there could be nobody anywhere, not even one man anywhere or one empty street or one dark window or one shut door because they didn't want to buy oranges and they wouldn't smile at him.

Two Days Wasted in Kansas City

✿ ✿ ✿

I PUT the dice into the cup and laughed at the man with the rake. I said, You don't know what kind of luck I have. Watch me make that number.

The number was four, one of the toughest numbers in the world. I was rattling the cup and laughing and telling myself I would lose and go away and lose again in another city and go away and lose again, when the door opened and a little girl came in, smoking a cigarette.

Watch me make that number, I said. You don't know what kind of luck I have.

Four, it said to me: Your number is four and you'll make it because of this girl, the world said to me.

I didn't say it. I didn't *think* it. I *knew* it. It happened while she was walking to the table, exhaling smoke and looking at the players.

I turned the dice loose and it was two deuces. I picked up the ten dollars and I was about to walk away because you can't beat them if you stay with them, but I didn't walk away because it kept talking to me and I knew I would be a fool to walk out on the world and everything else when it was all for me.

She came to the table and stood away from the men who were playing and watching and I felt located because she was in the room. That's exactly the way it was. I felt located. It went like this in my mind. Kansas City, August, 1928, on a side street, in a gambling joint, throwing dice, from San Francisco, headed for New York, two hours off the bus, staying in Kansas City three hours, and this girl.

I had been having the lousiest luck in the world.

Then, all of a sudden, I made a four.

Give me the dice, I said.

The man with the rake looked at the girl, twisting his cigar around.

Then he looked at me.

I knew he knew I knew what he was thinking. I could tell he knew what was happening and I could tell he didn't like it.

The girl stood very quietly. I could see she wasn't walking the streets yet, and I could see my good luck was happening at last *because* she wasn't walking the streets yet but would be in an hour or so if something didn't happen.

That's why I didn't go away with my money.

Just before a girl from a small city in a big city starts to walk the streets a condition is established in the world which is of pity, pride and humility; and no girl is ever so beautiful as a girl who has decided to live, even if she has to give over everything she has, and is waiting timidly to see if something in the world won't let her live the way she is and wants to be.

I could see she was very hungry, very sure everything would turn out for the worst, very angry, very proud, and at the same time very humble, very innocent, very faithful in her belief in the innate goodness of things.

I am not speaking of faith in God. I am speaking of faith in things. Maybe it is the same thing.

The man with the rake was like all gambling-joint workers. Tight-lipped and wise.

He looked at me, he looked at the girl, and then he decided there was nothing he could do. He knew he would lose and he knew there was nothing he could do because it wasn't cheating, although it was nearly the same thing. He knew I couldn't lose.

He could send the girl away and spoil everything, but he was a gambler and a gambler likes to watch a thing work out.

I think he really wanted to see if it would.

The girl was nobody. He could send her away and break down the whole arrangement. He didn't, though.

There were five spectators and one was drunk. He was the only spectator who was aware of what was going on.

The drunkard laughed quietly and happily.

Alcohol heightens the instinct for accuracy and makes real the darkest and most secret patterns of order.

I put the ten dollars on the table and began to rattle the dice, knowing it would be a seven, but that it would be a seven only if I believed, only if I remembered it was for this girl waiting to know if she could live the way she wanted to live, and not simply an acceptance of the implicit danger in things, not simply seeking and trying, the way gambling always is when only money is involved, and I knew if I remembered the girl nothing in all creation could keep the dice from rolling to seven, and it was so, the dice rolled to seven.

The man with the rake put ten dollars on my ten dollars and twisted the cigar in his mouth.

In San Francisco I had had the lousiest luck in the world. I had had nothing to win but money and nothing to lose but money, and I had always lost.

I'll play the twenty, I said.

If I win, I said, I'll quit. If I lose, I'll quit.

I said this to the world, to the girl, and to the man with the rake.

I wanted him to know I knew he knew. I wanted him to know I didn't want to spoil a good thing.

The drunkard laughed.

While I was rattling the dice the girl turned away from the table and went to the door.

I stopped rattling the dice.

She had her hand on the door and was opening it and there was time enough for me to ask her politely to come back and stand at the table and notice what I was doing, but I couldn't do it, and I saw her go away, and all I could think was, She doesn't know, she doesn't understand, she doesn't realize I want her to go on believing.

I lit a cigarette and laughed, knowing the arrangement was destroyed.

In San Francisco, I said to the man with the rake, I made seven passes in a row one night.

I was bluffing because I knew the arrangement was broken.

She doesn't know, I said. She is walking up a dark street in a strange city and she doesn't know I want her to believe. She is not here, she is lost again in the world and no one there will do anything for her, and I will lose, I will be sure to lose.

The drunkard stopped laughing.

I prayed for luck. She is not here, I said, but she *was* here, and I believe, I believe in everything, please let me make another seven, or an eleven, and I will run up the street and find her and give her the money, so she can believe, too. I never saw her before, but she's from a small town somewhere and she's waiting to find out if there is any good in anything, and I want her to know there is. I know there is and I want her to know there is, too.

I turned the dice loose and it was a six.

The drunkard came very close to me and said, Six, six, six, be a six.

There *is* good in everything, I said.

I rattled the dice and turned them loose and it came to nine.

Then it came to eight, then another eight, then five, and I said, One six, please, so I can run up the street with the money and find her and give her the money, and the next one was a six, a pair of threes.

I took the money and walked out of the joint.

The man in the cigar stand was reading *True Confessions*.

I said, Where did that girl go?

He looked up from the magazine and said, What girl?

I ran down the street and the only girls I saw were street-walkers. It was the district: dice and lust.

One of the girls said, What's the big hurry?

I'm looking for a girl, I said.

Don't go any further, said the girl.

This girl is from a small town, I said.

So am I, said the girl.

You don't get the idea, I said.

I get the idea, said the girl.

I ran across the street to a little restaurant, but she wasn't there.

I ran back to the gambling joint, and she wasn't there.

The bus would be going away in ten minutes and then there wouldn't be another bus till eight in the morning. I went to the bus station and got into the bus. About a minute before the driver started the motor I got off and went back to the gambling joint, but she wasn't there.

I spent most of the night looking for her in Kansas City, but it was no use. I went into all kinds of places, and then I rented a room for the night.

I spent the next day looking for her but I didn't find her.

I don't suppose it matters much, but I wish a little thing like this could turn out all right instead of going haywire. I wish everything wouldn't go haywire this way. I knew she was waiting to see if there was any good in the world, and there was, and then she was gone and I couldn't find her.

I wanted her to know all of it wasn't dirty. I wanted her to know some of it was decent sometimes.

I guess she found a place for herself, in some house. I guess she stayed alive all right, but I wish she hadn't gone away from the dice table when I was winning for her.

I wasted two days in Kansas City, hoping to find her. I only wanted to tell her I made my number because I knew how it was with her and wanted her to have the money so she could go on being alive the way she wanted to be alive. For a minute there, while she was in the gambling joint, we had the whole world and every idea of right on our side, and I wish to Christ she hadn't gone away and left me with only a lot of silly money in my pocket, instead of the real rich winning I had made.

Going Home

☼ ☼ ☼

THIS valley, he thought, all this country between the mountains, is mine, home to me, the place I dream about, and everything is the same, not a thing is changed, water sprinklers still splash in circles over lawns of Bermuda grass, good old home town.

Walking along Calaveras Avenue he felt glad to be home again. Everything was fine, common and good, the smell of earth, cooking suppers, smoke, the rich summer air of the valley full of plant growth, grapes growing, peaches ripening, and the oleander bush swooning with sweetness, the same as ever. He breathed deeply, drawing the smell of home deep into his lungs, smiling inwardly. It was hot. He hadn't felt his senses reacting to the earth so cleanly and clearly for years; now it was a pleasure even to breathe. The cleanliness of the air sharpened the moment so that, walking, he felt the magnificence of being, the glory of possessing substance, of having form and motion and intellect, the piety of merely being alive on the earth.

Water, he thought, hearing the whispering splash of a lawn sprinkler; to taste the water of home, the full cool water of the valley, to have that simple thirst and that good cold water with which to quench it, that was to live. He saw an old man holding a hose over some geranium plants, and his thirst sent him to the man.

Good evening, he said quietly; may I have a drink?

The old man turned slowly, his shadow large against the house, to look into the young man's face, amazed and pleased. You bet, he said; here, and he placed the hose into the young man's hands. Mighty fine water, said the old man, this water of the San Joaquin valley; best yet, I guess. That water up in San Francisco makes me sick, ain't got no taste. And down in Los Angeles, why, the water tastes like castor oil; I can't understand how so many people go on living there year after year.

While the old man talked he listened to the water falling from the hose to the earth. You said it, he said to the old man; you said it. Our water is the finest water on earth.

He curved his head over the spouting water and began to drink, and as he drank he thought, Now I *am* home. He could feel the cool water splashing into his gut, refreshing and cooling him. Losing his breath, he lifted his head, saying to the old man, We're mighty lucky.

He bent his head over the water again and began again to swallow the splashing liquid, laughing to himself with delight. It seemed as if he couldn't get enough of it into his body; the more he drank, the finer the water tasted and the more he wanted to drink.

The old man was amazed. You drunk about two quarts, he said.

Still swallowing the water, he could hear the old man talking. He lifted his head at last, saying, I guess so. It sure tastes fine. He wiped his mouth with a handkerchief, still holding the hose, still wanting to drink more.

Man alive, said the old man. You sure was thirsty. How long since you had a drink, anyway?

Two years, he replied. I mean two years since I had a drink of *this* water. I was born here, over on G Street in Russian town; you know, across the Southern Pacific tracks; been away two years and I just got back. I'm going to get a job and settle down.

He hung his head over the water again and took several more swallows; then he handed the hose back to the old man.

You sure was thirsty, said the old man again. I ain't never seen anybody anywhere drink so much water at one time. It sure looked good seeing you swallow all that water.

He went on walking down Calaveras Avenue, the old man staring at him.

Good to be back, he thought; greatest mistake I ever made, coming back this way.

Everything he had ever done had been a mistake, and this was one of the good mistakes. He had hitch-hiked south from San Francisco without thinking of going home; he had thought of going as far south as Merced, stopping there awhile, and then going back, but once he had got into the country, he hadn't been able to stop. He had had to keep going.

One little city after another, and here he was walking through the streets of his home town, at seven in the evening. It was great.

He wasn't far from town now, the city itself, and he could see one or two of the taller buildings, the Pacific Gas & Electric Building, all lit up with colored lights, and another, a taller one, that he hadn't seen before. That's a new one, he thought; they put up that one while I was away; things must be booming.

He turned down Fulton Street and began walking into town. It looked great from where he was, far away and nice and small, a real quiet little town, the kind of place to live in, settle down in, marry in, have a home, kids, a job, and all the rest of it. It was all he wanted. The air of the valley and the water.

In the city everything was the same: the names of the stores, the people walking in the streets, and the slow passing of automobiles; boys in cars trying to pick up girls; same as ever; not a thing changed. He saw faces he had known as a boy, people he did not know by name, and then he saw Tony Rocca, his old pal, walking up the street toward him, and he saw that Tony recognized him. He stopped walking, waiting for Tony to come into his presence. It was like a meeting in dream. He had dreamed of the two of them playing hookey from school to go swimming, to go out to the county fair, to sneak into a moving-picture theatre; and now here he was again, a big fellow with a lazy, easy-going walk, and a genial Italian grin. It was good, and he was glad he had made the mistake and come back.

The two boys shook hands and then began to strike one another, laughing and swearing. You old bastard, Tony said: where the hell have you been?

Old Tony, he said; good old punchdrunk Tony. God, it's good to see you. I thought maybe you'd be dead by this time. What the hell have you been doing? He dodged another punch, and struck his friend in the shoulder. He swore in Italian at Tony, using words Tony had taught him years ago, and Tony swore back at him in Russian.

I've got to go out to the house, he said at last. The folks don't know I'm back. I've got to go out and see them. I'm dying to see my brother Paul.

He went on down the street, smiling about Tony. They would be having a lot of good times together again.

Walking by stores, he thought of buying his mother a small gift. But he had little money, and all the decent things were expensive. I'll get her something later, he thought.

He turned west on Tulare Street. Crossing the Southern Pacific tracks, he reached G Street, then turned south. In a few minutes he would be home again, at the door of the little old house; the same as ever; the old woman, the old man, his three sisters, and his kid brother, all of them in the house.

He saw the house from a distance of about a block, and his heart began to jump. He felt suddenly ill and afraid, something he had forgotten about the place, about that life which he had always hated, something ugly and mean. But he walked on, moving slower as he came closer to the house. The fence had fallen and no one had fixed it. The house suddenly appeared to be very ugly, and he wondered why in hell the old man didn't move to a better house in a better neighborhood. Seeing the house again, feeling all its old reality, all his hatred for it returned, and he began to feel again the longing to be away from it, where he could not see it. He began to feel, as he had felt as a boy, the deep inarticulate hatred he had for the whole city, its falseness, its meanness, the stupidity of its people, the emptiness of their minds, and it seemed to him that he would never be able to return to such a place. The water; yes, it was good; but there were other things.

He walked slowly before the house, looking at it as if he might be a stranger, feeling alien and unrelated to it, yet feeling that it was home, the place he dreamed about, the place that tormented him wherever he went. He was afraid someone might come out of the house and see him, because he knew that if he was seen, he might find himself running. Still, he wanted to see them, all of them, have them before his eyes, feel the full presence of their bodies, even smell them. But it was too much. He began to feel hatred for everything in the city, and he walked on, going to the corner. There he stood beneath the street lamp, bewildered and disgusted, wanting to see his brother Paul, to talk to the boy, find out what was going on in his mind, how he was taking it, being in such a place, living such a life. He knew how it had been with himself when he had been his brother's age, and he hoped he might be able to give his brother a little advice, how to keep from feeling the monotony and the ugliness by reading.

He forgot that he hadn't eaten since breakfast, and that he had been dreaming for months of eating another of his mother's meals, sitting at the old table in the kitchen, seeing her, large and red-faced and serious and angry toward him, loving him, but he had lost his appetite. He thought he might wait at the corner; perhaps his brother would leave the house to take a walk and he would see the boy and talk to him. Paul, he would say, and they would talk together in Russian.

The stillness of the valley began to oppress him.

Still, he couldn't go away from the house. From the corner he could see it, and he knew that he wanted to go in and be among his people, a part of their lives; he knew this was what he had wanted to do for months, to knock at the door, walk across the floors of the house, sit in the old chairs, sleep in his bed, talk with his old man, eat at the table.

And now something he had forgotten while he had been away, something real but ugly in that life, had come up swiftly, changing everything, the appearance and meaning of the house, the city, the whole valley, making it all ugly and unreal, making him wish to go away and never return. He could never come back. He could never enter the house again and go on with his life where he had left off.

Suddenly he was in the alley, climbing over the fence, walking through the yard. His mother had planted tomatoes and peppers, and the smell of the growing plants was thick and acrid and somehow heart-breaking. There was a light in the kitchen, and he moved quietly toward it, hoping to see some of them without being seen. He walked close to the house, to the kitchen window, and looking in saw his youngest sister Martha washing dishes. He saw the old table, the old stove, and Martha, with her back turned to him; and all these things seemed so sad and so pathetic that tears came to his eyes, and he began to need a cigarette. He struck a match quietly on the bottom of his shoe, lighted a cigarette, and inhaled the smoke, looking at his sister in the old house. Everything seemed very still, very clear, terribly hopeless. He wished his mother would enter the kitchen; he wanted to have another look at her. Would she still have that old angry look? He felt angry with himself for not being a good son, but he knew it was impossible.

He saw his brother Paul enter the kitchen for a drink of water, and for a moment he wanted to cry out the boy's name. The boy seemed lost, bewildered, imprisoned. Looking at his brother, he began to whisper, O Jesus, Jesus.

He no longer wished to see his mother. He knew he would become so angry that he would do something crazy. He walked quietly through the yard, hoisted himself over the fence, and jumped to the alley. He began to walk away, his anguish mounting in him. When he was far enough away not to be heard, he began to sob, loving them passionately and hating the ugliness and hopelessness of their lives. He hurried away from home, from his people, sobbing bitterly in the darkness of the clear night because there was nothing he could do, not one confounded thing.

The Horses and the Sea

✿ ✿ ✿

DRINKING beer in *The Kentucky* on Third Street, I met a fellow named Drew, father English, mother Italian, and he said he had just got off the boat, straight from Australia, assistant engineer. He was a tall dark half-breed with a solid chin and a long horsey face. Like most seamen ashore he seemed to be in a daze, and although he'd hear something I'd say, he wouldn't understand the meaning immediately. It would take him thirty seconds or a little longer to make out what I was talking about. It seemed as if he had something important on his mind, but in reality he was only becoming adjusted to land, to the city, and what was going on. In reality he still had the sea in him and it was taking him time to get the land back into his brain. He wasn't liking it, either: it wasn't pleasing him very much. He had gone to sea when he was fourteen and, on and off, he had been to sea ever since. He was nearing his fortieth year, but appeared to be in his middle twenties: it is like this with some seamen: they lead a hard life, they drink, they go away in ships, they walk streets of alien cities, they do a lot of swift living, and yet they keep young. Drew was one of these men, and we were drinking beer together, talking.

We got to be friends casually, the way it happens in saloons, and Drew began to talk about himself, how it had been with him from the beginning, feeling restless, dreaming of cities, wanting to walk in them: a young fellow from inland longing for the sea.

All of a sudden he said, Do you understand horses? I want to gamble a little because I haven't much money and winter is coming.

I don't know anything about horses, I said.

But Mac winked at Drew and said, Don't believe it. He's the best handicapper on Third Street.

Drew wasn't very alert mentally, as I've said, and he wanted to know if I ever played the horses. I told him I had been playing the horses regularly for over seven years and that all in all I was about eleven dollars and sixty-five cents ahead of the game.

Drew said, I'm feeling lucky today. I'd like to make a little bet.

We went around to Number One Opera Alley, through *The Kentucky* to the alley. It was Belmont that day, Arlington Park in Chicago, and Tia Juana, across the border. I began to look over the racing sheets to get a line on distances, odds, weights, and jockeys, and it looked like a bad day at every track. Not one race looked like a business proposition: everything was even-stephen, three horses in every race that might win, and these kinds of races are no good. I want a horse to be there to win alone, by two lengths at least, at good odds. My object is not to make the bookies rich, but Drew came up with the name *Sea Bird*.

That horse, he said, sounds good.

What do you mean, good? I said.

The name, he said. *Sea Bird*.

I had to laugh: I happened to know. *Sea Bird* was a no-good worthless piece of female horse flesh. She hadn't won a race since she had gone to the barrier two years ago. I liked her name myself but horses with fancy names don't win races. Names have nothing to do with it, although once in a long while a man may win a few dollars by following name hunches. It isn't often, though. I told Drew to lay off the horse.

Nevertheless, he liked the name so much he bet a half dollar on her across the board, dollar and a half in all, four bits to win, four bits to place, and four bits to show, and *Sea Bird* ran eighth in a nine-horse race. If she had won, Drew would have got a potful of money. He made the remark himself.

Then he said, She sounded good to me. Too bad a horse with a name like that has to be so slow.

I said she was probably a very handsome horse, but not of the running breed, the fast running, the nervous, hysterical kind, the kind that know a race is a race and like to win.

Drew was holding a dollar in his hand and looking bewildered. All those names. It was confusing. What horse do you like up there? he asked.

I said that I didn't like any horse that day. Not one race looked O.K. to me. I told him I wasn't betting.

Well, said Drew, make a suggestion.

I asked if he had money and he told me he had about twelve dollars. He had been in town four days and he had bought a suit of clothes, a pair of shoes, and a few other things: he had been drinking a little and now all he had was twelve dollars. I suggested he ought to hang on to it and forget the horses for the time being, but no, he wanted to make another bet, at least one more.

I named the horse *Unencumbered*.

What's it mean? he asked. That word?

It means, I said, *un* encumbered. Do you know what encumbered means? Drew said he did not.

Well, I asked him what the hell difference it made what the word meant. The horse was pretty good. It ought to win. It probably would win.

The odds were six to one. I told him to bet a half dollar to win and quit whether the horse won or not.

Drew bet two dollars on *Unencumbered* to win: he was a gambler, I could see that. He said, You like this horse. I think she'll win.

Now I am sorry I ever suggested the horse because it did win and it sort of made a tramp of Drew. We left the joint and he was full of gratitude. Now, he kept saying, if we can make one bet a day like this, I can get through the winter in good style. He said, Will you meet me every noon at *The Kentucky?*

I told him I would, but that it wouldn't be wise for him to have too much confidence in the horses. It didn't always work out so nicely. Sometimes you didn't win a bet in a week, sometimes two weeks.

The next day he had very good luck. I gave him a horse that won, and Pete, the unemployed Southern Pacific engineer, gave him a horse that won, and Drew himself bet only two of his own hunches that lost, so that at the end of the day, he was three dollars to the good.

I could tell he was going haywire, though, because he bought a copy of *The Racing Form* and said he was going to go at the thing scientifically, and the next day when I saw him he said, I've got this racket all figured out. I've got eight winners for today.

It isn't impossible to pick eight winners in one day, but I never knew anybody who ever bet eight horses that won, and didn't bet any others.

I didn't say anything and Drew bet his eight horses and two of them won, and the two that won paid very little, and at the end of the day he was out seven dollars.

Afterwards he took it easier and made only one or two bets a day, and one day, about two weeks later, he was broke and I lent him a dollar.

I'm waiting for a boat, he said.

What happened to *your* boat? I said.

It went back to Australia, he said. Five days ago. I lost my job. They got another assistant engineer.

I didn't see him again for a month. Then he came tearing into Number One Opera Alley in a way that made me know he had money.

I been painting houses, he said. Making six, seven dollars a day.

He had on a brand-new suit and there was a smell of paint with him.

Giving up the sea? I said.

Sure, he said. Seven dollars a day is a lot of money.

He made three swift bets, the kind guys with lots of money and lots of faith in luck make, and lost.

He felt pretty good, though.

I thought I'd lose, he said. I just wanted to find out.

How much did you lose? I said.

Seventeen dollars, he said.

He went away in a hurry.

When I saw him again, about six weeks later, I knew he wasn't painting houses any more and didn't have much money, maybe five or six dollars.

He wasn't wearing a brand-new suit and he wasn't acting game. He was being very cautious about everything. He was looking at the form charts in a way that meant that he didn't want to make a bet just to find out if he was right in believing he would lose, he wanted to make a bet and win, although he was pretty sure no matter what horse he bet on he would lose, and he couldn't afford to lose, and looking at the form charts this way he was looking bewildered and confused and worried. Too many things could happen. He could bet on *Will Colinet* at two to one that ought to win, and it would lose; and *Bright Star*, at six to one, that ought to come seventh would win; or he could bet on *Bright Star*, and *Will Colinet* would win, and no matter which horse he played he would lose, and he kept looking at the form chart and trying to make up his mind.

Then he walked away from the form chart and we bumped into each other.

Any luck? I said, but I didn't mean horses.

Haven't made a bet yet, he said. Can't make up my mind.

He stayed around till the races were over and didn't make a bet, and I knew he had very little money.

So many things could happen, it was beginning to scare him because he believed only one thing could happen as far as he was concerned: he would lose all his money.

The next day he was busy all day studying the form charts and looking up the past performances of the various horses, but at the end of the day he hadn't made a bet. After each race he would be amazed that he didn't have sense enough to bet on the winner. And at the end of the day his senselessness in not having bet on every winner and become rich was disgusting to him, and he was all bawled up and couldn't make a bet, not even a small half-dollar one.

And it was the same the next day. All the races were run, and all the winners came in, and he didn't pay out or collect a nickel, because he couldn't make up his mind to accept the challenge of possibility and win or go broke, although one or the other would be better than trying to get along every day on forty or fifty cents, two small meals, and one small room to sleep in.

And it was like this for five or six days, and I knew it was getting worse and worse with him: afraid to make up his mind, and all his money being spent carefully for things he needed, and now hardly anything left, so I took him to an Italian restaurant for a big dinner.

My ship is three days out, he said.

I knew how he felt. Here he was in the stinking city, in the stinking places of the city, doing no work, fretting about the comparative nervousness of horses, fretting about the infinite possibilities of a single event, a horse race, and three days out of San Francisco, on the Pacific, was his ship, and on the ship were the men, working, doing the things that would bring the ship to port, doing the things that would bring about the happening of only one event, not a horse race, but a ship crossing an ocean from one city on one continent to another city on another continent, and no two ways about it, and all around the ship the clean sea, and above the ship the clean sky, and the certainty of deep sleep at night because he had worked and because the sea could be heard, even when it was very silent, and no confusion in his mind.

The next day he told me frankly he was broke, and I told him I would lend him as much money as he needed each day, and I did, and in a couple of days The Texan came to port, and he went down and talked to the Captain and the Chief Engineer, and got his job back. They told him he had missed one of the best voyages of the ship, and when he came uptown to Number One Opera Alley to pay me the money I had loaned him, he said, This voyage I missed because I stayed in the city, painting houses and betting horses, was one of the finest The Texan ever made. Four days out of Sydney they hit a big storm and the ship rolled all over the place. Everybody ate standing and the coffee would spill out of your cup while you were drinking it, and nobody could stay in his bunk to sleep, and then they hit the calmest sea anybody had ever seen, sunshine and warm breezes, and the tables steady as tables in restaurants.

And then I knew how it was. It was the *kind* of challenge that he didn't like: the city challenge was fake. It didn't need to be one way or another in the first place, and that was why he couldn't figure it out. They dared you to pick one horse out of six or seven or eight or nine or ten or eleven or twelve, and if you did, you were a fool, even if you picked the right one, and if you didn't but were interested you were a greater fool, and the whole thing was goofy. Who cared about a horse race, anyway? And what if you did win? What if you got rich? It was the same. And the challenge wasn't worth accepting in the first place. But with the sea, with the ship, it was different. There was work to do all the time, but it was reasonable. There could be a storm and trouble, but there was sense to it because you were working to get a ship to port and when the sea got rough, you liked it because it was clean, the sea was clean, the job of getting the ship to port was a clean job, and even if the ship sank and everybody drowned it was all right because it was reasonable and the challenge was sensible.

World Wilderness of Time Lost

✿ ✿ ✿

BEFORE dawn the blinds of houses on the streets where I walk are drawn and I know life sleeps, though I cannot. The heavens are pious with impending light and my eye finds morning, my flesh another beginning. My heart sings world's joy and my blood charges to symphony of living. The hill is ugly with the habitations of man, yet beautiful, and the smell of morning is clean as before civilization. The year is a truth I wish not to believe, and the moment is a moment of forever. I am alone with the universe on a dirty street in the city at dawn. I laugh, remembering pain and grief. My life is without emptiness and being well in one place I have been to the ends of the earth, and looking clearly into the face of structures I have seen the glory of the firmament. My laughter is the only language I know, and the *only* language. When I go down into the city and speak to the living my laughter waits for morning and silence.

The winding downhill street of asphalt is yet beneath the sky and it is the place of our latest walking. The flood of motorcars will swerve along the street when the sun is bright and I will be in another place, watching. The street is yet of the universe and I cannot see it and not see the curve of endlessness above it. And the tall mortality of myself upon the street, within the time, of the place, walking while the world sleeps, seeking tomorrow. No bird sings, for again it is winter and only the remembrance of singing birds is in the earth as a sadness and a joy. And the flight of them as a sentence of eloquence in the silence. If I walk into the day smiling I will live, and the wilderness of the world will grow into a garden before the clearness of my glance. And the waste of seasons will blossom into trees. Of love there is no end, and pity is the cure of all ugliness.

Here is a house my heart knows, and the curtains conceal the secrecy of new inhabitants. The configuration of the street smiles to the remembrance I feel, then weeps. Five years ago I walked here in loneliness and walking here again the years fall away to greet me, and the houses I saw then and see now groan with the sadness I know.

We are remembered, cry the houses. The sad one has returned at dawn and remembers our loneliness. He is older and wiser and more sad than ever, and cut with grief his mouth twists with laughter, and he stands at the door of 2378 Sutter Street, and stares, blinking. Do you remember his drunken stagger and his crazy oratory in the morning, crying, Oh, there is nothing in the world, only sadness and pain, and the way he used to sing Christian songs with bawdy words, and swear at the dark windows of houses?

No one is reading the story of life, and no one is writing it. The houses cry remembrance and the sky hangs low over the rooftops, and dark over my heart. I knew all these quiet houses and the faces of their people I knew. The Japanese tailor and his three kids, two girls and a boy, Americans. The shop is empty and the family is gone. The hollowness is the hollowness of wasted years. Aki, The Tailor. For Rent. This street is two miles from the place where I now live, and it is an eternity away. I used to talk to Aki. He was a small man with the manners of a king-peasant. Yes, tomorrow. Thank you. I will have your trousers, thank you. Yes, I will run the crease to the top, thank you. Good-bye, thank you. Little Aki who would never laugh because it would not be polite, but would smile, thank you. And his wife, quietly at the far end of the store, sewing, her head only rarely lifted, smile and nod, thank you, and the three kids, polite as their parents but alive as the city, the time, thank you. For rent.

The Cigar Store is closed, but through the window I can see the counter and the dice-board where I used to roll dice with Pat, from everywhere in the world. I hope you win, son, he would say and when I wouldn't he would be sad. Nobody ever wins, son. I been everywhere and I know what's what. Dice or anything else. You lose. Make them dance, son. Roll them hard, slap them down, and make the numbers jump for you. You can't win but I always like to see a man try. You only get to try but you might as well try with all your might. Bang hell out of them. Rattle the cup and make them dance. Put your heart into it and get sore. Take a poke at me if you think my heart's against you. Knock down anything or anybody that gets in your way. Cut loose and lay everything low. I've been to every foreign port in the world and I've seen everything there is to see, sin and death and decency, and you can't win. Flip them neatly, son, and if you have to cheat, cheat. Get all you can but don't be sore if you get nothing. This place is a jungle and don't let anybody tell you different. Get all you can because nobody ever gets anything.

Well, I have returned to the street, to the year of another life, to the wilderness of a world lost, to a time lost, and now regained. Day breaks with a smile, and the muscles of my body tighten with joy, and my heart sings, since I am not yet one of the dead. It is morning and I am yet alive. It is the eternal morning of life, and again I am walking. In this city which I love, my life is yet a truth, and the light of the sun builds a shadow out of my substance.

Fresno

✿ ✿ ✿

A MAN could walk four or five miles in any direction from the heart of our city and see our streets dwindle to land and weeds. In many places the land would be vineyard and orchard land, but in most places it would be desert land the weeds would be the strong dry weeds of desert. In this land there would be the living things that had had their being in the quietness of deserts for centuries. There would be snakes and horned-toads, prairie-dogs and jack-rabbits. In the sky over this land would be buzzards and hawks, and the hot sun. And everywhere in the desert would be the marks of wagons that had made lonely roads.

Two miles from the heart of our city a man could come to the desert and feel the loneliness of a desolate area, a place lost in the earth, far from the solace of human thought. Standing at the edge of our city, a man could feel that we had made this place of streets and dwellings in the stillness and loneliness of the desert, and that we had done a brave thing. We had come to this dry area that was without history, and we had paused in it and built our houses and we were slowly creating the legend of our life. We were digging for water and we were leading streams through the dry land. We were planting and ploughing and standing in the midst of the garden we were making.

Our trees were not yet tall enough to make much shade, and we had planted a number of kinds of trees we ought not to have planted because they were of weak stuff and would never live a century, but we had made a pretty good beginning. Our cemeteries were few and the graves in them were few. We had buried no great men because we hadn't had time to produce any great men. We had been too busy trying to get water into the desert. The shadow of no great mind was over our city. But we had a playground called Cosmos Playground. We had public schools named after Emerson and Hawthorne and Lowell and Longfellow. Two great railways had their lines running through our city and trains were always coming to us from the great cities of America and somehow we could not feel that we were wholly lost. We had two newspapers and a Civic Auditorium and a public library one-third full of books. We had the Parlor Lecture Club. We had every sort of church except a Christian Science church. Every house in our city had a Bible in it, and a lot of houses had as many as four Bibles in them. A man could feel our city was beautiful.

Or a man could feel that our city was fake, that our lives were empty, and that we were the contemporaries of jack-rabbits. Or a man could have one viewpoint in the morning and another in the evening. The dome of our court-house was high, but it was ridiculous and had nothing to do with what we were trying to do in the desert. It was an imitation of something out of Rome. We had a mayor but he wasn't a great man and he didn't look like a mayor. He looked like a farmer. He *was* a farmer, but he was elected mayor. We had no great men, but the whole bunch of us put together amounted to something that was very nearly great. Our mayor was not above carrying on a conversation with an Armenian farmer from Fowler who could speak very little English. Our mayor was not a proud man and he sometimes got drunk with his friends. He liked to tell folks how to dig for water or how to prune muscat vines in order to get a good crop, and on the whole he was an admirable man. And of course we had to have a mayor, and of course *somebody* had to be mayor.

Our enterprise wasn't on a vast scale. It wasn't even on a medium-sized scale. There was nothing slick about anything we were doing. Our enterprise was neither scientific nor inhuman, as the enterprise of a growing city ought to be. Nobody knew the meaning of the word efficiency, and the most frightening word ever used by our mayor in public orations was *progress*, but by *progress* he meant, and our people understood him to mean, the paving of the walk in front of the City Hall, and the purchase by our city of a Ford automobile for the mayor. Our biggest merchant was a small man named Kimball, who liked to loaf around in his immense department store with a sharpened pencil on his right ear. He liked to wait on his customers personally, even though he had over two dozen alert clerks working for him. They were alert during the winter, at any rate, and if they sometimes dozed during the long summer afternoons, it was because our whole city slept during those afternoons. There was nothing else to do. This sort of thing gave our city an amateur appearance, as if we were only experimenting and weren't quite sure if we had more right to be in the desert than the jack-rabbits and the horned-toads, as if we didn't believe we had started something that was going to be very big, something that would eventually make a tremendous change in the history of the world.

But in time a genius appeared among us and he said that we would change the history of the world. He said that we would do it with raisins.

He said that we would change the eating habits of man.

Nobody thought he was crazy because he wore spectacles and looked important. He appeared to be what our people liked to call *an educated man*, and any man who had had an education, any man who had gone through a university and read books, must be an important man. He had statistics and the statistical method of proving a point. He proved mathematically that he would be able to do everything he said he was going to do. What our valley needed, he said, was a system whereby the raisin would be established as a necessary part of the national diet, and he said that he had evolved this system and that it was available for our valley. He made eloquent speeches in our Civic Auditorium and in the public halls of the small towns around our city. He said after we got America accustomed to eating raisins, we would begin to teach Europe and Asia and maybe Australia to eat raisins, our valley would become the richest valley in the whole world. China! he said. He shouted the exact number of Chinese in China. It was a stupendous figure, and the farmers in the Civic Auditorium didn't know whether to applaud or protest. He said that if we could get every living Chinaman to place one raisin, only *one* mind you, in every pot of rice he cooked, why, then, we could dispose of all our raisins at a good price and everybody in our valley would have money in the bank, and would be able to purchase all the indispensable conveniences of modern life, bath-tubs, carpet-sweepers, house electricity, and automobiles.

Rice, he said. That's all they eat. But we can teach them to drop one raisin in every pot of rice they cook.

Raisins had a good taste, he said. People liked to eat raisins. People were so fond of eating raisins they would be glad to pay money for them. The trouble was that people had gotten out of the habit of eating raisins. It was because grocers all over the country hadn't been carrying raisins for years, or if they had been carrying them, the raisins hadn't been packed in attractive packages.

All we needed, he said, was a raisin association with an executive department and a central packing and distributing plant. He would do the rest. He would have an attractive package designed, and he would create a patented trade-name for our raisins. He would place full-page advertisements in *The Saturday Evening Post* and other national periodicals. He would organize a great sales force. He would do everything. If our farmers would join this raisin association of his, he would do everything, and our city would grow to be one of the liveliest cities in California. Our valley would grow to be one of the richest agricultural centers of the world. He used big words like *co-operation, mass production, modern efficiency, modern psychology, modern advertising,* and *modern distribution,* and the farmers who couldn't understand what he was talking about felt that he was very wise and that they must join the raisin association and help make raisins famous.

He was an orator. He was a statistician. He was a genius. I forget his name. Our whole valley has forgotten his name, but in his day he made something of a stir.

The editor of the *Morning Republican* studied this man's proposal and found it sound, and the editor of the *Evening Herald* said that it was a good thing, and our mayor was in favor of it, and there was excitement all over our valley. Farmers from all over our valley came to town in surreys and buggies. They gathered in small and large groups in front of our public buildings, and they talked about this idea of making the raisin famous.

It *sounded* all right.

The basic purpose of the raisin association was to gather together all the raisins of our valley, and after creating a demand for them through national advertising, to offer them for sale at a price that would pay for all the operating expenses of the association and leave a small margin for the farmers themselves. Well, the association was established and it was called the Sun-Maid Raisin Association. A six-story Sun-Maid Raisin Building was erected, and an enormous packing and distributing plant was erected. It contained the finest of modern machinery. These machines cleaned the raisins and took the stems from them. The whole plant was a picture of order and efficiency.

Every Thursday in those days I went down to Knapp's on Broadway and got a dozen copies of *The Saturday Evening Post*. The magazine was very thick and heavy. I used to carry a dozen of them in a sack slung over my shoulder. By the time I had walked a block my shoulder would be sore. I do not know why I ever wanted to bother about selling *The Saturday Evening Post,* but I suppose it was partly because I knew Benjamin Franklin had founded it, and partly because I liked to take a copy of the magazine home and look at the advertisements. For a while I even got in the habit of reading the stories of George Agnew Chamberlain. One Thursday evening I had a copy of *The Saturday Evening Post* spread before me on our living-room table. I was turning the pages and looking at the things that were being advertised. On one page I read the words, *Have you had your iron today?* It was a full-page advertisement of our Raisin Association. The advertisement explained in impeccable English that raisins contained iron and that wise people were eating a five-cent package of raisins every afternoon. Raisins banished fatigue, the advertisement said. At the bottom of the page was the name of our Association, its street address, and the name of our city. We were no longer lost in the wilderness, because the name of our city was printed in *The Saturday Evening Post*.

These advertisements began to appear regularly in *The Saturday Evening Post*. It was marvelous. People were hearing about us. It was very expensive to have a full-page advertisement in the *Post*, but people were being taught to eat raisins, and that was the important thing.

For a while people actually *did* eat raisins. Instead of spending a nickel for a bottle of Coca-Cola or for a bar of candy, people were buying small packages of raisins. The price of raisins began to move upward, and after several years, when all of America was enjoying prosperity, the price of raisins became so high that a man with ten acres of vineyard was considered a man of considerable means, and as a matter of fact he was. Some farmers who had only ten acres were buying brand-new automobiles and driving them around.

Everybody in our city was proud of the Raisin Association. Everything looked fine, values were up, and a man had to pay a lot of money for a little bit of desert.

Then something happened.

It wasn't the fault of our Raisin Association. It just happened. People stopped eating raisins. Maybe it was because there was no longer as much prosperity as there had been, or maybe it was because people had simply become tired of eating raisins. There are other things that people can buy for a nickel and eat. At any rate, people stopped eating raisins. Our advertisements kept appearing in *The Saturday Evening Post* and we kept asking the people of America if they had had their iron, but it wasn't doing any good. We had more raisins in our Sun-Maid warehouse than we could ever sell, even to the Chinese, even if they were to drop *three* raisins in every pot of rice they cooked. The price of raisins began to drop. The great executives of the Association began to worry. They began to think up new ways to use raisins. They hired chemists who invented a raisin syrup. It was supposed to be at least as good as maple syrup, but it wasn't. Not by a long shot. It didn't taste like syrup at all. It simply had a syrupy texture, that's all. But the executives of our Association were desperate and they wanted to dispose of our surplus raisins. They were ready to fool themselves, if necessary, into believing that our valley would grow prosperous through the manufacture and distribution of raisin syrup, and for a while they believed this. But people who were buying the syrup didn't believe it. The price of raisins kept on going down. It got so low it looked as if we had made a mistake by pausing in the desert and building our city in the first place.

Then we found out that it was the same all over the country. Prices were low everywhere. No matter how efficient we were, or how cleverly we wrote our advertisements, or how attractive we made our packages of raisins, we couldn't hope for anything higher than the price we were getting. The six-story building looked sad, the excitement died away, and the packing house became a useless ornament in the landscape. Its machinery became junk, and we knew a great American idea had failed. We hadn't changed the taste of man. Bread was still preferable to raisins. We hadn't taught the Chinese to drop a raisin in their pots of cooking rice. They were satisfied to have the rice without the raisin.

And so we began to eat the raisins ourselves. It was amazing how we learned to eat raisins. We had talked so much about them we had forgotten that they were good to eat. We learned to cook raisins. They were good stewed, they had a fine taste with bread. All over the valley people were eating raisins. People couldn't buy raisins because they were a luxury, and so we had to eat them ourselves although they were no luxury to us.

The Broken Wheel

✿ ✿ ✿

WE had a small house on Santa Clara Avenue, in the foreign district of Fresno where everyone moved about freely and where conversations were carried on across yards and alleys and streets. This house had been the home of a man who had been in the business of roasting and marketing all kinds of nuts. We found small and large pieces of his machinery in the two small barns, and in the cracks of the floors we sometimes found nut-shells and bits of nut-meats. The house had a clean wholesome smell. There were a number of crickets somewhere near the kitchen sink and quite a few house spiders, the kind that are called daddy-long-legs. There was also a cat. The cat was there when we moved into the house, so we took it for granted. It was a big black tom with a proud demeanor, an aristocratic air of superiority and indifference. At first it lived under the house in the dark, but later on when the weather got cold the cat moved into the house. We never bothered to give it a name, but referred to it simply as *Gatou*, which is the word for cat in Armenian.

Our trees were two sycamores at the side of the house, by the alley; an English walnut tree in the back yard that was perhaps twenty years old; a small olive tree; and three lilac trees that were growing close to the front porch. The porch was shaded by a thick honeysuckle plant. There were also geraniums, Bermuda grass and other weeds. After a while we planted two peach trees, a cactus tree, and a castor plant. The peach trees happened accidentally; we hadn't meant to plant them, we had only thrown peach-pits in the back yard and the trees had come up by themselves and we hadn't transplanted them. They were growing much too close to one another but they were either very lucky or very stubborn and after three years the leaves that fell from them in the fall were enough to rake into a pile and burn. They were growing just outside our yard but since we had no fence and no close neighbors, except for the family immediately across the alley, we considered the peach trees our trees. Once a year my sister

Naomi would bring some of the pink blossoms into the house and place them in a black vase.

We used to see the blossoms in the vase and suddenly laugh because winter was over. In the winter we laughed a great deal. We would be sullen and sorrowful for weeks and then suddenly all of us would begin to laugh. We would laugh fifteen or twenty minutes and then we would be sullen and sorrowful again.

My brother Krikor was responsible for the cactus tree. He came home one afternoon with a piece of thorny-cactus in his hands. He said, Did you know that all of this country was desert once and that cactus was growing everywhere?

Do you mean no one was living here?

Yes, said Krikor. No one but the lizards, I guess, and the snakes and the horny-toads and the chicken-hawks and things like that. No people.

I thought of our valley without people and streets and houses, and it seemed very strange.

Do you mean, I said, all the way to Selma and all the way to Clovis and away over to Kerman, past Skaggs Bridge?

I mean the whole valley, Krikor replied. I mean all this level land between the Coast Ranges and the Sierra Nevadas. All this country where the vineyards are growing now. It was dry here in those days, so they began to bring in the water in canals and irrigation ditches.

Krikor planted the cactus that afternoon and by the time I was ten it was producing red blossoms and a fruit no one knew how to eat; and it was taller than a tall man.

The castor tree happened accidentally too. An old castor tree was growing in the yard of our neighbors across the alley. One summer some of its seeds got into our yard, and the following summer we had a small castor tree of our own. It was a spurious sort of a tree, growing too rapidly, and being too delicate for a tree. A small boy couldn't climb it and the least little storm that came along would tear some of its branches away. But it had a nice leaf and a clean growing odor and it made a lot of shade. We hadn't planted it, but as long as it had started to grow we were glad about it.

In the summertime it would be very hot and we would have to get up early in the morning to feel a cool breeze. Every summer the city sent out a tractor to plow into the tar of Santa Clara Avenue and improve the condition of the street. This tractor made a lot of noise, pounding steadily, approaching and going away from our house. In the morning we would hear its far-away *boom-boom-boom*. We used to say, Here it is again. We sometimes asked what difference it made if the street was a little uneven. No one uses it, anyway, we said. Casparian, the man who sold watermelons each summer, passed over the street every afternoon with his old horse and his wobbly wagon, crying watermelon in Armenian, but there wasn't much other traffic. Those who wanted to get around in a hurry rode bicycles.

One year my uncle Vahan, then a young man, drove down from San Francisco in a brandnew Apperson roadster and stopped in front of our house.

How do you like it? he asked. There are only eleven Appersons in America and only one red one. His was the red one. We all laughed and my uncle Vahan smoked cigarettes. He took his sister, my mother, for a ride to Roeding Park. It was her first ride in an automobile and she felt very proud of her brother. We all thought he was great. It wasn't only the Apperson, it was also his nervousness and his energy and the way he laughed and talked. When he came back with my mother he took my sisters, Lucy and Naomi, for a ride to town. My brother Krikor sat on the front porch with a book, waiting nervously for his turn to ride. Krikor said the automobile could go fifty miles an hour. Rouben, our neighbor, was sitting on the porch with us. He said his uncle Levon had a Cadillac that could go sixty miles an hour.

Yes, I said, but is it red? He admitted that it was black. There is only one red Apperson in America, I said. It was like saying that one's great-grandfather had seen Lincoln or that one's ancestors had come over on the *Mayflower;* only it was more impressive. You knew that a great big piece of red junk on wheels would come around the corner, thundering, and stop before your house, and you felt that it was a big thing.

My uncle Vahan came home with Lucy and Naomi and went inside for a cup of Turkish coffee. We could hear him telling his sister how he had been getting along in San Francisco. He had passed his Bar examination and was now an attorney-at-law, but he had made most of his money selling watermelons wholesale. Eventually he hoped to open an office in the Rowell Building right here at home. My mother was very happy about her young brother and we could hear her laughing with him and asking him questions.

Krikor was very ill at ease because his uncle Vahan had not offered to take him for a ride and because he was too proud or too polite to *ask* for a ride, but I felt, There is a lawyer in our family and he has a red Apperson. We are an enterprising people. I was so happy about this that I couldn't sit still and kept walking on the porch-railing and jumping down.

When my uncle Vahan came out of the house Krikor was standing a few feet from the automobile, admiring it. He was admiring it so humbly, my uncle understood what it was that was eating him and said, Come on, you fellows. I'll give you a ride.

My uncle Vahan started the motor and we went off, making a lot of smoke and noise. I remember that my mother and Lucy and Naomi stood on the front porch and waved to us. We had an exciting ride through town and felt very elated. When we returned, my mother had cut two cold watermelons and we all sat in the parlor, eating watermelon and talking. It was very hot and we were all perspiring, but it was a clear moment in our lives.

My uncle Vahan said, We do not know how fortunate we are to be in such a country as this. Every man is free. He spoke in Armenian because it was easier for him. He had been thirteen when he came to America and now he was twenty-two. He asked Krikor if he had decided on a career for himself and Krikor became embarrassed. I hope, my uncle Vahan said, you will decide to study law. And my mother replied, Of course. I thought, Krikor wants to be a musician, but I didn't say anything. In a day or two my uncle Vahan drove away in his red Apperson and we began to remember all the little details of his visit that we hadn't paid much attention to at first.

Everything was solid and permanent in our house and we didn't notice the time that was passing. One afternoon Krikor came home with a small black satchel. He placed the satchel on the table in our dining-room and we all gathered around to see what was in it. We never knew what Krikor was likely to do and we were always prepared for anything. Krikor

was very excited and silent. He placed a small key into the key-hole of the satchel and turned it and opened the satchel, and we saw that it contained a cornet. My mother asked in Armenian, What is that, Krikor? and Krikor replied in Armenian that it was called a cornet.

As far back as I could remember we had always had a piano wherever we had lived. There would be times when no one would go near the piano for months and then suddenly all of us would be playing it. My sister Lucy had taken lessons and could play by note. She played the works of Chopin and Mozart. Naomi played by ear. She played the songs of the people, *Keep the Home Fires Burning; I Love You, California; There's a Long Long Trail; Smiles; Dardanella; Oh, What a Pal Was Mary;* and other songs like that. I couldn't play by note and I couldn't play by ear but I had managed to invent a few melodies from which it seemed I could never escape. In my despair I used to beat the keys of the piano, employing all the variations of tempo and volume I could devise. I was always being driven away from the piano by one of my sisters. I didn't know why I had to try to play the piano but it seemed to me that I had to. We were all living and it seemed to me that something should happen, but it always turned out that everything remained the same.

Krikor's cornet was a blunt and tangled affair, more a piece of plumbing than a musical instrument. He brought home a music stand and a book on how to play the cornet. By Christmas, he said, I'll be playing *Barcarole*.

He practiced a long time and we began to accept the horn as something permanent around the house, like the cat or the crickets or the English walnut tree; but he never learned to play *Barcarole*. Krikor had a very bad time of it from the beginning and gradually his ardor cooled and he began to be suspicious. He would fidget with his music and make a valiant effort to play only the printed notes and then suddenly he would go off and make all sorts of noises, and we knew that he could be heard as far south as the Rainier Brewery and as far north as the Court House Park because we had been told. After a while he would be too tired to blow any more and he would sit down and look miserable. He would say, I don't know what's the matter. I have done everything the book says to do and I have practiced regularly. He would look at the horn and ask, Do you think it's because this horn is so old or is it just that I haven't got any talent for cornet-playing? I wouldn't know what to think but I would understand how he felt because I felt the same way. There was something to be done, but we hadn't found out what it was.

Everyone for blocks around knew that Krikor had a cornet and when he passed people in the street they would whisper to one another, There he goes. The boy who is making all the noise. He has a cornet and he is trying to learn to play. We thought it was street cats, but cats don't make that noise in the daytime.

Every summer the long tractor came back and filled the days with its dismal hollow pounding, the nuts from the English walnut tree fell to the ground and we gathered them into boxes. Imperceptibly the change was always going on and each spring my sister Naomi placed peach blossoms in the black vase.

One day Krikor said, I have decided to give up the cornet. He spoke deliberately and, I thought, bravely. Less than a week later he came home on a bicycle, riding under the cross-bar because he couldn't reach the pedals from the seat. He was almost twelve but he was small for his age. When my mother saw him coming up our street, pumping under the cross-bar, his body all out of shape, she ran down the front porch steps to the sidewalk. What is this you've brought home? she said. Get out of that crazy thing. Do you want to cripple yourself for life?

Krikor took the bicycle to the back yard and began to lower the seat. He worked hard and after a while he got the seat down as far as it would go, but even at that the bicycle was too big for him and he had to go on riding it from under the bar. My mother carried the bicycle into the house one evening and locked it in a closet. Your father, she told Krikor, was an erect man and your mother is an erect woman and I am sure I am not going to let you make a cripple of yourself. If you must ride a bicycle you had better get one you can ride from the top.

Krikor had been selling the *Evening Herald* after school almost two years and he had been saving money. My mother encouraged him to save his earnings but she did not object to his spending as much as he felt he ought to spend. On his twelfth birthday he came home with a cake which had cost him seven dollars and fifty cents. When we asked why he had gone to such an unreasonable expense and why he had brought home such a large cake when there were only five of us to eat it, he said, This was the first cake the baker showed me and I hadn't ever bought a birthday cake before. I thought it was about the right size. Is it too big?

We had cake at every meal for a week and we never stopped talking about it.

So Krikor took the big bicycle back to the shop and traded it in for a smaller one. He had very little talent for making bargains and the only reason he had bought the big bicycle in the first place was that Kebo, the bicycle man, had insisted on selling it to him. He came home on a smaller bicycle, sitting on the seat where he belonged and my mother said, That's more like it. You look like something now.

It wasn't long before I was riding the bicycle more than Krikor was, and finally we got into a fight over it. We had had fights before, but this was our biggest fight because we had grown bigger. Krikor chased me around the house and then suddenly I turned and chased him around the other way. We were wrestling when my mother separated us and said that we could not have the bicycle at all if we could not keep from fighting over it. I knew, and I think Krikor knew, it wasn't the bicycle. We would have fought over something else. The bicycle just happened to be there. It was because we were brothers and because we had been together through so many different things. One day when Krikor and I were fighting silently in the back yard old man Andreas, who was passing through the empty lot next to our house, ran up to our front door and cried in Armenian, Ester, Ester, your sons are killing each other!

We began to use the bicycle together, hiking one another. Sometimes I hiked Krikor but most of the time he hiked me. There were many brothers in the town who were doing this. We had made a path across the lot, and at the end of the lot there was a steep bank of three or four feet. We used to start from our back yard and after picking up some speed we used to go down this bank.

One Sunday afternoon in November we decided to ride out to the County Fair Grounds. There was no Fair and no baseball game but we wanted to go out there and get on the dirt track with our bicycle. We had done this before and we had enjoyed being in the deserted Fair Grounds because it was different from being out there when all the people were there. It was finer and more private and we had lots more fun being alone. We liked the quiet and the enormity of the place, the strangeness of the empty grandstands. We used to take turns riding the bicycle around the mile track. Krikor had a watch and he would time me and then I would time him and we had a small book in which we kept a written record of our speed.

The castor plant had grown a lot and the peach trees had spread out. Easter and Christmas and Raisin Day had come around, we had thinned the honeysuckle plant to give it new life, we had bought new shoes and new clothes, we had got ill with the flu, but we hadn't noticed and we hadn't remembered. There were a few photographs of us in the family album, but to look at them it didn't seem as if we had changed. We had gone on quietly, sitting through the winter evenings, doing our school lessons, playing the piano, talking with one another, and laughing loudly for no reason. It had all happened and it was all there but we hadn't remembered about it and now we wanted to get on our bicycle and go out to the County Fair Grounds again.

I sat on the cross-bar and Krikor got on the seat and we went across the lot. Now for the big dip, Krikor said. We came to the bank, but while we were going down something happened. The fork of our bicycle cracked and broke and the front wheel sank on its side. It happened almost too slowly to be real and while it was happening, while the fork was cracking and the wheel was sinking, we seemed to be coming out of a long dream. This trivial occurrence ought to have been amusing, and we ought to have laughed about it, but it wasn't at all amusing and we didn't laugh. We walked back to the house without saying a word.

My mother had seen what had happened from the window of Naomi's room and when we went into the house, she said, Don't you boys realize you've grown? You're too big for one bicycle now.

We didn't speak of the matter all afternoon. We sat around the house trying to read, trying to feel that only the fork of our bicycle had broken. We had forgotten our lives. Now, because of the little accident, we were remembering all the details that marked the stages of our growth.

I remembered the time Krikor and I made a canoe of plaster laths and burlap and tar, because we wanted to float down a stream, and walked with it six miles to Thompson Ditch through a burning sun and saw it sink under us.

I remembered the time I nearly drowned in Kings River and Krikor swam after me shouting in Armenian. The time Lucy lost her job at Woolworth's and cried for a week. The time Naomi was ill with pneumonia and we all prayed she wouldn't die. The time Krikor came home with a small phonograph and two records: *Barcarole* and *O Sole Mio*.

And I remembered with a sickening sensation the day my uncle Vahan came to our house in a soldier's uniform and played *Johnny Get Your Gun* on his violin; my mother's cheerfulness when he sat at our table and her silence when he went away in a train. I remembered all the days she sat in the parlor reading the *Asbarez* and telling us about the misery and pain and dying in the old country.

And I remembered the day we learned that my uncle Vahan had been killed in France and we all sat at the supper table and couldn't eat and went to bed and couldn't sleep because we were all crying and talking about him.

I remembered that I had run down to the *Herald* office each noon for the extra edition about the War and had run through the streets shouting. I remembered the day it ended and the *Herald* printed a front-page etching of our Lord and the words *Peace on Earth, Good Will Toward Men*. How I came home, hoarse from shouting and sick in my soul because it was all over and my uncle Vahan was still in Europe, dead. I remembered the times I had walked alone, and suddenly burst into tears because life was so bright and clean and fierce.

All afternoon and almost all evening there was no talking in our house. My sister Lucy played the piano a few minutes and my sister Naomi hummed *Smiles* until she remembered that my mother had asked her never to hum that song because her brother Vahan had sung it. We all felt sullen and bewildered. We were getting ready to go to bed when Krikor said, Wasn't it funny the way the bicycle broke under us?

My mother and my sisters said it was the funniest sight they had ever seen and they began to laugh about it. They laughed softly at first. They would stop laughing and then remember how funny it had been and then they would start laughing again, only louder. Krikor began to laugh with them and it seemed as if everything in our world was all right. I couldn't decide what to do because I didn't think the incident had been funny at all, but after a while I began to laugh, too. All those things had happened and yet we were still living together in our house and we still had our trees and in the summer the city would send out the long tractor again and we would hear it and old Casparian would pass before our house in his wagon, crying watermelon in Armenian. I didn't feel at all happy but I laughed until tears came out of my eyes.

Then suddenly something strange happened; it happened inside of me, but at the same time it seemed to be happening all over the world. I felt that I was a part of life at last, that I knew how all things ended. A strange, desolating sadness seemed to sweep through the earth and for the first time in my life I was feeling it personally. It seemed as if I had just been born and become aware of the earth. I knew why I had always sat at the piano pounding the keys, why I had fought with my brother Krikor, and why we had laughed together. And because I had been laughing, and because tears had come from my eyes, I sat on my bed and began to cry.

Without saying a word, my brother Krikor began to cry, and after him my sisters began to cry.

My mother said in Armenian, It is no use to cry. We have always had our disappointments and hardships and we have always come out of them and always shall.

When we were all supposed to be asleep, I got up from my bed and went to the door that opened on our parlor and opened it an inch or two. I saw that my mother had taken her brother's photograph from the piano. She had placed it before her on the table. I could hear her weeping softly, and I could see her swaying her head from side to side the way people from the old country do.

The War

✿ ✿ ✿

THE War got into us. We were told not to eat too much, not to waste anything; everything was precious. We were told to buy War Stamps. We were sending thousands of soldiers across the Atlantic to the War, and it was taking money. We were encouraged to earn money and buy War Stamps, twenty-five cents each. Miss Gamma said we, the children, were soldiers just as much as the men in uniforms. There were parades. We saw soldiers marching. We saw them piling into trains at the Southern Pacific depot; we heard their mothers and sisters crying at the depot.

Germany was a criminal nation. The Germans were wiping whole nations off the map. The forests, the fields, the towns, were all being destroyed by big shells. Even in the Atlantic Germany was committing its crimes: down went the *Lusitania*. A submarine sent it to the bottom of the sea.

It was a thing a boy dreamed about. I used to be sick thinking of the *Lusitania*.

I began to hate. Yes, the Germans were criminals. They were not like us. We saw them in *Shoulder Arms* with Charlie Chaplin. At the Kinema Theatre we sat on the edges of our seats and cheered Charlie, the hero of the War. Charlie made mistakes, but in the end he won the War. We saw the Kaiser in the picture, and booed him. He was Germany. And Chaplin, made a monkey out of him. We laughed and laughed, but it was sad all the time, because we knew, they could never fool us, even if it was a comedy.

The world's villain, that was the Kaiser, and we hated him.

It was everywhere, this hate. I had a cousin, a small boy. His name was Simon, and as soon as he learned to talk he said, I will chop off the Kaiser's head. No one had taught him to hate the Kaiser. He had got it out of the atmosphere.

We used to climb the walnut tree in our back yard, a half dozen of us, and sitting in the tree, we used to think up various ways to destroy the Kaiser. There was a boy who was very good at inventing tortures. His name was Albert Savin, and he himself was a cry-baby, but he was the best inventor of tortures in our neighborhood. The major object of each of his tortures was to get the Kaiser as close to death as possible and then to leave off for a while, and then to begin again with another torture, only a little worse. In this way the Kaiser would die a thousand deaths and always stay alive to be tortured again. The least satisfying torture we invented was to have him shot. That was too simple. No one wanted him only to die. All the little boys wanted him to suffer enough to make up for all the suffering he had caused. Some of the tortures would be funny. We would be thinking of Charlie Chaplin and we would think up funny tortures, surprises and so on. We would invite the Kaiser to an important banquet, for example, and we would have a big chair for him to sit in. It would be an electric chair. The Kaiser would be sitting in the chair, eating food, and then we would turn on the current. We wouldn't turn it on enough to burn him to death right away, we would drag it out slowly, and everybody in the room would be standing around him, making faces at him, reminding him of the *Lusitania*. I do not know who invented this torture, but I remember the day it was invented. It was a clear summer day and all of us had felt very lively in the tree. For hours we had dwelt upon good ways of hurting a man without hurting him to death.

There was a family of Germans who had a house in our neighborhood, on San Pablo Street. They were fine people, clean and simple. There was a son named Herman, about the same age as my brother Krikor. He was a quiet boy, a bit sullen, who spoke with a slight accent in spite of the fact that he was a native of our valley.

When we got to talking about torturing the Kaiser, I did a little talking myself, but I thought it was a game and that we would never do anything cruel to anyone. But there were others, bigger boys, and after a while these boys got nervous and wanted to do something. Somebody mentioned Herman. Well, there are a lot of boys who are just like their fathers, and this cry-baby Albert Savin and another boy named Edgar Rife began to stir up hatred for Herman, who hadn't ever done anyone any harm.

It all started in our walnut tree, but it spread out to the whole neighborhood. A mob of these boys, nine or ten of them, decided to get Herman. My brother Krikor went along with them, and I went along too. I didn't want Herman to get hurt, but I couldn't get myself to stay home. I felt it would kill me if I stayed home and didn't see what happened. My brother Krikor walked with me, and we stayed behind the bigger boys. We were not really a part of the mob, but we felt that it had all started in our tree, and we wanted to see.

The mob went to San Pablo Street. Edgar Rife went up to the front door of Herman's house and knocked. The rest of the mob stood across the street, waiting. Herman's mother opened the door, Edgar Rife talked with her a moment, and then returned to the mob.

He's not home, Edgar said. His mother said she thought he went to town. He'll be along pretty soon.

My brother Krikor said in Armenian, I hope he doesn't come home.

But Herman came home. Somebody saw him walking up San Pablo Street, and the mob ran to him. Somebody said, Are you a German?

Herman said, Yes.

Somebody said, Do you hate the Kaiser?

Herman said, No, I don't hate anyone.

Then somebody hit Herman in the face. Somebody tripped him and he fell. Somebody jumped on him, and he was struck and kicked.

It didn't take two minutes. It was all over in no time. We were supposed to be little soldiers. We were supposed to be the defenders of decency. And they said to Herman when he was bleeding at the nose, *Now*, do you hate the Kaiser? And he shouted, No! I hate you! When they saw that he would not hate the Kaiser, they let him up. They laughed at him, and mimicked the way he was crying, and walked behind him, shoving him, striking him from behind, and kicking him. All the way to his house they did these things, and when he reached his house, he did not run. He was walking up the steps of the front porch when his mother came out of the house and saw him. She ran to her son and helped him into the house. She did not say anything to the boys; she was too amazed. The boys stood in front of the house a little while, shouting names and laughing, then went away.

That night when we were in bed I said to my brother Krikor, Krikor, do you hate the Germans? And my brother Krikor said, What? I said again, Do you hate the Germans, Krikor? He did not say anything for a little while, but I knew what he was thinking. No, I don't hate them, he said. I don't know what I hate, but I know I hate something. What they did today. I hate *that*. That is the thing I hate.

The Death of Children

✿ ✿ ✿

EMERSON SCHOOL was haunted. Its twin box-like structures of gray stone, with their high bare walls and small dark windows, were joined by a bridge of wood, and at night the school's appearance was dismal and depressing. Even in the light of day it had a desolate aspect and almost all of its pupils secretly hoped that it would burn down. It was a comparatively recent structure, and there was an Assyrian carpenter in our neighborhood who told us he had helped to construct the school, but we thought of it always as being very old in a way that something decayed and rotten is old. Around sundown every night bats swooped out of its cracks, and flew, in spasmodic jerks, about the school yard.

The western building contained the intermediate grades, and the eastern building contained the fourth, fifth, and sixth grades. Both buildings were haunted. It was said that if you were to pass between the two structures at night, you would hear dead teachers scolding pupils of many years ago. You would hear old lady Timanus saying, Now listen, class. Listen carefully. Two times eight is sixteen, is it not? Very well then, how much is two times sixteen? Then you would hear giggling and mischief, the ghosts of former boys and girls scurrying about the classroom.

Frank Sousa said that he himself had heard these things with his own ears. We took it for granted that he had and we stayed away from the school at night.

One winter evening on my way home from selling papers I came to the dark school and when I remembered that it was haunted I began to feel afraid. I had planned to take a short-cut by walking between the two buildings and cutting across the school grounds to Santa Clara Avenue, but when I remembered the unwholesomeness of the place at night, I decided to walk around it. From across the street I looked up to the small window of the room in which I was a pupil, the fourth-grade room, and just as I did so I heard much noise of a fearful sort, and the lights of the room went on.

I didn't stay to watch and listen. I ran.

Years later I decided it must have been the night janitor sweeping the room. But I could never account for the noise. One man could never have made so much racket, so it must have been my imagination. At any rate, no one believed the school was not haunted, and certainly we haunted it during the day.

We had all the dimensions of real beings, we had weight and form, and yet there was something unreal about us, the small boys, the small girls, the old and young teachers, the sitting with books, the smell of chalk, the asking and answering of all sorts of childish questions. There was something startling about the whole thing.

There were all kinds of us.

There was Rosa Tapia, the little Mexican girl who had more grace than anyone else in the school but no ability to learn, no understanding of grammar, no talent for arithmetic. She did not seem real. She walked as if she were not on earth or as if she were on earth by mistake, and she spoke softly, enunciating her words with the rhythm of song. When America entered the War, Miss Gamma's two brothers left the university at Berkeley to enlist in the army, and our teacher came to class with bloodshot eyes and a dazed expression on her face. She made an admirable effort to teach geography, and then announced that owing to the momentousness of the occasion our class would spend the remainder of the day at games, recitations, and singing. She asked if someone would volunteer to stand before the class and sing some patriotic song. No one offered to do this. Then Rosa Tapia stood in the aisle beside her desk and said, Meess Gamma, do you weesh I should sing *Juanita*?

Everyone in our class was astounded, but most astounded was Miss Gamma, herself. Her sad face was caught tightly with amazement, and she said, Why, of course, Rosa. Come to the front of the class. The little Mexican girl moved to the front of our room without embarrassment. She said, *Juanita*, and began to sing in her native tongue. She sang, not with her lungs and lips, but with the shape of herself that was invisible and could only be sensed, and only by us who were living with her midway between the reality of sleep and the reality of wakefulness, and all of us felt that she, certainly, was not real, not merely one more little girl. And we understood that it was all right and even proper for her not to know about grammar and arithmetic and all the other pointless things that we were being taught.

There was Carson Wampler, a sullen-faced boy, the son of no-account Southerners who had come West in a wagon, penniless, hungry, and mean. They lived in a tent somewhere south, by the Santa Fé Railroad tracks. Carson came to school, even in the winter, without shoes. In the summer it was traditional for all of us to go barefooted and only a few children of the rich wore shoes to maintain their superiority. A number of boys made fun of Carson and called him names, and in the end .it turned out that everyone disliked him and looked down upon him. He was always alone, silent, sullen, and without shoes. For a long time I saw his pinched face and for a long time I was on the verge of going up to him and speaking to him, but there was something about his loneliness and his defiance that was too noble to be touched, and I was afraid to speak to him. His feet were very large and the skin was thick and cracked. When it was very cold he stood alone in the school yard and shivered.

He stopped coming to school suddenly, and I began to wonder where he was and if he ever got a pair of shoes. He became in time the vague sort of identity I sometimes met in dreams. In remembering him it would seem that he had never lived, that I had known him only in the secrecy of my sleep. But I could never forget the defiance of his pinched face and the loneliness that stood with him, shivering.

When, after a number of years, I had almost forgotten him, I saw him again. I was riding in a Ford with an uncle through the vineyard country near Malaga. It was winter and the vines were without leaves. The landscape was brittle and bare but somehow precise with the quiet precision of dream, and therefore beautiful. Carson, grown taller but with the same pinched face, was standing over a vine near the edge of the road, and he was holding a hoe. I was so pleased to see him again that I called his name and greeted him.

Carson thumbed his nose at me and made a face. I felt sorry for him and angry with myself. It was partly the fault of the automobile. There was so little time for friendliness that Carson, doubtless confused and suspicious, automatically performed the swiftest and safest sort of gesture he knew.

I did not see him again.

There was Alice Schwab, a large-limbed, rose-cheeked, German-Jewish girl, the daughter of a watch repairer. She was the neatest and best-behaved girl in school and every morning she came to class with an apple, an orange, or some flowers for her teacher. Once she brought a large shiny eggplant to class, as big as her head. It was from her father's garden and Miss Gamma spent ten minutes praising the eggplant as a vegetable and Mr. Schwab as the father of the pupil who had brought the vegetable to class. We tried to paint the eggplant during our drawing period, but none of us seemed to be able to do it. The color of the eggplant was the most delightful thing about it and we found that none of us could make such a color. It had a delicious look and everyone thought it must have a sweet flavor, but Miss Gamma frowned and said it was not for eating, it was for admiration. The vegetable rested on our teacher's desk until it began to rot, and then it vanished without the slightest reference to the evanescence of all earthly and material things.

Alice was not a pretty girl. Her features seemed unrelated and she herself seemed to be an exaggeration of the idea of good girl. In spite of all this, there was something important about her. It was style perhaps, and even though there was a touch of the pompous and fraudulent about everything she did, she had the most impressive manners of anyone at school.

She wore her thick brown hair in braids hanging down her back, her face glowed with cleanliness, her eyes leaped with intelligence and alertness, she stepped primly, turned pertly, and spoke sharply and emphatically. There was nothing negative about her and she seemed to be the most wholly alive person in our class. She was hardly ever incorrect in her answers to questions, and if occasionally she appeared to be a shade misinformed, everyone, including Miss Gamma, felt that, no, the book must be wrong, Alice could not be. If we were to have taken a vote, she would have been unanimously elected the girl in the fourth-grade most likely to succeed in life. She was teacher's pet and everyone knew that she herself planned to become a teacher. No one liked her, and everyone thought she was a nuisance.

One morning Miss Gamma said:

Everyone will please rise and bow his head. Alice Schwab is dead.

Then all of us loved Alice, and wondered how it was that she of all people had not lived.

One winter morning the door of our classroom opened and our principal, Mr. Dickey, brought into our midst a boy in strange clothes who was small and frightened. There was something about his shy presence that made me ill with joy, for I knew that he had come from our country and that he had seen all that had happened there. I wanted to get up from my seat and speak to him in our tongue. I wanted to protect him from the strangeness of our room, from the eyes that were staring at him, and I wanted him to lift his head and know that here in this new country he was not alone, but I couldn't speak.

I went to him during recess when we were in the school yard. He told me of the things that had happened. He said that all of a sudden they were driving his father and mother and his brothers and sisters along a road at night. Their house was burning. He could see men being struck by soldiers with whips and blades, but he could not cry because it was not a small thing a boy could cry about. They killed his father before his eyes. His mother became insane with grief and could not keep on walking. His brothers became separated from him, and he could not find his sisters. For a long time he walked with the people who had been driven from their homes. Along the roads he saw the bodies of dead men and dead women, and the bodies of many dead children. All over the country it was the same. Everywhere were the bodies of children who had died.

I cannot tell you everything, he said. There are many things I cannot tell you, but I cannot believe that I am alive.

He came to school a year, and then my mother called me to her and she said, Do you know that little boy, Gourken, who came from the old country? He is dead. She showed me a photograph of him that had been printed in the *Asbarez* and she read the account of his life.

The Barber Whose Uncle Had His Head
Bitten Off by a Circus Tiger

✿ ✿ ✿

MISS GAMMA said I needed a haircut, my mother said I needed a haircut, my brother Krikor said I needed a haircut.

Everybody said, When are you going to get a haircut?

There was a grape shipper in our town named Huntington who used to buy an *Evening Herald* from me every day. He was a man who weighed two hundred and forty pounds, owned two Cadillacs, six hundred acres of Alicante vines, and had over a million dollars in the Valley Bank, as well as a small head, all bald. He used to make railroad men from out of town walk six blocks to see my head. There's California for you, he used to shout in the street. There's climate and health. Lord God, he used to roar, there's hair on a head.

Miss Gamma was pretty bitter about my head.

I'm not mentioning any names, she said, but unless a certain young man in this class visits a barber one of these days, he will be sent to Reform School.

She didn't mention any names. All she did was look at me.

What's the big idea? my brother Krikor said.

Remember Samson, I said. Remember the wrath of Samson when they took away his hair.

That was different, said my brother Krikor. You're not Samson.

Oh, no? I said. How do you know I'm not? What makes you think I'm not?

One day I was sleeping on the grass under the walnut tree in our yard when a sparrow flew down from the tree and sang into my ear, waking me up. It was a warm winter day and the world was sleeping. It was very still everywhere. Nobody was rushing around. The only thing you could hear was the joyous hush of reality. Ah, God, it was good to be alive. It was good to have a small house in the world: a big front porch for the long summer afternoons and evenings. Rooms with tables and chairs and beds. A piano. A stove. Pictures out of *The Saturday Evening Post* on the walls. It was good to be in the world.

I was so glad about everything I wanted to dream about the places I had never seen. The magic cities of the world: New York, London, Paris, Berlin, Vienna, Constantinople, Rome, Cairo. The streets, the houses, the people. The doors and windows. The trains and the ships at sea. The bright moments of all the years. In 1919 I dreamed a dream one day: I dreamed the living lived everlastingly. I dreamed the end of decay and death.

Then the sparrow flew down from the tree and woke me up.

I opened my eyes, but didn't move.

Never before in my life had I heard the talk of a bird so clearly. What I heard seemed very startling and new, but at the same time very simple and old. What I seemed to hear was, Weep! weep! weep! And yet the bird articulated this melancholy message in the most joyous spirit. There had been no sound in the world and then suddenly I had heard the music and oratory of the sparrow. For a moment, while I was still half-asleep, the whole business seemed altogether natural: the bird talking to me, and the remarkable contradiction in the meaning of the message and its spirit. On the one hand grief, on the other joy.

I jumped up, and the sparrow, properly frightened, flew as far away as it could go in one breath. As for me, I felt so good I decided to get a haircut.

There was an Armenian barber on Mariposa Street named Aram. He spent most of his time reading the *Asbarez* and other Armenian papers, rolling cigarettes, smoking them, and watching the people go by. I never did see him giving anybody a haircut or a shave, although I suppose one or two people went into his shop by mistake, in all innocence.

I went to Aram's shop on Mariposa Street and found him sitting at the little table with an Armenian book open before him.

In Armenian I said, Will you cut my hair? I have twenty-five cents.

Ah, he said, I am glad to see you. What is your name? Sit down. I will make coffee first. That is a fine head of hair you have.

Everybody wants me to get a haircut, I said.

That is the way with the world, he said. Always telling you what to do. What's wrong with a little hair? Why do they do it? Earn money, they say. Buy a farm. This. That. Ah, they are against letting a man live a quiet life.

Can you do it? I said. Can you cut it all away, so they will not talk about it again for a long time?

Coffee, said the barber. Let us sip a little coffee first.

There was a small gas-range at the back of the shop, a sink and faucet, a shelf with small cups and saucers, spoons, a can-opener, and other things.

He brought me a cup of coffee, and I wondered how it was I had never before visited him, perhaps the most interesting man in the whole city. He was about fifty and I was eleven. He was no taller than I was and no heavier, but his face was the face of a man who has found out, who knows, and yet loves and is not unkind.

When he opened his eyes, his glance seemed to say, The world? I know all about the world. Evil and miserliness, hatred and fear, uncleanliness and rot. Even so, I love it all.

I lifted the small cup to my lips and sipped the hot black fluid. It tasted finer than anything I had ever before tasted.

Sit down, he said in Armenian. We have nowhere to go. We have nothing to do. Your hair will not grow in an hour.

I sat down, and he began to tell me about the world.

He told me about his uncle Misak who was born in Moush.

We drank the coffee. Then I got into the chair and he began to cut my hair. He gave me the worst haircut I have ever gotten, much worse than the ones I got at the barber college across the S. P. tracks, free, but he told me about his poor uncle Misak, and none of the student barbers across the tracks could make up a story like that. All of them put together couldn't do it. I went out of his shop with a very bad haircut, but I didn't care about that. He wasn't a barber anyway. He was just pretending to be a barber, so his wife wouldn't bother him too much. He was just doing that to satisfy the world. All he wanted to do was read and talk to decent people.

My poor uncle Misak, he said, was born a long time ago in Moush. He was a very wild boy, although he was not a thief. He was wild with people who thought they were strong and he could wrestle any two boys in the whole city, and if necessary their fathers and mothers at the same time.

So everybody said to my poor uncle Misak, Misak, you are strong; why don't you be a wrestler and earn money? So Misak became a wrestler. He broke the bones of eighteen men before he was twenty. And all he did with his money was eat and drink and give the rest to children. He didn't want money.

Ah, the barber said, that was long ago. Now everybody wants money. They told him he would be sorry some day, and of course they were right. They told him to take care of his money because some day he would no longer be strong and he would not be able to wrestle, and he would have no money. And the day came. My poor uncle Misak was forty years old and no longer strong, and he had no money. They laughed at him, and he went away. He went to Constantinople. Then he went to Vienna.

Vienna? I said. Your uncle Misak went to Vienna?

Yes, of course, said the barber. My poor uncle Misak went to *many* places. In Vienna, my poor uncle could not find work, so he went to Berlin. Ah, there is a place in the world. Berlin. There, too, my poor uncle Misak could not find work.

The barber was cutting my hair left and right. I could see the black hair on the floor and feel my head becoming colder and colder and smaller and smaller. Ah, Berlin, he said. Cruel city of the world, streets and houses and people, but not one door open to my poor uncle Misak, not one room, not one table, not one friend.

It was the same in Paris, the barber said. The same in London, the same in New York, the same in South America. It was the same everywhere, streets and houses and doors, but no place in the world for my poor uncle Misak.

In China, said the barber, my poor uncle Misak met an Arab who was a clown in a French circus. The Arab clown and my uncle Misak talked together in Turkish. The clown said, Brother, are you a lover of man and animals? And my uncle Misak said, Brother, I love everything in God's holy firmament. The Arab clown said, Brother, can you love a ferocious jungle tiger? And my uncle Misak said, Brother, my love for the ferocious jungle tiger is unbounded.

The Arab clown was very glad to hear about my uncle's love for the wild beasts of the jungle, for he too was a very brave man. Brother, he said to my uncle, could you love a tiger enough to place your head into its yawning mouth?

My uncle Misak said, Brother, I could.

The Arab clown said, Will you join the circus? Yesterday the tiger carelessly closed its mouth around the head of poor Simon Perigord, and there is no longer anyone in the circus with such great love for the creations of infinite God.

My poor uncle Misak was weary of the world, and he said, Brother, I will join the circus and place my head into the yawning mouth of God's holy tiger a dozen times a day.

That is not necessary, said the Arab clown. Twice a day will be enough.

So my poor uncle Misak joined the French circus in China and began placing his head into the yawning mouth of the tiger.

The circus, said the barber, traveled from China to India, from India to Afghanistan, from Afghanistan to Persia, and there, in Persia, it happened. The tiger and my poor uncle Misak became very good friends. In Teheran, in that old decaying city, the tiger grew savage. It was a very hot day, and everyone felt ugly. The tiger felt angry and ran about all day. My poor uncle Misak placed his head into the yawning mouth of the tiger. He was about to take his head out of the tiger's mouth when the tiger, full of the ugliness of things living on this earth, clapped its jaws together.

I got out of the chair. All my hair was gone. I paid Aram the barber twenty-five cents and went home. Everybody laughed at me. My brother Krikor said he had never seen such a haircut before.

It was all right, though.

And I looked forward to the day when I would need a haircut again, so I could go to Aram's shop and listen to his story of man on earth, lost and lonely and always in danger, the sad story of his poor uncle Misak. The sad story of every man alive.

Antranik of Armenia

✿ ✿ ✿

WHEN my grandmother Lucy came to our house she sang about Antranik the soldier until I knew he was a mountain peasant on a black horse who with only a handful of men was fighting the enemy. That was in 1915, the year of physical pain and spiritual disintegration for the people of my country, and the people of the world, but I was seven and I didn't know. From my own meaningless grief I could imagine something was wrong in the world, but I didn't know what. My grandmother sang in a way that made me begin to find out, chanting mournfully and with great anger in a strong voice, while she worked in the house. I picked up the story of Antranik and Armenia in no time because it was in me in the first place and all I needed to do was hear the words to know the remembrance. I was an Armenian. God damn the Turks for making the trouble. (That is the way it is when you are an Armenian, and it is wrong. It is absurd, but I did not know. I did not know the Turk is a helpless man who does what he is forced to do. I did not know that hating him was the same as hating the Armenian since they were the same. My grandmother didn't know either, and still does not know. I know now, but I don't know what good it is going to do me because there is still idiocy in the world. Everybody in the world knows there is no such thing as nationality, but look at them. Look at Germany, Italy, France, England. Look at Russia. Look at Poland. Just look at all the maniacs. I can't figure out why they won't open their eyes and see that it is all idiocy. I can't figure out why they won't learn to use their strength for life instead of death, but it looks as if they won't. My

grandmother is too old to learn, but how about all the people in the world
who were born less than thirty years ago? How about all those people? Are
they too young to learn? Or is it proper to work only for death?)

In 1915 General Antranik was part of the cause of the trouble in the
world, but it wasn't his fault. There was no other way out for him and he
was doing only what he had to do. The Turks were killing Armenians and
General Antranik and his soldiers were killing Turks, but he wasn't destroying any real criminal because every real criminal was far from the scene of
fighting. An eye for an eye, but always the wrong eye. And my grandmother prayed for the triumph and safety of General Antranik, although
she knew Turks were good people. She herself said they were.

General Antranik had the same job in Armenia and Turkey that Lawrence of Arabia had in Arabia: to harass the Turkish Army and keep it from
being a menace to the armies of Italy and France and England. General
Antranik was a simple man who believed the governments of England and
France and Italy when these governments told him his people would be
given their freedom for making trouble for the Turkish Army. He was not
an adventurous and restless English writer who was trying to come to terms
with himself as to what was valid in the world for him, and unlike Lawrence
of Arabia General Antranik did not know that what he was doing was
stupid and futile because after the trouble the governments of England
and France and Italy would betray him. He did not know a strong government needs and seeks the friendship of another strong government, and
after the war there was nothing in the world for him or the people of
Armenia. The strong governments talked about doing something for Armenia, but they never did anything. And the war was over and General
Antranik was only a soldier, not a soldier and a diplomat and a writer. He
didn't fight the Turkish Army because it would give him something to
write about. He didn't write two words about the whole war. He fought the
Turkish Army because he was an Armenian. When the war ended and the
fine diplomatic negotiating began General Antranik was lost. The Turkish
government looked upon him as a criminal and offered a large sum of
money for his capture, dead or alive. General Antranik escaped to Bulgaria, but Turkish patriots followed him to Bulgaria, so he came to America.

General Antranik came to my home town. It looked as if all the Armenians in California were at the Southern Pacific depot the day he arrived.
I climbed a telephone pole and saw him when he got off the train. He was
a man of about fifty in a neat American suit of clothes. He was a little under
six feet tall, very solid and very strong. He had an old-style Armenian
moustache that was white. The expression of his face was both ferocious
and kindly. The people swallowed him up and a committee got him into
a great big Cadillac and drove away with him.

I got down from the telephone pole and ran all the way to my uncle's
office. That was in 1919 or 1920, and I was eleven or twelve. Maybe it was
a year or two later. It doesn't make any difference. Anyway, I was working
in my uncle's office as office boy. All I used to do was go out and get him
a cold watermelon once in a while which he used to cut in the office, right
on his desk. He used to eat the big half and I used to eat the little half.
If a client came to see him while he was eating watermelon, I would tell
the client my uncle was very busy and ask him to wait in the reception room
or come back in an hour. Those were the days for me and my uncle. He
was a lawyer with a good practice and I was his nephew, his sister's son,

as well as a reader of books. We used to talk in Armenian and English and spit the seeds into the cuspidor.

My uncle was sitting at his desk, smoking a cigarette.

Did you see Antranik? he said in Armenian.

In Armenian we never called him General Antranik, only in English.

I saw him, I said.

My uncle was very excited. Here, he said. Here's a quarter. Go and get a big cold watermelon.

When I came back with the watermelon there were four men in the office, the editor of the *Asbarez*, another lawyer, and two clients, farmers. They were all smoking cigarettes and talking about Antranik. My uncle gave me a dollar and told me to go and get as many more watermelons as I could carry. I came back with a big watermelon under each arm and my uncle cut each melon in half and each of us had half a melon to eat. There were only two big spoons and one butter knife, so the two farmers ate with their fingers, and so did I.

My uncle represented one of the farmers, and the other lawyer represented the other. My uncle's client said he had loaned two hundred dollars to the other farmer three years ago but had neglected to get a note, and the other farmer said he had never borrowed a penny from anybody. That was the argument, but nobody was bothering about it now. We were all eating watermelon and being happy about Antranik. At last the other attorney said, About this little matter?

My uncle squirted some watermelon seeds from his mouth into the cuspidor and turned to the other lawyer's client.

Did Hovsep lend you two hundred dollars three years ago? he said.

Yes, that is true, said the other farmer.

He dug out a big chunk of the heart of the watermelon with his fingers and pushed it into his mouth.

But yesterday, said the other lawyer, you told me he didn't lend you a penny.

That was yesterday, said the farmer. Today I saw Antranik. I have no money now, but I will pay him just as soon as I sell my crop.

Brother, said the farmer named Hovsep to the other farmer, that's all I wanted to know. I loaned you two hundred dollars because you needed the money, and I wanted you to pay me so people wouldn't laugh at me for being a fool. Now it is different. I don't want you to pay me. It is a gift to you. I don't need the money.

No, brother, said the other farmer, a debt is a debt. I insist upon paying.

My uncle swallowed watermelon, listening to the two farmers.

I don't want the money, said the farmer named Hovsep.

I borrowed two hundred dollars from you, didn't I? said the other farmer.

Yes.

Then I must pay you back.

No, brother, I will not accept the money.

But you must.

No.

The other farmer turned to his lawyer bitterly. Can we take the case to court and make him take the money? he said.

The other lawyer looked at my uncle whose mouth was full of watermelon. He looked at my uncle in a way that was altogether comical and Armenian, meaning, Well, what the hell do you call this? and my uncle almost choked with laughter and watermelon and seeds.

Then all of us busted out laughing, even the two farmers.

Countrymen, said my uncle. Go home. Forget this unimportant matter. This is a great day for us. Our hero Antranik has come to us from Hayastan, our native land. Go home and be happy.

The two farmers went away, talking together about the great event.

Every Armenian in California was happy about the arrival of Antranik from the old country.

One day six or seven months later Antranik came to my uncle's office while I was there. I knew he had visited my uncle many times while I was away from the office, in school, but this was the first time I had seen him in the office. I felt very angry because I could see how bewildered and bitter and disappointed he was. Where was the glorious new Armenia he had dreamed of winning for his people?

He came into the office quietly, almost shyly, as only a great man can be quiet and shy, and my uncle jumped up from his desk, loving him more than he loved any other man in the world, and through him loving the lost nation, the multitude dead, and the multitude living in every alien corner of the world. And I with my uncle, jumped up, loving him the same way, but *him* only, Antranik, the great man fallen to nothing, the soldier helpless in a world now full of cheap and false peace, he himself betrayed and his people betrayed, and Armenia only a memory.

He talked quietly for about an hour and then went away, and when I looked at my uncle I saw that tears were in his eyes and his mouth was trembling like the mouth of a small boy who is in great pain but will not let himself cry.

That was what came of our little part in the bad business of 1915, and it will be the same with other nations, great and small, for many years to come because that way is the bad way, and even if your nation is strong enough to win the war, death of one sort or another is the only ultimate consequence, death, not life, is the only end, and it is always people, not nations, because it is all one nation, the living, so why won't they change the way? Why do they want to go on fooling themselves? They know there are a lot of finer ways to be strong than to be strong in numbers, in war, so why don't they cut it out? What do they want to do to the people of every nation in the world? The Turk is the brother of the Armenian and they know it. The German and the Frenchman, the Russian and the Pole, the Japanese and the Chinese. They are all brothers. They are all small tragic entities of mortality. Why do they want them to kill one another? What good does it do anybody?

I cherish the exhilaration that comes from having one's body and mind in opposition to a strong force, but why should that force be one's own brothers instead of something less subject to the agonies of mortality? Why can't the war be a nobler kind of war? Is every noble problem of man solved? Is there nothing more to do but kill? Everybody knows there are other things to do, so why won't they cut out the monkey business?

The governments of strong nations betrayed Antranik and Armenia after the war, but the soldiers of Armenia refused to betray themselves. It was no joke with them. The governments of strong nations were busy with complex diplomatic problems of their own. Their war was ended and the time had come for conversation. For the soldiers of Armenia the time had come for death or great good fortune, and the Armenian is too wise to believe in great good fortune.

These were the Nationalists, the *Tashnaks*, and they fought for Armenia, for the nation Armenia, because it was the only way they knew how to fight for life and dignity. The world had no other way. It was with guns alone. It was the bad way, but these men were great men and they did what they had to do. They were dead wrong, but it was the only way. Well, they won the war. (No war is ever won: that is a technical term, used solely to save space and time.) Somehow or other the whole people was not annihilated. They were cold and hungry and ill, but these soldiers won their war and Armenia was a nation with a government and a political party, the *Tashnaks*. (That is so sad, that is so pathetic when you think of the thousands who were killed, but I honor the soldiers, those who died and those who still live. These I honor and love, and all who compromised I only love.) It was a mistake, but it was a noble mistake. It was a very small nation of course, a very unimportant nation, surrounded on all sides by enemies, but for two years, for the first time in thousands of years, Armenia was Armenia, and the capital was Erivan.

I know how silly it is to be proud, but I cannot help it, I am proud.

The war was with the Turks of course. The other enemies were less active than the Turks, but watchful. When the time came one of these, in the name of love, not hate, accomplished in no time at all what the Turks, who were more honest, whose hatred was unconcealed, could not accomplish in hundreds of years. These were the Russians. The new ones. They were actually the old ones, but they had a new theory and they said their idea was brotherhood on earth. They made a brother of Armenia at the point of a gun, but even so, if brotherhood was really their idea, that's all right. Very few of the Armenians of Armenia wanted to be brothers to the new Russians, but each of them was hungry and weary of the war and consequently the revolt against the new enemy was brief and tragic. It ended in no time at all. It looked as if the world simply wouldn't let the Armenians have their own country. They just didn't want the Armenians to have their nation. So it turned out that the leaders of the Armenian soldiers were criminals, so they were shot. That's all. The Russian brothers just shot them. Then they told the Armenians not to be afraid, the Turks wouldn't bother them any more. The brotherly Russian soldiers marched through the streets of the cities of Armenia and told everybody not to be afraid. Every soldier had a gun. There was a feeling of great brotherliness in Armenia.

Away out in California I sat in my uncle's office. To hell with it, I said. It's all over. We can begin to forget Armenia now. Antranik is dead. The nation is lost. The strong nations of the world are jumping with new problems. To hell with it. I'm no Armenian. I'm an American.

Well, the truth is I am both and neither. I love Armenia and I love America and I belong to both, but I am only this: an inhabitant of the earth, and so are you, whoever you are.

I tried to forget Armenia but I couldn't do it. My birthplace was California, but I couldn't forget Armenia, so what is one's country? Is it land of the earth, in a specific place? Rivers there? Lakes? The sky there? The way the sun comes up there? And the moon? Is one's country the trees, the vineyards, the grass, the birds, the rocks, the hills and mountains and valleys? Is it the temperature of the place in spring and summer and winter? Is it the animal rhythm of the living there? The huts and houses, the streets of cities, the tables and chairs, and the drinking of tea and talking? Is it the peach ripening in summer heat on the bough? Is it the dead in the earth there? The unborn? Is it the sound of the spoken language in all the places of that country under the sky? The printed word of that language? The picture painted there? The song of that throat and heart? That dance? Is one's country their prayers of thanks for air and water and earth and fire and life? Is it their eyes? Their lips smiling? The grief?

Well, I don't know for sure, but I know it is all these things as remembrance in the blood. It is all these things within one's self, because I have been there, I have been to Armenia and I have seen with my own eyes, and I know. I have been to *that* place. There is no nation there, but that is all the better. And I know this: that there is no nation in the world, no England and France and Italy, and no nation whatsoever. And I know that each who lives upon the earth is no more than a tragic entity of mortality, let him be king or beggar. I would like to see them awaken to this truth and stop killing one another because I believe there are other and finer ways to be great and brave and exhilarated. I believed there are ways whose ends are life instead of death. What difference does it make what the nation is or what political theory governs it? Does that in any way decrease for its subjects the pain and sorrow of mortality? Or in any way increase the strength and delight?

I went to see. To find out. To breathe that air. To be in that place.

The grapes of the Armenian vineyards were not yet ripe, but there were fresh green leaves, and the vines were exactly like the vines of California, and the faces of the Armenians of Armenia were exactly like the faces of the Armenians of California. The rivers Arax and Kura moved slowly through the fertile earth of Armenia in the same way that the rivers Kings and San Joaquin moved through the valley of my birthplace. And the sun was warm and kindly, no less than the sun of California.

And it was nowhere and everywhere. It was different and exactly the same, word for word, pebble for pebble, leaf for leaf, eye for eye and tooth for tooth. It was neither Armenia nor Russia. It was people alive in that place, and not people alone, but all things alive there, animate and inanimate: the vines, the trees, the rocks, the rivers, the streets, the buildings, the whole place, urban and rural. The automobile bounced over the dirt road to the ancient Armenian church at Aitchmiadzin, and the peasants, men and women and children, stood in bare feet on the ancient stone floor, looking up at the cross, bowing their heads, and believing. And the Armenian students of Marx laughed humbly and a little shamefully at the innocent unwisdom and foolish faith of their brothers. And the sadness of Armenia, my country, was so great in me that, sitting in the automobile, returning to Erivan, the only thing I could remember about Armenia was the quiet way General Antranik talked with my uncle many years ago and the tears in my uncle's eyes when he was gone, and the painful way my uncle's lips were trembling.

Little Miss Universe

✧ ✧ ✧

THERE were three authorities on the horses at *The Kentucky*, Number One Opera Alley in San Francisco: Mr. Levin, a fat gentleman of fifty who was affectionately called The Barrel because he resembled one; San Jose Red, a nervous, thin person of sixty-five; and a neatly dressed young man of twenty who was known as Willie. These three gentlemen knew more about race-horses than any other three people living, and for that matter, as someone had suggested, more than the horses themselves knew. Nevertheless, they were almost always out of funds with which to play the ponies. Each kept an accurate record of what he would have won if he had had money with which to bet, and the profit for each day was fairly amazing; for a month it was breath-taking. A month ago, for example, if Willie had had a half-dollar to bet on the nose of *Panther Rock*, today he would be worth—well, to be exact (he opened a small book full of neatly written figures)—ten thousand two hundred and eighty-six dollars and forty-five cents.

And, said Willie, I could use it, too.

Willie had a system. He looked up the horses in every race and chose the one with the worst record. That horse, he explained, has been loafing. He has been going around the track as a spectator, watching the race from a good position. But he'll win today. Even a horse has got to break the monotony. He'll win out of sheer boredom. His mother was *Ella Faultless*, and you know what she did.

No, somebody said. What did she do?

Well, said Willie, five years ago she started twenty times and wasn't once in the money. She ran beautifully but never exerted herself. Then all of a sudden she woke up and won six races in a row.

Willie looked into the faces of his small audience with an expression of profound wisdom, as if by divine grace he alone of all mortals had been blessed with the faculty of understanding such a remarkable performance.

Bang, he said with emotion.

One.

Two.

Three.

Four.

Five . . . SIX!

In a row. Think of it. He spoke the small words distinctly, sending them from his mouth with the pain and precision and pride of a hen producing an egg.

Somebody must have got the horse mad, said the young gambler named Blewett. He was a barber by profession.

Willie smiled at Blewett and whispered confidentially, That's just it— some horse must have got her mad. We can't figure these things out because they're not in the dope sheets. But it's a cinch one horse can get another horse sore. Remember *Mr. Goofus?* He was a card.

What'd he do? asked Mr. Blewett.

There was a horse, said Willie. He paused to catch his breath for the remarkable statement he was about to make. There was a horse, he repeated, that was almost human.

Ridiculous, said D. L. Conrad, an accountant who had passed out cards to several of his pals of the pool room. Who ever heard of such a thing? How can a horse be almost human?

Allow me to explain, said Willie with the imperial air of a duke addressing a peasant. It is characteristic of human beings to compete, is it not? In athletics. In commerce. In life itself. And, yes, in love, too, for that matter.

Granted, said Mr. Conrad, the accountant. But what has that to do with Mr. Goober, or whoever it was you mentioned?

Allow me, said Willie impatiently. If you will permit me to proceed for a moment, you will soon know. Now then: I said *Mr. Goofus* was almost human. I mean just that. There was a horse that had the soul of man. In short, he was vicious. He was a bully. Please do not interrupt me. If *Mr. Goofus* was leading the field and another horse tried to overtake him, why, he would turn around and bite the horse. It made him mad to have another horse pass him. He didn't like it. Of course they disqualified him a couple of times, but that didn't matter. He had all the horses scared, and it wasn't often they would try to get in front of him. He had a terrible eye, they say. One look and it was all over. *Mr. Goofus* won a lot of races and he beat horses that were a lot better-bred than he was. You've got to work on horse personalities. That is an element almost invariably overlooked by handicappers. Psychology. Horses have it. No use being old-fashioned. There isn't a single race-horse that hasn't better breeding than the average man. You can't expect such beasts to remain uncivilized for long. They're bound to get vicious after a while.

Nuts, said Mr. Conrad with a laugh. A horse is a horse. Tell me who's going to win the third at Arlington and we'll have a beer together.

I do *not* tout, said Willie with pride. I like *Miss Universe*.

Mr. Conrad made an ugly face. Why, he said, that horse has started eleven times in the past month and hasn't once been better than sixth.

I know, said Willie. I'm aware of the facts. Nevertheless, I like her just the same.

I'm playing *Polly's Folly*, said Mr. Conrad. This horse was what is known as a hot favorite; her odds were a paltry six to five to win, whereas the odds on *Miss Universe* were twenty to one. Nevertheless, Willie said: I hope you have luck.

Willie sat at a table and produced his notebook and a pencil. Under the classification *Tired Horses* he wrote the name *Polly's Folly*. Among other names under this classification was that of the great *Equipoise*. In Willie's humble estimation Equipoise was tired of everything; of winning, of racing, of the whole routine in general. Let it be known then that Willie, himself a superior by nature, disliked superior horses and cherished fondly those whom most bettors despised. For example, of the millions of ponyplayers in America, he alone had hopes for the ultimate success of the two-year-old maiden *Miss Universe*. To Willie this horse was not merely another horse. She was something more mystical. Along with the success of *Miss Universe* would date the success of Willie himself. She was his pet.

He loved her passionately. He had a special alibi for each of her miserable performances, a psychological alibi. Also: the name was beautiful. It was poetry. No other horse in the history of racing had had such a glorious name. Such a horse could not fail. It would be unnatural.

Mr. Levin, called The Barrel, also had a system. It was externally more complicated than Willie's, but a good deal less subtle. Willie's system was centrifugal, working outward from the brain, the soul, and the personality of the horse. The hub of Mr. Levin's system was the great panorama of the world itself. To him the horses were mere puppets, helpless and a bit foolish. His desire was to discover the dark secrets of owners, jockeys, and wise gamblers. His system took into consideration all the physical facts involved in a race: the distance, the weight and talent of the jockey, the tendencies of the owner and trainer of the horse, the weather at the track, the number of people at the track, the state of his own private stomach, and the amount of money on the person being touted.

In short, everything.

Mr. Levin was a drab realist. Willie, on the other hand, was a mystic. Which brings my document (for this *is* a document, as I shall soon show) to the case of M. San Jose Red. I have said he was a thin, nervous person of sixty-five. Do not imagine, however, that San Jose Red was an old man, for he was not. (A young man once addressed him innocently as *Pop* and was severely reprimanded for the indelicacy. Don't call me Pop, said San Jose Red. I don't like it. I go out of this joint every day with five hundred dollars. This was a preposterous exaggeration, but San Jose Red apparently had the idea that if a man made money on the races he could not possibly be old.) He had the slim figure of a boy, the voice of a boy, and, alas, the sense of one. He was Irish. He was angry. He puffed at his pipe with defiance. He uttered one fantastic falsehood after another, innocently, sinlessly, since he himself believed his most atrocious lies. He was never known to have a dime. Nevertheless, he maintained vigorously that he won no less than five hundred dollars per week, net. If you got him angry enough he announced, as I have already indicated, that he earned this sum *every* day. He was extravagantly careless with these sums, and threw vast figures about him with the heedlessness of the born spendthrift. Nothing definite was known about him, though from his name it is to be inferred that at one time he lived in or near the city of San Jose, which lies sixty miles south of San Francisco, in Santa Clara Valley.

Needless to say, San Jose Red also had a system. It was the laughing-stock of The Kentucky, but San Jose Red believed in it implicitly. After every race this fiery old codger would swiftly scribble the name of the winner on a small sheet of cardboard, and, flourishing this document wildly, rush through the crowd, grumbling insanely, but with a beatific smile on his magnificent Irish face, See? *Black Patricia.* I told you. Why, I picked that horse last night. And then he would go on to tell a stranger how much he cleaned up every day.

This system, of course, is nothing short of infallible; in fact, it is a good deal more than infallible, for there has not yet been a horse race in which at least one horse has not won. Under the circumstances, it must be designated a philosophical (and perhaps scientific) system, and San Jose Red must be identified as both a philosopher and a scientist, something in the nature of Albert Einstein with a bit of Oscar Spengler, Walter Lippmann, and the Associated Press thrown in for good measure. The philosophy accelerates on this scientific basis; one waits until a thing happens, and then declares that it has happened. You can't go wrong; science, statistics, legal documents, and everything else is on your side. It is, in its way, the only system known to man worth a tinker's toot, or whatever it is. But you've got to be unimaginative to fool with it. Or else, like San Jose Red, you've got to believe in the retrogression of events. In plainer terms, you've got to confuse the outcome of an event with the state of affairs immediately preceding the outcome. Or in still simpler terms, you've got—well, you've got to be sixty-five and Irish and broke and angry and frustrated and mad at the world. You've got to give yourself all the odds, a million to one, or to use figures generally related to the number of light years of the universe (or something), sixty trillion to one.

Now, perhaps, you are beginning to see that this *is* a document, and a profound one at that; a document with stupendous implications. For the unsubtle reader, and for children, I shall hint one of the implications.

Gambling, betting on horses, among other things, is a way of life. The manner in which a man chooses to gamble indicates his character or his lack of it. In short, gambling is a game, a philosophy, just as in Spain bull-fighting is these things, as Mr. Hemingway has pointed out in five hundred pages of small print and two or three dozen photographs. Of course this document would be richer if I accompanied it with photographs of San Jose Red, Mr. Levin, and Willie in various poses and at various crucial moments. I should like to have you see, for instance, an actual photographic reproduction of San Jose Red frantically flourishing the name of the latest winner, or one of Mr. Levin standing humbly behind his stomach telling a boy of eighteen how to play the ponies, or yet another of Willie in his elegantly pressed twelve-dollar suit, elucidating on the subtle make-up of horse-brains; but I regret that I cannot produce these pictures. Not that these men are not real flesh-and-blood people (you can go down to Number One Opera Alley any day and see for yourself that they are), but that the light in *The Kentucky* is dim indeed, and furthermore that my camera lies now in hock.

My document ought, properly, to end at this point, but such a termination would be artless. What sort of a story do you call that? readers would be saying to themselves. No plot, no outcome, no climax, nothing exciting.

All right then. I will proceed to a plot. I will manufacture an outcome, a climax, and produce excitement. (Mind you, nothing ever really happens at *The Kentucky*. Bets are made, a few lucky fellows collect, but in the long run everybody loses. These are the facts. Day in and day out Willie and Mr. Levin and San Jose Red arrive and wait for the races, but nothing ever happens, so if I make a tale it is not my fault, but the fault of art.)

Well, Willie is sitting at a table. The next race is the third at Arlington. Mr. Levin is rolling a cigarette of borrowed paper and tobacco. While he does so he is telling the man from whom he has borrowed the tobacco that a horse named *Wacoche* is going to win the race. He's going to win by six lengths, says Mr. Levin, feeling miserable and lonely.

San Jose Red is out of sight. He comes in after the race. No one knows where he goes between races, but he is always out of sight until the winner is announced.

Let the matter rest here for a moment. Anyone can see for himself that any number of tales are possible now. I could say, for instance, as a young man once actually said, speaking of himself, that Willie, in an idle moment, thrust his thumb and his forefinger into his upper right-hand vest pocket, an act of habit, and there felt a heavy coin, which instantly set

his heart to beating and proved to be a *bona fide* American half-dollar coin.
I can go on to say that Willie rushed up to Smithy, the bookie-clerk, and
bet the whole half-dollar right on the nose of *Miss Universe*, and that furthermore *Miss Universe* came to life and won the race, thereby placing in
Willie's neat trousers the vast sum of ten dollars. And I could continue,
saying that Willie's luck, as he himself dreamed, began at this point and
that from this meagre beginning in less than a week he became the pos-
sessor of four hundred and sixty-two dollars and eleven cents. I could say,
for the sake of romance, that he was in love with a beautiful young stenographer who would not marry him until he earned enough money to buy
a license and a cheap ring. And so on.

About Mr. Levin and San Jose Red I could say all sorts of things that
would make this tale interesting and exciting, but, forgive me, I *cannot*.
It is impossible for me to lie, even though Mr. Kipling has declared that
writers can never lie, that even when they do so, they unconsciously reveal
an even more profound truth. But about these men I cannot lie. Their
stories are exciting enough in themselves. Let us try to be content with the
paltry romance which lies pathetically in the ugly truth.

So we return. It is Thursday. One twenty-four P.M. In about six minutes
the third race at Arlington will be run.

There's the lay-out.

Now the fun begins.

I am strolling along Third Street, a melancholy-looking young writer seeking material for a tale. It is a bright day, the sun is warm, and even the
forlorn men on this drab street seem to reflect the brightness of the day in
their unshaved faces. I am idly eating California peaches, when suddenly
I notice three men hurrying in quick succession through a narrow doorway
marked *Cairo Club, Gentlemen*. There is something exciting about their
haste. I decide to find out where they are going and why. In less than half
a minute another man passes swiftly and impatiently through the same
portal. Then another. Then yet another. This last fellow is in a terrific
hurry; he is nervously jingling two coins in his right hand. I follow him
at a trot and find myself stampeding down a narrow and dark corridor,
close on the heels of my guide. We make two turns, open as many doors,
and finally emerge into the gloom of a paved crevice between the Winchester Hotel, Rooms 35¢ and Up, and the Westchester Hotel, same rates.

It is Opera Alley!

I read the sign *Number One Opera Alley* over the swinging doors of
The Kentucky, and hasten to enter. Number One Opera Alley is a large,
dark, square room containing five tables, fourteen chairs, six benches, and
thirteen spittoons; not to mention sixty-three men including Mr. Levin and
Willie. (San Jose Red, as I have already mentioned, is out of sight for the
moment.) I am there. I myself, the writer. I see that Mr. Levin is sadly
longing for someone to tout. And I see Willie seated at the table, impeccable, his face glowing with lack of character, his entire physical being a
picture of graceful lack of purpose. Still, he is the neatest person in the
room, so I take the chair beside him.

In precisely four minutes and twelve seconds *Miss Universe*, in company with seven other horses, will begin to scramble around the track at
Arlington Park, in Chicago. There is no time to lose, but I know absolutely nothing about horses or horse-racing.

For fully fifteen seconds I do not hear so much as an idle word from
the lips of my contemporary. (Nine out of ten gamblers are habitual talkers-

to-themselves. But not Willie.) I decide to offer him a cigarette. He replies: Thank you, I do not smoke.

I am astounded. What character! What discipline! Not to smoke in that atmosphere of hope and dread and spiritual fidgetiness. It is incredible.

Although I am aware of what is going on, I say to Willie in order to make conversation:

What is going on here, anyway?

He looks at me with eyes that are suddenly transformed. I detect in them the roar and surge of great hope. I am, bluntly, a greenhorn, and perhaps after all Willie will be able to bet on *Miss Universe*—with *my* money. Nevertheless, he is a subtle performer.

I beg your pardon, he says with elegance.

I repeat my question and Willie relates to me the entire history of horse-racing, the tricks of owners, the habits of jockeys, the idiosyncrasies of horses, and the thoughtlessness of most gamblers. And while he speaks with an air of great leisure, he nevertheless imparts all this information in something less than twenty seconds flat. A thoroughbred himself.

In the meantime I have dispatched my right hand to my vest pocket where I have carefully placed my last dollar, the dollar which is to keep me with food in my stomach another long week.

By this time, I have developed implicit confidence in the mystical omnipotence, etcetera, of Willie, and am itching to have him make a bet for me.

There is one horse in this race, says Willie, that is all but human. She hates to lose; it breaks her heart. She has been trying for all she's worth and today's her day. She is the daughter of *Lady Venus* by *The Wop*, and you know what *Lady Venus* did.

Of course I have no idea what *Lady Venus* did, and I say so.

Everything, says Willie. She did everything.

Well, I say, who is the horse?

Willie bends to whisper into my ear, so that no one will learn the good news. *Miss Universe*, he says passionately.

God, what a beautiful name, I think, and the next thing I know I have given Willie my last dollar. He rushes up to Smithy, the bookie-clerk, and plasters it on the nose of *Miss Universe*—and none too soon either, for no sooner had Smithy scribbled the bet on a slip of paper than the race began.

You see, everything worked perfectly and precisely.

Well, there I am in *The Kentucky*, and about two thousand miles away, in Chicago, eight horses are running around a track, one of them *Miss Universe*. And there beside me is Willie, neat and clean, piously hopeful.

A beautiful name, I keep thinking. A glorious name.

The phone clerk calls: At the quarter: *Stock Market, Dark Mist, Fiddler*. This means that these horses are leading the field in the order named.

Willie is pale. I'm paler. Willie says, She's running fourth. She starts slow but she'll come up. Then for an instant he is overcome and shouts to himself, Come on, *Miss Universe!*

I do the same.

The phone clerk announces: At the half: *Stock Market, Dark Mist, Fiddler*.

Willie is a little paler. I'm just a shade paler than he is.

Her mother, Willie gasps, lost eleven races before she got out in front. This is *Miss Universe's* eleventh race. You watch her tear loose in a minute.

The phone clerk, his voice rising (he knows everyone is excited and he wants to be sympathetic; he knows small histories are being made and unmade; he is not heartless and he *can* shout), shouts:

At the far turn: *Stock Market*, a neck, *Fiddler*, a half-length, *Dark Mist*, five lengths.

Cute Face is running fourth, he declares apologetically.

Willie is visibly nervous and a bit paler than before. I resemble a well-dressed ghost.

Come on, *Miss Universe*, Willie whispers madly.

Yes, I say to myself. Come on, *Miss Universe*, please come on, that's all the money I have and I have a terrible appetite.

It was a prayer, I admit. All horse-bettors are piously religious.

The phone clerk pauses dramatically and shouts:

The next is the winner.

Then he says:

Number 57, *Fiddler*, wins—by a neck. 51, *Stock Market*, is second—by three lengths. 53, *Dark Mist*, is third.

There you have it: the story. Nothing added, nothing taken away.

But wait: what's this? A mad man is tearing through the crowd. He is small and Irish, and he is shouting, See. Didn't I tell you? *Fiddler. Fiddler.* Why, I had him picked last night. He is holding a slip of cardboard on which is written the name of the horse.

It is San Jose Red, but, of course, you knew.

Willie is ill with disappointment. He falls exhausted into a chair.

I'm sorry, he says. Her father was never much to speak of.

It's all right, I reply.

Now I am walking up Third Street with an empty pocket, and I am telling myself, There is still half a loaf of rye bread, a quarter pound of coffee, a bit of cheese, and eleven cigarettes. *Miss Universe*. What a beautiful name! If I have one slice of bread twice a day and a cup of coffee for breakfast—well, I can make it, I suppose.

Our Little Brown Brothers the Filipinos

✿ ✿ ✿

I DON'T suppose you ever saw a two-hundred-and-fifty-pound Filipino. They don't come that size very often, but when they do, brother, look out. It's as bad as an earthquake or a hurricane. I guess I was just about the best friend Ramon Internationale had in the world, but do you think I could ever figure out what that crazy baboon was liable to do, especially in a wrestling match? I never could figure out anything. I used to sit in the little office on Columbus Avenue and worry about him all the time. He just wouldn't lose. He was the biggest and toughest and wildest gorilla that ever got out of the jungle into the world. The only difference between him and something goofy in a cage was that he could talk, and boy how he could talk. Perfect English. You know nothing, he used to say; you do not know anything.

Ramon Internationale? I said. Never heard of him.

Never heard of him? he said. Ever hear of Jimmy Londos, Strangler Lewis? Ever hear of Dempsey? Well, this baby was all of those guys in one large package. Not to mention Firpo. Where the hell were you two years ago?

I was right here in Frisco, I said.

Well, so was Internationale, he said. What were you doing, hiding? Didn't you ever read the papers? Don't you remember seeing his picture on the front page of every newspaper the day after he wrestled six police-men, one referee, two timekeepers, three reporters, and me?

No, I said. I don't remember. Who won the match?

Who won the match? Who else? Internationale won the match. The ligaments of my left leg were in a knot three weeks after that trouble. His heart was broken about that. He claimed he didn't know it was me. He said he thought it was some enemy of his people. He figured everybody in Frisco hated his people. Tom, he said, why didn't you stay out of that trouble? Who told you to jump in there when I was angry? I told him I had to do it to keep him from going to jail.

How come? I said.

I was his manager. That's how come. I couldn't let him mangle all them citizens without trying to quiet him down. The crowd thought it was the best wrestling match in the history of the game. That was the only thing that kept him from going to jail. The crowd was tickled to death because he knocked everybody out of the ring and then refused to move. He stood right in the middle of the ring and refused to move. The crowd was tickled to death. It was like some crazy giant challenging the whole world, and that's something that always goes over big with people who go to wrestling matches.

What started the trouble in the first place? I said.

What? he said. You don't mean what. You mean who. It wasn't any-thing. It was Internationale. He was supposed to lose a match to Vasili Ivanovitch, the Russian rock crusher, so Vasili wouldn't look like a punk. Vasili looked like a real tough guy, but Internationale could floor him in three minutes any day in the week. I agreed with Vasili's manager that Internationale should throw the match, but I didn't know very much about Internationale at the time. He didn't like the idea of losing to Vasili. He just didn't like the idea of losing at all. He couldn't understand such a thing. I had got five matches for him and he had won each of them easily because they weren't framed. This was his first big match, so of course it was framed. Well, he moped in the office four days in a row before the match. Tom, he said, I don't want to wrestle this Russian if I got to lose to him. I can floor that fellow in three minutes. I knew that. He didn't have to tell me, but the game has rules and if you don't want to starve you've got to play the game according to the rules. Internationale could floor any man in the world in three minutes, but that's no business. There's got to be a contest. The crowd likes it better when a strong man loses. I argued with him four days in a row and even then I didn't know for sure what he would do. I guess he himself didn't know. I guess he wanted to wait until he got into the ring with the Russian rock crusher before making up his mind. He was supposed to let Vasili floor him after eleven minutes the first time, and after seven minutes the second. Well, he let Vasili

floor him the first time after fifty-seven minutes. He nearly killed that poor
Russian in them fifty-seven minutes. Then he laid down in the middle of
the ring, flat on his back, and Vasili sprawled all over him, trying to act
tough. That was the first fall. It was two out of three.

Well, when they started the next one Vasili got a little careless with his
facial expression, figuring he was going to win anyway, and he got Internationale sore, and Internationale floored the Russian in seven minutes.
I was scared stiff and when I went to Internationale in the dressing room
I knew it was all over.

He was smoking a cigar. Tom, he said, you know nothing; you do not
know anything.

What's the matter? I said.

That Russian fool thinks he's tough, he said. He thinks he can have
fun with me.

No, I said. You're wrong, Ramon. He knows you can floor him in three
minutes.

You know nothing, he said. You do not know how it is with me in the
ring. It is not like out here, talking. When he starts thinking he is better
than I am, I got to show him he's wrong. I got to lay him out.

Don't be like that, Internationale, I said. Lose this match, so we can
get a return match at more money.

I don't want more money, he said.

Listen, Internationale, I said. Who was it took you out of the pea fields
down in Salinas and brought you up to Frisco and made a great wrestler
out of you? It was me, wasn't it? Well, you got to play ball. You got to
do me this little favor. You got to lose this match to Vasili Ivanovitch
because if you win, you and me both are just about through in this game.
No manager in the country will give us another match.

Why? he said. I can floor any of their wrestlers. Why do I have to lay
down for them?

Well, I said, that's the way the game is played, and we've got to play
the game according to the rules.

So it was time to go back to the ring. The crowd was yelling for more,
especially all the little Filipinos, not one of them more than a hundred ten
pounds in weight, but every one of them dressed in purple and red and
green clothes, every one of them smoking a long panetela cigar. There
must have been a thousand of them, but it looked more like a million.
Every one of them had bet money on Internationale to win, and me and
Vasili's manager and a couple of cops and the referee and the timekeepers
and the three newspaper reporters had bet on him to lose.

First Internationale took to throwing Vasili out of the ring, and Vasili
kept rubbing his bruises and groaning and looking around at everybody to
see why everything was going wrong. Internationale threw him out of the
ring three times, and then Diamond Gates the referee figured he'd stop all
the nonsense. Vasili was horsing around a little and Internationale fell on
his back. He was getting up, holding Vasili by the nose, eyes, ears, and hair
with one hand, and both feet with the other, all primed to throw him out
of the ring again, when Diamond Gates patted Vasili on the back and
called him the winner. Of course that was the only thing to do, but it
was a mistake. Internationale threw Vasili out of the ring, and then he
threw Diamond Gates out, and then the three reporters, who had been
drinking a little, jumped into the ring, and Internationale threw them out,
and then the cops jumped in, and the ones he didn't get to throw out, he

knocked out, and then I jumped in. Less than ten seconds later I was sitting in Harry White's lap, away back in the tenth row. By the time my head cleared Internationale was standing alone in the center of the ring challenging the world. And the crowd was tickled to death.

Didn't you ever read about that in the papers? he said.

No, I said. I guess I missed that. But what happened? How did it end?

Well, he said, Internationale kept waving at Vasili to come back into the ring like a man and finish the match, but Vasili wouldn't think of it. Then Internationale asked the cops to come back, and the timekeepers, and the reporters, but nobody would come back, and then he made a speech. Boy, that was the craziest speech I ever heard. Everybody in Dreamland was yelling and laughing and whistling, but everybody heard what Internationale said in his little speech. There were two ladies in the crowd and Internationale said, Ladies and gentlemen, you know nothing; you do not know anything. The referee says I am the loser of this match, but you know nothing. I am the winner. I challenge Vasili Ivanovitch, the Russian rock crusher, to return to this ring, and I challenge anybody else in this audience to enter this ring, and I will not leave this ring until the referee declares that I am the winner.

The crowd cheered louder than ever, because Internationale *was* the winner.

From a safe distance Diamond Gates shouted, The winner of this match is Vasili Ivanovitch. The bout is over. Everybody go home.

Well, nobody got up and left the building, not one solitary soul. Then somebody ordered the lights to be turned out. That was a crazy mistake. The little Filipinos thought it was a plot, so in the darkness they started hitting people on the heads with pop bottles, and when the lights went on, everybody in the crowd was slugging somebody else, including the two ladies. And Internationale was still in the center of the ring, alone.

He wouldn't budge. About two hundred police arrived with sawed-off shotguns, tear-gas bombs, clubs, and horses. The horse cops rode right into Dreamland on their horses, because they were afraid to get off. They ordered everybody to get out of the building, and after a half hour or so the building was empty except for two hundred cops, fifty of them on horses, the three reporters, Diamond Gates, Vasili Ivanovitch, his manager Pat Connor, the two timekeepers, and me. The cops pointed shotguns at Internationale and told him to get out of the ring or they would shoot. I was scared stiff. I knew the cops wouldn't really shoot, but I was afraid one of them might get nervous and kill him accidentally. I didn't want anybody to hurt Ramon Internationale because I knew he was right. So I ran up to the ring and begged him to get out. He said he wouldn't leave the ring until he was declared the winner, or at least until Vasili returned and went on with the match. Vasili returned from the shower room dressed in his street clothes, smoking a cigar.

It was the worst affair I ever saw. Little by little the little Filipinos started coming back into the auditorium to see the finish of the fight, and the horse cops would turn their horses around and run them out, and five minutes later they would come back in, anxious to learn the final result of the match. Their countryman Ramon Internationale was still in the center of the ring and still alive, and they wanted to know how the match was going to turn out. About fifty of them sneaked up to the balcony where the horse cops couldn't go, and they locked the doors, so the other cops couldn't reach them. It was the craziest thing I ever saw. Then they started to cheer Internationale. The cops pointed sawed-off shotguns at them and threatened to mow them down, but these fifty little Filipinos wouldn't move. They were as stubborn as their hero Internationale. And then somebody fired into the ceiling, and one of the little Filipinos fainted. This made the other forty-nine Filipinos sore, so they started throwing pop bottles at the cops. A couple of horses got scared and busted loose, falling all over seats and crying out with pain. And Internationale wouldn't budge.

I almost cried, begging him to get out of the ring. You know nothing, he shouted at me; you do not know anything.

Outside, people from all over San Francisco were rushing to Dreamland in automobiles, by street car, and by foot, and although we didn't know it, there was a crowd of over three thousand people in the streets, and more arriving every minute. People love to see one man, especially someone dark-complected, challenging the whole world, and nine times out of ten they are for him. This crowd was certainly on Internationale's side. Most of the people hadn't seen the match, but from what they found out about it from people who had seen it, they were sure Internationale was the winner. They started guessing how long he'd be able to hold out against the police, and wondered how the police would finally get him out of the ring. They believed he would die before he'd get out, unless they declared him the winner. Even people who had never before heard of Internationale. They just knew he would stand there in the middle of the ring and let them kill him because that's exactly what they themselves would do if they were as big as he was, and as crazy. The part that bothered every one of them was his being a Filipino. They couldn't understand how a Filipino could grow to be two hundred and fifty pounds in weight, but everybody was glad it had happened. You know how happy the world was about the successful birth of the quintuplets.

They had to get the chief of police out of bed at midnight to ask him what they should do, and, boy, was he sore? It took them over twenty minutes to explain just what had happened and what was going on, and even then he didn't know for sure. Finally, he got out of bed and put on his clothes and came down to Dreamland in a red automobile traveling sixty miles an hour through heavy traffic, with a half dozen motorcycle cops in front and a half dozen behind. I remember how amazed he was when he walked into the auditorium and saw all the horse cops riding up and down the aisles, and Internationale in the middle of the ring, and the fifty little Filipinos in the balcony, throwing pop bottles. One of the bottles busted on the cement floor right beside him, and that's when he turned around and saw the little Filipinos up there. He was scared to death.

What the hell are all the well-dressed Filipinos doing up there? he said.

Ha ha, said the reporter from the News. They've locked themselves in, and they're throwing pop bottles. So let's see you get them out. Go ahead, you're chief of police. Get them out. Let's see you get Internationale out of the ring, too. You're a brave man. Go in there and throw him out.

The chief took one good look at Internationale and decided to argue it out. He said they wouldn't put Internationale in jail if he got out of the ring peacefully and went home, but if he refused to do so, they would gas him out and put him in jail for ten years. Internationale said, You know nothing; you do not know anything, and one of the little Filipinos in the balcony threw a pop bottle that hit another horse and the horse jumped from the sixth row into the ring. The cop on the horse took one big leap and landed in the fourth row because Internationale was moving toward him. The horse, however, was too stunned to move, so Internationale got into the saddle. It was the craziest thing in the history of wrestling. I was afraid he was going to throw the horse out of the ring, too, but Internationale was too kind-hearted to do a dirty trick like that. He loved dumb animals.

Every once in a while we could hear the crowd outside booing, and we knew why, but the chief didn't. What the hell are they booing about? he said.

No cop would tell him, so the reporter from the *News* told him. Ha ha, he said, they're booing you and the cops, that's who. Every man, woman, and child out there is one hundred per cent for Internationale.

So the chief came over to me. He was disgusted.

You his manager? he said, and I said I was.

All right, he said. Get him out of there.

So I began begging Internationale to get out of the ring again. Well, this time that crazy frightened horse neighed at me. I nearly fell over. I guess the horse didn't want to get out of the ring either. Internationale said the same thing as before. You know nothing, he started to say, and I said, I know, I know, don't tell me again. I do not know anything. But for the love of Mike, Ramon, get the hell out of that ring.

He wouldn't budge.

So the chief and Vasili Ivanovitch and Vasili's manager and the referee and the timekeepers and the reporters and two dozen cops held a little meeting. They decided to send Vasili back into the ring to finish the match, but he wouldn't hear of it. He began to stamp his feet like a baby, pointing at the horse, but that was only an alibi. He was scared to death. He said he had been declared the winner once and that was enough. Then the chief sat down and started to groan. He would be disgraced. The whole city would laugh at him.

He jumped up, looking furious. Gas him out, he said. He looked up at the fifty little Filipinos in the balcony. Gas them all out, he said. Our little brown brothers, the Filipinos, he said. Gas them all out.

How about the horse? somebody asked.

Gas the horse out, too, said the chief.

Then he heard the crowd outside booing, and he changed his mind.

Wait a minute, he said. Aren't there fifty able-bodied men among you who are willing to go into that ring and arrest him?

There wasn't one, let alone fifty.

The chief was disgusted. He telephoned the mayor, and the mayor swore at him for five minutes. Then the mayor told him to leave the Filipino wrestler on the horse in the ring, and the fifty little ones in the balcony, and clear the streets and let the Filipinos stay in the auditorium until they got sleepy or hungry and went home. The chief thought this was a great idea until he found out the people in the streets wouldn't go away and kept rushing into the auditorium and sitting down and cheering, at least five thousand of them. It was a clear night in August and everybody was feeling great and didn't want to go home.

The chief was panic-stricken. This was worse than a strike. It was ten times worse.

He telephoned the mayor again and talked a long time. Then he told Diamond Gates to go into the ring and declare Internationale the winner. I can't do that, Diamond Gates said, and the chief said, Like hell you can't. You go on in there and declare that crazy Filipino the winner or there won't be any more wrestling matches in Frisco.

So Diamond Gates tried to get into the ring. Every time he ducked under the lower rope the frightened horse would stand on its hind legs and neigh very mournfully and Diamond Gates would run half way up the aisle, sweating and shivering. Finally he stood on a seat and declared Ramon Internationale the winner. Everybody in Dreamland cheered, especially the fifty little Filipinos in the balcony, and gradually the auditorium emptied. Then Internationale got off the horse and left the ring.

I never did find out how the horse got out of the ring. It was scared to death.

The Dark Sea

✿ ✿ ✿

IN the middle of the night when all the passengers were asleep I left my cabin and went upstairs to the highest deck to look at the sea.

I went inside again and asked for coffee and ham and eggs and sat down to eat. The waiter came to take the dishes away.

The sea, I said. How do you like it?

It is very pleasant sometimes, he said. I have been through some bad storms.

I went out on deck again and walked. I didn't look at the sea.

Then I looked again.

It is a body of water, I said.

The ship moved along a dark path through the empty water. The dark sea is never and forever.

Sleep.

It is everything and everywhere and nothing and nowhere.

It is the music we never hear. It is the heart. The lung. The liver. The eye. The brain.

It is darkness, music, laughter, danger.

I went to my cabin and said, Now I will sleep.

I dreamed eternity in ten seconds and sat up.

The sleep of this body is puny beside the sleep of the sea. There is no good in sleeping in this dream of nothing and everything.

I got up and put on my clothes and went upstairs again. The waiter was sitting in a chair, awake, staring into the gloom of night over sea. He turned quietly, amused, displeased, somewhat sorry.

What's the matter? he said.

I don't want anything more to eat, I said. I'm only curious about the sea.

It's nothing, he said. You get used to it.

What he meant by nothing was not the same as what I mean by it.

I went on deck and looked again. It was cold and the sea was warm with a warmth that had nothing to do with temperature.

I looked into the darkness and warmed myself in the cold, looking at the sea. It is the sleep of nothing beginning to be something. It is the dream of everything while it is nothing, beginning in a continuous eternity, which is always never, and always now, to be. The note of sound, out of the silence. The curve of shape, out of nothing. The splash of motion, out of immobility, rock. The warm sea. The dark sea. The time and the place, never and nowhere, here and now. And then darkness, and then silence, and the boat shifts forward and where we had been there is now only a level of the sea, without an eye upon it, at night, lost, unheard, asleep.

And it is death, it is the end, the never-to-be end of all things, the end which is now and can never be, the end which is only the beginning. It is only a body of water, it is only the Atlantic, and I went down to my cabin and closed the door and said, I am on a ship, crossing the ocean, moving in a vessel from North America to Europe, that's all.

I thought I would let it go at that because the sleep of the sea was deep in my life, from the beginning of it and before the beginning of it, all the dark nights on the dark sea were deeply within my life and I could not stay awake, I did not want to stay awake, and I put aside my life from the beginning and slept the sleep of the dark warm sea, the warm sleep of death, of life, and life-death, the dark warm sleep of time and space and all the lost eternities of all the dead and all the living, caught together in this vast body of black pulsing nothing, the sea.

On the Atlantic. May, 1935.

Malenka Manon

✿ ✿ ✿

LEMBERG, Poland, is a nightmare. It is supposed to be a city, a place where human beings hang around until they die, but it is nothing more than one of God's bad dreams. In the streets of Lemberg you can see the tortured face of God asleep. The sky over Lemberg is low and black, the air is stagnant and hard to breathe, and all the people of the city are dream-walkers.

It is a city of dirt. A configuration of rot. A monument to death and waste and ineffectuality.

And the small proud Polish soldiers passing one another in the streets salute with energy.

It is one of God's worst dreams, and this salute is that sad element of the comic which is always present in the tragic.

The streets smell, the buildings smell, and the people smell. There is no water anywhere. There is no clarity of earth and sky, and no clarity of mortal moment. There is no moment in all the twenty-four hours of the day and night. It is all out of time, out of space, out of reality.

The people seem to have work to do, and this is very strange. There are shops with signs. A tailor. A baker. A butcher. A barber. In Polish. In the printed words of that language. A book shop. A moving picture theatre. A department store.

And the people walk in the streets. Their faces are the faces of nothing. All their faces are nothing. It is God sleeping a bad dream. In all their faces is only one thing, emptiness. More than half the people are without shoes. Women and men and children. Many are cripples. Midgets twisting with evil forms. Vast heads on smashed bodies. Long thin fingers. Fat blue veins. Epileptic rhythms.

And the small proud soldiers salute with energy.

The streets rattle with old carts drawn by starved horses. The carts bounce around and the men sitting on the carts look at nothing. When the empty carts return to the city they are full of small unhealthy-looking potatoes. Food for the bad dream.

I went into a restaurant and sat down. The Polish waiter with the short arms and short legs and the twisted face came to the table, staring a question.

I want some food, I said in English, but first I would like a glass of water.

In Polish he said he didn't understand.

Wasser, I said, and I made the motion of pouring from a pitcher into a glass, shaping the pitcher, bending it, shaping the glass, and then lifting it to my lips.

He brought a pitcher of luke-warm water that tasted like something dead. I asked for ice, but I couldn't think of any motions to suggest ice, so I let it go.

The food was dead. The meat stank. The lettuce was wilted. The bread had dirt in it. The coffee was not coffee. I don't know what it was, but it was not coffee.

This place is very interesting, I said aloud to myself. I ought to spend a month here and try to find out why the people don't die.

The waiter was taking away the dishes. He asked in Polish what I was saying.

Everybody is dead in this town, I said.

He thought I wanted something else to eat.

Nothing, I said. Forget it. With the right gesture.

A blind man came into the restaurant holding the hand of a girl of twelve. He was not an old man and he was not a cripple, only blind. The girl was obviously his daughter. Each had the same desperate expression. He was carrying a case containing a musical instrument. It was something like a banjo, only its music was unlike the spurious music of the banjo. Of course the music had a lot to do with Poland. The place and the deep mood of the people.

I thought I was going to be amused with some bad music, but the music was not bad and I was not amused.

The first song he played and sang is the only song I shall talk about because it is the only one that belonged to Lemberg, to God's bad dream, and to the rotting life of the city.

It was full of the deep dark melancholy of an unhappy people. It was bitter and angry, impetuous and defiant, and at the same time it was warm and full of longing for life. It was an incredibly good song. The blind man sang a line or two and then his daughter joined him, making the melancholy a fuller melancholy.

There were only two people eating in the restaurant. The girl came to my table with a tambourine and I put two large Polish coins into it. I guess each was the equivalent of an American quarter, although I am not sure, maybe more, maybe less, but the girl was very grateful.

I said, Could you tell me the name of that song?

She did not understand. The name? I said.

I went to her father, but he understood less than his daughter, being blind. He thought I wanted him to sing other songs and he began to strum on the instrument. I sat down again, hoping he would play the song again, but he didn't, so I asked everybody who worked in the restaurant what the name of the song was but nobody could understand what I was trying to find out. The cook opened the doors of the stove and spoke in Polish about what a wonderful invention it was, the waiter brought out a bottle of wine, and so on.

So I left the restaurant.

In the street two small Polish soldiers passed one another and saluted with energy.

I saluted twice and said, What the hell.

I was glad to get out of Lemberg, and in a way I was sorry I couldn't stay and study the city.

On the train from Kiev to Kharkov in Russia three days later I heard a Russian soldier humming the song. He did not sing any words, but the mood of the song was much the same.

Ah-ha, I said. What is the name of that song?

And I hummed it with him.

All he did was give me the Russian word for song which I have forgotten. Uteson, or utreson, or something of the sort.

And he said in exactly these words, En Ahmerikah nietro utreson? Meaning of course, Have you no songs in America?

In Kharkov I heard a girl in a park humming the song.

Many people in Poland and Russia are humming the song.

I myself hummed the song to a girl in Kharkov who speaks English. Perfect English, so perfect in fact that it is difficult to understand what she is talking about.

Can you tell me the name of this song? I said.

Aaaaaaah, she said. Malenka Manon. Yes?

She hummed the song.

That's it, I said. What is it called?

Malenka Manon, said the girl. It is a Polish song.

What does it mean? I said.

It is the name of the song, she said.

What do the words Malenka Manon mean? I said.

Little Manon, said the girl.

This is all I have been able to find out about the song, and the whole thing comes to nothing, except that in the atmosphere of death and dead-dream in Lemberg the living asked for life, they asked to live only in the music of this simple little song, and they did so through a blind man and his little daughter. The soldiers saluted.

Kharkov, Russia. June, 1935.

The Proletarian at the Trap Drum

✿ ✿ ✿

ON the train from Lemberg, Poland, to Shepetovka, Russia, was an Austrian who could speak a little English.

I said, Every country looks alike to me.

He said, Please?

Alike, I said carefully. Every country.

I waved at the landscape.

Yes, he said. I like Russia.

Emphatically but politely I said nothing for a half minute.

How long do you plan to stay in Russia? I said.

Please? he said.

How many days? I said.

Please? he said.

So I laughed and spoke in English and he laughed and answered in German. We had a lively conversation this way because he got the general idea and I got the general idea, and the idea was this, mostly: You are an Austrian going to Russia and I am an American going to Russia and we are on the same train, so what the hell, we'll talk a little even though you don't understand what I'm saying and I don't understand what you're saying, *comrade*.

He smoked one of my Polish cigarettes and five minutes later I smoked one of his Austrian cigarettes, and then I went back to my place in the next car.

The big Ukrainian peasant lady was in my place, eating black bread and snorting to herself. I sat down on the opposite bench and remembered how much noise she made in the station at Shepetovka and how she kept a big bag of money and other junk between her breasts and brought out the bag when it was necessary and showed her breasts with the innocent unconcern of the noble and showed her money with the pride of the wealthy and shouted and laughed with the men and lifted her baskets and got aboard the train. Obviously, a great lady, and I was honored to be on the same train with her.

From behind a mouthful of black bread she flew into an impetuous oration, full of expressive modulations of the voice and dramatic gesturing.

I don't understand Russian, I said.

She stared at me with some amazement.

This was altogether too fantastic, so, pinching the left nostril of her nose and snorting, which is the same in any language, she returned to the black bread.

I went into the diner and ordered lunch in English with a Russian accent.

Soup, I cried from the depths of a Russian heart. Salat. Brod, meaning bread, I hoped. Meat. Cohfee.

The girl said, Da, da, and went away. She returned in a moment with a glass of water and three slices of black bread. Fine. I began to eat the bread and drink the water.

How about a little butter, Comrade? I said.

You know? I said. Btr. Swiftly. I thought that might be the way they said it in Russian.

She answered in Russian that she knew what I wanted, and I said to myself, These young proletarians are very intelligent.

She returned with a small plate of black caviar.

Well, the idea had never occurred to me, but I liked it very much.

I spread the caviar on the bread and ate heartily. The girl took a Russian worker soup. I pointed at the soup. She brought me soup. She took another worker something that looked like hamburger steak. I pointed at this and she brought me this.

In short, I ate heartily. And I found out about a Russian drink called citro or citron. It is like soda water, only it has a smoother and sweeter and more natural taste, as if it might actually be the juice of fruit, although it is only carbonated water with a little sugar and flavoring. It is very pleasant to drink, however. One bottle contains two and a half glasses. I have no idea what the cost is. I have no idea what the cost of anything in any foreign country is. All I could do was hold up a handful of coins and ask politely that the proper sum be taken. I am sure I was never cheated and even if I was what the hell of it and more power to them, there are a lot of poor people in the world and if they don't steal a little from strangers once in a while, what is the world coming to, anyway?

When I returned to my compartment the big Ukrainian lady was sadly studying her bare feet which were resting on the edge of the bench across the way. They were very husky feet and they were pretty dirty and the big lady was very melancholy. She paid no attention to my unimportant arrival, but finally sighed tragically, probably remembering the two sons she lost in the revolution, who, if they had lived, would now be thirty-four and thirty-five respectively, her own dear dead boys, Boris and Mikel, and perhaps very important men in the Union of the Soviet Socialist Republics. USSR.

Anyway, I figured she was remembering something. It may be, though, that actually she was remembering nothing which also makes one sad.

She turned to me once again and again spoke very rapidly and with even more passion than before. I knew she was friendly and only wanted to talk, so I said, I can't understand a word you are saying, but I think I know how you feel.

She seemed to understand what I meant and began to bend from side to side while she continued to tell me her story.

Yes, I said in English. Da, da, I said in Russian, and the big Ukrainian lady almost burst into tears.

So I returned to the young Austrian engineer.

We exchanged cigarettes again and when the train stopped at a little station we got down and walked along the platform.

An old man appeared and spoke to us in Russian. A worker from the train shouted at him bitterly and the old man went away, shouting back even more bitterly.

What did the old man say to us? I said to the young Austrian.

He said, said the young Austrian, I am an old man.

Ah, I said. What did the worker say to the old man?

He said, said the young Austrian, go away, he is an American, he does not understand.

Ah, I said. What did the old man say to the worker?

He said, said the young Austrian, I have no money, I have no bread, I am an old man, who do you think you are?

So we got aboard the train again and it began to move through Russia. I saw a fine clean rich landscape of grass, trees, brooks, cows, horses, and peasants, most of them bare-footed. Many children waved at the train. Many cows ran from it. I began to think deeply as a conscious artist should and I discovered this amazing truth, that nature is international and that everything natural is very closely related, especially people, so why should there be wars etcetera?

It was too warm and there was too much noise in the train for me to think any deeper, so I didn't discover why there are wars, although without thinking at all I seemed to understand that there are wars because if you give a small man a uniform and tell him this is his duty, the crazy jackass gets the idea he is somebody, and when you have a million jackasses with the same idea, and the idea has to do with guns and swords and horses and machines, well, then you have a war, but this is not an observation I should care to offer to the world as my own and I mention it here only to suggest how difficult it is for even a great thinker to think while traveling.

They told me our train would reach Kiev, the capital of the Ukraine, at exactly fifteen minutes to ten, and it did. I expected to find the world in black darkness by that time, so I was in the diner drinking citro or citron when the train arrived in Kiev. The little man in uniform who dusted the benches and examined the lavatories every once in a while came rushing into the diner and scolded me severely for being so inattentive to my private affairs, ignoring my baggage which might at any moment be snatched up by a thief, especially the machine, the typewriter, which he asked me to show him and which he admired very much, and also that I ought to pay closer attention to the fact that the train had stopped and was in Kiev, where I was supposed to get off.

I thought it was about six o'clock in the afternoon, but it was nine forty-five, and the summer days of the Ukraine are long and pleasant, and the nights very short but also pleasant.

I followed the little man at a trot and got my bags off the train. A lady was on the platform to meet me. She spoke English. Kiev, she said, is one of the most beautiful cities in the world. She spoke with an accent. I found out several minutes later that she was born in Kiev and had never traveled more than thirty miles away from it. Nevertheless, Kiev is very beautiful, and the Lavra Monastery is worthy of any traveler's careful study. There are many kinds of architecture in the city, mostly old, and mostly ecclesiastical. In the Lavra Monastery are catacombs. I thought I ought to mention this, although as it is it doesn't seem very impressive even to me, although the catacombs themselves are very impressive. These ecclesiastical places are used as museums of obsolete ways of life, with printed explanations on the silliness involved, and guides who explain that one monk had a lady love, as the Russians say, and was a very remarkable fellow with the women. Therefore, obviously, there is no God. There are signs explaining that a monk's fancy garment cost one thousand two hundred and eighteen pounds of wheat. The peasants are always astounded at this information, although personally I found some of the garments worth three pounds more.

So I rode up Karl Marx Street to my hotel and fought my way into a room with a shower. Then I took a walk with the lady who met me at the station through the Garden of May First. It is a pleasant garden, or park, and from hills in it there are nice views of the river Dnieper. The garden had another name before the revolution, but after the revolution nobody wanted to hear the other name because it had something to do with some such ridiculous and savage person as a Czar.

On the way to Kiev, I must say, at the various stations, I mean, when the train was not in motion, many children in rags came to the window and asked for money. I had only Polish coins, but I dropped one of these to each of the children. I discovered, however, that this sentimental indulgence was being noticed and severely disapproved, so I had to be very cautious and secretive about the whole matter.

It isn't like Hearst said of course, but there are a lot of poor people in Russia. There's nothing any of us can do about it, but when a small boy or girl comes to the window of the train and speaks very earnestly and politely about how hard times are I think it is a decent sort of Christian gesture to accept the story and drop a coin, large or small, depending upon one's own story.

And of course the country has direction, which is a lot more than other countries have. There is some pomposity, but you get that everywhere. There is as much humanity here as anywhere else, although they try to tell you there isn't, and it is a fairly satisfactory state of affairs. People hate people they do not like, and so on. There is envy and greed and everything else. Laughter and love. In the Garden of May First, just like in Central Park in New York. What the hell, human beings are human beings and you can call them anything you like and they can call themselves anything they like, but they are the same anywhere, anytime. Except trap-drummers. They vary, and they vary greatly.

Now, in America, a good trap-drummer, Negro or white, is *somebody*. I mean, he's the boy who keeps the music swinging the way jazz ought to swing, and if he is a colored boy, he sways around like nobody's business, even when he isn't making any musical or other sound at all, and it is very important. It is one of the things we remember about America when we are away. Our hot trap-drummers.

So I got out of the big Lincoln and fought my way into my room with a shower and took a shower and went downstairs to supper. Eleven at night. I heard soft jazz music and decided I must be getting homesick, which seemed very strange, since I felt completely at home. I listened carefully and decided no, I was not homesick, there was music somewhere nearby. I went to a door and the sound of the music increased. I spoke to the headwaiter and he pointed to the garden. I asked if I could sit out there and he said in Russian that I could sit in the garden, I could sit inside, I could have my food in my room, he was at my service, God Almighty, this place was no dump, it was better than places in Paris, Vienna, London, so I sat in the garden, right in front of the seven-piece orchestra, every member a worker, a proletarian, a student of Karl Marx, and an ardent admirer of Lenin and Stalin.

Well, the orchestra played jazz, good old American jazz, full of the rich old human American (and international) sentimental hooey that anybody could tell was hooey and still like it, only the orchestra couldn't quite put it over.

And the reason was the trap-drummer.

He was a young Russian of seventeen or eighteen. I guess he had seen trap-drummers in movies and he went through the motions, but it didn't work and the noises he managed to make were very bad, they were very sad, it was pathetic, and I wondered why proletarians should want to monkey with jazz in the first place, why in hell didn't they stick to *Dark Eyes* and the *Volga Boatman* and the gypsy dances and *Chardases* and stuff like that?

And I could tell from the sad way this young proletarian trap-drummer went about his business that his heart was not in it, and it was a pleasant relief when the melancholy sirens began to moan and the lights were turned out, and in the morning they told me it was *war practice*. If you were in the street at the time, they said, you would have to go into the nearest house and wait. It was a pity I wasn't in the street because the practice lasted over a half hour and I would have had a chance to study Soviet Russian home life.

But the whole point of course is that jazz doesn't mix with the thick sorrowful resentful mood of old man Karl Marx and the sooner the proletarians find this out the better off they will be.

Jazz is the comic and tragic expression of the poor of Capitalist countries, the moment of freedom, relief from labor and worry and all the rest of it, and it is music and rhythm of joyful despair, of glorious unhope, utter loss in the chaos of matter and energy, tin-can wholeness whooping itself laughingly out of disintegration and despair, weaving to hell and gone like old man river, like the ocean, and it is the product of those who are lost and do not know where they are going and don't much care, it is not the hymn of those who are found, who have a direction, and within it is no mood of brotherhood on earth, dictatorship of the proletariat, or classlessness among the living, and nothing is funnier or more fantastic than big Russia, full of its blind certainty, horsing around with that very quality of living, that very noble evasiveness of living, which enables the poor to go on forever being poor, and it seems to me they ought to leave jazz to those poor pitiable souls who need its crazy refreshment, and stick to their jolly Internationale.

Kiev, Russia. June, 1935.

The Black Tartars

✿ ✿ ✿

IN 1926 there were only twelve Black Tartars in Russia, and now, in 1935, there are only ten because of the deep love of Mago the soldier for Komi the daughter of Moyskan.

In 1926 Mago was nineteen years old. I met his brother and his brother's wife on the train from Kiev to Kharkov. Mago's brother Karachi is no soldier and he doesn't care if Black Tartars vanish from the world altogether because he believes it is wiser to live quietly than to live greatly and foolishly, and he would rather be a Russian, anyway. But Mago, no. He would live greatly.

Karachi spoke in Russian to the Jewish girl on her way to Tiflis and the Jewish girl translated his words to me. Karachi's wife was a Ukrainian girl. Karachi didn't care to marry a Black Tartar and preserve the race and the culture of the race. All he wanted was to live and have a girl near him when he didn't feel so good.

The Jewish girl translated and Karachi's wife smiled and moved closer to the young Black Tartar.

Moyskan, said Karachi in Russian to the Jewish girl and the girl in English to me, was an excellent singer. He not only sang the older Black Tartar songs but made new ones, especially when he was drunk. After beating his wife, his songs were full of lamentations and he would call on God to destroy him, and the next day he would complain bitterly to his friends, What can I do if God wills me to live?

Moyskan had five sons and one daughter. Three of the sons were killed in small wars or in banditry, one was in Siberia for no reason in the world, and the other was a worker in a Moscow tractor factory. Moyskan's daughter Komi was the most beautiful girl in the world, said Karachi. I fell in love with Komi, he said, my brother Mago fell in love with her, and all the officers and men of the Soviet Azerbaijan Army fell in love with her. Any man who saw Komi fell in love with her, he said.

He lit a Russian cigarette, inhaled deeply, and glanced impatiently at his wife and at the Jewish girl, and then said very politely, Komi was not like these, God forgive my crazy brother, wherever he may be. She was all beautiful things of the earth. Her heart was a dark sea. A black deep endless sea, and my brother wanted her for his wife.

Moyskan said *yes* with a new song. He sang the wedding of my brother Mago and his daughter Komi three days and three nights without stopping, except to drink.

Komi said to my brother Mago, said the young Black Tartar, I do not wish to love you.

My brother Mago stole a horse and brought it to her and again she spoke the same words.

It was a fine horse and any other girl would have loved my brother for stealing such a horse for her, but not Komi.

My poor brother stole a dress for Komi, and again she said she did not wish to love him. He stole a cow for her and Moyskan slaughtered it and ate it, and he stole a table for her, and still she did not wish to love him and he said he would steal an American automobile for her, only he did not know how to drive an automobile.

I am a year younger than my brother Mago, said Karachi. An older brother speaks to a younger brother. A younger brother does not say to an older brother, You must not do this, you must do *this*.

It is not this way with Black Tartars only, he said. It is the same with many people. Is it so with Americans?

In a way, yes, I said.

My brother, said Karachi, wished to steal an American automobile for Komi because he loved her so much. I loved Komi, too, but when a sea is dark and wild only a great man will wish to swim across the sea, or a crazy man, or a man who is not afraid to die, or who wishes to die, and I did not wish to die. My brother was not sleeping at night and he was not sleeping during the day, and I could see in his eyes that he could destroy the world in order to love Komi, that he could kill her so that no other man could love her, that he could do *anything*. It is foolishness, said Karachi, but it is greatness, too. Only my brother Mago is a real Black Tartar. Only he is a fool and not ashamed to be a fool. Only he would steal an American automobile for Komi. The officers of the Army would not do it and the soldiers would not do it. They knew fear. To steal an American automobile that belongs to the government is to die.

Mago stole a Cadillac and drove it into a hotel, said Karachi.

He wished to take Komi an American automobile, but he did not know how to drive, and he drove into the New Europe Hotel on Malygin Street, in Baku.

Karachi got up from the bench and shook his head slowly and sadly.

My brother, he said. My crazy brother. My poor crazy brother Mago. To love so deeply.

He sat down again and remained silent for some time, remembering his brother, looking at the floor sullenly.

Ahkh ahkh ahkh ahkh, he whispered.

Do you understand such a thing in America? he asked.

Ask the American, he said to the Jewish girl, if they understand such a thing in America.

He wants to know if you can understand such a thing in America, said the Jewish girl.

Tell him yes, I said to the Jewish girl. Tell him it is the same everywhere. Tell him it has nothing to do with the form of government, Capitalist, Fascist, or proletarian, it is the same everywhere.

The Jewish girl translated what I said, and the young Black Tartar said in Russian to me, Da, da.

My brother, said Karachi, drove the American automobile through the door of the New Europe Hotel on Malygin Street in Baku. He broke the door down. He broke the glass window to a thousand pieces. He frightened all the people in the hotel. He arrived in the lobby of the hotel in the American automobile with his head bloody from pieces of broken glass. My brother Mago sat in the automobile and smoked a cigarette and everywhere around him ran a hundred people, shouting and screaming, and then two hundred people, and then came Moyskan, and then Komi.

My brother said, Komi, is there another soldier in the Azerbaijan Army who would do this for you? Is there another man in all the world who would do this for you?

This was in 1926, said Karachi. The years go by, he sighed. The landscape of life changes. (He says, said the Jewish girl, the landscape of life changes. I do not know how to translate his words.) The dead are forgotten by the living. My poor crazy brother killed Komi. My brother who loved her more than any other man in the whole Azerbaijan Army. My poor brother who is now in Irak or Afghanistan or dead. Ahkh ahkh.

Everybody said my brother would be shot in the morning. To steal an American automobile. To steal from the government.

To the New Europe Hotel they sent one officer of the Army and one hundred soldiers.

The officer said to Mago, What are you doing in this automobile?

I am sitting in this automobile, said Mago.

The officer said, Where did you get this automobile?

My brother said, I got this automobile on Narimanovskaya Street, in front of the building of the People's Commissars.

The officer said, You know this automobile belongs to the Central Executive Committee?

Yes, I know, said my crazy brother.

You stole this automobile? said the officer.

Yes, said Mago, I stole it.

My brother was brave and crazy, said Karachi.

Do you know what is the punishment for such a crime? said the officer.

Yes, I know, said my brother. It is death.

Ahkh, Mago, Mago, Mago, said Karachi.

He turned bitterly to the Jewish girl and asked many questions. I knew they were questions from the intonation of his voice and from the expression on his face.

What is he asking? I asked the Jewish girl.

He is asking if I am translating every word, said the Jewish girl. He wants to know if you understand the deep love of his brother. He does not believe any man who has not seen Komi can understand why his brother stole the American automobile and drove it into the New Europe Hotel.

Tell him I understand, I said.

Da? he asked me. Yes? You understand?

Yes, I said.

Everybody, he said, is listening carefully to the officer and my brother, and when my brother says the punishment is death, everybody is talking out loud and saying, Listen, listen to him, did you hear? The punishment is death, he knows, he is not afraid.

Then why did you steal this automobile? said the officer.

Because I love Komi, said my brother.

Then everybody is being very quiet, only one man is speaking. This man is a man with a hunchback. He is saying, The whole world is in love with Komi, even I. And somebody is putting a hand over his mouth because it is true and the people are ashamed. They are ashamed to love a girl so beautiful and they are proud that my brother Mago is not ashamed to love such a girl and to steal an American automobile for her and drive it into the New Europe Hotel.

The officer was in love with Komi too, said Karachi.

The officer did not make any reply. He understood.

So they took my brother Mago to the military jail in Baku. In the morning they began to ask him many questions. To every question he answered the truth.

They said, Did you steal a horse?

And my brother said, Yes, I stole a horse.

Did you steal a dress? Did you steal a cow? Did you steal a table? Yes. Yes. Yes.

Why did you steal these things?

I stole them for Komi.

The military Judge was a big Captain. He was an old man with a big moustache.

Who is Komi? said this man.

She is a Black Tartar girl, said Mago. She is the most beautiful girl in the world. I am a Black Tartar. I love Komi and I want to live in the same house with her. There are not many Black Tartars in the world. I do not wish to see the tribe of Black Tartars to end in the world. I wish to love Komi.

You do not look very black, said the Judge.

I have not been in the sun very much lately, said my brother. I am in the Azerbaijan Army and I work where it is shady, in the stable. A month in the sun and I am as black as Komi herself. It is the shade of the stable that has given me this sickly white color. In times of war I ride in the cavalry, but in times of peace I work in the stable.

I never heard of Black Tartars, said the Judge. I have seen many white Tartars. Who are the Black Tartars?

They are the ones who are black, said my brother.

Ah, said the Judge. How many Black Tartars are there in the world?

In the world I do not know, said my brother. In Baku there are only nine or ten. Thirty years ago a Black Tartar named Kotova went to America. He is now an American and his children are not black any longer and they live in Pittsburgh.

What language do you speak? said the Judge.

Mostly other languages, said my brother. Arabic, Kurdish, Turkish, and lately Russian.

Have you any language? said the Judge.

Yes, we have a language, said my brother.

Is it a written language? said the Judge.

Of course, said my brother. Only there is no Black Tartar in the world who can read or write in our language or in any other language.

Ah, said the Judge. What is your word for *sun?*

We have no word for *sun* in our language, said my brother.

Have you any words at all in your language? asked the Judge.

Oh, yes, said my brother. We have many words. They are Arabic and Kurdish and Turkish and Russian, only we speak these words in our own language, as Black Tartars.

How is that? asked the Judge.

We speak as Black Tartars, said my brother. We *are* Black Tartars and any words we use are in our language.

And you stole the official automobile of the Central Executive Committee in order to give it as a gift to this Black Tartar girl you love. Is that so? asked the Judge.

Yes, it is so, said my brother.

Please bring this girl to me, said the Judge.

In the afternoon of the same day they brought Komi to the room where they were asking my brother questions. The Judge was looking at papers when she entered the room. Then he began to read aloud, opening the trial. He was reading aloud when he lifted his eyes and saw Komi. He stopped reading and stared at her.

Is this the girl? he said.

Yes, said my brother. This is Komi.

Give her a chair, said the Judge. He looked very excited. Why are you fools standing around? he said. Give her a chair.

After a while Komi stood before the Judge and he asked her some questions.

Do you understand what has happened? he asked.

No, said Komi.

This foolish young soldier, said the Judge, is in love with you. He has stolen a horse for you, a dress, a cow, a table, and finally the official automobile of the Central Executive Committee. Do you understand?

No, said Komi. Mago is my cousin.

Komi, said Mago. That is not so. I am not your cousin.

Silence, said the Judge. Do you realize you are on trial for your life?

I am not her cousin, said Mago. You can ask any Black Tartar in Baku.

Silence, said the Judge.

He turned to Komi, bending away over his desk in order to be closer to her.

Do you love this foolish young soldier? he said.

No, said Komi.

Now then, said the Judge, and he leaned way back in his chair.

Now then, he said, let me see.

You have stolen the official automobile of the Central Executive Committee, he said.

Yes, said Mago.

You were in love at the time, said the Judge.

Yes, said Mago. I am still in love. I shall always be in love with Komi.

Silence, said the Judge.

By law the punishment for such a monstrous crime, said the Judge, is immediate death.

He is my cousin, said Komi. You are not going to kill him, are you?

I am not afraid to die, said Mago.

Silence, said the Judge.

He turned to Komi again, leaning forward.

We shall do everything in our power to forgive this sorrowful misconduct of your cousin, he said. We shall examine his record and if he has murdered no man during the last five years, we shall return him to the ranks of the Army where his behavior will be closely watched.

Four days later, said Karachi, they returned Mago to the Army. Everybody in Baku was happy about this.

One evening my brother Mago saw Komi in an automobile with the Judge. The Judge was crowding over Komi, and Komi was laughing at him. The Judge was an old man and his children were older than Mago.

My brother Mago was very angry. First, he said, he would kill the Judge, then he would kill the Judge's wife, then each of his five children, the oldest first, the next oldest next, and so on down the line until all of them were killed.

Then he said he would not kill the Judge, he would steal two good horses, and tie Komi to one of the horses and take her into the hills where he would keep her until each of them died, either of old age, or starvation, or from loving one another too much and not wanting to be alive.

My brother Mago went to Komi and said, Why are you going around with this rotten old man?

Because I want to, said Komi.

He is not a Black Tartar, said Mago. If I see you with him again, I will kill him.

He saved your life, said Komi.

I will kill him, anyway, said Mago. You are a Black Tartar and you must love a Black Tartar.

I do not know what I am, said Komi. Maybe I am not a Black Tartar.

You are a Black Tartar, said Mago. I want you to live in the same house with me.

I do not wish to love you, said Komi.

You will love me, said Mago. You are a Black Tartar and I am a Black Tartar and you will love me.

Ahkh, ahkh, said Karachi. There are so many girls in the world. But my poor brother would not look at another girl as long as Komi was alive. Maybe you will understand this, but my poor crazy brother killed Komi and went away to Irak or Afghanistan, or maybe he killed himself, too. We do not know.

She would not love him, said Karachi. He was the one man in the world for her, and she would not love him. He drove the American automobile into the lobby of the New Europe Hotel for her and still she would not love him.

One morning before daybreak my brother Mago went to Moyskan's house with two of the finest horses from the stables of the Azerbaijan Army. He entered the house and tied Komi's arms and legs, kissing her lips and hands and hair. Moyskan helped him because he did not think it was good for Komi to go around with an old man, but Moyskan's wife cried and screamed until Moyskan knocked her down. Then my brother Mago tied Komi to one of the horses and took her with him into the hills.

Nobody knows what happened there, said Karachi.

No man in all the world loved a girl as deeply as my brother Mago loved Komi, he said.

They sent soldiers on horses into the hills. First ten soldiers, then twenty, then fifty, then a hundred, then the whole Aberbaijan Army. The old Captain was very angry. He said, Shoot that foolish young soldier, but bring back the young girl unharmed. But the soldiers did not find my brother and Komi.

One morning they found Komi dead. My brother Mago had held her under the water of a shallow stream. He did not want her to live if she would not love him.

In America, said Karachi, does a man love a woman so deeply?

I don't think so, I said.

He turned to the Jewish girl again and began to talk to her very rapidly.

He is saying, said the Jewish girl, that he wants you to understand it was not a crime. It was not hate, it was love. You have never seen Komi, he is saying. He wants you to know his brother was a great man. He was a man who wanted to live greatly. That is why he did all those foolish things.

Tell him I know how it was, I said.

And the Jewish girl told him.

He did not speak for many minutes.

Then he said, Ahkh, Mago, Mago, Mago. And many other words in Russian which I did not understand.

What is he saying? I asked the Jewish girl.

He is saying, To kill such a girl as Komi. To kill her. To end the life of such a one as Komi. A man must love deeply to do such a thing.

Kharkov, Russia. June, 1935.

The Little Dog Laughed to See Such Sport

✿ ✿ ✿

THERE was a little dog in Moscow that had an amazing face. It lived near the Kremlin where Lenin once lived and where Stalin now lives. The Moscow River saddened the little dog, and it would stand on the bank of the river, and howl, so that I myself, being near by, would be impelled to swing at real or imaginary evil forces in nature.

When I would whistle, the little dog would stop howling for a moment, turn and look at me (only another miserable soul in the world and certainly an enemy like everybody else), and go on howling. Who was I to interrupt such pure agony? Who was I to disturb the religious ferocity of river and moon and night?

And the dog would turn away from me and begin to howl again.

Vascha, Vascha, I would shout. You don't have to howl at the moon. This is Russia. We have learned the truth about everything. It is counter-revolutionary to notice that you are alive and that there is a river, an earth, a moon, days and nights, dwellings in the world, things alive, seasons, days of light and days of darkness, days of warmth and days of cold, days of rain and snow, and live things sleeping, and days of live things growing. It is no use to howl. Everything happens because a rich toy manufacturer wants more money with which to enlarge his business. This is so. It is all the result of a fat man's greed. The moon is nothing and neither is the river.

And I whistled the way we whistle to dogs in America, two notes rolling after each other many times. But the little dog would not understand, and in the end I would have to kick at a passing automobile, containing, no doubt, three executives of the Central Committee, and a Russian actress.

During the day, however, when there was no moon, and there was hunger to be satisfied, and places to go, the little dog would do a good deal of running about in the streets, following first one Russian and then another, and never make a friend, and at times it would trail along fearfully behind some elegantly dressed foreigners, perhaps Americans. It would know from the mere appearance of the foreigners that here, at last, was quality of some sort. Here was a special kind of the tribe, and just notice how swiftly they hurry about, puffing furiously at cigarettes, shouting to one another in an alien tongue, knocking over old women and cripples, spitting as far as six feet, waving their arms at buildings, especially St. Basil's Cathedral.

And it was at a time like this, during the day, that I first came face to face with the little dog and noticed what an amazing face it had.

At first I merely made the observation that the little dog had an amazing face, and let it go at that. Brother, I said to a beggar, dropping sixty kopecks into his hand, did you notice the dog?

God keep you wealthy, brother, said the beggar, and I went on to my room where, by way of balancing the discrepancies of life and the world and the universe, I was reading the Book of Job, one of the world's noblest fools. In the midst of Job's agonies, I suddenly remembered the little dog, but it was more than remembrance, it was the beginning of a fresh acquaintance with a universe I once discovered in sleep, inhabited, and then, growing older and wiser, forgot. The little lost dog of Moscow was the little lost dog of this universe, the small living thing lost in enormity, in endlessness of space and time, in the fantastic simultaneity of event, and after much exploration in the lost and recovered universe I found out why I was so much interested in the face of the little dog.

The dog looked exactly like me. It had the most sullen expression of anything alive in the world you ever saw, even a camel, and at the same time you saw in its eyes unlimited capacity for laughter because of much innate and instinctive wisdom. If you tried to run over the dog, for instance, in a sixteen-cylinder Packard, it would leap far beyond its normal powers, escape by an easy quarter of an inch, land safely on its four legs thirteen feet away, and turn around and bark at you. All this without thinking, without the least premeditation, although in many cases, especially when the barking would continue long after the Packard had disappeared, the anger and resentment would be deliberate and artful, and consequently there would be varieties of outbursts, furious growls, thunderous roars, and soul-piercing howls. God damn you sons of bitches, you rats and bastards in big automobiles, you heathens with power and money, you liars and thieves. And in this way, meeting each horrible danger with that amazing efficiency which is part of the divine in things alive, it would go on living to a ripe old age with innumerable illegitimate children running about in various parts of the country, all carrying on the tradition, and leaping to safety every time a danger arrived.

You can say of course that the trouble with me is that I am opposed to governments of any sort, and of course this is so, but you cannot possibly fail to observe that the only thing I am deeply interested in is order. The establishment of order, the revelation of it, and (if necessary) the improvement of such order as may already exist, though it be sadly confused and chaotic. It is mostly a private concern of mine of course, and like every private concern of any man it involves everybody and everything. I myself desire little: time in which to learn to live in a way that will somewhat amount to immortality. No mediocre intrusions, no polite interruptions, and only the elemental things as a beginning: the earth, the universe, the seasons, substances of life to satisfy hunger, water to satisfy thirst, air to breathe, and so on.

It is a private concern of mine. It is an altogether selfish concern of mine. I want to live while I am alive, that is all. I want at least to try. We have not yet been able to find out if it is possible for us to really live during all the seasons, all the changes of climate, all the stages of growth, each with its own fierce and magnificent problems, but we have the right to want to try. We don't really care if it kills us, just so we are allowed to try and are not interrupted by some irritating idiocy such as war which comes about through the same despair in duller men finding a different outlet. We want to go about it quietly, privately, without cannon booming, without oratory, without transportation, aviation, war tactics, abnormal pain, abnormal heroism, abnormal greatness. We want to go about it in some small part of the world we know, in which we have lived, and we want every part of this small landscape to be real to us, to become a part of us, and we want every God damn tree in the place, every patch of empty earth, every plant with leaves, every stream, every moment of sky, every hour of light in the world, every ounce of pressure of air, every mouthful of food and water and wine, to mean something to us, to be a part of our seeking to be alive immortally. We want to have the time it takes and we don't want any interruptions.

I speak for myself of course. Maybe you want something else, and if you do, good, go and have it. I know what I want, and I want it. I don't want any evasion because we have been alive in the world a long time and it is a long time since Jesus Christ lived and died, and I'll be God damned if I can see any decent change yet, and it looks to me as if it is about time we began trying to live. We have all the thought it takes. All the literature that goes with it. All the music. All the painting. All the sculpture.

So before the war starts (and everybody alive, from the cab driver to the Professor of Economics, at Columbia, will tell you the war will soon start), I want to tell the world that I am not interested. I am completely bored with the war. It has nothing to do with me. I have no quarrel of such a ridiculous nature, although I have quarrels enough. I want nothing of it. I refuse to accept its reality. Kill yourselves all you like. Do it artfully, with the finest guns and gases invented. Do it on a large scale. I am not interested, and I shall have no pity for the dead. Let them die. I don't care what impelled each one of them to accept the war, but whatever the reason, it was no reason to me, and I am not interested. They were alive. They are dead.

Well, let me tell you something. If they are dead from a war, they were never alive. They never lived. They never began to live. Let me say this before the cannons begin to boom and there is no small corner of the earth in which to escape their thunder. Let me make my little speech before the papers are full of it.

In my room at the New Moscow Hotel I remembered the old universe, and saw it again. It was not another place, though. It was this same place, our earth, only it was at the beginning. From this place and time I may proceed, I dreamed, to my world and my mortality. But when I wakened the world was full of confusion. So I dreamed again. This place, I dreamed, in which my dream of dreaming and my dream of reality are mingled together, will be the beginning of the world for me. But again when I wakened the world was about me and with me and it was not the beginning, it was the ending. This, I said, standing in the city, is not the end of the beginning I am making. I cannot want this, and I dreamed again. There, in the universe of sleep, would be myself, the earth, and for some crazy reason now and then the little lost dog with my face. In dream we used to pass one another, not speaking, as little lost dogs passed my corner in the city where I sold papers. You go your way, I'll go mine. In time, though, that dream ended, and I began to dream the world, growing older. I began to dream: I shall go to a far place in the world, I shall go among the strangers and be one of them, I shall do this, I shall do that, and so on. The world and its confusion were good enough for me because, what the hell, there was nothing else to have. This is so. But not the world. Forget the world. What *is*, is good enough. But forget the world. Stick to what's elemental because it is more than enough and there is no end to its potentialities. You can even become immortal. And I forgot all about the little lost dog until many years later, in the country of the strangers, after I had done many of the things I had wanted to do, the dog appeared again, the same as ever, with my face, and still, by the grace of God, alive.

Naturally, I was deeply concerned about the little dog. So of course I always went to the river and listened to the little dog crying with grief, and of course I always tried to make it stop crying. But it wouldn't. It couldn't. It was full of the wrath and bitterness of God, and it howled until all I could do was take swipes at evil forces in the air and kick at passing automobiles.

One night, however, the little dog laughed. It was delighted with the whole mess. The river, the moon, things alive, the cities, the governments, the ideas, the plans, the trembling, the oratory, the falsity, the pettiness and magnificence, and the little dog busted out into laughter. I dreamed the early universe again, and with heavy melancholy walked over a road through the desolation. Soon the little lost dog of Moscow appeared, walking fearfully behind me because I was an American in good clothes. I turned and saw that it was the little dog with my face, and it was more sullen now than ever before. O.K., I said, come along. It's a big world, and every dog has his day. I'm going nowhere as usual. You might as well come. And the little dog said nothing. It groaned a little and followed at my heels. After a while I reached the Moscow River. The moon looked down on Moscow. I went to the bank of the river and sat on a boulder, smoking a cigarette. The little dog began crawling on its stomach to me, the way street dogs do, and I said, Don't be a God damn fool, get up on your feet and walk like a dog.

And of course it did, because it was a dream. The little dog leaped to its feet and began wagging its tail wildly, its eyes sparkling with this amazing kinship and friendship, and I said, All right, take it easy. I just want to sit here and remember. Take it easy.

The dog quieted down and stretched out at my feet.

Pleasant evening, I said.

I always speak of the pleasantness of the evening when it is no use talking about anything else. Actually, however, I felt miserable because I was disgusted with everything.

The dog said, What of it? Who cares about that?

Well, I said, it isn't much, but it's something.

Sure, said the dog. Anything is something. So what?

The Russians are all right, I said. They mean well. The idea is to give everybody a chance to begin to be alive, even you.

Ha ha, said the dog, that's funny.

The only reason we have the same evils here as we have in Capitalist countries, I said, is that it takes time.

Ha ha, listen to him, said the little dog. Just listen to him.

There will be another war, of course, I said, and Russia will hop right into it and have a lot of Russian kids slaughtered, but it is not because Russia wants a war, it is because you can't extend Communism all over the world until there is one war after another, and half the people of the world are dead, and Capitalist governments are weakened, and then the people (*the people*) rise and take over everything.

Ha ha, said the dog. What's there to take over? Ha ha, they can have it. What are they going to do with it after they've taken it over?

Plenty, I said. Equal distribution of wealth, for one thing.

Ha ha, said the dog. You mean equal distribution of poverty.

And no classes, I said. All men equal.

Ha ha, said the dog, all men equally mediocre. That's what you mean, comrade.

And then, I said, there will no longer be any private ownership.

Ha ha, said the dog. There never has been any private ownership of property. There never has been any private ownership of anything.

No more hunger in the world, I said.

Ha ha, said the dog. There are kinds of hunger.

No more fear, I said.

Ha ha, said the dog. Not much, comrade, not much.

No more conflict, I said.

Ha ha, said the dog.

And in this fashion we carried on a long conversation. I was very serious and I wanted to be on the side that wanted everybody to be able to begin to be alive, but the little dog laughed at everything I said, so I got up and went away. When I got to the bridge I looked back and saw the dog lift its head toward the moon, and then it began to howl again.

London. July, 1935.

Train Going

✿ ✿ ✿

WHAT hearts break at railway stations, and how the tears fall. How the eye blurs with agony and the torn flesh aches. How the nerves tremble, the tongue goes dumb, the throat dries, and the million moments of yesterday roll away to death, the bell of the train ringing, the steel wheels beginning slowly to move, beginning slowly to carry away the tragic hours of a man's life with a woman. Stay, do not go: let us go back and mend the broken pieces. Let us return to the errors and make them right, so that we can breathe again. Let us go to each place of error and begin from the beginning. And before the train is too far away for him any longer to see her face, his heart rushes back to each place they knew together: the dull quiet rooms of morning and night: the chairs and tables: the windows: the restaurants: the theatres: the streets: the parks: the trees and lakes: the sky. And the conversations over the telephone. Before the train has gone too far, he has returned to the places of many moments, stalked through them like a maniac, a ghost seeking in the world her ghost, the lost in himself seeking the lost in her, and not finding. Before the wheels of the train have turned five times he has run through the world and destroyed all things of error, and he has left the dull quiet rooms roaring in flames: the world must end and begin again. And all he does is stand in one place and smoke a cigarette, knowing it can never be. Knowing the errors shall stand. Knowing the train will disappear in a moment, and he will return alone to the places they knew, and live, though it would be best to die, and he turns away and disappears in the world.

In one place it is a young Englishman, in another it is an Austrian or an

Italian or a Spaniard or a Russian. In every language *he* knows wordlessly it shall always be so: error and glory shall be together, inhale and exhale.

The bell ringing, the wagon beginning to carry away the long quiet moments of a mother's heart in a babe born, and now grown to the size of a soldier, a young man going away in a train: for England, for France, for Austria, for Russia, for Finland. To have a gun. To walk in line. To fire accurately. To obey. To salute. To sing the national anthem. To be brave. To love England France Austria Russia Finland. To love life. To love the earth. The poor woman's heart torn out of her flesh, and the boy smiling at her. It is the earth, it is not the nations. The nations are not loved, it is the small part of the earth each nation occupies, and it is the small part of each city or country in which the mother lived and saw the boy grow, and now she is crying, she cannot help it, it is too much, it is too strange, he is on a train and he is going away to be a soldier: he is in the national uniform, and now he is going away to begin to learn there may be war and it is best to forget home. But how can he forget Finland? How can he forget the streets of the French villages? How can he forget the woods of Vienna? And everywhere the train keeps moving: it is by schedule, and at first it moves slowly, making all who weep feel there is still time to change everything, the whole order of the world. No airplanes for bombing cities. No cannon. No tanks. No machine guns. No armies at all. The wars have all been fought. We have learned that death is the only answer, and we can wait till we die of old age. We have learned it is impossible to be brave, that it is weakness to be brave. We have learned that no conflict has ever existed between the soil of England and the soil of France, of Finland and Russia, of Japan and China. We have learned that ostentation is impressive but ridiculous, and all the poor mothers groan while the train begins to move.

The mothers of life stand in the railway stations of the world and weep. And they know, as the lover knows, that it shall ever be so. They will never understand what force it is that has made it so. They will never know why it is so, but they will know it will never change. They will go back to their houses and to the dull aching moments of life again bleeding.

And the same bell ringing, the same train beginning to go, and there he is in the station, the same as ever, eternally there, the small newsboy with no friend, the child of the world, the street-boy, standing in vast loneliness with eyes widened with love for the traveler: the lifted hand, to nobody, to everybody, good-bye, and the fierce smile of relationship: Jesus Christ, we are alive together in the same world, and now you are going away, good-bye. And he runs; to stay a little longer nearer you whom I do not know. And he keeps running, and the train begins to move faster, and he begins to run faster, waving at everybody, good-bye, we shall meet again, and this is not the end, good-bye.

Stockholm, Sweden. July, 1935.

The Whistle

✿ ✿ ✿

CARNIVAL NIGHT on the *Berengaria,* somewhere on the Atlantic between North America and Europe, at this latitude and that longitude, on June 1, 1935, I was given a toy whistle which has changed the history of the world.

There is a very bad poem in the world about Lenin which goes like this:

Once, twice in a century
A man arises
Once, twice in an historical epoch
A man changes the course of history
Once, twice amid suffering and struggle
A man breaks through misery and despair to light and happiness
Once twice in history the millions of commonfolk are thrilled out of their apathy, excited into selfless activity, purified by the glimpse of a splendid promise, glorified by the creation of a new world—
Thrilled, excited, purified, aroused, glorified by a great man.

And of course the answer is Lenin who is dead.

This bad poem goes on and on, saying that Lenin was this and Lenin was that, and then it says we see him here and we see him there, and it is very boring and very unfair to Lenin, even though he is dead. From now on of course Lenin will not be able to do anything about anything, but no one will say that he did not change the history of the world. No one will bother to say such a thing. No one will care if he did or didn't. Sometimes the history of the world changes by itself, but if they want to say it happened because of Lenin, that is fine, and no one will say it is not so.

The history of the world changes every minute, of course. It is Wednesday for example. Then Thursday, then Friday, then Saturday, and every day the history of the world changes. Every day everybody alive does this and that and after three days of such tremendous activity there is a definite change in the history of the world. Several people have died and several have been born. On one Wednesday or Thursday or other days it was his birth, and then his death. There was a definite change of course, but it would have been so if his name had been Vladimir Ilyich, which actually was his name, or any other name you please. It had nothing to do with Lenin himself. It was the simple physical presence of the man on earth, alive, and it would have been the same if he had been born an idiot. It is the comic miracle of shaped flesh alive on the earth. As the American song goes, *You call it madness, I call it love.*

But the truth is, it is God.

They do not believe in God of course, and that is all right because that is another way of believing in God, and it all comes out in good order in the end, some dead, some alive, some pregnant, and a multitude of young men strutting around on the verge of laying any likely young lady who comes along, keeping up the tempo.

One man alive changes the world only a little more than another man alive, and the difference is so small, it is not worth trying to estimate. In the morning the sun comes up if the weather is good. If the weather is bad, the sun does not come up. It comes up, but you can't see it. No mountain moves until it moves, and once, twice in a century, as the bad poet would cry out bitterly, there is an earthquake and the Kremlin and other fine buildings crumble to dust. But it isn't on account of Lenin. It isn't on account of Stalin either; or Hitler; or Mussolini; or you, or me, insignificant fools that we are. It *is*, and that's the end of it.

At the same time, no one will say Lenin did not fool with the idea of doing this and that, and thereby end private ownership, private enterprise, and anything else private, and no one will say nothing ever came of his efforts. I myself will say something happened, although it doesn't prove anything, least of all that Lenin is not dead.

I wish I could put this down very simply. All they fear is death and they do everything imaginable to say that death is cruel, that it is wrong, that it is too bad everybody and everything must die, but they put it in other words.

I am not violently opposed to this sort of fear of death. I am only mildly opposed to it, and a little amused.

There are this many people alive on the earth today. Seven thousand million of them, let us say. Maybe more. Seven thousand million will do, however. Each one is one person alive. Each one was born. Each one lives somewhere on the earth. Each one will die. Before each one will die each one will experience that amount of pain which is part of the delight and agony of living, and each one will laugh and weep. Each one will dream and love. One will die at the age of seventy-six years, another at the age of seven years, another at the age of seven days, another at the age of seven minutes. Another will be born dead. And whole nations of men will not even be born, and no one will know how to improve living conditions for them. No one will even be sad about them. They simply won't exist.

After the ones who are born are born, though, there is much alarm in the world about them. Everybody knows they are only going to die, and so they decide it will be a very good idea to change economic conditions and provide bread and water for everybody, and as a side line to provide literature, generally bad, and music, invariably bad these days, and to teach them not to believe in God because it is all a mess and there cannot be a God because the church always fools the people and collects the equivalent of five cents from everybody who wants to buy a candle and light it and place it in front of a picture or statue of Jesus or his mother Mary or some unfortunate saint who was burned at the stake or spit upon by greasy money-lenders or merchants.

This is all right in the long run because even in times of war mountains do not move until they move, and every morning the sun comes up, even in times of war. There is Spring and Summer, Fall and Winter, and you will die. This is all right, too. It is fine. The question is, How will you die? And of course that will depend on how you live, how you occupy the moments of your life, when you laugh, when you weep, when, where, how, why, and what you love, and so on.

Myself, I am in favor of a certain amount of laughter. I will go so far as to say I am heartily in favor of a certain amount of laughter. I cannot tell you why or when or where or how to laugh, or what to laugh at because God alone and you alone can determine that, but the time is ripe.

No matter what you do, though, you will change the history of the world. There will never be another person exactly like you in the world, and although your house may be occupied by another, although your house will perhaps stand in its place one hundred years after you are dead, no person will ever walk the streets of the world with your identity.

I am also in favor of pity. Anger also. Also daring. And many other things. In fact, everything. Actually, though, I am not fond of people who are proud and pompous, or cruel and cunning, or stupid and pretentious, or ugly and fat. They are all right of course, but I hate to think that such people have to be alive when much finer people could be alive instead, but who knows the mind of God? It is so broad and generous, so free with the substance and breath of life.

I am not one to say there ought not to be a place in the world for bastards. What the hell, it is a big world if you travel by foot, and there are many years ahead. Let them all live.

I could go on for weeks. What I want to say is that it is not good to be uncivilized in the world when there have been civilized men here and there. It is not good to have too much faith in Lenin dead and Stalin alive, and this man and that man. The idea ought to be this, according to my way of thinking: to be alive, you yourself, and to be genial about it. It is all right for anybody to have faith in anything he chooses, and actually I am not opposed to Lenin, dead or alive, or anybody else.

It is this maybe: that everybody seems to be getting away from themselves, as if they themselves were nothing at all, and they seem to be throwing themselves into fantastic configurations of other personalities, and into dark and dull theories that only make a man's hair fall out and spoil his appetite. This is wrong. I don't know why, but it is. After you are born you yourself are supposed to be the inhabitant of the earth and you yourself are supposed to do your living. You yourself are supposed to change the history of the world.

Nothing could be simpler. I will show you how easy it is to behave in such a manner that never again will the world be the same. Very little in the nature of apparatus is needed. Some people prefer heavy books and fat education. Let it be so.

A small whistle, however, will serve just as well.

Four days out of Manhattan everybody on board the *Berengaria* was bored to death with the sea, except myself. I was bewildered by it. I would wake up in the middle of the night and remember that I was on a ship in the middle of the ocean, and then I would try to understand the meaning of so much water on the earth. It is simply a mood no one has yet been able to gather into the germ of life. It is still a dark mysterious void. And so on. And I would get up and put on my clothes and go on deck and look at the sea. I would stand at the rail looking down at the sea for hours.

A million thoughts and half-thoughts, remembrances and dreams, moods and sufferings would be coming to life and dying while I stared at the sea. I would remember a gesture: the sea. A face: the sea. A way of looking at an object: the sea. A word: the sea. Something whole, then broken: the sea. Something alive, then dead: the sea. A single slender plant with large brown leaves deep in the jungle among millions of other plants: the sea. A lizard racing across a hot boulder: the sea. A staircase of black marble in a house, in Athens, a thousand years ago, and a dark bare-footed girl walking up the stairs: the sea. The face of the earth a thousand years from this night: the sea. The word *yea:* the sea. And the word *nay:* the sea.

And in the midst of such visions and remembrances would come and go the gay and tragic moods of my own small life, from its beginning in recent years, the day I first knew of the earth and the universe, and fixed myself in a place in its vastness, on the grass, by the eucalyptus tree, in the morning, under the sun; and the moment once at night when I saw the world end; and the evening I walked alone over an empty road through the country and was lost in the world and could not cry; and the times I laughed.

The times I laughed and laughed because I did not know and would never know and could never know, and yet somehow knew.

All this was the sea, and it bewildered me. I stared at the sea for hours during the day and for hours at night, and I couldn't understand why or where or when or how or what of anything. It is nothing, I thought. And I knew it was everything. This is the cradle. It rocks back and forth and out of its darkness and its rhythm all things emerge.

But I could not believe this, and I knew I was not translating the sea into language that had meaning that could never be changed, so when they gave me the little toy whistle I was pleased.

Everybody was bored and it would be pleasant to have a Carnival and do all the sad things people do when they do not know what else to do, and it was so, and everybody was happy in a mournful sort of way during the Carnival.

It was a very ordinary whistle, made of wood and painted three colors, white, black, and red. When you blew on it, it made a sound. Now, it is going to be difficult for me to describe this sound or to make you hear it, but I will try. It was one of those silly sounds that immediately cut into your heart and make you want to laugh because you are ashamed to cry. A ridiculous sound, somewhat like weeping, but more like a caricature of a child weeping, and yet also somewhat like laughter of one sort. The sort that is sometimes heard from small beautiful ladies who have never known any real happiness, although they have always sought the best in life, and are now married and have children and are no longer young, and deeply believe it was all a mistake and if they had gone to such and such a place on a certain night twenty years ago, they would have met someone else, who is now altogether lost, and everything would be different and much nicer. A very melancholy sort of laughter, I mean. There was only one sound in the whistle, but if you blew softly and not too long, it would be like children half-crying about something unimportant and at the same time half-laughing about the same thing, as when they fall down and hurt themselves while running to leap into the arms of their fathers, and their fathers have picked them up and are kissing them; and if you blew a little more strongly and kept on blowing a little longer, it would sound like the beautiful and unhappy ladies laughing sadly about the errors of their lives, but these are the subtleties of the whistle and not what I want to talk about.

You don't blow a whistle softly, and you don't try to make a musical instrument of it, and unless you have a lot of time to kill and nothing else to do, you don't relate its ridiculous sound to the whole reality or unreality of living.

You blow into it strongly, and then you get the real sound.

The real sound was funnier and more foolish, and yet a good deal more important. It was altogether a sound of no meaning. In its shrill silliness was the cry of nothingness. You blew it and there it was: nothing. In no language. In no real sound. Altogether a manufactured note, belonging to the scale of no music. And yet so very pertinent to all things. Nothing.

I am not at all exaggerating when I say I was very much delighted with this whistle. It was the very thing I needed to fill out the empty spaces in my character. It was the very means of articulation I had been seeking for years and years to express my feeling about those things in life which a man of honor and dignity will simply not articulate in words. In short, my vocabulary had been completely rounded out. I could now say anything I pleased in most unmistakable language, and at the same time not bother to utter a word.

I had found the lost word.

The sad and silly sound of this whistle saying nothing.

During the Carnival I tested the whistle on various people and carefully observed the effect it had. I wanted to make sure it was the lost word.

And it was. The sound of the whistle made everybody laugh at first and then quickly quiet down.

Deep, though. Quiet down very deep, and seriously, in spite of the silliness of the sound.

It said nothing. Unmistakably.

I was the last person to leave the saloon after the Carnival. I was sitting in the big leather chair in the corner of the saloon looking at God only knows what when the Irish porter came in.

It was three in the morning. The Irish porter was very tired and he had a lot of work to do and he began to do this work.

I brought the whistle out of my coat pocket and blew it.

The Irish porter was scrubbing the floor with a soapy rag, on his hands and knees. After I blew the whistle he laughed and got up and flopped into a chair that was exactly like the chair I was sitting in.

He waved at the floor, and at the whole room.

To hell with it, he said. (Nothing.)

And that was the beginning of something in the Irish porter, and in the world, too.

I could have talked to him for two hours and all it would have been would have been conversation, and nothing more. And nothing would have happened. But when he heard the sound of the whistle, he immediately understood, and he got up and waved the floor to hell, which was proper.

No one can say everything is going to be the same in the world from now on.

I walked out of the saloon and thought I would throw the little whistle into the ocean. The Carnival was over and a good time had been had by all, as the saying is, so I might just as well throw away such a childish toy. I, a philosopher and a writer. Such a thing would be silly to carry around.

But when I got to the rail I saw the sea and remembered that I did not understand it.

I blew the whistle at the sea, leaning away over the rail.

(Nothing, and to hell with it.)

And I decided to keep the whistle.

In the morning I found an officer of the ship bawling out the Irish porter. I blew the whistle. The officer forgot what he was saying, and that was the end of his little fever of indignation. He simply couldn't feel important after having had such a sound made at him. He went away feeling disgusted with such a simple and ferocious philosopher. What would happen to England if such a philosophy took hold of its people?

And again I changed the world. Never again will the world be the same after the expression on that officer's face.

In London I blew the whistle at the king's palace, and there will be no end of consequences.

In Paris I couldn't understand a word of what anyone was saying, and being obviously an American, I blew the whistle at everyone left and right wherever I went.

There was a Hungarian girl on the train from Paris to Vienna and with her was a small baby. The mother was quiet and timid, but the baby was in a sullen mood and was always crying. I blew the whistle at the baby and it laughed. And the mother laughed and spoke to me in Hungarian. You really don't need books to change the world.

In Poland I blew the whistle at two little army officers who were about to salute very pompously and throw the whole world into war, and it did something marvelous to their arms. They couldn't salute the way they liked to salute, and they turned around and looked at me with great nationalistic bitterness.

I blew the whistle at all sorts of people, under all sorts of circumstances, and of course the world will never be the same again. Nevertheless, when I die, I don't want any fool to come along and write a bad poem about once, twice in every century a man arises and takes a whistle and travels around the world blowing it at people. It is too silly.

Moscow, Russia. July, 1935.

Finlandia

☼ ☼ ☼

I WAS walking down Annankatu Street in Helsingfors when I saw two horns, a cello, a violin, and a picture of Beethoven in a store window, and remembered music. You go out into the world and all you see is telegraph poles and city streets, and all you hear is the train moving and automobile horns. You see multitudes of people trying to do all sorts of things, and in restaurants and in the streets you hear them talking anxiously. You forget music, and then all of a sudden you remember music.

Jesus Christ, you say. There is nothing else. After the train stops and you get off, or the ship docks and you walk down the gangplank, or the airplane comes down to the earth and lets you put your feet where they belong, there is nothing. You have arrived and you are nowhere. The name of the city is on the map. It is in big letters on the railway station. And the name of the country is on the new coins which buy bread, but you are nowhere and the more places you reach the more you understand that there is no geographical destination for man.

To hell with this, you say. London, and nothing. Paris, and nowhere.

Vienna, and nothing. Moscow. The same. Dialectical materialism. Class consciousness. Revolution. Comrades. Baloney.

Nothing. Nowhere.

There is no place to go in that direction. And it breaks your heart. Jesus, you say. This is the world. These are the places of the world. What's the matter? Everything is haywire. And in the streets of every new city you feel again the world's dumb agony.

In Helsingfors it is not so bad, although there is private ownership of property in Finland. People own small objects. In the market those who own fish, sell fish, those who own tomatoes, sell tomatoes. Maybe it is Capitalism, but even so you can't find anything wrong with the people.

When I saw the cornet and the trombone and the cello and the violin and the picture of Beethoven, I felt very mournful. The shape of the cornet is no small triumph, and even a tin violin is a poem of an idea.

I went into the store and asked the girl in English if I could listen to some phonograph records of Finnish music. The girls of Finland are quiet, healthy, beautiful. Their mothers and fathers are Lutherans and believe in God. The girls look as if they also believe, but even if they don't, they probably go to church every Sunday and sing, and it amounts to the same thing. They aren't fanatics, but they probably go to church because it is all right. It is rather nice. Everybody is there, and the old Sunday mood of the world quiets the harsh noises and irritations of week days, and by the time the sermon is over everybody feels less important than on week days and there are no hard feelings. You own the bank. Good. Keep it. I have a bicycle. You are the mayor. Good. I am a clerk in an office. No hard feelings, and the Sunday sun is bright.

In Russia, though, there is no such thing as Sunday. The girls of Russia burst into false laughter every time a movie puts over a little anti-religious propaganda because they know it is not true, there were never any saints, religion is the opium of the people, Karl Marx is the closest thing to a saint the world has ever known, Trotzky is a rat, Lenin was almost the second coming of Jesus, and Comrade Stalin is something amazing. As a result the girls of Russia don't look very good. They are so wise it has spoiled their complexions. All the same, Russia is at least a thousand years ahead of Finland. Look at the things they are doing. Building cities. Creating a classless society. Calling everybody Comrade. Years and years ahead. The girls look pretty bad, though.

The girl in the music store in Helsingfors was very old-fashioned. She was polite. She didn't know anything about creating a classless society, so she had time enough to do one small thing at a time, instead of doing nothing at all, and that loudly, the way it is in Russia. Not all the time of course. There are some girls in Russia who are almost like the girls of Finland, but these are the ones who are not militant. It's Dictatorship of the Proletariat, so it's Dictatorship of the Proletariat, and they go on living their private lives. These kind will never be leaders. They will never elevate the lives of the peasants. They are very unimportant. But most of the girls in Russia a traveler meets smell dialectical. It's something like the smell of a weed you know is poison.

Jean Sibelius, I said to the girl in the music store. *Finlandia.*

Two months ago Helsingfors was very far from where I was. I was in a room in the Great Northern Hotel in Manhattan, 517, with bath. Helsingfors? Where's that, anyway? Now I am in Helsingfors, and the only thing I know about the location of Manhattan is that you get into a boat and after six days, if the boat is fast, you see the skyline of Manhattan, and there you are. It is the same with Helsingfors or anywhere else. You are so many feet and so many inches off the cement pavement. The sky is over you. The sun comes up in the morning. In Manhattan, of course, it gets darker in the summer than it does in Helsingfors in the summer. It never gets very dark in the summer in Helsingfors. At midnight it is still pretty light, and a couple of hours later the sun comes up again.

And it is fine. It is tremendous. It is the crazy world. The urban corners of what is affectionately known as civilization. A cornet, a trombone, a cello, and a violin in a store window. And of course music is the most effective opium of the people there is, unless it is composed by a dialectical materialist. Then nobody knows what it is. But if it is good, then the boy who did the job is fooling somebody, maybe Marx.

All I wanted was music. No dialectics. Just the simple old-fashioned fury of one man alone, fighting it out alone, wrestling with God, or with the whole confounded universe, throwing himself into silence and time, and after sweating away seven pounds of substance, coming out of the small room with something detached, of itself, alive, timeless, crazy, magnificent, delirious, blasphemous, pious, furious, kindly, not the man, not all men, but a thing by itself, incredibly complete, an incision of silence and emptiness, and then sound and the shapes of things without substance. Music. A symphony.

Finlandia, I said. The word was strong and good, and I was there. I am in Finland, I thought. This store is on Annankatu Street in Helsingfors. Jean Sibelius lives in Finland. It was here that he composed *Finlandia*, and in America five years ago I heard *Finlandia*, and I have been hearing it ever since, and the ear of man will never cease hearing it.

It is no small thing to hear *Finlandia* in Helsingfors.

The girl was very pious, changing the needle, letting it touch the record, winding the phonograph. She went away six paces and stood humbly listening. After the silence the music began to leap out into the world again. Finland.

O Jesus Christ, there is no geographic destination for man. And the music charged into the chaos of the world, smashing hell out of error, ignoring waste, and creating a classless society. Last year in England the king listened and knew the truth, and tomorrow in Nebraska a child will listen and know the truth, and it will be the same with kings and children a hundred years from now, or a thousand.

I smoked four cigarettes, and then this great work of Jean Sibelius ended. The silence that had existed before the music began came into existence again, and now it was no longer *Finlandia* but Finland, Helsingfors. The girl could not speak English, but she also could not say anything in Finnish. She smiled, almost weeping. Then she hurried away and returned with an album containing the records of a whole symphony by Sibelius.

No, I said. It was very kind of you to let me hear *Finlandia* in Helsingfors. I cannot buy. I am only here on my way back to America. I am sailing tomorrow for Stockholm.

I brought some marks from my pocket and asked if I could pay for hearing *Finlandia*.

This, the appearance of money, spoiled everything. Now the girl not only did not understand what I was saying, she did not understand the *meaning* of what I was saying. She could not understand how I felt. With the music she knew and she didn't need to understand the words.

She wanted to give me something for the money.

No, I said. This money is for hearing *Finlandia.*

This was too much. She went away and returned with a girl who spoke English.

I explained everything, and the girl who knew English interpreted to the girl who did not, and we all laughed.

No no, said the girl who spoke English. Would you like to hear some more of Sibelius?

No, I said. I want to remember *Finlandia* in Helsingfors. Do you know Jean Sibelius?

Yes, of course, said the girl.

The other girl stood by watching our faces.

What sort of a man is he? I said.

Big, said the girl. He is very big. He comes to this store very often.

He lives in Helsingfors?

Yes.

Look, I said. I am in Helsingfors today and I may never be here again. Tomorrow I am going to Stockholm. I am an American, and I am supposed to be a writer. Do you think Jean Sibelius would see me?

But wait a minute. Let me explain.

The first time I heard *Finlandia,* five years ago in America, I got up from the chair, pushed over the table, knocked some plaster out of the wall, and said, Jesus Christ, who is this man? Now, it was almost the same. It is not every day that I am in Helsingfors, and it is not every century that Jean Sibelius is in Helsingfors the same day.

Yes, said the girl. Wait a moment, please. I will get the number.

And she went upstairs. She returned running.

Jean Sibelius is in Jarvenpaa, she said.

How far is that from Helsingfors? I said.

One hour, said the girl.

I wrote the name of the place on an envelope and hurried away. The two Finnish girls walked all the way to the door with me. They were almost as excited as I was. From America, and he has heard *Finlandia.* Music is international. (And it is. Even the word music is. If you say bread in English, many people will not know what you mean, but if you say music, they will know.)

I thought I would send a telegram. I tried to write one but it sounded lousy. It doesn't mean a thing in a telegram.

I asked the hotel clerk if I could reach Jean Sibelius by telephone. I felt like a fool. Such a thing is ridiculous.

Of course, he said.

And before I knew it I was talking to him over the telephone.

I am from America, I said. Everybody in America likes your music.

I am at this place in the country, he said in English. Come at seven.

It was half past four, and it took an hour to get to Jarvenpaa, so that left me about an hour in which to try to figure out what the hell was going on. Who am I to see Jean Sibelius? What can I say to the man who composed *Finlandia,* and what will he have to say to me? He is seventy years old and I am twenty-seven. I was born in America. I am a punk writer, and he is a great composer, Jesus Christ.

But that's music for you. I didn't know what I was doing.

It is *Finlandia.* And it was Finland. The girls were beautiful and very quiet and very polite. It is a writer's job to try to find out how these things happen: that music, and the clean innocent faces of the girls of Finland.

I went up to my room at the Torni Hotel and tried to think of some questions to ask Jean Sibelius, but nothing is more disgusting than a question, and the ones I wrote were the worst questions anybody ever thought of asking anybody else. They were long involved questions, asking if perhaps it is true that all art forms are inherent in nature and all the artist can do is reveal these forms, and what effect does the world of man, the world of cities, trains, ships, skyscrapers, factories, machines, noises, have on a composer, and if music should have a function, and what is the quality which most nearly makes a competent composer a great composer, his spiritual heritage, his race, the experiences and remembrances of his race, his own personal experiences, or simply much energy, some anger, and the will or impulse to declare his mortality at a certain time and thus to be immortal?

Jesus Christ.

And God forgive me I actually asked the questions.

It was an old Buick going like a bat out of hell through the clean landscape of Finland, and along the roads were boys on bicycles, girls walking, and farmers going home on carts. Clear air. Fresh green growing things. Clean sky. Cool clean lakes. Cool trees. Grass. The place of *Finlandia*.

It is not easy to explain. It is not only these things, but something more. Maybe it is because there is hardly any night at all during the summer. Maybe it is because they are Lutherans, and have a church, and believe. Maybe it is because Finland is north. Cool. Quiet. Blond. Blue eyes. I don't know what the hell it is.

It was a country house in this landscape. The cab-driver stopped the car in the country and asked three young girls where was the road to the house of Jean Sibelius. The girls told him he had traveled too far. It was about a quarter of a kilometre back. In Finland everybody knows about Jean Sibelius and many people in and around Helsingfors have spoken with him.

Don't get this wrong. I mean something. Don't get the idea I mean it is remarkable that many people have spoken with Jean Sibelius or that it is splendid of him to know so many people. I mean it is all the same. These are the people of Finland. Jean Sibelius is the big man who makes music, and the others are the others, and it is the same. They are all alive in Finland.

I went into the house all mixed up. The maid was waiting for me and welcomed me in Finnish. He was seated, talking to a young man, an American-Finn from California, and he got up, and then it was the thing I was after, *Finlandia*, Jean Sibelius, seventy years old, and timeless, and a child, the smile, the fury of politeness, *yes yes yes*, the strong hand, the introduction to his friend, the strong gesture, the energy, sit down, and Jesus Christ, what about those crazy questions? I couldn't talk, I had to say my piece and scram and I wanted to do so, so I began to explain about the questions, stumbling, a very big man, and I don't mean bulk alone, and I was from America, eleven hours in Helsingfors.

He answered the God damn questions, and it was great. Yes, yes, silence. Silence is everything. (He jumped up, his big hands trembling, and got a can of cigars. Cigar? And then he shouted for whiskey, and in a moment the maid came into the room with whiskey.) Music is like life. It begins and ends in silence. He made a wild gesture, every nerve of his body alive. Drink whiskey, he said. I didn't know what to do. I poured a drink for his young friend, and another for myself, and we drank.

The world of cities, I said. Trains, ships, skyscrapers, subways, airplanes, factories, machines, noises, what effect?

I felt like a fool.

He was furious and began to speak in his native tongue.

He cannot answer, said the young man. Music speaks for him. It is all in the music.

I am sorry about these questions, I said. I'll leave out some of them.

He spoke in Finnish, and the young man interpreted: Beauty and truth, but he does not like the words. Not the words. It is something different in music. Everybody says beauty and truth. He is no prophet. Only a composer.

And the angry-kindly smile in the ferociously stark face.

Drink whiskey, he said in English.

I went on to the one about what is it that makes the man great.

No, he said in English. You cannot talk about such a thing.

It was swell. It was the real thing. It was too silly to talk. He was too wise to fool with words. He put it down in music. I felt swell because he was so young, so much a boy, so excited, nervous, energetic, impatient, so amazingly innocent, and on the way back to Helsingfors I began to see in the landscape of Finland the clean clear music of *Finlandia*.

Helsingfors, Finland. July, 1935.

The Armenian and the Armenian

✧ ✧ ✧

IN the city of Rostov I passed a beer parlor late at night and saw a waiter in a white coat who was surely an Armenian, so I went in and said in our language, How are you, God destroy your house, how are you? I don't know how I could tell he was an Armenian, but I could. It is not the dark complexion alone, nor the curve of nose, nor the thickness and abundance of hair, nor is it even the way the living eye is set within the head. There are many with the right complexion and the right curve of nose and the same kind of hair and eyes, but these are not Armenian. Our tribe is a remarkable one, and I was on my way to Armenia. Well, I am sorry. I am deeply sorry that Armenia is nowhere. It is mournful to me that there is no Armenia.

There is a small area of land in Asia Minor that is called Armenia, but it is not so. It is not Armenia. It is a place. There are plains and mountains and rivers and lakes and cities in this place, and it is all fine, it is all no less fine than all the other places of the world, but it is not Armenia. There are only Armenians, and these inhabit the earth, not Armenia, since there is no Armenia, gentlemen, there is no America and there is no England, and no France, and no Italy, there is only the earth, gentlemen.

So I went into the little Russian beer parlor to greet a countryman, an alien in a foreign land.

Vy, he said with that deliberate intonation of surprise which makes our language and our way of speech so full of comedy. You?

Meaning of course I, a stranger. My clothes, for instance. My hat, my shoes, and perhaps even the small reflection of America in my face.

How did you find this place?

Thief, I said with affection, I have been walking. What is your city? Where were you born? (In Armenian, Where did you enter the world?)

Moush, he said. Where are you going? What are you doing here? You are an American. I can tell from your clothes.

Moush. I love that city. I can love a place I have never seen, a place that no longer exists, whose inhabitants have been killed. It is the city my father sometimes visited as a young man.

Jesus, it was good to see this black Armenian from Moush. You have no idea how good it is for an Armenian to run into an Armenian in some far place of the world. And a guy in a beer parlor, at that. A place where men drink. Who cares about the rotten quality of the beer? Who cares about the flies? Who, for that matter, cares about the dictatorship? It is simply impossible to change some things.

Vy, he said. Vy (slowly, with deliberate joy) vy. And you speak the language. It is amazing that you have not forgotten.

And he brought two glasses of the lousy Russian beer.

And the Armenian gestures, meaning so much. The slapping of the knee and roaring with laughter. The cursing. The subtle mockery of the world and its big ideas. The word in Armenian, the glance, the gesture, the smile, and through these things the swift rebirth of the race, timeless and again strong, though years have passed, though cities have been destroyed, fathers and brothers and sons killed, places forgotten, dreams violated, living hearts blackened with hate.

I should like to see any power of the world destroy this race, this small tribe of unimportant people, whose history is ended, whose wars have all been fought and lost, whose structures have crumbled, whose literature is unread, whose music is unheard, whose prayers are no longer uttered.

Go ahead, destroy this race. Let us say that it is again 1915. There is war in the world. Destroy Armenia. See if you can do it. Send them from their homes into the desert. Let them have neither bread nor water. Burn their houses and their churches. See if they will not live again. See if they will not laugh again. See if the race will not live again when two of them meet in a beer parlor, twenty years after, and laugh, and speak in their tongue. Go ahead, see if you can do anything about it. See if you can stop them from mocking the big ideas of the world, you sons of bitches, a couple of Armenians talking in the world, go ahead and try to destroy them.

New York. August, 1935.

The Man with the Heart in the Highlands

✿ ✿ ✿

IN 1914, when I was not quite six years old, an old man came down San Benito Avenue on his way to the old people's home playing a solo on a bugle and stopped in front of our house. I ran out of the yard and stood at the curb waiting for him to start playing again, but he wouldn't do it. I said, I sure would like to hear you play another tune, and he said, Young man, could you get a glass of water for an old man whose heart is not here, but in the highlands?

What highlands? I said.

The Scotch highlands, said the old man. Could you?

What's your heart doing in the Scotch highlands? I said.

My heart is grieving there, said the old man. Could you bring me a glass of cool water?

Where's your mother? I said.

My mother's in Tulsa, Oklahoma, said the old man, but her heart isn't.

Where *is* her heart? I said.

In the Scotch highlands, said the old man. I am very thirsty, young man.

How come the members of your family are always leaving their hearts in the highlands? I said.

That's the way we are, said the old man. Here today and gone tomorrow.

Here today and gone tomorrow? I said. How do you figure?

Alive one minute and dead the next, said the old man.

Well, what is your mother doing in Tulsa, Oklahoma? I said.

Grieving, said the old man.

Where is your mother's *mother?* I said.

She's up in Vermont, in a little town called White River Junction, but her heart isn't, said the old man.

Is her poor old withered heart in the highlands, too? I said.

Right smack in the highlands, said the old man. Son, I'm dying of thirst.

My father came out on the porch and roared like a lion that has just awakened from evil dreams.

Johnny, he roared, get the hell away from that poor old man. Get him a pitcher of water before he falls down and dies. Where in hell are your manners?

Can't a fellow try to find out something from a traveler once in a while? I said.

Get the old gentleman some water, said my father. God damn it, don't stand there like a dummy. Get him a drink before he falls down and dies.

You get him a drink, I said. You ain't doing nothing.

Ain't doing nothing? said my father. Why, Johnny, you know God damn well I'm getting a new poem arranged in my mind.

How do you figure I know? I said. You're just standing there on the porch with your sleeves rolled up. How do you figure I know?

Well, you ought to know, said my father.

Good afternoon, said the old man to my father. Your son has been telling me how clear and cool the climate is in these parts.

(Jesus Christ, I said, I never did tell this old man anything about the climate. Where's he getting that stuff from?)

Good afternoon, said my father. Won't you come in for a little rest? We should be honored to have you at our table for a bit of lunch.

Sir, said the old man, I am starving. I shall come right in.

Can you play *Drink to Me Only with Thine Eyes?* I said to the old man. I sure would like to hear you play that song on the bugle. That song is my favorite. I guess I like that song better than any other song in the world.

Son, said the old man, when you get to be my age you'll know songs aren't very important, bread is the thing.

Anyway, I said, I sure would like to hear you play that song.

The old man went up on the porch and shook hands with my father.

My name is Jasper MacGregor, he said. I am an actor.

I am mighty glad to make your acquaintance, said my father. Johnny, get Mr. MacGregor a pitcher of water.

I went around to the well and poured some cool water into a pitcher and took it to the old man. He drank the whole pitcher full in one long swig. Then he looked around at the landscape and up at the sky and away up San Benito Avenue where the evening sun was beginning to go down.

I reckon I'm five thousand miles from home, he said. Do you think we could eat a little bread and cheese to keep my body and spirit together?

Johnny, said my father, run down to the grocer's and get a loaf of French bread and a pound of cheese.

Give me the money, I said.

Tell Mr. Kosak to give us credit, said my father. I ain't got a penny, Johnny.

He won't give us credit, I said. Mr. Kosak is tired of giving us credit. He's sore at us. He says we don't work and never pay our bills. We owe him forty cents.

Go on down there and argue it out with him, said my father. You know that's your job.

He won't listen to reason, I said. Mr. Kosak says he doesn't know anything about anything, all he wants is the forty cents.

Go on down there and make him give you a loaf of bread and a pound of cheese, said my father. You can do it, Johnny.

Go on down there, said the old man, and tell Mr. Kosak to give you a loaf of bread and a pound of cheese, son.

Go ahead, Johnny, said my father. You haven't yet failed to leave that store with provender, and you'll be back here in ten minutes with food fit for a king.

I don't know, I said. Mr. Kosak says we are trying to give him the merry run around. He wants to know what kind of work you are doing.

Well, go ahead and tell him, said my father. I have nothing to conceal. I am writing poetry. Tell Mr. Kosak I am writing poetry night and day.

Well, all right, I said, but I don't think he'll be much impressed. He says you never go out like other unemployed men and look for work. He says you're lazy and no good.

You go on down there and tell him he's crazy, Johnny, said my father. You go on down there and tell that fellow your father is one of the greatest unknown poets living.

He might not care, I said, but I'll go. I'll do my best. Ain't we got nothing in the house?

Only popcorn, said my father. We been eating popcorn four days in a row now, Johnny. You got to get bread and cheese if you expect me to finish that long poem.

I'll do my best, I said.

Don't take too long, said Mr. MacGregor. I'm five thousand miles from home.

I'll run all the way, I said.

If you find any money on the way, said my father, remember we go fifty-fifty.

All right, I said.

I ran all the way to Mr. Kosak's store, but I didn't find any money on the way, not even a penny.

I went into the store and Mr. Kosak opened his eyes.

Mr. Kosak, I said, if you were in China and didn't have a friend in the world and no money, you'd expect some Christian over there to give you a pound of rice, wouldn't you?

What do you want? said Mr. Kosak.

I just want to talk a little, I said. You'd expect some member of the Aryan race to help you out a little, wouldn't you, Mr. Kosak?

How much money you got? said Mr. Kosak.

It ain't a question of money, Mr. Kosak, I said. I'm talking about being in China and needing the help of the white race.

I don't know nothing about nothing, said Mr. Kosak.

How would you feel in China that way? I said.

I don't know, said Mr. Kosak. What would I be doing in China?

Well, I said, you'd be visiting there, and you'd be hungry, and not a friend in the world. You wouldn't expect a good Christian to turn you away without even a pound of rice, would you, Mr. Kosak?

I guess not, said Mr. Kosak, but you ain't in China, Johnny, and neither is your Pa. You and your Pa's got to go out and work sometime in your lives, so you might as well start now. I ain't going to give you no more groceries on credit because I know you won't pay me.

Mr. Kosak, I said, you misunderstand me: I'm not talking about a few groceries. I'm talking about all them heathen people around you in China, and you hungry and dying.

This ain't China, said Mr. Kosak. You got to go out and make your living in this country. Everybody works in America.

Mr. Kosak, I said, suppose it was a loaf of French bread and a pound of cheese you needed to keep you alive in the world, would you hesitate to ask a Christian missionary for those things?

Yes, I would, said Mr. Kosak. I would be ashamed to ask.

Even if you knew you would give him back two loaves of bread and two pounds of cheese? I said. Even then?

Even then, said Mr. Kosak.

Don't be that way, Mr. Kosak, I said. That's defeatist talk, and you know it. Why, the only thing that would happen to you would be death. You would die out there in China, Mr. Kosak.

I wouldn't care if I would, said Mr. Kosak, you and your Pa have got to pay for bread and cheese. Why don't your Pa go out and get a job?

Mr. Kosak, I said, how are you, anyway?

I'm fine, Johnny, said Mr. Kosak. How are you?

Couldn't be better, Mr. Kosak, I said. How are the children?

Fine, said Mr. Kosak. Stepan is beginning to walk now.

That's great, I said. How is Angela?

Angela is beginning to sing, said Mr. Kosak. How is your grandmother?

She's feeling fine, I said. She's beginning to sing too. She says she would rather be an opera star than queen. How's Marta, your wife, Mr. Kosak?

Oh, swell, said Mr. Kosak.

I cannot tell you how glad I am to hear that all is well at your house over at 149 East Orange Avenue, Mr. Kosak, I said. I know Stepan is going to be a great man some day.

I hope so, said Mr. Kosak. I am going to send him straight through high school and see that he gets every chance I didn't get. I don't want him to open a grocery store.

I have great faith in Stepan, I said.

What do you want, Johnny? said Mr. Kosak. And how much money you got?

Mr. Kosak, I said, you know I didn't come here to buy anything. You know I enjoy a quiet philosophical chat with you every now and then. Let me have a loaf of French bread and a pound of cheese.

You got to pay cash, Johnny, said Mr. Kosak.

And Esther, I said. How is your beautiful daughter Esther?

Esther is all right, Johnny, said Mr. Kosak, but you got to pay cash, Johnny. You and your Pa are the worst citizens in this whole county.

I'm glad Esther is all right, Mr. Kosak, I said. Jasper MacGregor is visiting our house, and he asked me to ask you if you ever saw him on the stage. He is a great actor.

I never heard of him, said Mr. Kosak.

And a bottle of beer for Mr. MacGregor, I said.

I can't give you a bottle of beer, said Mr. Kosak.

Certainly you can, I said.

I can't, said Mr. Kosak. I'll let you have one loaf of stale bread, and one pound of cheese, but that's all. What kind of work does your Pa do when he works, Johnny?

My father writes poetry, Mr. Kosak, I said. That's the only work my father does. He is one of the greatest writers of poetry in the world.

When does he get any money? said Mr. Kosak.

He never gets any money, I said. You can't have your cake and eat it.

I don't like that kind of a job, said Mr. Kosak. Why doesn't your Pa work like everybody else, Johnny?

He works harder than everybody else, I said. My father works twice as hard as the average man.

Well, that's fifty-five cents you owe me, Johnny, said Mr. Kosak. I'll let you have some stuff this time, but never again.

Tell Esther I love her, Mr. Kosak, I said.

All right, said Mr. Kosak.

I ran back to the house with the loaf of French bread and the pound of cheese.

My father and Mr. MacGregor were in the street waiting to see if I would come back with food. They ran half a block toward me and when they saw that it was food, they waved back to the house where my grandmother was waiting. She ran into the house to set the table.

I knew you'd do it, said my father.

So did I, said Mr. MacGregor.

He says we got to pay him fifty-five cents, I said. He says he ain't going to give us no more stuff on credit.

That's his opinion, said my father. What did you talk about, Johnny?

First I talked about being hungry and at death's door in China, I said, and then I inquired about the family.

How is everyone? said my father.

Fine, I said.

So we all went inside and ate the loaf of bread and the pound of cheese, and each of us drank two or three quarts of water, and after every crumb of bread had disappeared, Mr. MacGregor began to look around the kitchen to see if there wasn't something else to eat.

That green can up there, he said. What's in there, Johnny?

Marbles, I said.

That cupboard, he said. Anything edible in there, Johnny?

Crickets, I said.

That big jar in the corner there, Johnny, he said. What's good in there?

I got a gopher snake in that jar, I said.

Well, said Mr. MacGregor, I could go for a bit of boiled gopher snake in a big way, Johnny.

You can't have that snake, I said.

Why not, Johnny? said Mr. MacGregor. Why the hell not, son? I hear of fine Borneo natives eating snakes and grasshoppers. You ain't got half a dozen fat grasshoppers around, have you, Johnny?

Only four, I said.

Well, trot them out, Johnny, said Mr. MacGregor, and after we have had our fill, I'll play *Drink to Me Only with Thine Eyes* on the bugle for you.

I don't want them living things killed, I said.

I'm mighty hungry, Johnny, said Mr. MacGregor.

So am I, I said, but you ain't going to kill no snake of mine and eat it. I caught that snake.

What's the use keeping an old gopher snake? said Mr. MacGregor.

I like that snake, I said.

Let's cook and eat that nice fat snake, Johnny, said Mr. MacGregor.

My father sat at the table with his head in his hands, dreaming. My grandmother paced through the house, singing arias from Puccini. As through the streets I wander, she roared in Italian.

Nobody's going to cook and eat that snake, I said.

All right, said Mr. MacGregor. Just as you say, Johnny, but I sure am hungry.

How about a little music, Mr. MacGregor? said my father. I think the boy would be delighted.

I sure would, Mr. MacGregor, I said.

All right, Johnny, said Mr. MacGregor.

So he got up and began to blow into the bugle and he blew louder than any man ever blew into a bugle and people for miles around heard him and got excited. Eighteen neighbors gathered in front of our house and applauded when Mr. MacGregor finished the solo. My father led Mr. Mac-Gregor out on the porch and said, Good neighbors and friends, I want you to meet Jasper MacGregor, the greatest Shakespearean actor of our day.

The good neighbors and friends said nothing and Mr. MacGregor said, I remember my first appearance in London in 1867 as if it was yesterday, and he went on with the story of his career. Rufe Apley, the carpenter, said, How about some more music, Mr. MacGregor, and Mr. MacGregor said, Have you got an egg at your house?

I sure have, said Rufe. I got a dozen eggs at my house.

Would it be convenient for you to go and get one of them dozen eggs? said Mr. MacGregor. When you return I'll play a song that will make your heart leap with joy and grief.

I'm on my way already, said Rufe, and he went home to get an egg.

Mr. MacGregor asked Tom Brown if he had a bit of sausage at his house and Tom said he did, and Mr. MacGregor asked Tom if it would be convenient for Tom to go and get that little bit of sausage and come back with it, and when Tom returned Mr. MacGregor would play a song on the bugle that would change the whole history of Tom's life. And Tom went home for the sausage, and Mr. MacGregor asked each of the eighteen good neighbors and friends if he had something small and nice to eat at his home and each man said he did, and each man went to his home to get the small and nice thing to eat, so Mr. MacGregor would play the song he said would be so wonderful to hear, and when all the good neighbors and friends had returned to our house with all the small and nice things to eat, Mr. MacGregor lifted the bugle to his lips and played *My Heart's in the Highlands, My Heart Is Not Here*, and each of the good neighbors wept and returned to his home, and Mr. MacGregor took all the good things into the kitchen and our family feasted and drank and was merry: an egg, a sausage, a dozen green onions, two kinds of cheese, butter, two kinds of bread, boiled potatoes, fresh tomatoes, a melon, tea, and many other good things to eat, and we ate and our bellies tightened, and Mr. MacGregor said, Sir, if it is all the same to you I should like to dwell in your house for some days to come, and my father said, Sir, my house is your house, and Mr. MacGregor stayed at our house seventeen days and seventeen nights, and in the afternoon of the eighteenth day a man from the old people's home came to our house and said, I am looking for Jasper MacGregor, the actor, and my father said, What do you want?

I am from the old people's home, said the young man, and I want Mr. MacGregor to come and live at our place because we are putting on our annual show in two weeks and need an actor.

Mr. MacGregor got up from the floor where he had been dreaming and said, What's that you said, young man?

My name is David Cooper, said the young man, and I am from the old people's home. They want you to come with me because we need a leading actor for our next production, *Old People's Follies of 1914*.

So Mr. MacGregor got up and went away with the young man, and the following afternoon, when he was very hungry, my father said, Johnny, go down to Mr. Kosak's store and get a little something to eat. I know you can do it, Johnny. Get anything you can.

Mr. Kosak wants fifty-five cents, I said. He won't give us anything more without money.

Go on down there, Johnny, said my father. You know you can get that fine Slovak gentleman to give you a bit of something to eat.

So I went down to Mr. Kosak's store and took up the Chinese problem where I had dropped it, and it was quite a job for me to go away from the store with a box of bird-seed and half a can of maple syrup, but I did it, and my father said, Johnny, this sort of fare is going to be pretty dangerous for the old lady, and sure enough in the morning we heard my grandmother singing like a canary, and my father said, How the hell can I write great poetry on bird seed?

Bitlis

✿ ✿ ✿

I FORGET everything until I hear again the melancholy and heart-sickening steamwhistle of the popcorn man's wagon passing in the street, and then I see the wagon again, and the street, and remember again, as if I were still a small boy of eight sitting on the steps of the house on Santa Clara Avenue, days I remembered then and still remember, but days nevertheless that were never in my life, that were days of the world of people in cities far away, a long time ago. Sitting on the steps of the porch, I would feel again the bitter ache of those ended moments returning to me, knowing they were mine, though I had never lived them.

The sky would be very high, yet very near, and clear, and bright with the tragic presence of many stars, the air would be warm and full of substances almost tangible, and it would be impossible, breathing, not to go back, turning in the warm moment, to the long years of sleeping, after birth, in the warm days of the warm months, August and September and

October, a small body alive in a house, dreaming the world, and it would be impossible not to live again all the dark warm hours of breathing this world, in sleep.

The horse and the popcorn wagon would go by in the street, moving slowly, and I wouldn't be able to know the substance of the days returning to me, and I would ask the questions, Where? Who? When? There was a city surely, and places, and men came to the city in carts drawn by oxen, or seated on camels, and they would enter the places of the city, places with tables and chairs, food and drink, and the men would sit at the tables and eat, and drink, and talk, and I would be there.

I would follow the popcorn wagon to the corner, asking, Who laughed? And I would follow the wagon another block, asking, Who roared with laughter?

And then I would remember danger, and be frightened by the world, and the inhabitants of the world, the multitudes of them. Then I would laugh at the fear, remembering the laughter of the one who laughed, and I would laugh. I would challenge it. It is so, I would laugh. There is danger in things seen, and in things unseen. Well, here I am. I'm not afraid.

I would go back to the house and sit on the steps and begin to wait again. Let it come. There would be a sea somewhere, and it would be desolate and full of danger, and then the wind would come up and rain would fall and there would be thunder in the darkness. The cold would be full of danger and there would be no bottom to the sea. But at the edge of the sea there would be land. There would be warm earth and clean fields of growing grass: trees, rocks, brooks, and all the living things of earth; animals with fur; eyes, feet. And birds with colored feathers; and eyes. On the earth. And there would be cities and streets and houses and people.

One night my father's younger brother Setrak came down the street on his bicycle. He put the pedal of his bicycle against the wooden curb and came up the walk.

Why are you so eager? he said.

Where did we live first? I said.

You were born here, he said. You've lived in this valley all your life.

Where did my father live? I said.

In the old country, he said.

What was the name of the city?

Bitlis.

Where was this city?

In the mountains. It was built in the mountains.

And the streets?

They were made of rock, and they were crooked and narrow.

Do you remember my father in the streets of Bitlis?

Of course. He was my brother.

You saw him? I said. You saw my father walking in the streets of the city in the mountains?

I got up and jumped down from the steps and walked in front of the house. I walked away from the house and turned around and walked back.

Like this? I said. You saw him walking in the old country? My father?

Of course, of course. He was my elder brother. Many times I walked with him.

You walked with my father? I said. What would he say?

Well, my father's younger brother said, he wouldn't talk much.

Sometimes he would, though, I said. When he'd say something, what would he say?

I remember one day, my father's younger brother said. We were walking together to church. Your father said, Ahkh, ahkh, look at it, Setrak. Look, look.

You heard him say that? I said. *Ahkh, ahkh?* What was it?

Nothing, my father's brother said. It was nothing. It was everything.

Ahkh, ahkh, I said like my father. Look, look.

My father's younger brother went away on his bicycle, and I sat on the steps of the porch and, breathing, the days of my father alive in the city in the mountains returned to me, and I knew he was not dead because, breathing, the sky very high, yet near, and clear, and the air warm and full of substances almost tangible, the moment was the timeless moment of all days and all men, and the world was the world of all who were ever born, the world of all who once dreamed through the long warm days of August and September and October.

Baby

☼ ☼ ☼

THE muscles of the American body tighten with remembrance. The heart opens deeply to fresh indrawn air of Montana. The eyes widen with vision. The giant stands large in Nebraska. The babe of Louisiana is boisterous with black blood and bravery. He leaps, laughing.

This is the American. Tom Sawyer, and myself, and yourself. The genial largeness of spirit. Across the continent strides the body. Through the panorama of loneliness, over the endless stretch of mirthful earth.

Here is the native dream. The street, the dwelling, the window. The stuff of this life. The juice. The muscle. The bone and flesh. The city sin. Mississippi. Tin Pan Alley. The beauty of the movies. The magnified faces, the glorious bodies. The gags. The vaudeville dancing. The comedy of daily news.

Inside, out. The hurry of Packards up and down the Lincoln Highway. The roar of subways. The leap of skyscrapers. The well-dressed poise of millionaires, the casual loping of peasants. Our style is the style of the earth: weed and flower, rock and reptile, tree and hill, path and plain, river and sea, city and furnished room.

The furnished room. I am in the heart of Manhattan. August, 1928. I am looking for a place to sleep. God Almighty, I never saw so many people in one place in all my life. I can't believe so many people are alive. The whole thing is a dream. The landscape isn't right. There is too much noise. I am walking up Broadway. No one knows when life begins. But I know. Or else I'm taking a lot for granted. It begins when remembrance begins, and death begins at the same time, so that living and dying are simultaneous beginnings.

This is a remembrance of my native land. The bridge. I walked across that bridge at nightfall once, Manhattan to Brooklyn, and laughed. To be there, on that bridge, alive, walking, Manhattan's million windows glowing, electricity and progress, night and sadness, to Brooklyn. Wherever you are, you are alone. If it isn't a symphony, it's a fox trot, or a waltz, or a tango, baby O maybe.

II

Fifteen years ago in my home town there was a boy named Casper who had a lot of rhythm. He used to wear candy-striped trousers and dark blue shirts. He used to dance all the time, even when he walked. At the County Fair he used to hold a little girl in his arms and go through so many joyous and crazy movements that farmers from away out in Hanford used to stand around and watch him with their mouths open.

Remember him. He is the rhythm boy of this moving picture.

He was the only boy in my home town who wasn't afraid to wear patent-leather shoes. God, what a hero, what an American.

His father was born in a village in Armenia.

III

The street of America is a long street, and the lost who walk along this street are many. There are those who drive up and down the old Lincoln Highway in automobiles. These are the rich. I am concerned with everybody and everything. The poor, the rich. The strong, the weak. The sane, the mad. The good, the evil. Morning and night. Summer and winter. Death and decay and disease. Life and love and laughter.

God is in this legend. He will be coming in through the open door. He will be sitting down and listening and smiling and going away. God is always lonely for a place and a moment in which to be at home. In Manhattan I was alone. A man is seldom not alone. He is not alone only when God is near by. I used to meet God in many places. In the subway. On Broadway, His gentle face in a mob of twisted faces. In the weary smile of an overworked stenographer, going wearily to her small furnished room. Baby, may the darkness of night fall sweetly about your naked body, may heaven kiss your naked spirit.

In the middle of the night I used to remember little things I hadn't remembered in years. A furious cat by the railroad tracks, howling and making a desolation in the earth. The runaway horse, down Mariposa Street. The burning church on Ventura Avenue at midnight. The quiet, early-morning talk between myself and a newsboy named Rex Ford who died three years later. And the coming up of the sun, filling the hollow streets with light. He died, I lived. Once we talked together before daybreak. Now I am in Manhattan, alive, and he is dead.

And romance: melodic and clean like winter snow: White. In the movies. The gentle glacé-fruit face of loveliness: the eyes wide with understanding: the hair warm and thick: the heart big with love. It is nowhere, and it is America.

The long street through the continent and through the heart.

In school I was always laughing. Everybody took me for the saddest boy in school, and maybe I was. Even the little pictures in the books saddened me. Holy God, what universe is this? Where is this shore of sea?

Who is this man and who are these two small boys? From what far and lonely place has this ship returned? Why shouldn't I have been sad? I had not been there. I had not been one of the boys. The ache of the past stabbed me with the longing to have lived always. To have known all life.

One sea, one continent, one city, one street, one dwelling, one door, one room, one man. Rooms conceal us, and the streets groan with the force of our loneliness. In Manhattan I heard much talk, with deep implication. The problems of an office, implying love of right and need of immortality. The worn words concealing the proud, undying desire.

We hardly ever notice the wheel, taking it for granted. The miracle of the subway escapes us. The turning of many wheels no longer startles us, but it will never cease to startle that within each of us which is timeless and deathless: the earlier life, the life of walking. We take for granted. I do not know who perish first, the weak or the strong. I think the strong. Timelessness in them cannot accept contemporary horror. They die. The weak turn away from themselves and are protected, living two lives at one time. The surface life and the inward one, the inward one waiting patiently for another century. It will come. Horror cannot exist forever. The inward life will lift its broken body out of the nightmare and breathe.

IV

The earth was white with winter frost the day she came to our school and walked into our room, bringing with her the cool wind of the Sierra Nevadas, the quiet attentiveness of mountain animals, the grace and silence of flying hawks, a tall American girl with a full round face and heavy black hair. To town in a wagon with her father. Eyes with the wisdom of having seen largeness. Strength of stance. Grace of motion. Hardness and gentleness of speech. America, and we all turned to admire our continent, North Dakota, Nebraska, Wyoming, the endless stretch of American earth, this girl, Betty.

Having the strength of hard land and high mountains, she was humble and smiled at us. We knew how to read and she didn't, but we knew less than she, for she talked with words hewn solidly from substance, and everything she said had deeper meaning than anything we said.

She hadn't been to school and already she was fourteen years old and bigger than a grown woman. Her hands were brown and big, and she said, I been keeping my father's house in the hills six years in a row now, but I guess I got to learn to read sooner or later, so I've come to learn from the books.

Everybody in our class was glad somebody from the mountains had come down to the valley, to our little city, over muddy roads in a wagon into our little world. She was bigger than anything and too old to be in the third grade, but she was neither ashamed nor embarrassed. Our teacher was embarrassed. Our teacher said, You mean you've never been to school? You mean this is the first time you've been inside a school building?

I been going around with my father, the girl said. We been going around in a wagon and I ain't had a chance to stop and go to school. We been traveling all over this country. One night we stayed at a hotel in Cheyenne, and in the morning we ate fried beefsteak and drank coffee.

Our teacher was amazed. This wasn't going to be easy for her. This girl had been traveling in another world. She hadn't been moving with the nation of children of her time, learning the alphabet and numbers. She was the daughter of a simple man, and she had come to greatness moving across the continent in a wagon with him, and our teacher was confused.

Where is your mother? she said.

Joe ain't never told me about my mother, the girl said, and God Almighty, right then and there I had the craziest idea any boy in the third grade ever had. I said to myself, This girl wasn't born of any woman. She just came up by herself out of all those places I've never seen, all the big level valleys, all the mountains, all the rivers, all the towns from one end of this country to the other.

I wanted to know her the way a bee wants to know a great bright flower, diving into it deeply where the sweetness is, and mystery, drawing honey out of the fire of color, and poise out of the miracle of shape.

All I could do was get sullen and be bad. All I could do was anger our teacher and say things out of turn and get sent to the office, being the worst boy at school, wanting this big mountain girl.

V

I want to bring into the open the germ of American magnificence, hold the glass over it, bring the sun close to it, watch it grow, see it stir with life, see the form of man spring from it, hear it laugh, leap, reach the big street, stalk down the street through Boston and Manhattan and Baltimore and Chicago and St. Louis and Kansas City, down every street of every city and town of this nation, down dark avenues everywhere, at night, seeking fulfillment, glory and truth, warmth and humor, being fearless, the way living should be, and is, with the great. Ladies and gentlemen, this is the time of America, from the Atlantic to the Pacific, Columbus to the latest birth. Here is Big Joe, born of flesh and ten centuries of loneliness, of going down dark streets of every city of every continent, of every day and night and year of time, a male here and a female there, the bone and blood of this man, and the tender, frantic union of this flesh and spirit and this flesh and spirit, love and kisses, there is no end to the legend of man on earth, and no beginning.

I want to set in motion. When lightning flashes the outline and temper of magnificence is revealed. The electric globe is lightning a million times tamed, flashes of revelation a million times repeated. All things lie dark in possibility. The lamp-lit street and the moon-lit desert. There is no substitute for the eye, inward or outward.

Stir to life. The tiger leaping. Rocks even may leap with living shapes if the mind will penetrate into the depths of them. Look upon the boulder and if your vision is clear, the giant of Georgia will leap from it and scramble two flights up in Atlanta to buy a fifteen-dollar suit, with two pairs of pants.

I can't help laughing about our great civilization.

VI

Socrates was a small Greek boy in my home town who used to steal raisins from Guggenheim's Packing House. He spoke English well, but whenever they caught him stealing raisins he would stop speaking English.

He would answer their questions in modern Greek. He would look bewildered.

They would say, What do you mean, getting into our freight cars and stealing our good muscat raisins?

Socrates would look dumb.

No speak English.

Don't you know it's against the law to steal?

Dumb look. Greek words.

They would always let him go. Walking home, he would talk to himself. Raisins, he would say. They got more raisins in that packing house than all the people in the world can eat. I like raisins myself. Who the hell do they think they are?

He had a cousin named Plato. This boy got caught stealing raisins and instead of acting dumb, he began to cry. They put him into a Ford roadster and drove out to his house and raised hell with his mother. She got scared and screamed in Greek at the little boy. Plato, she screamed. What have you done? Why have you become a thief?

She wept a long time, while the men from the packing house stood around, getting more and more involved in the little tragedy.

O my little Plato, she wept. I cannot believe you have become a thief.

Finally, the men from the packing house got tired of hanging around and went away.

Plato thought his mother was going to kill him.

She dried her eyes and looked at him bitterly.

Next time, she said, don't behave like a thief. They don't need all the raisins. I guess we can use a few of them. Next time don't cry. When they see you acting like a thief, they think they've got to do something about it. Stealing raisins isn't being a thief. They cheat the farmers, don't they? You don't ever see them acting like thieves, do you? Next time act ignorant. That's how *they* do it.

These Greeks of my home town were natural-born philosophers. Plato, though, was instinctively a Christian. He had to bawl when they caught him with stolen raisins in his pockets. He himself believed he had done wrong, so he cried.

Socrates wasn't older than Plato, but instinctively he was a pagan. He couldn't feel badly about being caught with stolen raisins in his pockets. What he wanted to know was, Who the hell did they think they were?

When Socrates was nine, I was about fifteen, and I had just discovered the other Socrates, the original.

I used to laugh about this every time I saw him. It was very funny. Socrates and Socrates.

VII

The finest rebel is the quiet man who knows the end of all things, yet is pleased to go on drawing breath. Only the mind cannot die, and the smiling mind makes an everlasting ripple in the void of the universe. And it is music of silence, motion of substance, light and color. Laughter is the only thing. Laugh down the cruel. Laugh down the evil. Gentlemen, I know the foulness of your acts. Good ladies, I know your greed.

It is the lust for material possessions which is so comical. The itch to own. The ache to have and hold. Including love, so evanescent, so deliciously swift in reaching the blood, blooming, and dying, so gloriously full of death. They would possess. Outwardly.

This boy Caspar was a dancing fool, a fellow of great animal wit, turning neatly on the highly polished dance floor with the country girl in his arms, making her scamper with him, making her bend, lifting her to heaven, letting her down to earth, pivoting, leaping, tearing loose in the great valley, electrifying the night with his pious acrobatics, making God roar with delight, a black Armenian of the vineyard country, a free slave in America, busting loose with the glory of his body, his black hair greased down, his patent-leather shoes sparkling, his candy-striped trousers long and neatly pressed, his arms strong with love of life, hugging the girl, embracing America, the new world, the loping easy-going world of the west.

The language of his movement was simple. I breathe. This body lives. These limbs move, this heart smiles, these eyes see, these ears hear, and with this big Hittite nose, ladies and gentlemen, I can smell the sweat of slaves ten centuries ago. With this nose I can smell heaven on earth.

Black Caspar bending his beak of Asia Minor over the glowing face of little Miss Nebraska, breathing his life into her life.

I said America. Every corner of the place. Every drop of blood. Every dream. All pain and all delight. I'll grab hold of this continent and reveal the dream of this life. I'll turn the whole place inside out and reveal the bright germ of our mortality. Tom Sawyer. Myself and yourself. Black Caspar. Big Joe coming to life. American music. American rhythm.

To hell with death. The races of this earth are many, and each of us is of every race, and this is a narrative of living, and subtly music will be heard, the face of man in stone will be seen, the body and the spirit. The cry of the hawk will be a stab in the heart, and the roll of the whale through sea will be an earth-turn in dream, upward toward light and air.

I used to wake up before daybreak and put on my clothes and jump on my bike and tear around town because I was alive. I used to whistle all the symphonies Bach and Brahms forgot to compose.

VIII

I was born. I was taught to walk. I learned to see and feel things in every known dimension and in several dimensions not known. I listened and heard silence, which is music. I was hungry and ate. I was tired and slept. I was refreshed and wakened. I was cold and made a fire and watched the flames and saw in them the leap of my own spirit. I sold newspapers and shouted in the city when there was war in the world. I jumped on my bicycle and rode pellmell through the city, sprinting, scaring old ladies, whistling everybody and everything out of my way, out of my way, brothers, dodging in and around traffic, delivering telegrams. I grew through all the centuries of life in a handful of years. I remembered. I dreamed, laughed, wept, waited, watched. I wanted to say something. I wanted to make. I wanted to bring about equilibrium in all things. I wanted to shape all essences into one imperishable body of grace and humor.

I saw the errors of man and wanted to correct those errors. A small boy wanting to change the way of the world. A small boy alive in a dull city.

For a sullen boy I laughed a lot. I laughed all the way through the journey in the wilderness of a small American city, seeking beyond its ugliness its magnificence. If one man is pure in heart, the earth is saved.

So I wrestled with God and laughed, and you should have seen me and God jumping all over one another and rolling crazily all over the city, raising hell in my home town, me in the city, selling papers, wrestling with God, on a bicycle early in the morning and late at night, the meanest rough-and-tumble fight of all time, God a presence in the men I saw, lost and almost forgotten, deep beneath the errors of man.

I will show them God in themselves, I said. I will teach them to remember. I will talk to them in the language of revelation. If they are deaf, I will give them hearing. If they are blind, I will give them sight. If they are crippled, I will make them whole. If they thieve, I will teach them charity. If they kill, I will teach them love. If they are mad, I will calm them with the music of silence. Their frowns I will turn into smiling. Their weeping I will change into laughter. Their envy I will change into goodwill. All who are upon the earth have life, but the germ of death is mighty in them. I will resurrect the germ of life in them.

And then I remembered. O Jesus, I remembered. This is now. This is here. This earth, this continent, this small dull city. And myself.

I? Who the hell am I? And the question leaped high in the world. I am a small boy who is always in trouble. Trouble at home, trouble at school, trouble in my heart.

Life is still blindness and ugliness. They have changed nothing. Who am I? You must be children again. The germ is cleanest in the child, in the child-heart, and the wisdom of the child is the wisdom of God. God, the angry giant, born of the world-irritations of the living.

I was born, so what? The bird breaks through shell of egg, lives, learns to fly, bursts into song, so what? In the bowels of the earth the mother-rodent brings forth her young and they live, so what? In the river and in the sea the fish comes to life in the pneumatics of water, and moves like the glory of God, so what? A race of the family of man blossoms to greatness, builds great cities, flourishes ten centuries, and dies, so what?

I want to know about these things. Life in all things. Insects, rodents, reptiles, fish, beasts, man. Do you realize how pure a gem is the living eye?

The germ, the germ. I want to understand the germ, the seed, the energy, the egg, the beginning, the timeless and imperishable force of being. Big Joe, the great American country boy, seeking God in the glory of the female body. O baby maybe.

IX

All things exist. Revelation is the only thing. Deep within the seed is beginning and end, the wondrous world of come and go, the moment of now, yesterday's eternity, lost. Life, death. All things are. A man moves directly through the chaos of miraculous simultaneity, through time unending, to place unbounded, and if he is humble, or mad, he finds the window and the door. He sees time and place, enters everywhere, and journeys there.

The seed is watchfulness and seeking.

Riding nowhere on my bicycle, I reached eternity. I rolled deeply into the universe and found it a godly emptiness, full of all things unknown, unseen, unshaped, all things of the world to be. Tomorrow, breathed coldly from the void, and today, a mirage of glory to come.

One afternoon I delivered a death message to the mother of a jockey. I rode to her house on Railroad Avenue, knowing the message.

Mother, your son is dead. He was a good jockey. He brought in a lot of winners. He rode like a gentleman. He was loved by trainers and touts alike. Today, in Chicago, he fell from his mount and was crushed under the hooves of seven horses. Your son John.

Jesus Christ, I said, what can I do about this?

I nearly lost my job trying to decide what to do. I rode out to the house. I ran up to the door, and then I couldn't do it. I couldn't knock. I ran down the stairs, jumped on my bike, and started racing around the block.

Jesus Christ, I said, I can't do it. She'll go crazy. She'll fall down and die. I can't just go up and knock at the door and hand her the telegram. Her boy is dead.

I rode around the block many times. I was losing my nerve, worrying about the old lady, worrying about my job. I loved that God damn job. It opened the door for me that led into the big world. My boss would be standing in the office, waiting for me to return. He'd say, For the love of God, son, where in Christ's name have you been? What the hell kind of a messenger do you call yourself?

I passed in front of the old lady's house many times.

I guess I'll go back and tell the chief I'm through, I said. I guess I'll go back and turn in my uniform. I guess I'll tell him I can't deliver any more death messages.

I never worked so hard in my life, trying to decide what to do. My legs were sore from pumping and I was scared to death. This was no ride to Railroad Avenue. This was no visit to the house of an old lady whose boy had been killed. This was a black chariot, swinging darkly out of the void, charging through our town, sixteen black horses charging through our town, stopping at the shy door of this little old lady's life. This was not myself, a small boy with a telegram in his hat, riding around the block, unable to let her know her son was dead, within himself dead, within herself dead, upon the earth dead, within the seed dead, without motion, without thought, without remembrance, without speech, without laughter, uneyed, unspirited, unborn.

What's the big idea, God? What's the big idea getting funny with this little old lady? You know I love you. What the hell do you call this? Why pick on her boy Johnny, seventy pounds in weight? Why make me miserable this way?

Little Mother, your boy Johnny is dead, every one of his seventy pounds. His eyes are blind with firelessness of spirit, his hands are cold with the winter of nowhere, his mouth is laughless with the shock of exit. Little Mother, I have a telegram for you. The words report the end of the world for your boy Johnny. Read these words, accept this horror, and weep. Weep till the end of time. Your boy is dead.

It was summer, August of the endless summer, and I was glad to be alive. Still, another's death is my death, another's grief is my grief.

I jumped off the bicycle and ran across the yard and up the stairs. I stood at the door, and knocked, and began to wait, my heart pounding in me like the havoc of Judgment Day. I heard the old lady stirring in the house, coming to the door. I wanted to go back to the office and tell the chief I was through. I saw the door open, and I saw her face.

She knew. She had heard the thundering of the black horses. She knew, only it was odd that I, a small boy, should bring the message.

Mrs. Krek, I said. I have a telegram for you.

My hand, trembling, placed in her hand, trembling, the sealed envelope. She opened the envelope and read the words, every nerve of her body trembling. Then she said, I can't read without my glasses. I must get my glasses.

She began walking in and out of the small rooms of her house, knowing her son was dead, having read that he was dead, looking for her glasses. She walked around this way a long time. Then she came back to the door and began to weep, looking at me and making me ask, Jesus Christ, what can I do? Is there anything I can do?

What does it say? she said. I can't find my glasses. What does the telegram say? Is it about my boy Johnny? Sometimes when he wins an important race they send me a telegram. Is my boy coming home to me? Read the telegram. I can't find my glasses.

She was sobbing like a child.

Mrs. Krek, I said. It says here Johnny is dead. (I couldn't cry, but God Almighty she was crying, and my heart was breaking.) It may be a mistake, Mrs. Krek, I said. Sometimes they make a mistake. Maybe another boy was killed and they thought it was Johnny, but it says Johnny. I can go back to the office and ask them to find out for sure. You just go in and lie down and I'll make them find out for sure.

She took me by the hand into the house and showed me a lot of old photographs of the boy. He was a little guy with a pinched face who looked very sad, even when he was a baby. She kept telling me ridiculous and tragic things about him, and she kept saying she couldn't find her glasses. I don't know how I ever got away. I thought she would fall down and die.

When I got back to the office, the chief was raving like a maniac. A fine messenger you are, he said. We thought you got killed out there on Railroad Avenue. I knew I never should have hired you. I knew I never should have given you a uniform. You're not old enough to be a messenger. You're thirteen and you told me you were sixteen. I knew how old you were, and I gave you a job, but I'll be damned if you'll ever make the grade. What happened to you, anyway? What the hell kept you so long? God Almighty, the delivery desk is overflowing with important telegrams that got to be delivered. What the hell happened to you out there on Railroad Avenue?

It was Mrs. Krek, I said. She couldn't find her glasses. It was a death message, I said. Mrs. Krek couldn't believe her boy Johnny is dead. She started to cry and asked me to stay in the house with her. She can't believe it. She wants us to make sure it's her boy. She got a letter from him yesterday saying he would be home for Thanksgiving. She can't figure it out at all.

Oh, said the chief. Oh, I see.

Yes sir, I said. She cried all the time I was there.

Oh, said the chief.

Yes sir, I said. Her boy Johnny was killed in Chicago today. That's what the telegram said.

Oh, I see, said the chief. Put a dozen of these telegrams in your hat and get them delivered. These aren't death messages. These are business telegrams. Just take them around and leave them. That's too bad. We'll find out for sure if there isn't some mistake. You hurry along and get these telegrams delivered.

Yes sir, I said. I made a big route for myself and ran out of the office with a hat full of telegrams.

X

Whisper and laugh, rise in the morning and remember, turn about and move deeply into the dark corridor of dream, walk and sleep, and sleep smiling, for the earth is an error of glory, and the universe a dream without a dreamer. Where, Lord, is this place? By what thought is this substance shaped? By what force animated? Whose rhythm is the ebb and flow of the sea? Whose order is the order of the seasons? Whose energy brings up the sun each morning? Whose grief spreads night upon the earth? Whose weeping is the cry of infant animal? Is truth within us, Lord? Whose purity lifts us tall as men? Whose sin trips us stumbling into depths? Where, Lord, is this place. When is it, Lord?

The river, Lord, and the plain, the shining city, the street, the dwelling, the door, the window, the stair, garments and gadgets, sword and gun, locomotive, ship, flight or bird, glide of reptile, echo, arrival, departure, height, the tower of Rockefeller, depth, the tunnel under the river, flight of steel, the bridge, the mine, width, the path of the airplane, hammer, spade, saw, the iron claw of surgery, the wheel, the automobile, highway, cow-path, destination, danger, drought, hurricane, the running of the fearful, the church, piano, piety, prayer, poverty, the grave. Sleep smiling, for the earth is the half-thought of man unborn.

XI

I do not know if we know, and I do not know if we need to know. I know we have wanted to know and always will, but I know we cannot know if we shall ever know, because the miraculous is forever inexplicable, the earth forever in motion, and when there is duration there is succession and when there is succession there is change and when there is change there is tentative knowing followed by tentative unknowing, and what was, no longer is, and what is, is no longer.

We have invented beginning and end, but I do not know if we know if there is beginning and end, or if there has ever been, or if there shall ever be.

We are not made of earth, shaped whole by the hand of God, given breath from wind and space, motion from revolving planets, heat from sun, laughter from God knows where. We do not enter this earth fresh from nowhere. We do not arrive here clean and whole. We are of earth's duration, earth's change, and each of us is the multitude of all living now dead. Thus and thus and everlastingly thus: great, small, strong, weak, noble, vicious, magnificent, maudlin, gentle, savage, divine, mortal, good, evil.

Silence is, space is, substance is, motion is, man is, but we do not know. Brother, we do not know. Our thought is no more than the folk-poetry of the earth and the universe, but, boy, that's plenty. We know what two times two is, but what the hell is laughter? I don't know, but between thought and laughter I'll take laughter any day, and vanilla. Rock is a form of fire, laughter is a form of grieving, weeping is a form of joy, a form of piety and prayer, death is a form of life, of blossoming birth, and wisdom is a form of idiocy, though I grant you it is a higher form.

Wahoo.

Before him lay the gray Azores, and Columbus came to the shore of this glorious continent. Behold the white towers of Manhattan, the Eighth Avenue subway, the Brooklyn Bridge, the burlesque beauty in glory of dim purple light, the Sunday morning funny papers, daily news, vital statistics, holy ha-cha, the genial broad grin of Big Joe Mefoofsky.

Sitting at the window of our little house on San Benito Avenue I used to wonder if I would ever know. We are not made of earth and we do not come here clean and whole. Multitudes inhabit us and journey through our blood.

XII

All presence we take for granted, and many shapes we no longer see, since we no longer look, having once, some years ago as children, looked, and having remembered. The shape of house we no longer see, yet the shape of house we inhabit. This is what I call magnificent blindness. The long street we no longer see, yet the street we walk. The subway tunnel we no longer see, and the subway train we no longer see, yet beneath the city we roar through the tunnel, sitting inside the train. The airplane we have not yet taken for granted, and still see. Of all the shapes we have made it is the most poetic, and at heart we are a race of poetry lovers. We still lift our eyes in wonder at the miracle of substance shaped by us moving across the sky by power we have made and controlled.

I think we must begin again to see. I think we must learn again to look. An apple is an apple, but for the love of God look at an apple before you eat it and you will have become a man alive and for a moment a man who cannot die.

The parts, inert, combine to make a whole, which is America, and the whole is a thing alive, breathing, in motion, men and plains and cities, our lovely contraptions, such as all things of wheels and motors, all things moved by steam and electricity and gasoline, all things miraculous and comical.

This age groans, but don't forget that it laughs too.

XIII

So this is the earth and the world and where we breathe. It is a jungle, a garden, a wilderness, a desert, and it is where we walk. It is the place Dante saw and swung wildly into hell. It is the configuration Shakespeare knew, or made. Who the hell are we, and what the hell are we doing?

I sing the glory of little things alive. The shy secretive gopher of the warm summer prairie. The field mouse. Movement in eternity of wind humming in tall grass, reality of shadow, that small eye seeing, and the everlasting instinct for life. Such is the glory of the earth. To be thus a mouse. In the cosmos, a mouse. By men despised. And yet with the ferocious instinct of mice to live. I laugh the splendor of the lowly despised. Timorous beastie, Scotland's peasant poet loved thee, and I love thee. Thy life is my life, and the life of all things living. You are born. You move. Your period of endurance in the field of grass is no less and no more than the period of my endurance in the city. My books rise no higher above my head than grass above thine. The course of my blood and mind through life is no lovelier than the shy movement of your body from nest to petal of meadow flower. If it could be known which of us is most truly God's, I think it would be you, shy heart-beat of earth. To breathe I need the poise of Socrates. You draw breath from the vast lungs of the universe. To stand I need the support of Jesus. The holy pneumatics of time and space and substance fix you lightly at the center of your world. To walk from my room to the city I need faith in God and man. You are moved by the everlasting motion of the universe. I can listen to the fury of Beethoven's heart in mortal music, but who knows what music shapes your nimble substance? My untutored eye can journey and dwell within the universe of Cézanne, but who knows what microscopic magnitude unfolds itself from grain of sand before your silent stare?

XIV

You cannot say our world is not a dream, quickened out of the swift passage of inestimable centuries, a moment of sudden actuality, this long highway across the world, this city, these inhabitants, their going and coming between day and night.

Our world is a dream and we are not the dreamers but the dreamed.

Time is our most useful delusion, and religion our finest rhythm. The rock of earth is our rock of ages, and out of the rock spring all mortal things: the breathing rock which is man. The breathing beast of the field and forest. The tree, the bush, the bough, the flower. Air and water and fire.

Can you believe city, subway, skyscraper, ship, bridge, locomotive? Can you dream the dream of native and contemporary unreality and make it real? Can you believe mob? The parade of the living? Across the world? Is the life of man a life on earth or a life within the dreaming heart of the universe? Within darkness of desperate and lonely dream? Can you believe what is laughingly called civilization? The pose of life?

Is this the earth of man?

What frantic need brought about the building of the path through the wilderness of the world? What bitter longing made the ship? What wild caprice sent motor and steel flying through heavens of clouds? Ah, yes, the bird, the bird. The wing. The eye. What brotherhood relates each subtle fragment to the subtler whole? Is glass the frightened eye in weary stare? Is door the broken heart locked tight against the world? The earth dreams and is dreamed. We have broken everlasting now into small units of sadness: the second, the minute, the hour, the day, the week, the month, the year, and eternity.

XV

Sang baby O maybe. Sang motors and wheels till Saturday night in America, and a hundred thousand jazz orchestras sang *So come sit by my side if you love me,* and the sad-eyed, weary-lipped Mexican girl silenced Manhattan uproar with soft, velvet-petaled singing of darkness and death, O heart there is no end to the river's flowing. Sang locomotive north through snow to Albany and west to Chicago, O baby maybe.

This is my own, my native land. Sang the heart, miledeep in Pennsylvania earth. O love, O weary love, these meadows lie in timelessness of thought. These hills. These streams. Sang Alabama summer afternoon. Sang Negro *Nobody knows the trouble I know.* My sunshine, sang. Blood drawn in, blood sent out, drawn in, sent out, the living heart beating, in, out, O love this is our earth, our life, O baby maybe. Grimace of American

grief, O what a pal was Mary. Shy mother of life, O what a pal was she.
Sang in the back room of the bawdy house, O bang away fair Lulu, bang
away good and strong. The sullen giant weeping. O baby maybe.

In and out, a hundred million faces of the man, Big Joe, the great
American, the rube from everywhere, weeping baby O maybe. The living
fire in all who have presence here, baby, baby, baby.

Big Joe, who laid the tracks across the continent, rushed the locomotives
through one city after another, lifted the skyscrapers out of the earth,
turned the wheels of American factories, brought forth coal, and on Saturday night sang baby O maybe. Who shaved his leathery face, put on his
Sunday clothes, and went looking for the loosest of women, or a wife. Who
fell dead with wounds of war. Leaped like a goat to God. Embraced heaven.
Who lived once and never died. My race, my native land, O baby maybe.
Who walked alone down all the alien streets of America. Who is Wop and
Hunky and Greek and Jew and Nigger. Who crept in secrecy of sleep like
mongrel dog to the feet of God, begging grace, O baby maybe. Who can
never die, since all who live are his body. This American Big Joe. Yourself
and myself. Who is a shadow even in the cosmos of the moving pictures.
The face in the background of newsreels. The unsung hero of the world.
The small boy running after the President's automobile. Seldom seen, yet
always present. In voices sometimes. In gestures sometimes. And always
in the staring. Our mortality, the darkly flowing stream in all who live, the
storm, the hurricane, the deluge, the dream unfolding, the seed and the
germ, and the darkly flowing river singing O baby maybe.

The Beggars

✿ ✿ ✿

I WAS a traveler once and I went to Europe.

I went right out and saw the world. Everywhere I went I saw the same
thing. The world and beggars. I saw every variety of beggar there is. I saw
rich beggars and poor beggars, proud beggars and humble beggars, fat
beggars and thin beggars, healthy beggars and sick beggars, whole beggars
and crippled beggars, wise beggars and stupid beggars.

I saw amateur beggars and professional beggars. A professional beggar
is a beggar who begs for a living. He begs for money with which to buy
bread.

Every man alive in the world is a beggar of one sort or another, every
last one of them, great and small. The priest begs God for grace, and the
king begs something for something. Sometimes he begs the people for
loyalty, sometimes he begs God to forgive him. No man in the world
can have endured ten years without having begged God to forgive him.

I saw gay beggars and sad beggars.

One of the gayest little beggars I ever saw was a Russian boy of nine or
ten who met the trains at the station of a little village south of Kiev on

the way to Kharkov. He met the train on which I was a passenger very early one morning and inasmuch as everybody aboard the train seemed asleep, he sang in a very loud voice and wakened a number of the passengers, including me. He sang like a gay cock in the morning. He sang like an angel. He was in rags and had no shoes, but his face was the shining face of an angel, and his voice was the voice of one. It was the loudest, purest, simplest, strongest, gayest, most fearless voice I have ever heard, and the song he sang was. I did not understand the words of the song but I understood the music. I guess the words came to just about the same thing: gaiety, joy, pride, delight, simplicity, poise, strength, fearlessness. A beggar boy, doubtless an orphan, a *bezhprizoni*, homeless, without father or mother, uncle or aunt, brother or sister or cousin or friend. Friend? He had as many friends as there were people in the world, good and evil.

I was sleeping on the wooden bench, in the third class section of the train, and early in the morning his voice wakened me and I got up, delighted with the world and the Soviet Socialist Union of Republics, or whatever it's called.

The black Caucasian peasant who slept on the opposite bench wakened too. He lighted a Russian cigarette, inhaled, yawned, and began to smile. He pointed, as if toward the voice, and said something in Russian.

The song this little Russian sang is impossible to describe, and impossible to forget: it began strong, almost violently, at the top of his voice; nevertheless, like the crow of a cock, which becomes at the end almost impossibly strong with morning delight, every now and then it reached a newer, an almost unbelievable, and greater, strength and gaiety and joyousness.

I got up and stretched my muscles and lighted a Russian cigarette. Then I hurried to the first window and lifted it and looked down on the singer, who was looking up at the train, singing, laughing, lifting himself upward exactly as the cock does. And until I arrived not a soul had come to the windows to see and hear him. He had been singing to the train.

There was sadness in the song but it was the kind of sadness which has not forgotten gaiety. The boy was tough, lithe, hard, supple, blond, and brown with exposure to sun and wind and the world. He sang the song through once and then stood smiling at me and I began to hurry through my pockets for Russian money. The black Caucasian peasant came to another window and lifted it and looked out and said a few words to the boy. I don't know what it was, but it was a question. He perhaps asked the boy what his name was. The boy answered the peasant in a few words, and then I showed the coins and when I dropped them he caught them neatly and thanked me in Russian and began to sing the same song all over again which was exactly what I had wanted him to do.

He wakened quite a few people before the train began to move away. Everybody was delighted with him. It is impossible to forget that kind of singing, and I daresay it is impossible to hear that kind of singing twice in a lifetime. That kind of singing comes out of the whole heart of a race, the whole strength and suffering of an age. I could go back to Russia a hundred times in the next fifty years and I doubt very much if I should ever again hear that kind of singing.

This was one of the things that pleased me very much about Russia.

I went to Edinburgh in Scotland and found a fairly good hotel on the slope of a hill, on a very old and narrow street, and my room had a view of the street. Edinburgh is a gray sombre city. There are beggars in Edinburgh too.

A group of three of them came around the curve of this street and stopped in front of my hotel and began to perform. These beggars were three young men. One beat a big drum, another played a banjo, and the third, who was the greatest artist of all, the greatest beggar of all, sang through a megaphone and then tap-danced. Right in the street. Right in the world. Right on the stage of the world-theatre. That kind of music is magnificent in the world. I don't know how it would be in a theatre, but I doubt very much if it would be half as magnificent. That kind of music needs the world for a stage. These are the things which delight the traveler. These are the human things. I didn't visit any of the places travelers visit. I wanted to know about people living in the world. These voices of the beggars are things I remember with gladness. And this team of beggars was a great team. The drummer, the banjo-player, and the singer and dancer. In that gray sombre city, Edinburgh, in that profound and noble city, these three beggars smashed the quiet of centuries with deep, melancholy, Scotch anger. They didn't play and sing Scotch music. There was no bagpipe. These young men were in ordinary every-day clothes, except the singer and dancer. The singer and dancer wore a cutaway coat and a derby.

He sang only the chorus of a song. The music would go along, reach the chorus, he would put the megaphone to his lips and sing; and after he had sung the chorus, he would dance the chorus. He danced like a man who was very angry, not waiting for his feet to fall after he had lifted them, but putting them down with great speed, great energy, great anger, and he didn't dance in one place, he went down the slope of the street, then turned around and danced up the slope, and it was great stuff. He sang something I tried very hard to remember, but all that I remembered was this: *Ha ya hika, waka ho*, and much more in this same kind of language.

The police drove away the three beggars and I got my hat and coat and ran downstairs and followed them. I gave the singer a half crown piece and talked to him. Did the police always go after them? Yes; only sometimes the police put them in jail. It all depended on the location. Couldn't get too close to business streets. Everywhere else the police only kept making them move on. The team went five blocks away and then stopped and again began to perform. They had only one song, this *Ha ya hika, waka ho*. I thought it must be some song these boys had made up, so I asked the singer and dancer. No, it was an American song. He named the song. Then when he sang the song again I listened very carefully, but it wasn't the American song; not any more. I knew the American song: it didn't go that way. It didn't have one-tenth of the anger in it that this song had.

In London I got a third-floor room in a traveler's hotel, and the room overlooked the street. There were a number of kinds of beggars who passed along this street. Organ-grinders mostly, but flower-sellers too. There was a big cockney lady of fifty or so who had a bunch of roses, and she passed along this street very slowly and called to the people in the hotels. The way she did it broke my heart. All she did was say, *Buy a pretty rose, a lovely garden rose*, and so on over and over again, but her voice, that is the unforgettable thing.

It was the saddest and loveliest and most tragic voice I have ever heard, and her language was cockney. She uttered her words half in speech and half in song. It was very touching, very sorrowing, very beautiful, and a thing to remember.

There were all kinds of beggars in the world when I left home and went traveling. Most of them irritated me very much, especially the rich ones, the fat ones, the whole ones, the pompous ones, but the real beggars, the noble beggars, the gay beggars, the angry beggars, either saddened or delighted me.

Their voices I shall never forget.

Quarter, Half, Three-Quarter, and Whole Notes

✿ ✿ ✿

THERE is only one way to write a story and only one way to write one sentence and that is to be pious and simple and inwardly isolated; above all things inwardly isolated. When you move through the mob you must move through it alone; otherwise there is a chance that your vision will be blurred. It is essential for anyone alive to establish a personal method of living and to impose personal limitations: one must possess one's identity fully and vigorously and steadily if one hopes to dominate time rather than be dominated by it. The year is empty because the moment was empty, and the moment *need* not be empty. There must be no evasion. Evasion occurs when one performs acts not pertinent to the ultimate object of one's activity in life, which is to achieve personal wholeness, and to give the material world reality and order. A story (or any other work of art) does not occur when one does the actual writing: it began to occur when one began to live consciously and piously. The writing, which is the least of it, follows inevitably.

A year or two ago I had a job for a while, and with part of my earnings bought some interesting books: *Anna Livia Plurabelle,* which is a small part of Joyce's *Work in Progress; In the American Grain* by William Carlos Williams, which contains some fine prose, especially *The Destruction of Tenochtitlan; An American Argosy* by Morley Callaghan, good short stories. I bought the books at less than half the original price. Then I lost my job. I sold about ten dollars' worth of books for a dollar and a quarter, and I bet a dollar of this money on a horse named *Prose and Poetry,* having great faith in the printed word, and the horse ran fifth in a seven-horse race.

Syncopation.

Geography of the Unmapped World.

I said yes, and I stood at the big desk, in front of the big man with the big job, and I said, yes sir, yes sir, because I want a bicycle and a phonograph, a wheel and music, and then the writing machine, a typewriter, one fellow in this desolation who is going to write, and I got the job.

They gave me a hat two sizes too large and a coat two sizes too small and they said, Son, do you know this town, do you know the ups and downs, where the big buildings are, and where the joints are, do you think you could go backstage right where big country girls take off their clothes and get into feathers and stuff, do you think you could do it? Son, do you know what a responsibility it is to carry telegrams to important people and to people who have just lost someone dear to them, and all that? And I said, I know anything, just let me start and I'll show you what I know, and they gave me a telegram and they said, Run out there and deliver it, this fellow's wife just got killed in an automobile accident and he's probably dying to hear the good news.

I took the telegram and jumped onto a borrowed bicycle (because they didn't want me to buy a bicycle until they were sure I was the boy for the job) and I began to tear through traffic, whistling for the right of way, bumping into the rumps of fat ladies, yelling at them, out of my way, ladies, a woman just got killed and she's got a lonely husband out there on Blackstone Avenue, and I'm carrying him the news, out of my way, all of you, and I tore through the town as if my pants were on fire, the fastest messenger in the San Joaquin Valley, and when I got back to the office, they said, Son, you're the boy for the job all right, only don't get killed the first day because it's a big world and if you live you're going to go places. And by God I lived.

Nothing is trite, if you choose to be vigorous. You can imply that life is sad, which is a platitude, and if you give the implication sufficient fullness there will be no platitude: you will have implied that life is sad. And it is this: that he who is able to take the oldest thoughts or moods of man and resurrect them is, I think, finally the greatest artist. Also: you can never say anything new. You can devise a new way of saying an old thing. No more. The writer's problem is to be so earnestly alive that nothing is old or dull to him. Nothing. And do not suppose that such a condition is impossible because it isn't.

The Green Earth Smiling.

Poem.

Alexandra, small with small quiet hands, small feet, soft black hair, a Jewess, walking alone in Paris, April 1802, the same sun, the same moment of breathing, Alexandra alive, and young trees, youthful with new leaf. Two or three carriages. Look. Alexandra. And the swift staring of three students: Tears for Courtesans.

Another and a better world.

Andalusia Eldorado.

Comic wonder.

Gloom and glory.

One by one the women.

A primer of the forgotten language.

Ha Ha Ha: thus: a child's talk, with especial emphasis on the *ha ha haaa*, drawn out: illness with an implication of death: a child, uttering this expression, still alive, innocent of its tragic condition, expressing naive pride in the possession of some childish object: a toy: the emotion of man in the infant: ha ha ha. O Jesus, I cried.

Trembling, Trembling, Trembling: subtle treatment of everyday life: affairs, petty complexities, fears, shadowy loves and hates, fears, climaxes.

Pictures of 1926.

Unfinished things.

Prose should get the simultaneity of events: of thought and incident. Things do not happen by themselves. They happen together with innumerable other events: thoughts, remembrances, moods, words, emotions, melodies, mingling, and generally unrelated. Sad and comic.

Pious Conversation: at the beach: Pacific: waves: gulls: fishing boats: the sea-sound: debris: walking.

I will be around, waiting to say what is essential. Nothing more.

Break down the stupid structure of the language and make it live.

Sometimes Gaiety, Sometimes Not: a story.

The Communist: you know. He begins to explain dialectical materialism and winds up with an account of his unhappy boyhood.

No one cares to walk any more, and it is too bad, because walking is one of the divine privileges of man. Each of my walks to the public library or the Pacific Ocean is divided into three sections, after the manner of a symphony. The first stage is devoted to reading, especially religious pamphlets; the second to studying architecture and faces; and the third to looking for nickels.

The Vacant Hour: a story.

A vocabulary of the earth.

Do I notice things? Are my powers of perception great? Did I notice the flower in his lapel? A pink sweet pea. Them pink peas were in the vase on her table. Is there something to this? Ask me. Is there a connection here? Well, look for yourself, the way each of them smile, the same sort of sinful secrecy. I know they have been together, in my house, in my own house, and what am I? Am I supposed to be the bright boy who sees all, hears all, and says nothing while my wife is sleeping with a common gigolo: the little bald bookkeeper with his pretty wife and the young Italian at Izzy's drinking beer.

Pennies? We dint used to keep pennies. We trew em away. (Punch-drunk Snorky, the syphilitic walk: hard times in the world, and only three years ago they used to throw pennies away.)

Destinies of the American people.

Limited space.

Distribution of blame.

Things without duration, cities, big events, dreams of money, love itself. There will be an earthquake and the banks will fail. Starved, but living none the less, Zagreb, the smiling Yugoslav, reaches through the long afternoon to pluck a blade of grass, for meditation and a taste, as of food. O blessed smell of bread. Nourish virtue and hatred: only the impure do not hate.

Cafeteria: a poem: Clatter of china and glass combine in chords of (business of swallowing, fish, tea, biscuits.)

One flight up, one ascension, smell of tobacco and blur of human talk, tables, chairs, spittoons, the men, the horses, and the races, at Coney Island, in Ohio, and Arlington Park, in Chicago, five Jews, five Greeks, two Germans, two colored gentlemen, one Armenian, the bookies, the betting, the waiting, smoking, coughing, spitting, laughing, and the God Almighty weeping, as of little ones amazed. No one wins, no one comes out ahead, no one can beat the horses. But hold on, hold on, there is a horse in the next race at Arlington, *Panther Rock*, Jockey Coucci up, and this horse is going to win: a story.

The Wreck of the Cadillac 12: a story.

Picture yourself dead in the hulk of a ship, floating and lost, a century after the crack of doom, waiting, when everyone has ceased to wait, for death out of mind.

Sufficiently varied to amuse.

And the earth bounced.

Show them your legs, Miss Digman: don't be afraid. We're all professional men. Etcetera.

Death coming up the stairs.

3:30 in the morning, singing: home on the range: this little piggy: inka dinka do.

Penitentiary Blues. A dream: listen, warden, them six dollars I stole: I'll give them back to the fellow. I'll give him six hundred dollars, warden. Only let me get to a street corner and start walking. Jesus, warden, let me walk in the city. The horror and agony of confinement.

A tender story of the sadness that comes over people who have known one another only slightly, when they part.

The boys on the little bridge: Koke says to Mose, I dare you to push me in. So Mose pushes him in, Mose's sister laughing. Koke swims out of the river and gets up on the bridge again. I dared you to push me in, he says, and you pushed me in. Do you dare me to push you in, Mose? Mose says, No. Mose's sister is still laughing. Koke gets sore: something's wrong somewhere. He pushes Mose's sister in. Funniest thing I ever saw. Mose's sister in the water, looking scared and crying for help.

Joy cometh with morning.

Hydrogen, oxygen.

Memories of the city: what a child sees and remembers at night: the lost city: it was here: now everything is different: the dimensions of growing perceptions.

The little red wagon Santa Claus forgot to bring: a story.

A menace to life and limb, said women who had very nearly fallen beneath the smash and roar of his wheeled contraption. A maniac and a fool. Boy on motorcycle. A story.

Fancy a perfect world, a god-like man, and an intelligent and severe order of nature, an order no less technically precise than our own order and yet in choice of matter infinitely wise: no waste of the fire of life in rotted substance, or in the diseased, or in the crippled, in short, no bad forms of life. All men whole and innocent and strong. And from this beginning move on to the nobler problems of the living, the newer tragedies of mortality.

Bad dreams: a realistic novel: the living are sleep-walkers, and by Christ they are.

Steel & Glass: prose.

Winter dancing. Folk tales from the mind of America. The body. Places, not people. American lullaby: winter white: the quiet winter mood of mortality. Snow. The poor man walking through desolation, a street in Chicago, another in St. Louis, another in Manhattan, and so on.

Good men and good things.

One thing against another: hydrogen, oxygen: the holy leap of anger and the polite smile of convention: hate and civility.

When the train whistles, the race of man wails. This is our contribution to music. A simple direct sound of grief. Our symphony.

How they live.

On a windy day like this when every particle of dirt in the whole blooming city finds its way into my eyes, generally my left eye, which is my best eye, the left side of my face being the side I use for observation, the place for me, I daresay, is the reference room of the public library, where, they tell me, I can learn more about the English language in two hours than in ten years of listening carefully to people in the streets, and where, I understand, I may be able most easily to give an impression of being a scholar, so of course I shall not go to the public library, since I have never wanted to give the impression of being a scholar.

I will go down to the city, biblically. I will walk through the thorough-fares of commerce.

And let the wind bring all the dirt of the city into my eye, I shall not mind. My shepherd is the Lord, and my cigarettes, they comfort me. And though I walk through the canyons of idiocy, I fear no evil, though they cry misery on every corner, crying headlines on every corner: love, murder, jealousy, death, birth, marriage, adultery, and holy fornication on every corner.

Molly. Constant remembrance. I wish you joy.

A few good words in his mouth.

This city at night is a young woman whose mouth is sad with the pain of lost men in the world, whose eyes are wise with the remembrance of many tragic scenes, whose ears have heard the secret cries of the lonely living, whose body has embraced their small naked forms, whose voice has lulled them to forgetfulness and sleep, a young woman of no morals, and the greatest morals, who laughs at the heart's desolation and weeps for those who want to live, who leads the lonely to small and ugly rooms where she watches them, who whispers remembrance of a better place and a better life, lost.

My city, last night all the girls were standing naked: laughing: smoking cigarettes: and the ocean came and went: and the ships moved over the surface of the water and went to China: and the little mothers of the lost tribes of the earth laughed at death: and it is a big night for the girls when the night is melancholy with fog: up the stairs come the forms of many men: and for each man there is a special nakedness: himself: the nakedness of his own soul: and I remember the full innocent breasts of Leah: and all the streets and all the faces moving over the streets: and the ocean coming and going: and the ships gliding to China: and the mortal cry of grief in the fog horns.

While infidels scoff, let us adore.

The race of writers needs to be the race of man at its best.

The ocean is the Pacific, at San Francisco. I am on the beach, and the ocean is rolling up to my feet, and then rolling away, back again.

I am seeking pebbles.

A pebble is a fact, a most remarkable kind of fact. And a poem. A mark of punctuation in the sand. Every pebble is the earth and the universe. The winter sun is bright and the pebbles shine as the ocean comes over them and then slips away: the pebble, water, and light: and the movement of the ocean, like breathing.

Pebbles are like eyes shining through eternity. They are of many colors.

Every pebble is old, from the beginning. It is this that is so important about them. In comparison with flowers and other evanescent things of beauty they are static. They change, especially in size. Every century or so, some small change takes place in every pebble on the earth. After a while a number of them get to have shapes that are sculptural, and it is pleasant to find such pebbles as these. To find them perfect, after all the centuries. They are small, detached, static, precise, and, to my way of thinking and perceiving, lovely. There is something pious about their precision. I do not intend to be mystical. I intend to be sensible, and I am saying there is something pious about the precision of pebbles. I mean this. There is. I have studied the matter. I can speak as an authority on the subject. Not as a geologist, but as one who wishes to perceive the unity of all matter. I know nothing of rocks, nothing scientific. What I am saying is new history and new science: maybe new religion. It is impossible not to be religious, seeking perfect pebbles. They are of the sea. And the sea is half of everything.

Everybody thinks I'm kidding, but all I want is a player-piano, one of those old-style player-pianos that make you laugh, and of course a little house to put the piano in, in the desert somewhere. I mean, the warmth of the desert and the comical music of the piano. And of course a quiet woman. Not a smart one. I mean some young peasant girl, if any of them are left. Some warm Mexican girl who knows how to cook and sing, and they think I'm kidding. God's my witness. I'm not.

Firmament.

A brother at a funeral, shouting the truth about the dead boy, and about those who are crying. Why are you telling lies? Did my brother have to die to become virtuous in your minds? You know he was rotten, and you know what killed him, and you know you never liked him. You know it was women and syphilis. You can't cry about my brother this way. He's dead now. I loved him while he lived, while he was rotten. You never loved him, never knew him. You do not love him now. A story.

Birth, baptism, crucifixion, and resurrection.

A funeral psalm.

I have fallen asleep and dreamed my end in time and eternity, and I have wakened and dreamed again the living of my flesh, now, as motion again, he who walks, whistling, over the cement sidewalk, and reaches the city, who enters its order, stands among its inhabitants, speaks, and returns, walking, to his room, and between these two dreams, the one of death to be and the other of life (which is) is the long road or the broad plain or the bright city of living, the lonely path through the rich forest of earth unborn, or the clean clear plain of the smiling heart, or the vast white city of strength, and for this reason, that I am so deeply caught and fixed within this order, which is not really tragic, though it sometimes is, I must laugh and feel that all is right, though all be wrong: that death is right, that pain is right, that disease is right, hatred, cruelty, mockery, sin, despair, fear, and only for this reason, that I (and yourself of course) am so deeply caught within this magnificent time and place of error and waste which we call life, so amazingly entered into the earth, upon it, standing, so magnificently related to the universe, so ridiculously the son and brother of God, so pathetically immortal, so sinfully innocent of all guilt, since the only guilt is *being*, having once been born, but not twice. The lives of all who once lived and are now dead and the lives of all who live tonight and the lives of all who shall come tomorrow, or next century, the sad, rain-saddened lives of all who breathed or breathe or shall breathe, the weary laughing tragic comic lives of the one great living body of the universe: God himself. Poor God, everywhere, everytime, all the time, forever and forever, here an Armenian, staring, there an Englishman, drinking tea, here a Chinese, smoking, there a Russian, working, here and there and everywhere, all the endless time.

Guns Firing: a novel. When there is peace, it is a good time to write of war. The machine-gun racket should be the basic theme of the greatest symphony of this age.

The Weather Has Something to Do with Everything: a story.

An untidy world.

Heaven & Civilization: a story.

Earth rotating.

Living matter.

The lovely moist face: the deep dark: and the dance of mood in lips: the gentle warm aroma of living flesh: Dorothy.

I'm Out of Ohio: a story.

What centuries whirl away within this drunken sleep.

You go everywhere in automobiles. You never walk. You are tangled in junk. And it spoils your sleep. Why are you amazed?

Scene: a public lavatory: men coming and going. Swinging doors. A young man shaving in the morning with cold water, carrying on a conversation. A few words with each. Unemployment. Travel. Police. Hunger. I got to keep up appearances, he says.

Sights & Lamentations.

A large assortment of gadgets.

Pain in the bowels of the earth.

Walking to the breadline.

Death of a Sparrow: a story. Great possibilities, especially for me.

On a day when the earth is sunless and skyless and mirthless, when the oldest of all moods of man returns to man, the mood of wonder and innocence, of loneliness on earth, of timeless and endless loneliness in life, it is difficult to move, to walk, or to sit in a motor car and drive. The world is still and the sky is on the verge of some profound grief, and even the thought of getting up suddenly and putting on one's coat and leaving the house and going down the street seems blasphemous, sitting at the open window, staring at the gloom and hearing the solemn solitude of the earth and the world, and the early hush of life beginning, the simple noble tragic *o sole mio* of the infant universe, the breaking of desolate and beautiful day, the coming of light through emptiness of worlds, the smiling rise of sun, the blossoming of great flowers in warm earth, the making and shaping of mortality, the male and the female, bone and flesh and blood, eye with which to see, ear with which to hear, nostrils through which to breathe, arms and legs, and the rich warmth of female substance, love, and proportion to all things.

The Big Sad Eyes of God: a novel.

A natural revolution.

Curl the lip and shoot the tongue with curse and ribaldry.

Look, honey, look look look look look, O God, look, honey, look, look, look at the trees, look at the houses, look at the little roads, O darling, look at the sky, the grass, the hills, O Jesus Christ, darling, look at everything: a story: a new automobile.

Big Chairs for Impressiveness: a story.

Talk: Your hands are warm, though. I've been walking. What about?

They've Got Me Going & Coming: a story.

The minutes and the hours and the years, the mornings and the noons and the nights, the Saturdays and the Sundays and the Mondays, the Januarys and the Junes and the Augusts and the Decembers: the change in the landscape: the new grass, the new buildings, the new faces: and the new voices, birds and men: and all the smiling of sky and pavement, all the anguish of house and door, all the despair of place in time.

Wisdom Crieth in the Streets: a story.

I have found one mob as bad as another, and I have put it down plainly, and a lot of the professional proletarians don't like it. This fool, they feel, is a mob himself, and how can you have a revolution when one man's mob is greater than the collective mob?

What revolution? Any revolution, *the revolution*, the one they are always talking about, writing bad poems about. You know: poor man walking into rich man's house without wiping shoes. Knocking over vases, and smoking expensive cigars: heaven on earth.
Well, I think mine is the better mob. And I think it will win the better revolution.

He made a world of the streetcar and explored it, pulling open the slide door, going around in the thing while it moved, and running back to his mother, with a rapt expression on his face, he told her how remarkable it was: a small boy: a story.

Hello, Rat.

Miseries of 1935.

Comparison of Pains.

The Man with the Glass Eye, Hare Lip, and Wooden Leg: a story. What a man.

A Brief Life: a short novel of a boy, born to poor parents, whose wisdom is instinctive and profound: he sees, understands, knows, wordlessly: with sensibility: he prefers death to life, and dies at the age of eight, swimming alone in Kings River, the chapter on his death closing the story: an historic death, the death of all things, through this boy who is all things: a great character: articulations of unworded wisdom.

Lady, You Were a Riot: a story.

A man is silly to walk in a parade unless he has a drum to beat, because it is no fun to walk quietly and gradually become sullen-faced, and have people look at you and maybe think you are a little loose upstairs, or maybe pity you, or maybe laugh, so when they told me I could have a drum in the parade I said all right, I would join the party and be a Communist, although at heart I am an Anarchist and believe the worst is yet to come. The drum: a story. (They'll kill me.)

Errors of Man: a story of people who steal or kill or perform cruel acts: as paining small animals or hurting the feelings of children. Theft and murder.

Pity, Awake.

Vultures in this world, evil-eyed, filthy, glutted, yet starving: rats, racing in the underparts of the body of man: snakes, frogs, spiders. Clammy things, half-plant and half-animal. Worms. A story of the filthiness in the heart of man. (A heart which is pure, too.)

Character: What I got is personality, I guess.

O Jesus, if you could see the things I am seeing in this crazy town you would get drunker than I am drunk and you would do crazier things than the things I am doing, running around everywhere trying to straighten everything out.

Streetcar to the sun.

Unwritten.

A number of sheets of paper bound or stitched together. A moment of a man. Something said. A word. The word. And silence. An implication. The smile of mortality. Holy, holy, holy, which was, and is, and is to come.

Night. Day. (Repeat endlessly.) If any have ears let them hear. Rivers. Seas. Continents. Cities. Plains. Hills. The face of one or two living. Arrangement.

Never there, the heart, sadly, and the sorrowing peasants springing from the hot earth, crying for one thing, to live, begging for it, Mexican life, turning, inwardly to themselves, outwardly, to the earth and to the Aztec sun, to the heart itself. Dark and mad with it, Mexican blood crying for Mexican life, weeping for it. The bleeding heart of the world-peasant.

Legs chorus-girls dancers whores movie-stars: parenthetical music: a novel.

So I visited my friend, and he was a great Wop, solid, all there, Italy itself, the broad geniality, the fine laughter, loud and easy, the clear thinking, the violent generosity, and he said he was of the streets, not of the polished floors, and I said I am of the streets, and we drank wine, being of the same universe, the everlastingly level street: Italy.

Brawn and birth: and gasp: and mighty wail. This is the moment of another face: mortality implied. And movement: pain and madness: the face distorted. Mortal suffering. Great expectations, although it is only another birth.

He died. She died. The earth swarms with him and with her, and each rots alone in the earth: unhappy ending.

If you laugh loudly, you are bound to weep bitterly. Walk in the valley, and through the dark city walk. See.

Suddenly the whole town was in motion, not only people running, but houses and streets. A big light in heaven. The church on fire. God and flame. How beautiful. How appropriate. Church Burning.

Sea burial. The cow and the train. The meadow and the track. Earth and steel. A sudden fury of train smash, meadow flash of flower, and myself walking up the aisle saying, You sons of bitches. Tree shadows across the meadow: my mortality. Sheep and anger. Waiting for arrival: the train going.

Pages lost. I said nothing. I thought nothing. My own unwritten works coming across the broad black valley of time, a mountain of silence in my ear, thick with snow and fog, and lost somewhere, in such and such a city: the great book unwritten, novel.

My country, it is of thee I sing: existence in space. Essence. Sweet land, thy rocks I love. To stand and to be and to have time in the flesh: let rocks their silence break. Let pebbles speak. They are thyself, and every morning the sun occurs and every evening the moon and every moment the face of man. This continent. These cities. And the big machines. They weep. They sleep. Thy rocks in silence weep. Thy pebbles sleep. America.

In 1926 they were singing Valencia, in my dreams. Do you remember the cigarettes? The traffic turning the corner? Mirage of earthfaces? Eyes of living stone? Whistle? Gasoline? The roar of sudden machinery? Boy, we have been alive: sweet land. Shadows calm upon the rocks. Summer carols.

Irish songs: Oh, didn't you hear the glorious news that happened at Ballyhooly? Dan Tutty the gauger was caught and thrashed by Paddy and Timothy Dooly. Farewell for evermore. O give me your hand. With my Ballinamona Oro, the girl of Cullen for me. Gaily we went and gaily we came. In the new-mown meadows. The dear black white-backed cow. Get up, my darling, and come with me. Go home, go home, dear heart. A kiss in the kitchen. Shall we ever be in one lodging? O Mary my darling. Last night I was thinking of the ways of the world. In deepest sorrow I think of home. When my old hat was new.

If I haven't got the best job in America, I'd like to know who has. The hours are lousy. There is no pay. Even so.

You do not have to be a composer in order to hear music everywhere, and it is impossible not to hear American music everywhere, wherever you may be. And you remember music that you once heard and you remember music that was never composed and never played by an orchestra or sung by a singer. It is the music of this continent and the music of these times and the music of these people who have their lives on this continent in the cities and in the small towns and in the country, on the farms, in the places of mobs and in the places of quiet, Manhattan and the great southwestern desert, the subway and the sleeping lizard, Carnegie Hall, and the wagonwheel road that leads to the abandoned house. Notes for an American symphony.

A work of prose may be said to be good (though not necessarily great) when it has wholeness, for it is wholeness that man instinctively desires in works of art, and this wholeness need not be purely technical, as many writers imagine. As a matter of fact, the logical growth of the story form would seem to be toward a dismissal, or at least a relegation to a position of minor importance, of technical virtuosity, and a more powerful emphasis of the spiritual or emotional intensity and wholeness of a piece of writing involving man. A narrative in order to be a narrative need no longer concern itself solely with physical events in the lives of men (this is history); on the contrary, it should concern itself with the subtlest and most evanescent of universal meanings evolving from all the facts which make for consciousness in man; that is to say, from his being conscious in the first place, which is certainly an immense thing alone, from his awareness of the world (and every man is aware of the world in a way of his own, which furnishes the sincere writer with an endless source of material), from his awareness of his fellow man, from his very chemistry (that is to say, his organic make-up, his physical structure, the thickness of his blood, the quality of his nervous system, the sharpness or dullness of his perception), from (and this is very important) the manner in which he dreams, the substances and rhythms of his sleep, and from the thoughts that run through his mind when he is not exactly the civilized being he would pretend to be when he is abroad in the world, and so on almost endlessly. So long as a work of prose is about man, and so long as it is brief and tends to emphasize one phase of the reality of man, it may be called a short story, provided it possesses this wholeness. Plot, atmosphere, style, and all the rest of it may be regarded as so much nonsense: it is impossible to write one paragraph about man without having plot, and atmosphere, and what is known as style.

The Living and the Dead

✿ ✿ ✿

I WAS in my room fast asleep at three in the afternoon when Pete the writer came in without knocking. I knew it was Pete from the extra nervous way the door opened and I didn't even need to open my eyes to make sure who it was *after* he was in because I could smell it was somebody who needed a bath and I couldn't remember anyone I knew who needed one, except Pete, so I tried to stay asleep. I knew he wanted to talk and if there was anything I didn't want to be bothered with at that hour of the day it was talk.

When you are asleep at an hour when everybody but a loafer is supposed to be awake you understand how foolish all the activity and talk of the world is and you have an idea the world would be a better place in which to suffer if everybody would stop talking a while and go to sleep, especially at three in the afternoon when sleeping is supposed to be immoral and an indication of the spiritual disintegration of modern man. You figure sleep is one of the extra special privileges of the mortal. You figure not being able to sleep is the basic cause of man's jumping around in the world, trying to do stuff.

It was a warm day and the light of the sun was on my face, going through my shut eyes to the measureless depths of the rest of it, the past of my life, the place where the past is assembled, lighting up this vast area, inside, and I was feeling quiet as a rock and very truthful. Try it sometime. Maybe you have no idea how far away you've been from where you are now, within your skull and skin, but if you are alive and know it, chances are you've been everywhere and seen everything and have just reached home, and my slogan is this: What this world needs is a better understanding of how and when to sleep. Anybody can be awake, but it takes a lot of quiet oriental wisdom to be able to lay your weary body in the light of the sun and remember the beginning of the earth.

Pete isn't a bad guy and in his own way he can write a simple sentence that sometimes means what he wants it to mean. Ordinarily, in spite of the smell, he is good company. He is excited, but that's because he is trying hard to say something that will straighten out everything and make everybody get up tomorrow morning with a clean heart and a face all furrowed with smiles.

Asleep, I am a pretty profound thinker. Consequently I get sore at people who have no consideration for the sanctity of prayer and the holiness of comfort. Awake, however, I am a picture of good breeding.

There were two quart bottles of cheap beer on the table, a bottle-opener, a glass, and a package of Chesterfields. Pete opened a bottle, poured himself a glass, took a gulp, lit a cigarette, inhaled, and I sat up and yawned, my only form of exercise.

God Almighty, Pete said, how can you sleep at a time like this? Don't you realize the world is going mad? The poor are perishing like flies. Starving to death. Freezing to death. And you stretch out here in this hole in the wall and act as if everything were jake. Do you mind if I have a drink?

I told him anything I had was his, and he said: The true bourgeois, all kindness, but you can't fool me. That sort of charity isn't going to stand in the way of the revolution. They are trying to buy us off with their cheap groceries and their free rent, but we'll rise up and crush them.

I yawned and opened the window. A little clean air moved past the curtain and I breathed it and yawned again. Who do you want to crush? I said.

Don't be funny, said Pete. This tyranny's got to end. They're trying to cram Fascism down our throats, but they won't get away with it.

Who are you talking about? I said.

The bosses, said Pete, the lousy bosses.

You haven't done an honest day's work in ten years, I said. What bosses?

The rats, said Pete. The blood-sucking Capitalists. Morgan and Mellon and them big pricks.

Them guys are just as pathetic as you are, I said. I'll bet ten to one if you could meet Morgan you'd appreciate how close to death he is. He'd give two or three million dollars to be in your boots, just so he wouldn't have to be a writer. He'd give every penny he has to be as young as you are. Morgan's an old man. He isn't long for this world. He'll be dead any minute now. You've got a good forty years ahead of you if you don't fall down somewhere and bust your head against a fire hydrant.

That's all bourgeois talk, said Pete. I'm talking about *twenty-five million hungry men, women, and children in America.*

Everybody gets hungry, I said. Even the rich get hungry between meals.

Don't get funny, said Pete. I'm talking about getting hungry and not having anything to eat.

He poured himself another glass of beer and spilled some of the foam onto his vest and wiped it off and said he wished to Christ I wouldn't be a Fascist and be an honest Communist and work toward international good will among men.

I'm no Fascist, I said. I don't even know what the word means.

Means? said Pete. (Very nervous writer: he spilled more beer on his vest and began to shout.) You don't know what Fascism means? I'll tell you what it means. It means muzzling the press. It means the end of free speech. The end of free thinking.

Well, that isn't so bad, I said. A man can always get by without free speech. There isn't much to say anyway. Living won't stop when free speech does. Everybody except a few public debaters will go right on living the same as ever. Wait and see. We won't miss the debaters.

That's a lot of hooey, said Pete. Do you mind if I have another cigarette?

You're excited, I said. What's on your mind?

Confidentially, said Pete, I've been sent out by the local chapter of the Party to get a dollar from you.

Oh, I said. I thought you were really upset about the poor.

I *am* upset about them, said Pete.

What do they want a dollar for? I said.

To help get out the next number of the *Young Worker*, said Pete.

Young Worker, my eye, I said. *Young Loafer*. You punks never worked in your lives, and what's more you don't even know how to loaf.

I got a story in the next number, said Pete.

That cinches it, I said. I hope they never raise the money to get the paper out.

It's the best story I ever wrote, said Pete.

And that's none too good, I said.

It's the sort of story that will tear out their rotten hearts, said Pete.

Have another beer, I said. Open the other bottle. That's what you think. You've got twenty or thirty dopes down there who want to be writers and not one of you know where the hell to begin and what to say. Communism is a school of writing to you guys.

I say plenty in this story, said Pete. I talk right out in this one.

What do you say? I said.

I say plenty, said Pete. Wait till you read it. It's called *No More Hunger Marches*.

I'll wait, I said, gladly.

You've got to let me have a dollar, said Pete. I haven't collected a dollar in six weeks and they're checking up on me.

Suppose you never collect a dollar? I said.

I'm supposed to be an active member, said Pete.

A militant member, I said.

Yeah, said Pete.

You boys are fighting *some* war, I said. I'm lousy with money. I'm the guy to go to for a dollar. Why don't you visit Montgomery Street? Why don't you be a militant Communist and try to get a dollar from Fleishacker or Spreckels?

They're our enemies, said Pete. They hate our guts.

And you just love them, don't you? I said.

We hate their guts, too, said Pete.

One big happy family, I said. Here's a dollar. Get the hell out of here. Bring me a copy of your story when it's printed. You may be Dostoyevsky in disguise. You smell bad enough to be somebody great. When are you going to take another bath?

Day after tomorrow, said Pete. Thanks for the dollar. Do you think I like going around this way, dirty clothes, no money, no baths? Under Communism we'll have bathtubs all over the place.

Under Communism, I said, you'll be exactly the way you are now, only you'll be just a little worse as a writer because there won't be anything to tear out their rotten hearts with and there won't be any rotten hearts to tear out. I was sleeping when you busted into this place. Why don't you guys send out circular letters instead of making personal calls?

Can't pay the postage, said Pete. Do you mind if I take three or four cigarettes?

Take the package, I said.

He went to the door and then turned around a little more excited than before.

They want you to come to the meeting tonight, he said. They asked me to extend a special invitation to you to attend tonight's meeting.

You guys make me laugh, I said.

This isn't one of those boring meetings, said Pete. This is going to be better than a movie. We've got a very witty talker tonight.

I'm going to be playing poker tonight, I said. I can learn more about contemporary economics playing poker.

I'll be expecting you at the meeting, said Pete.

I may drop around, I said. If I lose at poker, I'll *be sure* to drop around. If I win, I'll want to stay in the game and see if I can win enough to get out of town.

Everybody wants you to join the Party, said Pete, because they claim Communism is in need of guys who have a sense of humor.

They want dues, I said.

Well, you could do at least that much for your fellow-man, couldn't you?

I always tip the barber and the bootblack and the waitress, I said. Once a week I give a newsboy half a dollar for a paper. I'm doing my little bit.

That's bourgeois talk, said Pete. I'll see you at the meeting.

If I lose at poker, I said.

You'll lose, said Pete.

He closed the door behind him and hurried down the hall. I opened all three windows of the room and breathed deeply. The sun was still shining and I stretched out again and began to sleep again.

II

Then my grandmother came into the room and stared bitterly at everything, grumbling to herself and lifting a book off the table, opening it, studying the strange print and closing it with an angry and impatient bang, as if nothing in the world could be more ridiculous than a book.

I knew she wanted to talk, so I pretended to be asleep.

My grandmother is a greater lady than any lady I have ever had the honor of meeting, and she may even be the greatest lady alive in the past-seventy class for all I know, but I always say there is a time and place for everything. They are always having baby contests in this crazy country, but I never heard of a grandmother contest. My old grandmother would walk away with every silver loving cup and gold or blue ribbon in the world in a grandmother contest, and I like her very much, but I wanted to sleep. She can't read or write, but what of it? She knows more about life than John Dewey and George Santayana put together, and that's plenty. You could ask her what's two times two and she'd fly off the handle and tell you not to irritate her with childish questions, but she's a genius just the same.

Forty years ago, she said, they asked this silly woman Oskan to tell about her visit to the village of Gultik and she got up and said, They have chickens there, and in calling the chickens they say, *Chik chik chik*. They have cows also, and very often the cows holler, *Moo moo moo*.

She was very angry about these remarks of the silly woman. She was remembering the old country and the old life, and I knew she would take up the story of her husband Melik in no time and begin to shout, so I sat up and smiled at her.

Is that all she had to say? I said. *Chik chik chik* and *moo moo moo*?

She was foolish, said my grandmother. I guess that's why they sent her to school and taught her to read and write. Finally she married a man who was crippled in the left leg. One cripple deserves another, she said. Why aren't you walking in the park on a day like this?

I thought I'd have a little afternoon nap, I said.

For the love of God, said my grandmother, my husband Melik was a man who rode a black horse through the hills and forests all day and half the night, drinking and singing. When the townspeople saw him coming they would run and hide. The wild Kourds of the desert trembled in his presence. I am ashamed of you, she said, lolling around among these silly books.

She lifted the first book that came to her hand, opened it, and stared with disgust at the print.

What is all this language here? she said.

That's a very great book by a very great man, I said. Dostoyevsky he was called. He was a Russian.

Don't tell me about the Russians, said my grandmother. What tricks they played on us. What does he say here?

Everything, I said. He says we must love our neighbors and be kind to the weak.

More lies, said my grandmother. Which tribe of the earth was kind to our tribe? In the dead of winter he went to Stamboul.

Who? I said.

Melik, she shouted. My own husband, she said bitterly. Who else? Who else would dare to go that far in the dead of winter? I will bring you a bright shawl from Stamboul, he said. I will bring you a bracelet and a necklace. He was drunk of course, but he was my husband. I bore him seven children before he was killed. There would have been more if he hadn't been killed, she groaned.

I have heard he was a cruel man, I said.

Who said such an unkind thing about my husband? said my grandmother. He was impatient with fools and weaklings, she said. You should try to be like this man.

I could use a horse all right, I said. I like drinking and singing, too.

In this country? said my grandmother. Where could you go with a horse in this country?

I could go to the public library with a horse, I said.

And they'd lock you up in jail, she said. Where would you tie the horse?

I would tie the horse to a tree, I said. There are six small trees in front of the public library.

Ride a horse in this country, she said, and they will put you down for a maniac.

They have already, I said. The libel is spreading like wildfire.

You don't care? she said.

Not at all, I said. Why should I?

Is it true, perhaps? she said.

It is a foul lie, I said.

It is healthful to be disliked, said my grandmother. My husband Melik was hated by friend and enemy alike. *Bitterly* hated, and he knew it, and yet everybody pretended to like him. They were afraid of him, so they pretended to like him. Will you play a game of *scambile*? I have the cards.

She was lonely again, like a young girl.

I got up and sat across the table from her and lit a cigarette for her and one for myself. She shuffled and dealt three cards to me and three to herself and turned over the next card, and the game began.

Ten cents? she said.

Ten or fifteen, I said.

Fifteen then, but I play a much better game than you, she said.

I may be lucky, I said.

I do not believe in luck, she said, not even in card games. I believe in thinking and knowing what you are doing.

We talked and played and I lost three games to my grandmother. I paid her, only I gave her a half dollar.

Is that what it comes to? she said.

It comes to a little less, I said.

You are not lying? she said.

I never lie, I said. It comes to forty-five cents. You owe me five cents.

Five pennies? she said.

Or one nickel, I said.

I have three pennies, she said. I will pay you three pennies now and owe you two.

Your arithmetic is improving, I said.

American money confuses me, she said, but you never heard of anyone cheating me, did you?

Never, I admitted.

They don't dare, she said. I count the money piece by piece, and if someone is near by I have him count it for me, too. There was this thief of a grocer in Hanford, she said. Dikranian. Three cents more he took. Six pounds of cheese. And I had five different people count for me. Three cents more he has taken, they said. I waited a week and then went to his store again. For those three cents I took three packages of cigarettes. From a thief thieve and God will smile on you. I never enjoyed cigarettes as much as those I took from Dikranian. Five people counted for me. He thought I was an old woman. He thought he could do such a thing. I went back to the store and said not a word. Good morning, good morning. Lovely day, lovely day. A pound of rice, a pound of rice. He turned to get the rice, I took three packages of cigarettes.

Ha ha, said my grandmother. From thief thieve, and from above God will smile.

But you took too much, I said. You took fifteen times too much.

Fifteen times too much? said my grandmother. He took three pennies, I took three packages of cigarettes, no more, no less.

Well, I said, it probably comes to the same thing anyway, but you don't really believe God smiles when you steal from a thief, do you?

Of course I believe, said my grandmother. Isn't it said in three different languages, Armenian, Kourdish, and Turkish?

She said the words in Kourdish and Turkish.

I wish I knew how to talk those languages, I said.

Kourdish, said my grandmother, is the language of the heart. Turkish is music. Turkish flows like a stream of wine, smooth and sweet and bright in color. Our tongue, she shouted, is a tongue of bitterness. We have tasted much of death and our tongue is heavy with hatred and anger. I have heard only one man who could speak our language as if it were the tongue of a God-like people.

Who was that man? I asked.

Melik, said my grandmother. My husband Melik. If he was sober, he spoke quietly, his voice rich and deep and gentle, and if he was drunk, he roared like a lion and you'd think God in Heaven was crying lamentations and oaths upon the tribes of the earth. No other man have I heard who could speak in this way, drunk or sober, not one, here or in the old country.

And when he laughed? I said.

When Melik laughed, said my grandmother, it was like an ocean of clear water leaping at the moon with delight.

I tell you, my grandmother would walk away with every silver loving cup and gold ribbon in the world.

Now she was angry, ferocious with the tragic poetry of her race.

And not one of you *opegh-tsapegh* brats are like him, she shouted. Only my son Vahan is a little like him, and after Vahan all the rest of you are strangers to me. This is my greatest grief.

Opegh-tsapegh is untranslatable. It means, somewhat, *very haphazardly assembled,* and when said of someone, it means he is no particular credit to the race of man. On the contrary, only another fool, someone to include in the census and forget. In short, everybody.

And when he cried? I said.

My husband was never known to weep, said my grandmother. When other men hid themselves in their houses and frightened their wives and children by weeping, my husband rode into the hills, drunk and cursing. If he wept in the hills, he wept alone, with only God to witness his weakness. He always came back, though, swearing louder than ever, and then I would put him to bed and sit over him, watching his face.

She sat down with a sigh and again stared bitterly around the room.

These books, she said. I don't know what you expect to learn from books. What is in them? What do you expect to learn from reading?

I myself sometimes wonder, I said.

You have read them all? she said.

Some twice, some three times, I said. Some only a page here and there.

And what is their message?

Nothing much, I said. Sometimes there is brightness and laughter, or maybe the opposite, gloom and anger. Not often, though.

Well, said my grandmother, the ones who were taught to read and write were always the silliest and they made the worst wives. This soft-brained Oskan went to school, and when she got up to speak all she could say was, They have chickens there, and in calling the chickens they say, *Chik chik chik.* Is that wisdom?

That's innocence, I said in English.

I cannot understand such an absurd language, she said.

It is a splendid language, I said.

That is because you were born here and can speak no other language, no Turkish, no Kourdish, not one word of Arabic.

No, I said, it is because this is the language Shakespeare spoke and wrote.

Shakespeare? said my grandmother. Who is he?

He is the greatest poet the world has ever known, I said.

Nonsense, said my grandmother. There was a traveling minstrel who came to our city when I was a girl of twelve. This man was ugly as satan, but he could recite poetry in six different languages, all day and all night, and not one word of it written, not one word of it memorized, every line of it made up while he stood before the people, reciting. They called him Crazy Markos and people gave him small coins for reciting and the more coins they gave him the drunker he got and the drunker he got the more beautiful the poems he recited.

Well, I said, each country and race and time has its own kind of poet and its own understanding of poetry. The English poets wrote and your poets recited.

But if they were poets, said my grandmother, why did they write? A poet lives to sing. Were they afraid a good thing would be lost and forgotten? Why do they write each of their thoughts? Are they afraid something will be lost?

I guess so, I said.

Do you want something to eat? said my grandmother. I have cabbage soup and bread.

I'm not hungry, I said.

Are you going out again tonight? she said.

Yes, I said. There is an important meeting of philosophers in the city tonight. I have been invited to listen and learn.

Why don't you stop all this nonsense? she said.

This isn't nonsense, I said. These philosophers are going to explain how we can make this world a better place, a heaven on earth.

It *is* nonsense, said my grandmother. This place is the same place all men have known, and it is anything you like.

That's bourgeois talk, I said in English.

These philosophers, I said in Armenian, are worrying about the poor. They want the wealth of the rich to be shared with the poor. That way they claim everything will be straightened out and everybody will be happy.

Everybody is poor, said my grandmother. The richest man in the world is no less poor than the poorest. All over the world there is poverty of spirit. I never saw such miserliness in people. Give them all the money in the world and they'll still be poor. That's something between themselves and God.

They don't believe in God, I said.

Whether they believe or not, said my grandmother, it is still a matter between themselves and God. I don't believe in evil, but does that mean evil does not exist?

Well, I said, I'm going anyway, just to hear what they have to say.

Then I must be in the house alone? she said.

Go to a movie, I said. You know how to get to the neighborhood theatre. It's not far. There is a nice picture tonight.

Alone? said my grandmother. I wouldn't think of it.

Tomorrow, I said, we will go together. Tonight you can listen to the radio. I will come home early.

Have you no books with pictures?

Of course, I said.

I handed her a book called *The Life of Queen Victoria*, full of pictures of that nice old lady.

You will like this lady, I said. She was Queen of England, but she is now dead. The book is full of pictures, from birth to death.

Ah, said my grandmother looking at an early picture of the Queen. She was a beautiful girl. Ahkh, ahkh, alas, alas, for the good who are dead, and my grandmother went down the hall to the kitchen.

I got out of my old clothes and jumped under a warm shower. The water was refreshing to the skin and I began to sing.

I put on fresh clothes and a dark suit. I went into the kitchen and kissed my grandmother's hand, then left the house. She stood at the front window, looking down at me.

Then she lifted the window and stuck her head out.

Boy, she shouted. Get a little drunk. Don't be so serious.

A blue-ribbon old lady.

O.K., I said.

III

Now, a man's life begins from the beginning, every moment he is alive, wakeful or not, conscious or not, and the beginning is as distant in the past as the ending is in the future, and walking to town, alive and miraculously out of pain, I looked upon the world and remembered. Sometimes, even in the artificial and fantastic world we have made, we are able somehow to reach a state of *being* in which pain does not exist, and for the moment seems forever an unreality. Miraculously out of pain, I say, because in this place, in this configuration of objects and ideas which we call the world, pain in the living seems more reasonable than the absence of pain, and the reason is this: that *stress* (and not ease) is the basic scheme of function in our life, in this world. All things, even the most simple, require effort in order to be performed, and to me this is an unnatural state of affairs.

And I do not mean sloth which leads inevitably to degeneracy: I mean only ease and effortlessness. Grace. Which all living creatures, save man, naturally possess, the bird, the fish, the cat, the reptile. I mean inward grace, inherent freedom of form, inherent truthfulness of being.

I mean, *being*, but in this world ease and truthfulness are difficult because of the multitude of encumbrances halting the body and spirit of man on all sides: the heavy and tortuous ideas of civilization, the entanglement of the actual world in which we are born and from which we seem never to be able to emerge, and, above all things, our imprisonment in the million errors of the past, some noble, some half-glorious, some half-godly, but most of them vicious and weak and sorrowful.

We know we are caught in this tragic entanglement, and all that we do is full of the unholiness of this heritage of errors, and all that we do is painful and difficult, even unto the simplest functions of living creatures, even unto mere being, mere breathing, mere growing, and our suffering is eternally intensified by impatience, dissatisfaction, and that dreadful hope which is all but maddening in that its fulfillment seems unlikely, our hope for liberation, for sudden innocent and unencumbered reality, sudden and unending naturalness of movement, sudden godliness.

So we turn, somewhat in despair, to the visible in our problem, to matter, and we say if all men had food enough to eat, shelter and comfort, once again all would be well in the world and man would regain the truthfulness of his nature and be joyous.

Anyway, I was walking to town, whistling a comical American song, at five in the afternoon, feeling for a moment altogether truthful and unencumbered, feeling, in short, somewhat happy, personally, when suddenly and apparently for no reason, at least no *new* reason, the whole world, caught in time and space, seemed to me an absurdity, an insanity, and instead of being amused, which would have been philosophical, I was miserable and began to ridicule all the tragic straining of man, living and dead.

Worse still, I saw a child staring out at the world from a window and crying, and this, too, brought to me the essential error of our effort, since if a child, who is innocent, cannot see good in this world, then certainly there must be little good in it, and we do no more than grow and accept, since acceptance is easier than denial, and we deceive ourselves into believing all is well, though, actually, we suffer pain enough from day to day to know that all is not well.

I guess I'd better get drunk at that, I said, but this, of all evasions, is the most ignoble, since one escapes to nowhere, or at any rate to a universe even more disorderly, if more magnificent, than our own, and then returns with sickened senses and a stunned spirit to the place only recently forsaken.

The drunkard is the most absurd of the individualists, the ultimate egoist, who rises and falls in no domain other than that of his own senses, though drunkards have been, and will long be, most nearly the children of God, most truthfully worshippers of the universal.

Insanity, I said, idiocy and waste and error, cruelty and filth and deathfulness, pride and pomposity, pain and poverty, and birth, and the children of the world eternally at the window, weeping at the strangeness of this place. Sure. Teach them the gospel of Marx and have them born in Russia and they will not stare from the window, they will run through the streets of Moscow like mountain goats and laugh and never after will they know grief, because Marx is a nobler father than God, amen.

I began to feel down in the mouth. I began to feel lousy, or, as my grandmother would say in Armenian, melancholy, which is my natural state, except when I am among others and then my natural state is this: to oppose possible error with possible laughter, since laughter, though largely pointless, is at least less damaging than error, and less pompous than blind sincerity, which is infinitely more dangerous than utter irresponsibility. In fact, I admire most those men of wisdom who accept the tragic obligation to be irresponsible until the time when sincerity will have become natural and noble and not artificial and vicious as it is now.

I walked to The Barrel House on Third Street, the street in San Francisco where the misery of man stalks back and forth in the nightmare images of creatures once mortal and now dispersed, as a large seeded flower is dispersed by a strong wind, or mangled as a crushed insect is mangled, yet crawls, impelled by life in itself to move, these broken bodies, these slain souls, passing in the street, going nowhere, and returning nowhere.

And I stood in the street, clean and comfortable and secure and out of danger, and angry with myself and with the world that had done these things to these men, asking myself what I intended to do about it. The thick smell of fear in the air, of decay, the decay of flesh, of spirit, the waste of animal energy mingling with the rotten smells pouring out of the doorways and windows of the cheap restaurants, and I said, Breathe deeply, draw deeply into your lungs the odor of the death of man, of man alive, yet dead, most filthily dead, yet alive, and let the foul air of this death feed your blood, and let this death be your death, for these men are your brothers, each of these men is yourself, and when they die, you die, and if they cannot live, you cannot live, though you forsake the world and enter a world of your own, you die.

And what will you do about this? Here is one who may be saved. A boy, years younger than yourself, torn by the cruelty of the world, yet young enough to be saved, and what are you going to do about him? And the boy walked by, blind and deaf and dumb, yet alive, crawling like the crushed insect, pulling himself to another, one more moment of life, of misery, of fear.

And this old man who is crippled, whose legs are tied by the tightening pains of years of agony, whose face is the mask of one in hell, yet on earth, what are you going to do about him?

Be a gentleman and give him a dime for coffee and doughnuts. Humiliate him again and let his trembling hand close upon the small coin, his rotted heart close upon the cheap charity of the strong and secure, and the old man went by, and across the street the shabby saints of the Salvation Army preached and prayed and sang and asked the hungry men for alms with which to spread the holy gospel of truth, and the men gave no alms.

When the revolution comes, these men will be like gods, and their sons will come into the earth innocent and whole, and within them will be no germ of sin, no germ of greed or envy or cruelty or hatred, and they will grow to be greater gods than their fathers, and the daughters of these dead men will move upon the earth with the feline power and grace and poise of jungle cats, and when the revolution comes all misery on earth will end, and all error will end.

Indeed. And the thing to do is to get cockeyed, to be blind and deaf, to go stumbling through the filth of the world, laughing and singing.

I walked into The Barrel House and sat at a table.

Nicora, the waiter, came over and wiped the table clean, leaving the wood moist, standing sullenly, a little drunk, his dark Italian face weary and worried, yet indifferent, lots of trouble in the world, *paesano*, but I got a good job: all day I drink, what do I care about trouble? Wife, two kids, and himself, and when the revolution comes Nicora will serve drinks to his brothers in a big garden in the sun.

Hi-ya, Nick, I said.

O.K., kid, he said. Little shot, maybe?

Yeah, I said. How's your wife?

Oh, fine, he said. She's very sick, another kid coming.

Congratulations, I said, and he went to the bar and got a drink.

He put it down in front of me, talking.

I tell you, kid, he said, take my advice, don't get married, first the wife, then the kids, then the rent, then the bread, then the kid falls down and breaks the arm, then the wife cries, then you get drunk and break the window and the dishes, then the wife's brother comes and makes trouble, then you fight him, then the jail, then you sit inside the jail and think, and Jesus Christ, kid, don't be crazy and get married, I know, and I don't want to see another guy in trouble.

All right, Nick, I said.

I swallowed the whiskey and it burned all the way down and I began to feel all right all right, like a big gesture in the world, all right, and I began to feel gay and at the same time very proud, like, *who me?*

Don't worry about me, pals, just worry about yourselves, pals: I'm doing all right, pals, and I told Nick to get me another because I figured I'd get good and drunk and laugh the way my grandfather Melik used to laugh when he got drunk in the old country, and Nick brought another and I swallowed it, everything's jake, pals, and I told him to get another and he did and I swallowed this one, everything's O. K., pals, and another, and then I started to laugh, but not out loud, only inside, away back in the old country, on the black horse, riding through the hills, in the beginning, cussing and singing.

IV

Drink expands the eye, enlarges the inward vision, elevates the ego. The eye perceives less and less the objects of this world and more and more the objects and patterns and rhythms of the other: the large and limitless and magnificent universe of remembrance, the real and timeless earth of history, of man's legend in this place. Until, of course, one is under the table. Then the magnificence is succeeded by sensory riot and lawlessness, and the law of gravity comes to an end, amid comedy and tragedy. Distance is unreal, and flesh and spirit exist not alone in one place and in one time but in all places and during all times, including the future. In short, one achieves the ridiculous and glorious state of fool.

The gesture blossoms in the universe, dramatic and significant, saying *I know*, the language of limb in motion, artfully. The head wags yea and nay. The tongue loosens with the chaos of a million languages. The spirit laughs and the flesh leaps, and sitting at a small table in a dark saloon, one travels somehow to all the places of the world, returns, and goes again, gesturing and reciting, wagging the head and laughing, singing and leaping.

I got a little drunk, sitting at the small table, and Nicora came and went, telling me what to do and what not to do in order to be happy in the world, my spiritual adviser.

I wished Paula were getting drunk with me, sitting across the table from me, so I could see her round white face with the deep melancholy eyes and the full melancholy lips and the pert melancholy nose and the small melancholy ears and the brown melancholy hair, and I wished I could take her warm melancholy hand and walk with her over the hard melancholy streets of our dark melancholy city and reach a large melancholy room with a good melancholy bed and lie with her beautiful melancholy body, and all during the night have a quiet melancholy conversation between long melancholy embraces and in the morning waken from deep melancholy sleep and hide our melancholy nakedness with cheap melancholy clothes and go out for a big cheerful breakfast.

So I went to the telephone booth and dropped a nickel in the slot and dialed the number. I guess I dialed the wrong number or forgot the right one because the girl who answered wasn't Paula. She didn't have Paula's quiet melancholy voice: she had a loud melancholy voice.

This is fate, I said, or something like it, so I talked to the girl. The telephone is a great invention. If you get a wrong number, it doesn't make much difference because you get a girl anyway, even if it isn't the one you had in mind, and the whole thing amounts to fate, slightly assisted by the noble mechanics of our age.

What's the good of getting a wrong number if you don't talk a little? Where's the Christian kindliness and love of neighbor in hanging up on a girl with a loud melancholy voice just because you've never seen her?

Young lady, I said, I'm getting drunk on rotten whiskey at The Barrel House on Third Street. Jump into the first street car and come right down and have a drink. After a while we will take a taxi to The Universe Restaurant on Columbus Avenue and have a dinner of spaghetti and roast chicken. We will sit at the table and talk and then we will go through the city and see the sights. When we are tired we will go to a movie or if you prefer we will go to a Communist meeting and join our comrades in singing the Internationale and in hating the guts of the rich.

The girl hung up with a fierce melancholy bang. I dialed the number again and the bell rang once, twice, three times, four times, and then it was Paula.

We talked, over the wires, by electricity, our voices passing under the city and over it, each of us unseen by the other, while a thousand others talked with one another.

Hello, said Paula.

Hello, I said.

How are you? said Paula.

I'm fine, I said. How are you?

Fine, said Paula. What's the matter?

Nothing, I said. Something the matter?

You sound serious, said Paula.

Wait a minute, I said. I want to light a cigarette.

All right, said Paula. I want to light one too.

I inhaled smoke and began to feel less and less gay.

Hello, I said.

Hello, said Paula.

I heard her exhale smoke, and even this sounded melancholy. I could see her round melancholy face.

How are you, Paula? I said.

I'm fine, Mike, she said. How are you, Mike?

I'm fine, too, I said.

I guess we both feel lousy, said Paula.

No, I said. I feel great.

I went to a movie last night, said Paula.

Swell, I said. How was it?

Great, said Paula. It was just like life.

Did you cry? I said.

No, said Paula, I laughed. It was about a boy and a girl in love. A new idea in the movies. They had a lot of trouble at first, but in the end they were married.

Then what happened? I said.

The movie ended, said Paula.

That's bourgeois propaganda, I said. I saw a movie like that once. They got married, too.

Must have been the same boy and girl, said Paula.

The universal male and female, I said.

Then I got sore at myself for being smart again. I wasn't saying what I wanted to say, the way I wanted to say it, and I got sore.

Listen, Paula, I said, to hell with that stuff.

Sure, said Paula. To hell with it.

Paula, I said, come to town and have dinner with me.

Can't, said Paula. I'm going out.

Who with? I said.

Friend of mine, said Paula.

Sure, but who? I said.

Young lawyer, said Paula. You don't know him.

What do you want to go out with a young lawyer for? I said.

He's a very intelligent boy, said Paula.

That's not important, I said.

I know it, said Paula.

Tell him you're sick, I said, and come to town and have dinner with me.

Can't, said Paula.

What the hell you talking about? I said.

We're going to be married, said Paula. Just like in the movies.

You're kidding, I said.

Look in next Sunday's *Examiner*, said Paula. My picture, his name.

Jesus Christ, I said.

I'm in love with him, said Paula.

Sure, I said. You sound *madly* in love. You're crazy.

We're going to the Hawaiian Islands, said Paula.

Listen, Paula, I said. I want to see you tonight. Go ahead and get married. I don't care about that. But I want to see you tonight. What time will you be through with the young lawyer?

You can't, said Paula. When we come back from the Islands we're going to live in a big house in the hills, in Berkeley.

You're crazy, I said.

Maybe, and maybe not, said Paula. I'll know after a while.

Oh, I see, I said.

I'd like to meet the lawyer, I said.

You can't, said Paula.

Oh, I said.

We didn't talk for half a minute.

O.K., Paula, I said. I'll see you by accident in the street sometime.

Sure, said Paula. It's a small world. So long, Mike.

So long, Paula, I said.

I went back to the small table and Nick began bringing me drinks again. The more I drank the worse I felt. When I went outside it was raining. The rain was fine, and the air was clear and good. I walked through the wet melancholy streets to the Reno Club on Geary Street. I walked in and there was a seat open in a draw poker game. I sat down and bought ten dollars' worth of chips. I'm pretty lucky when I'm a little drunk. Apostolos, the Greek restaurant man, dealt the cards. I played two hours and came out four dollars ahead.

Then I went up to Fillmore Street to the Communist meeting, and began climbing the stairs.

I'm drunk, I said, and Paula's getting married to a lawyer, and Pete wants to save the world, and my grandmother is homesick for Armenia, and Nick's wife is going to have another baby, and listen, comrades, if I don't go easy climbing these stairs I'll fall down and bust my head, comrades. What good will it do when everybody has bread, comrades, what good will it do when everybody has pie, comrades, what good will it do when everybody has everything, comrades, everything isn't enough, comrades, and the living aren't alive, brothers, the living are dead, brothers, even the living are not alive, brothers, and you can't ever do anything about that.

Laughing Sam

✿ ✿ ✿

THERE was a boy in my home town fifteen years ago who was called Laughing Sam because he was always laughing. He was one of those extremely sensitive boys who, being afraid of everything in the world, try to laugh at everything and get into all kinds of trouble. He couldn't do anything without doing it at least partly wrong.

A lot of boys in my home town died before they were twenty, and Sam was one of these boys, but he even died wrong, and for all I know maybe he was laughing at the time, or at least right till he realized he was being killed by the elevator. The elevator crushed him. He was scared to death of elevators, so he was showing off to people he hated, who were always making fun of him, and he slipped and fell, and the elevator smashed his body.

He was sixteen years old at the time.

I knew him about four years.

I saw him for the first time coming down the cement stairs to the pressroom of the *Evening Herald* with Buzz Martin. Old Buzz Martin, who was circulation manager and a good amateur fighter, and very goosey, who was killed in an automobile accident in 1924 or 1925 at the age of twenty-seven, told Sam to wait somewhere till the Home Edition came off the press, and Sam began to wait as if waiting were an event of great activity. He kept looking around fearfully at all the newsboys, the Italians and Russians and Armenians, and he began looking at the big black press, and little by little he began to be panic-stricken.

I was nine or ten and he was a year or two older, but I could tell what was going on. He was just another poor boy in the world. The wrong kind too. I knew he'd have a lousy time of it all the time.

I felt bad about him and wished I could think of something to say to him, but I couldn't. I wanted to say, Now, wait; take it easy; don't get excited; don't let it scare you. There's nothing to it; take it easy.

I couldn't say anything, though.

I saw a flash of something like horror and agony in his eyes, and then I figured he'd start to cry.

He laughed instead.

He was some sort of a Jew, small and tense. He had a big beak, thick black hair, not much of a forehead, skin full of blackheads, thick lips, and uncommonly foolish-looking ears. He was the ugliest-looking boy I had ever seen, and yet there was something tragic and noble about his face, and his figure too, for that matter; tragic and noble and pathetic. His arms were short. His fingers were stubby. He had no shoulders at all, and he had very big feet. It was July, and he was without shoes, as all of us were. Seeing him for the first time, one felt, Here is man; here is the poor agonized body of the ancient slave, under-nourished, over-worked, ill, wounded, graceless, foolish; here is the body of Our Lord outraged by the world.

I didn't talk to him that first day. I was a little afraid of him; not of the boy himself, but of what he seemed to be: the victim of the world. The helpless, guiltless inheritor of centuries of every mortal cruelty and error.

But I watched him.

He was obviously lost, completely out of place; not simply out of place in the press-room, but out of place in the world, in time, in space, in history, in life. He seemed to be haunted by an instinctive tribal remembrance in his blood: *Get away, get out of it, go to another place, hide, run, do not stay among them, they will kill you.*

I heard him try to talk to Buzz Martin. Well, he couldn't talk. I mean, he didn't stutter, but when his lips and mouth began to shape a word they became paralyzed and you could see him trying to say the word, but you couldn't hear anything.

Where shall I wait? he asked Buzz Martin.

Buzz Martin was a great guy. He was tough. He used to cuff the boys around when they got out of line, but he was a great guy, and he never took advantage of a scared kid. He was an American, as we used to call them in my home town, but he wasn't like most Americans: in my home town fifteen years ago an American was an incompetent who despised people of other races because they weren't incompetent. Buzz Martin was O.K. He took the broader view: he didn't care what you happened to be, just so you were O.K., and if you weren't, he didn't blame it on your race. He just put you in your place with a clout on the ear.

So Buzz wasn't unkind to the boy, although he was a little bewildered by the boy's question.

Just wait right where you're standing, he said. Don't go anywhere. The Home Edition will be out in about five minutes and I'll give you ten papers and tell you what to holler.

Sam laughed and stood right where he was.

He began looking around for somebody to talk to, and picked out Nick Kouros, the Greek boy.

He said, How do you sell papers? (Then laughed.)

Kouros said, I don't know. (And didn't laugh: he was probably the most melancholy newsboy in town. He hated everything and everybody, and every now and then we used to see him crying, for no reason at all.)

I ain't never sold papers, Sam said. Do I have to holler? (He laughed again.)

Kouros said, No.

Do *you* holler? Sam said. (He laughed very much, and Kouros looked terrible.)

Yes, Kouros said.

How do you do it? Sam said.

I just open my mouth and holler, Kouros said.

What do you holler, Sam said, paper, paper, paper?

Yes, Kouros said, paper, paper, paper, *Evening Herald, Evening Herald,* and whatever the news is.

I ain't never sold papers, Sam said. My mother said we need money, ha ha ha ha, so I came down here. Do you make much money?

No, Kouros said.

Do you make *any* money at all? Sam said.

If you sell two papers, Kouros said, you make a nickel; for every two papers you sell you make a nickel.

How many do you think I can sell if I try hard? Sam said.

Ten maybe, Kouros said.

That's twenty-five cents, ain't it? Sam said.

Yes, Kouros said.

Then the press began to work and Sam said, Look, ha ha ha ha ha.

What's the matter? Kouros said.

Ha ha ha ha, Sam said, look at it.

The headline that day was about the War. Buzz Martin gave Sam ten papers and told him to holler the headline: *Allies Make Big Advance.*

We got our papers and ran to town. I had *The Post Office Corner.* The better you were at hustling the better the corner they gave you. My corner was sixth from best.

If you were new, they told you to walk all over town and do the best you could.

Sam didn't walk all over town, he ran, and he kept it up for hours. He was out to make good. He wanted to be a good hustler. He wanted to please Buzz Martin and the publishers of the *Evening Herald,* and he wanted to take home a little money to his mother. They needed money badly, so he wanted to sell his papers and take home a few coins. He was hollering and laughing and running around town as if he had to get somewhere just in the nick of time.

He was funny, and nobody could resist the temptation to have a little fun with him. The Italian kids got a big kick out of asking him questions and hearing him answer and laugh, and after a while they got a big kick out of pushing him over backwards and hearing him laugh, and they couldn't figure it out. They figured he'd either get sore and fight, or cry, but all he did was laugh. Then they took down his pants and smeared him with press ink, and again he laughed. The Italian kids didn't know what to make of it.

He stood at the center of a crowd of crazy kids and tried to get the ink off and he said, You put ink on me ha ha ha ha ha. It won't come off.

I felt terrible because I could tell how deeply hurt he was, and horrified, and how anxious he was to get along.

For a week everybody got a big kick out of him, but after a week the novelty of his laughter wore away and gradually his laughter began to be irritating. It wasn't right to laugh about *everything.* One day, coming down the cement steps in a hurry, he stumbled and fell and was hurt, and everybody ran over to him, wanting to help him, even the toughest of the kids wanting to be kind to him, and although his coat was torn and his arm was bleeding, he jumped up and began to laugh.

I fell downstairs, he said, ha ha ha ha ha.

And everybody, even the dullest of the boys, resented his laughing about it.

What the hell's the matter with him? they began to ask, and after a while nobody would go near him or talk to him and he was all alone in the press-room.

He used to come down every day and try to be friendly, but he couldn't talk very well, and he was always laughing.

One day the headline was about a collision on the highway at night, five people killed, two of them kids, and three injured. He went around town hollering the headline and laughing.

He went tearing around my corner hollering, *Five Killed in Highway Accident* ha ha ha ha.

I stopped him.

I neither liked nor disliked him. No matter how hard I tried I couldn't like him, but it was impossible to dislike him too. He wasn't simply another newsboy. He was man on earth, at his worst. Taking everything and laughing about it.

Wait a minute, I said. That's nothing to laugh about.

He came to a sudden inward halt.

I ain't laughing, he said.

Then I *knew* what the hell was going on: he *wasn't* laughing. It *sounded* like laughing, but he was crying. His heart was breaking about everything, and he was crying. He was doing it by laughing.

Listen, I said. You're not glad them people were killed, are you?

He tried very hard to stop smiling.

No, he said.

You're sorry, ain't you? I said.

I'm sorry all right, he said.

That's all I want to know, I said.

He ran on down the street, and I almost busted into tears.

He sold papers until he was fifteen.

Then he got a job in the warehouse of a van and storage company. Eight or nine dollars a week. I don't know what he was supposed to do in the warehouse, but I suppose every once in a while he was supposed to operate the freight elevator. I guess the other workers made him do it because he was so afraid of the contraption, and I guess he did it to try to get along. I guess he laughed too. I don't know just how it happened, but one day I read in the *Evening Herald* that he was smashed by the elevator and instantly killed. Everybody said it was his own fault. He got panic-stricken because the elevator didn't stop where it was supposed to stop and the other workers were laughing at him and he tried to get out of the elevator while it was moving and he didn't quite make it.

He lived sixteen years in this world and laughed all the time. He wept from the beginning of his life, ten centuries ago, to the end of it, fifteen years ago.

The Sunday Zeppelin

✿ ✿ ✿

LUKE was holding my hand and I was holding Margaret's. We had a nickel each for collection, and Luke said to me, Don't forget, Mark, drop the nickel: don't keep it like last time and buy ice-cream.

You too, I said.

Last time Luke didn't drop his nickel and I saw him. I bought an ice-cream cone in the afternoon when it was very hot. Schultz gave me two scoops. Luke saw me eating the ice-cream cone under the china-ball trees of Emerson School.

He acted like Hawkshaw the detective.

Ah-ha, he said.

Where'd you get the money, Mark?

You know where, I said.

No, he said. Where? Tell me.

Sunday School, I said. I didn't drop it.

That's a sin, Luke said.

I know it, I said. You didn't either.

I did too, Luke said.

No, you didn't, I said. I saw you pass the basket without dropping the nickel.

I'm saving, Luke said.

Saving for what? I said.

For a zeppelin, he said.

How much is a zeppelin? I said.

There's one in *Boys' World*, he said, that costs a dollar. It comes from Chicago.

A real zeppelin? I said.

Two people can go up in it, he said. Me and Ernest West.

I swallowed the last mouthful of ice-cream.

How about me? I said.

You can't go up, Luke said. You're too small. You're a baby. Ernest West is my age.

I ain't a baby, I said. I'm eight and you're ten. Let me go up in the zeppelin with you, Luke.

No, Luke said.

I didn't cry, but I felt sad. Then Luke got me sore.

You like Alice Small, he said. You're just a baby.

This was true. I *did* like Alice Small, but the way Luke said it made me sore.

I felt sad and alone. I liked Alice Small all right, but did I ever do any of the things I wanted to do? Did I ever walk with her? Did I ever hold her hand and tell her how much I liked her? Did I ever say her name to her the way I wanted to, so she'd know how much she meant to me? No. I was too scared. I wasn't even brave enough to look at her long. She scared me because she was so pretty, and when Luke talked that way I got sore.

You're a son of a bitch, Luke, I said. You're a dirty bastard, I said. I couldn't think of any of the other bad words I had heard big boys saying, so I started to cry.

I felt very bad about calling my own brother these names. In the evening I told him I was sorry.

Don't try to fool me, Luke said. Sticks and stones can break my bones, but names can never hurt me.

I never threw any sticks and stones at you, Luke, I said.

You called me those names, he said.

I didn't mean to, Luke, I said. Honest I didn't. You said I like Alice Small.

Well, you do, Luke said. You know you do. The whole world knows you do.

I don't, I said. I don't like anybody.

You like *Alice Small*, Luke said.

You're a son of a bitch, I said.

Pa heard me.

He was sitting in the parlor reading a book. He jumped up and came into our room, Luke's and mine. I started to cry.

What was that, young man? he said. What was that you just called your brother?

Sticks and stones, Luke started to say.

Never mind that, Pa said. Why are you always teasing Mark?

I wasn't teasing him, Luke said.

He was, I cried. He said I like Alice Small.

Alice Small? Pa said.

He hadn't even heard of Alice Small. He didn't even know she was alive.

Who in the world is Alice Small? he said.

She's in my class at school, I said. Her father's the preacher at our church. She's going to be a missionary when she grows up. She told us in front of the whole class.

Pa said:

Tell Luke you're sorry you called him a bad name.

I'm sorry I called you a bad name, Luke, I said.

Luke, said Pa, tell Mark you're sorry you teased him about Alice Small.

I'm sorry I teased you about Alice Small, Luke said. Only I knew he wasn't sorry. I was sorry when I told him I was sorry, but I knew he wasn't sorry when he told me he was sorry. He was only saying it because Pa told him to.

Pa went back to his chair in the parlor. Just before he sat down he said:

I want you boys to occupy yourselves intelligently and not get on one another's nerves. Do you understand?

Yes, sir, Luke said.

So we got a copy each of *The Saturday Evening Post* and started looking at the pictures. Luke wouldn't talk to me.

Can I go up in the zeppelin? I said.

He just turned the pages of the magazine and wouldn't talk.

Just once? I said.

I woke up in the middle of the night and started thinking about being up in the zeppelin.

Luke, I said.

Finally he woke up.

What do you want? he said.

Luke, I said, let me go up in the zeppelin with you when it comes from Chicago.

No, he said.

That was last week.

Now we were on our way to Sunday School.

Luke said: Don't forget, Mark. Drop the nickel.

You too, I said.

You do what you're told to do, Luke said.

I want a zeppelin too, I said.

Who said anything about a zeppelin? Luke said.

If you don't drop your nickel, I said, neither will I.

It looked like Margaret didn't even hear us. She just walked along while me and Luke argued about the zeppelin.

I'll give half, Luke, I said, if you let me go up.

Ernest West is giving the other half, Luke said. We're partners.

Eight more weeks, Luke said, and the zeppelin will come from Chicago.

All right for you, I said. *Don't* let me go up. I'll get even with you some day. You'll be sorry when you see me going around the world in my own boat.

Go ahead, Luke said.

Please, Luke, I said, let me go up in the zeppelin. I'll let you go around the world with me in my boat.

No, Luke said. You go alone.

Ernest West and his sister Dorothy were standing in front of the church when we got there. Margaret and Ernest's sister went into the churchyard together, and me and Luke and Ernest stayed on the sidewalk.

Palka eskos, Ernest said to Luke.

Immel, said Luke.

What's that mean, Luke? I said.

Can't tell you, Luke said. That's our secret language.

Tell me what it means, Luke, I said. I won't tell anybody.

No, said Ernest.

Effin ontur, he said to Luke.

Garic hopin, Luke said, and then they busted out laughing.

Garic hopin, Ernest laughed.

Tell me, Luke, I said. I promise never to let anybody else know what it means.

No, said Luke. Invent your own secret language, he said. Nobody's stopping you.

I don't know how, I said.

The church bell rang, so we went inside and sat down. Luke and Ernest sat together. Luke told me to go away from them. I sat in the row behind them, the last row. In the first row was Alice Small. Her father, our preacher, walked down the aisle and then went upstairs to his private study. That's where he made up his sermons. He was a tall man who smiled at everybody before and after the sermon. During the sermon he never smiled at all.

We sang some songs, then Ernest West called for *At the Cross*, only he and Luke sang, *At the bar, at the bar, where I smoked my last cigar, and the nickels and the dimes rolled away, rolled away.*

I felt jealous of Luke and Ernest West. They knew how to have fun. Even at church. Once in a while Ernest would look at Luke and say arkel ropper, and Luke would answer haggid ossum, and then both of them would try to keep from laughing. They would hold themselves in with all their might until the loud singing began, then they would bust loose with all the laughter that was part of their secret language. I felt miserable being out of all that fine stuff.

Arkel ropper, I said and tried to feel how funny it was, but it wasn't. It was terrible not knowing what arkel ropper meant. I could imagine it meant something funnier than anything else in the world, but I didn't know what it was. Haggid ossum, I said, only it made me feel sad. Some day I would invent the funniest language in the world and not let Luke or Ernest West know what the words meant. Every word would make me feel happy and I would talk no other language. Only me and one other person in the world would know *my* secret language. Alice Small. Only Alice and me. Ohber linten, I would say to Alice, and she would know what a beautiful thing that meant, and she would look at me and smile and I would hold her hand and maybe kiss her.

Then Harvey Gillis, our superintendent, got up on the platform and told us about the Presbyterian missionary work we were helping to pay for in many foreign and heathen countries of the world.

In Northern Africa, my dear young people, he said in a high-pitched voice, our shepherds of the Lord are performing miracles every day in the name of Jesus. The native savage is being taught the holy gospel and the pious life, and the light of our Lord is penetrating the darkest depths of ignorance. We can well rejoice and pray.

Umper gamper Harvey Gillis, Luke said to Ernest.

Luke could barely keep from laughing.

I felt all alone.

If I only knew what they knew. Umper gamper Harvey Gillis. That could mean so many things about our superintendent. He was a sissy and he talked in a high-pitched voice. I don't think anybody, except maybe Alice Small, believed a word of what he said.

Our noble heroes in the field are healing the sick, he said. They are sacrificing life and limb to prepare the world for the Lord's second coming. They are spreading His truth to the far corners of the earth. Let us pray for them. Will Miss Valentine pray?

Would she? She'd been waiting all week for a chance to pray.

Miss Valentine got up from the organ bench and took off her glasses and wiped her eyes. She was a skinny woman of forty or so who played the organ at our church. She played it as if she were sore at somebody and wanted to get even, pounding the keys and turning around every once in a while to take a quick look at the congregation. It seemed as if she hated everybody. I only stayed for the sermon twice in my life, but both times she did those things, and once in a while she nodded very wisely at something our preacher said, as if she was the only person in the whole church who knew what he meant.

Now she got up to pray for our heroic missionaries in dark Africa and other heathen places of the world.

Exel sorga, Ernest said to Luke.

You said it, Luke answered, and more besides.

Almighty and merciful Father, she prayed. We have erred and strayed from Thy ways like lost sheep.

And a lot of other stuff.

I thought it was supposed to be for our noble workers in the field, but all she talked about was straying away and doing wrong things, instead of right ones. She prayed too long too.

For a while I thought Harvey Gillis was going to touch her arm and make her open her eyes and tell her, That will be enough for this morning, Miss Valentine. But he didn't. I opened my eyes the minute she started to pray. You were supposed to keep your eyes shut, but I always opened mine to see what was going on in the church.

Nothing was going on. All the heads were bowed except Luke's and Ernest's and mine, and Luke and Ernest were still whispering funny things to one another in their secret language. I could see Alice Small with her head bowed lower than anybody else's, and I said, O God, some day let me talk to Alice Small in our own secret language that nobody else in the world will understand.

Amen.

Miss Valentine finally stopped praying and we went to the corner of the church where boys between seven and twelve studied the stories in The Bible and dropped their Sunday offering in the basket.

Luke and Ernest sat together again and told me to get away from them. I sat right behind them to see if Luke would drop his nickel. Every Sunday they gave each of us one copy of a little Sunday School paper called *Boys' World*. It told about little boys doing kind things for old people and the blind and the crippled, and it had advice on how to make things. Me and Luke tried to make a wheel-barrow once, but we didn't have a wheel. After that we didn't try to make anything. On the back page were the advertisements with pictures.

Our teacher was Henry Parker. He was a fellow who wore thick glasses and had some red pimples around his mouth. He looked sick and nobody liked him. I guess nobody liked going to Sunday School at all. We had to go because Pa said it would certainly do less harm than good. Later on, he said, when you get to be older you can stop going or keep on going, as you choose. Right now, he said, it's good discipline.

Ma said, That's right.

So we went. Maybe we got used to it because we never asked not to go. There wasn't much else to do Sunday morning anyway. Ernest West had to go too, and I guess that's why Luke never tried to get out of it. He could always talk their secret language with Ernest West and laugh about everybody.

The story was the story of Joseph and his brothers, Joseph with the brightly-colored coat, and then all of a sudden the whole class started talking about the movies.

Ah-ha, Luke said to Ernest West.

Now, said Henry Parker, I want each of you to give me one good reason why no one should go to the movies.

There were seven of us in the class.

The movies, said Pat Carrico, show us naked women dancing. That's why we shouldn't go.

Well, said Henry Parker, yes, that's a good reason.

They show us robbers killing people, said Tommy Cesar, and that's a sin.

Very good, said our teacher.

Yes, said Ernest West, but the robbers always get killed by the police, don't they? The robbers always get theirs in the end, don't they? That's no reason.

Is too, said Tommy Cesar. It teaches us how to steal.

I would be inclined to agree with Mr. Cesar, said Henry Parker. Yes, he said, it sets a bad example for us.

Oh, all right, Ernest West said.

He looked at Luke wisely and was about to say something in the secret language, only this time he didn't need to because Luke laughed out loud anyway, and then Ernest laughed with him. It seemed as if Luke knew what Ernest was going to say and it must have been something very funny because they laughed like anything.

What's this? said our teacher. Laughing in Sunday School? What are you two laughing about?

I'll tell on them, I thought. I'll tell him they've got a secret language. Then I decided not to. That would spoil it. It was such a funny language. I didn't want to spoil it, even if I couldn't understand any of the words.

Nothing, Luke said. Can't a fellow laugh?

Then it was Jacob Hyland's turn. Jacob was the dumbest boy in the world. He couldn't think up anything. He couldn't make up *any* kind of an answer. He couldn't even guess.

Now, said Mr. Parker, *you* tell us why we shouldn't go to the movies.

I don't know why, Jacob said.

Come, now, Mr. Parker said, surely you know one good reason why we shouldn't.

Jacob started to think. I mean, he started to look around the room, then down at his feet, then up at the ceiling, while all of us waited to hear what he'd think up.

He thought a long time. Then he said:

I guess I don't know why, Mr. Parker. *Why?* he asked.

I'm asking *you,* our teacher said. *I* know why, but I want *you* to know why for yourself. Now, come, give me one reason, Mr. Hyland.

So Jacob started thinking all over again, and all of us felt sore at him. Anybody could make up some small reason, anybody but a dumb boy like Jacob. Nobody knew what made him so dumb. He was older than anybody else in our class. He kept squirming around in his chair and then he started picking his nose and scratching his head and looking at Mr. Parker like a dog looks at somebody it wants to be friends with.

Well? said our teacher.

Honest, said Jacob. I don't know why. I don't go to the movies much.

You've been to the movies once, haven't you? said our teacher.

Yes, sir, he said. More than once, but I forget quick. I don't remember.

Surely, said our teacher, you remember one little thing you saw in the movies that was a bad example, and a good reason why we should never go.

All of a sudden Jacob's face lighted up with a big smile.

I know, he said.

Yes? said our teacher.

It teaches us to throw custard pies at our enemies and kick ladies and run.

Is that all you remember? said Mr. Parker.

Yes, sir, Jacob said.

That's no reason, Ernest West said. What's wrong about throwing a custard pie?

It gets all over you, Jacob said, and he busted out laughing. You remember, he said, how it drips down a man's face.

It is certainly wrong to kick a lady, said Mr. Parker. Very fine, Mr. Hyland, he said. I knew you would remember a good reason if you thought carefully enough.

Then it was Nelson Holgum's turn.

It's expensive, he said. It costs too much.

Only a nickel at the Bijou, I said. That's no reason.

You can buy a loaf of bread with a nickel, Nelson said. A nickel is a lot of money these days.

True, said Mr. Parker. A very good reason indeed. There are much nobler ways for us to spend our money. If our young people would stop going to movies and give their money to missionary work, think of the tremendous progress we would make in only one year. Why, we could convert the whole world to Christianity in one year on the money spent annually for frivolous amusements like the movies.

Mr. Parker nodded at Ernest West.

The movies teach us to be dissatisfied with what we've got, Ernest said. We see people riding around in big automobiles and living in big houses and we get jealous.

Envious, said Mr. Parker.

We start wanting all them things, Ernest said, and we know we can't have them because we haven't got the money to buy them with, so we feel bad.

A splendid reason, said Mr. Parker.

It was Luke's turn, and next it would be mine.

The music is bad, Luke said.

Not at the Liberty, Tommy Cesar said. Not even at the Kinema. That's no reason.

It's bad at the Bijou, Luke said. They play one song over and over again on the player-piano, he said. It gets monotonous. *Wedding of the Winds.*

That's not true, Tommy Cesar said. Sometimes they play another song. I don't know the name. Sometimes they play six or seven songs.

They all sound alike, Luke said. It gives you a headache.

Now we're getting somewhere, said our teacher. It gives us headaches. It harms our health. And we shouldn't do anything that is harmful to the health. Health is our most precious possession. We must do those things which improve our health rather than those which harm it.

I said we shouldn't go to the movies because when we got out of the theater we didn't like our town.

Everything seems silly in our town, I said. We want to go away.

Then it was time to pass the basket around. Mr. Parker made a little speech about how urgently money was needed and how much better it was to give than to receive.

Tommy Cesar dropped two pennies, Pat Carrico three, Nelson Holgum one, Jacob Hyland a nickel, and then the basket reached Ernest West. He handed it to Luke and Luke handed it to me and I handed it back to Mr. Parker. We didn't drop anything. Mr. Parker took a purse from his pocket, jingled some coins, picked out a quarter so all of us could see it, and dropped it among the other coins. He looked very noble. Everybody hated him for the way he looked, even a dumb boy like Jacob Hyland. He looked as if he was saving the whole world with that quarter.

Then he gave each of us a copy of *Boys' World*, and class ended.

Everybody jumped up and ran out to the sidewalk.

Well, said Ernest West to Luke, aplica till we meet again.

Aplica, said Luke. Then my little sister Margaret came out of the church and we started walking home.

I turned to the last page of *Boys' World* and saw the advertisement of the zeppelin. The picture showed two boys high in the sky, standing in the basket of the zeppelin. Both of the boys looked sad; they were waving good-bye.

We went home and had Sunday dinner. Pa and Ma were very cheerful at the table and we ate till we couldn't get any more down. Pa said, What was the lesson, Luke?

Evils of the movies, Luke said.

What are they? Pa said.

Naked women dancing, Luke said. Robbers killing police. Expensive. Teaches us to throw custard pies.

I see, said Pa. Very evil.

After dinner I couldn't think of anything to do. If I wasn't so scared I would go to Alice Small's house and tell her I liked her. Alice, I would say, I like you. But I was scared. If I had my boat I would go around the world in it. Then I thought of the zeppelin. Luke was in the yard, nailing two pieces of wood together.

What are you making? I said.

Nothing, Luke said. I'm just nailing.

Luke, I said, here's my nickel. When the zeppelin comes let me go up with you.

I tried to give him the nickel but he wouldn't take it.

No, he said. The zeppelin's for me and Ernest West.

All right for you, I said. I'll get even.

Go ahead, he said.

It was very hot. I sat on the cool grass under our sycamore tree and watched Luke nail the boards together. The way he was hitting the nails you'd think he was making something, and I couldn't believe he wasn't until he was all through. He nailed about ten boards together, and that was all. They were just nailed together. They didn't make anything.

Pa heard all the hammering and came out smoking his pipe.

What do you call that? he said.

That? Luke said.

Yes, said Pa. What is it?

Nothing, Luke said.

Splendid, Pa said, and he turned around and went right back in.

Splendid? Luke said.

It ain't anything, I said. Why don't you *make* something?

I could hear Pa singing inside. I guess he was drying the dishes for Ma. He sang very loud, and after a while Ma started singing with him.

Then Luke stopped nailing and threw the boards over the garage.

He ran around the garage and came back with the boards and threw them over again and went and got them again.

What are you playing? I said.

Nothing, Luke said.

Luke, I said, let's go to the Bijou together.

Me and *you?* Luke said.

Sure, I said. You got your nickel and I got mine. Let's go see Tarzan.

I got to save up for the zeppelin, Luke said. I got a dime now. Eight more weeks and it'll be here, and then good-bye.

Good-bye? I said.

Yes, said Luke, good-bye.

You ain't going away, are you, Luke? I said.

Sure, he said. What did you think I wanted it for?

You mean never to come back again, Luke?

I'll come back all right, he said. I'll go away for a month or two, but I'll come back.

Where will you go, Luke? I said.

Klondike, he said. North.

Up there in that cold country, Luke?

Sure, Luke said. Me and my partner Ernest West. Palka eskos, he said.

What's it mean, Luke? I said. Tell me, please. What's palka eskos mean?

Only me and my partner know, Luke said.

I won't tell anybody, Luke. Honest I won't.

You'll go and tell somebody, Luke said.

Cross my heart, I said. Hope to die.

Needles through your tongue, if you do?

Yes, I said, needles and hot irons too, Luke.

On your word of honor?

Yes, Luke. What does it mean?

Palka eskos? he said.

Yes, Luke. Palka eskos.

Good morning, he said. It means good morning.

I couldn't believe it.

Is that all, Luke?

That's all palka eskos means. We got a whole language, though.

Palka eskos, Luke, I said.

Immel, he said.

What's immel mean, Luke?

Immel?

Yes, Luke.

You won't tell?

Same as before, I said. Hot irons through my tongue.

Hello, said Luke. Immel means hello.

Let's go to the Bijou, Luke, I said. We got a nickel each.

All right, he said. The music doesn't really give you a headache. I just said that.

Tell Ma, I said.

Maybe she won't let us go, Luke said.

Maybe she will. Maybe Pa will tell her to.

Luke and me went inside. Pa was drying the dishes and Ma was washing them.

Can we go to the Bijou, Ma? Luke said.

What's that? Pa said. I thought the lesson was the evils of the movies.

Yes, sir, Luke said.

Well, is your conscience clear? Pa said.

Oh, what's playing? Ma said.

Tarzan, I said. Can we go, Ma? We didn't drop our nickels. Luke is saving up for a zeppelin, but he won't let me go up with him.

Didn't drop your nickels? Pa said. What kind of religion do you call that? First thing you know them Presbyterian missionaries will be packing up and leaving Africa if you boys don't keep them supplied with nickels.

I guess so, Luke said, but me and Ernest West are saving up for a zeppelin. We *had* to do it.

What kind of a zeppelin? Pa said.

A *real* one, Luke said. It travels eighty miles an hour and carries two people, me and Ernest West.

How much does it cost? Pa said.

One dollar, Luke said. It comes from Chicago.

I'll tell you what, Pa said. If you clean out the garage and keep the yard in order next week, I'll give you a dollar Saturday. All right?

I'll say, Luke said.

Provided, Pa said, you let Mark go up.

If he'll help me with the work, Luke said.

He'll help, Pa said. Won't you, Mark?

I'll do more than Luke, I said.

Pa gave us ten cents more each and said to go to the movies. We went to the Bijou and saw Tarzan, chapter eighteen. Two more chapters and it would be all over. Tommy Cesar was there with Pat Carrico. They made more noise when Tarzan was cornered by the tiger than all the rest of us put together.

Me and Luke cleaned out the garage and kept the yard in order all week, and Saturday night Pa gave Luke a dollar bill. Luke sat down and wrote a nice letter to the people in Chicago who sold zeppelins. He put the dollar bill in an envelope and dropped the letter in the mailbox on the corner. I went to the mailbox with him.

Now, he said, all we got to do is wait.

We waited ten days. We talked about all the strange and faraway places we would go to in the zeppelin.

Then it came. It was a small flat package with the same picture we saw in *Boys' World* stamped on the box. It didn't weigh a pound, not even half a pound. Luke's hands shook when he opened the box. I felt sick because I knew something was wrong. There was a slip of paper with some writing on it in the box. It said:

Dear Boys: Here is your zeppelin, with instructions on how to operate it. If every direction is carefully followed this toy will ascend and stay aloft for as long as twenty seconds.

And a lot more like that.

Luke followed every direction carefully, and blew into the tissue-paper sack until it was almost full and almost the shape of a zeppelin. Then the paper tore and the whole shape collapsed, the way a rubber balloon does.

That was all. That was our zeppelin. Luke couldn't figure it out. He said, The picture shows two boys standing in the basket. I thought the zeppelin was coming out in a freight train.

Then he started talking in his secret language.

What are you saying, Luke? I said.

Good thing you can't understand, he said.

He smashed what was left of the zeppelin and tore the tissue-paper to pieces, then went out to the barn and got a lot of boards and nails and the hammer and started nailing the boards together. All I could do was say to myself, Them people in Chicago are sons of bitches, that's what they are.

Corduroy Pants

✿ ✿ ✿

MOST people hardly ever, if ever at all, stop to consider how important pants are, and the average man, getting in and out of pants every morning and night, never pauses while doing so, or at any other time, even for the amusement in the speculation, to wonder how unfortunate it would be if he didn't have pants, how miserable he would be if he had to appear in the world without them, and how awkward his manners would become, how foolish his conversation, how utterly joyless his attitude toward life.

Nevertheless, when I was fourteen and a reader of Schopenhauer and Nietzsche and Spinoza, and an unbeliever, a scorner of God, an enemy of Jesus Christ and the Catholic Church, and something of a philosopher in my own right, my thoughts, profound and trivial alike, turned now and then to the theme of man in the world without pants, and much as you might suppose they were heavy melancholy thoughts no less than often they were gay and hilarious. That, I think, is the joy of being a philosopher: that knowing the one side as well as the other. On the one hand, a man in the world without pants *should* be a miserable creature, and probably would be, and then again, on the other hand, if this same man, *in* pants, and in the world, was usually a gay and easy-going sort of fellow, in all probability even without pants he would be a gay and easy-going sort of fellow, and might even find the situation an opportunity for all manner of delightful banter. Such a person in the world is not altogether incredible, and I used to believe that, in moving pictures at least, he would not be embarrassed, and on the contrary would know just what to do and how to do it in order to impress everyone with this simple truth: namely, that after all what is a pair of pants? and being without them is certainly not the end of the world, or the destruction of civilization. All the same, the idea that I myself might some day appear in the world without pants terrified me, inasmuch as I was sure I couldn't rise to the occasion and impress everybody with the triviality of the situation and make them know the world wasn't ending.

I had only one pair of pants, my uncle's, and they were very patched, very sewed, and not the style. My uncle had worn these pants five years before he had turned them over to me, and then I began putting them on every morning and taking them off every night. It was an honor to wear my uncle's pants. I would have been the last person in the world to suggest that it wasn't. I knew it was an honor, and I accepted the honor along with the pants, and I wore the pants, and I wore the honor, and the pants didn't fit.

They were too big around the waist and too narrow at the cuff. In my boyhood I was never regarded as well-dressed. If people turned to look at me twice, as they often do these days, it was only to wonder whose pants I was wearing. There were four pockets in my uncle's pants, but there wasn't one sound pocket in the lot. If it came to a matter of money, coins given and coins returned, I found that I had to put the coins in my mouth and remember not to swallow them.

Naturally, I was very unhappy. I took to reading Schopenhauer and despising people, and after people God, and after God, or before, or at the same time, the whole world, the whole universe, the whole impertinent scheme of life.

At the same time I knew that my uncle had honored me, of all his numerous nephews, by handing down his pants to me, and I *felt* honored, and to a certain extent clothed. My uncle's pants, I sometimes reasoned unhappily, were certainly better than no pants at all, and with this much of the idea developed my nimble and philosophical mind leapt quickly to the rest of the idea. Suppose a man appeared in the world without pants? Not that he wanted to. Not just for the fun of it. Not as a gesture of individuality and as a criticism of Western civilization, but simply because he had no pants, simply because he had no money with which to buy pants? Suppose he put on all his clothes excepting pants? His underwear, his stockings, his shoes, his shirt, and walked into the world and looked everybody straight in the eye? Suppose he did it? Ladies, I have no pants. Gentlemen, I have no money. So what? I have no pants, I have no money. I am an inhabitant of this world. I intend to remain an inhabitant of this world until I die or until the world ends. I intend to go on moving about in the world, even though I have no pants.

What could they do? Could they put him in jail? If so, for how long? And why? What sort of a crime could it be to appear in the world, among one's brothers, without pants?

Perhaps they would feel sorry, I used to think, and want to give me an old pair of pants, and this possibility would drive me almost crazy. Never mind giving me your old pants, I used to shout at them. Don't try to be kind to me. I don't want your old pants, and I don't want your new pants. I want my own pants, straight from the store, brandnew, size, name, label, and guarantee. I want my own God damn pants, and nobody else's. I'm in the world, and I want my own pants.

I used to get pretty angry about people perhaps wanting to be kind to me, because I couldn't see it that way. I couldn't see people *giving* me something, or *anything*. I wanted to get my stuff the usual way. How much are these pants? They are three dollars. All right, I'll take them. Just like that. No hemming or hawing. How much? Three dollars. O.K., wrap them up.

The day I first put on my uncle's pants my uncle walked away several paces for a better view and said, They fit you perfectly.

Yes, sir, I said.

Plenty of room at the top, he said.

Yes, sir, I said.

And nice and snug at the bottom, he said.

Yes, sir, I said.

Then, for some crazy reason, as if perhaps the tradition of pants had been handed down from one generation to another, my uncle was deeply moved and shook my hand, turning pale with joy and admiration, and being utterly incapable of saying a word. He left the house as a man leaves something so touching he cannot bear to be near it, and I began to try to determine if I might be able, with care, to get myself from one point to another in the pants.

It was so, and I could walk in the pants. I felt more or less encumbered, yet it was *possible* to move. I did not feel secure, but I knew I was covered, and I knew I could move, and with practice I believed I would be able to move swiftly. It was purely a matter of adaption. There would be months of unfamiliarity, but I believed in time I would be able to move about in the world gingerly, and with sharp effect.

I wore my uncle's pants for many months, and these were the unhappiest months of my life. Why? Because *corduroy pants* were the style. At first *ordinary* corduroy pants were the style, and then a year later there was a Spanish renaissance in California, and *Spanish corduroy pants* became the style. These were bell-bottomed, with a touch of red down there, and in many cases five-inch waists, and in several cases small decorations around the waist. Boys of fourteen in corduroy pants of this variety were boys who not only felt secure and snug, but knew they were in style, and consequently could do any number of gay and lighthearted things, such as run-

ning after girls, talking with them, and all the rest of it. I couldn't. It was
only natural, I suppose, for me to turn, somewhat mournfully, to Schopenhauer and to begin despising women, and later on men, children, oxen,
cattle, beasts of the jungle, and fish. What is life? I used to ask. Who do
they think they are, just because they have Spanish bell-bottomed corduroy
pants? Have they read Schopenhauer? No. Do they know there is no God?
No. Do they so much as suspect that love is the most boring experience
in the world? No. They are ignorant. They are wearing the fine corduroy
pants, but they are blind with ignorance. They do not know that it is all
a hollow mockery and that they are the victims of a horrible jest.

I used to laugh at them bitterly.

Now and then, however, I forgot what I knew, what I had learned about
everything from Schopenhauer, and in all innocence, without any profound philosophical thought one way or another, I ran after girls, feeling
altogether gay and lighthearted, only to discover that I was being laughed
at. It was my uncle's pants. They were not pants in which to run after a
girl. They were unhappy, tragic, melancholy pants, and being in them, and
running after a girl in them, was a very comic thing to see, and a very
tragic thing to do.

I began saving up every penny and nickel and dime I could get hold of,
and I began biding my time. Some day I would go down to the store and
tell them I would like to buy a pair of the Spanish bell-bottomed pants,
price no consideration.

A mournful year went by. A year of philosophy and hatred of man.

I was saving the pennies and nickels and dimes, and in time I would
have my own pair of Spanish style corduroy pants. I would have covering
and security and at the same time a garment in which a man could be
nothing if not gay and lighthearted.

Well, I saved up enough money all right, and I went down to the store
all right, and I bought a pair of the Spanish bell-bottomed corduroy pants
all right, but a month later when school opened and I went to school I
was the only boy at school in this particular style of corduroy pants. It
seems the Spanish renaissance had ended. The new style corduroy pants
were very conservative, no bell-bottoms, no five-inch waists, no decorations.
Just simple ordinary corduroy pants.

How could I feel gay and lighthearted? I didn't *look* gay and lighthearted. And that made everything worse, because my pants *did* look gay
and lighthearted. My own pants. Which I had bought. *They* looked gay
and lighthearted. It meant simply, I reasoned, that I would have to be, in
everything I did, as gay and lighthearted as my pants. Otherwise, naturally,
there could never be any order in the world. I could not go to school in such
pants and not be gay and lighthearted, so I decided to *be* gay and lighthearted. I was very witty at every opportunity and had my ears boxed, and
I laughed very often and discovered that invariably when I laughed nobody else did.

This was agony of the worst kind, so I quit school. I am sure I should
not now be the philosopher I am if it were not for the trouble I had with
Spanish bell-bottomed corduroy pants.

The First Day of School

✧ ✧ ✧

HE was a little boy named Jim, the first and only child of Dr. Louis Davy, 717 Mattei Building, and it was his first day at school. His father was French, a small heavy-set man of forty whose boyhood had been full of poverty and unhappiness and ambition. His mother was dead: she died when Jim was born, and the only woman he knew intimately was Amy, the Swedish housekeeper.

It was Amy who dressed him in his Sunday clothes and took him to school. Jim liked Amy, but he didn't like her for taking him to school. He told her so. All the way to school he told her so.

I don't like you, he said. I don't like you any more.

I like *you*, the housekeeper said.

Then why are you taking me to school? he said.

He had taken walks with Amy before, once all the way to the Court House Park for the Sunday afternoon band concert, but this walk to school was different.

What for? he said.

Everybody must go to school, the housekeeper said.

Did you go to school? he said.

No, said Amy.

Then why do I have to go? he said.

You will like it, said the housekeeper.

He walked on with her in silence, holding her hand. I don't like you, he said. I don't like you any more.

I like you, said Amy.

Then why are you taking me to school? he said again.

Why?

The housekeeper knew how frightened a little boy could be about going to school.

You will like it, she said. I think you will sing songs and play games.

I don't want to, he said.

I will come and get you every afternoon, she said.

I don't like you, he told her again.

She felt very unhappy about the little boy going to school, but she knew that he would have to go.

The school building was very ugly to her and to the boy. She didn't like the way it made her feel, and going up the steps with him she wished he didn't have to go to school. The halls and rooms scared her, and him, and the smell of the place too. And he didn't like Mr. Barber, the principal.

Amy despised Mr. Barber.

What is the name of your son? Mr. Barber said.

This is Dr. Louis Davy's son, said Amy. His name is Jim. I am Dr. Davy's housekeeper.

James? said Mr. Barber.

Not James, said Amy, just Jim.

All right, said Mr. Barber. Any middle name?

No, said Amy. He is too small for a middle name. Just Jim Davy.

All right, said Mr. Barber. We'll try him out in the first grade. If he doesn't get along all right we'll try him out in kindergarten.

Dr. Davy said to start him in the first grade, said Amy. Not kindergarten.

All right, said Mr. Barber.

The housekeeper knew how frightened the little boy was, sitting on the chair, and she tried to let him know how much she loved him and how sorry she was about everything. She wanted to say something fine to him about everything, but she couldn't say anything, and she was very proud of the nice way he got down from the chair and stood beside Mr. Barber, waiting to go with him to a classroom.

On the way home she was so proud of him she began to cry.

Miss Binney, the teacher of the first grade, was an old lady who was all dried out. The room was full of little boys and girls. School smelled strange and sad. He sat at a desk and listened carefully.

He heard some of the names: *Charles, Ernest, Alvin, Norman, Betty, Hannah, Juliet, Viola, Polly.*

He listened carefully and heard Miss Binney say, Hannah Winter, what *are* you chewing? And he saw Hannah Winter blush. He liked Hannah Winter right from the beginning.

Gum, said Hannah.

Put it in the waste-basket, said Miss Binney.

He saw the little girl walk to the front of the class, take the gum from her mouth, and drop it into the waste-basket.

And he heard Miss Binney say, Ernest Gaskin, what are *you* chewing?

Gum, said Ernest.

And he liked Ernest Gaskin too.

They met in the schoolyard, and Ernest taught him a few jokes.

Amy was in the hall when school ended. She was sullen and angry at everybody until she saw the little boy. She was amazed that he wasn't changed, that he wasn't hurt, or perhaps utterly unalive, murdered. The school and everything about it frightened her very much. She took his hand and walked out of the building with him, feeling angry and proud.

Jim said, What comes after twenty-nine?

Thirty, said Amy.

Your face is dirty, he said.

His father was very quiet at the supper table.

What comes after twenty-nine? the boy said.

Thirty, said his father.

Your face is dirty, he said.

In the morning he asked his father for a nickel.

What do you want a nickel for? his father said.

Gum, he said.

His father gave him a nickel and on the way to school he stopped at Mrs. Riley's store and bought a package of Spearmint.

Do you want a piece? he asked Amy.

Do you want to give me a piece? the housekeeper said.

Jim thought about it a moment, and then he said, Yes.

Do you like me? said the housekeeper.

I like you, said Jim. Do you like me?

Yes, said the housekeeper.

Do you like school?

Jim didn't know for sure, but he knew he liked the part about gum. And Hannah Winter. And Ernest Gaskin.

I don't know, he said.

Do you sing? asked the housekeeper.

No, we don't sing, he said.

Do you play games? she said.

Not in the school, he said. In the yard we do.

He liked the part about gum very much.

Miss Binney said, Jim Davy, what are you *chewing?*

Ha ha ha, he thought.

Gum, he said.

He walked to the waste-paper basket and back to his seat, and Hannah Winter saw him, and Ernest Gaskin too. That was the best part of school.

It began to grow too.

Ernest Gaskin, he shouted in the schoolyard, *what* are you *chewing?*

Raw elephant meat, said Ernest Gaskin. Jim Davy, what are *you* chewing?

Jim tried to think of something very funny to be chewing, but he couldn't.

Gum, he said, and Ernest Gaskin laughed louder than Jim laughed when Ernest Gaskin said raw elephant meat.

It was funny no matter what you said.

Going back to the classroom Jim saw Hannah Winter in the hall.

Hannah Winter, he said, *what in the world* are you *chewing?*

The little girl was startled. She wanted to say something nice that would honestly show how nice she felt about having Jim say her name and ask her the funny question, making fun of school, but she couldn't think of anything that nice to say because they were almost in the room and there wasn't time enough.

Tutti-frutti, she said with desperate haste.

It seemed to Jim he had never before heard such a glorious word, and he kept repeating the word to himself all day.

Tutti-frutti, he said to Amy on the way home.

Amy Larson, he said, *what, are, you, chewing?*

He told his father all about it at the supper table.

He said, Once there was a hill. On the hill there was a mill. Under the mill there was a walk. Under the walk there was a key. What is it?

I don't know, his father said. What is it?

Milwaukee, said the boy.

The housekeeper was delighted.

Mill. Walk. Key, Jim said.

Tutti-frutti.

What's that? said his father.

Gum, he said. The kind Hannah Winter chews.

Who's Hannah Winter? said his father.

She's in my room, he said.

Oh, said his father.

After supper he sat on the floor with the small red and blue and yellow top that hummed while it spinned. It was all right, he guessed. It was still very sad, but the gum part of it was very funny and the Hannah Winter part very nice. Raw elephant meat, he thought with great inward delight.

Raw elephant meat, he said aloud to his father who was reading the evening paper. His father folded the paper and sat on the floor beside him. The housekeeper saw them together on the floor and for some reason tears came to her eyes.

The Man Who Got Fat

✿ ✿ ✿

NATHAN KATZ was an easy-going, roly-poly, hard-working Jew of thirty-six or thirty-seven who was said to be the world's fastest telegraph operator when I was fourteen and No. 1 messenger at the telegraph office in my home town where Mr. Katz and I used to work.

They used to call me *Speed*. I used to be able to travel by bicycle from our office to any other place in the city faster than any other messenger in town, or anywhere else. I used to be considered intelligent by some people too. These, however, were relatives. In an elevator, nevertheless, I always removed my hat, and I knew how to behave in what used to be known as a house of ill-repute.

Nathan Katz came to my home town from San Francisco. He was not a regular telegraph operator, he was a contact man. My home town used to have a generous population of Armenians and I liked everything about it but the location. It was too far nowhere. So when this medium-sized, amiable Jew came walking into our office from Frisco I was mighty glad to see him. I was mighty glad in those days to see anybody from anywhere just so it wasn't the other side of the railroad tracks or the exclusive residential district. The exclusive residential district was a place where an Armenian couldn't buy a house even if he had the money.

They used to argue in my home town that the average Armenian didn't have any manners, so I always went out of my way to take off my hat in elevators and be kind to people in trouble. I used to be one of the kindest fourteen-year-old boys in the whole San Joaquin valley. I used to help drunkards home. I used to do little favors for young and unhappy men who were having trouble with their sweethearts, their wives, or somebody else's wife. I used to break my neck to be a gentleman. I didn't want any white riff-raff making cracks about the manners of Armenians.

Nathan Katz could sit at a table and put his hand around the old bug and flash telegrams faster than anybody anywhere, and he was a roly-poly Jew. I could get from our office to anywhere else in town faster than anybody anywhere, and I was an Armenian. I could get there politely too. I kicked a cop once, but he got sore and knocked me off my bicycle.

On the whole, however, I was a model young man. I was practically a Boy Scout.

What I mean is, there we were the fastest two guys in the world in our fields, a Jew and an Armenian. So what? What else? We got along fine. We got along first-rate.

Katz was contact man: his job was to take people to lunch or dinner and get palsy-walsy with them and the next day, by God, they would be sending their telegrams by Postal Telegraph instead of by Western Union.

We worked for Postal Telegraph. That is a magnificent organization. That is as cold and heartless an organization as Western Union.

Katz used to take his roly-poly person around town and bust loose with his warm laugh and pass out cigars and get business for that noble organization. I've got no use for any organization. They're all O.K. and lousy to me. They allow slaves to go on being slaves all their lives and that's O.K. too. May God have mercy on all organizations. May God forgive them for the lousy bargains they make with men. May they go bankrupt and may their machines rust and may God forgive them. They take a man's life and give him a penny. May the Creator of the Universe and All Things forgive them.

I've got no use for machines that kill. I've got no use for men who become machines. I've got no use for machines that get fat with the time out of the lives of men, with the blood out of their lives. I've got no use for that kind of stuff.

If a machine makes a lot of money the money belongs to the slaves who *are* the machine. That's my theory. Postal Telegraph is all right. Western Union is noble and fine. Every American organization is O.K. The money belongs to the slaves. They're being gypped now, but don't forget who the money belongs to.

Poor Katz. How alive he was, how loudly he used to laugh, how joyously he used to go to lunch and look over the menu and order. How happy he was to be in the warm valley, in the fine little town. Poor Katz who went away, the way of them all.

By God, I love that crazy town. I love all them fine ordinary people. They didn't want us to move in among them on account of we were Armenians. Our poor friends and neighbors. God Almighty.

Those years. All those splendid years. Did I get the hell out of that town in a hurry? And do I love them? Am I fond of them fine noble white people? Them superb superior specimens of mortality?

Armenians are white. Some are black too, but they are sun-burned. The sun started burning them centuries ago, but it's nothing more than that: they are sun-burned. The ones who are white, though, are white for just about as good a reason. I guess the sun didn't burn them. I guess they didn't get out into the sun enough. Black or white, though, they didn't like the manners of Armenians. They didn't like the loud way Armenians laughed.

Well, Katz was very good at it. He got a lot of business for that fine organization and we were a couple of pals. I was smart, although my relatives didn't stop at that: they claimed I was downright over-bright. I knew all the calls that came into the office the way fire alarms go into a fire station. I knew them all by heart. I knew how to typewrite. I knew how to answer the telephone and take a telegram over the telephone. I knew all the rates. I knew how to take a telegram over the counter. And I was learning telegraphy too.

All I was, though, was a messenger. I was only figuring on working my way up from the bottom to the top: from messenger to sixteenth vice-president. That was the top. Sixteenth vice-president was the top, unless you were related to Clarence Mackay. His picture was on the wall of our office. He himself, though, never came to our office. He never even came to our town, not even for the heat, not even to see all the Armenians. Dozens of millionaires used to come to our town to see the Armenians. Not old Clarence Mackay, though.

My home town used to be and is now the center of the grape, raisin, and dried fruit industry of California. Every summer hundreds of small men used to come out from Chicago, Pittsburgh, Philadelphia, New York, and Boston, and ship carloads of grapes to those cities and make the railroads rich. They used to send a lot of telegrams too and it's a good thing Katz was on hand because a lot of them couldn't write in English, they could barely talk in English, and that's where Katz and me came in.

We came stalking right in at that point.

There was one hotel in my home town where these business men lived and killed time. In this hotel old Katz set up a miniature telegraph office with me as the guy. All it was was a table, a typewriter, and me. A chair for me, and a chair for anybody who wanted to send a telegram. If the man couldn't speak English old Katz would tell me what to put down on the telegraph blank. We got all kinds of business.

We kept it up three years.

Then Katz found out all there was to know about the shipping racket and he stepped out of the telegraph racket and got into the shipping racket and I found out all there was to know about any racket and stepped out of all of them at once and left town. I went to Frisco. I had a lousy time of it, but I got by.

I didn't see Katz again for three years. He had become lousy with money by that time. He had a great big black Packard and he was putting on weight and losing his hair. I only saw him for a minute. He was busy as hell making money. He shipped grapes and cleaned up. He shipped peaches and cleaned up. Then he branched out into all kinds of things and he shipped lettuce, celery, potatoes, onions, and everything else that grew, only something went haywire and little by little he began to lose all his money, and then four years later I was in El Centro, in the Imperial Valley, and old Katz was there too. He was at the best hotel in town, the Barbara Worth.

I went up to see him.

He was very fat. He was at least twice as fat as he had been in the old days. It was very hot. He didn't have on a shirt. He was sweating. He could barely breathe. The light in the room was the very bright kind. The kind we used to have in the telegraph office. He had a table up there and a typewriter. There were papers all over the room and a carton of cigarettes and a couple of bottles of whiskey.

He was broke. His back was to the wall, he said. He was sick too. It was the fat. He was very sick with it.

We talked along and it was terrible, old Katz fat that way, lousy with fat, sick with it, unable to breathe because of it, hardly able to walk, broke, and he said, I don't know, I guess I'm dying.

I knew he wasn't kidding either. I knew exactly how truthful he was being.

We had some drinks and I noticed he was very nervous. How can a fat man be nervous? He told me he never slept any more. He worked all the time and smoked cigarettes all the time and drank a lot.

When I went downstairs I almost cried. Jesus Christ, poor Katz. How can a fat man make anybody want to cry? How can one be moved to grief by a fat man? I could barely keep from crying.

Poor Katz.

This is no story. I'm not writing anything. That swell roly-poly Jew got fat and died.

He's dead now.

I remember the day he came into that telegraph office in my home town from San Francisco. I remember the way he talked and laughed and how he could sit at a table and make the old bug rattle and carry on a conversation at the same time. I remember all them years.

He got fat and died. That's all. It's nothing. He got fat and died. What the hell does it come to? I don't know. He was the fastest telegraph operator in the world. He got wise to a better racket and cleaned up a lot of money. The next thing I knew he was rich. Then he got fat and one night I went up to his room in a hotel in El Centro and he told me he was dying. He just said it. And a couple of months later he died. The night I saw him he could barely breathe.

It doesn't mean a thing. It's just like I said. Every bit of it. I don't know anything about anything, but I've got no use for six or seven things in the world, and dying of this sort is all seven of them.

The Messenger

✿ ✿ ✿

CLARENCE ACOUGH was ten years old and on his way home from school, in 1918, when Jeff Willis called him into the drug store on Mariposa Street and said, Son, Judge Olson's mother is dying and I want you to run over to Doc Gregory's house on Blackstone Avenue and tell him to come right down for the medicine and then hurry out to Malaga to Judge Olson's house. Doc Gregory'll probably be drunk, but splash some cold water on his face and if he sicks the dog on you, call the dog by its name, Hamilton, and it won't bite you. Otherwise it will. Splash six or seven cups of cold water on Doc's face and get him into the Ford and come back to the store with him. I'd go myself, but I got to stay in the store and take care of the soda fountain trade.

The little boy was pretty confused. In the first place, he hadn't ever talked to Jeff Willis before, although he had seen him in the window of the drug store many times, changing the attractions around, especially the mechanical dummy boy that licked an ice-cream cone and shook its head from side to side, delighted with the taste of ice-cream. Otherwise Clarence didn't know Jeff, and Jeff didn't know Clarence, and the little boy was confused and excited about the whole thing, especially the dog.

Hamilton.

He would have run right out of the store and done his duty, but he didn't like the part about Hamilton the dog, although he was somewhat anxious about Judge Olson's mother in Malaga. It was exciting all right, but it was just a little too exciting. So many names of people and places were involved that Clarence didn't know who or where, so he made for the door, then turned around, almost moving in two directions, wanting to get the good deed done, wanting to do it right, remembering the dog Hamilton, and said, *What?*

Judge Olson's old lady, Jeff Willis said. She's dying, son. She's had another stroke and it looks like she ain't going to pull through and see another County Fair. Out in Malaga. She's a hundred and two. The Judge is over seventy himself, and he's all upset, and the only man in the world who can keep her alive until the Judge takes her to another County Fair is Doc Gregory, and you got to run right out to his house on Blackstone Avenue and splash cold water on his face. You can't miss it. It's the house with the two cement lions on the front lawn.

On his way home from school, Clarence had been dreaming about adventure, and he had been feeling melancholy about the dullness of everything, and he had been kicking pebbles along the sidewalk and street, dreaming of adventure and being melancholy about being a small boy and having to go to school every day and never being able to really enjoy living. He had kicked one pebble two blocks out of his way, and that's how he had gotten on Mariposa Street.

Yes, sir, he said to Jeff. The house with the two cement lions on the front lawn.

Is it a big dog?

It's the biggest kind of dog there is, the druggist said. A St. Bernard, but if you call it by its name, Hamilton, it won't bite you.

Yes, sir, the boy said. Hamilton. Splash water on his face and tell him Judge Olson's mother is dying.

Now you got it, the druggist said. Run right out there. It's only six blocks. You'll be there in no time. What's your name?

Clarence, the boy said.

All right, Clarence, the druggist said. Here's a package of chewing gum for you.

I don't want anything, the boy said. I'll run right out there.

He ran out of the store, looking back six or seven times in two seconds, and ran into the middle of a large lady who immediately exhaled a mournful groan. He begged the lady's pardon and began running up the street full speed.

While the boy was running up the street, Jeff tried to comfort the lady.

Judge Olson's old lady, Jeff said. She's dying. I sent the boy to Doc Gregory's house. Doc'll probably be drunk, but I told the boy what to do.

I'd go for the doctor myself, Jeff said, only I got to take care of the soda fountain trade.

Well, Jeff Willis never served more than three drinks a day over the soda fountain and there was no trade. Not more than seven people ever passed his store in an hour. He just thought he was running a business, and he didn't want to change his opinion at the last minute after ten years of sustained effort.

The lady asked for a glass of water, please. Jeff raced around behind the counter and got a glass and filled it with luke-warm water and placed it neatly on the tiled counter.

Clarence Acough got very tired after running a block, but he couldn't so much as think of slowing down. At the end of the second block, though, he couldn't keep it up, so he sat on the curb to rest. It was very warm and he was sticky with sweat, and all of a sudden everything that had always seemed common and dull to his eye now seemed exciting and wonderful. Out in Malaga the poor old lady was dying and most likely she wouldn't live to see the next County Fair. She would be *dead*. She wouldn't be able to see *anything*. Consciously, he studied the fine white house across the street, with the two enormous eucalyptus trees, and the telephone poles, and the street, and everything else visible.

It was good to be alive.

He was breathing hard, feeling how swell it was to be able to look around and see things, when Doris Barnes and Grover Stone came across the street and stood before him. Well, Doris Barnes was the one magical person in the world to Clarence Acough, and Grover Stone was the one boy in the world Clarence couldn't tolerate. When Clarence saw the boy and girl together he began again, in less than a fraction of a second, to feel melancholy about the way things were, especially Doris walking home with Grover. The trouble with Grover, primarily, was that he always wore good shoes and always had five or ten cents in his pocket. Consequently, he imagined he was something.

The little girl said, What's the matter?

If Clarence hadn't been sore about the way Grover was standing over him and looking down, he would have explained about Judge Olson's mother dying in Malaga, Doc Gregory, Jeff Willis, the County Fair, and the dog Hamilton. Clarence would have jumped up and gone on down the street, toward the doctor's house, with the two cement lions on the lawn. He would have done his duty, but he began to forget about the old lady in Malaga and he began to feel bitter about Doris walking home with a guy like Grover.

It was very warm. He was sticky, and nothing ever happened.

Nothing's the matter, Clarence said. I guess I can sit down and rest if I feel like it.

Clarence figured maybe Doris would have sense enough to know from the way he talked how much he loved her, but he was wrong. Doris didn't like the way he talked, and neither did Grover. Grover thought he would have some fun, being smart, and he said, Clarence Acough thinks he's tough.

Clarence jumped up and said, You think you're smart.

In the drug store on Mariposa Street Jeff Willis was walking around in a circle when the telephone rang. It was Judge Olson, in Malaga. He wanted to know where in hell Doc Gregory was.

I just sent a boy to get him, Jeff said. Doc'll be out to your place in no time. How's your mother?

I don't know for sure, Judge Olson said. She seems to be dead, but I guess she's sleeping.

Is she breathing? Jeff Willis said.

I don't know for sure, Judge Olson said. I don't think so.

Are you sure? Jeff Willis said.

She doesn't seem to be breathing, Judge Olson said. Where in hell is Doc Gregory?

I sent a boy named Clarence to get him, Jeff said. I told him what to do about the dog.

Grover Stone said, I *am* smart.

And he made a very smart face.

Clarence couldn't help it: he hit Grover on the left ear, and Grover hit him on the nose. Clarence felt the pain very sharply and began chasing

Grover toward town, away from the house with the two cement lions on the front lawn. Clarence chased Grover four blocks, but Grover got away. Clarence was too tired to go on chasing him.

Doris Barnes hadn't kept up with them. She was probably home, sitting on the front porch.

She herself.

Clarence began walking toward her house and when he reached the house, she *wasn't* sitting on the front porch. He sat on the curb across the street and waited for her to come out of the house. She was the loveliest creature in the world. And she was in the house. She was somewhere in the house, and maybe she would come out, and he would see her. He would see the neat white dress she wore, and he would see her clean round face with the amazing eyes and nose and lips and the amazing brown hair. Doris Barnes. Maybe she would come out of the house and go to the store for a can of peaches or something. Maybe she would talk to him. Maybe she would *like* him.

When it began to be dark, he decided maybe she wouldn't come out of the house. Then he decided maybe she *would*.

She didn't, though, so he got up, feeling very tired, and confused, and began walking home. He was almost home when he began to remember that he had forgotten something. He began to walk very slowly and little by little it came back to him: the old lady out in Malaga, dying. Doc Gregory in the house with the two cement lions on the front lawn, drunk, and the dog Hamilton.

He was very hungry, very tired, and very sleepy, and Doc Gregory's house on Blackstone Avenue seemed very far away. He guessed he ought to turn around and run like anything all the way to Doc Gregory's house and splash six or seven glasses of water on his face and call the dog Hamilton and get Doc into the Ford and rush down to Jeff Willis's drug store and get the medicine and drive forty miles an hour down the highway to Judge Olson's house in Malaga and give the old lady the medicine and keep her alive long enough to see the next County Fair, but maybe she was already dead, or maybe Doc Gregory wasn't at home, maybe he was somewhere in town, drinking, or if the old lady wasn't dead, maybe she'd be dead by the time Doc Gregory got out to the house in Malaga with the medicine, if he was at home, and Clarence was so tired he didn't think it would make much difference if Doc Gregory *did* keep her alive a year or two more, she would be sure to die after a year or two anyway, so he didn't turn around and run back to the house on Blackstone Avenue.

She'd probably die in a year or two anyway.

He staggered home and ate supper and right after supper he fell asleep, and in the morning he forgot all about it, remembering Doris Barnes, and he kept on forgeting all about it, and three months later his father moved the family a hundred miles up the highway to Modesto, and Clarence Acough kept on forgetting the old lady in Malaga, and after a while he even forgot Doris Barnes, and then one day in August, in 1926, eight years later, when he was eighteen years old, he remembered Doris, and three seconds later he remembered the old lady in Malaga, dying, and he was driving a second-hand Studebaker home from Junior College, and he drove right past his house, and on down the highway, and three hours later just before it got to be dark he reached the old home town and drove down Mariposa Street, looking for Jeff Willis's drug store, and found it.

He went in and Jeff was standing behind the counter, taking care of the soda fountain trade. Jeff was delighted to see a young man parking a car in front of his store and coming in and sitting on a stool at the counter.

What'll it be? Jeff said.

What I want to know, Clarence Acough said, is: *Did she get to see the County Fair?*

Who? Jeff said.

You don't remember me, Clarence said. I'm sorry I didn't get out to Doc Gregory's house on Blackstone Avenue, but something happened on the way.

What? said Jeff.

Don't you remember? Clarence said. You told me to run out to Doc Gregory's house on Blackstone Avenue. The house with the two cement lions on the front lawn. And throw six or seven glasses of cold water on his face if he was drunk. And to be careful about the dog Hamilton. Remember?

Jeff thought about it carefully, making a face.

Oh, yes, he said. I remember. That was *ten fifteen* years ago.

No, Clarence said, eight years ago.

Judge Olson's mother, Jeff said. I remember. Sure.

I'm sorry I never did get out to Doc Gregory's house, Clarence said. I feel pretty bad about that. Did she ever get to see the County Fair? Did Doc Gregory come down in his Ford and pick up the medicine and drive out to the house in Malaga and save her life? How did it turn out?

She was stone dead before you left this store, Jeff Willis said. Coroner Fielding claimed she had been dead three days. They took Judge Olson up to Napa to the asylum. They claimed he was crazy from old age, but he wasn't much over seventy. He's still up there for all I know.

I don't suppose the medicine would have done her any good, Clarence said.

Well, I don't know, Jeff Willis said. Coroner Fielding claimed she had been dead three days, but Judge Olson claimed she wasn't dead at all. He claimed she was sleeping. Coroner Fielding was the kind of man to exaggerate a good deal, and I don't know for sure if a little medicine wouldn't have straightened everything out.

What about Doc Gregory? Clarence said. I never did get to see Doc Gregory.

Well, nobody's seen much of Doc Gregory lately, Jeff said. He don't go out much. He just stays home and drinks.

How about the dog? Clarence said. Hamilton.

Hamilton died about three years ago, Jeff said.

The young man looked up at the signs over the mirror and read the descriptions of the magnificent things Jeff Willis prepared for the soda fountain trade. He felt pretty sad about everything, a mournful nostalgia for something impossible to define, great loneliness, partly because it was nightfall, partly because he didn't know whatever became of Doris Barnes, partly because the old lady had been dead three days anyway, partly because Judge Olson was in the asylum, partly because Doc Gregory didn't go out any more: nevertheless, he said, I'd like a special de luxe chocolate sundae with walnuts, and Jeff, after waiting eighteen years, started jumping around with glass dishes, ice-cream scoops, and fancy spoons.

My Uncle and the Mexicans

☼ ☼ ☼

JUAN CABRAL was a tall Mexican who worked for my uncle, pruning vines. He was a poor man with a number of possessions: his wife Consuela, his sons Pablo and Pancho, his three daughters, his lame cousin Federico, four dogs, a cat, a guitar, a shotgun, an old horse, an old wagon, and lots of pots and pans.

I was in the farmyard talking to my uncle the morning Juan came up the road in his wagon to ask for work.

What's this? my uncle said.

Mexicans, I said.

How can you tell? he said.

The dogs, I said. The Mexicans are a noble and simple people. They are never so poor they cannot keep a pack of hounds. They are Indians, mixed with other noble races.

What do they want? he said.

Work, I said. It will break their hearts to admit it, but that's what they want.

I don't need any help, my uncle said.

They won't care, I said. They'll just turn around and go on to the next vineyard.

The wagon came slowly into the farmyard and Juan Cabral said good morning in Mexican. *Buenos dias, amigos.* In bad English he said, Is there work on this vineyard for a strong Mexican?

Who? said my uncle. (For instance, he said to me.)

Me, said Juan Cabral. Juan Cabral.

Juan Cabral, said my uncle. No, there is no work.

How much is the pay? said Juan.

What'd he say? said my uncle to me. He lit a cigarette to help him through his bewilderment.

He wants to know how much the pay is, I said.

Who said anything about pay? my uncle said. I'm not hiring anybody.

He wants to know anyway, I said. He knows you're not hiring anybody.

My uncle was amazed.

Well, he said, I'm paying the Japs thirty cents an hour. Most farmers are paying twenty and twenty-five.

The pay is thirty cents an hour, I said to Juan.

That is not enough, said the Mexican. There are many mouths to feed this winter.

What's he say? said my uncle.

My uncle was pretty sore and wouldn't understand anything Juan said until I said it over again.

He says thirty cents an hour isn't enough to feed all the mouths he's got to feed this winter, I said.

Who's he got to feed? my uncle said.

All them people in the wagon, I said.

Where they going to live? my uncle said.

I don't know, I said. They'll find a place somewhere, I suppose.

Juan Cabral did not speak. One of his dogs came over to my uncle and licked my uncle's hand. My uncle jumped and looked around fearfully. What's this? he said.

It's one of the Mexican's dogs, I said.

Well, get it away from me, said my uncle.

I told the dog to go back to the wagon and it did.

My uncle watched it go back. He not only watched the dog go back, he studied the dog going back.

That's an ordinary dog, he said. You see hundreds of them in the streets.

That's right, I said.

That dog ain't worth a penny, my uncle said.

It ain't even worth a lot less than a penny, I said. You couldn't give that dog away with two dollars.

I wouldn't take that dog with three dollars, my uncle said. What can it do? Can it catch a jack rabbit or anything like that?

No, I said.

Can it scare robbers away? said my uncle.

No, I said. It would go out and lick the hands of robbers.

Well, what good is it? my uncle said.

No good at all, I said.

What do they want to keep a lot of dogs like that for? my uncle said.

They're Mexicans, I said. They're simple Mexican people.

I hear Mexicans do a lot of stealing, said my uncle.

They'll take anything that ain't got roots in the earth, I said.

I got thirteen mouths to feed, not counting my own, said Juan. Thirty cents an hour isn't enough.

Thirteen mouths? said my uncle.

He's counting the animals, I said.

I don't suppose he knows how to prune a vine, my uncle said.

Do you know how to prune a grapevine? I said to Juan.

No, señor, he said. I am a soldier.

What'd he say? said my uncle.

He says he's a soldier, I said.

The war's over, my uncle said.

The Mexican brought out his shotgun and was lifting it to his shoulder by way of demonstrating his being a soldier when my uncle noticed what he was fooling with. My uncle jumped behind me.

Tell him to put that gun away, he said. I don't want any Mexican shooting me accidentally. I believe him. I believe he's a soldier. Tell him to put that God damn gun away. He'll shoot me just to prove he's a soldier.

No, he won't, I said.

I don't need any help, my uncle said to Juan Cabral.

Thirty cents an hour is not enough to feed thirteen mouths, not counting my own, said the Mexican.

He put the gun away, and the first thing my uncle knew five young Mexican faces were looking up at him. He almost lost his balance.

Who are these people? he said.

These are the children, I said. Two boys and three girls.

What do they want? said my uncle.

Beans and flour and salt, I said. They don't want much.

Tell them to go away, my uncle said. He don't know how to prune a vine.

Anybody can learn to prune a vine, I said.

He'll ruin my vineyard, my uncle said.

And steal everything that ain't got roots in the earth, I said.

I'm paying ten cents an hour more than most farmers are paying, my uncle said.

He says it ain't enough, I said.

Well, said my uncle, ask him how much *is* enough.

Señor Cabral, I said to the Mexican, will you work for thirty-five cents an hour? My uncle does not need any help, but he likes you.

Have you a dwelling for my family and the animals? said the Mexican.

Yes, I said. It is modest but comfortable.

Is there much work to do? said the Mexican.

Very little, I said.

Is it pleasant work? said the Mexican.

It is pleasant and healthful, I said.

Juan Cabral stepped down from the wagon and came over to my uncle. My uncle was pretty scared. The dogs walked behind the Mexican, and his children were already surrounding my uncle.

Señor, said the Mexican to my uncle, I will work in your vineyard.

I am honored, said my uncle.

He was all mixed up. It was the dogs mostly, but it was also the five Mexican children, and the Mexican's magnificent manners.

It was certainly not the gun. My uncle wouldn't let any power in the world intimidate him.

By three o'clock in the afternoon the Mexicans were established in their little house, and I took Juan Cabral, followed by Pablo and Pancho and his lame cousin Federico, to a vine to teach him how to prune. I explained the reasons for each clip of the shears. To keep the shape of the vine. To keep it strong. To let its fresh branches grow upward toward the sun. And so forth. I moved down the row of vines to the next vine. I handed him the pruning shears and asked if he wouldn't enjoy trying to prune the vine. He was very polite and said it would be a pleasure. He worked thoughtfully and slowly, explaining to his children and his lame cousin, as I had explained to him, the reasons for each clip of the shears. His lame cousin Federico, who was a man of sixty or so, was very much impressed.

I suggested that he go on pruning vines until dark and returned to my uncle who was sitting at the wheel of the Ford, dreaming.

How does it look? he said.

Excellent, I said.

We drove back to the city sixty-six miles an hour, as if my uncle wanted to get away from something frightening, and all the way he didn't speak. When we were coming into Ventura Avenue near the Fair Grounds he said, All four of them dogs ain't worth a penny put together.

It ain't the dogs, I said. Mexicans just look at it that way.

I thought that dog was going to bite me, my uncle said.

No, I said. He wouldn't think of it. Not even if you kicked him. His heart was full of love. The same as the Mexicans. The stealing they do never amounts to anything.

Them kids looked pretty healthy, my uncle said.

They don't come any healthier, I said.

What do they eat? my uncle said.

Beans and Mexican bread, I said. Stuff that ain't supposed to be good for you.

Do you think he'll ever learn to prune a vine? my uncle said.

Sure, I said.

I don't suppose he'll go away with the tractor, will he? my uncle said.

No, I said. It's much too heavy.

I lost money on that vineyard last year, my uncle said.

I know, I said. You lost money on it the year before too.

I've been losing money on that vineyard ever since I bought it, my uncle said. Who wants grapes? Who wants raisins?

It may be different this year, I said.

Do you think so? my uncle said.

I think this Mexican is going to do the trick, I said.

That's funny, my uncle said. I've been thinking the same thing. If he feeds them thirteen mouths this winter, not counting his own, it won't be so bad this year.

You can't lose more than you lost last year, I said.

The Japs are all right, my uncle said, only they don't look at things the way Mexicans do.

The Japs wouldn't think of keeping four ordinary dogs, I said.

They'd drive the dogs away, my uncle said.

They'd throw rocks at the dogs, I said.

I think I'm going to have a good year this year, my uncle said.

We didn't say anything more all the way into town.

Countryman, How Do You Like America?

✪ ✪ ✪

THERE was a man by the name of Sarkis who came to America from the village of Gultik, in Armenia, in 1908 when he was not yet thirty years of age. He was a big peasant with thick heavy hair and a large black mustache. He weighed about two hundred pounds but wasn't fat, and had an unusually melancholy expression. In Gultik he hadn't been very important —no one in Gultik had been very important—but he had gotten along very well and had had many friends: Armenians, Kurds, Turks, Arabs, Greeks, Bulgarians, and men of many other tribes and nations. He had spoken in Armenian, Kurdish, Turkish, and Arabic with these people of Asia Minor, and when he had left Gultik he had left many friends behind him.

He reached New York in May, in 1908.

It was a very bewildering place and there was no one to talk to. There were very few people in New York in 1908 who could speak so much as three words of Armenian, Kurdish, Turkish, or Arabic. It was very lonely.

He went up to Lynn, Massachusetts, and got a job in a shoe factory and began to learn a little English.

It was very hard work, especially for a big man. It wasn't work that a man did with his legs and shoulders and trunk, it was exasperating work, with the fingers and with some of the muscles of the arm. And with the eye.

He worked in the shoe factory a year and his loneliness grew and grew. There were a number of Armenian families in Lynn, but he didn't like them. They weren't like the people of Gultik.

One night he got drunk and an Armenian priest found him staggering through the streets. They went together to the priest's home.

My son, the Armenian priest said, what is your trouble?

I am lonely, the peasant groaned.

God is your father, the priest said.

That is all very well, the peasant said, but Little Father, I am lonely. There is no one I can talk to. In Gultik I knew everybody, Christian and heathen alike. Ah, Little Father, how lovely was life in Gultik.

You should take a wife, the priest said.

That is so, the peasant said. Little Father, find me a woman of beauty who can cook food and speak Armenian and at least one other language. Kurdish, Turkish, or Arabic, and I will marry her.

The priest took the peasant home and put him to bed, and a week later the peasant got a letter from the priest, which he read many times. In the letter the priest said that he had found a good girl for the peasant, and asked the peasant to visit him very soon. The peasant read the letter fifty times; it wasn't a long letter.

Then he put on his best clothes and went to the priest's house.

Little Father, he said, can she cook? That is what I want to know. Can she cook? My stomach has gone crazy with the food of these people. Can the girl cook? Can she sing? Is she in your house, Little Father?

No, my son, the priest said. She is not in my house. We will go to her house.

They walked a mile to the house in which the girl lived.

She was rather ugly, to say the least.

The peasant stood in the house, his heart breaking because of so many unhappy things in his life: the loss of Gultik, the loss of his many friends, the wretched work in the shoe factory, his loneliness, his longing for good food, his need of someone good and beautiful to sing to him, and then, this woman, an Armenian, to be sure, doubtless a woman of the noblest character, perhaps an excellent cook, perhaps expert with thread and needle, but all the same—no, he did not want her, he did not like her, she made him lonelier than ever.

He brought a cigarette from his pocket and striking the match cried out, Little Father, forgive me, I must smoke.

Here, the priest said, leave your hat here. Let us go in and sit down. I have not yet told you her name. It is Elizar Iskanderian.

The peasant put down his hat and inhaled deeply on his cigarette.

That is so, he said. That is her name, Little Father. I will take your word for that. It is an honor, he said to the woman.

You shall meet her father and mother, the priest said. They are excellent people.

I can see that, Little Father, the peasant said. It is true, they are fine people, as this room itself proves. I would not hesitate a moment to grant that they are people of the first order.

He inhaled deeply, looked at the woman again, and said, *The very first order.* Forgive me, Little Father.

The mother and father of the girl came to meet the peasant and asked his name.

Sarkis Khatchadourian, he said. From Gultik. Torn from the warm breast of the homeland. Fifteen months in America. Lost in the wilderness. A slave. Miserable and lonely. Forgive me, Little Father, how disgraceful is the world.

The girl cooked Turkish coffee: it tasted very bad. She sang: it sounded very bad.

The peasant sat in his chair mournfully dreaming of home.

He brought out his gold watch and looked at it.

Forgive me, countrymen, he said, I have been delighted. I must go. God keep you. Good night.

The priest left the house with him.

So? said the priest. How is it?

Little Father, the peasant said, I cannot tell you how deeply unhappy I am. She is a fine woman; she cooks good coffee; her voice is the voice of a nightingale, as it were; but, Little Father, there is something about her, a small speck of something which saddens me. No, I should not like to be in the same house with her. In the same bed, Little Father, completely out of the question.

You will learn to love her, the priest said.

Little Father, the peasant said, I do not want to learn. Forgive me, I am very unhappy.

It is only a question of time, the priest said. One week, two; one month, two; one year, two; a child, and then another, and then, what is it? You are married, you have children, the years go by.

Forgive me, Little Father, the peasant said. I am grateful to you. That small speck of it. No. Not one week. Not two. Good night, Little Father.

Good night, my son, the priest said.

An Armenian from California came to Lynn and one evening Sarkis Khatchadourian met this man in a coffee house and drank *rakki* with him and the man told Sarkis about California.

It is Armenia again, the man said. Sunshine, vines, meadows, olive trees, fig trees, brooks, cows.

Cows, my countryman? the peasant cried. Did you say cows?

Hundreds of them, the man said.

My God, the peasant said. Cows.

And work? he said. What is the nature of the work?

Farm work, the man said.

My God, the peasant said. In the sun, he mused. My beloved countryman, he cried, are there many of our people in California? That is the question.

There are many, said the man.

My God, the peasant said. Then I shall go to California.

And he did.

He reached California in August, just in time to pick grapes. It was better work than working in a shoe factory, but it had its bad points too. The workers were mostly Mexicans and Japs. Strange people. He wanted to talk, but nobody could understand him so he had to work and not talk.

The work was to cut a bunch of grapes at the stem and place it on a timber tray which remained under the sun, and the grapes, drying, became raisins. After the grapes had been dried on one side two workers went down a row, lifting a tray and turning the grapes over onto another tray, so that the sun would dry the other side.

It was not pleasant to do this work with a Mexican, a man one could not talk to.

It was very mournful to turn trays hour after hour with a Mexican.

He did this work all summer, and in the winter he plowed the earth and pruned the vines, and on Sundays he went to the city, to an Armenian coffee house on Mariposa Street where he drank *rakki* and coffee and played *scambile* and *tavli* and talked with his countrymen. They were all new people, men he had met in California.

One Sunday a man came to this coffee house while the peasant was there, and this man was Arshag Dombalian, who was from Gultik. Arshag Dombalian had known Sarkis Khatchadourian in the old country. In the old country they had spoken to one another. It was very pleasant for Sarkis to meet this man from Gultik in America.

They shook hands solemnly, and almost cried.

Ahkh, brother Sarkis, Arshag Dombalian said, how are you?

I am well, brother Arshag, Sarkis said mournfully. I am well indeed. How are you?

Ahkh, I am very well, my beloved brother, said Arshag. And how do you like America, my friend from Gultik?

Ahkh, America, said Sarkis. How do I like it? What shall I say? Go; come; and with men known and unknown turn trays. That is all. Go, come; go, come; known, unknown; and turn trays. Who are they? How should we know, my brother? We have never seen them before. What nation are they of? What tongue do they speak? Who can tell?

Sarkis Khatchadourian took a wife the year after he reached California. She was from less distinguished people than the girl of Lynn, but she was rounder, darker, lovelier. This girl bore him a son the following year. He worked hard and saved three hundred dollars and made a down payment on a ten-acre vineyard. He was now a farmer in his own right. He owned horses, a cow, he had a house, a good wife, and a son.

As the priest had said, one became two, two became three, three became four: days, months, years, and children. It was all very good indeed; he would not say it was not good, but he did not know. He was prospering. As he earned money, he bought more land, plowed, planted, pruned, irrigated, harvested. His vineyard of ten acres grew until it was a vineyard of thirty, then forty, then fifty.

And he put up a new house, with electricity; he bought a phonograph; he bought an automobile; he took his wife and his children to the city for ice-cream; soda-water; he took them into moving picture theaters. The years went by. His first son graduated from high school and the peasant sat in the auditorium of the school and saw the boy get his diploma and his eyes filled with tears. It was all fine. He knew it was all splendid. His first son married an Armenian girl born in California and the boy bought a small vineyard of his own and at the wedding there was real Armenian and Turkish and Kurdish music and singing and dancing. Fine, fine. His second son not only graduated from high school, he went to Berkeley and graduated from college. It was splendid.

It was all marvelous. The change he had seen in life and in the world, right before his very eyes. The telephone. The automobile. The tractor. Carpet-sweepers. Vacuum cleaners. Washing-machines. Electric refrigerators. The radio. His sons and daughters speaking English, writing English, learning many things. It was a great age, a great time.

Still, it was sad. He did not know. In Gultik it was fine too. One knew the man one spoke to. Arab, Arab; Kurd, Kurd; Turk, Turk; one knew. One knew the face, the eye, the nose, the very smell. It was home. One talked and knew who one was talking to; but in America what was it? He could never forget what it was in America.

Sometimes important Armenians, professional men, visited him. Sometimes, sipping coffee, they said, Well, countryman, how do you like America? And always he looked mournfully into the face of the man he knew, into the eyes he knew, and he said, What do I know? Go, come; and with men known and unknown turn trays.

Where I Come from People Are Polite

✿ ✿ ✿

ONE morning I walked into the office and the bookkeeper was putting on her hat and coat and tears were coming out of her eyes. It was April and what did I care if I was only a fifteen-dollar-a-week clerk in a lousy cemetery company? Didn't I have a new hat and a new pair of shoes and wasn't the Southern Pacific sending special trains at special low rates down to Monterey every week-end and wasn't I going down to Monterey tomorrow? Wasn't I going to take a train ride down the peninsula tomorrow?

I was going to work until noon Saturday and then I was going to get a de luxe hamburger for fifteen cents at Charley's and then I was going to hurry down to the Southern Pacific depot at Third and Townsend and buy me a special week-end round-trip ticket to Monterey and get on the train and be free in the world from Saturday afternoon till Monday morning. I was going to buy me a copy of *The Saturday Evening Post* and read stories all the way down to Monterey.

When I walked into the office, though, Mrs. Gilpley, the bookkeeper, was putting on her hat and coat and tears were coming out of her eyes.

I stopped whistling and looked around. It was very quiet. The door of Mr. Wylie's office was just a little open, so I figured he was at his desk. Nobody else was around, though. It was twenty minutes past eight, and the clock was making a lot of noise for a clock you could hardly hear ordinarily.

Good morning, Mrs. Gilpley, I said.

Good morning, Joe, she said.

I didn't go straight to the locker and hang up my hat and go to my desk because I knew something was wrong and I figured it wouldn't be polite to just go and hang up my hat and sit at my desk and not try to understand what was wrong and why Mrs. Gilpley was putting on her hat and coat and crying. Mrs. Gilpley was an old lady and she had a mustache and she was stoop-shouldered and her hands were dry and full of wrinkles and nobody liked Mrs. Gilpley, but it was April in the world and I had a new hat and a new pair of shoes and I had worked in the same office with Mrs. Gilpley from September till April, right straight through Winter, and maybe I didn't exactly love her, maybe I wasn't exactly crazy about her, but she was a good-hearted old lady, and I couldn't just go and hang up my hat and start another day. I had to talk to her.

Mrs. Gilpley, I said, is something the matter?

She pointed at the partly open door of Mr. Wylie's private office and made a sign that told me not to talk and just hang up my hat and go to work.

I see, I thought. He's fired her.

After all these years.

Mrs. Gilpley, I said, you haven't lost your job, have you?

I've resigned, she said.

No, you haven't, I said. I wasn't born yesterday. You can't fool me.

Mrs. Gilpley's salary was twenty-seven-fifty per week. It was eight a week when she first started to work for the cemetery company. They taught me to do Mrs. Gilpley's work. My salary was fifteen a week, so they were giving the old lady the gate. Well, I was pretty lucky to have a job and I wanted to go down to Monterey and I felt fine in a new pair of three-dollar shoes and a new hat, but I didn't like the idea of making Mrs. Gilpley cry at her age.

Mrs. Gilpley, I said, I came in this morning to quit my job and I'm *going* to quit. I got an uncle in Portland who's opening a grocery store and I'm going up there to handle his accounts for him. I ain't going to work for any cemetery company all my life. I'm quitting.

Joe, Mrs. Gilpley said, you know you ain't got no uncle in Portland.

Is that so? I said. You'd be surprised where I got uncles. I'm through with this job. Keeping track of dead people's addresses. That's a hell of a career for a young man.

Joe, Mrs. Gilpley said, if you quit your job, I'll never speak to you again as long as I live.

I don't need no job in a cemetery company, I said. What do I want to be keeping track of dead people for?

You got no friends in this town, Joe, Mrs. Gilpley said. You told me all about where you're from and what you're doing out here in Frisco, and I know how it is. You need this job, and if you quit it, I'll be deeply hurt.

Mrs. Gilpley, I said, how do you think I feel? Coming in here and taking your job? It ain't right. You been doing this work twenty years or more.

Joe, Mrs. Gilpley said, you go on now and hang up your hat and go to work.

I won't, I said. I'm quitting right now.

I walked straight into Mr. Wylie's office. Mr. Wylie was the vice-president. He was an old man with a nose that was squeezed down at the end. He was tall and absent-minded and he wore a derby. And he was mean.

I walked straight into his office. Mr. Wylie, I said, I'm quitting my job beginning this morning.

What's that? he said.

Quitting, I said.

What for? he said.

I ain't getting enough money, I said.

How much do you want? he said.

Boy, was I surprised? I thought he'd throw me out. I figured I'd have to ask for plenty to make him throw me out, so I did.

I want thirty dollars a week, I said.

But you're only eighteen, he said. Such a salary would be a little premature, but perhaps we can arrange it.

What the hell. If I had tried to put over a thing like that, if I had wanted to put over something like that, and get more money, it never would have worked. Thirty dollars a week was enough to buy me all the stuff I always wanted, in less than six months. Why, Jesus Christ, I'd be able to buy a Harley-Davidson in no time at thirty a week.

No, I said. I'm quitting.

Why are you quitting? he said. I thought you liked your work?

I used to, I said. But I don't any more. Mr. Wylie, I said, did you fire Mrs. Gilpley?

Mr. Wylie leaned back in his chair and looked at me. He looked sore. Who the hell was I to ask *him* a question like that?

Young man, he said, a check for you will be made out in full this morning. You can come back for it in an hour.

I was sore too.

I want my check *now*, I said.

Then wait in the outer office, he said. Behind the rail.

I went out behind the rail and leaned on the counter.

Mrs. Gilpley looked excited.

I quit, I said.

She couldn't talk.

He wanted to give me thirty dollars a week, I said, but I quit.

She gulped a couple of times.

Mrs. Gilpley, I said, they'll have to give you your job back because they ain't got anybody else to do your work.

Joe, she said, you've hurt me very deeply.

That's all right, I said. Where I come from a young man doesn't take a lady's job. I come from Chicago and I guess I can always go back.

Go back to Chicago? Not me. I liked California. I always liked California. But that's what I said.

Joe, said Mrs. Gilpley, suppose you can't find another job?

I snapped my fingers.

I can get another job just like that, I said.

Mr. Wylie stood in the doorway of his private office and nodded at Mrs. Gilpley and she went into his office and he closed the door. She didn't come out till it was a quarter to nine. She took off her hat and coat and got out the check book and wrote a check and took it to Mr. Wylie.

The check was for me. It was a check for thirteen dollars.

Here's your check, Joe, Mrs. Gilpley said. I tried to get him to give you fifteen, but he said you were insolent.

Did he give you your job back? I said.

Yes, she said.

Mrs. Gilpley, I said, I'm very glad you've got your job back. What did he say I was?

Insolent, said Mrs. Gilpley.

What's that mean? I said.

Impolite, Mrs. Gilpley said.

I ain't impolite, I said. Where I come from people are courteous. Who does he think he's calling impolite?

I went into Mr. Wylie's office and asked him.

Mr. Wylie, I said, who do you think you're calling impolite?

What are you talking about? he said.

You can't call me impolite, I said. Where I come from people are courteous.

People in Chicago aren't really courteous; not in every part of Chicago, but most of the people in the neighborhood where I lived were pretty polite. Most of the time anyway. I guess I was just sore.

You can't say I ain't got good manners, I said.

Where do you come from? Mr. Wylie said.

Chicago, I said. Didn't you know that?

No, he said.

I used to work on South Water Market Street, I said.

Well, said Mr. Wylie, you've got a lot to learn. You're going to learn it doesn't pay to bite the hand that feeds you.

I didn't bite no hand that fed me, I said.

You quit, didn't you? he said.

Yes, sir, I said. I quit all right, but I didn't bite nobody.

Well, what do you want now? he said.

I just want to say goodbye, I said. I just want you to know I've got good manners.

All right, said Mr. Wylie. Goodbye.

Goodbye, I said.

I went out of the office and said goodbye to Mrs. Gilpley. Mr. Wylie came out of his private office while I was saying goodbye to Mrs. Gilpley. She got all excited when he came out of his office, but I wouldn't stop talking.

Mrs. Gilpley, I said, all my life I've wanted to buy a Harley-Davidson and ride around and see a lot of small towns and I guess I could have done it if I had wanted to keep my job here, but where I come from a man don't keep a job and buy a Harley-Davidson and get somebody else who needs a job worse fired.

What's a Harley-Davidson? Mr. Wylie said.

It's a motorcycle, I said.

Oh, he said.

And don't think I won't get along all right, Mrs. Gilpley, I said, because I will.

What do you want with a motorcycle? Mr. Wylie said.

I want to ride it, I said.

What for? he said.

To get somewhere, I said. Travel.

That's no way to travel, Mr. Wylie said.

It's one of the best ways in the world, I said. Mr. Wylie, I don't suppose you've ever driven a motorcycle.

No, I haven't, he said.

There ain't nothing like it, I said. A good motorcycle can go eighty miles an hour, easy.

Mrs. Gilpley, I said, if I ever get a motorcycle with a side-car, I'd be very happy to take you for a little ride through Golden Gate Park, just to give you an idea how pleasant motorcycle riding can be.

Thank you very much, Joe, Mrs. Gilpley said.

Goodbye, I said.

Goodbye, said Mrs. Gilpley.

Goodbye, said Mr. Wylie.

I went out and rang for the elevator. It was the Greek George.

Where you going? he said.

Portland, I said.

Portland? he said. What the hell you going to do in Portland?

I don't know, I said.

What's the matter? he said.

I just quit my job, I said.

What the hell you want to quit your job for? he said.

I didn't like it, I said. I don't like keeping track of dead people.

You're crazy, he said.

I ain't crazy at all, I said.

I walked out of the elevator, out of the building, and up Market Street. I don't know how it happened, but I went straight to the Harley-Davidson agency, and they showed me the new model. I asked the salesman if I could try one out for a little while, and he talked it over with somebody in an inside office and then he said I could try one out if I would leave some money in the office. In case, he said.

Well, I had the check, so I gave him the check.

It was a beautiful machine. I tore down Market Street and stopped at the building where I used to work and went upstairs and walked into Mr. Wylie's office.

He looked dumbfounded.

Mr. Wylie, I said, I got a beautiful Harley-Davidson downstairs and if you'd like to go for a ride, I'd be more than glad to let you sit behind me. It's a big seat and if I move up toward the front, you'll be comfortable.

I don't want to ride no motorcycle, he said.

I thought maybe you would, I said.

I went out of the office, and then I went back.

Well, would you care to *see* it? I said.

No, he said.

All right, I said, and I went on downstairs and got on the motorcycle and drove away. It was a beautiful job. The motor was great. I got out on the Great Highway at the beach and then I remembered Monterey and I figured maybe I ought to let her out and tear down to Monterey and then tear back, and then give them back their motorcycle and start looking for another job. They'd maybe give me back some of the money, and maybe not, but even if they didn't, I figured it would be worth it, so I let her out. It was the real thing. April. And the Harley-Davidson under me, and the Pacific Ocean beside me. And the world. And the towns. And the people. And the trees. And I roared down to Monterey in no time.

It was a fine town. There were some old buildings in the town, and ships. Fishing ships. There was a fine smell of fish down there, and a lot of sunlight. The fishermen talked very loud in Italian. I drove the Harley-Davidson all around town and right out onto the wet sand of the beach and along the beach for quite a way. I scared a lot of sea gulls and then I stopped at a place and had three hamburgers and two cups of coffee.

Then I started back for Frisco.

It was a great trip, going and coming. It was the most beautiful machine I ever saw. I could do anything with it. I could make it go anywhere, and I did. And I could make it go slower than a man walking, and faster than any expensive car on the highway. I'll bet I passed at least sixty millionaires on the highway. I could make it roar too. I could drive it zig-zag. I could ride it leaning away over on one side. I guess I scared a lot of people on the highway. I drove it a mile no hands. I stood on the seat a long time, holding the handlebars. People think that's dangerous, but it isn't if you know how to do it.

I had a great time with the Harley-Davidson. Then I took it back and turned it in. The salesman said, Where did you go?

I went down to Monterey, I said.

Monterey, he said. We didn't know you wanted to go that far. We just thought you wanted to find out how it worked.

Well, I said, I always wanted to go down there. Can I have my money back?

Are you going to buy the motorcycle? he said.

How much is it? I said.

It's two hundred and seventy-five dollars, he said.

No, I said.

I ain't got that much.

How much have you got? he said.

I got that check, that's all, I said. Then thirteen dollars.

We thought you were going to buy the motorcycle, he said.

I would have bought it if I hadn't quit my job, I said. Can I have my money back?

I don't think so, the salesman said. I'll talk to the manager.

He went into an office and talked, and then he came out and another man was with him. The other man looked important and sore.

What do you mean by taking a new bike and riding it to Monterey and back? he said.

What? I said.

I didn't know what to say. What did *he* mean, *what did I mean?* I didn't mean anything.

You can't do that, he said. We thought you just wanted to ride the motorcycle around the block or show it to somebody or something.

I showed it to a few people, I said. Can I have my money back?

I'm afraid *you* owe *us* money, said the manager. That machine's a new machine. It's for sale. It's second-hand now.

Can't I have *some* of my money back? I said.

No, said the manager.

It's a swell motorcycle, I said.

I walked out of the place and walked up to my room and I didn't even stop to think where I'd ever be able to find a job. I was feeling too happy about the ride to Monterey and back.

The Trains

☼ ☼ ☼

HE used to stand for hours at the window, staring, more asleep than awake, forgetting everything, deeply troubled by a feeling of homelessness which was all the more saddening in that he *was* home: in the warm valley where he had entered the world, where he had lived the first seventeen years of his life. He had been home four months now, from June to September, and was still homeless, in spite of the summer temperature which was perfect; in spite of the places he remembered which were delightful to see; in spite of the faces he had known long ago which, though they had journeyed much through time, had remained essentially unchanged; in spite, even, of the summer sky, daytime and nighttime, the summer odors which never during his travels had he ever forgotten, and which, when he first breathed them in again to his heart and spirit, his heart laughed and his spirit leaped; in spite, even, of the absurd sounds of the absurd city: the water-sprinklers on the miserable lawns, the popcorn wagon whistles, the sound of the streets, in the morning, at high-noon, and at the peak of evening; and then after the people had gone home and the streets grew cold and empty; he was still homeless in spite of the chaotic, and often comical, presence of home in every fragment of time and place about him and within him, and it was this unfriendly condition which had brought about his deep inward bewilderment and stupor; his spiritual listlessness; his day-dreaming; his inability to work.

The child had come home from the world to be a child again: the child had opened the door of the house of home, and entered, and stretched out upon the bed of home, and slept, and awakened, and was still homeless. Home was not home. He was home: everything was in place, and yet he was a stranger. He was alone. And little by little a profound silence had come over his spirit, so that when he slept, it was not sleep, and when he wakened, it was not wakefulness. And he found it very difficult to speak, either with the people of the town, which ordinarily would have been the easiest thing in the world for him; or through his work, in his paintings:

he could think of no word to say to anybody in the town; and no meaning-ful silence or poise or precision or accuracy or purity to articulate in his paintings. He would go out in the evening and look about him for someone to speak to, and after many hours, walking, sitting in cafés, drinking, he would return silently to his two rooms; and this would be so, amazingly, even when he was drunk, when ordinarily he would be garrulous with goodwill and gaiety. Once he staggered upstairs into a cheap whorehouse, went to a room with a girl, stared at her foolishly for several minutes, laughed out loud, begged her pardon with a bow and a gesture, gave her three dollars instead of two, and staggered down the stairs.

Now, after many hours of it, many hours of many days and many nights, he found solace only in standing at the window and staring down at the trains. The Santa Fe Station was across the street, and this pleased him because, although he did not know it, he was very close to the beginning of going.

The departure of trains saddened him very much, but the arrival of them gladdened him: and he wondered a good deal about the people who got off the trains, who they were, where they had been, why they had come to this place, and so on and so forth.

Once he saw a young girl with a small black satchel descend from a train, and she seemed so lonely and frightened that he wanted to shout to her and run down to her and smile and tell her, My name is Joe Silvera. I was born in this town, but I went away when I was seventeen and stayed away seven years. I've been back four months. I live across the street. I'm a painter. Come on up to my place and rest; I've got some wine.

All he did, though, was stare at her, and finally when she disappeared, walking down Tulare Street, he wanted very much, even then, to run down to the street and catch up with her; and a day later he wanted to look for her all over town; and a week later he wondered where she might be.

The silence was getting him; it was really getting him the worst way. And he was just crazy enough to give it every advantage, to stay with it, to watch it, if only out of a sense of curiosity. To escape, all he had to do was throw everything together, get aboard a train, and in less than seven hours be in San Francisco, where his homelessness would be thorough and consequently much easier to endure, much easier to accept and dismiss. He knew how small the world was: he had been to the magic cities of the world that every small-town boy dreams about and seldom reaches. He knew that arrival in the magic cities was purely a question of train and ship sched-ules, and having the fare, or being willing to hitchhike, ride the freight trains, or work on ships. It was nothing. The cities weren't really magic. The people in them were exactly like the people in other cities, like the people in this town.

He wanted to give the thing every advantage because he knew how it was: the magic was not in the world. It was in a dimension made out of the longings of the inhabitants of the world: and that's where home was too. If home were a place, then he was home. But it was not a place: it was a synchronization of a multitude of subtle and constantly changing substances and rhythms and perceptions and values in a number of people together, as a family; or in two people, as himself, and the lost girl, for instance; or himself and a friend, like old Otto Bennra in Vienna.

Maybe it was; maybe it wasn't too. He didn't know. Maybe it was another of the mirages the heart was constantly creating. He was afraid it was a mirage; and he was afraid home was movement for the body, travel; and he was sorry this might be so. He could feel that he was very close to a beginning of some sort, but he couldn't tell what sort it would be: to stay or to go. It would have to be one of the two, and he wanted to stay. He wanted to stay and paint, and be in the valley a long time. He felt too near death, constantly, away from the valley, as if all his strength were necessary for only one thing, to keep off death a little longer. And he believed his strength could be put to better use.

The trains would come and go. He would watch for the appearance, far in the south, of the crack passenger trains from Los Angeles. And listen for their cry of arrival: the whistle desolating and full of human anguish, like the ungodly anguish of the heart after possessing flesh and losing spirit; and the last minute haste, the roar, the fire and smoke; and then, almost meaninglessly, sadly, the slow stop, the tentative pause, the swift-ending moment of rest; and then the going again, unlike the movement of the spirit, the train going from city to city, place to place, climate to climate, configuration to configuration. Unlike the going of the spirit, which traveled ungeographically, seeking absurdly magnificent destinations: all places, the core of life, the essence of all mortality, eternity, God. And, he thought bitterly, seeking everything else, in one big bright package.

It was very warm and pleasant during August and September, but within himself was the paralysis of indecision and bewilderment on the one hand, and on the other the slow-growing impulse to run inwardly amuck, getting cockeyed, and letting himself have half a chance to fight the thing, which he believed he could lick with alcohol and physical comedy: like doing any crazy thing that reached impulse, being obscene, fighting. The temperature of the valley during August and September was swell, but he couldn't enjoy it.

He was very nearly caught, although he knew escape ultimately would be very easy; even though, he knew, it would not be permanent.

One Sunday in September he was sure the time had come to make a decision: one way or another. To stay and go still deeper into the gloom of inaction and despair, or to find his way out to the light; or to go away by train, geographically, right out into the outward light, which of course was the easiest way, and the one he hoped, even yet, to be able to avoid.

He got up around six in the morning and after watching the arrival and departure of the morning passenger train, he went downstairs and walked to town, looking into its silly Sunday face, listening to its sorrowful Sunday stillness.

After breakfast at a Greek place on Mariposa Street he walked around town and then went into the White Fawn on Broadway and began drinking beer. It was very warm in the city and very cool in the White Fawn. After an hour of beer he suddenly shouted across the room at the bartender.

Hey, Mac, bring me six bottles of Pabst.

How many? the bartender said.

Six, he said. No, make it seven. Seven bottles of Pabst.

One at a time? the bartender said.

No, he shouted, all at once.

And he knew he was on his way; he was already beginning to feel that he was awakening, and every now and then he would shake his head, as one who had been suddenly wakened does.

What day is this? he shouted. What month? What year? What's the population of this town? Anything exciting happening around here these days?

And so on and so forth.

He emerged from the saloon a little after one in the afternoon, glowing with the warmth of beer, staggering slightly, full of good-will, amiable, and inclined to be overcourteous. Especially toward lamp-posts. He was full of bowing, gesturing, clicking the heels together.

It was very pleasant, superficially, to be busting loose again, even at midday.

He went to the Court House Park and challenged the horseshoe players to a contest, which was great sport until the physical exertion began to sober him; and then he became self-conscious and apologetic. While he was drunk, though, he played a beautiful game, pitching the shoes either much too far, or only three or four feet in front of him, which was very amusing. When he began to be sober, he began really trying to pitch, and the effort was not at all comical.

His departure from the game was not grand, as it would have been had he been drunk. It was, rather, a little ridiculous. He thanked the players for letting him play. If he had been drunk, he would have told them to remember what he had taught them about the game.

He went across the park and stretched out under a magnolia tree and immediately went to sleep, dreaming mournfully, the expression of his sleeping face one of long weariness, long unhappiness.

He slept what seemed to be many days and many nights and many weeks and many months, but when he awakened it was not yet four o'clock. He sat up and yawned, and when he opened his eyes and began looking out of them sharply, he saw the girl. He shook his head and looked again because he thought he might still be asleep.

She was seated on the lawn under the same tree, very near him, and had no doubt been watching him while he slept.

Without thinking, without even smiling, as if he were speaking to nothing, or to the world, he said, Hello.

Hello, the girl said.

Then, for some crazy reason, he stretched out again and closed his eyes. With his eyes closed he said, My name is Joe. And then just to be comical he almost shouted, I'm a painter. A *great* painter.

He sat up again and again opened his eyes.

Now, he was completely awake.

The girl was real.

She was very nice; not altogether too nice, but neat and cool-looking and with good hands.

The girl smiled, and he wondered if she might be a hooker who'd come to the park for a little Sunday afternoon quiet.

She wasn't knitting though, so he supposed she wasn't.

Joe Silvera, he said. I've been all over hell, but even so, this is my home town. Is it yours?

No, the girl said.

Where are you from? he said.

The girl hesitated a moment, thinking, and he said, Any place; it doesn't have to be the truth. Texas maybe?

That's right, the girl said.

I've always liked Texas, he said.

Any place is all right, the girl said.

If, he said. If?

If you've got money or a job, the girl said.

That's right, he said. I'm hungry and I'd like to go on with this conversation. Would you care to have supper with me?

The girl hesitated again.

At a restaurant, he said.

Christ, he thought, what the hell's she being coy about? I'll kiss her when I help her up.

All right, the girl said, and he got up and took her hand and helped her up and was about to kiss her when she bent down to pick up her handbag.

Only she had known what he intended to do.

Her face was very nice, her expression calm and cool; and he figured she was as splendid a girl as any man might wake up in a park and find sitting in front of him on a warm September Sunday afternoon in a small town; statistically, she was really very remarkable. But all this spoofing was only superficial and he knew it: he was rather delighted with her, and regarded her as something extraordinary, most desirable, and perhaps the means for him to synchronize all the vagrant moods within himself and achieve a state of being home; a state of inward contentment and delight.

He might have to discount her conversation here and there, he believed, but deeply he believed that she might be something extraordinarily important to him; and to his return to the valley. He hoped so; he hoped so very earnestly.

He enjoyed a pleasant, long supper, slowly eaten, quietly, with much quiet conversation and much quiet laughter, and much drinking of wine; and gradually he came to be delighted with the girl. Effortlessly, he learned all he wished to learn about her, and knew that she would go with him to his rooms across the street from the Santa Fe Station. There, he would show her his paintings, and after a while stand with her at the window and look down at the trains, and a little later he would try to find out, through her, whether he should stay or go.

When he had awakened in the morning he had known he would decide which he would do, but he had imagined that he would make the decision alone, and now this accompaniment, this presence of the girl beside him, was a pleasant improvement.

She did not like his paintings very much, and wanted to know what they were about.

They were about everything, he said.

When he heard the whistle of the northbound passenger train, arriving from Los Angeles, he led the girl to the window, and together they watched the train come into the station and stop. He said nothing for some time, but held the girl beside him, inwardly frantic about her reaction to this common event, which to him had become uncommonly significant and touching. If she said nothing, if she did no more than turn to him with any sort of a satisfactory glance, he would take her in his arms, and know that he would stay, and he hoped desperately that this communion would be established between himself and the girl.

He waited fearfully, not daring to speak, and then the girl walked away from the open window, and with her back turned to him, she said, The trains certainly make a lot of noise, don't they?

He sat down and lit a cigarette.

Across the street the train hissed and began to move, and suddenly he

wanted to be aboard it and on his way, away; he went to the window alone
and watched it go north. The house shook while the train passed beside it,
and the sound of the locomotive was very sorrowful. After a moment the
room was still again; the train had come and gone.

He sat down and smiled at the girl; then began to laugh.

The girl got up, perhaps to move toward him, and he said, Must you go?
She hadn't thought of going.

Can I take you home in a cab? he went on. I'm very grateful to you.
I've enjoyed talking with you very much.

When the girl was gone, he turned on the electric light in his room and
began getting his paintings together because he knew he wouldn't have
time to do so in the morning.

One of the Least Famous of the
Great Love Affairs of History

✢ ✢ ✢

ONE thing I never could get enough of used to be candy. Another used to be bananas. I also used to have a tremendous appetite for pies of all kinds. Ice cream was something I always wanted, and in the summertime I was very fond of watermelon. I used to get small amounts of each of these things now and then, but large amounts, enough for my appetite, I never used to get. Consequently, during most of the years of my boyhood I went around with a hungry look in my eye. There was bread, but what I wanted was cake.

I got it too.

I mean I didn't go without. I went *with*. If anybody went with I did. If anybody had an inalienable right to go with, it was me. I had the proper appetite for going with, and for not going without.

I used to feel the same way about shoes, and when the style was button shoes I had me a pair of red button shoes. The buttons were green. It was the leather that was red.

People used to stand off six or seven paces and admire my shoes. They used to either admire them or just stand horror-stricken. You could tell I was coming from a distance of three blocks. It wasn't the squeak alone, it was the flash of color too.

Them shoes scared more than half the horses that used to pass down Ventura Avenue at high noon. That was when the flash was at its height. Many a day-dreaming horse used to get that flash and take a big jump and keep moving for as many as seven miles in at least seven directions.

Years later, perhaps three years later, around 1919, after the Armistice, them kind of shoes went out of style. They went completely out of style. Only vaudeville comedians kept on wearing them.

What I had in mind wearing shoes like that was to keep society in its place. Society, for some dark and secret reason, was out to humiliate me in the world, and I was out to keep society in its place. I wanted shoes and society wanted me not to have shoes. So I had shoes.

Society isn't really malicious. It doesn't really single anybody out and make a monkey out of him, but way back there in 1917 I used to believe that for all I knew society was hounding me like a wolf hounding a lame tiger and I figured society had one major objective: to keep me from having my share of everything.

By society I used to mean society *people*. That is to say, people with money: the fathers, the mothers, and the well-fed kids. I used to resent the fathers, the mothers, and the kids. I not only used to resent the kids, I used to refuse to talk to them. I wasn't on talking terms with any boy who had all the good clothes he wanted, all the good things to eat he wanted, and money in his pockets besides. I couldn't figure out one of them boys having all them things without having to work for them the way I was working for them, selling papers. By what right did they get all the good stuff without doing anything for it?

That was the basis of the argument. Who the hell were they?

I wouldn't talk to them. One year, though, I fell in love with a girl who was society. I talked to *her* because, after all, a girl shouldn't work for anything anyway, but what good did it do me?

She wouldn't talk to me.

That cinched it.

To hell with society and watch me get my share.

Well, I was going along there flashing my red button shoes and going over to Chatterton's Bakery on Broadway and buying me two pies for a quarter, one loganberry and the other peach, and I was sitting down on the running board of one of them old automobiles they don't make any more, one of them Appersons or Hendersons that society people used to affect in them days, and I was slowly and thoughtfully putting away them pies, getting up, and giving out a terrific whoop that was supposed to be a headline about the War.

I was eating two whole pies alone and unassisted, and I was getting up and giving out the terrific whoop.

My headline hollering used to be the next to the loudest noise in my home town. The loudest was the fire alarm.

In the summertime watermelon used to be a thing I was practically a colored boy about. I used to be crazy about cold watermelon away back there in the early days of the world. I used to steal a watermelon out in the country and eat the heart. It used to be warm and not as good as a cold watermelon, but it used to be all right too. That was because it used to be stolen and as far as I was concerned society could try to stop me, or keep me supplied with cold watermelons. I used to place the cards on the table: one way or another.

That year that I fell in love with that beautiful society girl was a funny one. It was one of them goofy years that never happen but once in a life-time and always before a man is twelve. When I say goofy I mean it was a sad year. I mean the weather was sad: it was cold. The sky was sad too. It was dark. Everything was cold and dark and what I wanted was cake. I wanted warmth and light, and it was dark and cold. Another thing it was was awful. I mean it was stark raving mad awful day after day. School was lousy. The War was still going on.

This society girl that I fell in love with had a brother my age whose name was Vernon. Old spic-and-span impeccable gentlemanly polite Vernon. He was O.K. Vernon was mighty like a rose and as for being the sweetest little fellow, faith and he was that too. He had better manners than anybody you ever saw and he was really being brought up. He was not going without either. He had shoes, clothes; this, that, and the other, and when I say he was being brought up I mean he was being brought right smack up. And no dilly-dallying. Vernon's parents, as he used to say, were giving him a real honest to God bringing up. Well, I went and plumb lost my head and fell in love with Vernon's sister Mary Lou. That used to be a popular name in the society world in them days. Mary Lou Smith and Mary Lou Carter and Mary Lou anything else.

What it was was the awful weather and the ghastly (*ghastly*, I mean: I mean, with the society intonation) state of affairs in the world. It was cold and dark and the world was mean, so as a last resort I went ga-ga and fell in love with Mary Lou.

That love affair was one of the least famous of all the great love affairs of history, literature, art, music, and our time. That poor love affair got nowhere. It just came to a dead halt and froze right there in the middle of nowhere. Of all the spectacular love affairs of the machine age that small love affair was the least furious and all-consuming. Lord, that there love affair stepped in, stepped out, closed the door behind it, and said, O.K., sister, you go your way and I'll go mine.

And I did. I went my way lock, stock, barrel and whole hog.

I really liked Mary Lou but I couldn't tolerate her attitude. I was pretty broken-hearted the day I got acquainted with her attitude. I mean, her society attitude. She just didn't care about mingling with the hoi-polloi. She just didn't want any truck with poor white trash. I went down to the paper offices and got my papers and went through town hollering the most broken-hearted, grief-stricken headline ever hollered. I just couldn't make head nor tail of anything. I sold all my papers in no time and got ten more. I sold them in no time too. They just went like nothing. I guess it was that broken-hearted howl about the War. They just couldn't resist buying a paper from a boy who could feel contemporary tragedy so deeply, to the very roots, as it were.

I was very sad when the gloom of that winter day darkened to the deeper gloom of winter night and the street lights came on and everybody in town started going home. I felt awful. I went over to Chatterton's Bakery on Broadway and bought me two of the day-old pies for a quarter and I went outside and stood in the empty street and slowly ate the pies. I ate every bit of each of the pies and then I sat down for a moment to review the whole situation. I sat down on the running-board of one of them old cars they don't make any more and I reviewed the situation from beginning to end. I reviewed the situation inside and out, left and right, north and south, east and west, vice and versa, coming and going, and from every other angle. It was just like I thought.

It was *exactly* like I thought. The whole thing came to exactly what I figured it ought to come to. It was a tie score, no matter how you looked at it. It was lousy and great. It was as much one thing as another, and all you could do was choose carefully and be careful where you stepped.

It was crazy but it was all right too.

I got up and gave out a terrific whoop, and then I started walking home.

The La Salle Hotel in Chicago

☼ ☼ ☼

THE philosophers were standing around the steps of the Public Library, talking about everything. It was a clear dreamy April day and the men were glad. There was much good will among them and no hard feelings. The soapboxes were not supercilious towards the uninformed ones as they ordinarily were. The Slovak whose face was always smoothly shaven and whose teeth were very bad and who was usually loud and bitter and always in favor of revolution, riot and fire and cruelty and justice, spoke very quietly with a melancholy and gentle intonation, his bitterness and sadness still valid, but gaiety valid too.

I don't know, he said with an accent. Sometimes I see them in their big cars and instead of hating them I feel sorry for them. They got money and big houses and servants, but sometimes when I see them, all that stuff don't mean anything, and I don't hate them.

The listeners listened and smiled. The eccentric one, who was religious in an extraordinary way, and old, who hated three kinds of people of the world, Catholics, Irishmen, and Italians, scratched his beard and didn't make an argument. He hated Catholics because he had once been a Catholic; he hated Irishmen because Irishmen were cops and cops had hit him over the head with clubs several times and pushed him around and knocked him down and taken him to jail; and he hated Italians because Mussolini was an Italian and because an Italian in New York had cheated him thirty years ago.

Now he listened to the Slovak and didn't make an argument.

The young men, who were always present but never joined the meetings, stood among the old men and smoked cigarettes. One of them, who was in love with a waitress and wanted to get married, said to the small anarchist who was violently opposed to everything in the world, A lot of people that are married—both of them work.

The anarchist was usually high-strung, impatient, and sarcastic, but on this day he did not mock the young man or laugh out loud in the peculiar way he had that was neither natural nor artificial.

That's true, he said. And the young man was glad to have someone to talk to.

The anarchist was a man of forty-five or so. He had a well-shaped head, thick brown hair, and his teeth were good. He thought Communists were dopes. You God damn day-dreamers, he said to them one day. I know all about your Karl Marx. What was he? He was a lousy Jew who was scared to death by the world. (The anarchist himself was a Jew, but his love of Jews was so great that it had turned to hate and mockery.) You think you've got a chance, he said, but you've got no more chance than anybody else. Nobody's got a chance. Even after you have your lousy revolution you won't have a chance. What will you do? Do you think anything will be different?

Then he became very vulgar and the Slovak said, What's the use talking to you? You've got your mind made up.

On this day, though, the anarchist was very kindly and allowed the young man who was in love to tell his story.

I only had a quarter, the young man said, so I walked into that cheap hamburger joint—Pete's on Mason Street, right around the corner from the Day and Night Bank—because I figured I could get a lot for my money. It was around midnight and I hadn't had anything to eat since breakfast. That was last week, Friday. I ain't been working lately and on top of everything else I got kicked out of my room. The landlady kept my stuff because I owed her two dollars. I got the quarter from a rummy-player on Third Street who'd been lucky. Well, my insides were groaning and I felt sick, but all I wanted was a big sandwich and a cup of coffee. It's funny the way things go. I didn't have any place to sleep either, and when I sat down on the stool at the counter and she came up to take my order I didn't even look at her. She put a glass of water down and I said, A hamburger with onions and everything else and a cup of coffee. The Greek started to make the hamburger and she brought the coffee. I took two sips and looked up. I had been looking down at the spoon and fork and knife. She was standing to one side looking at me and when I looked up she smiled, only it was different. It looked like she had known me all her life and I had known her all my life and we hadn't seen one another for maybe ten or fifteen years. I guess I fell in love. We started talking and I didn't try to make her or anything because I was so hungry and tired I guess, and maybe that's why she liked me. Any other time I guess I would have tried to make her and just have a little fun. She took me up to her room that night and I been staying there ever since, five nights now.

Here the young man began to be confused. The anarchist was very kind, however, and the young man explained.

I haven't touched her or anything, but I really love her and she really loves me. I kissed her last night because she looked so tired and beautiful, and she cried. She's a girl from Oklahoma. I guess she's had a few men, but it's different now. It's different with me too. I used to do office work, but I ain't got a job any more. I been going around to the agencies, but it don't look very good. If I could get a job we could get married and move into a small comfortable apartment.

A lot of people that are married—both of them work, he said. But I ain't got a job. When one of them works, he said, it's usually the man. I don't know what to do.

That's true, the anarchist said. Maybe you'll get a job tomorrow.

Where? the young man said. I wish I knew where. Everything's different with me now. My clothes are all worn out. I saw some swell shirts in the window of a store on Market Street for sixty-five cents; I saw a blue-serge suit for twelve fifty; and I know where I can get a good pair of shoes for three dollars. I'd like to throw away these old clothes and begin all over again. I'd like to marry her and get rid of everything old and move into a small comfortable apartment.

The anarchist was very sympathetic. He didn't care about the young man himself, who was miserable-looking and worried and undernourished and yet rather handsome because of this new thing in his life, this love of the waitress. He was delighted with the abstract purity and holiness of the event itself, in the crazy world, the boy starving and going into the dump for a hamburger and running headlong into love.

Maybe you'll get a job tomorrow, the anarchist said. Why don't you try a hotel?

The young man didn't quite understand.

No, he said, I don't think we'd care to live in a hotel. What we'd like to get is a small comfortable apartment with a bathroom and a little kitchen. We'd like to have a neat little place with some good chairs and a table and a bathroom and a little kitchen. I don't like these rooms that ain't got no bath in them, and you've got to go down the hall to take a bath and nine times out of ten there ain't no hot water. I'd like to fill a tub with warm water and sit in it a long time and then clean off all the dirt and get out and put on new clothes.

I don't mean to live in, the anarchist said. I mean to get a job at. I was thinking of these fine hotels that I'm accustomed to visiting the lobbies of.

Oh, the young man said. You mean to go to the hotels and ask for work?

Sure, the anarchist said. If you could get a job they'd give you a regular weekly salary and on top of that you'd make a little on tips.

I ain't had no experience being a bell-boy, the young man said.

That don't make no difference, the anarchist said.

Some of his old impatience began to return to him, and he believed nothing in the world should stop this boy from getting a job in a hotel and earning a regular weekly salary and making a little more on tips and marrying the waitress and moving into a small comfortable apartment with a bath and filling the tub with warm water and cleaning off all the dirt and getting out and putting on new clothes, the sixty-five-cent shirts and the twelve fifty blue-serge suit.

That don't make a God damn bit of difference, the anarchist said. What does a bell-boy have to know? If they ask you have you had any experience, tell them sure, you were bell-boy at the La Salle Hotel in Chicago five years.

The La Salle Hotel in Chicago? the young man said.

Sure, the anarchist shouted. Why the hell not?

Maybe they'll be able to tell I ain't had no experience being a bell-boy, the young man said. Suppose they find out I ain't never been in Chicago?

Listen, the anarchist said. What if they do find out you ain't never been in Chicago? Do you think the world will end? (The anarchist himself was beginning to think the world would end if the young man didn't go out and get a job and move into an apartment with the girl.) Do you have to tell the truth, he said, when it doesn't make any difference one way or another if you've had any experience as a bell-boy or not or if you've ever been in Chicago or not, except that they *won't* give you a job if you *do* tell the truth and *might* if you don't?

The young man was a little bewildered and couldn't speak. The anarchist was so angry with the world and so delighted about this remarkable love affair that he himself didn't know what to say, or how to put what he meant.

He became a little unreasonable.

How the hell do you *know* you've never been in Chicago? he shouted.

The Slovak heard him shouting and stopped talking to listen. The eccentric one, the man of God, whose God was unlike anybody else's, moved closer to the anarchist and the young man, and little by little all the men gathered around the two.

What? said the young man.

He was beginning to wake up, and at the same time he was beginning to be embarrassed. He had been telling secrets, and now everybody was near him, near the secret, and everybody was listening and wanting to know what it was all about; why, on such a day as this, when everybody was glad and without ill will, and quiet, the anarchist was shouting.

How the hell do you know it? the anarchist shouted. Catch on? he said. You were *born* in Chicago. You lived there all your life until three months ago. Your father was born in Chicago. Your mother was born in Chicago. Your father worked in the La Salle Hotel in Chicago. Your mother worked in the La Salle Hotel in Chicago. *You* worked in the La Salle Hotel in Chicago.

The listeners didn't understand. They looked around at one another, smiling and asking what it was all about, and then they looked again at the anarchist who was suddenly so different and yet so much the same, and then they looked at the young man. It was all very confusing. But they knew it would be dangerous to interrupt the anarchist and ask a question or say something witty. They listened religiously.

There are a lot of good hotels in this town, the anarchist said. Begin at the beginning and go right on down the line and don't stop until they give you a job. Get up in the morning and shave cleanly and go down and talk to them and don't be afraid. Them hotels are full of people that got plenty of money and not one of them in the whole city has got better use for a little lousy money than you have. Not a lousy one of them, he shouted. What the hell makes you think you ain't never been in Chicago? Start with the St. Francis Hotel on Powell Street. Then the Palace on Market Street. Then the Mark Hopkins. Then the Clift. Then the Fairmont. What the hell do you mean you ain't been in Chicago? What the hell kind of talk do you call that?

Now the young man was completely awake, as the anarchist was awake. He seemed to understand what the anarchist was trying to tell him and he was ashamed because the men were near him and could feel, even though they didn't *know* what it was all about, what it was all about.

The anarchist took the young man by the arm. His grip was very strong and the young man felt as if the man might be an elder brother or a father.

You understand what I'm telling you, don't you? he said.

Yes, the young man said.

He moved to go.

Thanks, he said.

He hurried down the street, and the anarchist stamped into the Public Library.

The men were very silent. Then one of them said, What the hell was he shouting about anyway? What the hell was all that stuff about the La Salle Hotel in Chicago? What *about* the La Salle Hotel in Chicago?

Ah Life, Ah Death, Ah Music, Ah France, Ah Everything

✿ ✿ ✿

STUDENTS all over America are deeply indebted to the postage stamp on the envelope from Chicago: how I, uneducated, in six easy lessons learned to play the piano and speak fluent French, and I, a Greek, learned, in less than two weeks, to write poetry: O Texas, O Alamo, O People, O God, and I, shunned by society girls on every side, rose, in less than five years, to assistant bookkeeper of Mifflan, Mofflan, Incorporated, and won the friendship, not to say respect and admiration, of numerous debutantes, as well as several of their mothers.

Ah life, ah December, ah Alexander Woollcott, ah Victor Phonograph Records, ah citizens, comrades, patriots, traitors, ah Harvard, ah Yale, ah all the colleges I never did go to, ah all the courses in literature and medicine and mathematics and French and Latin I never did take, ah literature, ah medicine, ah mathematics, ah French, ah Latin, ah all the stuff I didn't learn.

Behind all the comedy in this world and behind all the laughter is a horse of another color, ah cattle in Wyoming, ah Texas, O compendium, O ether, O Columbia, O history and machinery.

And behind the horse which is behind all the comedy in this world, and the laughter, is the old saga, ah Iceland, ah snow and darkness, ah music. For this grief, Lord, let the game go on, ah disease, ah whiskey.

All over the world, ah world, ah city after city, ah street after street, ah face after face, ah mischief, ah sex, ah perfume at night, ah Greece, ah Athens, how I, a Greek, learned, in less time than the years of the earth, to carve poetry in stone: O birth control, O Zola, O Spain, O Christianity, ah music.

Ah France, ah Paris, ah religion, ah George Santayana.

The hero is a young department store clerk who is studying engineering by mail. The theme is lofty. Ah loftiness. It is the story of a man's struggle against odds. Ah gambling. There is a false background of tenement houses and a fake smell of frying steaks. Ah meat, ah food. The style is simple, fake, colorful, false, vigorous, spurious, ah style, ah simplicity, O falsity, O color, ah vigor, ah mathematics.

There are a number of love scenes. Ah love.

The characters are out of the telephone book, ah modern science, ah commercial law. They act and talk just like the people who occupy the flat upstairs, ah stairs. They love jazz and hamburgers, ah America.

The story is the story of every man, ah literature.

There is tea-drinking, and fancy talk.

Mr. Giles, Mrs. Gripe. Mrs. Gripe, Mr. Giles. Mr. Gripe, Mrs. Giles. Mrs. Giles, Mr. Gripe. Ah death, ah Chesterfields.

One of the characters is high-minded, warm-hearted, heavy-handed, and half-cracked. Ah Ethiopia, he says. Ah Italy. Ah war.

And he stares around the room at the tangible blessings of life, ah time and space, ah architecture.

The path is a good path. It travels straight across the bare and bleak landscape, through tenements, and back again to slums, ah freedom, ah liberty.

In many cases the young student will go so far as to deprive himself of food and clothing in order to continue his studies, ah fame, ah fortune. He will eat canned beans and read the seventh lesson of a correspondence course on how to speak impressively, and the day will come when he will speak. Ah oratory. It will be a gloomy day, but the young student will speak his line and be fired.

Ah grammar, the young student will be fired and he will take another correspondence course, ah art. He will study hard and try to be a success, ah Illinois and Ohio. He will break his neck trying to be a success, ah Michigan. He will wear out his brain trying to learn what he thinks he ought to learn, ah Louisiana. He will wind up in the gutter trying to be a great American, ah South Carolina.

And there will be a revolution, ah Moscow. There will be cheerless running, ah victory. After the revolution everything will be the same. Everything will be exactly the way it was before the revolution, only the young student will be dead, ah death, ah poetry. Every lousy thing in the world will be lousy the same way as before, ah lousy lousiness. Ah fraudulence, ah treachery. Every cockeyed thing in the whole universe will be the same except the young student who will be dead, ah sadness, ah misery, ah music.

Ah Iceland, ah snow and cold and fear and pain, ah God, why in Christ's name don't you just let it smash? Ah God, why don't you let them sleep again in the darkness and not want to know how to be polite and how to play the harmonica and how to speak in public and how to be a success? God Almighty, God, why don't you just let them sleep again?

The Genius

✧ ✧ ✧

UP at Izzy's one night a young genius in corduroy pants came up to me and said, I hear you're a writer. I've got a story that'll make a great movie, only I need somebody with experience to write it for me. I'd write it myself, only I've got to make a living working and when I get through working I'm too tired to write.

I was a little drunk, but I'm never too drunk and never too busy to listen to a fellow-artist, and I said, Go ahead, tell me the story. If it's good I'll write it and we'll get Metro-Goldwyn-Mayer to make a movie out of it. What happens?

If you've ever had a story printed in a national magazine and been around at all you've met all kinds of people with stories that will make great movies. The world is full of people with movie stories, all unwritten, but it seems the people who manufacture movies never meet these people, or if they do, never let them tell their stories, consequently the average movie manufactured is lousy, even in technicolor, even starring Clark Gable, John Barrymore, Norma Shearer, or anybody else. The people who manufacture movies just simply don't care to manufacture good movies.

Up at Izzy's as many as eighty-seven good movies are related in one night, but not one of them is ever filmed.

I told the boy to go ahead and tell me the story.

Shall I begin at the beginning? he said.

Not necessarily, I said. Begin anywhere. Begin at the end and work backward to the beginning. You might even sit down if you like.

Thanks, he said, I'd rather stand.

Take all the time you need, I said.

There ain't much to say, he said. The idea is this. Says, I'll do something. I won't be a clerk all my life. Ships out on a boat to Shanghai.

Who? I said.

The fellow, said the boy. Clark Gable.

Oh, I said. Clark Gable. Says he'll do something. Do what?

Coming up on deck he bumps into the girl.

The girl? I said.

Joan Crawford.

Ah, Joan, I said. What's it come to?

They fall in love.

So the boy does something?

Not right away. That's at the end.

I know, I said. Anything special?

He marries the girl.

How about the money? I said. Who's got the money?

She has. That's where the trouble comes in.

Oh, I said, the trouble.

Yeah, the boy ain't a gigolo, so he won't marry the girl when he finds out she's rich.

Why? I said.

He figures he can't marry a rich girl, even if he is in love with her, so they quarrel.

Just in fun, of course, I said. Nothing serious.

Plenty serious. The girl's got to marry somebody before the boat reaches Shanghai or she won't inherit the eighteen million dollars.

The how many million? I said.

Eighteen.

Do you think that's enough? I said. For all practical purposes?

It's a tidy sum.

A trifle, I said. How does it turn out?

Well, the man who is engaged to the girl is a middle-aged banker. He ain't very good-looking. She don't want to marry him. That's where she gets a chance to do some acting.

Boy, I said.

After the boy and the girl fight, the girl says she's going to marry the banker, just to make the boy jealous.

That's another spot for some fancy acting, I said.

Yeah, so the Captain makes plans for a ship wedding. This is where it gets exciting. One thing after another happens, in quick succession. Chinese pirates take over the ship, and a Chinaman decides to marry the girl himself, without the formality of a wedding of course. The banker doesn't care, because he's scared, but the boy hates the Chinaman. He's a young educated Chinaman and speaks better English than anybody else on board the ship.

So? I said.

The Chinaman gets the girl in her cabin and starts chasing her around.

That's bad, I said.

The Chinaman is chasing the girl around the room, when the boy breaks the door down. The Chinaman and the boy have a fight. The Chinaman gets the boy flat on his back and gets out his dagger and is about to stick it in the boy.

Where? I said.

Right in the heart. The girl hits the Chinaman over the head with a chair.

That's love for you, I said.

In the meantime, a cablegram is received by the ship, asking the Captain to put the banker in chains for grand larceny and bigamy.

Just two little misdemeanors? I said.

And possible murder. The picture ends with the boy kissing the girl.

Boy, what an ending, I said.

How is it? he said.

It's fine, I said.

Is it exciting enough?

It's breath-taking, I said, especially where the Chinaman chases her.

I thought you'd like it, he said. First I think you ought to make a book out of it, and then sell it to the movies.

By God, I said, I'd do that little thing, only I gave up writing day before yesterday.

What for? he said.

I got bored, I said. Same old stuff over and over again.

This is different, he said. Think of the Chinaman. East against West.

Even so, I said. I gave up writing day before yesterday. *You* write it.

Do you think they'll print the book? he said.

They'd be fools not to, I said.

What style should I use? he said.

Oh, I said, don't worry about style. Just put it down on paper the way it comes to you after work and you'll find it'll be full of style. There'll be enough left over for two more movies.

My grammar ain't so hot, he said.

Neither is mine, I said. You don't need to worry about that. That'll be part of your style, part of your originality. Unless I'm badly mistaken, you're a genius.

No, he said. I just get these ideas for books and movies, that's all. I've forgotten enough ideas for books and movies to make a dozen books and a dozen movies.

Write them down, I said. Don't let them get away. You're losing money every minute.

Got a pencil? he said.

I'm afraid not, I said. I gave up writing day before yesterday.

What the hell for? he said.

My stuff's no good for movies, I said. I sell a story for thirty or forty dollars every now and then. I don't get movie ideas. I thought I would after a while, but I didn't, so I gave it up.

That's tough, he said. I get movie ideas left and right.

I know it, I said. All you got to do is get them down on paper and I know you'll be famous and rich in no time.

I'll tell you another idea I got for a movie, he said.

Joe, I said.

Joe came over to the table.

Joe, I said, here's a dime. Go get me a pencil.

Joe went over to Izzy and Izzy looked around and found a pencil. A little tiny one. Joe brought the pencil over to me. I handed it to the boy.

Listen, George, I said, you got no time to lose. Here's a pencil, all sharpened and everything. You take this pencil and go home and write them ideas down on paper. Any old kind of paper. Lincoln wrote his famous speech on the back of an envelope.

He took the pencil, but didn't start to go.

I thought I'd take it easy tonight and start writing tomorrow, he said.

No, I said, that ain't right. You go right home and go to work while the ideas are still fresh in your mind.

All right, he said.

He put the pencil in his inside coat pocket, pulled his hat down over his eyes, and went down the stairs.

Joe, I said, bring me three beers.

The Fire

✧ ✧ ✧

IT was so cold in the world, beyond the warm room, and the air was so clear you could hear it and when the Santa Fe crossing bell rang it was like churches, Sunday and peace in the world, quiet, and then the whole house, like the soft laughter of his father Jesse, trembled with the heavy weight and movement of the passing train.

It seemed as if the only safety in the world was in the red and yellow and white flames of the fire in the stove, the color and the heat, the whole house trembling like a sad man laughing, the whole world cold and sad, and nothing in the world, only the flowers of the fire, blossoming a hundred times a minute, a whole world full of flowers, and outside, beyond the room, the whole world frozen and hushed, so still you could hear the hush.

They said to sit in the kitchen and keep the stove going so he would be warm until they got home in the evening, and not open the door of the stove, be sure not to open the door of the stove, especially Beth, always telling him what to do, and Jesse telling him to mind her because now *she* was his mother. His father asking him if he couldn't be nice to her and act like she *was* his mother.

Well, they couldn't fool him. The door of the stove was open, his mother was dead, they couldn't put anything like that over on him, she was dead. It was so quiet in the world you could hear it and the ringing of the Santa Fe crossing bell was like churches. He guessed he was old enough to know his mother was dead, he guessed he knew who saw them put the big box at the front of the church, and the way the house trembled while the train moved was the way Jesse laughed when it was all over and the house was empty, and little pieces of the fire, like petals of flowers, flew out of the stove to the floor and disappeared.

He knew. There was nothing in the world. It was empty and she was dead. Empty as a pitch black night, and nothing to have but fire, no light and no warmth and no color and no love. They asked him to keep the door of the stove closed. What did he care about any of that stuff? He was cold, he was almost freezing. At the same time he seemed to be burning. It was the first time in his life he felt cold and hot at the same time. It was the first time in his life he noticed things like the crossing bell being like churches, the trembling house being like Jesse laughing, the fire being like flowers, and everything being nothing because the house was empty.

Nothing in the whole world could make her come back and be alive and come up to the front door of the house and put the key in the lock and open the door and come in and be there with him and be his mother and talk to him again.

It was the first time in his life he knew about everything. They couldn't fool him. Beth was all right. She was swell. She even brought him candy and toys. That was all right. He liked candy sometimes. He liked the little colored whistles and marbles and different kinds of toys that did all sorts of things and he liked Beth too, but he knew all about it. There was a bag of candy on the table in the parlor. He didn't want any of it. The toys were in the parlor. He didn't want to blow any of the whistles or shoot the marbles or wind up the toy machines and watch them work. He didn't want anything. There *wasn't* anything. There wasn't one little bit of anything. All he wanted was to be near the fire, as close to it as he could be, just be there, just see the colors and be very near. What did he want with toys? What good were toys? The whistles sounded sadder than crying and the way the machines worked almost made him die of grief.

In the fire, though, there was laughter, and not only that, there was singing and every kind of music he had ever heard. There was no end of laughter and singing in the fire, only the laughter was not like the times at school when he used to laugh at the funny way the kids talked and acted, and the singing was sadder than the singing at church. Everything was not the way it used to be. He used to think a whistle was something and he used to blow a whistle until it wouldn't make a noise any more. He didn't want anything. Beth was in town working in the department store, and Jesse was at the factory. Jesse worked with big machines and made all kinds of stuff out of iron.

He guessed Jesse was making nothing. What could Jesse make? What could anybody make? Jesse could make a part of a machine, but even after he had made it, what good was it? What good was the whole machine, after it was put together? Maybe it would be an automobile, maybe a Ford. Who wanted a Ford? Who cared about getting into an automobile and going down the highway? Where could you go? What place was there in the world to go to?

Bright petals of yellow and red flew from the blossoming flower to the floor and disappeared, and he knew. Nothing in the whole world could happen to make her be there again. Jesse figured he was doing stuff at the factory, but he wasn't doing anything. There wasn't anything to do. Could Jesse do something that would make her be in the house again where she belonged? Could anybody do anything in the world that would make something like that happen? Not one man in the whole world could do anything like that. Jesse could go ahead and make every crazy kind of piece of machinery he felt like making and after they had put all the pieces together nothing would happen, except maybe smoke would come out from some pipe and some wheels would turn and the big machine would do something that nobody cared about, maybe move, but nobody in the whole world could make anything that would do something everybody in the world would like to see done. Jesse could work hard and save money and fill the house with new furniture, like the new tables and chairs in the parlor, but the house would always be empty. He could try to live in the house with Beth, but he knew it couldn't be, it could never turn out that way, and he knew this from the quiet way Jesse laughed when Beth wasn't around. Jesse just didn't know what to do. That's why he brought Beth to the house. He just didn't know what *else* to do. Before Beth came to the house Jesse used to sit in the parlor and do nothing and say nothing. Jesse figured maybe there was something he could do. He knew, though. He knew exactly how it was. He didn't like to know, it scared him, but he knew.

The fire. That was all. The laughter. The singing. The blossoming of the flower. The color and the sadness, and the bright petals falling to the floor and ending. The ending, especially. Even though one petal followed another endlessly. The house was no good any more. It was no place she would come to again. The world was no good. She was not there. It was no use getting well again and going back to school and laughing at the kids. He didn't want that again. He didn't want to learn to read and write and answer the questions. They were fooling everybody. The questions were nothing. They asked you about apples and eggs. That was nothing. They asked you about a word. They never asked you a real question, so how could you give them a real answer? They didn't even know the real question, how could anybody tell them the answer? They couldn't fool him. None of them, not Miss Purvis, not Jesse, not Beth, not any one of them.

He knew. The question was, Can you do it? Any of you? Here or in any other place of the world? Can you do it by doing something in the world or by praying or by doing anything anybody alive can do? He knew the answer too. He knew it was no. So what were they doing? What good did it do them? What good was anything in the world when you couldn't do it? When you could never be able to do it? What good did it do you to do a million other crazy things that had nothing to do with it? What was the sense in answering a million other questions and never even *asking* the real question?

They told him to sit still and keep warm and not to open the door of the stove. They told him to be a good boy and wait for them to come home in the evening. They told him he was ill but all he needed to do was sit by the stove and keep warm.

He knew what *he* could do. It was right too. It was the only thing to do. It was a good thing, and he knew he would do it. He knew there would never again be any house for them to come to. And he wished a strong wind would carry the color and heat and fury of the fire to every house in the world and destroy every house and make them all know nothing in the world they could do could ever do it.

When the day darkened and he knew they would be coming soon, he took the fire on burning paper into the parlor and let it eat into the new table. The fire crept slowly up the leg of the table, and then he took the fire into each of the other rooms and planted it in the things of the house, so the whole house would burn, and when they found him across the street staring at the burning house, crying, they thought he was crying because the house was burning, they did not know he knew.

The Filipino and the Drunkard

✿ ✿ ✿

THIS loud-mouthed guy in the brown camel-hair coat was not really mean, he was drunk. He took a sudden dislike to the small well-dressed Filipino and began to order him around the waiting room, telling him to get back, not to crowd up among the white people. They were waiting to get on the boat and cross the bay to Oakland. If he hadn't been drunk no one would have bothered to notice him at all, but as it was, he was making a commotion in the waiting room, and while everyone seemed to be in sympathy with the Filipino, no one seemed to want to bother about coming to the boy's rescue, and the poor Filipino was becoming very frightened.

He stood among the people, and this drunkard kept pushing up against him and saying, I told you to get back. Now get back. Go away back. I fought twenty-four months in France. I'm a real American. I don't want you standing up here among white people.

The boy kept squeezing nimbly and politely out of the drunkard's way, hurrying through the crowd, not saying anything and trying his best to be as decent as possible. He kept dodging in and out, with the drunkard stumbling after him, and as time went on the drunkard's dislike grew and he began to swear at the boy. He kept saying, You fellows are the best-dressed men in San Francisco, and you make your money washing dishes. You've got no right to wear such fine clothes.

He swore a lot, and it got so bad that a lot of ladies had to imagine they were deaf and weren't hearing any of the things he was saying.

When the big door opened, the young Filipino moved swiftly among the people, fleeing from the drunkard, reaching the boat before anyone else. He ran to a corner, sat down for a moment, then got up and began looking for a more hidden place. At the other end of the boat was the drunkard. He could hear the man swearing. He looked about for a place to hide, and rushed into the lavatory. He went into one of the open compartments and bolted the door.

The drunkard entered the lavatory and began asking others in the room if they had seen the boy. He was a real American, he said. He had been wounded twice in the War.

In the lavatory he swore more freely, using words he could never use where women were present. He began to stoop and look beyond the shut doors of the various compartments. I beg your pardon, he said to those he was not seeking, and when he came to the compartment where the boy was standing, he began swearing and demanding that the boy come out.

You can't get away from me, he said. You got no right to use a place white men use. Come out or I'll break the door.

Go away, the boy said.

The drunkard began to pound on the door.

You got to come out sometime, he said. I'll wait here till you do.

Go away, said the boy. I've done nothing to you.

He wondered why none of the men in the lavatory had the decency to to calm the drunkard and take him away, and then he realized there were no other men in the lavatory.

Go away, he said.

The drunkard answered with curses, pounding the door.

Behind the door, the boy's bitterness grew to rage. He began to tremble, not fearing the man but fearing the rage growing in himself. He brought the knife from his pocket and drew open the sharp blade, holding the knife in his fist so tightly that the nails of his fingers cut into the flesh of his palm.

Go away, he said. I have a knife. I do not want any trouble.

The drunkard said he was an American. Twenty-four months in France. Wounded twice. Once in the leg, and once in the thigh. He would not go away. He was afraid of no dirty little yellow-belly Filipino with a knife. Let the Filipino come out, he was an American.

I will kill you, said the boy. I do not want to kill any man. You are drunk. Go away.

Please do not make any trouble, he said earnestly.

He could hear the motor of the boat pounding. It was like his rage pounding. It was a feeling of having been humiliated, chased about and made to hide, and now it was a wish to be free, even if he had to kill. He threw the door open and tried to rush beyond the man, the knife tight in his fist, but the drunkard caught him by the sleeve and drew him back. The sleeve of the boy's coat ripped, and the boy turned and thrust the knife into the side of the drunkard, feeling it scrape against rib-bone. The drunkard shouted and screamed at once, then caught the boy at the throat, and the boy began to thrust the knife into the side of the man many times, as a boxer jabs in the clinches.

When the drunkard could no longer hold him and had fallen to the floor, the boy rushed from the room, the knife still in his hand, blood dripping from the blade, his hat gone, his hair mussed, and the sleeve of his coat badly torn.

Everyone knew what he had done, yet no one moved.

The boy ran to the front of the boat, seeking some place to go, then ran back to a corner, no one daring to speak to him, and everyone aware of his crime.

There was no place to go, and before the officers of the boat arrived he stopped suddenly and began to shout at the people.

I did not want to hurt him, he said. Why didn't you stop him? Is it right to chase a man like a rat? You knew he was drunk. I did not want to hurt him, but he would not let me go. He tore my coat and tried to choke me. I told him I would kill him if he would not go away. It is not my fault. I must go to Oakland to see my brother. He is sick. Do you think I am looking for trouble when my brother is sick? Why didn't you stop him?

Jim Pemberton and His Boy Trigger

✿ ✿ ✿

Pa came into Willy's Lunch Wagon on Peach Street where I was sitting at the counter talking to Ella the new waitress from Texas and eating a hamburger and drinking a cup of coffee. He threw his hat on the pinball machine and took off his coat and folded it and put it by his hat and he said, Trig, I'm going to knock your head off. You told Mrs. Sheridan I wasn't in the army.

I nearly choked on hamburger and coffee and Ella told me to hold up my left arm because that would stop me from coughing, and Pa said, Trigger, get up off of that stool.

Let me finish this hamburger anyway, Pa, I said.

All right, Pa said. You told Mrs. Sheridan I never killed anybody in my life and now she don't want to see me any more.

Well, let me finish this hamburger, Pa, I said. You never killed anybody and you know it.

How do you know? Pa said. Are you sure?

I ain't exactly sure, I said, but gosh, Pa, what would you go to work and kill anybody for?

Never mind that, Pa said. I ain't got time to explain about what for. Go ahead now and swallow that last bite of hamburger and stand up. I'm going to knock your head off.

He turned to Ella.

Hello Ella, he said politely. Fix me up a sirloin steak. Kind of rare.

Yes, Mr. Pemberton, Ella said. Are you going to fight Trigger again?

He can't go around telling lies about me, Pa said.

It ain't no lie, Pa, I said. Who'd you ever kill? Name one man.

One hell, Pa said. I could name fourteen men on the tips of my fingers.

You ain't got fourteen fingers, Pa, I said. You ain't even got ten. You've got eight. You lost them last two fingers of your left hand in Perry's Lumber Mill.

I lost them fingers in the War, Pa said. For my country.

Pa, I said, you know you never did go over to Europe. It's your imagination getting the best of you.

I'll show you what's getting the best of me, Pa said. Mrs. Sheridan claims I ain't no hero.

You ain't, Pa, I said.

All right, stand up then, Pa said. If that's the way you feel about it, I'm going to knock your head off.

You know I can whip you, Pa, I said. Don't make me do it again.

Again? Pa said. When did you ever whip me?

Why Mr. Pemberton, Ella said, Trigger whipped you yesterday right here in front of Willy's.

Fix me a side order of fried onions, Pa said. How've you been, Ella? Has my son been passing insolent remarks to you? I won't stand for it, you know. I'll knock his head off.

Why Mr. Pemberton, Ella said, Trigger's been as nice as nice can be. Trigger is the best-behaved and nicest-looking boy in Kingsburg.

I won't stand for anybody passing insolent remarks to an innocent girl like you, Ella, Pa said. If my son Trigger asks you out to the country, you just let me know and I'll knock his head off.

Why I'd love to go to the country with Trigger, Ella said.

Don't you do it, Pa said. Trigger would have you down in the tall grass in two minutes.

He wouldn't either, Ella said.

He would too, Pa said. Wouldn't you, son?

I don't know, I said.

I looked at Ella and figured maybe Pa was right for once in his life. For once in his life Pa wasn't letting his wild imagination run away with him.

It looked like maybe Pa was going to forget to fight about Mrs. Sheridan and that made me feel pretty good. I didn't want to be spoiling the best years of Pa's life all the time pushing him around in what he thought were fighting contests.

Ella, Pa said, whatever you do, don't let Trigger carry you away with his fine talk and nice manners.

I been in town since day before yesterday, Ella said, and I ain't seen anybody I like half as much as I like Trigger.

She turned the steak over.

How's that look, Mr. Pemberton? she said.

Perfect, Pa said.

He sat down on the stool beside me.

Trigger, he said, would you mind waiting outside till I've had my supper? I can't put up any kind of a fight on an empty stomach.

I've got to go down to The Coliseum, Pa, I said.

You can wait five minutes, Pa said.

I've got an appointment to play Harry Wilke a little snooker, I said. What's on your mind, Pa?

I want you to drop over to Mrs. Sheridan's, Pa said, and tell her I killed seventeen Germans in the War. She's sitting on the front porch. I can't stand this kind of excellent weather without the affection and admiration of a handsome woman.

Gosh, Pa, I said, Mrs. Sheridan won't believe me.

Yes, she will, Pa said. She'll believe any crazy thing you say. Seventeen, now. Don't forget.

But you didn't really do it, did you, Pa? I said.

What difference does *that* make? Pa said.

Ella put the steak on a plate and set the plate on the counter between a tablespoon and a knife and fork. Pa cut off a big piece of steak. It was bloody red. He put it in his mouth and smiled at Ella.

You're a good innocent girl, Ella, he said. You'll be wanting to get married one of these days, so don't be going out to the country with Trigger.

Why I'd love to, Mr. Pemberton, Ella said.

All right then, Pa said. Go ahead and get yourself knocked up if you've got your heart set on it.

Pa turned to me.

Will you do that little thing for me, Trigger? he said.

Gosh, I felt proud of Pa.

Sure Pa, I said. I'll tell Mrs. Sheridan you killed a whole troop of machine-gunners.

You go right on over to Mrs. Sheridan's, Pa said. You'll find her on the front porch, in the rocking chair. Tell her I'll be over just as soon as I've had my supper.

Sure Pa, I said.

Good-bye, Trigger, Ella said.

Good-bye, Ella, I said.

I went out to the curb and got on my Harley-Davidson and rode six blocks to Mrs. Sheridan's Rooming House on Elm Avenue.

Mrs. Sheridan was sitting on the front porch just like Pa said, only Ralph Aten was there with her. Mrs. Sheridan was sucking strawberry soda pop through a straw out of a bottle.

I leaned my motorcycle against the curb and walked up to the porch. Mrs. Sheridan looked comfortable and pretty, but Ralph Aten looked sore, especially about me. I never did like his daughter Effie, though. He just thought I did. He tried to make me marry her, but I asked him to prove it was me and not Gabe Fisher. He claimed it didn't look like Gabe Fisher, and I claimed it didn't look like me either. He got sore and said he would take the case to the Supreme Court, but he never did.

Good evening, Mrs. Sheridan, I said.

Good evening, Trigger, Mrs. Sheridan said. Come on up and sit down.

Good evening, Mr. Aten, I said, and Ralph Aten said, Son, what brings you here at this hour of the evening?

Come on up onto the porch and sit down, Mrs. Sheridan said. Me and Ralph want to talk to you.

I went up onto the porch and sat on the railing, facing Mrs. Sheridan and Mr. Aten.

Here I am, Mrs. Sheridan, I said. What do you want to talk to me about?

Well, said Mrs. Sheridan, about your son Homer out of Effie, Ralph's youngest daughter.

Homer ain't my son, I said.

You're wrong there, Ralph Aten said. Trigger, you're dead wrong in that opinion. Homer is the spitting image of you, and your father, and your grandfather before him. Homer is a real Pemberton.

Mr. Aten, I said, I'm afraid you're letting your imagination get the best of you.

No, I ain't, Trigger, Mr. Aten said. Homer is your son. He's talking now, and he even talks like you.

Trigger, Mrs. Sheridan said, I think you ought to show a little more interest in your children.

Why Mrs. Sheridan, I said, how can you say a thing like that? What children? I ain't got no wife.

Wife or no wife, Mrs. Sheridan said, you've got over four children in these parts. You get around so easily on that motorcycle, Trigger. I don't suppose you realize how much time that machine saves you in reaching innocent girls and getting away from them in a hurry.

I use this machine to deliver the San Francisco papers to farmers who live in these parts, I said. That's what this motorcycle is for.

I ain't saying it ain't primarily for delivering papers, Trigger, Mrs. Sheridan said, but you only deliver papers an hour or so early in the morning. Your children are the nicest-looking kids in Kings County, and I think it is very unkind of you to pay no attention to them.

Trigger, Mr. Aten said, why don't you marry my daughter Effie and settle down and make a name for yourself?

What kind of a name do you mean, Mr. Aten? I said.

A great name, Mr. Aten said. Why don't you settle down and be somebody?

Yes indeed, Trigger, Mrs. Sheridan said, I think with a little effort on your part you could develop into quite a personage.

I figured it was about time for me to begin working on Mrs. Sheridan, but I couldn't do it in front of a man like Mr. Aten, a man Pa never did like, so I figured I'd get him out of the way in a hurry.

Mr. Aten, I said, before I forget I want you to know I came here to tell you Charley Hagen wants to see you down at The Coliseum about a private matter. He said to hurry right down.

Mr. Aten jumped three feet out of his chair.

You mean Charley Hagen the banker, son? he said. You mean the richest man in Kings County, Trigger?

Yes sir, I said. Mr. Hagen claims he has something important to talk over with you.

Well, who would have guessed it? Mr. Aten said. Excuse me, Mrs. Sheridan?

Of course, Mrs. Sheridan said.

Mr. Aten scrambled down the steps of the porch, jumped across the front yard, and began running down Elm Avenue.

Mrs. Sheridan, I said, you may not believe it, but my Pa destroyed a whole regiment of crack German machine-gunners in the war. He crept up on them while they were asleep. That's how he did it.

Mrs. Sheridan put down the bottle of soda pop and straightened out her large front, wiggling with amazement.

Trigger, she said, what in hell are you talking about?

My Pa, I said. I'm talking about Jim Pemberton, The Lone Wolf of Kings County, The Terror of Thieves and Pickpockets, The Protector of Children and Innocent Girls, that's who.

What did you say your crazy Pa did in the War, Trigger? Mrs. Sheridan said.

I said he killed seventeen crack German machine-gunners single-handed, that's what.

I don't believe it, Mrs. Sheridan said.

All I can say is, I think you're letting your imagination get the best of you, Mrs. Sheridan, I said. It's the truth. Pa had papers to prove it, but he lost them. He had seven medals, but he had to sell them. Pa is a hero, Mrs. Sheridan.

Trigger, Mrs. Sheridan said, who sent you here with that crazy story? Yesterday you told me your Pa never went to Europe at all. Yesterday you told me your Pa wasn't even in the army.

Mrs. Sheridan, I said, I was misinformed at the time. I was grossly misinformed.

Well, how did your Pa ever do such a brave thing? Mrs. Sheridan said. How in hell did he ever do it?

He crept up on them, I said. He killed eleven of them while they were asleep, hitting them over the head with the butt of his rifle. Then the other six woke up and started making trouble for Pa, but he turned one of their own machine-guns on them and mowed them down. He got seven medals for doing it, and two days later the War ended.

Mrs. Sheridan rocked back and forth very beautifully.

Well, what do you know about that? she said. Trigger, here's fifteen cents. Go down to Meyer's and get me a package of Chesterfields. This calls for some heavy cigarette smoking.

I ran half a block to Meyer's and bought Mrs. Sheridan a package of cigarettes. When I got back Pa was sitting on the porch, telling Mrs. Sheridan how he happened to do it. Pa was telling her in very tender and affectionate language.

Here, Trigger, Mrs. Sheridan said, give me them cigarettes.

I looked at Pa to see how he was making out while Mrs. Sheridan tore open the package of cigarettes, got one out and lighted it. Pa smiled and made a certain movement with his right hand that I knew meant everything was going along very nicely and many thanks. I made the movement back at Pa and Mrs. Sheridan inhaled deeply, looking exciting and lovely, so I knew my work was done.

Good night, Mrs. Sheridan, I said. It's been awful nice being in your company.

Not at all, Trigger, Mrs. Sheridan said. The pleasure's been mine.

Good night, Pa, I said.

Good night, Trigger, Pa said.

I went down to the curb and got on my bike. Before I started the motor I heard Pa start talking in a low warm affectionate tone of voice and I knew he was all set for the rest of the night at least.

The Insurance Salesman, the Peasant, the Rug Merchant, and the Potted Plant

✿ ✿ ✿

ARSHAG GOROBAKIAN was a small man who earned his living as a salesman for the New York Life Insurance Company. He worked exclusively among his own people, the Armenians. In twenty years, he often told a new client, I have sold three hundred policies, and so far two hundred of my clients have died. He did not utter this remark with sorrow and it was not intended to be a commentary on the sadness of life. On the contrary, Gorobakian's smile indicated that what he meant by two hundred of them dying was simply that these were men who had cheated death of its awful victory, and at the same time made a monkey out of the New York Life Insurance Company. All shrewd men, he often told a new client. Men like yourself, in all things practical and brilliant. They said to themselves, Yes, we shall die, there is no way out of that, let us face the facts.

Here the insurance salesman would bring the printed charts and statistics out of his inside coat pocket and say, Here are the facts. You are forty-seven years of age, and by the grace of God in good health. According to the facts you will be dead in five years.

He would smile gently, sharing with the new client the thrill of dying in five years and earning thereby an enormous sum of money. In five years, he would say, you will have paid my company three hundred and eighty-seven dollars, and on dying you will have earned twenty thousand dollars, or a net profit of nineteen thousand six hundred and thirteen dollars.

That, he would say, is a fair profit on any investment.

Once, however, he talked to a peasant in Kingsburg who didn't believe he would be dead in five years.

Come back in seventeen or eighteen years, the peasant said.

But you are sixty-seven years old now, the insurance salesman said.

I know, the peasant said. But I shall not be swindled in an affair like this. I shall be alive twenty years from now. I have planted three hundred new olive trees and I know I shall not be dead until they are full grown. Not to mention the mulberry trees, and the pomegranate trees, and the walnut and almond trees.

No, the peasant said, the time is not ripe for a bargain of this sort. I know I shall be alive twenty years from now. I can feel it in my bones. Shall I say something?

Yes, the insurance salesman said.

I shall live *thirty* years longer, not twenty. You will admit I should be cheated in a deal of this sort.

The insurance salesman was small, courteous, quiet-spoken, and never aggressive.

I can see, he said, that you are a man of giant strength—

Giant strength? the peasant roared. Shall I say something?

The insurance salesman nodded.

What you say is the truth, he said. I am a man of giant strength. What death? Why should I die? For what reason, countryman? I am in no hurry. Money? Yes. It is good. But I am not going to die.

The insurance salesman smoked his cigar calmly, although inwardly he was in a state of great agitation, like a routed cavalry officer trying desperately to round up his men and organize another offensive.

Death to you? he said to the peasant. God forbid. In all my life I have never wished another man's death. Life is what we enjoy. The taste of the watermelon in the summer is the thing we cherish.

May I say something? the peasant interrupted.

Again the insurance salesman nodded.

What you say is true, he said. The thing we cherish is the taste of the watermelon in the summertime. And bread and cheese and grapes in the cool of evening, under the trees. Please go on.

I do not wish any man's departure from this warm scene of life, the insurance salesman said. We must face the facts, however.

He shook the documents in his hand.

Our world is a crazy world, he said. You are a strong man. You enjoy the taste of the watermelon. You are walking in the city. An automobile strikes you and where are you? You are dead.

The peasant frowned.

Ah, yes, he said. The automobile.

In the event that you are killed accidentally, which God forbid, the insurance salesman said, you will be rewarded doubly.

The confounded automobiles, the peasant said. I shall be very careful in the streets.

We are all careful, the insurance salesman said, but what good does it do us? More people are killed every year in automobile accidents than in one year of a great war.

May I say something? the peasant said.

Say it, the insurance salesman said.

I have half a mind to be protected, the peasant said. I have half a mind to take out an insurance policy.

That is a wise plan, the insurance salesman said.

The peasant purchased a policy and began making payments. Two years later he called the insurance salesman to his house and reprimanded him severely, although politely. He complained that although he had spent several hundred dollars, he had not so much as come anywhere near being killed, which he considered very odd.

I do not want the policy any longer, he said.

The insurance salesman told the ironic story of another man who gave up his policy after two years, and three weeks later was bored to death by an angry bull. But the peasant was not impressed with the story.

May I say something? he said. There is no bull in the world strong enough to gore me. I would break his neck. No, thank you, I do not want to be insured. I have made up my mind not to die, even for a profit. I have had a hundred chances of walking in front of an automobile, but always I have stepped back cautiously and allowed it to go by.

That was fourteen years ago, and the peasant, a man named Hakimian, is still alive.

The insurance salesman, however, preferred people more enlightened than peasants. He himself was a graduate of college. His preference was for men with whom he could talk for hours about other things, and then little by little move in with the insurance speech. He would often drive two hundred miles to San Francisco to talk with a dentist who had graduated from college.

Once he decided to drive his Buick across the country to Boston. It was a journey of ten days. Along the way there would be much to see, and in Boston he would visit his sister and her husband and their eleven children. He drove to Boston, visited his sister and her family, and met a rug merchant who was a college graduate. Three times in ten days he called at this man's home and carried on pleasant conversations. The man's name was Haroutunian and he was extremely fond of conversation. The insurance salesman found him brilliant on all subjects. But when the subject of life insurance was introduced he discovered that his friend was, bluntly, in no mood for it. At least, not for the present.

The time came for the insurance salesman to return to California. Before departing he was paid a visit by the rug merchant, Haroutunian, who was carrying a small potted plant.

My friend, the rug merchant said, I have a brother in Bakersfield which is near where you live. I have not seen him in twenty years. Will you do me a favor?

Of course, the insurance salesman said.

Carry this plant to my brother with my greetings, the rug merchant said.

Gladly, the insurance salesman said. What plant is this?

I do not know, the rug merchant said, but the leaf has a wonderful odor. Smell it.

The insurance salesman smelled the plant and was disappointed in the smell of the leaf.

It is truly a heavenly smell, he said.

The rug merchant gave the insurance salesman the name and address of his brother, and then said:

One more thing. The agricultural department in each state demands that a plant being transported be examined for plant insects. There are none on this plant, but the law is the law. You will have to stop a minute at the agricultural department of each state. A formality.

Oh, the insurance salesman said.

His word had been given, however, so he put the plant into his car and made his departure from Boston.

He was a very law-abiding man and the plant caused him quite a little trouble. Very often even after he had found the agricultural department of each state, the inspector was out of town and wouldn't be back for several days.

The result of the whole thing was that the insurance salesman got home in twenty-one days instead of ten. He drove a hundred miles to Bakersfield and found the rug merchant's brother.

The plant was safe and was now growing small red blossoms that gave off an odor which to the insurance salesman was extremely unpleasant.

Three thousand six hundred and seventy-eight miles I have carried this wonderful plant, the insurance salesman said, from the home of your brother in Boston to your home in Bakersfield. Your brother sends greetings.

The rug merchant's brother liked the plant even less than the insurance salesman did.

I do not want the plant, he said.

The insurance salesman was a man who was hardly ever amazed by anything. He accepted the brother's indifference and took the plant home with him.

He planted it in the finest soil in his back-yard, bought fertilizer for it, watered it, and took very good care of it.

It is not the plant, he told a neighbor. It nauseates me. But some day I shall perhaps be going back to Boston to visit my sister and when I see the rug merchant again I know he shall ask about the plant and I shall be pleased to tell him that it is flourishing. I feel that I have as good a chance as any man to sell him an insurance policy some day.

The Year of Heaven

✿ ✿ ✿

THERE is a whole year of my life that's not included in the years I've been alive. It is a year that is back there in the days of the streets, and while the *real* year that year was like the one before, 1916, and the one after, 1918, another year took place at the same time and was more or less lost for ten or eleven years. Then I dreamed the movie and got it back.

It was a wonderful year, that separate year of 1917. It was the year of the movies. It was the year in which I left the world and went to heaven in the picture theaters. That was the only time I ever went to heaven and I went in rags, as it were, and by foot. I went with a dirty face, not a face glowing with holy light; and sometimes I went with a face wet with the rain of winter; with hands cold and dirty; sometimes even my shoes would be wet, all soft, and my coat too.

The movie was the one of the world, the one that never ended. It was the dream being dreamed, outside in the city, in the dirt and rain, and inside in the picture theater, in the darkness, with the pictures moving in front of you, the pipe organ saying how it was, and the dream unfolding in front of you until you got up and walked right into it and on into heaven, with Theda Bara and Mary Pickford, William Farnum and Two-Gun Hart, Fatty Arbuckle and Charlie Chaplin, and all the others who were in heaven in those days.

That year in heaven I forgot after the Armistice, and then one night while I was dreaming I dreamed the movie again and the whole year came back to me. It was a bright day in the dream and I was back in the streets selling papers and everybody was buying them, instead of not buying them, the way it had been in 1917. Everybody was buying them and I think I made a dollar and forty cents in no time.

I'm dreaming, I said in the dream. It wasn't a bright day: it was raining. They didn't buy any papers either. All it did was rain and the people hurried home. I went to George Koriakle's on Eye Street and traded a paper for four chunks of fudge. I ate the fudge and then went over to the Liberty Theater and gave Joe a paper and he let me in free. I went in just as Jimmy Valentine jumped up onto the chandelier. I'd seen the picture four times in the last four days and knew the story by heart. It didn't stop being heaven, though, because Jimmy Valentine, although once a safe-cracker, was at heart a man of great nobility, and when the girl got locked in the safe accidentally, Jimmy rubbed his fingers on stone until they bled and then when his fingers were sensitive that way he went to work and cracked that safe and saved the girl.

That year is the year I began to get over cowboy pictures. If they were being shown I'd see them through, of course, but I didn't like them. I liked comedies, but especially the ones with Snub Pollard in them, and a young zany named Al St. Joy. I liked love stories too. I liked the outdoor ones where the girl would be somebody wonderful and good like Mary Pickford and it seemed like the whole world was against a little kid like that with nothing but goodness in her heart, and then it would happen, the little girl's goodness would knock hell out of all the viciousness and she'd get the bad ones put in jail where they belonged. And all like that.

Before I got over cowboy stories, they were the best. The way to do it was with a gun. Draw quickly, fire accurately, duck and, if hurt, fall slowly, and go on firing. The worst it would ever be would be a flesh wound that would never keep you from getting on the horse and riding across the plains to the small house, leaping off the horse, stamping across the porch just in time for her to run out of the house into your arms, crying, O Danny, Danny. I didn't exactly see through that stuff. It was simply that I couldn't get a horse and even if I could buy a gun, I wouldn't know who to use it on, might not be able to shoot accurately, might be slow on the draw, might get shot through the head instead of through the flesh of my left leg, above the knee, and might accidentally shoot somebody who wasn't guilty.

The streets in our city were pretty much paved and nobody seemed to be arriving on horseback anyway, and I never saw anybody carrying a gun, except the cops, who were being paid to do it. And I never saw a cop draw a gun and do anything about anything. I saw a guitar-player of a marimba band draw a pistol in front of the Sequoia Hotel and wave it at the five other members of the band and a white woman, but he didn't fire, and I didn't know what it was all about. One of the other boys coaxed him into putting the gun back into his pocket and they all went into the lobby of the hotel as if nothing had happened.

So it didn't seem as if a gun would be any good. The only thing that seemed to be any good at all was wit, daring and forthrightness. But most important of all was virtue. If you had all the wit in the world, and a lot of daring and plenty of forthrightness, but no virtue, you were still on the wrong side and no good.

All I did that year was turn away from the city and walk into the theater and on into heaven. There was nowhere else to go. It was a year of London, New York, War, Love, Comedy, Newsreels and Heaven. It got so I didn't even think the newsreels were real. It got so I thought they were part of the movie too, the pictures of soldiers marching, and Generals striding about mechanically, turning feverishly, their lips moving, their arms rising and falling like the arms of men made of machinery. It couldn't be anything more than a movie. It was all part of the dream. The people walking along country roads, carrying small bundles, leaving bombed villages. It was all part of the great endless moving picture. The wounded in hospitals, with Royalty and Actresses and Generals going around mechanically from one bed to another, nodding, bowing, shaking hands and all that stuff. The trains going with all the faces looking out, and the others, not going, waving. If it wasn't a movie, I didn't know what it was.

It got so that even outside of the theater it was all a movie. Even *I* was one of the unnamed ones in the movie. One of the faces you saw for just a moment among a hundred faces.

I forgot about that strange year until I dreamed the movie and it had stopped raining and there seemed to be a sudden absence of miserliness and error in the world.

I guess the people will always be leaving the world and going to heaven. There's really nowhere else to go.

1924 Cadillac for Sale

✿ ✿ ✿

ANY time you think you can go out and pull something over on somebody, like selling them a bad used car, you're kidding yourself because people don't believe lies any more unless they've got their heart set on having the used car anyway. I used to sell an average of two used cars a week five years ago, but nowadays I'm lucky if I don't sell two a day. People who buy used cars these days would kill anybody who tried to stop them from buying. They just naturally want a used car. I used to try to argue them into believing they *ought* to have a used car, but that was before I found out I was wasting my time. That was before I found out people don't like to be fooled any more.

All I do now is hang around this used car lot and wait for people to come around and start asking questions about the jalopies we're showing. I tell them the truth.

I let them know exactly what they're getting, but it don't seem to stop them any when they've got their hearts set on going for a ride in an automobile. They just naturally insist on making a down payment and driving away. It used to make me feel real proud and smart to sell a used car in the old days, but nowadays I feel a little hurt every time somebody comes up and forces me to sell him one of these out-of-date broken-down heaps. I feel kind of useless and unnecessary, because I know I ain't selling anybody *anything*. I'm just letting the tide of humanity rush where it pleases or must.

They come here by the hundreds every day, men, women, and children, wanting a used car, and all I do is let them have their way. I don't put up any kind of an argument, because it's no use. An old lady who doesn't know how to drive a car wants to buy an old Hupmobile because it's green, so why should I interfere with her wishes? I let her know the truth about the old heap, but she buys it anyway, and the next day I see her going down the street forty-three miles an hour. She's in sports clothes, and the radio's going full blast, with a crooner hollering: *Deep in the heart of me.*

My God, it's beautiful and awful.

And then again a small boy, no more than twelve, comes in here with eleven dollars he's saved up, and he wants to know how much is the cheapest car on the lot; and I show him that 1922 Chevrolet we've been offering for fifteen dollars for seven years now, and he hops in, holds the wheel and says he'll go home and get the other four dollars. He comes back with his big brother, who signs the papers for him, and the next thing I know they've got the hood lifted and they're repairing the motor. In my opinion the old heap's got no more chance of moving than a bronze horse in a park; but three hours later something happens, and the whole lot is full of smoke and noise.

It's the old Chevrolet.

By the time the smoke clears I can see them walloping down the street, and I know deep in the heart of me, as the song goes, that either the people of this country are natural-born heroes or that the average used car, for all any of us knows, is part human and will respond to tender and loving care, just as anything else will.

There was a young Filipino came in here last April who'd been doing farm work down around Bakersfield, and he'd saved up a small amount of money which, he said, I wish to purchase a sports model Packard touring car with. Well, I had that great big battleship of a Packard that had been abandoned in the middle of the desert just south of Pixley about seven years ago, and I didn't want to see the boy gypped, so I told him I didn't have a sports model Packard touring car except one old one that had something fundamentally wrong with the motor and wouldn't run.

You wouldn't be interested in that car, I said.

I would appreciate it very much if you would allow me to look at it, the Filipino said.

His name was Vernon. I'm telling you this because I remember how amazed I was when he signed the papers. Vernon Roxas. The other boys who sat in the car with him when he drove out of the lot had names that were even worse. One of the boys was called Thorpe; another was named Scott, and another Avery. My God, them ain't names you ever see attached to people, native or alien, and me hearing them little men calling each other names like that made me stop in my tracks and wonder what the world was coming to. I mean I felt awful proud of them young citizens. I like people just so they're sensible and honest and sincere, and I like Filipinos as much as I like any other kind of people. I was just profoundly impressed by their superb adaptability. Them boys had not only adjusted themselves to our world: they'd fitted themselves out in the best style of our clothes, and they'd taken over our most impressive names. I felt awful proud of that condition in America among the boys from the Island.

Of course I was a little worried about their wanting that old Packard.

I showed the car to this boy Vernon Roxas, and he began crawling all over the car, trying out everything but the motor.

What is the price? he said.

Well, there was no price. I'd never bothered to give it a price because I was satisfied to have it in the lot as a sort of decoy, just to take space. I figured I'd do the boy a favor and name a big price so he wouldn't buy it.

Well, I said, it's pretty expensive. That'll run you about $75.

You mean $75 is the first payment? the boy asked.

Well, right there I guess I could have swindled him, and for a moment I was tempted to do it; but I just couldn't go through with the idea.

No, I said; $75 is the total cost.

I'll take it, the boy said.

He brought all kinds of money from his pockets, and we counted. He had a little over $75. I drew up the papers, and he signed. He said he would come back later that afternoon with several of his friends. He'd take the car then.

He came back in two hours with eleven well-dressed Filipinos named Thorpe, Scott, Avery, and other names like that. Each of them was carrying a satchel containing tools and other stuff. Well, they took off their coats and rolled up their sleeves and went to work. One of them started working on the motor, and the others started working on other parts of the car. In less than two hours they had that old warship looking like the car the Governor rides around in when there's a parade. And they had smoke coming out of it too.

I mean they'd fought their battle and won.

I stood in the lot with my mouth open, because never before in my life had I seen such beautiful co-operation and strategy. They just naturally fell on that pile of junk and tightened and cleaned and greased and oiled until it looked like a five-thousand-dollar job. Then they all got into the car and slowly drove out of the lot with the motor barely making any sound at all, like the motor of a car just out of the factory.

I couldn't believe my eyes. Or my ears, either.

I walked beside the boy at the wheel, Vernon Roxas, while the car moved out of the lot.

Vernon, I said, you boys have just taught me the greatest lesson any man can learn.

It is our opinion, Vernon said, that this Packard will travel fifty thousand miles before its usefulness is exhausted.

Well, I said, I don't doubt it the least. I'm more or less convinced that it will keep moving as long as you boys want it to.

And don't ever think it's the car. Don't ever think it's machinery. It's people. It's America, the awful energy of the people. It's not machinery, it's faith in yourself. Them boys from the Island went to work and changed that worthless heap of junk into a beautiful and powerful automobile with a motor that hummed.

When they drove out of this lot in that magnificent Packard my heart cheered this great country. People with no money having the polite impudence to want class and get it at no expense and to insist on getting it no matter how run-down and useless it might seem at first glance.

I don't *sell* used cars any more.

I just stand around in this lot and admire the will of the people, men, women, and children, as they take over a bankrupt and exhausted piece of machinery and breathe new and joyous life into it. I just stay here and admire this great and crazy race of adventure-loving people who can't be stopped by truth or expense. I just watch them throw themselves into a cause and come out with a roaring motor that five minutes ago was a piece of dead and rusted junk.

You're the first man who's come to this lot in six months and not *forced* me to sell him a car. I want to shake your hand. Like yourself I'm an honest man, and I believe as you do that every car in this lot is worthless, useless, and incapable of moving. I believe as you do that anybody who buys one of these cars is a fool and ought to have his head examined. It's my job to let the people have what they want, but I believe as you do that the most they can find here is junk, so naturally I admire somebody who agrees with me. This old 1924 Cadillac you've been looking at, in my opinion, isn't worth five cents, but we're asking sixty dollars for it. I don't think you're the type of man who could bring this car to life; and I wouldn't care to see you try, because if you failed I'd feel unhappy and maybe lose my faith in people.

But if you *want* to give it a try after all I've told you, well, that's your affair. I won't try to stop you. I'm telling you in all sincerity that this car is no good, but if you think you can fall on it like the others who buy cars here every day, and make it go, why go ahead. Nothing can amaze me any more, and if you've got your heart set on driving a Cadillac, well, here's a Cadillac, and good luck to you.

The Love Kick

✿ ✿ ✿

LOTS of people in Coalinga don't like Clip Rye just because he kicked Miss Alice Pfister on Oilfield Street in front of Joe Kolb's barber shop at high noon, but most of them don't understand Clip. Any other place but a little run-down town like this, Clip would be appreciated by upper-class people, but what happens to him in this Godforsaken neck of the woods? He's disgraced. He's in jail. What the hell for? Because he done it. Because he busted loose and let her have it. He kicked her. I ain't got nothing against Miss Pfister or anybody like her, only I don't want any truck with them kind of ladies, weekdays, Sundays, or holidays. Clip busted loose and kicked her. Lots of people don't like him.

The only trouble with Clip's kick was that it was a love kick. A lady like Miss Pfister don't deserve a love kick from a man like Clip, the most famous lover in Tulare County. What I say is, he was too kind to her.

Let me tell you how it happened. Clip ain't no brother of mine. He ain't no cousin of mine. We ain't even close friends. I ain't prejudiced in Clip's favor and I ain't one to say kicking a lady is exactly in keeping with the rules on how to behave in public. I kicked a lady once myself, and *nearly* kicked a dozen others. The lady I kicked claimed I was a loafer. She claimed I was lazy. My first wife. I didn't do it in public the way Clip did. You're the first man in the world knows I kicked a lady. I don't go around bragging about it because lots of people are sensitive on the subject and don't like to hear of a lady being kicked. Nine out of ten of them don't ever stop to think it over carefully. They just don't like the idea. I didn't want to kick my first wife. Not even after she almost drove me crazy nagging at me. She wanted me to take a correspondence course on how to increase the brain's capacity for thinking. My brain has a better than average capacity for thinking already, and I don't like it. I don't sleep good, on account of thinking. I keep thinking all the time. I think how different everything in the world would be if I had two or three hundred dollars. Then I start thinking along the political line, and I start thinking how wonderful it would be if I was a Senator or maybe Vice-President.

I'm thinking all the time, night and day, and my first wife had the impudence to ask me to take a correspondence course on how to increase the capacity of my overworked brain. Even then, though, I didn't *want* to kick her, my right leg just got out of control and the first thing I knew my first wife was sitting on the parlor floor calling me dirty names.

You may not believe me, but I'm still sorry about that. Ordinarily I'd only have clouted her, but my right leg got out of control. I apologized on the spot, but she wouldn't listen to me. She was mortified with shame. I told her I was sorry. I lifted my right leg to show her how out of control it was. She saw it trembling and aching to kick again, but she wouldn't understand. Honey, I said, it wasn't me, it was my leg. I didn't mean to do it.

She went right home to her mother and I never saw her again.

Clip Rye did it at high noon, though, and right in the street. A lot of people saw it happen. A lot of people were eye-witnesses. That's why they took Clip to jail. They claimed they not only saw it, they heard it. They claimed it made a lot of noise, especially when Miss Pfister sat down on the sidewalk.

Clip Rye is a natural-born lady-kicker. I reckon every man in the world is a natural-born lady-kicker if he'd be honest about it. I never yet knew a man who wasn't aching to kick some lady or other. I guess most men go through life keeping their right leg under powerful control. The average man wastes a Niagara of energy holding back his kicking leg.

What I say is, Kick a lady if it's the only thing to do. Let her have it.

For all we know, my friend, maybe the ladies themselves are asking for it. Maybe they want to be kicked. Maybe deep down inside they're just begging for a strong, healthy kick. I got a feeling Clip Rye's kick did Miss Pfister more good than harm. I just bet that kick was the starting point of a new era in Miss Pfister's love life.

Miss Pfister's love life is just about as interesting as the love life of the desert horned-toad. Miss Pfister ain't had a lover. She don't know what a man smells like. She ain't had a man's hands go over her the way a man's hands ought to go over a lady. Consequently, her love life has taken a half dozen special directions. First she was in the choir at the Presbyterian Church. Nothing happened. So she went over to the Baptist Church as a Sunday School teacher. Nothing happened. So she went in for astrology and studied the stars. Then she went in for professional gossiping. She spent all her time discussing the immorality of the people of Coalinga, especially Clip Rye, and the immorality of movie stars, and that's all she cared to do. She used up *most* of her energy talking about the immorality of Clip Rye, though. Every time she met Clip Rye in the street she lifted her nose at him.

She was flirting, of course. She was crazy about Clip Rye. Anybody but a fool could see how crazy Miss Pfister was about Clip Rye.

She acted as if she wouldn't look at Clip Rye if he was the last man in the world, but that was her way of flirting. Clip knew it, too. He knew what she wanted, even if she herself didn't, and Clip resented it. He didn't resent her gossiping about him, he resented her passion. It drove him crazy. That old hag's in love with me, he used to say.

Clip was sitting in Joe Kolb's barber shop getting a haircut. Last Saturday. He was minding his own business sitting there and staring out of the window at the people passing in the street. Then Miss Pfister went by in the street. Then she went by again, going up the street, and looking in at Clip and lifting her nose. I'm giving you the evidence. I'm trying to prove Clip don't deserve social ostracism. Then Miss Pfister went down the street, lifting her nose. Then up, then down, looking at Clip, adoring him, and lifting her nose, and then Clip's right leg got out of control and he jumped out of Joe Kolb's barber chair and ran out into the street and grabbed Miss Pfister by the arm. He was disgusted. Miss Pfister was so delighted she screamed. Clip bawled hell out of her. She bawled hell out of Clip. It sounded like a man and a woman who had been married sixteen years and knew all about one another, and Clip knew it and it burned him up. He was disgusted and sore and embarrassed. And then it was all over.

Miss Pfister was sitting in front of Joe Kolb's barber shop, on the sidewalk, at high noon, and everybody in town was running to the scene of the crime, and Miss Pfister didn't want to get up.

Clip was so sore he didn't know what to do. If Miss Pfister had gotten up he would have kicked her again, but she didn't get up. A couple of church-people started complicating Miss Pfister's love life, and the result of it was they had Clip Rye taken to jail and he's there yet and everybody in town is sore at him for kicking Miss Pfister.

Myself, I'd say Clip shouldn't have done it, if for no other reason than that it made Miss Pfister so happy. She didn't deserve such affection from a man like Clip Rye. I didn't see Clip kick her, but I showed up in time to hear Miss Pfister crying, and I know the kinds of crying there is, and Miss Pfister's kind was the joyous love variety. She was just thrilled to tears.

So they took Clip Rye to jail. They took him to jail for doing a noble kindness like that.

Joe Kolb never did get a chance to finish Clip's haircut.

The Warm, Quiet Valley of Home

✿ ✿ ✿

MY cousin drove the broken-down Ford to the front of the house and pulled the emergency brake because the regular brakes were no good. The car skidded, choked and stopped. He got out and came around the house to the back yard and stood a little while looking up at the sky. Then he came up the steps and on into the kitchen.

I was almost through shaving.

It's going to be a swell day, he said.

That's fine, I said.

He poured himself a cup of coffee and sat down and began to have breakfast. Bread and butter and coffee and Armenian cheese and black olives.

I dried my face and poured coffee into the other cup on the table and began to eat.

It was a big percolator. He drank four cups and I drank three; I would have had four cups myself, only there wasn't any more coffee in the percolator.

It was still dark when we left the house.

We've got a swell lunch, he said. I fixed it myself.

Anything to drink? I said.

Beer, he said. Six bottles. I've got them in a box with wet burlap on the bottom and top, so they won't get too hot.

Can't we get some ice? I said.

Well, sure, he said. But it'll melt.

That's all right, I said. We can drink the beer before we have lunch. It won't melt before ten in the morning, will it?

It gets pretty hot after daybreak, he said.

I don't like warm beer, I said.

I know where we can get some ice at this hour, he said.

Is it very far out of the way? I said.

No, he said.

I'll crank, I said.

No, he said. Let me crank. I know how to get this motor going.

He cranked, the motor started, we got in and drove away.

I don't suppose there are any streams up that way, I said.

There used to be a brook somewhere up there, he said. It might be dry this time of year, though.

Did you bring the guns? I said.

Hell yes, he said. If you hit anything with that twenty-two, it'll be luck, though.

Why? I said.

Something's the matter with the sight, he said.

Maybe it's your eye, I said.

I got a good eye, he said. It ain't my eye. I aimed at a cotton-tail not more than twenty yards away and missed.

It's probably your eye, I said.

How about the shot-gun?

It's O.K., he said.

Anything the matter with the sight? I said.

No, but you don't need the sight, he said.

Oh, I said.

The old Ford rattled down Ventura Avenue and then slowed down. My cousin pulled the emergency brake and the car skidded and stopped in front of a Coal & Ice place that had an office up front and a light on in the office. My cousin went up and tried the door, but it was locked. He looked through the window and saw a man sleeping in a chair, so he knocked at the door. After a while the man opened the door and said, What do you want?

Pennsylvania coal, my cousin said.

Ain't got no coal this time of year, the man said.

O.K., my cousin said, we'll take ice, then.

How much ice do you want? the man said.

Give me a dime's worth, my cousin said.

The man disappeared and came back half a minute later with a cube of ice in a canvas bag.

Got a pick? my cousin said.

Sure, the man said.

The man brought the ice to the car and my cousin took the ice out of the canvas bag and put it on the running board. Then he took the ice pick from the man and began chipping the cube and putting the pieces between the wet burlap around the bottles of beer.

My cousin gave the man a dime, and the man went back to his office and chair.

My cousin chipped the cube into small pieces and put all the pieces in the wet burlap; then he cranked the car and got in.

We turned north near the County Hospital. It began to be day. The sky was very fine and the hospital looked very sad.

Were you ever in a hospital? my cousin said.

Yes, I said.

What did you have? he said.

Nothing, I said. I was visiting.

Visiting who? he said.

Do you remember Kerop who died? I said. You weren't very old when he was around.

I remember, he said.

Well, I was visiting him, I said.

What did he have? my cousin said.

T.B., I said.

What sort of a guy was he, anyway? my cousin said.

He was O.K., I said. I used to take him grapes and figs and peaches. He wasn't very old when he died. He wasn't forty. I was ten or eleven.

When we reached Clovis the sun was up and the town was very pleasant-looking. My cousin drove around town four or five times, looking at the place.

Then my cousin pulled the emergency brake and the car stopped in front of a general merchandise store. There were no people in the town.

Do you want to walk around in this town? he said.

How about some more breakfast? I said.

Got any money? my cousin said.

About a dollar and twenty cents, I said.

All right, if we can find a place, he said.

We got out of the car and walked along the main street of the little town. There wasn't much to the town. It was just a lot of sad-looking wooden buildings facing a couple of sad-looking streets, a lot of sad-looking store windows, a lot of sad-looking doors and signs and second-story windows. And just beyond the town you could see the vineyards. It was just a little place in the country surrounded by vines, but it was very pleasant being there early in the morning.

My cousin went behind a shack that was empty and for rent.

Did I ever tell you about the colored boy who went up to the doctor? my cousin said.

No, I said.

That's a funny one, my cousin said. I like the jokes of this country more than the serious things. The serious things are funny too, but they're funny because they ain't supposed to be funny. Do you remember that guy who came to town and pitched a big tent and preached?

You mean that revivalist? I said. Sure I remember him.

He was all right, my cousin said. I didn't like the sawdust on the floor and the wooden benches and the canvas roof. That didn't seem like a church. He was an earnest man, though. It was very funny when he prayed. I could hardly keep from busting out laughing. The people were a lot funnier than the preacher. They were scared to death.

We went back to the main street of the town and found a restaurant, only it was closed.

There wasn't a soul in town, even though the sun was up and it was beginning to be hot.

Shall we wait for this place to open up, my cousin said, or shall we go on and eat some of the lunch and drink a bottle of beer each in the country?

This place may not open up for hours yet, I said.

I don't know why they ever opened this place in the first place, my cousin said. I'd like to meet the guy who did it.

What sort of a guy do you think he'd be? he said.

I figure he'd be a sort of an amiable sort of a guy, I said.

I don't mean amiable, my cousin said. I mean what the hell do you figure made him go and open up a restaurant in a town like this?

Maybe he's got a big appetite, I said. Maybe he takes care of that.

I'll bet ten to one that's the answer, my cousin said. He's a little guy with a big appetite. He doesn't want to go hungry, *any time*. He wants to have stuff near by all the time. So he has the restaurant. If the worst comes to the worst, he can eat all the hash himself.

I think we've solved the whole problem, I said, so we don't need to wait.

We went back to the hack and my cousin cranked it and we drove out of the town.

The hills were brown and dry. The grass was all dead and dry. We traveled about ten miles and then it was the place my cousin said was fine. It was a good place. It was cool and very pleasant, although the weather was very hot. There were trees that had grown up by themselves, on the slopes of the hills, and beneath the trees was grass that wasn't dry. We ate three beef sandwiches each and drank a bottle of beer each, and then we took the guns and the rest of the lunch, except the beer, and began to walk.

We walked about an hour and didn't see anything to shoot, so my cousin shot at a white butterfly with the twenty-two and missed.

See? he said. Something's the matter with the sight.

Give me that gun, I said.

I shot at a butterfly and missed too.

Sounds all right, I said.

Sounds just like a twenty-two, my cousin said.

Where the hell's that brook? I said.

What brook? my cousin said.

What do you mean, what brook? I said. *The brook.* Didn't you speak of a brook this morning?

I don't think there's any water in it, my cousin said.

It ain't a brook unless there's water in it, I said.

All of a sudden my cousin fired the shot-gun and I saw a jack-rabbit jump and run.

Something's the matter with the sight on that shot-gun, I said.

No, my cousin said, on second thought I decided not to kill an innocent animal. After all, what good would it do me?

We walked two hours before we found the brook. There was a little water in it, but the water was stagnant and stank. Nevertheless, we sat down on the cool grass and talked.

My cousin wanted to know some more about the man who died in the County Hospital. Kerop, our third uncle, I told him, and then he told me about a boy who drowned in Thompson Ditch. A friend of his named Harlan Beach.

He was a good guy, my cousin said.

It was very quiet and pleasant. I laid flat on my back and looked up at the sky. A lot of crazy years had gone by all right. A lot of crazy things had happened all right. It was September again and it was very pleasant. It was very hot, but it was very pleasant too. This was my valley, where I had been born. This earth and sky was home. This temperature was. My cousin was. The way he talked was. The memories he knew were part of it. The people he remembered. I looked up at the sky and remembered New York. I had lived there less than a year ago, when I was twenty years old, but it seemed as if it were *ten* years ago, or twenty, or a hundred. And it seemed as if I had never lived there, or had only dreamed of having lived there, a long summer and winter dream of sultriness and stickiness and crazy buildings and crazy crowds and crazy subways, and then bitter cold, snow and wind, and the black sunless sky.

My cousin talked in English, and I talked partly in English and partly in Armenian. Then he began to talk partly in English and partly in Armenian, and after a while we talked in Armenian only.

Poor Kerop, my cousin said. Poor, poor, poor. He used to walk; now he does not walk.

My cousin moved the palms of his hands together which is the Armenian symbol of the ending of a thing.

Let us eat bread, I said.

Let us eat bread and remember, my cousin said.

We ate all the sandwiches.

Then we started walking back to the car so we could drink the beer.

There were no animals or birds to shoot along the way. There were a number of small singing birds, but we did not shoot at them.

Let us salute the absent inhabitants of the world, my cousin said.

That's a noble thought, I said.

We lifted the guns to our shoulders and pointed them at nothing in the sky.

To the dead, my cousin said.

We fired the guns.

The sound was half-crazy and half-tragic.

To Kerop, I said.

We fired again.

To Harlan Beach, my cousin said, and again we fired.

To everybody who once lived on this earth and died, my cousin said.
We fired the guns.
The shot-gun made ten times as much noise as the twenty-two.
Give me the shot-gun for this next one, I said.
My cousin gave me the shot-gun and I gave him the twenty-two.
Who will it be? he said.
To my father, I said. I squeezed the trigger of the shot-gun. It had a powerful kick.
To *my* father, my cousin said.
We fired again.
To my grandfather, I said.
To *my* grandfather, my cousin said.
To Gregory the Illuminator, I said.
To Bedros Tourian, my cousin said.
To Raffi, I said.
We would walk a little way and stop and name someone who was dead, and fire the guns.
To Antranik, my cousin said.
To Khetcho, I said.
Poor Khetcho, my cousin said in Armenian.
To Mourad, I said.
We saluted many Armenian soldiers and scholars and writers and priests. We saluted many great men who were dead.
We made a lot of noise in the hills, but it was all right because there was nobody around.
When we got back to the car the beer was not quite as cold as it had been in the morning, but it was cool and good to drink.
We drank the beer, my cousin cranked the car, we got in and drove out of the hills into the warm, quiet, lovely valley that was our home in the world.

A Number of the Poor

✿ ✿ ✿

ONE summer I worked two months in a grocery store. I worked from four in the afternoon till midnight, but after eight o'clock there wouldn't be any business to speak of and all I'd do was look out the window or go around the store and keep things in order. It was a little store on Grove Street, in the slums. The people who came to the store were all interesting and poor.
Only two or three of them didn't steal things, not counting little children. Almost all the others stole more than they bought. It was just that they needed the stuff and didn't have enough money to buy it. They'd put a package of chewing gum in a pocket when my back was turned, or a small cake, or a can of tomato soup. I knew all about it, but I never let on. They were all good people, just poor.
Once in August a lady tried to hide a cantaloupe in her waist. That

was one of the saddest things I ever saw. She was a woman of fifty or so. It was obvious that she had a lot more under her waist than herself and I guess she just had to have a cantaloupe. That evening she didn't buy anything. I guess she was broke. She spent about five minutes in the store, asking about the prices of a lot of things, and tasting apricots and peaches and figs. I'd tell her figs were ten cents a dozen and very good and she'd say they looked good but were they really? Then I'd tell her to taste one. She'd hesitate a little and then lift a very big one out of the crate, peel it and very thoughtfully swallow it in three bites, tasting it carefully. She was always a lady. With a little money to go with her charm I believe she would have cut an impressive figure in a grocery store, but she never seemed to have any. I thought it was wonderful the way she got the cantaloupe without losing her dignity.

One of the few who came to the store and never stole anything was a little Spaniard named Casal. You had to know which stole and which didn't. Casal was one of those small men with big heads and sad faces that you notice right away and wonder about. He used to come to the store almost every night at ten and stay for a half hour or so to talk. He was quiet-spoken and solemn and dignified. If you're no bigger than a boy of eleven, and weigh about ninety-two pounds, it's no cinch to be dignified.

I always had a lot of respect for Casal. He didn't seem to know anything. I don't suppose he'd read a newspaper in ten years. He had no ideas and no complaints about anything. He was just a very small man who had managed to stay alive forty-eight years. Little by little I came to know why he was so dignified and had no need to complain about anything.

It was because he was a father. He had a son of sixteen. This boy was six feet tall and very handsome. He was Casal's boy all right; there was no getting around that. He had his father's head. Casal was very proud of him; that's what kept him going. One evening he said: You know my boy? He is a fine boy. So big and good. Do you know what? Every night when I come home from work my boy says, Pa, get on my shoulders. I get on his shoulders and he carries me all around the house. Then we sit down and eat.

What can you make of something like that? That small father and that great son, the boy carrying the father around on his shoulders? There's something there, I think.

Another night Casal said, I'll tell you why my boy is such a good boy. His mother died when he was born. That's the reason. He never knew his mother. He was always alone. Even when he was a baby. I used to go home in my lunch hour to see how he was. Sometimes he'd be crying. Sometimes he'd be through crying and he'd be all alone waiting. He stopped crying when he was just a little baby. He learned to know how it was. After he was two years old it was a lot easier for him and for me too. You should have seen the way he grew. Do you like him?

I think he's a fine boy, I said.

Well, I'll tell you, Casal said. Do you know what? He wants me to stop working. He wants to work for me now. He says I've worked enough. He's good with machines. He can get a job as a mechanic in a repair shop. You know what I told him? I told him no. I told him, Joe, you're going to college. He gets along fine everywhere. He's a good boy. I'm going to send him through college. He's got a right. I like to work for him.

Sure, I said.

Casal was one of the fine ones who came to that store when I worked there.

There was a little red-head, about twelve, who was another. Her name was Maggie. She was very powerful, the way some kids of the poor are, and full of the swellest laughter in the world.

She used to come into the store and bust out laughing, right out of a clear sky, no preliminaries, no explanations or anything. She'd just come in and laugh. That always pleased me, but I'd never let her know it. So she'd laugh some more.

All right, I'd say. What do you want?

You know, she'd say.

Laughter.

A loaf of bread?

Bread! she'd say.

Well, what *do* you want?

Out of the corner of her eye, a glance.

What have you got?

There wouldn't be anything else to do with somebody like that, so I'd toss her a peach which she would catch and eat very daintily. Spoofing, though, of course, with her little finger extended.

They say I look like Ginger Rogers, she'd say.

They're liars.

I do, she'd say. You know I do. Do you like her?

She's swell, I'd say.

I look just like her, she'd say.

Twelve years old.

The country's full of them too, and it's no use worrying about them. They're all in the big movie.

Another was the little boy who never had a penny but always came to look. About four years old. I used to call him Callaghan. He was great. He'd spend an hour looking at the penny candies and never say a word, except maybe to himself. People would stumble over him but he'd stick to his spot and keep looking.

One evening the lady who stole the cantaloupe patted him on the head.

Your son? she said.

Yes, I said.

A fine boy, she said. He resembles you. How much are figs today?

Ten cents a dozen, I said.

Are they really good?

Yes, they are. I ate one five minutes ago. Please try one.

She did; and tried also a peach and an apricot.

She didn't buy anything that night either. She stayed ten minutes and I know she wanted to ask if she might borrow twenty-five cents till to-morrow, but didn't dare. At last she said, We're lucky to be living in California, aren't we?

I've never been out of the state, I said. I've never been out of this city. Is it different in other places?

Oh terribly, she said. Why, there are places you can hardly breathe in in the summertime. Chicago. And look how wonderful it is here.

She was at the open door and waved her arm gently outward at the sky. The *air* is so fine here, she said.

When she was gone I called Callaghan. He came over immediately.

Would you like a licorice strap?

No answer.

He would, of course, but he wouldn't say so.

Come over here and take what you like, I said.

He came over behind the candy case but didn't reach to take anything.

Take anything you like, I said.

He looked at me, a little uncertain.

Sure, I said. You can have anything you like.

He couldn't believe it and was a little scared.

It's all right, I said.

He reached out and took a licorice strap.

Take something else, I said.

He put back the licorice strap and reached for a wax dog.

No, I said. Keep the licorice strap, too.

In all he took four different kinds of penny candies, but it took a lot of encouragement from me to get him to do it.

Okay, Callaghan, I said. Now go home and eat them. Take them with you.

Without a word, but still amazed, he went away.

The next day when he came back he said very quietly, The best is the licorice strap.

In that case, I said, I'll try one myself.

So I got him one and one for myself and together we ate them.

It was a good job while it lasted because of the fine, funny, tragic, little poor people who came there for things to eat or somebody to talk to.

Peace, It's Wonderful

✿ ✿ ✿

THE Judge said he was sorry but the young man was guilty of hopping.

Two eager, middle-aged, slum-dwelling, white women with memories got up in the first row and said, Thank you, Father. Peace, it's wonderful.

The Judge ducked, called for order, and said, Never mind that Father stuff. You ladies are old enough to be my mother. I will now pronounce sentence.

The sentence was five years in the Federal Penitentiary.

That ought to hold him a while, the Judge thought.

The young man told reporters he was happy and at peace with the world. He said powerful vibrations had been coming to him from New York. He said he was exhausted and looked forward to spending the next five years in holy seclusion. He told the reporters he had been wanting to write a book, and now he was going to have his chance.

Thank you, Father, he said. Peace, it's wonderful.

The Judge was disgusted.

It ain't right, somebody said. A good honest religious young man like that with nothing but love in his bones don't deserve punishment like that.

What is dis stuff? Manuel the pool shark said. Everywhere I go everybody saying Peace.

We went around the corner to Pete's and had two beers and a steak
sandwich each. Then we went across the street to the North Beach Branch
of that religious order. In the window was a picture of the man and
beneath the picture was the opinion that the man was God.

It was eleven o'clock at night. Two American girls of the half-wit school
came out of the place and stood on the porch. Behind them was a large
good-natured Negro woman who might have been a maid in any one of
the whorehouses in that neighborhood. There was a bunch of bananas in
the room, as well as a shelf of canned goods, mostly beans.

O.K., Sport, Manuel said. Flash de smile. Give out de personality.

These girls? I said.

Sure, Manuel said.

Good evening, I said to the Negro woman. How much are the bananas?

Thank you, Father, she said.

The two girls said, Peace, it's wonderful.

Oh boy, Manuel said.

Bananas are thirty cents a dozen, the Negro woman said. Peace.

I'll take a dozen and a half, I said. Thank you.

We went into the hall. The girls moved to go. Manuel said, Amen, and
gave the girls the religious eye. They smiled piously and vibrated.

I helped the Negro woman count out a dozen and a half bananas. When
I turned around Manuel was gone. I saw him at the corner with a girl
on each arm.

He turned around and hollered, Hurry up, Joe. Peace, it's wonderful.

I went back to Pete's and gave the bananas to a Chinese newsboy.

Manuel showed up a little before two in the morning.

Peace, I said.

It was lousy, he said. What is dis stuff?

Piano

✧ ✧ ✧

I GET excited every time I see a piano, Ben said.

Is that so? Emma said. Why?

I don't know, Ben said. Do you mind if we go into this store and try
the little one in the corner?

Can you play? Emma said.

If you call what I do playing, Ben said.

What do you do?

You'll see, Ben said.

They went into the store, to the small piano in the corner. Emma
noticed him smiling and wondered if she'd ever know anything about him.
She'd go along for a while thinking she knew him and then all of a sudden

she'd know she didn't. He stood over the piano, looking down at it. What she imagined was that he had probably heard good piano playing and loved that kind of music and every time he saw a keyboard and the shape of a piano he remembered the music and imagined he had something to do with it.

Can you play? she said.

Ben looked around. The clerks seemed to be busy.

I can't play, Ben said.

She saw his hands go quietly to the white and black keys, like a real pianist's, and it seemed very unusual because of what she felt when that happened. She felt that he was someone who would be a long time finding out about himself, and someone somebody else would be much longer finding out about. He should be somebody who could play a piano.

Ben made a few quiet chords. Nobody came over to try to sell him anything, so, still standing, he began to do what he'd told her wasn't playing.

Well, all she knew was that it was wonderful.

He played half a minute only. Then he looked at her and said, It sounds good.

I think it's wonderful, Emma said.

I don't mean what *I* did, Ben said. I mean the piano. I mean the piano itself. It has a fine tone, especially for a little piano.

A middle-aged clerk came over and said, How do you do?

Hello, Ben said. This is a swell one.

It's a very popular instrument, the clerk said. Especially fine for apartments. We sell a good many of them.

How much is it? Ben said.

Two hundred forty-nine fifty, the clerk said. You can have terms, of course.

Where do they make them? Ben said.

I'm not sure, the clerk said. In Philadelphia, I think. I can find out.

Don't bother, Ben said. Do you play?

No, I don't, the clerk said.

He noticed Ben wanting to try it out some more.

Go ahead, he said. Try it some more.

I don't play, Ben said.

I heard you, the clerk said.

That's not playing, Ben said. I can't read a note.

Sounded good to me, the clerk said.

Me, too, Emma said. How much is the first payment?

Oh, the clerk said. Forty or fifty dollars. Go ahead, he said, I'd like to hear you play some more.

If this was the right kind of room, Ben said, I could sit down at the piano for hours.

Play some more, the clerk said. Nobody'll mind.

The clerk pushed up the bench and Ben sat down and began to do what he said wasn't playing. He fooled around fifteen or twenty seconds and then found something like a melody and stayed with it two minutes. Before he was through the music became quiet and sorrowful and Ben himself became more and more pleased with the piano. While he was letting the melody grow, he talked to the clerk about the piano. Then he stopped playing and stood up.

Thanks, he said. Wish I could buy it.

Don't mention it, the clerk said.

Ben and Emma walked out of the store. In the street Emma said, I didn't know about that, Ben.

About what? Ben said.

About you.

What about me?

Being that way, Emma said.

This is my lunch hour, Ben said. In the evening is when I like to think of having a piano.

They went into a little restaurant and sat at the counter and ordered sandwiches and coffee.

Where did you learn to play? Emma said.

I've never learned, Ben said. Any place I find a piano, I try it out. I've been doing that ever since I was a kid. Not having money does that.

He looked at her and smiled. He smiled the way he did when he stood over the piano looking down at the keyboard. Emma felt very flattered.

Never having money, Ben said, keeps a man away from lots of things he figures he ought to have by rights.

I guess it does, Emma said.

In a way, Ben said, it's a good thing, and then again it's not so good. In fact, it's terrible.

He looked at her again, the same way, and she smiled back at him the way he was smiling at her.

She understood. It was like the piano. He could stay near it for hours. She felt very flattered.

They left the restaurant and walked two blocks to The Emporium where she worked.

Well, so long, he said.

So long, Ben, Emma said.

He went on down the street and she went on into the store. Somehow or other she knew he'd get a piano some day, and everything else, too.

The Sweet Singer of Omsk

✧ ✧ ✧

THERE is a Russian from Omsk in this town, Hollywood, who is a singer. He has read my books and claims I do not know what I have written. He claims *he* knows. He claims he is my best reader and he says I myself, Saroyan, Wheelyam Sar-o-yan, as he says, do not understand my stuff, which I wrote.

He is a serious man, an excellent singer of Russian songs, expert on the guitar, deeply sorrowful, extremely courteous, extraordinarily unhappy. He claims he is dead, not alive. He asks how I, writing as I do, saying what I say, am able to be so much alive. I tell him I don't know.

He then declares that I do not know what I write.

He plays the guitar like a crazy man, and I swear he knows less about the way he plays the guitar than I know, and I swear I write my stuff exactly the way he plays the guitar. In short, we are brothers.

He is, strictly, at heart, one who knows. He knows all things. His knowing is sharp and swift and to the dead center of it all: he knows it is all death. He knows it is all nothing. He is a big, sorrowful-looking fellow in excellent American clothes who plays the guitar the way I write.

Each time we meet at a party, this great Russian, this great singer who is truthfully my brother comes to me and very bitterly, in his deep voice, says to me, roaring deeply, very hurt about everything, a truly tragic man, a truly noble one, Wheelyam Sar-o-yan, *you* will understand.

I don't try hard to understand because it seems I almost always understand without trying, and I bust out laughing, and he tells me he cannot understand how I understand, how I write what I write. Sometimes, believing what I say, I say, sincerely but with a smile, that it is true, very often I do not know what I write, what I say. I simply write, something perhaps more significant than I know, which falls in place by itself, rather strangely. And oddly enough, or not oddly at all, he brings out his guitar, takes his stance, which is practically tragic, truthfully a thing to see and remember, and after a suitable half minute of reverent silence, he begins easily, effortlessly, as I begin each of my pieces, to sing and play the guitar. And before you know it, before you've had a chance to understand anything about anything he's singing and playing like one who was placed in this world to sing and play a guitar; and in no time at all the room is full of electrical, I might go so far as to say holy, splendor, magnificence, tragedy, and comedy; all at once, all together, all of it together in one piece. Eat, eat, eat, he sings in Russian, only the Russian word is not so flat, *kossi, kossi, kossi*. This Russian word for eat is the warm, kindly, gentle one of the mother to her child, the endearing one, *kossi, kossi, kossi*.

I do not believe there is a better singer of this kind in the world, nor for that matter, of my kind, a better writer. This man is possessed. And, unless I am badly mistaken, I am too. Most people meeting me, talking with me, do not get the impression that I am a great writer, and often do not believe me when I tell them so. Very often, even after I have told them six or seven times, they do not believe, and I beg them to read my stuff. I know they will know, while they are reading my stuff and afterwards, that everything I have said to them is true, and I beg them because I know it will be a splendid and extraordinary and funny experience for them. To hear me bragging, and then to read my stuff and know that I *am* a great writer. I beg them to read my stuff, so it will be complete.

I admit it. I am possessed. Most of the time not violently so. But often enough. Not haunted, mind you. The presence is not an evil one. It is often angry and bitter and furious, but most of the time it is warm and friendly and amiable and gentle and courteous, and at times a little gallant, even. It is a good presence, and in varying degrees it is with me always. I do not mind it at all, and am on the contrary on excellent terms with it. We sometimes have quarrels. I am sometimes strongly inclined toward one thing, such as loafing and having an easy-going time, and this presence is inclined toward another thing, such as sitting down somewhere and putting two or three thousand words on paper, making a story, or something else. As I say, I do not know a great deal about what the words come to, but the presence is always anxious that I take time out to say something. I say, What's there to say? And the presence says, Now don't get funny;

just sit down and say anything; it'll be all right. Say it wrong; it'll be all right anyway.

Half the time I *do* say it wrong, but somehow or other, just as the presence says, it's right anyhow. I am always pleased about this. My God, it's wrong, but it's all right. It's really all right. How did it happen?

Well, that's how it is. It's the presence, doing everything for me. It's the presence, doing all the hard work while I, always inclined to take things easy, loaf around, not thinking, not paying much attention to anything, much, just putting down on paper whatever comes my way.

The Russian singer told me about this. Wheelyam Sar-o-yan, he said, I know what you are saying, but *you do not know*.

This is, unfortunately, or fortunately, true. I think fortunately. Because I like being alive. And being dumb this way allows me to stay alive. By rights I should have died long ago. This is no fancy phrase. It is the truth. By all rights I should have died long ago.

Two years ago, at three in the morning, when I fell down a flight of cement stairs into the basement of a Greek restaurant on Market Street in San Francisco and should have been instantly killed, why did I get up and yell at Pete the short order cook, What the hell's the big idea putting these stairs where the toilet's supposed to be?

How did that happen? How did it happen that I was not even scratched?

I could give seventeen other instances. All those years, all that crazy stuff, all those years when I had no money, why didn't I die? How did it happen that I didn't even lose my hair?

I have always suspected that what I am doing is not the work of one man, but I have never given the matter much thought. Then I met this Russian singer, and he told me, and now I know for sure.

The Russian Writer

✿ ✿ ✿

IN Russia I ran into a small, undernourished, high-strung, mournful-looking young writer who spoke better English than I do, only with an accent, and he said, Comrade, I have read everything. I have read many of your American writers. I know the works of John Dos Passos, Ernest Hemingway, Jack London, and many others. Still, I know nothing. I know nothing about anything. I am twenty-seven years old. I am a writer too. You are a writer too. Still, if I may say so, Comrade, do you know anything?

If memory serves, he was only an inch taller than a midget. He smoked one Russian cigarette after another, inhaled deeply while he talked, and even more deeply while he remained silent. The other Russian writers in that city were taller men, or fatter, or quieter, or dumber. One of them was a giant. This small writer told me this big one was the worst of the lot, although they were all bad.

Forgive me, he said, if what I say seems counter-revolutionary, but we are the worst writers in the world. We are the very worst. We are the ultimate of worseness.

Here, he said. Here are six of my books. You cannot read Russian, thank God. Look at the print. All of it is the worst writing in the world. Where is Chekov? Where is young Gorky? Where is Tolstoy? Where is Andreyev? Have they all died in us? I have read your stories, he said. You are a very bad writer. My God, you write badly, but everybody is not dead in you. You are not bad as we are. We are the way we are because they are all dead in us. In you two or three of the Americans are alive. That is why you are so bad. You are always jumping around because they are all so alive in you. My God, everything you write is awful, but it is much less awful than everything we write. Comrade, he said, do you know anything at all?

Well, I said, I know when it's raining.

So, he said. Again. Again you can laugh. It is not funny, though. *I* do not even know when it is raining. Yesterday the sun was shining and I sat in this room writing a story and I did not know the sun was shining. I thought it was raining. I tell you I thought it was raining all the time. It is because we are so sad. You have heard them laughing. It is false. Listen to them next time they laugh and you will know it is false. It isn't false when *you* laugh. It is crazy, but it isn't false. How can you laugh, Comrade?

I'll tell you an American joke, I said. It will make you laugh. I told him the one about the father and the beautiful daughter on the train to Cleveland that was held up by train robbers. You know the one. Where the father says, If only your mother had been here, Alice, we would have been able to save the luggage. Every time I tell this story it makes me roar with laughter. Every time somebody else tells it I've got to laugh too. It's a great, goofy, American joke. I laughed all over the room, and the young writer went into hysterics, slapping his knee, bending over, running around the room, and bumping his head against the walls.

When he stopped laughing, there were tears in his eyes.

Did you hear me laughing? he said. Did you feel the grief of that laughter? Do you know another?

I told him the one about the two Forty-second Street fleas that went out adventuring one summer night. Remember?

The little writer went crazy over this one. His face got red from too much laughing and then suddenly he sat down on the floor and began to cry.

My God, he said, we can't even laugh. Please forgive me, Tovarich. Please tell another.

I knew a hundred more, but I didn't want to upset him like this. If I had known these jokes were going to upset him this way I wouldn't have told them. It was sad, the way he laughed like a young American who'd spent all his life in the slums of some big city; he sounded like a kid who'd been brought up in the slums of New York or Pittsburgh or Chicago or Frisco.

You must tell me a Russian joke, I said.

He looked at me with an amazed expression on his face.

A Russian joke? he said. We have no jokes. The people do not make up such stories as these. We have some comedy. There are many comical peasants, and many pompous executives who are very funny to observe, but no jokes. We do not tell jokes. We won't admit it, he said, but everybody is dead in us. We are the very worst writers in the world.

I told him I didn't believe it. Late that night I asked the other writers about him. They spoke of him with the humbleness of inferiors. He is a great writer, they said. He is one of the very greatest. We believe that he will be greater than Chekov. He is only a baby now. He writes like a crazy man.

That's what I thought, I told them.

That same night I left that city and continued my journey.

The Journey and the Dream

✿ ✿ ✿

NAGASAKI, Bull, Mr. Isaac, Dynamite, Hollywood Pete, and a kid in a leather coat who looked like a college student were playing stud when I walked into the joint with money burning holes in my pockets.

Well, said Bull. Where the hell have you been? Sit down and go broke.

Thanks, Bull, I said. I'll sit down, but I'll try not to go broke.

It was September, raining, and I had just come home from Europe and New York. Months ago when I got up from the game and left town, the players were sitting in the same seats they now occupied. Only Curley was out of sight.

Where's Curley? I said.

Nagasaki the Jap told me. Curley die, he said. Curley win big pot.

You're kidding, I said.

That's right, said Hollywood Pete. He tried to bluff out of that spot, but they called him.

Too bad, I said. Curley was O.K.

The best, said Bull. He broke me as many times as I tried to bluff him.

Waiter, I said. Perry the waiter came running over. Bring me some whisky, I said. I want to drink to the memory of Curley.

Make it three, said Bull. And then everybody at the table except the kid in the leather coat decided to drink to the memory of the old gambler.

I sat down, and Flash, the Irish tenor who used to sing in burlesque, came over to find out how much worth of chips I wanted to buy.

Where you been? he said.

I just got back from Russia, I said.

I was born in Russia, said Dynamite. He was a smart Jew.

What city? I said.

Kiev, he said.

I stayed at the Karl Marx hotel in Kiev, I said.

God damn it, said Dynamite. You ain't kidding, are you?

No, I said.

I left Kiev when I was ten years old, he said. How's the river? Dnieper.

Swell, I said.

Did you see Stalin? said Mr. Isaac. He was a little Jewish tailor.

No, I said. I went to see Russia. How's it going, Flash?

Bluffing the best way I know how, he said.

Bring me thirty dollars' worth, I said.

Fat Laramie was dealing and the first card he gave me was the Ace of Spades, which was swell. Perry came back with the drinks.

To Curley, I said.

To Curley, said the gamblers.

The kid in the leather coat was sitting on my left. Who's this guy Curley? he said.

He used to play here, I said. Usually he sat in the chair you're sitting in now. He was a great guy.

That calls for a drink, said the kid. Bring me the same.

How old a man was he? said the kid to the players.

He was a young man, said Bull, himself over sixty.

He was in his sixties, I said.

What the hell killed him? said the kid.

Bad heart, said Hollywood Pete.

Well, said the kid, I'm sitting in his chair. I don't suppose the game stops when a player dies.

No, said Nagasaki. Game go on all the time, night and day.

Neither night nor day nor storm nor war nor revolution interferes with this game, said Dynamite.

Where'd you get that? said Fat Laramie.

It's the truth, ain't it? said Dynamite.

Where'd you get it, though? said Fat Laramie.

I'm not as dumb as some of the players around here, said Dynamite. I know when to retreat. I got it out of a book.

I thought so, said Fat Laramie. I thought it didn't sound natural. What you mean is, this game goes on all the time.

It's a good game, said Nagasaki.

Yeah, said Bull. You haven't worked in two years. You've been in this game two years now. You never lose, do you, Nagasaki?

Sometimes lose very bad, said the Jap.

Yeah, said Fat Laramie, I know.

Somebody's got to lose, said the kid in the leather coat. I'm about twenty dollars in the hole right now.

One night, said Bull, I saw Curley lose eighty dollars in one pot to Crazy Gus who was drunk. Gus drew out on him. Curley had aces back to back and Gus had treys back to back. Curley bet everything in front of him on the fourth card. He wanted the poor fool to know he had the best, but Gus was too drunk to know anything; or maybe drunk *enough* to know everything. Anyway, he called and made two pair.

That was tough, said the kid.

Wait a minute, said Bull. Curley fished into his pocket and brought out a quarter and a dime. He bought seven white chips. Two hours later Crazy Gus got up from the table broke, and Curley had all his chips.

That's *luck* for you, said the kid.

Luck nothing, said Bull. Curley knew how to play. They can draw out on you once in a while, but not all the time.

Mr. Isaac said something, then Nagasaki said something, and then Hollywood Pete, and one after another each of the players said something while the game moved along into the night and the year. It was great and I knew I was home again. Somebody went broke and got up and went away and somebody else sat down in his chair, and I began to forget everything. It was fine. It was perfect because I wanted to forget everything. I played the way the cards demanded that I play and the cards were full of kindness. They didn't race after me, and they didn't trick me.

It was a little after midnight, and I was home again from Europe. The streets of all the cities I had visited, and the people of these streets, and the words of the foreign languages, began to return to the wakeful dream, and I began to return to each place I had visited for a day, or an afternoon, or an hour, and I began to see again each face I had seen, each street, each configuration of city and village.

I knew I'd be playing poker till the journey ended. All winter, most likely.

I drank whisky all night and left the game sober and hushed early in the morning. I went into the cafeteria on the corner and ordered buckwheat cakes with bacon and hot coffee. Then I walked three miles to my room through rain. I took off my wet clothes and got into bed. I slept and dreamed the journey, almost wakening now and then to listen more consciously to the sound of the train rushing from Paris to Vienna, through the Swiss and Austrian Alps. To look more clearly upon the green fields of Europe. To breathe more deeply the clear cold air of dawn in Austria. And when I got up at three in the afternoon, I felt stronger and wiser and more melancholy than ever before in my life.

I was beginning to forget everything, and the only way you can do that is to remember everything in the conscious dream and return everything to the living void of memory.

Then you'll be born again. Then you'll waken from the sleep of unbirth to the wakeful sleep of mortality.

The game lasted a long time, longer than the reckoning of days on the calendar, longer than time pulsing to inhale and exhale of breath, and the come and go of sea-tide, every moment wakeful and dreamed, inhabiting present and past, absorbing all movement over sea and continent, bringing the world together into one swiftly perceived reality and truth, and one morning when I got up from the game I knew the journey was ended and when I walked into the street I was laughing because it was so good to be in the world, so excellent to be a part of the chaos and unrest and agony and magnificence of this place of man, the world, so comic and tragic to be alive during a moment of its change, the sea, and the sea's sky, and London, and London's noise and fury, and the cockney's lamentation, the King's Palace, the ballet at Covent Garden, and outside Covent Garden the real ballet, and France, and the fields of France, and Paris, and the streets of Paris, and the stations, and the trains, and the faces, and the eyes, and the grief, and Austria, and Poland, and Russia, and Finland, and Sweden, and Norway, and the world, man stumbling mournfully after God in the wilderness, the street musicians of Edinburgh crying out for God in the songs of America, dancing after Him down steep streets, the tragic dream stalking everywhere through day and night, so that when I walked into the street I was laughing and begging God to pity them, love them, protect them, the king and the beggar alike.

The Tiger

✿ ✿ ✿

I

ONE day in January I was drinking beer in a little joint on Montgomery Street, talking to a lady who was drunk.

It was a nice day, it was a nice place, and the beer was good. I had come into the place to thank God for the world.

To hell with it, the lady said.

Lady, I said, let's not rush into this blindly.

To hell with it, she said.

Lady, I said, one of these days you'll be getting up and yawning and hailing a taxi and riding to the Southern Pacific depot and buying a ticket and getting aboard a train and going away at night to New Orleans and you will be delighted.

I drank ten of them and went away. The lady was immortal.

That was one of the days of the year.

II

One day in February I slept in the park on the grass, my face turned to the sky. The air of the earth was clear and I couldn't keep my eyes open. The book dropped from my hands and I began to dream. I dreamed the earth. Then I dreamed the world and wakened. An old lady was standing over me, looking down at me with great bitterness, although she was not my grandmother.

Good afternoon, I said.

Young man, said the old lady, you ought to be ashamed of yourself.

Why? I said.

This is no time to be sleeping, she said.

I didn't know, I said.

Why aren't you working? she said.

I am opposed to it, I said. My name is John Brook. I am a writer. I live in a furnished room on Pacific Street. My uncle, who is also opposed to work, pays my rent.

You ought to be ashamed, said the old lady.

She was a divine old lady, and I loved her when she was a girl, and forever after, even when she stood over me while I was dreaming. I couldn't help loving her when she was a girl because I could tell from her eyes how splendid, how innocent and good she had been. I knew she used to bathe Sunday morning and put on fresh clothes and walk down a quiet street to church and go in and sing. I knew how lovely she used to be. That would be in a small town somewhere. I could see the magnificent and lonely buildings and streets of the town in her eyes.

Of course I wanted to please her: that is how it is when you love a beautiful girl who is now an old lady.

Is there anything I can do? I said.

You might at least get up off the grass and stand, she said.

That was asking too much, but I got up off the grass and stood before the old lady anyway.

What do you write? she said.

English, I said.

English of course, said the old lady. Certainly not Chinese.

Chinese too, I said.

I don't believe it, said the old lady.

It is true, I said.

I was very humble about my writing Chinese. There are those who take pride in writing Chinese: these are the bad ones, who cannot write at all.

Speak to me in Chinese, said the old lady.

I cannot speak a word of Chinese, I said. You see, when I write English I write Chinese, Japanese, Italian, French, and every other language. You see, I said, I am a writer. I write in every language, in English.

Young man, said the old lady, I think you are crazy.

Is there anything I can do? I said.

You can tell me what you write, said the old lady. Do you write poems, stories, essays, novels, plays, history, biography, or what?

Yes, I said.

Yes, what? said the old lady.

I write everything, I said.

What did you say your name is? said the old lady.

John Brook, I said.

I have never heard of you, said the old lady.

Hardly anyone has, I said. I am very happy.

What books have you written? said the old lady.

I have not written any books, I said. I am writing *one* book. It will end when I die.

What is the name of the book you are writing? said the old lady.

John Brook, I said.

That's your *name*, said the old lady.

And the name of the book I am writing, I said.

What is the book about? said the old lady.

It is not yet written, I said. I do not know.

What is the plot of the book? said the old lady. Surely the book has a plot.

The plot is very simple, I said. Everything is the plot.

Is it a detective story? said the old lady.

Yes, I said. It is full of detectives.

Is it a love story? said the old lady.

Yes, I said. Love is in every word and sentence and paragraph and page of the book.

Young man, said the old lady, do you believe in God?

Lady, I said, could I disbelieve in that which I once was, and even now sometimes am?

Well, said the old lady, I don't know. You *seem* crazy. Yet I can see that you are in earnest.

I am delighted, I said.

Is there anything in the book about West Virginia, young man? said the old lady.

There are hours and days and years of West Virginia in the book, I said. It is the part where I name the places I have never visited.

I was born in West Virginia, said the old lady.

I am delighted, I said. Charleston?

Oceana, said the old lady.

This is indeed an honor, I said.

That was many years ago, said the old lady.

An honor, nevertheless, I said.

I had a long talk with the old lady. She told me to stop my nonsense and put on a clean shirt and go to town and look for a job, but I knew she wanted me to go on writing my book. I knew she wanted me to name Oceana, West Virginia. She pretended to be very angry with me, but I knew she knew I loved her as a girl. She knew I knew *she* loved me too.

III

One day in March I was in Los Angeles. It was almost a mistake. For one thing, I had no clean socks or shirts, and I didn't know the streets.

After a while, though, it was the same. I met a young man in the public library named Patrick Hogan. He was a writer. I mean, he wrote on paper. He wasn't really a writer. He wasn't writing Patrick Hogan. He was writing proletarian propaganda in the form, he said, of short stories, novels, plays, and poems.

We talked about one thing and another.

That is to say, I talked about Monday Tuesday Wednesday Thursday Friday Saturday Sunday Monday January February March April May June July August September October November December January everywhere, and Hogan talked about Fascism. It worked perfectly.

He said Hitler was a rat, and I said even so, he was born and he would die, Monday or Tuesday, January or February.

On the other hand, he said, Stalin is not a rat, but a great man, a lover of humanity. It was a warm day, the public library was well ventilated, and I was inclined to make no issue of it. I was inclined to agree that it was true: Stalin was a great lover of humanity, a man of nobility and strength, although diseased.

Diseased? said the young man.

Yes, I said.

How diseased?

I told him: by unbelief, by ambition, and by notoriety.

I see, he said. You are a Fascist.

I? I said.

He nodded.

My name is John Brook, I said.

He nodded again.

I live in a furnished room on Pacific Street in San Francisco, I said.

He nodded.

I am studying timeless and contemporary idiocy in man and in myself, and timeless and contemporary poise and dignity in beasts, plants, rocks, rivers, seas, and myself, and I am translating the universe, time and space, pneumatics, size, relativity, sleep, anger, despair, energy, motion, sound, texture, memory, and many other things into English. So far I have written one word.

One word? said the young man. What is that word?

God, I said. I wrote over two million false words before I achieved this one word.

God? he said. The word is meaningless.

It is not meaningless to me, I said. You must not forget the two million words which, although false by themselves, are true in this one word.

Have you no other word? he said.

Not completely, I said. I have two more words, but each is only partly achieved.

What is the second word? said the young man.

Is, I said.

Is?

Yes.

And what is the third?

Love, I said.

The last two words are not yet completely achieved, I said.

Your translation is a little trite, isn't it? said the young man.

On the contrary, I said.

All the same, he said, you are a Fascist.

My name is John Brook, I said. Would you care for some beer?

I don't drink, he said.

Not even one glass? I said.

Not even one glass, he said.

I wish you luck then, I said.

Wait, he said.

Yes? I said.

What do you intend to do about Fascism?

It is one of the false words, I said. I intend to wait for it to end. It began and it must end. The true word neither begins nor ends, *is*. I intend to have a couple of glasses of beer. What do you intend to do?

I am writing an essay for *The New Republic*, he said.

I hope the editors of *The New Republic* will have sense enough to buy your essay and publish it, I said.

I went down the long corridor and left the building.

The editors of *The New Republic* did not accept the essay of the young man, nor did the world accept the young man, nor did the young man himself accept the young man, nor did he accept Patrick Hogan, nor did Ireland accept him, nor America, nor the public library, and he did not get to be alive, although he was a writer. Brother, I mean death. The dream with no dreamer. The word, unwritten. The man, unborn. The tiger, unseen.

IV

Another day I walked from Main Street in Los Angeles to Hollywood. At the corner of Hollywood and Vine I saw Marlene Dietrich step out of a green Packard, like a chick out of an egg. It was not a moving picture, although she was alive and beautiful, divine and dying. The thing I noticed about her face was the sullen feline dreaminess, the melancholy stare of loneliness and regret and anger, the dark halo of grace and death. And I saw her walk. It was swift, angry, feminine movement, across the sidewalk to the doorway, through the afternoon and the year. And I saw the tiger follow her, aching with the warmth and perfume of her body.

I saw one of the Marx brothers too. He was sitting in a black Packard, pressing the button that made the horn sound, calling a friend. It was Chico, the one who plays the piano and talks with an Italian accent. The horn sounded many times but the friend did not appear. He drove the black Packard around the block and stopped in front of the restaurant again, and again sounded the horn, but the friend did not appear.

It wasn't a moving picture either. It was the world and the street of the world and Chico the clown. Neither tragedy nor comedy, and the friend did not appear. I waited many minutes and the clown drove the big automobile around the block many times and sounded the horn many times, and then it began to be mournful.

Brother, the only friend is the tiger, and even if she *had* come tripping out of the restaurant and even if she had stepped into the black Packard and gone away with you, brother, the tiger would be with her.

On the other hand, maybe it *was* a moving picture. I thought it was *better* than a moving picture. I thought it was Shakespeare. The sound effects were excellent and the cry of the horn was angry and desolating, the silence ferocious.

There was a place on Hollywood Boulevard where books were sold, and it was a place where writers arrived and departed. I went to this place for the view. It was a lonely place and the view was excellent. The whole panorama of the undiscovered universe was visible there.

A writer of detective stories entered this place and complained about Paramount. He also complained about America, which he identified as the public; and the tiger. He complained most about the tiger.

The tiger was almost caught up with him.

How much do you earn every week? I said.

One thousand dollars, said the writer of detective stories.

One thousand dollars is more money than I can understand, I said. What do you buy with the money?

Bread, he said.

Do you eat the bread? I said.

No, he said. None of us eats the bread. We have forgotten how to eat bread. We put the loaves into a large room and when we go to the room for bread to eat, each of the loaves is full of mold.

How about the detective? I said. Can't the detective help you? Can't he guard the loaves?

Not against mold, said the writer of detective stories. None of the loaves disappears, but each is with mold.

And your house? I said.

It is large, he said.

And your bed?

It was once the bed of a king.

And your automobile?

I have seven.

And when you enter your house?

I enter emptiness.

And when you go to bed?

I cannot sleep.

(The dream without a dreamer.)

And when you sit at the wheel of your most expensive automobile? I said.

The motor hums, he said. The wheels turn, and I go nowhere, and I return to my house and enter emptiness.

My name is John Brook, I said. I live in a furnished room on Pacific Street in San Francisco. I have not done an honest day's work in my life, nor a dishonest one. Where were you born?

In Fargo, North Dakota, said the writer of detective stories.

What day of what month of what year? I said.

The seventeenth day of September, 1898, said the writer of detective stories.

Go back to that day and that place, I said.

I am famous, said the writer of detective stories.

Go back to that day and place, I said. Go back and sleep. Go back and be born before you die.

The view of that day and place was excellent, uncluttered by detectives.

I also talked to a writer of love stories who hated himself, his wife, his daughter, the newsboy at the corner, and everybody alive. His stories appeared regularly in *The Saturday Evening Post*. He complained bitterly about the tiger.

A man in overalls entered the place and said he wanted to buy a book.

The clerk couldn't be bothered.

What is the name of the book you wish to buy? I said.

I don't know, said the man in overalls. I just thought I'd buy a book.

What do you want with a book? I said. Are you unhappy?

No, said the man in overalls. I feel fine.

Are you able to eat bread?

Yes.

Are you able to sleep?

Yes.

What do you want with a book?

I just thought I'd have a book in the house.

What for?

Well, he said, I just thought it would be nice to come home at night and just see the book.

He couldn't fool me, though. I knew all about it before he opened his mouth.

You're a carpenter, I said.

How did you know? he said.

I have just been talking to a writer of detective stories, I said.

I have always wanted to talk to a writer, he said.

Well, I said, this man over here is a writer. He writes love stories for the biggest magazines in America.

I pointed to the writer of love stories. He was standing in the corner, turning the pages of one of his books, and weeping.

He doesn't look like a writer, said the man in overalls. Besides, he's crying. What's he crying about?

What are you crying about? I said to the writer of love stories. This man wants to know.

Everything, said the writer of love stories.

Everything, I said to the man in overalls.

He doesn't look like a writer, said the man in overalls. He looks like a clerk in a department store.

This was the truth.

I shook hands with the man in overalls.

He sells, I said. He buys and sells.

I have always wanted to talk to a writer who looks like a writer, said the man in overalls.

My name is John Brook, I said.

My name is Jim Smith, said the man in overalls.

By God, I said, I am delighted. I live in a furnished room on Pacific Street in San Francisco.

I'm buying a house on North Orange Grove Avenue, he said.

By God, I said.

We could hear the writer of love stories sobbing.

By Jesus, said the man in overalls.

I am a writer, I said.

I have always wanted to talk to a writer who looks like a writer and talks like one, he said. By Jesus, he said, I'll buy one of *your* books. That will be a good book to have in the house I am buying on North Orange Grove Avenue.

I haven't written any books, I said.

By Jesus, he said, neither have I.

By God, I said, you can buy one of the books of this man in the corner who is crying.

By Jesus, no, he said.

By God, I said, he is known from coast to coast and his stories have been translated into seven European languages.

By Jesus, said the man in overalls, that's too bad. What the hell did they want to go to work and do that for?

By God, I said, they like it.

Well, by Jesus, said the man in overalls, what the hell's the matter with them?

By God, I said, everything.

By Jesus, he said, I believe you can tell me the name of a book I ought to have in the house on North Orange Grove Avenue.

By God, I said, you're right.

By Jesus, he said, what is the name of the book?

By God, I said, it's Jim Smith.

By Jesus, he said, that's *my* God damn name.

By God, I said, you're the greatest writing son of a bitch I have ever had the honor of meeting.

By Jesus, he said.

He walked out of the place and the tiger turned eighteen different kinds of somersaults following him.

By Jesus, said the tiger.

I walked two miles to Paramount. The lawn was green and cool, so I stretched out and stared up at the sky. A man in a uniform with brass buttons told me to get up and go away.

I work here, I said.

What do you do? he said.

I act, I said.

What parts do you play? he said.

I play the hero in the newsreels, I said. The President, the Greek waiter who won seventy-five thousand dollars on an Irish sweepstakes ticket, the winning jockey at Lexington, and all the others.

You can't sit on the lawn of Paramount Pictures Incorporated, he said.

My name is John Brook, I said.

You can't sit on the lawn anyway, he said.

I live in a furnished room on Pacific Street in San Francisco, I said.

If you don't get up and go away, he said, I'll blow this whistle.

By God, I said, I shall be delighted to hear you blow that God damn whistle.

A dozen Paramount Police armed to the teeth will come and *carry* you away, he said bitterly.

By Jesus, no, I said. I won the Army-Navy football game and the World War.

It wasn't a moving picture either, although the plot was better than most plots and the players better than most players.

The dialogue was good too. Best of all, though, was the setting: Paramount Pictures Incorporated, the lawn, and the sky. The sound effects were remarkably appropriate.

By God, I said, what's your name? *My* name is Cecil B. De Mille. Go ahead and blow your whistle.

Never mind my God damn name, he said. Get off the lawn of Paramount Pictures Incorporated, and get the hell out of here.

I could see the tigers playing and I could hear them laughing. They were having a hell of a time.

Blow your God damn whistle, I said.

Get off the lawn, he said.

There was no beautiful leading lady in the picture, so I got up and walked out of town, and the newsreel began. I hitch-hiked to San Francisco and when I reached the furnished room on Pacific Street it was very late at night.

V

My uncle was sitting at the table, reading the morning paper.

Where the hell have you been? he said. I've been sitting here since yesterday. I've read this paper from cover to cover. What the hell's going on?

That paper's six years old, I said.

I thought it was yesterday's paper, he said.

It's a good number, I said.

It's full of murder, if that's what you mean, he said.

No, I said. I mean the weather forecast. Clear and warm.

By God, he said, let's go out and buy a copy of *this* morning's paper.

It's no different, I said.

By God, he said, I've been reading Shakespeare all these years.

He's still writing for the newspapers, I said.

By God, my uncle said, that's what I thought. A lot of it sounded familiar.

I stretched out on the floor and went to sleep.

VI

One day in April I made a study of gambling and won eighty dollars on two horse races, by mistake. I made a parlay of *Old Judge*, 737, and *Claremore Clara*, 767. The numbers attracted me, not the names, and not the horses. I had intended to bet on *Lady Agatha*, 733, an excellent horse, and *Danny Deever*, 759, another excellent horse, but the numbers sounded bad, so I bet on *Old Judge* and *Claremore Clara*, two of the laziest horses in America, and each of them won. For three dollars, across the board, I got back eighty, so I went to my room on Pacific Street and put some shirts and stuff into a little satchel and paid my rent for three months in advance and told the landlady I was going away, perhaps to New Orleans, for a vacation.

A vacation from *what?* said the landlady.

You know me, I said.

Now you be careful, she said.

Good-bye, I said.

What's in New Orleans? she shouted bitterly.

Streets, I said.

In El Paso I ran into a dust storm. It was funny and tragic, the city far away and lost in the desert and dark with soft dust. The people went on breathing and walking and eating with great bravery. They eyes were full of dust, and every time they blowed their noses their handkerchiefs would be black with it. I was in the city six hours. Everybody wanted rain.

When the train rolled out of El Paso I looked into the empty landscape. The scene was glorious and full of wrath and agony: the earth and the sky were one. The earth solid and dry, the sky dark and thick with the substance of the earth. It was a picture one could only dream, only there was no dreamer.

The streets of New Orleans were narrow, crooked, dark, and lazy. The structures were old and they smelled. It was the smell of the place, the tribe there, the hours of living. I rented a room at the St. Charles Hotel and got under the shower to wash the dust of Texas out of the pores of my skin.

In the afternoon I went through the streets of the city and came to a cemetery that looked like a city. I walked through the cemetery and finally sat on the steps of one of the white marble houses to smoke a cigarette.

An old Negro passed before the house. He was crying.

Have you got loved ones buried in this cemetery? I said.

I got loved ones buried in many places of the world, said the old Negro. I don't know where. I come here to mourn. My boy Jephro is dead somewhere, and my other boy Sam, and my sister Dahlia, and my old Ma, and my old Pa, and my cousin Rufe Jackson, all dead. I come to this nice clean cemetery to mourn my dead.

Would a cigarette comfort you? I said.

A cigarette would comfort me more than anything in the world, said the old Negro.

He took a cigarette from the pack and I lit it and he sat down beside me, not crying any more.

He inhaled the smoke and exhaled many times, saying every time he exhaled, *Dead*, all gone from the world, all dead.

The tiger ran back and forth.

A small bird curved out of space and stopped on the roof of the dead-house across the way. Then it convulsed and the old Negro and I heard it cry.

He smoked the cigarette until it burned his fingers and lips.

Then he got up to go.

Here, I said, please take these cigarettes. My name is John Brook. I live in a furnished room on Pacific Street in San Francisco.

Thank you, my boy, he said. There's a heap of comfort in cigarettes.

I went back to the city. It was now early morning. I stretched out on the big bed and began to dream.

The tiger was restless in the dream. Sleep, I said, and it sank to the warm earth and slept.

When I wakened it was past midnight and the year was very still, the universe hushed, the tiger warm and drowsy. It rose to its feet, stretched its muscles, then roared, while I yawned, groaning.

VII

After April came May and after New Orleans New York. Then June and the sea, Atlantic. Then Europe and the cities there, and I mean death, the tiger following each who lives, brother.

I walked through London, and then through Paris, and Vienna, and Lemberg, and Kiev, and Moscow. I walked all over the world.

In August I returned to New York. In September I returned to San Francisco. I dreamed through October and November and December. One day the year ended, and the tiger ran amuck in the streets.

I went into the offices of a steamship company and asked for a calendar for the coming year.

Sweetheart Sweetheart Sweetheart

✿ ✿ ✿

ONE thing she *could* do was play the piano and sing. She couldn't cook or anything like that. Anyhow she didn't like to cook because she couldn't make pastry anyway and that's what she liked. She was something like the pastry she was always eating, big and soft and pink, and like a child although she was probably in her late thirties. She claimed she'd been on the stage. *I was an actress three seasons* is what she told the boy's mother. His mother liked the neighbor but couldn't exactly figure her out. She was married and had no kids, that's what his mother couldn't figure out; and she spent all her time making dresses and putting them on and being very pretty.

Who for? his mother would ask his sister. She would be busy in the kitchen getting food cooked or making bread and in English, which she couldn't talk well but which she liked to talk when she was talking about the neighbor, she said, What for, she's so anxious to be pretty? And then in Italian she'd say, But my, how nice she plays the piano. She's a good neighbor to have.

They'd just move from one side of town to the other, from Italian town to where the Americans were. This lady was one of them, an American, so his mother guessed that was the way they were, like fancy things to eat, sweet and creamy and soft and pink.

The neighbor used to come over a lot because, she said, it was so refreshing to be among real people.

You know, Mrs. Amendola, she used to say, it's a pleasure to have a neighbor like you. It's so wonderful the way you take care of all your wonderful children without a husband. All your fine growing girls and boys.

Oh, his mother used to laugh, the kids are good. I feed them and take care of them. Headache, toothache, trouble at school, I take care of everything; and his mother roared with laughter. Then his mother looked at the neighbor and said, They're my kids. We fight, we yell, we hit each other, but we like each other. You no got children?

No, the neighbor said. The boy became embarrassed. His mother was so boisterous and abrupt and direct. It was about the third time she'd asked if the neighbor had no children. What she meant, he knew, was, How come you haven't got any? A big woman like you, full of everything to make children?

The neighbor used to come over often when her husband was away. He covered the valley from Bakersfield to Sacramento, selling hardware. Sometimes his wife went with him, but most often not.

She preferred not to because travel was so difficult. And yet whenever she didn't go that meant that she would be in the house alone, and that made her lonely, so she used to visit the Italian family.

One night she came over sobbing and his mother put her arms around the neighbor as if she was one of his mother's kids, and comforted her.

But one thing he noticed that kind of puzzled him; she wasn't *really* crying. It wasn't honest-to-God crying; it was something else; she wasn't hurt or sorry or in pain or anything; it seemed like she just felt like crying, so she cried, just the same as if she might have felt like buying a dozen cream puffs and eating them. That's the impression he got.

Oh, Mrs. Amendola, she said. I was sitting all alone in the house when all of a sudden I began to remember all the years and then I got scared and started to cry. Oh, I feel so bad, she said and then smiled in a way that seemed awfully lovely to the boy and awfully strange. She looked around at his sister, and then, smiling, she looked at him and he didn't know what to do. She looked a long time. It wasn't a glance. And he knew right away something he didn't understand was going on. She was awfully lovely, big and soft and full of everything, and he felt embarrassed. Her arms were so full.

The little kids were all in bed, so it was only his mother and his sister and him. His mother said, You be all right. You sit with us and talk, you be fine. What's the matter?

I feel so sad, the neighbor said. When I remember all the years gone by, the times when I was a little girl, and then when I was almost grown-up at high school, and then on the stage, I feel so lonely.

Oh, you be all right, his mother said. You like a glass of wine?

His mother didn't wait for her to answer. She got out the bottle and poured two drinks, one for herself and one for the neighbor.

Drink wine, his mother said. Wine is good.

The neighbor sipped the wine.

Oh, it's wonderful, she said. You're a wonderful family, Mrs. Amendola. Won't you come to my house for a visit? I'd like to show you the house.

Oh, sure, his mother said. His mother wanted to see what her house looked like. So they all went to the house next door and room by room the neighbor showed them the house. It was just like her, like cream puffs. Soft and warm and pink, all except *his* room. He had his own room, bed and everything. There was something fishy somewhere, the boy thought. Americans were different from Italians, that's all he knew. If he slept in one bed and she in another, something was funny somewhere. Her room was like a place in another world. It was so like a woman that he felt ashamed to go in. He stood in the doorway while his mother and sister admired the beautiful room, and then the neighbor noticed him and took his hand. He felt excited and wished he was with her that way alone and in another world. The neighbor laughed and said, But I want *you* to admire my room, too, Tommy. You're such an intelligent and refined boy.

He didn't know for sure, maybe it was his imagination, but when she said he was intelligent and refined it seemed to him she squeezed his hand. He was awfully scared, almost sick. He didn't know about the Americans yet, and he didn't want to do anything wrong. Maybe she *had* squeezed his hand, but maybe it was as if she was just an older person, or a relative. Maybe it was because she was their neighbor, nothing else. He took his hand away as quickly as possible. He didn't speak about the room because he knew anything he'd say would be ridiculous. It was a place he'd like to get in and stay in forever, with her. And that was crazy. She was married. She was old enough to be his mother, although she was a lot younger than his mother. But that was what he wanted.

After they saw the house she cooked chocolate and brought them a cup each. The cups were very delicate and beautiful. There was a plate full of mixed pastry, all kinds of it. She made each of them eat a lot; anyway, for every one she ate, she made them eat one, too, so they each ate four, then there were two left. She laughed and said she could never get enough pastry, so she was going to take one of the last two, and since Tommy was the man present, he ought to take the other. She said that in a way that more than ever excited the boy. He became confused and deeply mournful about the whole thing. It was something new and out of the world. It was like wanting to get out of the world and never come back. To get into the strange region of warmth and beauty and ease and something else that she seemed to make him feel existed; by her voice and her way of laughing and the way she was, the way her house was, especially the way she looked at him.

He wondered if his mother and sister knew about it. He hoped they didn't. After the chocolate and pastry, his mother asked her to play the piano and sing and she was only too glad to. She played three songs; one for his mother; one for his sister; and then she said, This one for Tommy. She played and sang *Maytime*, the song that hollers or screams, *Sweetheart sweetheart sweetheart*. The boy was very flattered. He hoped his mother and sister didn't catch on, but that was silly because the first thing his mother said when they got home was, Tommy, I think you got a sweet-heart now. And his mother roared with laughter.

She's crazy about you, his sister said.

His sister was three years older than him, seventeen, and she had a fellow. She didn't know yet if she was going to marry him.

She's just nice, the boy said. She was nice to all of us. That's the way she is.

Oh, no, his sister said. She was *nicer* to you than to us. She's falling in love with you, Tommy. Are you falling in love with her?

Aw, shut up, the boy said.

You see, Ma, his sister said. He *is* falling in love with her.

Tell her to cut it out, Ma, the boy said.

You leave my boy alone, his mother told his sister.

And then his mother roared with laughter. It was such a wonderful joke. His mother and his sister laughed until he had to laugh, too. Then all of a sudden their laughter became louder and heartier than ever. It was *too* loud.

Let's not laugh so loud, the boy said. Suppose she hears us? She'll think we're laughing at *her*.

He's in love, Ma, his sister said.

His mother shrugged her shoulders. He knew she was going to come out with one of her comic remarks and he hoped it wouldn't be too embarrassing.

She's a nice girl, his mother said, and his sister started laughing again.

He decided not to think about her any more. He knew if he did his mother and sister would know about it and make fun of him. It wasn't a thing you could make fun of. It was a thing like nothing else, most likely the best thing of all. He didn't want it to be made fun of. He couldn't explain to them but he felt they shouldn't laugh about it.

In the morning her piano-playing wakened him and he began to feel the way he'd felt last night when she'd taken his hand, only now it was worse. He didn't want to get up, or anything. What he wished was that they were together in a room like hers, out of the world, away from every-body, forever. She sang the song again, four choruses of it, *Sweetheart sweetheart sweetheart.*

His mother made him get up. What's the matter? she said. You'll be late for work. Are you sick?

No, he said. What time is it?

He jumped out of bed and got into his clothes and ate and got on his wheel and raced to the grocery store. He was only two minutes late.

The romance kept up the whole month, all of August. Her husband came home for two days about the middle of the month. He fooled around in the yard and then went away again.

The boy didn't know what would ever happen. She came over two or three times every week. She appeared in the yard when he was in the yard. She invited the family over to her house two or three times for chocolate and pastry. She woke him up almost every morning singing *Sweetheart sweetheart sweetheart.*

His mother and sister still kidded him about her every once in a while.

One night in September when he got home his sister and mother had a big laugh about him and the neighbor.

Too bad, his mother said. Here, eat your supper. Too bad.

We feel sorry for you, his sister said.

What are you talking about? the boy said.

It's too late now, his mother said.

Too late for *what?* the boy said.

You waited too long, his sister said.

Aw, cut it out, the boy said. What are you talking about?

She's got another sweetheart now, his sister said.

He felt stunned, disgusted, and ill, but tried to go on eating and tried not to show how he felt.

Who? he said.

Your sweetheart, his sister said. You know *who.*

He wasn't sorry. He was angry. Not at his sister and mother; at *her.* She was stupid. He tried to laugh it off.

Well, it's about time, he said.

He comes and gets her in his car, his sister said. It's a Cadillac.

What about her husband? the boy said. He felt foolish.

He don't know! his mother said. Maybe he don't *care.* He's dead, I think.

His mother roared with laughter, and then his sister, too, and then he, too. He was glad Italians laughed, anyway. That made him feel a little better. After supper, though, he was strangely ill all the time. She was a stupid, foolish woman.

Every night for a week his mother and sister told him about the man coming and getting her every afternoon, driving off with her in his Cadillac.

She's got no family, his mother said. She's right. What's the use being pretty for nothing?

He's an awful handsome man, his sister said.

The husband, his mother said, he's dead.

They told him about the neighbor and her lover every night for a week, and then one night she came over to pay another visit. She was lovelier than ever, and not sad any more. Not even make-believe sad.

He was afraid his mother would ask about the man, so he tried to keep her from doing so. He kept looking into his mother's eyes and telling her not to make any mistakes. It would be all right across the tracks, but not in this neighborhood. If *she* wanted to come out with it herself, *she* could tell them. She didn't, though. The boy waited five minutes and then he decided she wasn't going to say anything.

He got his cap and said, I'm going to the library, Ma.

All right, his mother said.

He didn't say good night to her. He didn't even look at her. She knew *why,* too.

After that she never played the piano in the mornings, and whenever she *did* play the piano she didn't play the song she'd said was for him.

The Brothers and the Sisters

✿ ✿ ✿

BROTHER MATTHEW from Tennessee was the youngest of the Brothers. He was like any man, not like a churchman. The other Brothers were fond of him, but felt superior. They were all professors of this and that and the other thing. As far as the young man Jack Towey was concerned, they were bores.

Jack Towey was twenty-one and very big. One day he lifted Brother Garcia off the floor and held him overhead. Brother Garcia was a very dignified man who weighed around one hundred and fifty pounds. The young man did not lift Brother Garcia off the floor until Brother Garcia had given him permission to do so.

Brother Garcia, the young man had said, do you know I can lift you off the floor and hold you overhead?

Brother Garcia was, of course, somewhat stunned.

No, he said. I'd never given it a thought.

I can, Jack Towey said. Will you let me?

If you wish, Brother Garcia said.

I won't hurt you, the young man said.

Lord in Heaven, Brother Garcia said, I believe you. Please let me down.

It's easy for me, the young man said. I won't drop you. I could hold you up this way for an hour, I guess.

I'd rather you let me down, Brother Garcia said.

The young man put the Brother on the floor extra gently, as if the Brother were something that might break if jarred.

The others were eating lunch in the sunlight, sitting outside on the steps of the building. The young man wasn't with them because Brother Matthew was out of town. Brother Garcia had stayed upstairs during the lunch hour in the hope of doing some reading. After the young man had lifted him and let him down Brother Garcia felt strangely dissatisfied with himself. He felt that he ought to exercise more and develop his body. There was some dignity in having one's spirit housed in strong substance. He rather envied the young man's strength.

All right, he said. You'll have to excuse me now. I have some reading to do.

Don't you get tired of reading all the time? the young man said.

I don't read all the time, Brother Garcia said.

Brother Garcia sat down with his book. The young man went to the window where he remained standing for some time.

Brother Garcia lifted his eyes from the book now and then to watch the young man.

Brother Garcia, the boy said.

Yes? the Brother said.

Have you noticed the hotel across the street?

I know it's there, the Brother said. What about it?

Brother Garcia knew all about the hotel across the street. All the Brothers knew about it. It was one of many places of its kind in the North Beach.

I think they've got some girls upstairs, the young man said.

Is that so? the Brother said.

I think so, the young man said. Every day I've seen men come and go. Have you ever seen any of the girls?

I don't believe I have, the Brother said.

I saw one of them yesterday evening, the young man said. She was just a kid. That's what I can't understand.

What do you mean? the Brother said.

I mean, the young man said, why didn't she marry some young fellow instead? There are a lot of young fellows who'd like to marry a girl like her if they knew she was a good girl. She was very pretty. If you weren't a Brother, Brother Garcia, and you liked a girl like her, would you marry her anyway?

I don't know, the Brother said.

It sure surprised me when I saw how young and pretty she was, the young man said. She looked like a good girl. If I hadn't seen her come out of the hotel I would have believed she was a good girl. She smiled at me. I'd hate to fall in love with a girl like her.

Yes, the Brother said, that would only make you unhappy.

I feel unhappy now, the young man said. I'm not in love with her or anything, but it makes me sore to think she'd love anybody who'd pay for it. Have you ever gone up to any of those places?

Lord in Heaven, no, the Brother said.

I mean just to look around, the young man said. Maybe a Brother could do something about it.

I'm afraid not, the Brother said.

I don't know, the young man said, but I've got a feeling I ought to do something.

What could you do? the Brother said.

I don't know, the young man said, but I've got a feeling I ought to do something. It don't seem right.

After lunch the Brothers came upstairs and went on with their work. The only other worker in the winery who was not a Brother was old Angelo Fanucci. He worked with the young man, Jack Towey. He was a small man of fifty-seven whose life had been ruined by an unfortunate event of many years ago.

Angelo, the young man would say, did you see the fleet come in?

What do I care about the fleet? the old man would say. Will it go to the Bank of Italy and get my *tirteen tousand* dollars?

It was the same with everything.

Angelo, the young man would say, have you walked across the Golden Gate Bridge?

Why should I walk across the bridge? the old man would say. On the other side will I find my *tirteen tousand* dollars? Some day I will get that woman.

Then he would swear violently in Italian.

After work that evening the young man stayed in the winery until all the Brothers had gone home. The janitor and night watchman, Louis Getas, noticed him standing at the window.

Why you no go home? he said.

I'll be going in a little while, the young man said.

What you looking? the janitor said.

Nothing, the young man said.

He saw a man hurry into the doorway, press the button, and a moment later turn the knob of the door, open it, and hurry upstairs.

He felt a great hatred for the man because he was afraid the man might choose the girl he had seen yesterday and for a moment he wanted to go across the street, upstairs, and throw the man out of the place.

The following day Brother Matthew returned to the winery from the country. He had arranged to purchase many tons of wine grapes from vineyardists of the San Joaquin valley.

The young man was glad to see him back. When he was alone with the Brother he said, Brother Matthew, you know about this place across the street.

Sure, the young Brother said. Don't tell me you want to take me up there with you to spend some money.

The young man laughed. It was pleasant to talk with a Brother like Brother Matthew.

I'd like to go up there, the young man said.

Well, said Brother Matthew, for all I know maybe I would, too, but I'm not going to.

I don't mean to spend money, the young man said. There's a girl up there I'd like to talk to.

What do you want to talk to her for? the Brother said.

Well, I don't think she should be in a place like that, the young man said. It burns me up.

Who is this girl? the Brother said.

I don't know, the young man said. I saw her in the street a couple of days ago. Do you think maybe you could go up there with me?

What do you want to talk to her about? the Brother said.

I don't want her to stay in a place like that, the young man said.

I don't believe the girl would be interested in hearing that kind of talk, the Brother said.

She smiled at me, the young man said.

It may be, the Brother said, that she smiles at every man. It is possible that she would even smile at me. You're not in love with her, are you?

I've never been in love, the young man said. I don't know how it feels to be in love. I feel sore at everybody. What I want to know is what kind of a world is this when a girl like that has to be in a place like that? Will you go up there with me tonight after work?

Why don't you forget you ever saw her? the Brother said.

I guess I ought to, the young man said, but ever since I saw her I've felt sore at everybody.

Why don't you go up alone? the Brother said.

I'm afraid to go up alone, the young man said.

What are you afraid of? the Brother said.

I don't know, the young man said. If you go with me, I'll feel better.

The Brother thought it over a moment.

All right, he said. I hope nobody sees us. We'll have to be very careful.

That evening after work the young man and Brother Matthew took a walk until it was dark. Then they returned to the winery and when nobody was in sight they hurried across the street to the doorway of the hotel and the Brother pressed the button. Each of them was frightened.

Shall we go up? the young man asked the Brother.

There's still time to go away, the Brother said. Perhaps we'd better.

They heard the electric lock buzz. The Brother took the door knob and opened the door two or three inches.

Somebody's coming down the street, the young man said.

The Brother pushed the door open and the two young men hurried up the stairs.

There was a nauseating odor of powder and perfume in the place. At the top of the stairs was a middle-aged woman in a green tight-fitting dress with no sleeves.

Good evening, boys, she said.

Good evening, Brother Matthew replied.

When the woman noticed the Brother's clothes, she smiled.

She led the young men to a waiting room. They did not sit down.

I've always wondered what the inside of one of these places was like, the Brother said.

It wasn't much unlike any other small hotel, except for the way it made you feel. The odor of the place and your knowing what kind of a place it was made you feel any number of ways at once. You felt ashamed and foolish and amused and sorrowful, but more than anything else you felt that living was an ugly thing, and then because you knew this was so you felt the absurdity of trying to be good and you wondered if living the heedless life wasn't more true and real than living the good one.

When the girls came into the room they saw two excited young men, one of them a Catholic Brother. This embarrassed the girls and brought to an end something in them which was an essential part of their work, a partly-artificial and partly-genuine mood of gaiety, daring, recklessness, and good-humor. They became inwardly and outwardly clumsy. The innocence in the girls returned in them to meet the same thing in the young men. They were like three sisters. The young Brother's momentary feeling of wickedness fell away from him and instead of being excited by the girls as he had imagined he might be he felt more truly immune to sin than ever before in his life. He was, in fact, rather delighted that he had come.

The young man, however, could not take his eyes away from the girl who had smiled at him. Now, in this place, she did not smile, and he tried to understand this. He seemed to feel that what she had shared with him in the street was a thing which did not come with her to this place, a thing which nothing could take away from her, and which needed no guarding.

The Brother looked at each of the girls and then at the young man, asking with his glance if the young man wished to talk to the girl. The young man answered with an almost imperceptible shaking of his head.

The young Brother felt strangely happy.

We work in the winery across the street, he said at last. My friend and I thought we'd come in and say hello and ask if we might bring you some wine.

This broke down the feeling of awkwardness in everyone. The girls and the young men began to talk and laugh. The young men offered the girls cigarettes and everyone but the girl who had smiled at the young man smoked. The young man asked the girl if she'd like to go for a walk with him some evening and she said perhaps she would. This made him very happy.

The Brother and the young man promised to return soon with wine, and then went away.

In the street the two young men felt lively, but at the same time, for some reason, deeply sorrowful.

They're wonderful people, aren't they? the young man said.

Yes, they are, the Brother said. I don't believe I've ever met such truly innocent people.

I want to thank you for going with me, the young man said. If I didn't go, I'd feel bad all the time.

I'm glad you asked me to go, the Brother said.

They hurried along the street in silence for two blocks, and then suddenly the young man wanted to vomit. He began to cry, and the Brother, for the first time in his life, understood how difficult living would always have to be for everybody.

The Ants

✿ ✿ ✿

WE moved into a house once that the real estate man said was wonderful. What it had that was all right was a front porch Grandma could sit in a rocking chair on all day, which she began to do the day before we moved into the house, all eleven of us, counting Sam. Grandma liked the front porch so much she had me go seven blocks to our old house on Peachtree Street for her rocking chair and began sitting there the rest of the day. After sunset she came home for supper and after supper went back to the chair, smoking cigarettes and rocking. It was summer and the night was warm, so Grandma rocked in the rocking chair all night.

In the morning, when we began to arrive with the furniture, we woke her up. All eleven of us, counting Sam, had to make four trips before we moved all our stuff. By two o'clock in the afternoon we had all our stuff in the new house, and my uncle Woffard, or Louie, as we used to call him instead of Woffard, went to town to see about having gas and water and electricity turned on. By sunset we were all in the new house, the water was running out of the kitchen faucet, the gas in the stove was heating stew, and the electricity was brightening the ten-cent mazda lamps from Woolworth's.

Sam, whom we always included in our estimates of number of people on hand, regardless of his attitude, complained all day about everything, and around supper time threatened to run away from home again.

Sam, Grandma said, you ought to be ashamed of yourself, always threatening to run away from home, a grown man of forty talking like that in front of the kids; what kind of an example do you think you're going to be setting them?

Well, it ain't fair, Sam said, and you know it, Ma. You ain't got no right to shove me around like I was nobody.

We ain't saying you ain't somebody, Louie said. We're just saying cut out your fooling and buckle down like the rest of us and get somewheres in the world.

Where've you ever gotten in the world? Sam said.

Where? Louie said. I went to town, didn't I, and had them turn on water, gas, and lights, didn't I? I walked right in and gave them the address and gave them a new name, didn't I? Where've I ever gotten? I've rubbed shoulders with a few people here and there, and don't ever forget it.

We had no business moving out of our old house, Sam said. That's all I know. Just because we couldn't pay the man his rent.

That wasn't the reason at all, Grandma said. The house was too small. There wasn't any front porch to set this rocker on either. That's why we left.

You're all selfish, Sam said. Every last one of you are selfish, with no consideration for my art, all over the walls of the old house. All my poems and stories written on the walls. What about them?

Oh, write some new ones on the walls of this house, Grandma said. You go ahead and find yourself a good pencil and start at the top of the kitchen wall and write all the poems and stories you like.

Oh, hush, Sam said.

Well, Louie said, you'll just have to get along in this new house the best you can, Sam, that's all, because we've got water, gas, and lights here, and we'll have them two months before the companies shut them off.

So we started living in this new house with the front porch. We started living in it the minute we got there. Some of us started living right in the house and some of us outside in the yard, and my cousin Merle started living up on the roof, where, he claimed, you got a better view of practically everything.

It was a fine house except for the ants. They were all over the place, and the first morning of our living in the house, they were *on* us, and *in* the food we ate, and everywhere. At first we got all peeved, every one of us, and kept telling one another what an awful liar the real estate man was, telling us it was a fine house and not saying one word about the ants. They were all over us, crawling around under our clothes, in our hair, on our hands, around our eyes, and everywhere. At first we kept pinching them and squeezing them and stamping on them and drowning them, but after we found out it didn't do any good we just let them come and go as they pleased.

That was the only thing to do, although it had us all kicking and jumping and wiggling and flicking them off our hands and off the ends of our noses. But that was all you could do, except take a bath.

Well, Sam said, I guess *now* you'll all move back to the old house on Peachtree Street where we belong.

We *will* not, Louie said. We'll stay right here and face the music. What are we, men or what?

Well, Sam said, I can speak for myself only, and I say it's awful humiliating to have ants walking all over you all day and all night, and if any of you had any pride you'd do something about it.

Louis wiggled, kicked, jumped, and flicked two ants off his nose and said, We are doing something about it all the time. We've got just as much pride as you have.

So we not only began to live in the house, we began to live and suffer in it. We kept living and suffering in it every minute of every day and night, kicking, jumping, wiggling, flicking them off, and eating them with everything we ate.

I've seen ants before, Grandma said, but I ain't never seen them like this.

Cousin Velma kicked, jumped, bended, twirled, laughed, threw her arms into the air, and hollered *whoa*.

It was awful beautiful hearing her holler that way.

Folks from the other side of town came over to find out what it was all about.

They watched us from the street and shook their heads and went away, but one day a young fellow in a red and blue striped sweater hollered at Velma.

Sister, he hollered, what's going on up at your house?

Ants, Velma hollered back.

Why don't you kill them? the boy hollered, and Velma hollered back, Too many of them. We do kill them, but they're faster than we are.

I figure I can kill all the ants in your house, the young fellow hollered. Ain't no sense suffering the way you are.

We ain't suffering any more, Velma hollered. We've gotten used to it.

Must be awful tiring to be jumping around the way you are all the time, the young man said.

Not particular, Velma said.

In this manner their romance began. His name was John Tarhill and he was a sailor by trade. Leastaways that's what he said. Grandma liked him for his daring, and his reckless attitude toward the world. He'd been to San Francisco and had gotten on a docked boat once. He'd gone right down to the engine room and seen the boilers and the pipes and all the stuff and then he'd gone right up again and come back to Kingsburg. But he'd been on a boat. It was a great big one, too. It was called *The Vasco Da Gama*.

Do you believe me, Grandma, John Tarhill said, when I tell you that that boat I stood on the deck of and went down into the engine room of had gone to China and away over to places like that?

My, my, Grandma said, all the way to China. How did it smell?

On deck it smelled like spoiled coffee and oil, John Tarhill said, and down in the engine room it smelled like influenza with high fever. That's why I didn't take the trip to South America.

My, my, Grandma said, South America. You certainly came close to traveling an awful far distance, didn't you, son?

I certainly did, Grandma, John Tarhill said. Do you reckon if I get hold of two dollars somewhere I can marry Velma and raise ourselves a family?

I reckon so, son, Grandma said. You seem to come from a good family. Where else did that boat journey to, that you heard about?

Well, Grandma, John Tarhill said, I heard a man say it went to Liverpool once. That's in Ireland somewhere, I guess. It went to other places in that direction, too.

Well, landsakes, Grandma said. It certainly is interesting to sit here and talk to a young man who's seen his share of the world.

Cousin Velma and John Tarhill had a courtship of two weeks and then they got married. Sam performed the ceremony and Merle played something like wedding music on his mouth organ. John didn't get any two dollars anywhere for a license, so Velma and John got married without one.

I don't suppose anybody'll mind if you get your license later when you can afford it, Grandma said, just so it's legal, and Sam here will see that it's legal.

So then there were twelve of us in the house, jumping with the ants. They were awful interesting little things to watch, busy all the time, and funny too. Velma and John Tarhill spent their honeymoon on the left side of the front porch lying on their stomachs and watching them and laughing all the time, except when Grandma inquired further concerning the various places that that boat had at one time or another gone to.

One day cousin Velma came to Grandma and couldn't say a word.

Why, what's the matter with you? Grandma said, and Velma jumped and giggled.

Oh, that, Grandma said. Well, praise God, is what I always say. He knows best. It won't be for some time of course. I'm glad for you.

So we all knew Velma was going to have a young one from John Tarhill, our relative by marriage.

It was truly a pleasant two months we spent in the new house, what with the ants, the ship that John Tarhill stood on the deck of, and Velma's romance with him. After two months the different companies shut off the water and the gas and the lights and for a week we got along without them modern conveniences, but after a week the real estate man came and said we had to pay rent or get out and Grandma said, Pay rent? Why, boy, the house is full of ants. So that afternoon we moved to another house.

The Great Leapfrog Contest

❄ ❄ ❄

ROSIE MAHONEY was a tough little Irish kid whose folks, through some miscalculation in directions, or out of an innate spirit of anarchy, had moved into the Russian-Italian-and-Greek neighborhood of my home town, across the Southern Pacific tracks, around G Street.

She wore a turtle-neck sweater, usually red. Her father was a bricklayer named Cull and a heavy drinker. Her mother's name was Mary. Mary Mahoney used to go to the Greek Orthodox Catholic Church on Kearny Boulevard every Sunday, because there was no Irish Church to go to anywhere in the neighborhood. The family seemed to be a happy one.

Rosie's three brothers had all grown up and gone to sea. Her two sisters had married. Rosie was the last of the clan. She had entered the world when her father had been close to sixty and her mother in her early fifties. For all that, she was hardly the studious or scholarly type.

Rosie had little use for girls, and as far as possible avoided them. She had less use for boys, but found it undesirable to avoid them. That is to say, she made it a point to take part in everything the boys did. She was always on hand, and always the first to take up any daring or crazy idea.

Everybody felt awkward about her continuous presence, but it was no use trying to chase her away, because that meant a fight in which she asked no quarter, and gave none.

If she didn't whip every boy she fought, every fight was at least an honest draw, with a slight edge in Rosie's favor. She didn't fight girl-style, or cry if hurt. She fought the regular style and took advantage of every opening. It was very humiliating to be hurt by Rosie, so after a while any boy who thought of trying to chase her away, decided not to.

It was no use. She just wouldn't go. She didn't seem to like any of the boys especially, but she liked being in on any mischief they might have in mind, and she wanted to play on any teams they organized. She was an excellent baseball player, being as good as anybody else in the neighborhood at any position, and for her age an expert pitcher. She had a wicked wing, too, and could throw a ball in from left field so that when it hit the catcher's mitt it made a nice sound.

She was extraordinarily swift on her feet and played a beautiful game of tin-can hockey.

At pee-wee, she seemed to have the most disgusting luck in the world.

At the game we invented and used to call *Horse* she was as good at *horse* as at *rider*, and she insisted on following the rules of the game. She insisted on being horse when it was her turn to be horse. This always embarrassed her partner, whoever he happened to be, because it didn't seem right for a boy to be getting up on the back of a girl.

She was an excellent football player too.

As a matter of fact, she was just naturally the equal of any boy in the neighborhood, and much the superior of many of them. Especially after she had lived in the neighborhood three years. It took her that long to make everybody understand that she had come to stay and that she was *going* to stay.

She did, too; even after the arrival of a boy named Rex Folger, who was from somewhere in the south of Texas. This boy Rex was a natural-born leader. Two months after his arrival in the neighborhood, it was understood by everyone that if Rex wasn't the leader of the gang, he was very nearly the leader. He had fought and licked every boy in the neighborhood who at one time or another had fancied himself leader. And he had done so without any noticeable ill-feeling, pride, or ambition.

As a matter of fact, no one could possibly have been more good-natured than Rex. Everybody resented him, just the same.

One winter, the whole neighborhood took to playing a game that had become popular on the other side of the tracks, in another slum neighborhood of the town: *Leapfrog*. The idea was for as many boys as cared to participate, to bend down and be leaped over by every other boy in the game, and then himself to get up and begin leaping over all the other boys, and then bend down again until all the boys had leaped over him again, and keep this up until all the other players had become exhausted. This didn't happen, sometimes, until the last two players had traveled a distance of three or four miles, while the other players walked along, watching and making bets.

Rosie, of course, was always in on the game. She was always one of the last to drop out, too. And she was the only person in the neighborhood Rex Folger hadn't fought and beaten.

He felt that that was much too humiliating even to think about. But inasmuch as she seemed to be a member of the gang, he felt that in some way or another he ought to prove his superiority.

One summer day during vacation, an argument between Rex and Rosie developed and Rosie pulled off her turtle-neck sweater and challenged him to a fight. Rex took a cigarette from his pocket, lighted it, inhaled, and told Rosie he wasn't in the habit of hitting women—where he came from that amounted to boxing your mother. On the other hand, he said, if Rosie cared to compete with him in any other sport, he would be glad to oblige her. Rex was a very calm and courteous conversationalist. He had poise. It was unconscious, of course, but he had it just the same. He was just naturally a man who couldn't be hurried, flustered, or excited.

So Rex and Rosie fought it out in this game Leapfrog. They got to leaping over one another, quickly, too, until the first thing we knew the whole gang of us was out on the State Highway going south towards Fowler. It was a very hot day. Rosie and Rex were in great shape, and it looked like one was tougher than the other and more stubborn. They talked a good deal, especially Rosie, who insisted that she would have to fall down unconscious before she'd give up to a guy like Rex.

He said he was sorry his opponent was a girl. It grieved him deeply to have to make a girl exert herself to the point of death, but it was just too bad. He had to, so he had to. They leaped and squatted, leaped and squatted, and we got out to Sam Day's vineyard. That was half-way to Fowler. It didn't seem like either Rosie or Rex were ever going to get tired. They hadn't even begun to show signs of growing tired, although each of them was sweating a great deal.

Naturally, we were sure Rex would win the contest. But that was because we hadn't taken into account the fact that he was a simple person, whereas Rosie was crafty and shrewd. Rosie knew how to figure angles. She had discovered how to jump over Rex Folger in a way that weakened him. And after a while, about three miles out of Fowler, we noticed that she was coming down on Rex's *neck*, instead of on his back. Naturally, this was hurting him and making the blood rush to his head. Rosie herself squatted in such a way that it was impossible, almost, for Rex to get anywhere near her neck with his hands.

Before long, we noticed that Rex was weakening. His head was getting closer and closer to the ground. About a half mile out of Fowler, we heard Rex's head bumping the ground every time Rosie leaped over him. They were good loud bumps that we knew were painful, but Rex wasn't complaining. He was too proud to complain.

Rosie, on the other hand, knew she had her man, and she was giving him all she had. She was bumping his head on the ground as solidly as she could, because she knew she didn't have much more fight in her, and if she didn't lay him out cold, in the hot sun, in the next ten minutes or so, she would fall down exhausted herself, and lose the contest.

Suddenly, Rosie bumped Rex's head a real powerful one. He got up very dazed and very angry. It was the first time we had ever seen him fuming. By God, the girl was taking advantage of him, if he wasn't mistaken, and he didn't like it. Rosie was squatted in front of him. He came up groggy and paused a moment. Then he gave Rosie a very effective kick that sent her sprawling. Rosie jumped up and smacked Rex in the mouth. The gang jumped in and tried to establish order.

It was agreed that the Leapfrog contest must not change into a fight. Not any more. Not with Fowler only five or ten minutes away. The gang

ruled further that Rex had had no right to kick Rosie and that in smack-
ing him in the mouth Rosie had squared the matter, and the contest was
to continue.

Rosie was very tired and sore; and so was Rex. They began leaping and
squatting again; and again we saw Rosie coming down on Rex's neck so
that his head was bumping the ground.

It looked pretty bad for the boy from Texas. We couldn't understand
how he could take so much punishment. We all felt that Rex was getting
what he had coming to him, but at the same time everybody seemed to
feel badly about Rosie, a girl, doing the job instead of one of us. Of
course, that was where we were wrong. Nobody but Rosie could have figured out that smart way of humiliating a very powerful and superior boy.
It was probably the woman in her, which, less than five years later, came
out to such an extent that she became one of the most beautiful girls in
town, gave up tomboy activities, and married one of the wealthiest young
men in Kings County, a college man named, if memory serves, Wallace
Hadington Finlay VI.

Less than a hundred yards from the heart of Fowler, Rosie, with great
and admirable artistry, finished the job.

That was where the dirt of the highway siding ended and the paved
main street of Fowler began. This street was paved with cement, not asphalt. Asphalt, in that heat, would have been too soft to serve, but cement
had exactly the right degree of brittleness. I think Rex, when he squatted
over the hard cement, knew the game was up. But he was brave to the
end. He squatted over the hard cement and waited for the worst. Behind
him, Rosie Mahoney prepared to make the supreme effort. In this next
leap, she intended to give her all, which she did.

She came down on Rex Folger's neck like a ton of bricks. His head
banged against the hard cement, his body straightened out, and his arms
and legs twitched.

He was out like a light.

Six paces in front of him, Rosie Mahoney squatted and waited. Jim
Telesco counted twenty, which was the time allowed for each leap. Rex
didn't get up during the count.

The contest was over. The winner of the contest was Rosie Mahoney.

Rex didn't get up by himself at all. He just stayed where he was until
a half dozen of us lifted him and carried him to a horse trough, where
we splashed water on his face.

Rex was a confused young man all the way back. He was also a deeply
humiliated one. He couldn't understand anything about anything. He just
looked dazed and speechless. Every now and then we imagined he wanted
to talk, and I guess he did, but after we'd all gotten ready to hear what
he had to say, he couldn't speak. He made a gesture so tragic that tears
came to the eyes of eleven members of the gang.

Rosie Mahoney, on the other hand, talked all the way home. She said
everything.

I think it made a better man of Rex. More human. After that he was a
gentler sort of soul. It may have been because he couldn't see very well
for some time. At any rate, for weeks he seemed to be going around in a
dream. His gaze would freeze on some insignificant object far away in the
landscape, and half the time it seemed as if he didn't know where he was
going, or why. He took little part in the activities of the gang, and the

following winter he stayed away altogether. He came to school one day wearing glasses. He looked broken and pathetic.

That winter Rosie Mahoney stopped hanging around with the gang, too. She had a flair for making an exit at the right time.

The Acrobats

✿ ✿ ✿

DOWN in the street we could see them from the second-floor window of the dentist's, L. R. Dorgus, as he had it on the door. What they were doing wasn't easy to say until the littlest of the three, who was no bigger than a big midget, began to get himself thrown into the air, somersaulting, right in the street.

Look, Mr. Dorgus, Emmie said.

What's the matter? the dentist said.

Emmie's brother Harry closed his mouth when the dentist turned away from him and gave his sister a mean look.

Will you stay away from the window while I'm getting killed around here? he said. It's bad enough when he keeps his mind on his work, without you calling him to the window. What's going on, anyhow?

They're throwing the littlest man in the air, Emmie said.

Probably a family quarrel or something, Harry said. Ain't no sense poking into other people's affairs.

It ain't no quarrel, Emmie said. They ain't hitting him or anything. It looks like he likes to get thrown around. He lands on his feet like a cat. He bounces every time he comes down.

I didn't know what to make of it. They seemed to me the most alive people I had ever seen. They weren't like people at all for that matter; more like animals. They had dark faces with eyes you could see even from away up on the second floor and strong arms and nimble bodies.

The dentist came over to the window just in time to see the two biggest ones who weren't very big themselves, but the same size, take the littlest one and swing him into the air for three somersaults. He came down, circling, landed lightly on his feet, bounced up and down twice, and then, just out of high spirits most likely, jumped away up into the air. The other two twirled around while he jumped. People were beginning to come from across the street. The dentist stood over me and Emmie and said, Well, what do you know about that?

What is it, Doc? Harry said. You going to take out this tooth or stand at the window all day?

Come and see, Harry, Emmie said. People are coming from all over now.

Harry got up out of the dentist's chair and came over to the window. The three little men were dancing now, in single file, and leaping, and then they stopped, turned around, and began to move their lips.

The dentist pushed us out of his way to open the window.

By God, he said, I think they're singing. Right on Cotton Street; right across the street from the Court House. That ain't happened in Reedley before.

They *were* singing, too. They had loud voices, and sang in a language nobody had the slightest idea what it was. The song seemed to be funny and sad at the same time.

Well, what do you know? Harry said. What are they, anyhow?

Search me, the dentist said. I've been in this office here eleven years, going on twelve, and I've never seen anything like this before. Listen to them.

About twenty people gathered around the acrobats. Some of them I knew, especially Jim Hokey who used to be my best pal till we fought about cheating at *Cincinnati*. I could see him standing on the inside of the circle around them, with his eyes popping out. He looked scared, too, and so did everybody else. *We* were afraid ourselves. I couldn't figure out *what* we were afraid of, unless it was people like that coming into a little town like Reedley from some strange faraway place and tumbling around, leaping, dancing, and singing in a language we couldn't understand. Unless it was that, I couldn't understand what it could be. Unless it was their jumping around in the quiet street and singing in the morning, in the summertime.

Can I go down to the street? Emmie said.

You stay right here, Harry said.

I want to see them, Emmie said.

You stay right here where I won't have to worry about you, Harry said. How do I know who them crazy people are?

Well, what do you know? the dentist said. Listen to them. Can you make out what they're singing, Harry?

Let me go down, Emmie said. *Please* let me go down, Harry.

Harry, who was fourteen, took his sister by the arm and shook her.

You're lucky to be here at the Doc's at all, he said. Now just be satisfied to look down at them from up here where you're safe. This ain't no time to be running out into the street. How do we know who they are?

Emmie's lips began to quiver. Then she became ashamed and went away from the window and began to cry without making a sound.

There you go, Harry said. God Almighty, what do you want, anyhow?

I don't want anything, Emmie cried. I don't want anything, *ever*.

Stop crying, Harry said, and come back here to the window and watch them. You get a better view from here anyhow.

I won't, Emmie said. You just don't want me to have anything, ever.

She cried bitterly, her face all wrinkled, while the acrobats sang in the street. We could hear them clearer than ever when they started singing their second song. It was livelier and sadder than the first one and I wanted to go down and see them close, too, even if I was a little scared about the whole thing. Emmie was standing away from us, all tense, crying, and the acrobats were singing, and then I couldn't help it, I started to cry, too. I didn't know what was making me cry, but it just seemed I had to. I went over to the other side of the dentist's office.

Now, what are *you* crying about? Harry said. I suppose you want to go down, too. Well, you can't. I came here to get the Doc to pull out this bad tooth. This ain't no holiday.

Well, what do you know? the dentist said.

He was a dried-out, dry-mouthed, dry-skinned man of forty-five or so. He was very tall but stoop-shouldered and his breath was hot from smoking cigarettes all the time. He lit one from another and kept it up all the time he wasn't working over somebody's mouth. He was never busy and spent most of his time sitting in the chair and looking out the window at the sky and smoking cigarettes, winter and summer and all the year around.

Well, I never saw anything like *that* before, he said. Listen to them, will you?

How can I, Harry said, with these babies crying?

I'm not a baby, Emmie said. *You're* a baby. You're *afraid* to go down and see them close.

I came here to get this bad tooth out of my mouth, Harry said.

You're afraid, Emmie said. You just know you're afraid they'll look at you, or something.

I ain't either afraid, Harry said. We ain't got time to go down to the street, have we, Doc?

It wouldn't be exactly right for *me* to go down, the dentist said. I've got a certain reputation to uphold.

He was scared, too, a big man like him. He was afraid of three dark little men just because they weren't like other people; just because they were acrobats and dancers and because they weren't afraid to sing in the street.

You see, Harry said to Emmie.

I wasn't crying any more because I was too busy noticing how scared Harry and the dentist were. They were awfully scared and I wondered why. I was scared myself and I knew Emmie was, too, but I knew we weren't anywhere near as scared as Harry and the dentist. The dentist was most scared of all.

I'd say there's a city ordinance of some kind against that sort of thing, he said.

You'd think so, wouldn't you? Harry said. You can't just come into a town and find the main street and start doing acrobatic tricks and stuff like that. Come on back here, Emmie, and watch them; they're jumping around again.

I won't, Emmie said.

All right, Joe, Harry said. *You* come back and watch them.

No, I said.

There was no reason in the world for me to be stubborn that way but somehow I couldn't help it.

What do you say, Doc? Harry said. Let's get back to this bad tooth in my mouth.

Not just yet, Harry, the dentist said. It's my duty to be a witness to this sort of thing. I'm pretty sure there's some kind of an ordinance against it somewhere in the books.

There ain't, either, Emmie said.

Well, it hasn't happened before, the dentist said, and there must have been some reason.

I'd like you to get this bad tooth out of my mouth, Harry said. He was getting kind of nervous.

In due time, the dentist said. I want to be prepared to report what happened, after it's all over. Well, what do you know? he said suddenly. Now they're passing the hat around.

Emmie hurried back to the window to see, so I went back, too.

The two biggest ones were standing together at attention and the littlest one was going around on the inside of the circle, putting his hat in front of the people. He was doing it in a way that made you know he wasn't *asking* them to give anything, he was giving them a chance to give something if they felt like it. He was hurrying around the circle and nobody was dropping a coin in the hat. Not a single one of them. They were all turning away as he came up with the hat and pretending to be looking across the street somewhere, or they were moving one row back. He was hurrying around the circle when Emmie bolted and ran out of the office before Harry could grab her.

You come back here, Emmie Selby, he hollered.

We saw her running in the street toward the crowd around the acrobats. She was lovely to see. Her yellow hair was all loose and exciting. We saw her push into the center of the circle just in time to meet the littlest one, holding out the hat to them.

Then we saw her drop the coin. Everybody stood stunned and alarmed and the little man stepped back a pace, bowed to Emmie, then flipped backward three times, a thing he hadn't done before. Then he bowed to Emmie again. Then Emmie turned and ran across the street toward the Court House Park.

Without a word the acrobats moved out of the center of the crowd and disappeared around the corner, while the people stood together talking about them.

Well, what do you know about that? the dentist said. I think there's a law somewhere against that, but the sheriff didn't do anything about it. They're gone now.

A few of the people in the street went away, but most of them formed small groups and talked about what they had seen.

Wait till she gets home, Harry said. She'll get hers. She was the only one who gave them money.

She shouldn't have done that, the dentist said. That ain't the sort of thing to encourage in the streets.

For a minute or two Harry and the dentist stood at the window looking down at the people.

What about this bad tooth in my mouth, Doc? Harry said after a while.

I'll have it out in a jiffy, the dentist said.

Harry and the dentist went back to the chair and I stayed at the window until the tooth was out. There were still three small groups of loafers in the street when Harry was ready to start home.

All right, Joe, he said. Let's go. Emmie'll get hers when she gets home.

When we got home, Emmie wasn't there.

Harry told Mrs. Selby all about it.

She's scared to come home, he said.

Emmie didn't get home till it was almost night. I knew she'd been crying and I guessed maybe she'd walked a good deal all day. Harry was there in the living room waiting for her to come home, waiting to have Mrs. Selby punish her. Emmie saw him and was ashamed of the way he had been afraid, and ashamed of the way everybody hadn't wanted to give them something.

I don't care, she said. I gave them all I had. A quarter. If I had had more, I'd have given them that, too.

You'll get yours, Harry said.

Mrs. Selby came out of the kitchen and stood a moment, looking at

Emmie. She was a sight: tired, hungry, angry, and proud. All of a sudden Mrs. Selby smiled and held out her arms to Emmie. Emmie ran to them, and Mrs. Selby started to laugh and Emmie started to cry, and Harry got up and said, Well, for the love of Mike.

I'm glad you did it, Emmie, Mrs. Selby said. I would have done it, too. Tell me about them.

But Emmie was so happy she couldn't do anything but cry while Mrs. Selby roared with a warm strong laughter that made me feel fine, even if I was only her brother's son. It made me feel fine to hear her laugh while Emmie cried.

Citizens of the Third Grade

☼ ☼ ☼

TOM LUCCA was incredible. Only eight years old, he was perhaps the brightest pupil in the third grade, certainly the most alert, the most intellectually savage, and yet the most humane. Still, his attitude seemed sometimes vicious, as when Aduwa was taken and he came to class leering with pride, the morning newspaper in his pants pocket, as evidence, no doubt, and during recess made the Fascist salute and asked the colored Jefferson twins, Cain and Abel, what they thought of old King Haile Selassie now.

Same as before, Miss Gavit heard Abel say. You got no right to go into Africa.

And Tom, who wouldn't think of getting himself into a fist-fight since he was too intelligent, too neat and good-looking, laughed in that incredible Italian way that meant he knew everything, and said, We'll take Addis Ababa day after tomorrow.

Of course this was only a gag, one of Tom Lucca's frequent and generally innocent outbursts, but both Abel and Cain didn't like it, and Miss Gavit was sure there would be trouble pretty soon no matter what happened.

If General Bono *did* take Addis Ababa and Tom Lucca forgot himself and irritated Cain and Abel, there would surely be trouble between the colored boys in the Third Grade and the Italian boys, less brilliant perhaps than Tom Lucca, but more apt to accept trouble, and fight about it: Pat Ravenna, Willy Trentino, Carlo Gaeta, and the others. Enough of them certainly. And then there were the other grades. The older boys.

On the other hand, if Ras Desta Demtu, the son-in-law of Emperor Haile Selassie, turned back the Italian forces at Harar, Cain and Abel, somewhat sullenly, would be triumphant without saying a word, as when Joe Louis, the Brown Bomber of Detroit, knocked out and humiliated poor Maxie Baer, and Cain and Abel came to class whistling softly to themselves. Everybody, who normally didn't dislike the boys, quiet and easygoing as they were, deeply resented them that morning. No matter what happened, Miss Gavit believed, there would be trouble at Cosmos Public

School, and it seemed very strange that this should be so, since these events were taking place thousands of miles away from the school and did not concern her class of school-children, each of whom was having a sad time with the new studies, fractions and English grammar.

Tom Lucca was impossible. He had no idea how dangerous his nervous and joyous behavior was getting to be. It was beginning to irritate Miss Gavit herself who, if anything, was in favor of having the ten million Ethiopians of Abyssinia under Italian care, which would do them much less harm than good and probably furnish some of the high government officials with shoes and perhaps European garments.

It was really amazing that many of the leaders of Abyssinia performed their duties bare-footed. How could anybody be serious without shoes on his feet, and five toes of each foot visible? And when they walked no important sound of moving about, as when Americans with shoes on their feet moved about.

Of course she hated the idea of going into an innocent and peaceful country and bombing little cities and killing all kinds of helpless people. She didn't like all the talk about poison gases and machine guns and liquid fire. She thought it was very cruel of the Italians to think of killing people in order to gain a little extra land in which to expand, as Mussolini said.

Miss Gavit just bet ten cents the Italians could do all the expanding they needed to do right at home, in the 119,000 square miles of Italy. She just bet ten cents with anybody that Mussolini didn't really need more land, all he wanted to do was show off and be a hero. It was dreadful the way some people wanted to be great, no matter how many people they killed. It wasn't as if the people of Abyssinia were pagans; they were Christians, just like the Italians: their church was the Christian church, and they worshiped Jesus, the same as Pope Pius.

(The Pope, though, was a man Miss Gavit didn't like. She saw him in a Paramount News Reel, and she didn't like his face. He looked sly for a holy man. She didn't think he was really holy. She thought he looked more like a scheming politician than like a man who was humble and good and would rather accept pain for himself than have it inflicted upon others. He was small and old and cautious. First he prayed for peace, and then Italy went right ahead and invaded Abyssinia. Then Pope Pius prayed for peace again, but it was war just the same. Who did he think he was fooling?)

She guessed every important man in the world was afraid, the same as the Pope. Poor loud-mouthed Huey got his, and for what? What did poor Huey want for the people except a million dollars for every family? What was wrong with that? Why did they have to kill a man like that, who really had the heart of a child, even if he did shout over the radio and irritate President Roosevelt by hinting that he, Huey Long of Louisiana, would be the next President of the United States? What did they want to invent guns for in the first place? What good did guns do the people of the world, except teach them to kill one another? First they worried about wild animals, and then Indians, and then they began worrying about one another, France worrying about Germany, Germany worrying about France and England and Russia, and Russia worrying about Japan, and Japan worrying about China.

Miss Gavit didn't know. She couldn't quite understand the continuous mess of the world. When it was the World War she was a little girl in grammar school who thought she would be a nun in a convent, and then a little later, a singer in opera: that was after the San Carlo opera troupe came to town and gave a performance of *La Bohème* at the Hippodrome Theatre and Miss Gavit went home crying about poor consumptive Mimi. Then the war ended and the parades ended and she began to forget her wilder dreams, like the dream of some day meeting a fine man like William Farnum and being his wife, or the still more fantastic dream of suddenly learning from authoritative sources that she was the true descendant of some royal European family, a princess, and all the other wild dreams of sudden wealth and ease and fame and importance, sudden surpassing loveliness, the most beloved young lady of the world. And sobering with the years, with the small knowledge of each succeeding grade at school, she chose teaching as her profession, and finally, after much lonely studying, full of sudden clear-weather dreaming of love, she graduated from the normal school, twenty-two years old, and was a teacher, if she could get a job.

She was very lucky, and for the past five years had been at Cosmos Public School, in the foreign section of the city, west of the Southern Pacific tracks, where she herself was born and lived. Her father was very happy about this good luck. The money she earned helped buy new furniture, a radio, and later on a Ford, and sent her little sister Ethel to the University of California. But she didn't know. So many things were happening all over the world she was afraid something dangerous would happen, and very often, walking home from school, late in the afternoon, she would suddenly feel the nearness of this danger with such force that she would unconsciously begin to walk faster and look about to see if anything were changed, and at the same time remember poignantly all the little boys and girls who had passed through her class and gone on to the higher grades, as if these young people were in terrible danger, as if their lives might suddenly end, with terrific physical pain.

And now, with this trouble between Italy and Abyssinia, Benito Mussolini, Dictator of Italy, and Haile Selassie, the Lion of Judah, Miss Gavit began, as Tom Lucca's joyousness increased, to feel great inward alarm about the little boy because she knew truthfully that he was very kind-hearted, and only intellectually mischievous. How many times had she seen him hugging Mrs. Amadio's little twenty-month-old daughter, chattering to the baby in the most energetic Italian, kissing it, shouting at Mrs. Amadio, and Mrs. Amadio guffawing in the loudest and most delightful manner imaginable, since Tom was such a wit, so full of innocent outspokenness, sometimes to the extent even of being almost vulgar. The Italians. That's the way they were, and it was not evil, it was a virtue. They were just innocent. They chattered about love and passion and child-birth and family quarrels as if it were nothing, just part of the day's experience. And how many times had she seen Tom Lucca giving sandwiches from his lunch to Johnny Budge whose father had no job and no money? And not doing it in a way that was self-righteous. She remembered the way Tom would say, Honest, Johnny, I can't eat another bite. Go ahead, I don't want this sandwich. I already ate three. I'll throw it away if you don't take it. And Johnny Budge would say, All right, Tom, if you're sure you don't want it. That was the strange part of it, the same little Italian boy being fine like that, giving away his lunch, and at the same time so crazy-proud about the taking of Aduwa, as if that little mud-city in Africa had anything to do with him, coming to class with the morning paper and leering at everybody, stirring the savage instincts of the Negro twins, Cain and Abel Jefferson.

Miss Gavit believed she would do something to stop all the nonsense. She wouldn't sit back and see something foolish and ugly happen right under her nose. She knew what she would do. She would keep Tom Lucca after school.

When the last pupil had left the room and the door was closing automatically and slowly, Miss Gavit began to feel how uneasy Tom was, sitting still but seeming to be moving about, looking up at her, and then at the clock, and then rolling his pencil on the desk. When the door clicked shut, she remembered all the little boys she had kept in after school during the five years at Cosmos and how it was the same with each of them, resentment at accusation, actual or implied, and dreadful impatience, agonized longing to be free, even if, as she knew, many of them really liked her, did not hate her as many pupils often hated many teachers, only wanting to be out of the atmosphere of petty crime and offense, wanting to be restored to innocence, the dozens and dozens of them. She wondered how she would be able to tell Tom why she had kept him after school and explain how she wanted his behavior, which was always subtle, to change, not in energy, but in impulse. How would she be able to tell him not to be so proud about what Mussolini was doing? Just be calm about the whole business until Italy annexed Abyssinia and everything became normal in the world again, at least more or less normal, and Cain and Abel Jefferson didn't go about the school grounds apart from everybody, letting their resentment grow in them.

What's the matter now? Tom said. He spoke very politely, though, the inflexion being humble, implying that it was *he* who was at fault: he was ready to admit this, and if his offense could be named he would try to be better. He didn't want any trouble.

Nothing's the matter, Miss Gavit said. I want to talk to you about the war, that's all.

Yes, ma'am, he said.

Well, said Miss Gavit, you've got to be careful about hurting the feelings of Cain and Abel Jefferson.

Hurting their feelings? he thought. Who the hell's hurting whose feelings? What kind of feelings get hurt so easily? What the hell did I ever say? The whole world is against the Italians and *our* feelings ain't hurt. They want to see them wild Africans kick hell out of our poor soft soldiers, two pairs of shoes each. How about our feelings? Everybody hates Mussolini. What for? Why don't they hate somebody else for a change?

He was really embarrassed, really troubled. He didn't understand, and Miss Gavit noticed how he began to tap the pencil on the desk.

I don't know, he began to say, and then began tapping the pencil swifter than before.

He gestured in a way that was very saddening to Miss Gavit and then looked up at her.

You are an American, said Miss Gavit, and so are Cain and Abel Jefferson. We are all Americans. This sort of quarreling will lead nowhere.

What quarreling? he thought. Everybody in the world hates us. Everybody calls us names. I guess Italians don't like that either.

He could think of nothing to say to Miss Gavit. He knew she was all right, a nice teacher, but he didn't know how to explain about everybody hating the Italians, because this feeling was in Italian and he couldn't translate it. At home it was different. Pa came home from the winery and sat at the table for supper and asked Mike, Tom's big brother in high school, what the afternoon paper said, and Ma listened carefully, and Mike told them exactly what was going on, about England and the ships in the Red Sea, and France, and the League of Nations, and Pa swallowed a lot of spaghetti and got up and spit in the sink, clearing his throat, and said in Italian, All right, all right, all right, let them try to murder Italy, them bastards, and Ma poured more wine in his cup and Pa said in American, God damn it, and Tom knew how the whole world was against Italy and he was glad about the good luck of the army in Africa, taking Aduwa, and all the rest of it, but now, at school, talking with Miss Gavit, he didn't know what to say.

Yes, ma'am, he said.

Miss Gavit thought it was wonderful the way he understood everything, and she laughed cheerfully, feeling that now nothing would happen.

All right, Tom, she said. Just be careful about what you say.

You may go now.

Jesus Christ, he thought. To hell with everybody.

He got up and walked to the door. Then he began walking home, talking to himself in Italian and cussing in American because everybody was against them.

Tom was very quiet at the supper table, but when Pa asked Mike how it was going in Abyssinia and Mike told him the Italians were moving forward very nicely and it looked like everything would turn out all right before the League would be able to clamp down on Italy, Tom said in Italian, We'll show them bastards. His father wondered what was eating the boy.

What's the matter, Tom? he said in American.

Aw, Tom said, they kept me in after school just because I talked about taking Aduwa. They don't like it.

His father laughed and spit in the sink and then became very serious.

They don't like it, hey? he said in Italian. They are sorry the Italian army isn't slaughtered? They hate us, don't they? Well, you talk all you like about the army. You tell them every day what the army is doing. Don't be afraid.

The next day Cain Jefferson swung at Tom Lucca and almost hit him in the eye. Willy Trentino then challenged Cain Jefferson to a fight after school, and on her way home Miss Gavit saw the gang of Italian and colored and Russian boys in the empty lot behind Gregg's Bakery. She knew for sure it was a fight about the war. She stood in the street staring at the boys, listening to their shouting, and all she could think was, This is terrible; they've got no right to make these little boys fight this way. What did they want to invent guns for in the first place?

She ran to the crowd of boys, trembling with anger. Everybody stopped shouting when Miss Gavit pushed to the center of the crowd where Willy Trentino and Cain Jefferson were fighting. Willy's face was bloody and Cain was so tired he could barely breathe or lift his arms. Miss Gavit clapped her hands as she did in class when she was angry and the two boys stopped fighting. They turned and stared at her, relieved and ashamed.

Stop this nonsense, she said, panting for breath from excitement and anger. I am ashamed of you, Willy. And you, Cain. What do you think you are fighting about?

Miss Gavit, said Cain Jefferson, they been laughing at us about the Ethiopians. All of them, teasing us every day.

How about you? said Willy. How about when Joe Louis knocked out Max Baer? How about when it looked like Abyssinia was going to win the war?

Then three or four Italian boys began to talk at once, and Miss Gavit didn't know what to think or do. She remembered a college movie in which two football players who loved the same girl and were fighting about her were asked to shake hands and make up by the girl herself, and Miss Gavit said, I want you boys to shake hands and be friends and go home and never fight again.

Miss Gavit was amazed when neither Willy Trentino nor Cain Jefferson offered to shake hands and make up, and she began to feel that this vicious war in Abyssinia, thousands of miles away, was going to bring about something very foolish and dangerous in the foreign section. In the crowd she saw Abel Jefferson, brooding sullenly and not speaking, a profound hate growing in him, and she saw Tom Lucca, his eyes blazing with excitement and delight, and she knew it was all very horrible because, after all, these were only little boys.

And then, instead of shaking hands and making up as she had asked them to do, Willy Trentino and Cain Jefferson, and all the other boys, began to move away, at first walking, and then, overcome with a sense of guilt, running, leaving the poor teacher standing in the empty lot, bewildered and amazed, tearing her handkerchief and crying. They hadn't shaken hands and made up. They hadn't obeyed her. They had run away. She cried bitterly, but not even one small tear fell from her eyes. When old Paul Gregg stepped from the bakery into the lot and said, What's the trouble, Miss Gavit? the little teacher said, Nothing, Mr. Gregg. I want a loaf of bread. I thought I would come in through the back way.

When she got home she took the loaf of white bread out of the brown paper bag and placed it on the red and blue checkered table-cloth of the kitchen table and stared at it for a long time, thinking of a thousand things at one time and not knowing what it was she was thinking about, feeling very sorrowful, deeply hurt, angry with everybody in the world, the Italians, the Pope, Mussolini, the Ethiopians, the Lion of Judah, and England.

She remembered the faces of the boys who were fighting, and the boys who were watching. She breathed in the smell of the bread, and wondered what it was all about everywhere in the world, little Tom Lucca kissing Mrs. Amadio's baby and giving Johnny Budge his sandwich and leering at everybody because of the taking of Aduwa, the Negro twins joyous about Joe Louis and sullen about Abyssinia. The bread smelled delicious but sad and sickening, and Abel Jefferson watching his brother fighting Willy Trentino, and the *Morning Chronicle* with news of crime everywhere, and the *Evening Bee* with the same news, and the holy Pope coming out on the high balcony and making a holy sign and looking sly, and somebody shooting poor Huey Long, and none of her pupils being able to understand about English grammar and fractions, and her wild dreams of supreme loveliness, and her little sister at the University of California, and the day ending. She folded her arms on the table and hid her head. With her eyes closed she said to herself, They killed those boys, they killed them, and she knew they were killing everybody everywhere, and with her eyes shut the smell of the fresh loaf of bread was sickening and tragic, and she couldn't understand anything.

A *Prayer* for the *Living*

✿ ✿ ✿

I HAVE heard lately that there are two thousand *million* human beings in the world. Lord, my God, feed them, clothe them, guard them against fire and tigers. About half of them live in China and India, I hear. Nobody knows accurately or scientifically where they come from, why, or where they're going, or what the *élan* is. Every now and then a river rises making a flood, and anywhere from one to one hundred thousand of them drown.

It doesn't seem to make any difference.

They're a miserable lot. They're badly born. Their parents before them were badly born. They've always been badly born. They have neither the innocent unconsciousness of the animal nor the deliberate awareness of the human. They're diseased and stupid and dirty and the best of them, the very best of them, the noblest, the strongest, the gayest, the finest, are punks, Lord love them. God in Heaven protect them. Provide for them in Asia, in rural places and in villages, in agricultural regions and in industrial cities, in the big cities of Europe and in the small towns of America, in Iceland and in Greenland, Lord God be nice to them.

The college graduate at the gasoline pump says, Let us Marfak your car. My cousin says, This ain't our car. Marfak you. Ha—ha—ha.

God in Heaven let them at least laugh once in a while, and if it isn't asking too much let them play a little before the flood comes, before the tigers come down from the mountains, before the black birds darken the sky. Let them be together in innocence or in sin, in beauty or in ugliness, in pain or in delight, in delight or in despair, in rural places and in villages, in Iceland and in Greenland. Before they die let them at least feel that the whole thing is personal, although without meaning and somewhat in the nature of a swindle.

But first of all give them food. Give them a decent livable temperature. Let them have dwellings. Provide them with garments of some kind, except in tropical places. Shower them with shoes, button or lace. Give them a break, after any manner your little heart desires. Do it through Communism or Capitalism or Fascism or Christianity or willy-nilly. Any little manner your little heart desires. Just be kind to them, O saucy valentine of the emptiness, two thousand million of them are present in thy image, so do it, even if only willy-nilly, as heretofore.

Now about this trouble in Spain, I say to my cousin. How long do you think it's going to last and how many of the two thousand million are going to exit, walking?

Phft, phft phft, says my cousin.

That's a bold answer for times like these. Lord God, indeed it is. Guard them against machine-gun fire, if you feel inclined; and if it pleases you, against shrapnel; and if you are in the mood, against bombs; and if you aren't too busy, against gases. There are many of them but each is one and one is extraordinary, even if haphazard. One is approximately an eternity of *élan*, an enormity of region, rural or industrial, as well as a head upon a body. Even if there is no point to it and it doesn't make any difference, protect them, and if that is impossible love them, on either side, right or wrong.

Have you two nickels for a dime? I say to my cousin. I want to make a snappy phone call, dialing from left to right.

Phft phft, he says.

Son, I say, what is the world seeking?

The answer of course is love and love alone, but my cousin says, Phft.

It is a true answer, and if it isn't there never has been, and there never will be, Christian, Marxist, or willy-nilly.

Memories of Paris

✿ ✿ ✿

THE year I went to Europe I was so anxious to see everything, I moved about in a hurry and didn't stay long in any place. I stayed a few days in London. In Paris I stayed only from seven o'clock in the evening until noon the following day, Sunday. That was all.

I couldn't speak a word of the language and didn't run into any Americans. I saw one Englishman, but I didn't care to try to talk to him. He didn't look like the kind of an Englishman I'd care to talk to. He looked like the kind I'd go six blocks out of my way to avoid, so I avoided him. I had heard of lots of Americans being in Paris, but I didn't see any, even though it was Saturday night.

I had only American Railway Traveler's Cheques, and wanted to cash some of them. They were small ones. I went into one place after another.

I remember breaking into a shop, which was all but closed, in which, in a back room, the shopkeeper was having a quiet supper with, I believe, a woman he did not know very well as yet and wished to impress. I remember his confusion when I explained in English, which he did not understand, what I wanted: that is, to have him cash an American Traveler's Cheque for me. His woman came out to see me and have some fun and I carried on a long conversation with the two people, which in the end got nowhere. The man was forty or so, tall, and slightly fat. He had little hair on his head and seemed to be a man who loved food and was crazy about women. The girl was the first French girl I had seen in France for any length of time. The first one I had seen, that is, who was not walking toward me on the sidewalk. She was not very beautiful, which I couldn't understand. She was, in fact, quite plain, but generously made, and her laughter was splendid. It was hearty and coarse and trivial and yet extremely feminine. I put her down for one who had been around and liked it.

This man was in some sort of business, but I neglected to try to find out what that business was. I mean the place was some sort of a place people could enter without knocking. He may have been a notary, as there was a counter, a table with ink and pen, several chairs, but nothing in view that one could sell.

I was in a great hurry, but at the same time, because of the clarity of the air that evening, and because I was in Paris at last, and because the world seemed so full of amazing and delightful people, such as these two, who were obviously on the threshold of one of those unimportant but gay French romances, or affairs, I seemed to be completely at home, and not at all at a disadvantage for not knowing the language. I laughed a good deal, and very loudly, and this man and this young woman laughed with me and chattered to one another about me. Finally, the young woman asked if I had American cigarettes, which of course I had. She was coquettish about asking and when I lighted one for her, her eyes twinkled in a way which I took to be typically Parisian and wicked. The man accepted a cigarette also. I thanked them for trying to help me find a bank, which the man had done, and went away.

The man's directions for reaching a bank were so involved and the bank seemed so far away and there seemed to be so great a possibility that all the banks in Paris were closed that I decided to try some other place, a store, for instance.

Here, the storekeeper was an old Frenchman with a big white mustache. He was a small man, with very broad shoulders and a powerful voice, one that was almost a continuous grumble. I think he lisped also which made his speech very amusing to hear.

He said he had money but that he did not know me, did not know what I was up to, did not know if my cheques were genuine, and asked where I was headed for. I said Russia. He nodded and said something that was either about Russia being a long way for a young man to go or about Russia being a good place for a young man to go. He was a remarkably peaceful sort of old man, not irritable, but shrewd and cautious. He examined the traveler's cheques at least seven times, studying the signatures, mine and the vice-president's, I suppose, and each time shook his head. It was too bad, but he didn't know how many francs he ought to give me for each cheque, and in the event of making an uneven exchange, he was fearful that he might not get the best of it, assuming of course that the cheques weren't spurious in the first place, which was quite likely.

He gave me a plum, however.

The next place I went to was a fashionable hotel somewhere near the Opera House. I forget the name of the place. It was a very bright place and people in evening clothes, speaking French of course, which is great to hear, especially from pretty women, were walking about. The man at the desk was a young man who understood no English. He hurried about and found a middle-aged man wearing pince-nez glasses and behaving very pompously who did.

And now, he said, what is it you wish to sell?

I was feeling pretty good, even though I hadn't had a drink since I'd left London, and I said, I've been sent over here by the Curtis people of Philadelphia to get subscriptions for *The Saturday Evening Post*. My name is Lloyd Timkin. Call me Bud.

I see, the man said. They are now sending young men around the world to get subscriptions to magazines.

Yes, I said, fifty or so are selected from around a quarter of a million applicants. We are working our way through college, as a rule, although in my case, I'm working my way through high school.

I see, the man wearing the pince-nez glasses said. We do not wish to subscribe to your magazine.

We have a premium to offer, I said. When you learn what it is, I am sure you will change your mind. With every seven-year subscription to the magazine, at sixty cents a year which is our special Paris rate, we are giving away free of charge one latest model Harley-Davidson. Are you the manager of this hotel?

I am not, the man said. Do you wish to speak to the manager?

It is most imperative that I do so, I said.

The man wearing the pince-nez glasses disappeared into an office, and I disappeared into the night.

He would have caused an international situation, involving the United States fleet, before he would have cashed a five-dollar traveler's cheque.

I found a police, or gendarme, and told him my problem. He listened carefully, if not eagerly, and blew a whistle. This caused two taxis to come to a halt and three dozen people sitting at a sidewalk café to look in our direction. A fellow-gendarme came running and for a moment it looked like I was going to be arrested, in connection, I think, with the Stavisky case. I brought out my passport and tried my best to look the way I looked in the photograph. That is to say, angry at Capital. The fellow-gendarme spoke a little English. He suggested trying the hotel which I had just left. I told him I'd rather not trouble such a high-class establishment. Some little out-of-the-way hotel would be better. He thought deeply and remembered a place where he believed a deal could be made, provided of course we could find out how many francs each five-dollar cheque was worth. He spoke intimately to the other gendarme, who, I gathered, was beginning to be pretty suspicious, not mentioning any names of course. What he wanted to know was why I did not wish to go to the hotel which had been suggested. It was the sort of place which might be able to take care of my problem, so why didn't I wish to go? Something was wrong somewhere, he said.

The officer who could speak a little English began, for some reason or other, perhaps because he had never liked the other officer, to take my side, and a small, subtle, French argument developed between the two. My friend insisted that I had a right to avoid the big hotel, and the other officer insisted that if I had any occasion to wish to avoid such a fine French hotel something was wrong somewhere and it was his job to find out what. My friend lost the debate. The other officer, who, I believe, was a superior officer, or at least a superior debater, ordered my friend to go with me to the big hotel, the one I had just left.

When we reached the main desk the man with the pince-nez glasses was returning from the private office.

He said immediately, We do not wish to accept your offer. We have discussed the matter at great length and we do not wish to accept.

I'm sorry, I said. Then perhaps you may be able to cash a traveler's cheque for me.

My friend, the gendarme, spoke in French to the man with the pince-nez glasses, and so effectively, so sincerely, so convincingly, that the hotel clerk took one of my cheques and said that, with luck, he believed he might be able to take care of the matter, provided he could learn the rate of exchange at that hour of the night. I believe he did considerable telephoning. At any rate, he returned after ten minutes or so, with an authentic report from a reputable member of the Bank of France on the exact rate of exchange for that day, and the proper number of francs. My friend, the gendarme, was delighted. So was I. I shook hands with the man with the pince-nez glasses, and with the young clerk who didn't speak English.

It may please you to know, the man with the pince-nez glasses said, that I was in favor of accepting your offer, and pleaded with my superior to accept. He would not do so. One thing I would like to know.

Yes? I said.

What is that premium? he said.

You mean the Harley-Davidson? I said.

Yes, he said.

The Harley-Davidson, I said, is a motorcycle.

May we reconsider? he said. I have made a sorrowful error. I told my superior it was a hat.

Perhaps some other time, I said. I'm very hungry and want to eat.

I gave my friend the gendarme five francs and went on with my exploration of Paris. This lasted until four in the morning and most of it was something like what I have already written, so I'll let it go at that.

The Job

✿ ✿ ✿

FELIX came into the O.K. Lunch on Kearney Street where I was having a hamburger and a cup of coffee, and he said, Guess what happened, Fritz? I got a job.

I nearly choked.

The waitress came running with a glass of water and Felix slapped my back.

He was humming *Les Preludes*, the part where Liszt really got going.

Are you all right? the waitress said.

Thanks.

I swallowed some water.

I'm fine, I said.

What happened? the waitress said.

He says he got a job.

Felix was going to town on *Les Preludes*. He was tickled to death.

The waitress, who was a large flabby-armed German girl with eyes that were barely open, looked at Felix and listened to him humming.

What is he? she said. A singer?

A sad-looking little Greek gambler came into the place and sat down and the waitress hurried away to take his order.

You're kidding, I said to Felix.

He was playing the trombone now: *My Ohio Home*.

I want to wake up in the morning, he sang, and the little Greek gambler turned around and said something to himself.

Sit down and shut up, I said.

Felix sat down and began to drum on the counter with a knife and fork.

Where'd you get a job?

Some lousy little building on Geary Street.

What kind of a job?

The waitress came back and began looking at Felix all over again. She just couldn't figure him out. She just couldn't figure out anybody human being so happy.

Is he a singer? she said.

Tell her, Felix said. Go ahead, Fritz. Tell her.

Well, I said, I don't want to shock you or anything, but this young man is a composer of music.

I thought it would be nice to please the waitress.

What the hell, Felix said. *Tell* her. Don't be conservative.

Well, I said, this young Jew is probably the greatest composer of music in America.

Jesus, Felix said, is that the best you can do for a pal? Listen, he said to the waitress. Listen, sister, he said. My name is Isadore Schwartz. That don't mean anything. All right. I was born in the Bronx nineteen years ago. That don't mean anything either. O.K. My father was a push-cart peddler from Vienna. That don't mean anything either. O.K. He died when I was five years old. That don't mean anything either. O.K. My mother died when I was two years old. O.K. I had two older brothers and an older sister. My sister committed suicide when she was seventeen and I was seven. One of my brothers is in Sing Sing. O.K.

Take it easy, I said.

The waitress was getting pretty scared. The short-order cook was listening carefully, and the Greek gambler was listening too.

Wait a minute, Felix said. I don't get a chance every day to tell people who I am. I want this girl to know.

There was a piano in the Jewish orphanage, he said to the girl.

I finished the hamburger and swallowed all the coffee in the cup and lighted a cigarette.

I was playing Chopin when I was seven, Felix said to the girl. He was happier than he'd been in months.

He began to hum a little Chopin.

I have composed three symphonies, two operas, four ballets, seven concertos, eleven tone poems, and forty-six songs, he said.

That's fine, I said. Let's get going.

The waitress was almost trembling.

Isadore Schwartz, Felix said to the girl. We walked up to the cash register. The Greek gambler's eyes were almost popping out of his head. He was scared too.

Isadore Schwartz, Felix said to the Greek, and shook his hand vigorously.

I dropped a dime and a nickel on the counter beside the cash register, stuck a toothpick in my mouth, and we walked out.

In the street I had to smile about him.

Wow, Felix said.

What did you want to go and tell that poor girl all them lies for? I said.

What lies?

What did you want to go and shout at that poor innocent girl for?

Who shouted? You told her I was a composer, didn't you?

Some day, I said, some sensitive person is going to get so awful excited while you're telling lies about yourself that he's going to bust loose and kill you.

What the hell, Felix said. I'm happy. Can't I have a little fun?

Is that your idea of having fun?

I like music.

Lots of people like music.

I *could* be a great composer. If I could *write* music, I could be a great composer. I wasn't lying *much*.

We walked down Kearney to Market, and then up Market to Eddy, and then up Eddy to the poolroom. There were chairs in the poolroom. It was a cool dark place. It was a pleasant place to be. It was only a small place and we knew the night floor man. He was a nervous man of fifty who had a very kind heart. He used to leave the back door open for us and after the place closed we used to go in through the back door and sleep on the pool tables. We used to make pillows out of crumpled newspapers and put our coats over the paper. It wasn't bad. We had been sleeping in the pool room five nights. In the morning we used to go out the back door before the poolroom opened, so nobody would know we had been sleeping on the pool tables. We used to walk around town till around eleven or eleven thirty and then we used to go back and take a seat and stay there most of the day and night. We used to earn coffee money helping the day floor man any time he needed somebody to give him a hand. But our best friend was the night floor man.

We went into the pool room and sat down.

What kind of a job? I said.

Elevator, Felix said.

What do you mean, *elevator*?

I'm supposed to run it.

Do you know how to run an elevator?

It's an old-style elevator. It's an old-style building.

How much are you going to get?

Eight dollars.

Eight dollars a *what*? A day, a week, a month, a year, or what?

A week.

It's an old-style salary, too, I said. But it's better than nothing.

I'm an old-style Jew, Felix said. Wahoo. Am I happy?

Do you get Saturday afternoons off?

No.

Sundays?

I don't think so.

How the hell did you do it?

I don't know, he said. I was walking down Geary Street and I saw this sign in the doorway of this little building: *Elevator Boy Wanted.* So I went in and rang the elevator bell and after a while the little old-fashioned elevator came down and an old man opened the old-fashioned door and I told him I wanted to apply for the job.

That's great, I said.

I start working Monday. Today's Saturday.

He went back to the old mood of triumph in *Les Preludes.*

Well, I said, I guess I'll be going along now.

What the hell you talking about? Felix said.

I don't like Frisco, I said. It was all right when I had money and was gambling and winning. It was all right six months ago. I guess I want to try Seattle for a while. I think maybe my luck will pick up again if I go to a new city.

You ain't got a dime. Next Saturday I'll have eight dollars cash. You can do plenty with eight dollars.

I ain't lucky any more in this town. I don't want to take your money.

It ain't my money. I owe you plenty. You kept me going six months, didn't you?

You brought me a lot of luck.

Sure. I brought you so much luck you ain't got a dime to your name now.

That was my own fault.

Your own fault, my eye. You kept me going six months. I got a job now and you can do plenty with eight dollars next Saturday.

My luck's no good any more in this town.

What the hell am I going to do with them lousy eight dollars next Saturday? he said.

Well, I said, you *could* do plenty. You could rent a room with a bed in it and sleep in a bed for a change and you could eat a few decent meals for a change and maybe buy a new shirt and maybe after a week or so a new pair of shoes.

You kept me going six months. I don't want that lousy money. How the hell are you going to get to Seattle without any money?

I can get along.

I don't want the lousy money.

Listen, I said. I want you to get some sense in your head. Jobs are not easy to get.

You're a hell of a brother, Felix said.

I want you to keep that job. I want you to get a room with a bed in it and I want you to get some decent meals.

All right.

We walked together to the street.

I'll be back here in a couple of months.

All right.

Take it easy.

O.K., he said.

He stood in the doorway of the pool room while I walked down the street. I wouldn't let myself turn around, but I knew he was standing there and I kept saying, All the luck in the world, kid, you'll need it.

The Vision

✧ ✧ ✧

KYRIE ELEISON, said the priest. *Kyrie eleison,* answered the clerk. *Kyrie eleison,* said the priest again. *Christe eleison,* said the clerk. *Christe eleison,* answered the priest. *Christe eleison,* said the clerk again.

. . . .

Et cum spiritu tuo, said the clerk.

Then he removed the Mass book and knelt at the altar.

The priest said:

Dominus vobiscum.

Et cum spiritu tuo, answered the clerk.

The clerk was a young man of eighteen. The priest was a short old man of sixty who was growing fat and listless. The priest went through the Mass as if he didn't have much faith in what he was doing, but the clerk served him humbly and with energy, giving the priest wine and water, preparing the basin and cloth, removing the basin and cloth when the priest had washed and dried his hands, kneeling and moving about, crying out humbly yet passionately the Latin words he had memorized but did not understand. The young man felt, nevertheless, that he was saying words of some importance and certainly of great dignity. *Et cum spiritu tuo,* he cried with youthful passion, and the priest felt dimly: This boy is an ox: he bellows; he does not chant.

It was James Giordano. He was a new clerk at St. Anne's. He came from somewhere in the North Beach, and seemed to be a more than normally serious young man. The priest thought he would have a little talk with the boy some time soon and find out why he was so serious. Some of the Irish boys who served the priest were no less efficient than James Giordano, and yet they were more amusing to have around. They made him feel there was still liveliness and mischief in the living, and even when they forgot their lines or said them wrong or out of place, he didn't mind, and on the contrary smiled to himself, keeping, all the while, a most pious face.

The boy all but ran into the church only an evening later, and he was almost out of breath when he found the priest.

Father, he said, I want to talk to you. I don't want to confess because I haven't had any new sins since last confession. I only want to talk to somebody.

The priest walked with him out of the church. It was a clear winter evening.

And I want to talk to *you,* the priest said. We will take a little walk together.

They walked down Nineteenth Avenue toward the park.

Something is troubling you, the priest said.

Yes, Father, said the boy.

What is it, my boy?

Father, I have visions.

Visions? cried the priest. What do you mean?

And he thought: Now I begin to understand. I know these young men. Night and day they think of only one thing, and the serious ones are worse than the others. And in his mind he saw the young man dreaming all day and night of the great body of woman, the gigantic female of the instincts. He would talk to the boy quietly. Find yourself a good companion, he would say. The Lord created you to share your life with another. There is no evil in love.

And rather than pity the boy, the priest envied him. Which way of life is holier than the simple and innocent way? he wondered. Unknowing, and in ignorance, they achieve godliness.

They walked in the park. The tall eucalyptus trees made deep shadows and the stillness was soothing to the priest. It was good to be walking beside a young man, one who would soon enter life in all its fullness.

Tell me what you see, said the priest.

Father, said the boy, I see the world ending. For weeks now I have been seeing the end of the world. I am not frightened, but I want to talk to you.

This angered the priest. He was a man of little faith, and he did not believe it was possible for an ignorant young man, an Italian, to have such a terrible and glorious vision.

What happens? he said.

Father, said the boy, everything ends. The cities burn and fall, and the living die.

What nonsense, thought the priest.

I thought I ought to tell you, the boy said.

Well, said the priest, it is because you are young. There is nothing to fear.

Father, said the boy. He was very anxious.

Father, he said, I am not afraid for myself. I am prepared to die. I am afraid for the others who are not prepared, the worldful of them. They do not know. I thought I ought to tell you. I see the world ending all the time. When I close my eyes to sleep I see everything ending, and when I open my eyes I see all the people dying. I thought I ought to tell somebody.

The priest took the boy by the arm.

It is nothing, he said.

Nothing? the boy said.

It is all right, the priest said.

The boy did not understand. Father, he said, I see them dying. I thought somebody ought to tell them.

How old are you? the priest said.

I am eighteen, Father.

Have you a job?

Yes, Father. I am a waiter at the Fior D'Italia on Broadway.

Have you had a loss recently?

A loss, Father?

Has someone dear to you passed away? Your mother or father, a sister or a brother?

No, Father, they are all alive.

Have you a girl?

A girl, Father?

Are you in love?

No, Father.

I thought so, the priest thought.

He believed he had reached the bottom of the whole thing, and was quite pleased.

It is nothing, he said. There are many nice girls in the church, he said.

What shall I do, Father?

Find a good girl, the priest said.

Father, he said, do you mean that I should find a girl and tell her about the vision? Do you mean I should tell only one person to be prepared? Not all of them?

Good Lord, the priest thought.

Why do you feel you must tell everybody about the vision? he said.

I see the world ending, Father, he said. I see everybody dying.

Everyone alive will some day leave his mortal flesh, the priest said.

This dying is not the same, Father, the boy said. They go on moving around the same as ever, but there is death in them. I cannot explain it, Father. I see them dying all the time, and they *will* die.

Nonsense, the priest thought. What shall I tell him?

Oh, he said.

What shall I do? the boy said.

The priest himself wanted to know what *he* should do. The boy was certainly in earnest. He was certainly seeing the world ending and the living dying. He was not anyone sly or mischievous. He was not playing a joke.

The priest wondered what *he* would do if he were eighteen and very ignorant and very faithful and was having visions of the world ending and the living dying. It would be a very awkward experience, to say the least.

There is nothing to do, he said. You must be patient, and I think it would be very nice if you found a good Catholic girl.

They walked together in silence out of the park. The priest was not altogether pleased with himself because he knew the boy's vision was no common thing. If the truth were known, it was a most remarkable thing. But good Lord, what could he do about it? What could anyone do about it?

In the street the young man said, I thought I ought to tell you, Father.

You did right in telling me, the priest said.

I will be patient, the boy said.

That's right, the priest said.

I will find a good Catholic girl, Father, the boy said.

I think that would be very nice, the priest said.

Good night, Father, the boy said.

Good night, the priest said.

That was all. But walking away from the boy, the priest was deeply troubled, deeply angry with himself, but even more deeply jealous of the boy. Who was he, a boy of eighteen, to have such a vision? It was ridiculous.

We Want a Touchdown

☆ ☆ ☆

ONE day three years ago my cousin came over to this place on Carl Street and began playing phonograph records. He came up the stairs into this room where I work, where I've written most of my stories, and asked if he could hang around a while. I was typing a letter to a critic who'd said I wasn't a writer to take seriously and I was pointing out to the critic that he was mistaken. My first book had just been published. All quietness had been driven out of me by the strange feeling of beginning to be at last no longer one unknown among the many unknown. As you probably remember, I wasn't the quietest new writer of that year, 1934, and on the contrary was, by a great margin, the noisiest, and probably one of the noisiest that ever broke into print.

My cousin, on the other hand, was altogether unknown. Like myself, though, he didn't like being unknown because he knew he was somebody who ought to be known. I was always trying to discover means for him to break out of the shell of anonymousness into the world in which the record is kept. The world in which they put your name on paper and keep putting it there. At best you are known to *all* kinds of people, some worth being known to, and others not, but it is better, in some ways, than not being known at all, or only to your relatives, the kids you were brought up with, and the girls you've known.

Before the beginning of my fame the only people in the world who knew me were women, most of them not overbright. What they used to say was, Well, I like that. I never saw anybody so conceited. Who do you think you are? And so forth and so on. On trains sometimes a half-drunken old-timer would get to know me from the way I'd talk, especially after everybody in the smoker had gone to sleep. In that early-morning hour, I used to tell these old-timers about everything. Even as a kid, I had that way. By the time I was eleven or twelve, I had it strong.

My cousin, who'd come along six years after me, had it too, although differently. I had it noisily and he had it quietly. I kept telling him this was no world in which to be quiet. When you make a beginning, I kept telling him, in any field, make sure you make the kind that everybody in that field will have to notice, and make sure it's the kind that will enable you to go on for a long time. Make your beginning with style. That's the thing that counts. By style I meant combining in your behavior an awareness of your talent and an attitude concerning it that was honestly certain, if not downright conceited. You've got to do that, I told him, or else they won't know the truth about you because they aren't very bright.

In those early days I hadn't met any of the ones who were supposed to be bright, any of the famous ones, but since those days I have met many of them, and I know I was right. Even the famous ones are insignificant. That's the truth. There's nothing to them. At best they've had industry where a better man hadn't had it. At best they've been hard workers. When you meet them, they are tired and dull. Their labors have left them weary and less alive than men who do the more unimportant kinds of things. When you meet them, they are not strong in body or spirit and they are in no mood for comedy of any sort.

I was writing this letter to this critic in New York on a Saturday afternoon in November. This house on Carl Street is on the slope of one of the fourteen hills of San Francisco. It overlooks the Kezar Stadium in which, during the season, football games are played. In the fall of each year the stadium opens its gates, people go in and sit down, the players come out onto the field, and a football game begins. At the front of this house, in this room, I hear, all during the fall of each year, the cheers of the football fans. Before the Girls' Gymnasium was built behind this house, it was possible to see the east half of the football field, but after the Gymnasium went up, there was nothing to see except a narrow strip of the field somewhere in the vicinity of the eastern forty-yard line.

When my cousin came into this room that afternoon, Gonzaga was playing S.F.U., and the fans were cheering. It was a typical fall day. Gray, still, cold, and pious. There was a holy stillness in the air.

At a time like this, my cousin said, what do you think you're doing? Why don't you go down and see the game?

The game will be over in fifteen minutes, I said. In two months the *season* will be over. At the moment the game seems to be the most important thing going on in this vicinity, but as far as I'm concerned it isn't. In fifty years at the most I'll be dead. I'm not likely to be remembered as somebody who went with fifty thousand people to a football game.

Oh, I see, my cousin said.

He began to smile, making fun of me. I see, he said.

All right, I said. But remember this. These next two or three months are important ones for me. After them, the next three or four years are going to be even more important. I've made a beginning and it isn't a bad one. What I've got to do now is follow through. I can't be fooling around with watching football games. Not for a while, anyway.

How are things going? my cousin said.

Great, I said.

How's the book going?

It's a best-seller, I said. How are things going with you?

I'm writing a novel, my cousin said.

How many pounds do you weigh? I said.

One hundred and thirty-nine, my cousin said.

You'll lose twenty pounds before you finish the novel, I said, and right now twenty pounds is too many for you to lose. It would be different if you weighed around a hundred and eighty or ninety. What's the novel about?

I don't know yet, my cousin said. It's called *We Want a Touchdown*.

You'll lose too many pounds trying to write a novel, I said.

Then I realized what a good title he had.

Will you let me buy that title? I said.

Why? he said.

I like it, I said. I'll give you a handsome copy of *Moby Dick*, illustrated by Rockwell Kent, for that title.

No, my cousin said. I want that title myself. If the novel's good, Simon and Schuster will publish it and I'll be as famous as you are. I have a personal letter from Simon and Schuster.

I'll give you the complete works of William Blake too, I said.

No, my cousin said. You've got more good titles than any other writer in the country. I want this one for myself.

All right, I said. I hope you have the best luck in the world. It's a great title. I could do a couple of fine things in a story with that title. Everybody wants a touchdown. Is that it?

That's right, my cousin said.

And all the other people in the world are out to keep him from making a touchdown, I said.

That's it exactly, my cousin said. How did you know?

How did I know? I said. It's only by the grace of God that that title came to you instead of to me. I know all about that title. The touchdown is as many kinds of things as there are people with desires, and there are no people without them.

That's right, my cousin said. Tell me more.

Sure, I said. I'll help you write the novel.

Do, my cousin said.

All right, I said. When they go into the stadium, which is a structure of the subtlest beauty, being oval, shaped like an egg, which is the holiest of all shapes, they enter a region of worship. They sit in an *elevated* place and look *down*. That lifts their spirits. Church is never like that. In church you are a miserable creature looking upward toward God and light. In the football stadium you are still a miserable creature, with this difference: position. You are *up*, looking *down*. That helps a lot. The field is the symbol of the world. The yard lines and the boundary lines simplify the struggle which in the world is never simplified. Carrying the ball through the opponents, who themselves want to do the same thing, is what everybody in the stadium wants to do some day *in the world*.

Thanks, my cousin said. Anything more?

Sure, I said. If I were to concentrate on the theme I could do something great. For instance, I'd go close to a great variety of people in the stadium, look at them closely, look through them, and put down everything I saw. That would be a great part of the story. I'd give a complete history of every person, and I'd put down all the statistical facts about him such as height, weight, condition of health, etcetera.

That's really fine, my cousin said. I think I'll go right home and write the novel.

All the luck in the world, I said. You want a touchdown yourself.

Sure I do, my cousin said. So do you.

Everybody in the world wants a touchdown, I said. That gives me an idea.

I wrote a few words on the back of an envelope from a critic who'd answered my letter to him, in which I pointed out that he was mistaken when he believed I wouldn't write another book. I hadn't written another book, and I didn't know for sure if I would write one, but I told him he was mistaken because after making a ninety-nine-yard run through a broken field to a touchdown, you like to imagine that it wasn't an accident and that all you need to do to do it again is to receive the ball and go tearing down the field again. I wrote, *The Man Who Didn't Care to Make a Touchdown.*

What's that? my cousin said.

Just the title for a story, I said. I may never write it.

What is the title? my cousin said.

The Man Who Didn't Care to Make a Touchdown, I said.

Funny story? my cousin said.

You know how my stuff is, I said. There's something funny in everything I write. That's because there's something funny in everything.

Well, my cousin said, I guess I'll go home and go to work.

O.K., I said. Good luck.

He stood at the door a moment.

It's lousy, he said. I wish I didn't want to make a touchdown.

In the stadium the people were cheering. My cousin listened.

You're a lucky guy, do you know it? he said.

Do I? I said. I'm one of the luckiest guys in the world.

I want you to know I've been telling a few girls I'm you, he said.

That's all right, I said. Does it help?

You ought to know.

Any touchdowns to speak of?

None to speak of. It's because I know I'm lying. I just wanted to tell you.

I don't tell them I'm a writer, I said. I tell them I'm a gambler. That explains my not having any ready money.

You *are* a gambler, aren't you? my cousin said.

I've followed the horses a long time, I said. Any time I've got five dollars you'll find me in a poker game.

Do you think that's helped you?

I think so, I said.

I'm no gambler, my cousin said.

That's something you ought to learn to be, I said. It helps all along the line.

I imagine it would help, my cousin said, but I can't take it.

You've got to learn to take it, I said. If you don't know how to take it when you lose, you'll never know how to behave when you win.

I never win and I never lose, my cousin said. I don't gamble.

That's something to cultivate, I said. When five dollars is all the money you've got in the world and you are in a game trying to win five more, or ten, or twenty, or thirty, and you lose the five you started out with, you have the swellest chance in the world to understand a little more about everything than you could ever understand if you didn't gamble, or won. If you gamble and lose, you'll gamble and win some day. You'll lose a little weight at first, but after a while you won't. It'll be the same when you write too. If you've never gambled and are a writer who writes you'll lose a lot of weight when you write, but if you've gambled and lost until you've learned to take it without losing any weight, when you write and it doesn't go very well, you won't lose any weight to speak of, and after a while you'll be able to write in a way that will be easy, and you won't lose any weight at all.

You ought to give a course on writing, my cousin said. They'd put you in an asylum.

You're my cousin, I said. I don't mind telling you a few things I know. I wouldn't tell anybody else, unless I was drunk. I feel generous and friendly toward everybody when I'm drunk.

I'll try to remember what you've told me, my cousin said. So long.

So long, I said.

My cousin went home and for all I know worked all night on the novel. I wrote a few more letters and put on my coat and went downstairs to mail them.

The street was full of the people who had been in the stadium. They were wonderful people. They were still excited and there was a lot of humor in them. A lot of them had been drinking from bottles and flasks and were half-drunk. There was hurrying, loud outspoken talking, and laughter. There was much comedy of physical movement too. I myself was a little drunk from the writing I had been doing, so in the street, among the people who had just left the football stadium, I began to have fun.

A group of five small boys who had a two-dollar football were playing a game of football on the sidewalk. They were doing it in slow-motion, which I thought was a great idea. They were passing the ball and going through each play in slow-motion, their natural expressions growing with the passing of a few moments to expressions of determination, fierceness, bravery, and horrible pain.

The boy who was carrying the ball fumbled it just as I arrived. I picked it up and began very slowly to run for a touchdown, headed for the mailbox. A young man, probably a clerk, coming in the opposite direction, became my opponent and very slowly began to block my way. I was joined by another young man and a girl, and my opponent was joined by three or four others. At the line of scrimmage there was a very slow tangle in which everyone played a great game. Then there was much amusement while the audience cheered. All this began and ended in no time, and when I got to the mailbox I dropped my letters and went on down the street.

In five minutes the street was empty and it was very still everywhere. The people had all gone home and it was now night. I walked all the way to town, around town, and then down to Embarcadero, along the waterfront. Then I spent ten of the fifteen cents I had for a hamburger and rode a streetcar back to Carl Street. In my room I began to play the phonograph without turning on the light. I listened to music until around midnight and then I got up and went to bed.

Today, three years later, the people in the stadium are cheering again. They are the same people, although some of them who were in the stadium three years ago, the day my cousin visited me, are dead. This is the sad and wonderful thing about the game. It goes on all the time. There are always players.

There is always religion too. There is always longing in people to do a difficult thing, against great odds, in a fine way, with goodhumor if possible.

This is the thing about people I like most of all.

Saroyan's Fables, IX

✿ ✿ ✿

The Tribulations of the Simple Husband Who Wanted Nothing More than to Eat Goose but was Denied this Delight by His Unfaithful Wife and Her Arrogant but Probably Handsome Lover.

A SIMPLE husband one morning took his wife a goose and said, Cook this bird for me; when I come home in the evening I shall eat it.

The wife plucked the bird, cleaned it, and cooked it. In the afternoon her lover came. Before going away he asked what food he could take with him to his friends. He looked into the oven and saw the roasted goose.

That is for my husband, the wife said.

I want it, the lover said. If you do not let me take it, I shall never love you again.

The lover went off with the goose.

In the evening the husband sat at the table and said, Bring me the goose.

What goose? the wife said.

The goose I brought you this morning, the husband said. Bring it to me.

Are you serious? the wife said. You brought me no goose. Perhaps you dreamed it.

Bring me the goose, the husband shouted.

The wife began to scream, saying, My poor husband has lost his mind. My poor husband is crazy. What he has dreamed he imagines has happened.

The neighbors came and believed the wife, so the husband said nothing and went hungry, except for bread and cheese and water.

The following morning the husband brought his wife another goose and said, Is this a goose?

Yes, the wife said.

Am I dreaming?—No.

Is this the goose's head?—Yes.

Wings?—Yes.

Feathers?—Yes.

All right, the husband said, cook it. When I come home tonight I'll eat it.

The wife cooked the goose. The lover came.

There is another goose today, he said. I can smell it.

You cannot take it, the wife said. I had a terrible scene with my husband last night, and again this morning. It is too much, I love you but you cannot have the goose.

Either you love me or you don't love me, the lover said. Either I take the goose or not.

So he took the goose.

Bring the goose, the husband said.

My poor husband, the wife screamed. He's stark raving mad. Goose, goose, goose. What goose? There is no goose. My poor, poor husband.

The neighbors came and again believed the wife.

The husband went hungry.

The following morning he bought another goose in the city. He hired a tall man to carry the goose on a platter on his head. He hired an orchestra of six pieces, and with the musicians in a circle around the tall man carrying the goose, he walked with them through the streets to his house, calling to his neighbors.

When he reached his house there were many people following him.

He turned to the people and said, Mohammedans, neighbors, the world, heaven above, fish in the sea, soldiers, and all others behold, a goose.

He lifted the bird off the platter.

A goose, he cried.

He handed the bird to his wife.

Now cook the God damned thing, he said, and when I come home in the evening I will eat it.

The wife cleaned the bird and cooked it. The lover came. There was a tender scene, tears, kisses, running, wrestling, more tears, more kisses, and the lover went off with the goose.

In the city the husband saw an old friend and said, Come out to the house with me tonight; the wife's roasting a goose; we'll take a couple of bottles of *rakki* and have a hell of a time.

So the husband and his friend went out to the house and the husband said, Have you cooked the goose?

Yes, the wife said. It's in the oven.

Good, the husband said. You were never really a bad wife. First, my friend and I will have a few drinks; then we will eat the goose.

The husband and his friend had four or five drinks and then the husband said, All right, bring the goose.

The wife said, There is no bread; go to your cousin's for bread; goose is no good without bread.

All right, the husband said.

He left the house.

The wife said to the husband's friend, My husband is crazy. There is no goose. He has brought you here to kill you with this enormous carving knife and this fork. You had better go.

The man went. The husband came home and asked about his friend and the goose.

Your *friend* has run off with the goose, the wife said. What kind of a friend do you call that, after I slave all day to cook you a decent meal?

The husband took the carving knife and the fork and began running down the street. At length in the distance he saw his friend running and he called out, Just a leg, my friend, that's all.

My God, the other said, he is truly crazy.

The friend began to run faster than ever. Soon the husband could run no more. He returned wearily to his home and wife. Once again he ate bread and cheese. After this plain food he began to drink *rakki* again.

As he drank, the truth began to come to him little by little, as it does through alcohol.

When he was very drunk he knew all about everything. He got up and quietly whacked his wife across the room.

If your lover's got to have a goose every day, he said, you could have told me. Tomorrow I will bring TWO of them. I get hungry once in a while myself, you know.

Saroyan's Fables, XXIV

✧ ✧ ✧

How the Hair of Women is Long, the Understanding Short, and What a Ghastly Lack of Appreciation There is in Them For Genius.

A MAN had a cello with one string over which he drew the bow for hours at a time, holding his finger in one place. His wife endured this noise for seven months, waiting patiently for the man to either die of boredom or destroy the instrument. Inasmuch as neither of these desirable things happened, however, one night she said, in a very quiet voice, too, you may be sure: I have observed that when others play that magnificent instrument, there are four strings over which to draw the bow, and the players move their fingers about continuously. The man stopped playing a moment, looked at his wife wisely, shook his head, and said, You are a woman. Your hair is long, your understanding short. Of course the others move their fingers about constantly. They are looking for the place. I've found it.

Dear Baby

✧ ✧ ✧

THE room was a large one on the seventh floor of the Blackstone Hotel on O'Farrell Street in San Francisco. There was nothing in it to bring him there except the portable radio-phonograph, the one record, and darkness.

He came into the room smiling, and walked about, trying to decide what to do. He had six hours to go, and after that a time so long he didn't like to think about it.

He no longer saw the room. During the day the blind of the only window was drawn to keep the place dark. At night he turned the light of the bathroom on and kept the door almost shut so that only enough light came into the room to keep him from walking into something. It happened anyway. It wasn't that he couldn't see as well as ever. It was simply that he was alone again all the time and wasn't looking. There was no longer any reason to look.

He remembered everything.

At the core of everything was his remembrance of her.

He walked about quietly, turning, bumping into the edges of doorways and chairs and other objects in the room, moving unconsciously, his eyes unable to see because of the remembrance. He stopped suddenly, removed his hat and coat, stretched and shook his head as he did when he was confused in the ring.

It was nothing.

He could go on as if he had never known her. He could be boisterous in act and loud in laughter, and some day be all right again. He could go on like everybody else in the world, but he didn't know if he wanted to. Lazzeri said he was in better shape than ever, but Lazzeri didn't know what he knew.

The odor of her hair, the taste of her mouth, and the image of her face came to him. His guts sickened. He smiled and sat on the bed. After a moment he got up, went to the portable machine, turned the knob, and put needle to disc. Then he stretched out on the bed, face down, and listened to the music, remembering her, and saying: "Dear baby, remembering you is the only truth I know. Having known you is the only beauty of my life. In my heart, there is one smile, the smile of your heart in mine when we were together."

When the telephone rang he knew it was Lazzeri. He got up and turned off the machine.

"Joe?" Lazzeri said.

"Yeah."

"Are you all right?"

"Sure."

"Remember what I told you?"

"What did you tell me?"

"I want you to take it easy."

"That's what I'm doing."

"Don't go haywire."

"O.K."

"What's the matter?"

"I've been sleeping."

"Oh," Lazzeri said. "O.K. I'll see you at nine."

"O.K."

"Something's the matter," Lazzeri said.

"Don't be silly."

"Something's the matter," Lazzeri said again. "I'm coming right up."

"I've been sleeping," Joe said. "I'll see you at nine."

"You don't sound right," Lazzeri said.

"I'm fine."

"You haven't got somebody in that room with you, have you?"

"No."

"Joe," Lazzeri said, "what's the matter?"

"I'll see you at nine," Joe said.

"You're not going haywire on me again, are you?"

"No."

"O.K.," Lazzeri said. "If you're all right, that's all I want to know."

"I'm all right," Joe said.

"O.K.," Lazzeri said. "If you want to be alone, O.K. Just don't go haywire."

"I'll see you at nine," Joe said.

He went back to the machine, turned the knob, and then decided not to listen to the music any more. That's what he would do. He wouldn't listen to the music any more. He would break the record. He would give the machine away. He would lift the blind of the window. He would turn on all the lights and open his eyes. He would come to the room only to sleep. He would go down to the poolroom on Turk Street and find a couple of the boys. He would shoot pool and listen to the boys talking about cards and horses and the other varieties of trouble they knew. He would go up to a couple of the places he used to visit and find some girls he used to know and buy them drinks and ask how they'd been and hear them tell of the troubles *they* knew. He would stop being alone.

He began to laugh, at first quietly and then out loud. He laughed at himself—the wretched comedy of his grief. Then he laughed at everybody alive, and began to feel everything was going to be all right again. If you could laugh, you could live. If you could look at it that way, you could endure *anything*. While he was laughing he heard *her* laughing with him, as clearly as if she were in the room. He became sick again and stopped laughing, knowing it was no use.

He remembered her as if she were still alive, walking beside him along one of many streets in one of many cities, her face childlike and solemn, her movement beside him shy and full of innocence, her voice so young and lovely he would stop anywhere to hold her in his arms while she said seriously: "Joe, people are looking."

He remembered her alone with him in one of many rooms, her presence the first goodness and beauty in his life. He remembered the sweetness of her mouth and the soft hum of her heart growing to the sudden sobbing that brought out in him a tenderness so intense it was ferocious, a tenderness he had always hidden because there had never been anyone to give it to.

He walked about in the dark room, remembering how unkind he had been to her the night he had come home and found her listening to the record. He pointed at the machine and said, "Where did that come from?"

He remembered the way she ran to him and put her arms around him and the way he pushed her away. He remembered the way she moved away from him and said, "I only made a down payment on it. I'll tell them to come and take it back if you want me to. I thought you'd like it."

The record was playing, and although he knew it was something he liked very much, and needed, and should have known long ago, he went on being unkind. She was on the verge of crying and didn't know where to go or what to do. She went timidly to the machine and was going to shut it off when he shouted at her to let it play. She hurried, almost ran, into the other room, and he stood in front of the machine with his hat on and listened to the record until it finished. Then he shut off the machine and went back to town and didn't come home till after five in the morning. She was asleep. He couldn't understand what right he had to know her, to speak to her, to live in the same house with her, to touch her. He bent over her and touched her lips with his own and saw her eyes open. "Please forgive me," he said.

She sat up smiling and put her arms around him, and he kissed her lips and her nose and her eyes and her ears and her forehead and her neck and her shoulders and her arms and her hands, and while he was doing so he said, "Please remember one thing, baby. No matter what I say to you,

I love you. I'm liable to go haywire any time, but don't forget that I love you. Please remember that."

He took off his clothes, got into his bed and went to sleep. When she got in beside him he woke up and embraced her, laughing, while she whispered his name the sorrowful, serious way she always did when she knew he was all right again.

That was in Ventura, where they had taken an apartment because he had three fights coming up in that vicinity: one in Los Angeles, one in Hollywood, and one in Pismo Beach. He let her come to the fight in Hollywood the night he fought Kid Fuente, the Indian, because he knew how much she wanted to see him in the ring. He got her a ringside seat and after the fight she told him she had sat next to Robert Taylor and Barbara Stanwyck and they had been very nice to her.

"I hope you didn't ask them for an autograph," he said, and she became embarrassed and said, "Yes, I did, Joe."

"Well," he said, "they should have asked *you* for one."

"Oh, they were swell," she said. "They sure liked you."

"Oh, sure," he said. "Sure. Sure. That dumb Indian almost ruined me. I don't know how I won. I guess he got tired trying. I'll be punch-drunk in another three or four months."

"You were wonderful in the ring," the girl said.

He remembered the fight because she had talked about it so much. It was six rounds. He was almost out in the fourth. She had known it and kept talking around it, but one day she said, "I almost cried."

"What are you talking about?" he said.

"I mean," she said, "at the fight. Everybody was yelling and I didn't know whether they were for you or against you and I almost cried."

"When was that?" he said.

"I don't know," she said. "I was so excited. He was fighting hard and you were in a corner and everybody stood up and was yelling. I thought he was hitting *me*."

He remembered being in the corner, taking a lot of bad ones, not being able to do anything about them, not knowing if he wasn't going to be out and saying to himself, "You'll be punch-drunk in no time at this rate." He kept trying to move away, but there was nowhere to go, and all of a sudden the Indian slowed down, he was tired, and he remembered saying to the Indian, "O.K., Kid, that's all." He knew he was going to be all right now because there weren't more than fifteen seconds to that round. He gave the rest of the round everything he had. The Indian was tired and couldn't do anything, and just before the bell the Indian stopped a bad one and fell backward, looking up at him with an amazed expression because the Indian couldn't understand how anybody could take so much punishment and come up so strong.

The bell saved the Indian, but for the rest of the fight the Indian was no good, and he knocked him down once in each of the last two rounds.

"That was a bad spot," he told her. "By rights I should have been out, but the Indian got tired. You can't start slugging that way in the middle of a round and expect to keep it up till the end of the round."

"You looked fine," she said, "and you didn't look sore. Don't you get sore?"

"Sore?" he said. "Who's there to get sore at? That poor Indian is only out to earn a little money, the same as me. He's got nothing against me and I've got nothing against him. If he can floor me, he's going to do it, and if I can floor him, I'm going to do it."

"Well," she said, "I almost cried. You looked so fine all the rest of the fight, but when you were in the corner the only thing I could see was somebody being hit over and over again."

"I didn't like that myself," he said.

He was glad she hadn't seen some of his bad fights—the earlier ones, the ones in which he had taken a lot of punishment. Lately he'd learned enough about the racket not to get into a lot of trouble. He seldom took advantage of a chance to clinch, but if the worst came to the worst and there was nothing else to do he would do it, rest a few seconds and try to figure out what to do in the remaining seconds of the round. He usually ended every round nicely, coming back if he had been hurt earlier. Of course he had the reach, his legs were good, and even when he was hurt they didn't wobble and he could stay solid.

After seeing the fight with Kid Fuente she didn't want to see any more. The day of a fight she would be sick, sick in bed, and she would pray. She would turn on the phonograph and listen to the record, which had become their music, the song of their life together. And when he'd come home he'd find her pale and sick and almost in tears, listening to the song. He would hold her in his arms a long time, and he would hear her heart pounding, and little by little it would slow down to almost normal, and then he would hold her at arm's length and look into her eyes and she would be smiling, and then he would say, "It only means fifty dollars extra, baby, but I won." And she'd know there was no vanity in him, she'd understand what he was talking about, and she would ask him what she could get him. Ham and eggs? Scotch and soda? What would he like? She would rush around in an apron and fool around with food and dishes and put the stuff on the table.

He used to eat even if he wasn't hungry. Just so he hadn't lost. If he'd lost, he'd be mean, he'd be so sore at himself that he'd be mean to her, and she wouldn't know what to do, but in the midst of being mean to her he would suddenly say in a loud voice, "And don't be a fool, either; don't pay any attention to anything I'm saying now because I'm out of my head. I made a mess of the whole fight."

When he came home from the fight with Sammy Kaufman of New York he was pretty badly hurt. His head was heavy, his lips were swollen, his left eye was twitching, every muscle of his body was sore, and he was swearing all the time, even though it had been a good fight and a draw. He wasn't mean to her that night, though, and she said, "Joe, please give it up. You can make money some other way. We don't need a lot of money."

He walked around the apartment and talked to himself. Then suddenly he calmed down and shut off the lights and put the record on the machine and sat down with her to listen to their song. It was a piece by Jan Sibelius, from the *King Kristian Suite*, called "Elegie." He played the record three times, then fell asleep from exhaustion, and she kept playing the record until he woke up a half-hour later. He was smiling, and he said, "I'd like to quit, baby, but I don't know any other way to make money."

The following week he tried gambling and lost.

After that he had stuck to fighting. They had traveled together up and down the coast—north to San Francisco, Sacramento, Reno, Portland, and Seattle, and then south to the towns along the coast and in the valley that were good fight towns, and Hollywood and Los Angeles and San Diego—when he found out about it. From the beginning he was scared to death, in spite of how good it made him feel. He tried his best not to be scared and tried to keep her in good spirits, but he was worried about it all the time. She was a child herself. She was too little. He didn't know what to do. He remembered her saying one night, "Please let me have it, Joe. I want it so badly."

"Do you think I don't want it?" he said. "Do you think I don't want you to have it? That's *all* I want. That's all I've ever wanted."

Then he began to mumble, talking to himself.

"What, Joe?" she said.

"Do you feel all right?" he said. "Do you feel you can do it? You're not scared, are you?"

"I'm a little scared," she said, "but I guess everybody's scared the first time."

The months of waiting were the happiest of his life. Everything that was good in him had come out—even though he was worried all the time. Even in the ring he had been better than ever. His fights were all good, except one, and that was the fight with the champion, Corbett, which had been a draw, but very close, some sports writers saying he had won and others saying that Corbett had won, and everybody wanting a rematch, especially Lazzeri.

So tonight he was fighting Corbett again. He had six hours to go. If he won this fight he and Lazzeri would be in the big money at last. He believed he could take the fight, but what if he did? What did he care about money now? Suppose he did take the fight? Where could he go *after* the fight?

"I'm dead," he said. "What's the use bluffing?"

Remembering the girl, he fell asleep, and when he woke up he went to the telephone, without thinking, and asked the hotel operator to get him Corbett at Ryan's Gymnasium, and call him back. A moment later the telephone rang. He answered it, and Corbett said, "Hello, is that you, Joe?"

"Ralph," Joe said, "I want to tell you I'm out to win tonight. I think it's about time you retired."

At the other end of the line Corbett busted out laughing and swore at his friend in Italian.

"I'll take care of you, kid," he said. "You know I like an aggressive fighter."

"Don't say I didn't tell you," Joe said.

"See you in the ring," Corbett said.

In the ring, when they shook hands, Joe said, "This is going to be your last fight." Corbett didn't know he was talking to himself.

"O.K., Joe," he said.

The first round was fast and wild. Even the sports writers couldn't understand. Lazzeri was sore as hell.

"Joe," he said, "what do you think you're doing? You can't beat Corbett that way. Take it easy. Fight *his* fight."

The second round was faster and wilder than the first. They were probably even, but that was only because he wasn't tired yet. The music was humming in him all the time, getting into the roar of the crowd and sweeping along in him, while his heart kept talking to the girl, dreaming that she was still alive, at home listening to their song, waiting for him to come home and take her in his arms.

Lazzeri wanted to hit him after the second round. "Joe," he said, "listen to me. Fight Corbett's fight. He'll kill you."

("That's O.K. with me," his heart said. "Dear Baby, that's O.K. with me.")

The third round, if anything, was faster than the first and second, and coming out of a clinch Corbett said, "What do you think you're doing, Joe?"

"I'm knocking you out," Joe said.

Corbett laughed at him and they began slugging again, one for one, with the sports writers looking at each other, trying to figure out what was going on.

Lazzeri was furious.

"Joe," he said, "I'm not talking to you. I've worked with you six years. I changed you from a punk to a great fighter. Now you're throwing away the championship—the chance we've been working for all these years. You can go to hell, Joe. I hope he floors you in the next round."

During the fourth round things began to go haywire. Corbett's left eye was cut and bleeding badly, and it seemed he was bewildered and less strong than he had been.

("What the hell," his heart said. "Is Corbett going to go haywire at a time like this?")

After the round Lazzeri said, "Joe, I think you've got him—but I'll talk to you later. Your next fight will be in Madison Square Garden. We'll go to Florida for a while. But I'll talk to you later."

In the fifth round Corbett was slow, his punches were weak and he seemed confused. Toward the end of the round he fell and stayed on one knee to the count of nine.

"You're fighting the most beautiful fight you've ever fought," Lazzeri said. "The sports writers are crazy about you. You're a real champion, Joe."

The fight was stopped near the end of the sixth round because Corbett's eye was so bad.

Lazzeri was crazy with joy but unable to understand what had happened. It was obvious that Joe had fought a great fight—that his style had been perfect for *this* fight. And yet Lazzeri knew something was wrong somewhere.

"Joe," he said in the cab, "you're a champion now. What's eating you?"

"I'm not fighting for three or four months, am I?" he said.

"Two or three, anyway," Lazzeri said. "Why?"

"We've got more money than we've ever had before, haven't we?"

"We've got enough for both of us for two years at least," Lazzeri said. "But why? What are you driving at?"

"Nothing," he said. ("Dear Baby," his heart said.) "I think I'm entitled to a little celebrating."

"Sure, sure," Lazzeri said. "I don't want you to go stale. What do you want?"

"I want laughs," he said. "I'll go up to my room. Get a couple of girls. Bring some Scotch. I want *laughs*."

"Sure," Lazzeri said. "Sure, Joe. We'll have a little party. I need laughs myself after the scare you gave me."

When he got to his room he turned on all the lights, took the record off the phonograph, and for a moment thought of breaking it. He couldn't, though. He put the record under the bed, as if to hide it. He walked around the room until the sickness caught up with him again, only now it was worse than ever, and he sat down on the bed and began to cry.

When Lazzeri and the two girls came into the room it was dark except for a little light coming from the bathroom. The phonograph was playing, and the fighter was sitting on the bed with his head in his hands and he was crying.

"Get the hell out of here," he said softly.

Without a word Lazzeri led the two girls out of the room. "He'll be all right," he said.

"Dear Baby," the fighter kept saying over and over again.

The Hummingbird That Lived Through Winter

✿ ✿ ✿

SOMETIMES even instinct is overpowered by individuality—in creatures other than men, I mean. In men instinct is supposed to be controlled, but whether or not it ever actually is I leave to others. At any rate, the fundamental instinct of most—or all—creatures is to live. Each form of life has an instinctive technique of defense against other forms of life, as well as against the elements. What happens to hummingbirds is something I have never found out—from actual observation or from reading. They die, that's true. And they're born somehow or other, although I have never seen a hummingbird's egg, or a young hummingbird.

The mature hummingbird itself is so small that the egg must be magnificent, probably one of the most smiling little things in the world. Now, if hummingbirds come into the world through some other means than eggs, I ask the reader to forgive me. The only thing I know about Agass Agasig Agassig Agazig (well, the great American naturalist) is that he once studied turtle eggs, and in order to get the information he was seeking, had to find fresh ones. This caused an exciting adventure in Boston to a young fellow who wrote about it six or seven years before I read it, when I was fourteen. I was fourteen in 1922, which goes to show you how unimportant the years are when you're dealing with eggs of any kind. I envy the people who study birds, and some day I hope to find out everything that's known about hummingbirds.

I've gathered from rumor that the hummingbird travels incredible distances on incredibly little energy—what carries him, then? Spirit? But the best things I know about hummingbirds are the things I've noticed about them myself: that they are on hand when the sun is out in earnest, when the blossoms are with us, and the smell of them everywhere. You can hardly go through the best kind of day without seeing a hummingbird suspended like a little miracle in a shaft of light or over a big flower or a cluster of little ones. Or turning like gay insanity and shooting straight as an arrow toward practically nothing, for no reason, or for the reason that it's alive. Now, how can creatures such as that—so delicately magnificent and mad—possibly find time for the routine business of begetting young? Or for the exercise of instinct in self-defense? Well, however it may be, let a good day come by the grace of God, and with it will come the hummingbirds.

As I started to say, however, it appears that sometimes even instinct fails to operate in a specie. Or species. Or whatever it is. Anyhow, when all of a kind of living thing turn and go somewhere, in order to stay alive, in order to escape cold or whatever it might be, sometimes, it appears, one of them does not go. Why he does not go I cannot say. He may be eccentric, or there may be exalted reasons—specific instead of abstract passion for another of its kind—perhaps dead—or for a place. Or it may be stupidity, or stubbornness. Who can ever know?

There was a hummingbird once which in the wintertime did not leave our neighborhood in Fresno, California.

I'll tell you about it.

Across the street lived old Dikran, who was almost blind. He was past eighty and his wife was only a few years younger. They had a little house that was as neat inside as it was ordinary outside—except for old Dikran's garden, which was the best thing of its kind in the world. Plants, bushes, trees—all strong, in sweet black moist earth whose guardian was old Dikran. All things from the sky loved this spot in our poor neighborhood, and old Dikran loved *them*.

One freezing Sunday, in the dead of winter, as I came home from Sunday School I saw old Dikran standing in the middle of the street trying to distinguish what was in his hand. Instead of going into our house to the fire, as I had wanted to do, I stood on the steps of the front porch and watched the old man. He would turn around and look upward at his trees and then back to the palm of his hand. He stood in the street at least two minutes and then at last he came to me. He held his hand out, and in Armenian he said, "What is this in my hand?"

I looked.

"It is a hummingbird," I said half in English and half in Armenian. Hummingbird I said in English because I didn't know its name in Armenian.

"What is that?" old Dikran asked.

"The little bird," I said. "You know. The one that comes in the summer and stands in the air and then shoots away. The one with the wings that beat so fast you can't see them. It's in your hand. It's dying."

"Come with me," the old man said. "I can't see, and the old lady's at church. I can feel its heart beating. Is it in a bad way? Look again, once."

I looked again. It was a sad thing to behold. This wonderful little creature of summertime in the big rough hand of the old peasant. Here it was in the cold of winter, absolutely helpless and pathetic, not suspended in a shaft of summer light, not the most alive thing in the world, but the most helpless and heartbreaking.

"It's dying," I said.

The old man lifted his hand to his mouth and blew warm breath on the little thing in his hand which he could not even see. "Stay now," he said in Armenian. "It is not long till summer. Stay, swift and lovely."

We went into the kitchen of his little house, and while he blew warm breath on the bird he told me what to do.

"Put a tablespoon of honey over the gas fire and pour it into my hand, but be sure it is not too hot."

This was done.

After a moment the hummingbird began to show signs of fresh life. The warmth of the room, the vapor of the warm honey—and, well, the will and love of the old man. Soon the old man could feel the change in his hand, and after a moment or two the hummingbird began to take little dabs of the honey.

"It will live," the old man announced. "Stay and watch."

The transformation was incredible. The old man kept his hand generously open, and I expected the helpless bird to shoot upward out of his hand, suspend itself in space, and scare the life out of me—which is exactly what happened. The new life of the little bird was magnificent. It spun about in the little kitchen, going to the window, coming back to the heat, suspending, circling as if it were summertime and it had never felt better in its whole life.

The old man sat on the plain chair, blind but attentive. He listened carefully and tried to see, but of course he couldn't. He kept asking about the bird, how it seemed to be, whether it showed signs of weakening again, what its spirit was, and whether or not it appeared to be restless; and I kept describing the bird to him.

When the bird was restless and wanted to go, the old man said, "Open the window and let it go."

"Will it live?" I asked.

"It is alive now and wants to go," he said. "Open the window."

I opened the window, the hummingbird stirred about here and there, feeling the cold from the outside, suspended itself in the area of the open window, stirring this way and that, and then it was gone.

"Close the window," the old man said.

We talked a minute or two and then I went home.

The old man claimed the hummingbird lived through that winter, but I never knew for sure. I saw hummingbirds again when summer came, but I couldn't tell one from the other.

One day in the summer I asked the old man.

"Did it live?"

"The little bird?" he said.

"Yes," I said. "That we gave the honey to. You remember. The little bird that was dying in the winter. Did it live?"

"Look about you," the old man said. "Do you see the bird?"

"I see humming*birds*," I said.

"Each of them is our bird," the old man said. "Each of them, each of them," he said swiftly and gently.

The Stolen Bicycle

✿ ✿ ✿

THIS movie of 1919 was full of high spirits, recklessness, and excellent timing, so that when Ike George left the theater he himself was like a man in a movie: full of energy, afraid of nothing, and eager to get on with his life.

As if it were not himself, as if it were not wrong to do so, he took the brand-new bike out of the bicycle rack in front of the theater, and, in full view of the whole world, rode away on it.

Johnny Faragoh, who sold bicycles for Kebo the Jap, was standing in front of his house on L Street.

As the boy rode by, Johnny noticed the new bike.

"Hey, kid!" he called up.

The boy turned in the street and coasted up. He knew Johnny. If he called you, you had to stop. It was a pleasure for the boy, though: he had always admired Johnny, who was like somebody in a movie himself.

"That's a swell bike," Johnny said. "Where'd you get it?"

"Mr. York gave it to me for my birthday," the boy said.

"You mean the guy who's in charge of street sales for *The Herald?*"

"Yeah."

The boy got off the bike and let the older one take the handlebars. Johnny lifted the bike, bounced it, sat on it, and very easily began riding around in a small circle.

"He gave you a good one, boy. What's your name?"

"Ike."

"Ike what?"

"Ike George," the boy said.

"You anything to *Cookie* George?"

"He's my cousin."

"First or second?"

"First."

"Cookie's a good friend of mine," Johnny said.

"He's always in trouble," Ike said.

"Where'd you steal it?" Johnny said. "You can tell *me.*"

"I didn't steal it," Ike said. "Mr. York gave it to me for my birthday."

"Cookie's my pal," Johnny said. "Somebody else gave it to you. That guy York wouldn't give you a bike if you saved his life."

"He gave me *this* bike," the boy said.

"Tell them Cookie gave it to you," Johnny said. "Somebody'll go and ask York and you'll get in trouble."

"Cookie's got no money," the boy said.

"Sometimes he has and sometimes he hasn't," Johnny said. "I'm going to see him tonight," Johnny said. "I'll tell him about it. Go on home now."

The boy got on the bicycle and rode home.

When his father saw the bicycle he said, "Haig, where did you get that bicycle?"

"Cookie gave it to me," the boy said.

"You mean your cousin Gourken?"

"Yes," the boy said.

"Gourken has no money," the boy's father said. "You've borrowed it, haven't you?"

"No," the boy said. "It's mine."

"Go inside and eat your supper," the father said.

The boy went inside and ate his supper. It took him less than five minutes. When he came out of the house his father was riding the bike in the yard.

"Haig," the father said, "take the bicycle back where you got it. You're no thief."

"Cookie gave it to me," the boy said.

The next day he rode the bicycle to school, just the way it was. He didn't turn it over and hammer out the numbers the way you were supposed to do. The numbers were 137620R. After school he rode the bicycle to *The Evening Herald,* and told everybody his cousin Cookie had given it to him for a birthday present.

"What's your birthday?" his friend Nick Roma asked him.

"September 7, 1909," the boy said.

"This is May," Nick said. "You'll get in trouble, Ike."

He rode the bicycle to his corner, Mariposa and Eye, and sold papers all afternoon. Cookie came to the corner in the evening. "Is this the bike?" he said.

"Yeah," the boy said.

"I sure gave you a good one, didn't I?"

"Yeah. Thanks."

By October he had almost forgotten how the bicycle had come into his possession. In November the chain broke while he was sprinting. The rim of the front wheel broke and the fork buckled. It cost him a dollar-and-a-quarter for a new rim. Another dollar to have the buckled fork replaced by a straight secondhand one, and fifty cents for labor.

After that the bike was his, out and out.

One day a year after he had taken the bike from the rack in front of the Liberty Theatre, he put it back into the rack, and went on in and saw the show.

When he came out, the bike was gone. He walked home, and when he saw his father he said, "They stole my bike."

"That's all right," his father said. "Go inside and eat your supper."

"I'm not hungry," the boy said. "If I catch the fellow who stole it, I'll give him the worst beating he ever got."

"Go inside and eat," the boy's father said.

"I don't want to eat," the boy said.

He stood before his father, very angry, and then suddenly turned and ran. He ran all the way to town and walked along every street looking for his bike. After an hour he walked home, ate his supper, and went to bed.

He was now eleven years old.

One evening in August he was playing handball with Nick Roma against the wall of the Telephone Building. Nick made a man-killer, a truck turned into the alley, bumped the ball, and carried it down the alley. The boy went after the ball. It had fallen down a small flight of stairs into a narrow passageway where there were garbage cans and boxes full of ashes. He looked for the ball. In a corner he saw a bicycle frame, with the paint scratched off. He turned the frame upside down and read the number. It had been hammered, but he could still read the 13 and the R.

He stood in the dark passageway, holding the old frame. His friend Nick Roma came up and said, "Where's the ball?"

"It's lost," the boy said. "I found my bike. They took everything off of it."

"Is the frame all right?" Nick said.

"It's all right," the boy said, "but what good is a frame without the other stuff?"

"It's worth *something*," Nick said.

"I'd like to get the guy who stole it," the boy said.

Paul Armer came walking down the alley and saw the two boys with the bicycle frame.

He examined the frame with them.

"What do you want for it, Ike?" he said.

"I don't know," the boy said.

He was angry and broken-hearted.

"It was my bike," he said to Paul. "Then they stole it. We were playing handball, I went to get the ball and I found the frame. They took everything off of it and threw it in here."

"Where did the ball go?" Nick said.

"To hell with the ball," Ike said.

"I'll give you a dollar for it," Paul Armer said.

"All right," the boy said.

A week later when he saw the bike again, painted and with new parts, he became angry again and said to himself, "If I ever get the guy who stole it!"

The Story of the Young Man and the Mouse

✿ ✿ ✿

A WEEK of drinking turned the young man's fancy to mice, *the* mouse, the one and only, the mouse of all mice, the city mouse, the brilliant mouse, the genius of mice, the Great Northern Hotel mouse.

He, or it, arrived one night prancing in the manner of an overjoyed retriever. The mouse came fearlessly to the young man and dropped the money at his feet. The money was four ten-dollar bills which the mouse carried in its mouth. The mouse carried the money so dexterously, or rather so magnificently, so thoughtfully, so delicately that not even slight teeth marks impaired the beauty of the money. The young man picked up the money casually, examined it, and studied the mouse, which stood by in perfect harmony with everything.

The young man moved two paces and also stood by in perfect harmony with everything.

"Well," he said. "This *is* delightful."

He looked at the mouse thoughtfully.

"Stealing, hey?" he said.

The mouse nodded the way a clown nods when he acknowledges the commission of some petty but delightful crime.

"All right," the young man said. "I believe in live and let live. You bring me money this way so I can live and I'll try not to improve your morals. If you want to steal, that's all right with me."

This arrangement appeared to be all right with the mouse, which continued exploring the rooms of the hotel, going to those places where traveling people or retired army officers or people taking a shower like to leave their folding money. Almost every day the mouse returned to the room of the young man to deposit various foldings of American currency: sometimes tens, sometimes fives, sometimes a five and a couple of ones, and one day four ones, which was a crisis and a bitter disappointment to the young man, who was drinking a great deal.

"Live and let live of course," he said to the mouse, "but you can do better than that. Now, let me explain. This number. That's ten. That's good. Get that kind when you can. This is five. Half as good. If you can't get tens, get fives. This is a two. Bad luck. Don't leave them, but they aren't so good. This is one. Awful. Try for tens."

The mouse accepted this simple instruction and was lucky enough to enter rooms where guests who were having showers had left big folding money lying around here and there, so that for many days the young man lived pretty much like a king. He bought clothes. Odds and ends. Ate well. And drank exceptionally well.

The mouse, however, lived on very feeble fare. Old stockings.

"Now," the young man said one day to the mouse, "this may get around. Folks may begin to get suspicious. There is no law against a mouse stealing money, and you'll always be innocent according to the statutes. There isn't a jury in the country that would convict you. But some busybody somewhere may take a long-shot chance and set a trap. They're horrible things, but very attractive outwardly. Cheese is involved. With only one of these pieces of paper which you have just fetched I could buy, I believe, close to twenty pounds of the finest cheese imaginable—which, I daresay, you wouldn't like. They'll try to attract you with cheap cheese. Ten cents a pound. Something like that. Something I haven't eaten in months. Don't be a fool. Don't get taken in. Don't swoon and move into the trap because the smell of the cheese is so wonderful. I'm counting on you to stay in good health."

The mouse had never heard.

Cheese?

Traps?

He didn't know. It was all very exciting.

Money, for some reason, he *did* know. It didn't smell good. It was tasteless and official, but even so.

The young man might have furnished the mouse a little cheese, but he was afraid that if he did the mouse would cease to appreciate anything but food. That, he didn't want. It would be better for the mouse to fend for itself.

"But," he said clearly, "stay away from little pieces of cheese artfully attached to gadgets which appear to be perfectly static and harmless. Once you swoon, you're a goner. It may mean death."

Death?

The mouse hadn't heard.

The drinking continued. Many times the mouse went away and returned with money, but one day the mouse didn't return. Soon the young man began to be poor again. He began to be a little worried, too. First he worried about how he was ever going to be able to keep up appearances without money, but little by little he began to worry about the mouse. In a psychic or alcoholic way, he was able to trace the mouse's course from his room two days ago to where it had fallen into a trap.

This was room 517, one floor down, two doors to the left. The room was inhabited by an old woman whose children sometimes took her to Larchmont for week-ends.

It was a little difficult getting in through the window, but he made it, and sure enough in the corner of the room was the mouse. The old woman was in Larchmont.

The young man burst into tears.

"I told you," he wept. "You see what happens? Now look at you. Here. Let me get you out of this God-damned gadget."

He got the mouse out of the trap and carried it carefully in the palm of his left hand to his room, taking the elevator and weeping.

The elevator boy burst into tears with the young man, but suggested heat and quiet.

Heat and quiet were provided the mouse, and five cents' worth of cheese, which the mouse did not wish to eat.

This frightened the young man.

"Those ungodly people," he said again and again.

The mouse watched the young man quietly for five days and five nights, and then it died.

The young man wrapped it carefully in hotel stationery, appropriately white, and carried it to Central Park where he dug a small grave with the toe of his right shoe, and buried it.

He returned to the hotel and checked out, complaining bitterly about the type of people inhabiting the world.

The Struggle of Jim Patros with Death

✿ ✿ ✿

JIM PATROS is a waiter at Omar Khayyam's in San Francisco. He is a good-natured Greek of forty-four who seems a good deal younger. He is a little under medium-size, but not quite small enough to be a small man. He is well-built, and waits table with efficiency and style. He knows how to be helpful without being obtrusive, and his manners are naturally good.

Like many people who work for a humble living, he is a gambler and feels that some day he is going to make a killing and have all the money he wants. He follows the horses every day, and sits down to a game of stud now and then. So far his luck hasn't been the best in the world, but every six or seven days one of his long-shots comes in and keeps his faith.

And like most people who have always been too busy to loaf, Jim is full of stories about himself.

I like best his story of the time he nearly died of influenza, in Chester, Pennsylvania, in 1918.

I was sick, he said. When I got up in the morning I felt weak, but I put on my clothes, to go to work. When I was putting on my pants I fell down, but I got up. When I was walking to the door I fell down again. I didn't know what it was. I couldn't stand up. The rule was if you was working for the government and you didn't show up for work, they sent somebody to ask what's the matter? I tried to get up but I was too weak. I crawled to the bed and fell on it. The next day the nurse came and said, "What's the matter?"

"I don't know," I said. "I'll come to work tomorrow."

She gave me an examination and said I must go to the hospital. I got up from the bed and said, "I will go to work now." But I fell down, so the nurse helped me and said, "Well, stay in bed, anyway."

In the afternoon, the landlady came and said, "My boy, how are you?"

"Mother," I said, "I do not know."

There was a Greek doctor from Smyrna, so I said, "Mother, tell the doctor to come and look at me."

When the doctor from Smyrna came, the government doctor with the nurse was telling the landlady I must go to the hospital, but I said, "Let my countryman see me."

So the Greek doctor looked at me. He told me to go to the hospital. So. If I am sick, I got to go to the hospital, but I said, "No. I will stay here."

They went away, but an hour later came the police patrol and the government doctor and two policemen, and the nurse, and she said, "Get up."

"What for?" I said. "I work for the government."

"We know," they said. "We got orders. We must take you to the hospital."

"No," I said. "I want to go back to work."

So I got up again, but I couldn't walk. So. If I am sick, I got to go to the hospital.

"Take me in a boat to the best hospital in Philadelphia," I said.

"All the hospitals in Philadelphia are full," the doctor said. "We'll take care of you."

So they took me in the police patrol to the hospital. But what is the hospital?

Stable. One big room, with an *aisley* down the middle and beds on both sides. They put me in a bed and I began to wait. Three days they gave me nothing to eat and no water to drink. Only smashed ice. One night I see the nurse bringing food, but what is it? Fishes' tails. The nurse put down the dish and I looked at the fishes' tails.

"What is this?" I said.

"Food," the nurse said.

"Food?" I said. "Please. Take it away."

I began to look around and think about it. "What kind of a place is this?" I said. "What's the fishes' tails for?"

There was a dark nurse there who looked like a Greek, so I called her. "Are you Greek?" I said.

"I am Serbian," the nurse said.

"I don't like this place," I said. "Do they want to kill us?"

She told me in this place they pushed them out. They were all too sick. All the hospitals were full, and everybody was dying. But this place was the worst. If I'm going to die, I'm going to die at home, not in a slaughterhouse.

"I am Greek," I said to the nurse. "I want to go home. Tonight you bring my clothes and I get dressed and go home."

"If I lose my job," the nurse said, "I will do it. Do you think you will be able to walk?"

"I'll walk," I told her. "Please bring my clothes."

So. In the night she brought my clothes and helped me put them on. When I tried to stand up I began to fall, so she helped me. Everybody was sick, but they knew what I was doing.

"Jim," they said. "Where you going?"

"I'm going home," I said. "If I'm going to die, I'm going to die at home."

I tried to walk but I fell down, and the Serbian girl began to cry.

"Please try to walk," she said.

She walked with me to the door. In front of my eyes I couldn't see, but she stayed by me until I got a little fresh air. Then I could see, but what could I see?

All snow.

"How will you get home?" the girl said.

"I'll get home," I said.

She closed the door and went back. I sat down on the steps and my eyes began to close. I began to dream about the days in Greece when I used to run in the hills and eat berries and drink water from the rivers. Then somebody put his hand on my shoulder. It was an officer in the army.

"What's the matter?" he said.

"I'm going home," I said.

"Do you belong in this hospital?" he said.

"This is not a hospital," I said. "This is a slaughterhouse."

"Come to my office," he said.

In the office he said, "Sit down." He telephoned and told them when the bus was leaving for Chester to come and get me, and when the driver came into the office he said, "Take this man home. Walk with him to his door."

The bus was full of different-different workers going home. In the bus I went to sleep and fell in the lap of an Italian fellow. The Italian said, "That's all right, my friend. That's all right."

When the driver woke me up the bus was empty. He walked with me to the door. The Greek doctor from Smyrna told the Greeks I was going to die, so a Greek fellow told the landlady I was dead. When she opened the door she didn't know if it was me or my spirit. You know Lazar? I was like Lazar. My face was all beard and bones. He told her I was dead. "You know that little fellow?" he said. "I buried him yesterday with my own hands. Jim Patros. Do not wait for him." She was very scared. So.

"Do not be scared, Mother," I said. "It is me. Jim Patros. I am not dead."

"My boy," she said, "How are you?"

"I am sick, Mother."

She took me to my room and put me in my bed. My eyes closed, but I could hear. "My boy," she said, "what can I do for you?"

"Mother," I said, "please go downstairs and get me some chicken broth."

So she went downstairs and got me a bowl of chicken broth. I drank the broth and closed my eyes to sleep. In the night something began to come up inside, very cold, so all night I didn't sleep.

Something told me to stay awake. In the morning the landlady came and said, "My boy, tell me what I can do for you."

"Mother," I said, "please go downstairs and get me some chicken broth."

So she got me some chicken broth. About an hour later she came and said, "My boy, if there is anything in the world you want, please let me know."

She was crying. So.

"Mother," I said, "don't cry for me. If I am going to die, I'm going to die. We come into this world to live one life. Please get me some chicken broth."

Every hour until nighttime she brought me chicken broth.

In the night the Greek doctor and the government doctor came to look at me again. My eyes were closed, so they thought I couldn't hear. They said I was going to be dead by nine o'clock in the morning. "Well," I said to myself, "I don't know. Maybe the doctors know." When they went away the landlady came to me and began to cry.

"My boy, my boy," she said.

"Mother," I said, "it's all right. Don't cry for me."

She went away and after an hour she came back. "My boy," she said.

"Mother," I said, "don't waste your sleep for me. Go to bed. I heard what the doctors said. It's all right."

She went away but after an hour she came back. I could hear her walking around in the house.

"My boy," she said, "can I do anything for you?"

"It's all right, Mother," I said. "You go to sleep."

So this time she went to sleep. Inside my body the cold came up higher. I felt scared because I didn't know anything like that. I didn't know what it was. Then my nose began to bleed. At first I didn't know it was bleeding, but when I put my hand to my face my hand was warm and wet and I could smell the blood. It was coming fast. Under the bed I bent down for the pot and the blood dropped in for a long time. All the time it was falling, I began to feel better. Everything went away, came out of my nose with the blood. The room was dark but I knew I could see again. The cold was gone from the inside too. I was hungry but it was nighttime, so I sat up in bed and waited for morning. In the morning I could hear the landlady walking past my door. She walked past many times, and then she stopped, so I said, "It's all right, Mother. I'm not dead. You can come in."

So she came in, but she was very scared. I showed her the blood. I was ashamed and I said, "Please forgive me, Mother. I couldn't help it."

"My boy," she said. "My boy. How are you? Are you all right?"

"I am very hungry, Mother."

She went downstairs and brought me some chicken broth. But I was very hungry, so she went upstairs and downstairs all morning bringing me chicken broth. When the doctors came I was sitting up in bed. They expected to see a dead body.

"What's this?" they said.

They examined me again, but now I was all right.

I didn't like them and they didn't like me.

The government doctor wrote down in his book and went away. The doctor from Smyrna walked around in the room. Then he said, "I am going to ask you one question. Please tell me the truth."

"What is it?" I said.

"How old were you when you left the old country?"

"Seventeen," I said.

"All right," he said. "This is the question. How old were you when you began to wear shoes?"

"My father bought me shoes when I was three years old," I said. "But I threw them in the closet and ran into the hills in my bare feet. I didn't wear shoes as long as I was in Greece."

"That's the reason," the doctor said.

Then he went away.

You see, Jim said. From the earth to my feet came the strength of the old country. If I had worn shoes in the old country I would be dead now, not alive.

Sailing Down the Chesapeake

☼ ☼ ☼

COME on, Nancy, put your best dress on!" the man on the radio sang. He had a plain nasal voice that was very appropriate for the song. He sounded silly, but the song itself had a strange enormous sadness.

"Dear Nancy," the boy in the hospital said. "Sweet Nancy."

It was Sunday now and it was still raining. It had been raining since Thursday night when he had come to the hospital. Now, in the East, where the man was singing, it was probably snowing. It was winter now, and all over the country, the streets were wet and cold, but on the radio, in a warm room somewhere in the East, the man was singing to Nancy. He was telling her to put on her best dress. That would be in a small town on the East coast somewhere, on the Chesapeake Bay. That would be a bay of blue, with a blue sky over it. Walking down the street of that small town twenty years ago, he was calling on the girl.

The young man looked up at the nurse, who wasn't like the girl of the song at all. She was the ugliest girl he had ever seen. "My luck," he said. "My miserable luck." The nurse was reading a big book. She'd been reading it since eight in the morning, and now it was late in the afternoon.

"What's it about?" he asked her.

"Fellow named Rhett Butler," the nurse said.

"What about him?"

"It's about people down South."

"Tell me about them," he said.

"I'm not anywhere near started yet," the nurse said. "It's an awful long book."

"Well," he said, "I guess I'll never know then."

"You'll be all right."

"I'm all right *now*."

"Just rest."

"I'm resting all the time," he said. "I feel so at peace with the world. I'm living in my memories all the time now."

"How can you smile?" the nurse said.

"Why shouldn't I smile?"

"Aren't you sorry?"

"I am. I am *truly* sorry."

"Then how can you smile?"

"I don't know."

"Your poor mother," the nurse said.

"My poor mother," he said. "My poor, poor mother."

"That's more like it," the nurse said when she saw the tears in his eyes. They were the tears of a small boy who was truly sorry about what he'd done, and even though the nurse hadn't liked him from the beginning *because* of what he had done and the way he had talked before they had operated on him, she had felt forgiving.

"That's better," she said.

"I'm not crying about my mother," he said with anger. "I'm crying about my dirty filthy f—g luck."

The nurse got to her feet, trembling with rage.

"Sit down," he said. "Sit down and wait for me to die. That's what you're here for."

He smiled suddenly.

"Take it easy," he said. "I don't like people to be sorry for me, that's all. It's bad enough when I'm sorry for myself."

"You ought to be ashamed," the nurse said.

He laughed softly.

"Don't get sore," he said.

Two police came to ask if he had anything to give anybody.

"Nothing," he said.

It was a good thing everything was out in the open and he didn't have to protect anybody by keeping quiet. The two cops stood around, hating him, seeming to have something to say, not saying it, seeming to be on the verge of going, and then staying, as if they ought to shoot him. He turned their hatred back to them, smiling the way he knew they hated him for, only he wasn't acting, he wasn't trying to be tough, he was really sorry. He hadn't meant so much trouble. He hadn't meant so much trouble at all.

He was sorry about the poor police; about his friends; about his mother; and about himself. He was sorry about everybody, even the poor nurse. He was especially sorry about her.

The cops stood around, bringing to the small white room a smell of wet clothes, a smell of the world, that he was grateful for. They were good guys. He didn't hate them. He didn't hate anybody. Bad luck, that's all. Bad luck.

"What's your real name?" the one who hated him most said. He was big, Irish and rough, but probably underneath it all, kindly.

"Joe Renna."

"You're no Italian."

"You've got all my papers," he said. "My name's Joe Renna."

"You're no more Italian than I am," the cop said. "You're an American."

"Sure I'm an American," he said. "I was born on Columbus Avenue."

"What number?"

"I don't remember."

"Your mother or somebody will want to know about this," the cop said. Tears came to his eyes again.

"They're all dead," he said.

"You've got somebody, haven't you?" the cop said.

The young man thought of naming the girl. She had surely read about it in the papers, but she hadn't even telephoned. It might be a nice joke to name her as the one to mourn him.

"I've got three hundred dollars in the bank," he said. "That ought to be enough for a funeral. You've got the book. If there's anything left over, give it to some boy in the street."

"How about your clothes?"

"I'll want to wear what's left of them. A good tailor can fix them up."

"How about the stuff where you live?"

"All I've got is what I had on me."

The cops went out, and once again he wanted to cry. It was no good to be going.

The nurse herself, after the cops had gone, turned on the radio.

All of a sudden the man on the radio began to sing about sailing down the Chesapeake, and the boy began to dwell in a time before he had been born, in a place he had never seen. He was walking down a summer street toward a girl he didn't know, and he didn't have much time. He stared at the nurse until she lifted her eyes from the pages of the book she was reading and *saw* him.

"Come here," he said.

The nurse got up and said, "What do you want?"

"I want you to know I love you," he said. (Come on, Nancy, put on your best dress and we'll go sailing down the Chesapeake. Oh, murder, murder.)

The nurse stood over him a moment and then put her hand on his forehead.

"Not there," he said. "On my mouth."

The nurse placed her hand over his mouth and the boy kissed it. (Oh, Nancy, Nancy.)

The radio singer was coming to the last chorus of the song.

"Bring your lips close to mine," he said.

The nurse bent over him, taking her lips so close that while he talked his lips touched hers.

"Just because you don't love me," he said, "don't ever think I don't love you. I love you more than any man has ever loved any woman."

The singer came to the last chorus. The boy closed his eyes and began in a fury of trembling to sleep, standing cocky and confused in many places, turning, looking about, moving everywhere. Then, hurrying in a mob, he got to the little town on the East coast, twenty years ago, and went walking down the street under the blue sky, alive all over, his mouth full of thirst for cool water and for the taste of the lovely one, the whole world full of nothing but celebrations of love.

When his trembling stopped and his mouth fell open, the nurse hurried into the hall to fetch a doctor.

I Know You Good

✧ ✧ ✧

ONE Saturday night in New York's Eastside a boy of thirteen named Irving went to his mother and said, "Ma, can I have a little money?"

"A little money?" his mother said. "How much money?"

"A dollar, Ma?"

"A dollar yet," the boy's mother said. "What for a dollar?"

"I need some new stuff at school," the boy said.

"New stuff?" his mother said. "What new stuff?"

"I need a new geography book, Ma."

"Geography?" his mother said. "What's geography?"

He was a good-looking young Jew, and it was summertime. He was getting interested in girls.

"Geography's all about places, Ma," he said.

"All about places," his mother said. "What places?"

"Australia, China, Ohio," the boy said.

"Australia, China, Ohio," the boy's mother said.

She gave him a very sharp look. "I know you good," she said.

She gave him ten cents.

Last Friday, in the San Joaquin valley, Yep and I got up at four in the morning and drove out to Riverdale to see how the barley was making out. We stopped along the highway every two or three miles to shoot at jack rabbits. The gun was a Winchester .22 repeater, borrowed from Yep's cousin Ara. I tried out the sight on a little bird that was perched on a telegraph wire, and dropped it. In no time at all I ended life in three of the lanky rodents, too. One of them I stopped while it was running. We enjoy this sort of thing. I think it's much less the lust to kill than the love of accuracy. I apologized to every rabbit of the desert that I killed. One, whose bowels had been spilled, sorrowed me deeply and made me ashamed of myself. I should have shot it in the head. The reason I didn't was that it was too far away.

I tried several times to get close enough to some crows that were in a couple of scrub trees, but as soon as I got too close they quietly took flight. (I know you good.)

A couple of miles north of Huron at eight in the morning we asked a boy on a threshing machine if he knew how we could reach Tuck's place. The boy had a mouthful of tobacco and stuttered. He was new in that region. He'd come down from the Tehachapi Mountains to drive the tractor that pulled the threshing machine around. Something had gone wrong with the machine, so that it cracked the barley. He was doing some work on the machine while someone was driving forty miles to Fresno for a new part. He said he disliked this new level country, preferred the mountains. I asked him where he was from originally, and he said Texas. He had punched cows in Old Mexico. His name was Will Young. He was twenty.

I shot two blackbirds that were in trees on an overflowing stream and the water carried their bodies away.

I went after some water birds of some sort. There were five of them. They were white and very beautiful from a distance standing in the swamp water, and even more beautiful in flight. While going near them I felt it would be wrong to shoot and kill one of them but at the same time I felt that I would try to do so. When we got about four hundred yards away from them, they all flew away quietly. Perhaps it was more than four hundred yards. It was too far away, at any rate, to shoot with accuracy.

Walking about out-of-doors, however, is an activity that pleases the heart. Five minutes ago, I decided to do it more often. (August 31, 1939. Delayed.)

THE NEW YEAR

It was raining, the third or fourth or fifth day of January, and I hadn't yet gotten over three or four things of December. I had money, I was bored, and what I had was either the flu or something like it. So I went into the restaurant, wobbling a little, still drunk from December, and frowning from the many sadnesses, irritations, and amazements of the year gone. In the back room where the bar is I found Tom, also drunk from December, and the two girls Mary and Emma.

It was ten minutes to twelve, midnight. The restaurant was empty except for the waiters. Even the back room was empty, except for Tom and Mary and Emma, and, of course, Joe, the Italian bar-boy, and Ben, the headwaiter.

It was a celebration. Tom was drunk but well-behaved, and the girls were drunk and full of high spirits. They screamed when they saw me, and Mary embraced and kissed me. Then Emma drew Mary away, and she embraced and kissed me. I kissed each of the girls as if only they knew the fable of the years lost, as if in all the world they were the only people who meant anything to me.

THE JOURNEY TO NEW YORK

The whole year he planned to go to New York, but didn't. He would be a little drunk as a rule whenever it occurred to him that he had planned to go and hadn't. He didn't even begin to lose faith in the journey, however, until one morning in August. He had been up all night and was waiting for a streetcar when day broke and made him wonder what had happened.

"New York?" he said. "——— New York. What's in New York?"

He turned, as if to someone with him, and said, "Which way did they go? You know. The years."

Then he gave the world a quiet cussing and decided all he wanted to do was sleep. ——— everything.

After that he knew he wasn't going, and whenever he remembered New York it wasn't with any impulse to get there. "I'll go on rotting out here," he said.

He would get up around noon every day and go through the tiresome ritual of becoming alive again, shaving, bathing, putting on fresh clothes, and glancing with terrible distaste at the headline of the morning paper he had brought home with him. No matter how thoroughly he brushed his teeth and scraped his tongue, the taste he wakened with would stay foul until he had had two cups of coffee and a couple of cigarettes. He would feel better after that and would drink beer in the parlor until evening. He would have the blinds up for sunlight, if there was any, and sometimes he would sit at the piano and imagine he might get in the mood to play, but it always turned out that he didn't. Ordinarily, though, he wouldn't bother to notice the piano. Early in the evening he would take a streetcar to town and go to a quiet restaurant for the only meal of the day. It would be a very big one, and he would eat slowly, reading around in some pocket-size novel, or anthology of poems, or stories, or essays. From the restaurant he would go to a quiet bar and begin drinking. More often than not, people he had met somewhere would recognize him and come over to greet him. He would be polite but not enthusiastic, and they would know he wanted to be alone. After a moment they would leave, wondering what had come over him.

Drinking, he went to New York every night, and prowled through all the streets, looking for her, as if he didn't know she was not there, either.

FOO

"Now, about Chicago," he said. "If I go there, will I lose my hair?"

"Oh, you want to lose your hair?" the other said.

"No, I *don't* want to. That's what I want to know about Chicago. I've been thinking of going there. If I won't lose my hair, I'll go."

"Well," said the other, "take a look at my head."

He took off his hat and showed his head, which was bald, except around the sides.

"That started," he said, "in Chicago." Pause. "I went there on business."

Another pause, while the man with hair regretted the other's misfortune.

"In 1928," the bald one said, "my hair started falling out the first day I was in Chicago."

"If you don't want to lose your hair," he said, "don't go to Chicago. But if you do, that's the place to go."

The man with hair, who was forty but much more youthful looking, almost boyish, an Italian from a family which had buried all its men with full heads of hair, whose own hair in fact was as thick as hair ever is, and probably couldn't have been torn out of his head, listened attentively and signified with a puckering of his lips, and a lifting of his eyebrows that he understood. The world, his expression seemed to say. What a place! If you go to Chicago, you lose your hair.

"I thought you might want to lose your hair," the other said.

"No," the Italian said with a smile. "I'll go somewhere else."

"You never know when it's liable to start falling out," the other said.

The Italian signified that he understood, perfectly.

"Nothing you can do about it, either," the other said. "I tried everything. It just kept right on falling out."

It was very hot. The two men had come to the back room of the cigar store because of the lower temperature there, and to have themselves a cool drink. The Italian was drinking Dr. Pepper, and the other, an American, was drinking Coca-Cola. They had never met before and had hit upon Chicago as a subject of conversation more or less accidentally.

The American had said the heat was sultry—something like the heat of Chicago.

They finished their drinks, as they talked, put the empty bottles in the crates, and stood for a moment, cooling off.

The Italian was the first to go. Without a word, but not impolitely, he walked out to the street and the heat. The other lingered a moment and then followed the Italian.

The clerk behind the counter hadn't listened to their conversation, but when they were gone he said to himself, "Foo." It was a word he had been throwing about a good deal lately. He'd heard it from a tobacco salesman who'd come in one morning and said, " 'A stitch in foo saves foo.' "

"What's that?" the cigar-store clerk had asked.

"Foo, that's all," the salesman had said. "It's from the funnies. I got it from my kid. He's seven. Here's another, 'A foo and his money are soon parted.' "

"Say," the clerk had said, "that's good."

"No," the tobacco salesman had said, "not good, foo."

"O.K.," the clerk had said, "foo."

"Not O.K.," the salesman had said, "foo."

"Well, for crying out loud," the clerk had said, "at that rate you'd be saying 'foo' for everything."

"Foo," the salesman had said, meaning sure.

That's how it had started. The clerk had found the word useful, but lately it had begun to be a little difficult to control. Instead of saying thank you to a lady who had purchased a package of Herbert Raleigh cork tips he had said foo, and she had said I beg your pardon, and given him a very dirty foo. He meant look.

Well, foo to her. She was just a foo anyhow.

The world was foo, the human race was foo, love was foo, hate was foo, and above all things a man himself was foo.

* * *

How It Is to Be

☼ ☼ ☼

WHEN George Gershwin died, I believed I ought to have an X-ray picture taken of my head, but the doctor told me it wouldn't be necessary.

"It's something we don't know anything about," he said. "All we know is that there are two kinds of growths, benign and malignant. We don't know why there is either. That's the part you're supposed to find out about."

"Me?" I said. "What do you mean, me?"

"I mean," he said, "your guess is as good as anybody's, maybe better."

"Thanks," I said, "but how about these pains in my head every once in a while?"

"Well," he said, "how about the pains in my head every once in a while? Get the idea? It's nothing, or at any rate nothing that isn't a natural or at least an inevitable part of living."

"That's different," I said. "Just so everybody has them. Just so it's not because I'm a writer."

"It's not because you're a writer," he said. "It's because you're dying, so forget it, because everybody's dying."

"My God," I said, "is that true?"

"You know it is," he said. "You know better than I do that it's true. None of us is more than a minute from death at any time. You know that. Absence of oxygen and hydrogen, as when a man is drowning, can carry us out in almost no time at all. Loss of relationship, equilibrium, or position, as when a man is falling, can do it in two or three seconds. Collision, as when a man is carried swiftly to an object composed of firmer substance than himself, can do it instantaneously. These are the accidental and more violent passages, but even normally none of us is more than a minute from death."

So I decided to ignore the pains in my head.

Even so, that was the saddest news I'd heard in years because one night in New York I'd met him and talked to him and he'd played the piano for a couple of hours. He was only a boy. Nobody wants anybody like that to die at the age of thirty-five or thirty-six. Nobody wants anybody who can hear music to die while he's still a boy. I talked to Sibelius once. That's *how* we want it to be. Sibelius was close to seventy.

I was in my home town when I heard about it. One of my cousins told me about it. He came over to my grandmother's in his Chevrolet roadster and we started driving to Kingsburg. When we got out on the highway near Malaga he turned on the radio. There was an orchestra swinging around, and all of a sudden my cousin remembered.

"Gershwin's dead," he said.

Well, all he had to do was say it and I knew it was true. If my cousin said it, it was true. I couldn't believe it, but I knew it was true. Remembering Gershwin in New York I believed my cousin when he said Gershwin was dead. By God, it was true. There it was. He was dead. I looked at the grapevines in the beautiful light, the lovely trees, and the quiet roads.

"Did you know him?" my cousin said.

"I met him one night in New York," I said. "It was a big party and there were a lot of people and everybody was drinking and talking, but I guess I knew him."

We went out to the vineyard in Kingsburg and saw the vines and the grapes on them.

Then we went back to my grandmother's and had lunch: grape leaves wrapped around lamb and rice, Armenian bread and cheese, and cold watermelon. Then we drove out to the park and I kept looking at everything. I kept wondering how it is to *be*. How it *is*. How incredible and splendid it is. How strange and mournful and fine: having all the quiet things that were painted by great men who painted when *they* wanted to know how it is: the still-lifes, the forms of the quiet things, the pear, the peach, the cluster of grapes, the fish on the plate, the loaf of bread, the bottle of wine, the real things, in light. How magnificent and good and mysterious the living things are that all men have loved.

At two in the morning that night I took the train for San Francisco and went on looking at everything: the darkness of the landscape and the sky, waiting for the coming of light, the wan arrival of morning, the coming up of the sun, lighting up the world we have made, the ugly lovely world we have put on the earth, the railroads and industrial buildings, and the quiet sorrowing dwellings of poor people. I dreamed all night of how it is.

I'll try to tell you how it is. If I can remember, I'll go to all the places I have gone to by train or ship, and if I can remember what happened, I'll tell you, because if the pains in my head aren't because I'm a writer, what it is to me is what it is to you, and what it is to you is what it is to all the others who are still alive, who have not yet traveled, in wars or accidents or disease, to the other side. If I can keep from trying to say everything at once, I'll tell you how it is, or at least give you an idea.

I'll go back to the beginning, if I can. That's got to be, otherwise it won't be whole. The beginning is when *you* begin, and that isn't when you're born, except in a matter-of-fact statistical way. When you're born is the beginning all right, but not the one I'm thinking about. The beginning I mean is the one when you yourself *look* and for the first time *see*.

The beginning I mean is when you come out of the dream being dreamed by the universe and feel the lonely, fierce glory of being, of being out of emptiness, of being related to, and a part of, the great source of energy, of being an entity, whole and perishable, benign and malignant.

The beginning I mean is when you know the difference between what men pretend to be and what they are: not anything but visitors of the world, borrowers of time, coming and going. Not possessors of anything but the privilege of inhabiting substance and enduring time. Men are miraculously living things, never more than a day from death, never far from glory, and as long as they live children, because living is in its infancy. Men who travel the last moment to death at the age of seventy, or eighty, or ninety, travel as children. They go as they came, helplessly.

Let them have been great in the eyes of their fellows, or small, or unknown, or in the eyes of God let them have been noble and good and true, men, when they travel that last moment, go as men *coming* here travel the *first* moment. Those moments, that of coming to this place and that of leaving it, are the moments of mystery and miracle, benign and, if we choose to put it the other way, malignant, although coming is no more benign than going is malignant. Each is simultaneously malignant and benign.

They are always *together*, except for climate, and light, and the fragments of time each man knows that are of glory, of reaching destination in the opposite of one's kind. Benign and malignant are one in the living, in all things, except for these moments when the moving of time is halted by the infinite rise of heart, the immeasurable lift of spirit, the momentarily unending expansion of truth seeking truth, and finding it.

This is a suggestion of how it is, a suggestion of how *some* of it is. The parts are so numerous and so variable that no man may say how *all* of it is. Even for himself no man, no child here, great or small, or in the eyes of God noble and true, may know how *all* of it is, or even how all of it *may* be. It may be for now, as the ballad goes, or it may be for ever. For now or for ever, no man may know.

356 THE SAROYAN SPECIAL

The evening of that day, in my home town, my cousin and I rode around the Sunday streets and suddenly saw one of the opposite of our kind, born in that place, walking through the evening, as lovely as a cluster of grapes. My cousin roared. He drove the roadster up and down the street, keeping the girl in sight, roaring with delight and adoration, slapping the side of his head with sorrow, groaning in Armenian, and saying in English, "Oh, my God."

The girl was no more than sixteen or seventeen, or maybe no more than fourteen or fifteen, but as lovely as all young things of our earth are, as charged with grace and proportion as all things coming into this life are: the coming of day, fruit to the bough, sea to the shore, humor to the heart. And with my cousin, I was smitten with that grief which comes from delight and adoration of substance so lovely it is holy, though it be possessed by the daughter of a drunkard or an idiot or any man, great or small. My cousin and I saw mortal loveliness, and when it disappeared into a hovel on a desolate street by a railroad track, my cousin, still groaning, looked about furiously and shouted, "Let's go get a root beer."

We drove to a place on Ventura Avenue and had two of them. Then we drove out to his house. A dozen of us, all from the same sources, sat around and talked. The older ones remembered the old country and those who had died; the early days in this country, and how beautiful everything had been, how beautiful and different, and the same. The hard times and the times when one of us, still alive, was on his way to the last moment and the others prayed and swore and finally the one who was journeying turned and came back to us and at last all the others fell down and slept and in the morning the journeyer slept peacefully and a week later, or two or three, was back with us again, still one of us, talking with us, aged three or twenty, or forty, and laughed with us, and we were together still and there would be tables together still, food and drink together, seasons together still, and light in the world still. We talked of the dead as if they were not dead, as if the years had not gone by, as if Dikran was among us still, brilliant and swift and full of comedy, roaring with laughter, hugging the children of his sisters, bringing them gifts. We talked of Hovagim and his old rattletrap Buick and his ferocious anger when somebody was unkind or a liar, his fury one day when a neighbor lied to him, and how he lifted the neighbor's Ford and tipped it over on its side and shouted, "There! Now lie some more!" And all of us roared with laughter.

Later that night my cousin and I drove to town again and went to a bar. "Do you remember the men they were talking about?" my cousin asked. "A few of them I remember," I said. "Some were before my time, but I remember Hovagim. He took me and my brother out to his vineyard once in his rattletrap Buick. He took us hunting and played Armenian records on his old phonograph, and tears came down his face. He used to bring us grapes and peaches and watermelons. I remember this man, but I don't remember Dikran. I remember *hearing* about him from his sister, my mother, and from his mother, our grandmother. I like him. He seems to have been a solemn man, even though he was always comical."

We went to the Basque saloon on Tulare Street. There was a nickel-in-the-slot phonograph there and for two hours we sat around drinking Scotch and listening to Spanish tangoes and love songs. It was a good place. It was one of the best places of drinking I ever drank in, and I kept thinking of the night in New York when I met George Gershwin and he told me how it was with him when he composed.

Drinking, I knew how it is, but I couldn't say. It's the way nobody knows. He had journeyed past the last moment, but he was with us still because while he possessed substance he journeyed back and forth, into the darkness and back to the light, looking and listening, going into the region just beyond all of us, and coming back. I knew it was *that* way. But for the grace of God any of us is to be dead before we have come or gone, before we have begun, before we have reached any moment to remember, we are earth again, or rock, or nothing.

On the train going home I was a sad Armenian, as they say of Indians. It wasn't because Brahms had died, or Bach, or any of the others, Renoir, or Goya, or Dostoyevsky, or Dickens, or Robert Burns, or Byron, or Daniel Boone, or Tolstoy, or Andrew Jackson, or Mark Twain, or any of the others we love. It was because that's how it is, malignant and benign, by the grace of God, by the mercy of God.

The Declaration of War

✿ ✿ ✿

ON September the third, 1939, a boy by the name of John came running into the barber shop on Moraga Avenue where I was getting a haircut.

"War's been declared in Europe," he said.

Mr. Tagalavia dropped the comb from one hand and the scissors from the other.

"You get out of this shop," he said. "I told you before."

"What's your name?" I said to the young man.

"John," he said.

"How old are you?" I said.

"Eleven," John said.

"You get out of this shop," Mr. Tagalavia said.

I was under the impression that Mr. Tagalavia was talking to John, but apparently he wasn't. He was talking to me. He wasn't talking to *himself.*

John had left the shop.

The barber untied his apron and threw it aside.

"Who?" I said.

"You," Mr. Tagalavia said.

"Why?"

"I try to run a respectable barber shop."

"I'm respectable."

"You talked to that foolish boy," the barber said. "I don't want people like you to come to my shop."

"He didn't *seem* foolish," I said.

"He is a foolish, foolish boy," the barber said. "I don't want foolish people to come here."

"I suppose it *was* a little foolish of me to ask the boy his name," I said. "I'm sorry about that. I'm a writer, you see, and I'm *always* asking people questions. I apologize. Please finish my haircut."

"No," the barber said. "That's all."

I got out of the chair and examined my head. My haircut was less than half finished. The shape of my head wasn't exactly what it might be, but I could always walk three or four blocks and have the job finished by an ordinary barber. I put on my tie and coat.

"Excuse me," I said. "How much do I owe you?"

"Nothing," the barber said. "I don't want money from people like you. If I starve—if my family starves—all right. No money from foolish people."

"I'm sorry," I said, "but I believe I owe you *something*. How about thirty-five cents?"

"Not a penny," the barber said. "Please go away. I will make a present of the haircut to you. I *give* to people. I do not take. I am a man, not a fool."

I suppose I should have left the shop at this point, but I felt quite sure that what he *really* wanted to do was talk.

I have a power of understanding which is greater than the average, and at times uncanny. I sense certain things which other people, for one reason or another, are unable to sense.

(Sometimes what I sense is wrong and gets me in trouble, but I usually manage to get out of it. A kind word. A friendly tone of voice. A worldly attitude about such things. We are all brothers. The end is death for each of us. Let us love one another and try not to get excited.)

I sensed now that the barber was troubled or irritated; that he wished to speak and be heard; that, in fact, unless I missed my guess, his message was for *the world*. Traveling thousands of miles he could not have found anyone more prepared to listen to the message or to relay it to the world.

"Cigarette?" I said.

"I don't want anything," the barber said.

"Can I help you with the towels?"

"You get out of my shop."

Here, obviously, was an equal if I had ever encountered one. I have at times been spoken of by certain women who follow the course of contemporary literature as enigmatic and unpredictable, but after all I am a writer. One expects a writer to be impressive along the lines of enigma and so on, but with barbers one usually expects a haircut or a shave or both, along with a little polite conversation, and nothing more. Women who have time to read are likely to believe that it is natural for a writer to have certain little idiosyncrasies, but perhaps the only man in the world who can allow a *barber* similar privileges is a writer.

There is little pride in writers. They know they are human and shall some day die and be forgotten. We come, we go, and we are forgotten. Knowing all this a writer is gentle and kindly where another man is severe and unkind.

I decided to offer the barber the *full* cost of a haircut. Sixty-five cents, instead of thirty-five. A man can always get a haircut. There are more important things than making sure one has not been swindled.

"Excuse me," I said. "I don't think it's fair to you for me not to pay. It's true that you haven't finished my haircut, but perhaps some other day. I live near by. We shall be seeing more of one another."

"You get out of my shop," the barber said. "I don't want people like you to come here. Don't come back. I have no time."

"What do you mean, people like me? I am a writer."

"I don't care what you are," Mr. Tagalavia said. "You talked to that foolish boy."

"A few words," I said. "I had no idea it would displease you. He seemed excited and eager to be recognized by someone."

"He is a foolish, foolish boy," the barber said.

"Why do you say that?" I said. "He seemed sincere enough."

"Why do I say that!" the barber said. "Because he *is* foolish. Every day now for six days he has been running into my shop and shouting, War! War! War!"

"I don't understand," I said.

"You don't understand!" the barber said. "War! I don't know who you are, but let me tell you something."

"My name is Donald Kennebec," I said. "You may have heard of me."

"My name is Nick Tagalavia," the barber said. "I have never heard of you."

He paused and looked me in the eye.

"War?" he said.

"Yes," I said.

"You are a fool," the barber said. "Let me tell you something," he went on. "There is no war! I am a barber. I do not like people who are foolish. The whole thing is a trick. They want to see if the people are still foolish. They *are*. The people are more foolish now than ever. The boy comes running in here and says, 'War's been declared in Europe,' and you talk to him. You encourage him. Pretty soon he believes everything, like you."

The barber paused and looked at me very closely again. I took off my hat, so he could see how far he had gone with the haircut, and how much he had left unfinished.

"What do you write?" he said.

"Memoirs," I said.

"You are a fool," the barber said. "Why do you encourage the boy? He's going to have trouble enough without wars. Why do you say, 'How old are you'?"

"I thought he was rather bright," I said. "I just wanted him to know I was aware of it."

"I don't want people like you to come to my shop," the barber said.

"People like me?" I said. "I *hate* war."

"Shut up," the barber said. "The world is full of fools like you. You hate war, but in Europe there *is* a war?"

The implication here was a little too fantastic.

"Excuse me," I said. "*I* didn't start the war."

"You hate war," the barber said again. "They tell you there's a war in Europe, so you believe there's a war in Europe."

"I have no reason to believe there's peace in Europe," I said.

"You hate war," he said. "The paper comes out with the headline War. The boy comes running into the shop. War. You come in for a haircut. War. Everybody believes. The world is full of fools. How did you lose your hair?"

"Fever," I said.

"Fever!" the barber said. "You lost your hair because you're a fool. Electric clippers. Comb. Scissors. You've got no hair to cut. The whole thing is a trick. I don't want any more fools to come here and make me nervous. There is no war."

I had been right in sensing that the barber had had something to say and had wanted someone to say it to. I was quite pleased.

"You are a remarkable man," I said.

"Don't talk," the barber shouted. "I'm no foolish boy of eleven. I'm fifty-nine years old. I am a remarkable man! Newspapers. Maps. You've got no hair on your head. What am I supposed to cut? The boy comes running in. You can't sit still. 'War is declared in Europe,' he says. 'What's your name? How old are you?' What's the matter? Are you crazy?"

"I didn't mean to upset you," I said. "Let me pay you."

"Never," the barber said. "I don't want anything. That's no haircut. Not a penny. If a man with a head of hair comes in here and sits down, I will take the electric clippers and give him a haircut. The hair falls down on the floor. No trouble. No excitement. No foolishness. He gets out of the chair. His head is in good shape. Ears feel fine. Sixty-five cents. Thank you. Good-bye. The boy comes running in. I say, 'Get out of my shop.' The boy runs out. No trouble."

"*Other* barbers give me haircuts," I said.

"All right, he said. "Go to other barbers. Please go to other barbers. Remember one thing. There is no war. Don't go around spreading propaganda."

I was now satisfied that I had successfully gotten to the bottom of the man's irritation, and had obtained fresh and original material for a new memoir, so without another word, I sauntered out of the shop and down the street.

I feel that I have effectively utilized the material; that I have shaped it into a work which, if anything, will enhance my already considerable fame.

Highway America

☼ ☼ ☼

I HAVE been to Secaucus. I have crossed the Passaic.

That was the day after I bought the car. That was that rainy Sunday. I remember a lot of churches in one of those Jersey towns. I remember a couple of trees and a lot of lawn somewhere. I remember rain and a Greek or Roman Catholic Sunday service of some kind over the radio, with no word known, but good voices and considerable chanting. Later the radio broke.

What's the use being a writer if you aren't going to have a car and see the United States? Where does it ever get you? My cousin drove for me. He is a natural-born comedian. Another thing about him that's fine is that he talks Armenian. That's a great funny language. American is another great funny language, and when you put the two together you get something that's really casual.

The hardest thing of all is to get out of town. It's worth it, though. Down Fifth Avenue to the Holland Tunnel into Jersey and onto Pulaski Skyway. Pulaski was a Pole who fought the red-coats, I think. On highway Nine past the Newark Airport onto 22. Right on down to Galloping Hill Park and onto 29, to Watchung Mountain, Copper Hill, Ringoes, New Hope. Well, look at that. Lahaska. 202 now. Paoli and the freckle-faced, ripe and bursting beauty in the highway restaurant bringing the spare ribs and sauerkraut to the swing of nickel-in-the-slot. A couple of the boys from Fresno, California. Arminimums, my cousin explains. Lost—Westchester County. This is a county of some social importance, even though we're off the road, I inform my cousin. In Armenian he makes appropriate reply by word and gesture, and we recover the road over 322 at Downington. Black Horse, Paradise, Bird-in-Hand. People have no idea how wonderful they are. And as for you, child, you are an angel. She waved. The Delaware! Isn't there something important about this river? He wants to know isn't there something important about the Delaware. Listen, boy, Washington *crossed* the Delaware.

We cross the Susquehanna.

Just outside Gettysburg we bought three old rifles and one old little revolver that a girl wanted $14 for that I couldn't afford which she said another man bought one just like it only a month ago.

"Who was he?" I said.

"He was a stranger," she said.

Now about this little revolver I bought for a dollar and a half. Well, it's hard to say, but it seems they were playing cards and the man who had this gun concealed in his upper left-hand vest-pocket suspected another man of cheating. He drew this gun, fired it, and stung the other man in the cheek. The other man said ouch and killed the man who, probably sixty-seven years ago, owned my gun.

We had a few minutes in Maryland. "This is Mencken's state," I said, and together we sang "Maryland, My Maryland." "That's Wagner," my cousin said. Thus, we crashed headlong into Virginia and new adventure. We saw pigs on the side of the road looking like dogs, red and furry. Off the highway a mile to the Shenandoah Caverns. "We'll see these awful wonders of the world if it costs us fifty cents each," my cousin said. "A dollar sixty-five each," the man said. "We'd see it," I said, "if it was a dollar seventy, but first let us eat." The waitress was also the cook. "Those pigs," I said. "They look like dogs. What are they called?" "Piggies," she said. We saw the caves. Forty or fifty million years old, just like the dirt upstairs. We got through an hour-an-a-half lecture tour in ten minutes, instructing the guide along the way.

Little Rock, Malvern, Arkadelphia, Texarkana, and then Texas. You forget a lot. It's a big country. It's beautiful. Big Spring for sleep. Rain all the way in. Through Fort Worth. Nine cars, three trucks, tipped over in the mud on the side of the highway. We got to El Paso around six-thirty the next day. Mexican supper. Mexican music on the phonograph. Across the border to Juarez. Entering Juarez the Mexican Customs man arrived and said:

"Wharr gee wanna go?"

"Juarez."

"Wharr gee wanna do?"

"Drive around."

"Where gee wanna drive around?"

"Just around around."

"Where gee wanna drive around around?"

"Just around around around."

"Nineteen cents please," he said, letting us into Old Mexico.

On into New Mexico. The highway dips every half mile. Dips are cheaper than bridges. Into Arizona. Safford for the night. In Arizona we improvised on themes of Armenian folk music, and finally put words to something called Automobile, Automobile. This was sad, but wonderful, going ninety miles an hour and looking. The hills, the valleys, the streams, the trees, the rocks, the towns, the people. The heart chanting, "*Aye vakh!*"

After we forgot the song of the automobile, we put a few simple American words to an Armenian theme of music. The fellow says, "Come on to my house. I'm gonna give you candy."

Down the American highway into the valley of home. "Home," my cousin says. In the valley he busts out laughing. "Hey, look. The vines." (I'm looking. Don't worry. I'm looking.)

It's a beautiful country, but the most beautiful thing about it is that it's just like every country in the world—on account of the people, most likely.

My Home, My Home

✿ ✿ ✿

OF the unchanging things, the town in which you first saw the light is one of the most unchanging. It is always a place of monotony but at the same time, as you grow, change, go away, remember, return, and go away again, it is one of the most inexhaustibly rich places. And yet what it is is so nearly nothing, except for the dull, drab, lonely, lost objects of it, that you never know, each time you return to it, what it is that holds you so strongly to it.

What is it but an ordinary American town, no different from ten thousand others, where thirty million others were once born and where once they knew childhood and youth, and went away or stayed?

What is it more than a place where two or three dozen rested one day of one year and stayed, and others came, and stayed, and still others came out of their staying?

What is it more than two depots, one on each side of town, east and west, the city in between, the streets and houses all around, the dwellers never out of hearing of the trains coming and going?

What is it more than the beginning of the world, with winter coming?

Is it anything more than waking one morning and knowing presence in this place?

Or more than sitting at a desk at school and wishing to learn from the simplest lesson of arithmetic what *all* of it is, who all of them are?

Is it ever a place more than where, not in dream, the streets occurred and yourself came about in them, walking?

Is it anything more than longing, summer and winter? Loneliness you do not know shall never end?

Is it anything more than beholding beauty in the face of a small girl and adoring it and not knowing that never shall the light of that face go out of your sleep?

Is the small town a place, truly, of the world, or is it no more than something out of a boy's dreaming? Out of his love of all things not of death made? All things somewhere beyond the dust, rust, and decay, beyond the top, beyond all sides, beyond bottom: outside, around, over, under, within?

Is it a boy's knowing that, although this is a place of sorrowed trying, of sorrowful men trying for the best, it is also a place where in the midst of things seen and men known moves the race that never was born, and within the crying grief of its streets and structures is the whole towering world which almost came to be? To his nostrils just beyond the stench of sweat and rot, the holy scent of all things with only loveliness in them and no death? To his ears, the stillness of silence staying within and around all things? The soft, listening silence of the continuous beginning?

Once again I am back in my home town. Last night I learned that a great part of what this town is, wherever I go: is the nighttime sky: clear, sudden, and infinitely spacious.

Early this morning I walked to town down Ventura Avenue over streets I walked twenty years ago. I found nothing changed but a few signs on a few buildings, a few trees lost, a few new ones come, a few grown greater, a house fallen into disrepair but still inhabited, the porch in decay. The silence is the same, and it is broken the same as twenty years ago, by the coming and going of trains.

From Ventura Avenue to Tulare Street I walked on the Santa Fé railroad tracks, and from the north going south came the freight train. When it reached me I couldn't believe the years had gone, and I knew a man will go out of this world without ever finding that largeness and wholeness in the living and in himself which was the cause of all his longing when he was no more than ten years old.

While the train was going by, I knew that a man will go away without ever having reached anywhere, and never will the image of loveliness just beyond all things, all ends and edges, over and above and within, cease to be in his sleep until he is truly one who is no longer alive, and no longer able to sleep at all.

The Grapes

✿ ✿ ✿

THESE were the earliest grapes of the year, excepting the very earliest ones from Imperial Valley. On the vines the grapes might not be ripe enough in the morning, but by three in the afternoon they would be all right, so the Mexicans and Filipinos and Oklahomans would cut the bunches from the vines and put them in boxes, and seven days later the grapes would be in New York. They would ripen in six hours of that kind of heat and their color would change from a soft transparent green to a light brown, and then the government inspector would take a half-dozen bunches and mash them and test them for sugar. They would be sweet enough, or so close to it that he wouldn't make any trouble. A new inspector would always make trouble, or start to, but an old one would let the grapes go into the refrigerator car, just so they were close to the mark. The grapes would be packed in crates, about twenty-eight pounds to a crate, although some shippers would pack the crates heavy and run it up to thirty-two pounds. The railroad didn't like that because the maximum weight per crate was supposed to be twenty-eight, but a lot of the shippers loaded the crates and put them in the cars and rolled them. The railroads would send out a young man to weigh the crates and usually they would be around thirty or so, but he wouldn't make a fuss if he'd been on the job a season or two.

It was just no use trying to enforce a rule with grape shippers. They always got their way, within reason, and when you got down to it, they had a right to. They gave the railroads their best business and it was a tough racket. Usually the shipper lost money, one season or the next, so it was wise to be casual about the crates being heavier than they were supposed to be.

Everybody who was supposed to enforce some kind of a rule discovered sooner or later that it was wisest to take it easy and not try to be an enforcer of law, or obnoxious. An old-time railroad man, a vice president or a general manager, would tell a young man just out of college and going to work for the first year, "I know you know the rules, Jim, but let me tell you about Melikian out there at Magunden—well, he knows the rules, too, but you can't keep them, that's all. Sometimes it's just impossible to keep the rules, except you go to work and lose yourself ten thousand dollars, and we figure it's better to break the lousy rule than make a good shipper lose all that money—so take it easy."

I loafed around the packing shed at Magunden where Melikian was loading. Magunden's just outside of Bakersfield and isn't anything but a couple of loading sheds, and a store which is also a lunch room. Of course there is a marble game in the store and a phonograph that plays one of twenty records for a nickel each.

There were three dozen girls and women packing grapes for Melikian, three truckers hauling grapes from the field, a dozen men and boys working with hand trucks, and a half-dozen lidders and loaders. The lidders worked the machine that nailed the lid on the crate; the loaders nailed the crates in the boxcar, over a thousand crates in each car. The grapes were Thompson Seedless, Red Malagas, and Ribiers. Ribiers are those large black grapes that are so good to look at. A well-packed crate of them is something you feel ought to sell for five or six dollars in New York. It is a grape of great beauty, excellent color, and fine flavor, and it is one of the first to ripen. The Thompson is that grape you see at fruit and vegetable markets all the time, either greenish or light brown, and at its best very sweet. In fact you can't eat a lot of this grape because of its sweetness. The Red Malaga is not deep red or anything like that, just something close to red, actually closer to a shade of purple. Ribiers are black with a bloom of dust that makes you admire nature, if you care about such things at all.

All this is in terrific heat which can be delightful if you make no mistakes in eating and drinking. Hard liquor is stupid, and even beer is no good. Soda pop is all right, but best of all is water if you can get good water. The tap water is flat, though, so you have to drink soda pop until you get to a place where there is spring water, out of a jar. Best of all is plain bread and grapes which have been cooled, and once a day a little cold meat. Otherwise in two days you'll feel dopey and the excellent weather will seem fierce—just in case you intend to visit Magunden in August some day and see how the grapes get to market. You probably won't be bothering because in all probability you weren't brought up in the valley and you don't care how they get to market.

The most interesting thing about the grapes getting to market, however, is something I haven't even got close to so far. The innocence. That is, the sort of pardonable unimaginativeness of the people involved, the Mexicans in the vineyards, the truckers on the road, the shippers in the sheds, the packers, the loaders, the railroad men, the inspectors, and all the others, even the farmers. All these people go to work and get the grapes to New York and other far-away cities without any appreciation for the elemental significance of the ritual. This is so of course because each is troubled by the matter of money. The farmer is worried about what he's going to get, the shipper is always gambling on the market, and the workers of course are working in that heat because they need money to live on. Before the season is half started, though, even the workers have forgotten about living, and are giving everything they've got to the ritual of getting the grapes packed, loaded into the cars, and onto the chain of freight cars that travels across the continent to market. *That* becomes their living. You have only to watch them working around eleven o'clock at night, after twelve or thirteen hours of work, to realize that some of the significance of what's going on has touched them and given them fresh energy to get the last car loaded. They are all simple people, but after many hours of it, the time of year, the temperature, the clearness of the air, and all the other things make them begin to feel that what is happening is not completely an event of business. They work furiously, and nobody stands over them with a whip, nobody tells them what to do or how to do it: they just do it. Melikian told me it could be the slowest-thinking, slowest-moving man in the world, and after three days of it, he would be part of the whole ritual, swift-acting, accurate, and pretty much delighted, if nearly exhausted.

Only two or three of the three dozen girls and women will seem attractive at first; all the others will seem worn-out, dried-out, ugly and everything else unpleasing, but after you get to know them just a little, you know how truly beautiful each of them is, even the ones who are, at first glance, ugly. The ones which seemed attractive at first will seem almost incredibly intelligent and beautiful after two or three days, which of course is an illusion—the summertime sharpness coming out of all things and bringing them to the top of their form, ripening the grape on the vine in six hours, and intensifying any good thing in anybody almost to the point of perfection.

I'm thinking about the vines in the heat, the bunches of grapes ripening on them, the color and flavor of them, and how they get to the millions of people in the big cities in the East, before summertime ends—giving each of them who wishes to know the taste of the grape a chance to hold a bunch of them by the stem and pluck the berries off and eat them, before it is winter again, before the season is over and there are no grapes anywhere and the vines are all bare. The toughest thing in the world is to feel the summertime depth of ripeness, and then to separate the obvious part of it from the part of it that's truly the truth.

That is the tough part of it, for anybody: the young government inspector who is supposed to see that, when the clerk buys a bunch of grapes in New York, he won't taste sour grapes; the railroad inspector who is supposed to keep the shipper from gypping the railroad out of tariff by loading the boxes too heavily and making the railroad haul a ton extra, free; the girls and women packing the grapes for three cents a crate in order to have a hundred dollars or so at the end of the season; the Mexicans in the field; the truckers; and everybody. To get to the image of the bunch of Ribiers three thousand miles from where they were grown and what they mean to the eye of the Italian bootblack who has brought them home, or anybody.

All this is in the midst of all the other things, each of them of some importance, and yet all of them overlooked, everybody too busy to bother, or too tired, or too poor, or too rich, or too old, or too young, or something else. If it isn't grapes, it's one of the other things, each of them needing to be known about, so that people will know what counts and what doesn't.

But it's too tough a job. What I *wanted* to get was the grapes, the way they are, the way it is, and what I got is something I can't figure out. That was so, most likely, because of the people involved, and what they've been wanting to get, the ones in the heat of the valley, and the ones in the big cities in the East.

They are good people, though, and you know it when you stand in the sharp heat of summertime there and look at the grapes hanging from the vines.

My Witness Witnesseth

✿ ✿ ✿

A NUMBER of things have been asking to get on paper, but they have been asking at unusual hours, so that by the time I have been ready to get them down on paper, they have been forgotten.

They ask, for instance, at two or three or four in the morning when I want to sleep.

Naturally, I refuse to get up and go to work, so by way of compromise I turn over, and in the morning remember that I knew the truth, but forgot it.

Last night, for instance, I knew the word: I knew it: and how smiling and kindly it was: how simple: how much a part of every man's heart: how miraculous and ordinary: how beautifully commonplace and, until last night, inexpressible.

An industrious writer, even in his youth, even in his old age, would have gotten up in the middle of the night with a vision like that, taken it by the tail, and out of it written a book.

But what do *I* do? I turn over and go to sleep.

Well, such is the life of the lazy writer. The fool puts sleep above revelation. In the morning he rises and seeks to write the foolish story of the foolish waste of everybody, naming, for argument's sake, the world as the criminal, naming the story The Criminal World, itemizing the misdemeanors, taking inventory of the mayhem, the arson, the theft, the false witness, the murder, the rape, the sodomy of it, or anything at all: telling a story that gets nowhere and means nothing.

My witness witnesseth that at the age of twelve I was a better writer than I am now at the age of thirty, except that I did not know how to write then, and now, knowing how, I must say I have lost the way, lost the vision, lost the world I knew must be made real, lost the realm of truth I knew was in myself, lost everything in fact except the few odd fragments of the commonplace world which so easily fit themselves into the so-easily written words.

"You write of yourself," they say—the critics, my relatives, my friends, and people who aren't friends at all. That is what they all say. "It reads well enough. It is all entertaining enough. It is all quite interesting, but it is always about yourself. Why is that?"

The way I write now instead of the way I should have written, from the beginning, is unbelievable. And the millions of books, which were written by men at one time or another, which they sat down and deliberately wrote, which were printed and bound and for a time read—they are all the same: nothing, bloody nothing.

And nothing in the world is easier than to be a writer. Nothing is more stupidly flattering to one's self. Nothing is more pointless than to be another writer: anybody can be that: anybody at all. I can teach any man in the world to be that. That is a thing not worth teaching, I might say. And no one can blame me for the way I feel when the young men arrive and say with blushes or with firmness or with faith or with bitterness or with despair, "I want to write. I know I can write. How is it done?" I feel like a fool.

Anybody can be a writer. There is no middle-class boy in England or America who cannot be a writer. All he needs to do is work: just work: just muddle through.

I am sure of one thing: I am sure nothing is known. It is all to come when our eyes open; and something wonderful happens to our ears; and something incredible to our nostrils and lungs; and something to the pores all over us.

My witness witnesseth, but I wish to sleep, so by morningtime truth is lost, or at best in such a miserable state as this.

What can any writer born to write write when there isn't time enough in the years after twenty, or skill enough in the years before?

Even if you were born to write, even if you were born to look and see, listen and hear, feel and understand, sense and know, even then, by the time you're in command of the language, you're off in the jungle everybody's in, and you can write, but not really; you can write as they write and always have written; you can say everything that means nothing; you can do it expertly; you can make it a pleasure to read; but you can't carry them along to the living they want, you can't take them by the ear to life, you can't move the hour one second forward from where it was a million years ago; you can't say the word because you've forgotten it; you can't do anything but wait, the same as the others—making the pathetic stab at living the others are making, never coming to life, arriving dead from the dead, out of death creating the new dead, putting them on their feet, putting them into the streets, turning them loose into the mouse-trap world.

This is most certainly a sad transcript of the things that have been asking to get down on paper, but it is certainly the best I can do with the language I know, the body I inhabit, the mind I tried to educate. This is most certainly not the word. I, Saroyan, am most certainly not the man to say the word, but I know it is there, waiting to be said, and I hope to God somebody will do me a favor and say it.